The Thorpe Brothers Collection

His Captive Lover
His Unexpected Lover
His Secretive Lover
His Challenging Lover

Elizabeth Lennox

www.ElizabethLennox.com

Note to readers: The Introductions provided in this book were originally published on ElizabethLennox.com and distributed to our mailing list subscribers. They have never been included in the e-book or paperback versions of the books until this collection. The Introductions describe events much earlier in the main characters' lives and are meant to provide additional context.

To register for free introductions and news of upcoming book releases, please visit http://www.ElizabethLennox.com/subscribe/.

CONTENTS

CONTENTS (CONT'D)

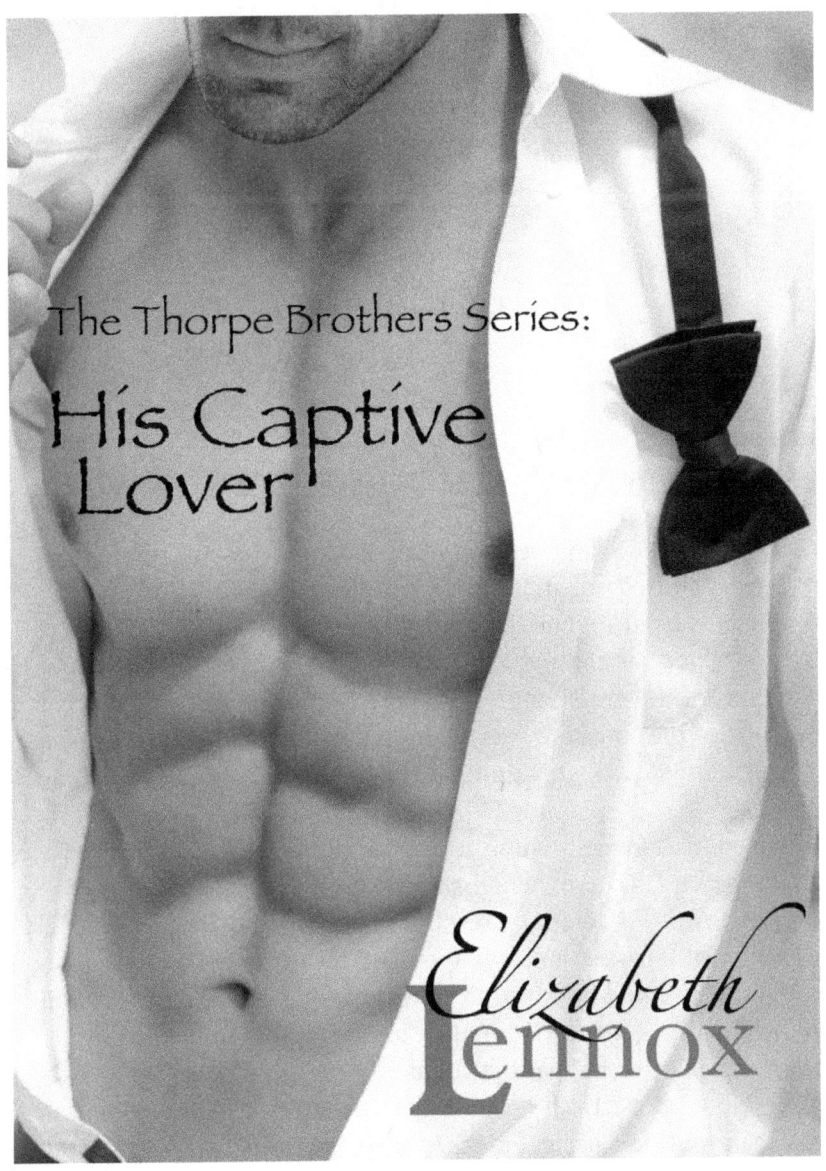

The Thorpe Brothers Series:

His Captive Lover

Elizabeth Lennox

Book 1:
His Captive Lover

INTRODUCTION

Ash's Story…

"Hold up," Ash said to his friend, putting a hand in front of him to stop any movement.

Jeremy stilled, looking back at Ash. When they were silent for a long moment, Jeremy shifted impatiently. "What's wrong?"

Ash tilted his head slightly. "Don't you hear it?"

Jeremy listened for another long moment. "Hear what?" he asked. He heard only the sounds of the grasshoppers chirping in the weeds and the occasional tree frog. The heat of the sunshine was beating down on their heads, causing sweat to roll down Jeremy's back, making him eager to get home and back into air conditioning.

Ash wiped his forehead with the bottom of his shirt, then was still again. A moment later he said, "There!" and listened. "Did you hear that?"

Ash didn't wait for Jeremy's response but moved off to the left. He ignored the possibility of snakes and other biting critters, following a sound that, apparently, only he could hear. "Can't you hear that?" he asked, assuming Jeremy was right behind him. He hurried in the direction of the sound.

Jeremy was startled to hear the slight mewling sound and his heartbeat picked up. "Yeah. Now I do." Both boys hurried towards the sound, racing through the underbrush and pushing aside branches in their hurry to find the source of the sound.

After running through the brush, the sound became louder, the whimpering sounds more heart-rending. "Look!" Ash said, pointing towards a hole in the ground where a small, furry head was poking out. "He's hurt!"

Jeremy shook his head in amazement. "Only you would've heard that sound," he said to Ash.

Ash dropped to his knees and started digging, trying to loosen the limb that had fallen on the dog that was obviously scared and in pain. "Can you find a stick? Maybe that will help us dig him out."

Jeremy immediately handed Ash a stick and the two boys slowly dug the dog out of the hole. When the heavy branch was finally pushed off of the scruffy dog's hind legs, they discovered that the poor animal was more hurt than they'd expected. It was a mangy mutt with blood on the fur of both his ears and the skin obviously torn up on the leg that had been trapped.

"We need to get him to a vet," Ash said, immediately taking off his shirt to cradle the dog. "It's okay, boy. We'll take care of you," he soothed, stroking his head and neck to try and give the animal some reassurance.

The dog looked up at Ash adoringly, but with pain in his eyes. He whimpered a bit more when Ash got behind him, but didn't make a sound as they carried him out of the woods and down the street to the only veterinarian's office they knew of.

As Ash moved as quickly as he could with his hands full with the wounded canine, Jeremy raced ahead, burst into the clinic, and held the door open.

"Can you help us?" Ash asked the receptionist. He tried to hide his anxiety with a façade of toughness, because boys were supposed to be tough and strong, not worried. "We found him in the woods over by the school and he's pretty badly hurt."

The young-looking receptionist quickly picked up the desk phone and called the vet, who came rushing out from a swinging door. The doctor, a man in his late fifties with thick glasses and a grandfatherly beard, looked at the dog and nodded. "Bring him back here," he said.

Ash laid the wounded animal on the metal table, then stepped back. When the dog whimpered again, the vet turned around to see what was going on. "He seems to trust you. Can you come closer while I get things ready? Just keep your hands on him so he can sniff your scent."

Ash immediately moved closer, rubbing the wiry fur on the dog's ears until the poor animal calmed down. "Okay, step back now. We need to give him a shot to help him with the pain, but I don't want the dog associating you with the pain. So let us hold him down for a moment, then you can come closer. Okay?"

Ash nodded, feeling angry for whatever had happened to this obviously neglected dog. No living thing deserved to be put through this. And the more he thought about it, the more the hole where he'd found the animal looked like something someone had dug on purpose. The idea that someone had done this deliberately infuriated him even more.

"There," the vet said, laying a soothing hand on the dog's head, scratching his ears gently. "He should be numb from the pain in just a moment. Why don't you wait in here until he falls asleep, then go wait outside in the waiting room while we fix him up."

Ash nodded slowly, his hands gently ruffling the fur on the dog's head, ears and back. When the dog's eyes closed, Ash bent down low, whispering in the animal's ear, "Don't worry fella. We'll take care of you."

The vet nodded with a warm, reassuring smile, indicating that Ash and his friend should head outside. Ash paced back and forth in the waiting room, his mind going over all the problems the dog might encounter over the next few weeks because of this injury. And that brought to mind the image of his mother, who probably wouldn't approve of bringing another animal home. He had a tendency to find strays but, in his defense, Ash had found good homes for each of the animals. Besides, he couldn't leave the poor animal here. He'd have to take it home. Surely his mother would understand this time.

His cell phone rang and he looked down at the window, cringing when he saw his mother's phone number come up. "Hi Mom," he said. "I know I'm late for dinner but I have a problem." He finished explaining all of it, relieved when she told him to stay with the dog. He sighed with relief at her words and comforting reassurance that she'd keep his dinner warm for him. As he hung up the phone, he smiled with relief. His mom had endured many trials raising four boys, and this wasn't going to be one of them, Ash promised himself mentally.

Twenty minutes later, the doors to the clinic swung open and Ash almost laughed when his three older brothers walked in, one of them carrying a small plastic container. "Mom told you what's going on?" he asked.

Ryker handed him the container which held his dinner of meatloaf, potatoes and broccoli. "Mom says you have to eat the broccoli."

In true brotherly solidarity, Xander simply took the container and popped the broccoli into his mouth then handed it back to Ash. "All eaten," he said, then clapped his brother on the arm.

Ash was relieved. He absolutely hated broccoli, while Xander didn't mind the repulsive vegetable. "What are you guys doing here? I thought you had a date with Emily," he said to Axel.

Axel shrugged his already broad shoulders and smiled, a mischievous twinkle in his eye appearing. "I told her what's going on. Now I'm her hero since I won't abandon the dog."

Ash rolled his eyes, chuckling at his brother's genius. "Good angle."

Axel's grin was huge. "I thought so. That's why I'm here. All the girls will be fawning over me tomorrow when they hear about this."

Ash snorted in disbelief. Axel might be saying he was here for the attention, but Ash knew better. The four of them might fight about everything from the last glass of milk to the front seat of the car, but when a problem came up, they were a solid wall of support.

Xander pushed him out of the way as only a brother could do. "How's the dog? And where did you find him?"

"Over behind that old abandoned barn near the school," Ash explained. Jeremy had already left, his mother demanding that he come home, so it was great that his brothers had arrived to help with the vigil.

The vet came out at that point, wiping his hands on his scrubs. "The dog's going to be okay. He's going to need antibiotics for a while, but he was in relatively good health so the wound won't put him back too far."

Ash swallowed, relieved for the good news. Then he squared his shoulders, bracing himself for the tough question. "How much is it going to cost?" he asked, nervous because he only had the money he earned mowing lawns. He and his brothers worked each Saturday around the neighborhood mowing the grass of several neighbors, trimming their bushes, and weeding out the gardens.

The vet hesitated. "I gather this isn't your dog, correct?" he asked.

Ash shook his head warily. "No. My friend and I found him this afternoon."

"How about if I throw in my cost for free and you guys pay for the medicine? Will that work out for you?"

Ash blew out the breath he'd been holding. "Sounds great, Doc. How much will the medicine cost?"

The vet named a price and Ash nodded. "Can I pay you half now and half in a few weeks?"

"No need," Axel said from behind Ash. "Here," he said and plunked down his own handful of money. That was the same amount that Ash had. Ash spun around and shook his head. "You can't do that. You have homecoming with Emily next week."

Axel punched Ash's arm. "I'll get Dad to drive us," he said.

Ryker and Xander both smacked their money down. "Here's our share," Xander said firmly.

Ash took a deep breath, swallowing the lump of emotion that welled up. He was grateful for these three guys. He knew he'd still get a pounding about whatever was coming around the corner, because that's what brothers do. He'd probably even deserve it, because he loved annoying his brothers on a regular basis. It was chaos central with all of them teasing and playing tricks on each other.

"Thanks," he said, bowing his head slightly until he got himself back under control.

The vet counted out some of the money, then handed the rest back to the boys. "This will cover it," he said with admiration tinging his tone. "Let me keep him here overnight. Can you come back tomorrow?"

Mia's Story....

5

"If you multiply these two numbers," Mia explained, looking up at Josh to see if he understood, "then you can…" she stopped, sitting back in her chair. "Josh, you're not paying attention to the paper."

The smile he bestowed upon Mia made her skin crawl. "I think you're one of the prettiest girls in school. How about if we go to the school dance together this weekend?" he suggested.

Mia wanted to laugh when Josh tilted his head and shoulders slightly, as if he were trying to look like a movie actor. Unfortunately, it only made him look silly. "I already have plans this weekend," she told him. "And if you don't learn this algebra, you're not going to be able to play in the game Friday night."

Josh chuckled. "They won't take me out of the game," he replied with complete confidence. "We're playing to get in first place."

Mia tried hard not to roll her eyes, but it was a strain. "So you're saying that the coach will ignore your failing grade simply so he can win the state championship?"

"Absolutely," he said with a laugh. "They need me." He paused and leaned forward, pasting what he probably thought was a charming smile onto his handsome features. But to Mia's mind, it just looked smug. She really hated smug men.

"Josh, don't you want to learn this stuff just for your own education?" she asked him carefully. "I mean, this is really basic stuff. People use this formula on a daily basis."

"Not when we're playing football," he replied with a laugh. "So how about it? Come to the dance with me? We can celebrate winning the game together."

"I already have plans." She turned the notebook towards him. "Why don't you try number six on your own?"

Josh looked down at the paper, barely even acknowledging the algebra problem. "After you agree to go to the dance with me."

Mia bit her lip, trying to come up with a way to get him to concentrate. "How about this," she offered. "If you'll get an A on Thursday's algebra test, I'll go to the game and cheer you on."

He made a rude sound and shook his head. "You never come to the games," he argued.

"Exactly. So this would be huge, right?"

"Would you really go?" he asked, his eyes bright with hope. "You wouldn't understand what was going on, so you might not enjoy it."

She considered that, trying to figure out what would motivate him. "Then let's do a trade." She watched his eyes and knew that she'd captured his attention. "You figure out algebra today. If you get an A on Thursday's test, then Thursday afternoon you can teach me the fundamentals of football and I'll go to the game on Friday night. Is it a deal?" she asked.

Josh considered her proposal carefully. "Will you cheer for me when I make every touchdown?" he clarified.

She smiled brightly, realizing in that moment that she'd won. "I'll scream so loud, you'll be able to hear me on the field."

His eyes brightened even more. "It's a deal," he told her. "Let's do this!"

He actually leaned forward then and focused on what she was telling him. It took another hour and a half but he finally figured out how to do the problems.

She worked with him about how to catch simple mistakes, different ways to check his work and even went on to the next chapter which built on the current concepts.

By the time Thursday afternoon rolled around, she was a nervous wreck! She had calculus first thing in the morning while Josh had algebra during the last period. By the time the last bell rang, she was hopping from one foot to the next, nervous about how Josh's test went. His coach had already spoken to Josh's algebra teacher, letting him know that Josh couldn't play in the game Friday night if he didn't pass the test. Josh had been stunned when the coach had backed up the school board policy of all athletes needing a B average in all classes to participate in school activities. So he was pretty nervous as well.

Mia stood outside Josh's classroom, while Josh stood beside his algebra teacher's desk, watching as his test was graded. When the teacher handed Josh the test back and Josh bowed his head, Mia's heart broke. She felt horrible and tried to figure out what he could have done wrong. She'd thought he'd really learned the concepts, so she berated herself for not doing something differently, not helping him in a way that he'd understood.

He walked out of the room and Mia didn't know what to do to make him feel better. "Josh, I'm so sorry," she said, laying a hand on his arm to comfort him.

And then he looked up at her, his grin widening. A fraction of a second later, he lifted her into his arms and spun her around. "I got an A minus!" he crowed, thrilled with his test results. "Now you have to go to the game!"

Mia's jaw dropped and she glanced back at the math teacher who was chuckling in the classroom doorway. "Really? Let me see!" she said, pushing against his broad shoulders so she could check the work herself. As she looked at the paper, her heart soared. "You really did it!" she said and hugged him. "This is awesome!"

Josh preened, proud of himself for the results. "Now you have to learn about football," he said and took her hand, pulling her out of the school. He waved to his algebra teacher, the test still in his hand. "Come on. You've got a lot to learn."

Thirty-six hours later, Mia was in the stands, wrapped up in a sweater and scarf as she screamed her head off. Josh was grinning from ear to ear as he tossed the football to the referee from the end zone. He looked up at Mia, saluting her as he moved over to the sidelines.

Mia and her friends high-fived each other, then settled down to watch the end of the game. Mia felt like she was in a bubble of happiness as she continued to watch the game, explaining third down conversions, pass interference, or interceptions to anyone who would listen.

CHAPTER 1

Autumn looked at the list, her eyes casually skimming down the cases. When her eyes caught one name in particular, she looked again, shocked and not believing her eyes. When she looked one more time, she gasped, still not sure she believed that this name was on this particular list. Sure enough, the name hadn't changed when she refocused.

Panic filled her and she looked around, wondering what she could do. This couldn't be happening! Of all the names that might have popped up on the court's docket roster, this one was the only one that Autumn never would have expected.

"Ash!" she whispered, suddenly knowing exactly what she needed to do.

Running down the stairs then through the long hallway, she burst into the office on the left corner. The large, intimidating man sitting behind the steel and glass desk seemed to be the day's super hero, at least when it came to this impossible situation. "Help!" she cried out as she burst into his office, not even bothering to knock as she normally would.

Ash looked up, his black eyebrows rising above his strange, blue eyes. "What's wrong?" he asked of the normally ultra-professional, uber-polite-except-when-a-certain-brother-was-around office manager. She rushed into his office, her eyes wide with an emotion that didn't make sense on her beautiful features. Ash watched as she hurried around his desk, remaining calm despite Autumn's panic.

"Please, you have to get her out of there!" she rushed over to his desk and slapped the list down in front of him then immediately turned to figure out what he might need to solve this horrible problem. She hurried behind his desk and grabbed the suit jacket that had been draped across the back of his chair, grabbing his hand and sticking it into the sleeve even while he read the paper she'd slapped in front of him seconds ago.

Ash looked down at the paper, still remaining calm even while he allowed her to help him into his jacket. "This is a list of the people being arraigned this morning." He transferred the paper to his other hand, still reading. With practiced coordination, Autumn grabbed the other hand to stuff it into the sleeve, then pushed the jacket onto his enormous shoulders.

Autumn didn't even bother to look at the paper again, too frantic to get the impossibly large man moving. "Correct. The person you're going to save is the third name down on that list." She grabbed his briefcase and haphazardly stuffed some papers into it, then looked around to see if there was anything else he might need.

Ash looked at the name. "Mia Paulson?"

"Yes! You have to go help her!" She ordered him and shoved his leather chair out of the way while she put her hands up on his shoulders, pushing his enormous body around his desk and out the door. She'd never been so bold before, but she didn't have time to be nice. This was an emergency.

Ash stopped moving and turned around to look down into Autumn's worried, chocolate eyes. "Looks like she's being arraigned for first degree murder."

Autumn looked up at the man who was the only one who could save her friend. Unfortunately, she had to take a precious moment to explain because Ash was too large and too muscular to move when he didn't want to. "She's my best friend and I guarantee that she's innocent. But more importantly, she's probably trying to do this all on her own because she naively believes in the justice system and probably thinks her claim of innocence will get her out of this mess." Autumn was already shaking her head and waving her hands in the air. "There's no way Mia could have killed anyone. She composts all of her plants. She scoots bugs out of her house instead of stomping on them like a normal person. When we're walking down the sidewalk, she'll actually stop and help earthworms get across so they don't dehydrate in the sunshine and die. So killing a human being is completely outside the realm of possibility. Unfortunately, you're her only hope and you've got to do something!" she explained, her voice rising towards the end as her patience in explaining things to Ash wore thin. There wasn't time to talk. The court would be in session in just a few minutes so Ash had to hurry and get over to the courthouse now!

Ash couldn't help it. The image of Autumn with her three inch heels and her pencil skirts, her long, dark hair looking so prim and proper walking with someone who helped earthworms and bugs was just amusing and he let out a deep chuckle. "So she's a saint. But even saints have a breaking point and, when provoked, can kill someone if rage or passion takes over."

"First of all, that wouldn't be first degree murder, would it? Besides, you're thinking of normal people like me when I'm talking to your obnoxious brother, Xander. Not Mia! We've known each other since elementary school," she said, gathering up his planner and extra pens, stuffing everything into his case in a haphazard manner. She walked behind him again, trying to shove him out of the office which was impossible unless Ash Thorpe was willing to be pushed. He was simply too big.

Thankfully, he allowed himself to be moved along, then pushed out the door. "You have to hurry. She's being arraigned any minute now and she's probably terrified. She definitely doesn't understand the process because she's a school teacher. The woman doesn't even have a parking ticket to her name so she has no clue how harsh the justice system can be. She needs you and you have to hurry!"

Ash grabbed another file on the way out, shaking his head at the odd situation. "If she's being charged with murder, where was she at the time of the crime? What is the evidence the police have on her? What's the motive?" he asked.

"I don't know!" she snapped, pushing him from behind now, picturing her friend's worried face as she sat in a jail cell with all the other criminals who might hurt her because Mia was such a nice, innocent woman who believed in human kindness. "Stop asking questions and move faster!" she ordered him, completely forgetting that she was the office manager while Ash Thorpe was one of the partners of the illustrious Thorpe Group legal team that consisted of four brilliant brothers who all worked in different areas of the law. Not to mention Ash Thorpe was also the best criminal attorney in the country. People hired Ash from all over the United States to get him to defend them.

"Don't you need your coat?" he asked, looking down at her silk blouse. He rarely saw Autumn without her matching suit jacket. She might take it off in her office, but she slipped it on if she had any reason to step out of her area. They were out in the cool October morning with a definite bite to the air.

She shook her head, barely even acknowledging his question in her urgency to get him out the door. "Not now." She led him over to her small car with a combination of forceful nudges, pulls and racing ahead of him to challenge him to keep up with her. When they finally arrived at her car, she opened the passenger seat and practically pushed him in, ignoring the humor of seeing his large, muscular frame sitting inside her tiny vehicle. At his questioning look, she said, "I'll drive. You'll be too slow. We might not make it in time."

He looked at her askance even as he whipped his foot out of the way before she slammed the door on it. "I'm too slow?" he asked with astonishment, but only the dust inside her car heard him since she was almost running around to the driver's side. He chuckled slightly as he shook his head. No one had ever accused him of being slow. He stepped out of the car and she froze, her wide, chocolate eyes begging him to get back into the car.

"Autumn, what's going on here? I'm never slow and court is almost in session."

She was becoming frustrated with his delays and questions. "Stop messing around! Mia needs your help! You're the one who always thinks that justice has to be done and here you are just standing here mocking me." She paused a moment, tears threatening her eyes. "Please, Ash. You're really the only one I would trust. She's my best friend and I know she's terrified right now and probably very confused."

Ash took pity on her and turned serious. Looking at her from across the roof of her car, he smiled reassuringly. Or as soothingly as he could without any knowledge of the situation. "Don't worry, Autumn. I'll help your friend. Judge Rooney is on the bench today. If your friend is third on the docket, we still have plenty of time to meet up with her. You can drive and on the way, I'll call some of my sources and find out what's going on, get the evidence against her and find out who is prosecuting. Okay?" he asked with that famous Ash Thorpe confidence.

She smiled, instantly relieved that he was finally on board with the issue. "Thank you!" she replied. But a moment later, she pointed for him to get back into the car and, even in her rush, gracefully slid in behind the wheel.

She ignored Ash as he made some phone calls, only hearing his end of the conversation as she focused on the early morning traffic. Thankfully, The Thorpe Group's offices were close to the courthouse but downtown Chicago traffic was still obnoxiously difficult.

Fifteen minutes later, Autumn swallowed painfully as she pulled into the courthouse parking lot. The expression on Ash's face scared her more than anything. "What's wrong?" she asked, parking in one of the empty spaces near the courthouse.

"Pretty much everything," Ash said and opened the car door. All signs of humor and resistance were gone now, replaced by that cold, logical determination that had made him so famous in previous trials. The man certainly loved his job, but when he grasped onto a situation, he was like a pit bull, not stopping for anything until he'd succeeded. "Come on. We have our work cut out for us." With that, he strode up the steps of the courthouse and worked his way through security. Once he was clear, he and Autumn rushed through the doors of the courtroom.

Right before he entered, he touched Autumn's arm to stop her. Looking down into her worried eyes he said, "Autumn, you need to let me do my job. I know this is your friend, but I'm going to treat her just as I would any other client. I have to in order to get her out of there."

Autumn swallowed, painfully aware that Mia was still waiting. She had no idea what Ash was telling her, but she nodded in agreement. When he started to turn back to enter the courtroom, she stopped him with a hand on his arm. When he was once again looking down at her, she explained the harsh truth to him. "She can't pay," Autumn said softly. "I'll pay your fees. Please, just help her."

Ash sighed, the issue becoming more complicated. Autumn might look professional and tough and she fought his older brother tooth and nail on anything she considered an important issue, not afraid to stand up for what she believed in. But Ash had worked with this woman for several years now. He knew that, deep down inside, Autumn was a soft, sweet, kind person which made her vulnerable to the harshness of life. "And what if she's guilty?" he asked carefully, needing her to face the possibility.

Autumn shook her head. "No. She isn't. You'll see. Wait until you meet her before you make a judgment. You'll know as soon as you look into her eyes. She's just a thoughtful, gentle person who teaches kids and loves her job and gardens as a hobby. She doesn't do anything wrong except stand up for the little guy."

Ash looked at her for a long moment. This would be a complicated case and if it weren't for Autumn's personal involvement, Ash wouldn't even take it. It seemed like an open and shut case from what his police source said. The only issue in their favor is that the police hadn't found the body of the victim yet.

He sighed, turning to fully face her so he could ensure that she understood how bad this looked for her friend. "Autumn, there's an eyewitness that said Mia Paulson and the victim were in a fight the day the victim went missing. The man your friend is accused of killing? It's her ex-fiancé. Your friend apparently was jilted for another woman." He shook his head and sighed. "Her fingerprints are even on a piece of evidence that has the victim's blood on it. It's an old baseball trophy with one of those heavy bottoms and the police think it is the murder weapon. It's a pretty tight case for the prosecution. If I were on the jury, I'd vote to convict her without even hearing the prosecution's arguments."

Autumn's eyes hardened as she listened to Ash's recitation of all he'd learned on the drive over here. And it just made her angrier. "If that bastard did this, you make him pay, Ash! Mia wasn't dumped. She broke up with him. Not only did she get rid of him, but their breakup was a while ago. Mia isn't mean or petty but she'd discovered some irritating things about her ex-fiancé and broke up with him. He wouldn't accept the breakup though. He stalked her and drove her nuts. Please, hurry and you'll see!" she begged.

Ash shook his head, wondering why he was even entering into the courtroom under these circumstances. "Autumn, you have to…"

She held up her hand to stop him. "If the evidence is that bad against her, then she needs your talents all the more. Please," she begged once again, "you're her only hope. You're the only one I know of that could help her get out of this mess."

Ash sighed and nodded his head. "Just don't get your hopes up, okay?"

Autumn's bright smile struck him and he wondered why his older brother Xander didn't do something about his feelings for this woman. Autumn was extremely intelligent, stunningly beautiful and obviously in love with Xander. In Ash's mind, the two made a perfect couple. And if the sparks flying around the office between the two combatants lately were any indication, there was either going to be a wedding to attend, or a funeral. Although he wasn't sure which.

"Let's do this," he said and stepped through the doors. Normally, he would spend time with his clients before their arraignment, find out any extenuating circumstances and get control of the courtroom. But because his new "client" was about to be announced any moment, he didn't have time for that today.

"People versus Mia Paulson, murder in the first degree," the court clerk at the front of the courtroom announced with his loud, bellowing voice.

As always, the courtroom was chaotic and filled with people milling about, attorneys speaking with their clients, family members moving around and talking amongst themselves, police officers conferring with district attorneys as well as the prosecuting and defense attorneys calling out their cases to the judge. It wasn't like the old fashioned courtrooms one saw on television but an ultra-modern room where the back was darker than the front and the judge sat on his throne-like chair in front of all the chaos, looking bored and irritated by the bother.

Into this mix stepped Ash while Autumn sat down in one of the rows, feeling better now that Ash was on board and taking charge. She scanned the room and tried to smile reassuringly as the police officer brought Mia forward.

Mia stepped up to the defense table, her eyes wide with fear and her whole body trembling. She couldn't believe this was actually happening. How had her life gotten so out of control?

She was wearing jeans and a tee-shirt instead of a professional looking suit. Since the police had banged on her door in the early hours of the morning, she didn't have any make-up on, her hair was a mess and she was terrified out of her mind. The police had arrived with a warrant for her arrest about four o'clock in the morning, waking her up out of a sound sleep and tossing questions and a piece of paper at her moments before they started rummaging around in her house. She'd answered the door in her robe, pushing her brown curls out of her eyes and trying very hard to focus. And now she stood in front of a busy courtroom, her mind frantically trying to figure out what was happening.

"Do you have counsel?" the judge barked out over the noise of the audience.

Mia looked around, finally figuring out that the judge was talking to her. A lawyer? Was this really happening to her? "Umm…" she started to say but she didn't have a chance to answer the judge. She was about to open her mouth but was stopped by someone behind her.

"Ash Thorpe here to represent Ms. Paulson, Your Honor," a deep, commanding voice said.

Mia looked around, her grey eyes scanning the crowd. A super tall man was stepping out of the crowd and her eyes widened in shock. She looked up into his blue eyes, wondering why he was here, who he was and why he was coming forward. A man this gorgeous shouldn't be in a courtroom. And he definitely shouldn't be standing next to her. But then, she shouldn't be here either! She should be rushing out of her little cottage home, dropping her keys onto the wooden steps and grumbling as she bent down to pick them up again as she raced down the stairs so she could get to school before her kids started arriving. She should be worrying about spilling her coffee on her suit as she fought the traffic into the city.

Instead, because of some weird, unexplainable twist of life, she was standing here, defending herself against a murder charge. Surely this was some sort of nightmare and she'd wake up in a moment. The sky would be lightening on the horizon and she'd figure out that she needed to wear a lighter suit instead of a wool one because it was going to be a hot, fall day instead of those delicious, cool ones that made her feel more motivated.

No, this horrible moment wasn't happening to her.

"How does your defendant plead?" the judge demanded over the din.

"Not guilty, Your Honor," the gorgeous man stated confidently. He stood right next to her, but didn't even bother to consult her on any of the issues. "We request that the defendant be released on her own recognizance," the crazy-tall man was saying.

The prosecutor spoke up and Mia's eyes swung over in that direction, completely confused about what was being said. Was this about her or another case? "The defendant is accused of murdering her ex-fiancé out of jealousy. The people request that the defendant be remanded until trial."

Tall-Gorgeous-Dude shook his head, his eyes glaring at the prosecutor. "Ms. Paulson doesn't have even a parking ticket to her name," the tall, muscular man called back, his voice confident and deep, sexy and Mia couldn't believe that she was thinking something like that while her entire life was at stake. "She hasn't been engaged to the supposed victim in four months, nor does the prosecution even have the body of which Ms. Paulson might have murdered."

The judge swung his eyes back to the prosecutor with irritation, stunned that the prosecutor would bring a murder charge without a body. "Is that true?" he asked.

The prosecutor shook his head, "The victim has been missing for more than a week. His blood was found on the murder weapon with Ms. Paulson's fingerprints."

The judge shook his head. "If there's no body, it sounds like you can't even prove that there's a murder. The man might have just left and gone to an island somewhere," the judge grumbled, obviously wishing he could do the same thing.

Tall-Gorgeous-Dude stepped in at that moment. "Since there's no body and the prosecution can't prove that there's even been a murder, I request that the charges against my client be dropped, Your Honor." Mia's eyes swung from the tall man beside her to the judge, praying with hope that the man in the black robes would agree with this stranger.

The prosecutor spoke up quickly. "The current fiancée to the victim swears that the victim wouldn't disappear. He's a principal at the local high school with enormous responsibilities. And there was a great deal of blood in the victim's house. Too much blood for there not to be foul play. We currently have investigators at Ms. Paulson's house digging up her back yard, searching for the body. We are confident that we will find it by mid-morning."

The judge considered the opposing arguments and came to a speedy conclusion. "Since there's no body, I won't hold the defendant. But the case can continue to trial and I'll let the presiding judge hear whether there's enough evidence to move forward. Defendant is released on her own recognizance, but must surrender her passport to the court until trial." The gavel banged down and another voice was calling out the next case.

Mia felt her arm grasped in a firm, demanding grip and she was pulled out of the courtroom. She still wasn't sure what was going on, but she felt the tall man's body next to hers, felt the trembling start up but for a completely different reason this time.

And then she saw Autumn and the tears burst out of her. "You're here!" Mia exclaimed and rushed forward, grabbing her friend around her shoulders and hugging her with all her strength. "I can't believe this is happening!" she sobbed out. Mia was shorter than Autumn, but only because of her best friend's love of spike heels.

Autumn held Mia in her arms and mouthed the word, "Thank you," to Ash who was still standing behind the slender woman.

Ash looked down at the two women hugging each other. The one he'd just been defending was sobbing and he felt only somewhat guilty to notice that the woman looked exceptionally fine in her tight jeans that hugged her bottom so perfectly. He stood there waiting, wanting to see if the woman looked as good from the front as she did from the back. She had softly curling brown hair that ended at her shoulders and his fingers actually ached to touch one of those curls. She was too slender, he thought. While she hugged Autumn, her shirt pulled against her back and he could see her ribs through the thin material. She needed to gain a good ten pounds and he wondered if she'd lost weight because of her recent breakup. He knew women generally either stopped eating when emotionally distraught, or they ate everything in sight. At least, that was the stereotype. He actually had no idea if it were true or not, steering clear of women during emotional upheavals. He preferred the happy, fun and sexy type to the drama queen.

Mia pulled back from her friend, her worried eyes looking up at her. "Thank you!" she said with heartfelt sincerity.

Autumn shook her head as she continued to hold Mia close, still not over the horror of watching her friend come into the courtroom from the menacing holding cells. "Why didn't you call me this morning? I only found out about these ridiculous charges about twenty minutes ago and we had to rush over here to help. I practically had to kidnap Ash to get him over here in time."

Ignoring the reference to the name "Ash", suspecting he was the tall, intimidating man standing behind her, Mia sighed and looked down. "I guess I was pretty ashamed. I don't know what's going on, but I can't figure out what happened to Jeff and nor can the police. They found blood on something and now they assume I killed him." She looked frantically at her friend, desperate for Autumn to not think she could have done something like that. "I haven't spoken to him for over a month and that was only to tell him to leave me alone."

Autumn put her arms around her friend and shook her head, silently reassuring her friend. "I told you that guy was a loser."

Mia laughed but it sounded more like a cry. "I know. Everyone told me that but I didn't listen. I'll definitely listen the next time." She looked around at the people milling all over the wide hallway. "Although, I honestly can't imagine being interested in a guy after this. I didn't even know that Jeff was dead until the police were handcuffing me this morning." She put a hand to her mouth, trying to control the emotions that were threatening to overwhelm her.

Autumn smiled and straightened up. "Don't worry. If anyone can get to the bottom of this situation, it will be Ash. He's the best criminal defense attorney in the world."

Mia turned around, ready to thank the man who had gotten her out of that horrible holding cell. But as soon as she turned around, she froze. Looking up at the man while her life was being threatened was one thing. But looking up at him now, she was stunned by both his height and his breadth. It wasn't that the man was fat. Quite the opposite in fact. His stomach was flat and his legs long and apparently muscular. But those shoulders! She'd actually stood next to this behemoth for all that time? Surely not! She would have noticed those shoulders before. He must be about six foot, four inches tall!

And those eyes! They were a clear, amazing blue, but there was a ring of yellow around the iris, causing her to blink as she looked up at him.

"This is Ash Thorpe," Autumn was saying. "Ash, this is your new client, Mia Paulson."

Ash looked down at the woman and gritted his teeth. Mia was not just a pretty woman. She was stunning! Her soft, grey eyes complimented her pale skin. Her lips were pale right now, but he suspected that was only due to the shock she'd just endured. And she was smiling at him! This woman had just been arrested and accused of murder, and she was smiling warmly at him, looking up at him with admiration and joy.

"It is a pleasure to meet you," Mia said, forcing her face to form a smile despite the fact that she wanted to just melt into a pool of humiliation. This man was so sophisticated, so elegant and so amazingly gorgeous and he'd just gotten her out of jail! Here she was in her worn out jeans and a tee-shirt that had definitely seen better days while he stood in front of her wearing a suit that probably cost more than she made in a whole month.

She felt like she might actually be drooling as she took in the suave, sophisticated giant of a man but then her circumstances occurred to her. She was off men as of four o'clock this morning. She'd made that vow while curled up in a jail cell, trying to get the black stuff off from her fingers after being fingerprinted and her mug shot taken. Her mug shot! How humiliating!

All that had occurred this morning was because she'd found one man cute and adorable. Jeff Richardson had been sweet and charming and had the silliest grin but now he was gone, missing, and everyone thought she'd killed him. Of all the things she did not need in her life at this moment, it was a gorgeous man who looked like he knew his way around a bedroom with his eyes closed.

Ash tore his eyes away from the lovely brunette and glared at his office manager. Autumn was smiling up at Ash, then at her friend and back again, trying to gauge their reactions to each other. That look told him that she knew exactly what was going through his mind.

Looking back down at the other woman, he extended his hand and enveloped her tiny one in his hand. He felt her trembling and every instinct inside of him ordered him to pull her into his arms and hold her tight, to reassure her that he would take care of everything. Where this protective instinct had come from, he had no clue. Women were nice and soft and warm and he loved when one was in his bed. But Mia Paulson didn't appear to be that kind of woman. Which was a problem, because not only did he want to hold her close, taste those full lips and discover all the secrets of her slender figure, but he wanted to hold her close and tell her that all this craziness would go away.

But he couldn't guarantee that. This woman might be a murderer. He knew almost nothing about her, about her case or about her past.

So why was he feeling like someone could tip him over with a feather?

Clearing his throat and pulling his eyes away from those soft, grey ones, he straightened up and told himself to not be fooled by a pretty face. "Let's go back to my office," he grumbled. He dropped the woman's hand and pushed his way through the crowd, grabbing onto the lovely Ms. Paulson's arm to make sure she stayed close to him. It wasn't that he thought she would spirit away from him. No, it was more that he needed the physical connection. Strangely, after holding her hand in his, he didn't feel right without that link. He'd touched her hand and now he wanted to touch all of her. He didn't want her out of his sight. Not because he thought she was guilty. Only because he wanted to feast his eyes on her beautiful features for the next....twenty hours or so. Yes, perhaps that would be enough time to get over the impact of those pretty, soft, grey eyes.

Mia scrambled to keep up with the taller man's longer stride but she couldn't seem to break his hold on her arm and she was practically running to keep pace with him. Even Autumn had problems matching his pace as they raced through the marble hallways and her friend was looking at her boss as if he'd just grown a second and third head.

"Ash, wait up!" Autumn called out, trying to slow him down. She couldn't keep up in these shoes and she caught Mia's desperate, confused look as well.

Ash didn't listen. He walked out to Autumn's car and opened the back door, placing the mystery woman in the back. "I'll drive," he said and plucked the keys out of Autumn's fingers.

Thankfully, Autumn didn't argue but got into the passenger seat while he walked around to the other side.

"I have no idea what's gotten into him, Mia," she said while both women watched his long stride as he walked around the engine of the car. "He's usually much more charming."

Mia wanted to reply, but the man she'd just thought of as handsome and delicious, but now knew was arrogant and a big, huge jerk, was now getting into the driver's seat and pushing back the seat to accommodate his longer legs. Did he care that Mia had to swiftly move her legs to the other foot well because there was now so little room in the back seat? Of course not!

They drove in silence to Autumn's office. Mia had been to this building before, but only to pick up Autumn for lunch or happy hour. She'd never actually been inside. She wanted to ask questions, figure out what was going on, what the man knew and what he wasn't telling her. He drove through the streets of Chicago and she watched his hands, unaware that she was forming silly, romantic dreams or, even worse, sexual fantasies about those hands until the sun disappeared and she blinked, coming back to the present with a thud.

CHAPTER 2

They parked in the underground parking garage and Mia took a deep breath as she followed her friend, who smiled reassuringly as they walked to the elevators, and her new lawyer, who looked like he was sucking on lemons, inside the elegant, granite and glass office building.

Stepping out of the elevators, she blinked at all the signs of wealth and success as she looked around. The law offices of The Thorpe Group were all black granite, shiny steel and sparkling glass with intelligent looking people bustling around in every direction as if they had an urgent purpose in life. Autumn had spoken of her co-workers before, but only in general terms, telling her that there were four brothers who partnered in the firm.

In Mia's mind, this wasn't a law firm. This was an enormous corporation. She had no idea how many floors each brother occupied, but it was intimidating to walk into the beautifully decorated office area wearing only jeans and a pink tee-shirt while everyone else wore immaculate, sophisticated suits with silk shirts or power ties. Mia tucked her hair behind her ears, wishing she could have put on something more sophisticated herself, or even done her hair, but she followed meekly along behind these two, wishing she were anywhere else other than following this disturbing man into his opulent office in her jeans and tee-shirt. Just a little lipstick, she thought as she stepped into the elegantly masculine room, would make her feel a bit more in control and presentable.

"Wait in here," the horrible man said, opening a door for her and waiting until she was inside before he closed it once again, with her on the inside and everyone else on the outside.

Mia stared at the closed door, her throat closing with the returning fear of being locked up for the rest of her life. Taking several deep breaths, she pushed the panic back down. She'd never been afraid of closed spaces before, but after this morning's experience, she suddenly felt clammy and nervous, as if the air around her were thicker somehow.

She backed to the center of the room and looked around, telling herself mentally that he hadn't locked her in here.

He probably thought she was guilty and should be in prison, Mia thought as she wandered around the room, concentrating on anything other than the fact that he might have locked the door. Had he put her in here to keep her from stealing the office supplies? She was being ridiculous, she knew. The door most likely locked from this side so the possibility that he'd locked her into his office was pretty low. That thought calmed her down a great deal and she was able to think more clearly.

Looking around, she noted all the various items in his office. And since he'd closed the door and told her to stay put, she wasn't above snooping. She told herself it was just her way of finding out if the man was any good at his job, but a small part of her also accepted that she wanted to know more about him personally.

The degrees on the wall caught her attention and she wandered over to look at them. Hmm…she thought, Stanford Law School. Impressive! Why were these over in the corner where most people wouldn't see them? She'd always thought people who went to the big, high-profile schools would broadcast their degrees as loudly as possible.

Wandering over behind his desk, she saw the pictures on the bookshelf. There weren't any children or women, so she assumed that Ash Thorpe wasn't married and didn't have kids. There were several pictures of four men, one of whom was Ash and the other three must be his brothers since they all looked so similar. There were several with the four men, one on a boat in crystal blue waters, another with snow falling around them, obviously a ski trip to some mountain she couldn't identify from the picture, another picture with all four men in tuxedos….she looked at each of the pictures slowly and grudgingly had to acknowledge that Ash Thorpe really was the most handsome of the group.

With a sigh, she ignored the pictures, not wanting to think of Ash Thorpe as a handsome man any longer. Looking around, she bit her lower lip and wondered how in the world she was going to be able to afford this man's hourly rate. She'd bet it was about two or three hundred dollars per hour, and there was no way she could cover that.

Of course, this was her life she was dealing with. If the man was willing to take her case, shouldn't she let him? She stared out the window but didn't see anything. Her mind was going over her assets. She had a retirement account, but she was only twenty-six so there wasn't a great deal in there yet. She could mortgage her house, but since she'd only bought it last year, there wasn't a whole lot of equity there either. In other words, she didn't have a big savings or huge assets to fall back on. These ridiculous charges were going to bankrupt her, she realized with sadness.

She'd been so careful all her life. She'd worked her way through college, saved as much as she could and bought a house because every investment expert said that real estate was the best investment. So she'd followed their advice. She'd wanted to get married and have a house full of children. Jeff had looked like the perfect candidate for a husband and father. How could she go wrong with a high school principal? But she'd slowly realized that she was going to marry him simply because she wanted the fantasy of a house and kids, not because she loved him with all her heart and soul. So she'd broken off the engagement, wanting to be honest and kind, to do the right thing so that Jeff could find someone who could love him like he deserved to be loved.

But after she'd given him back his ring, he'd gotten nasty, flinging insults at her. When she'd walked out on him during one of those conversations, he'd gotten even angrier, to the point that she'd had to block his calls on her cell phone. A month after she'd broken up with him, he'd reverted to sending her flowers, which she'd refused, candies, which she'd returned, small gifts which she'd sent back to him with a note telling him to not contact her again.

The entire fiasco had been one bad nightmare after another. She'd thought it would stop when she'd heard through one of her friends that he'd become engaged to another woman. Mia had relaxed her guard, which obviously had been a mistake. That was how she ended up here, standing in a stranger's office, snooping and fighting down panic.

She sat down in one of the comfortable chairs set up in a square by the window, her head falling into her hands as she contemplated how this was going to completely derail her life. Jeff had done this to her somehow. She didn't think he was dead. There was just something about this situation that didn't smell right and Jeff had been warning her to come back to him or he'd punish her. But for the life of her, she couldn't figure out what to do or how to prove her innocence or even her suspicion that he was behind all of this. How could she tell the police that the man they thought she'd killed probably wasn't even dead?

This was definitely a conundrum!

Ash ignored the chaos of his department, knowing that there were several high profile cases underway. Mia Paulson's case had suddenly become a higher priority, although he didn't completely understand his reaction as he walked up the stairs to the top floor. The Thorpe Group worked off of the top four floors of this building, each of his brothers having a separate floor with their staff of lawyers and support personnel filling in all the available spaces. The top floor was where his brother, Ryker, worked and was where he was headed now. He'd called an emergency meeting a moment ago and he knew that all of his brothers would drop what they were doing and get to the top floor conference room within the next five minutes.

He'd been wrong. As soon as he'd stepped into the room, his three brothers were already there.

"What's going on?" Ryker asked as soon as the door was closed. The oldest, and most emotionless, stepped forward, concern written all over his features.

"I'm taking a case pro bono," Ash said without preamble.

The three other men continued to look at Ash. "And?" one of them asked, prompting more information.

Ash was relieved. All three of his brothers were supporting him, not a single word voiced against such an action. He knew they'd always been there for each other, but this was an unusual circumstance. He wasn't even sure he could explain it to himself, much less his brothers. Ash looked at the table, his hands fisted on his lean hips. "It's a murder case where a woman is involved."

Xander crossed his arms over his chest. "Is this woman in some sort of danger?"

Ash hadn't thought of that. He knew he wasn't thinking clearly on a number of subjects, which also meant he probably shouldn't take this case. But he was going to anyway. "She isn't in danger that I know of, but I'll keep you informed as the information unfolds."

"So what's special about this case?" Axel asked, watching his brother curiously.

Ash took a deep breath before finally saying the words that might invite a different reaction but he had to be honest with his brothers. They'd never lied to each other outside of the normal sibling teasing and joshing. And he wasn't going to pussy-foot around this. Something inside of him was signaling that this was too important. "This is personal. To me."

The three men looked at their brother, stunned. "How personal?" Ryker finally asked, voicing the question they were all thinking, including Ash himself.

Ash considered his words carefully. "I don't know. My gut instinct is 'very'."

All three men thought about that. Then slowly, as they always did, nodded their heads indicating their full support. "You'll let us know how we can help," Axel came back. It wasn't a question, it was a command. The brothers were close in age, only about a year or a year and a half apart. Their parents had died in a car accident several years ago and it had brought them closer together, forming a family unit instead of letting their relationships disintegrate. Ash was the youngest at thirty-three. Axel, the next oldest, was thirty-four and always laughing about something. He was the tease in the family, but also the one that received and gave out the most poundings at the gym. They worked out together frequently in the boxing ring, a sport at which all four excelled. Xander was thirty-five and constantly fighting with their office manager, Autumn, who the three other brothers suspected that he was in love with. None of them were brave enough to step into that minefield though, afraid of the explosion that might occur. Ryker, the oldest and now the head of the family, was heading into old-man territory at thirty-six. But his old-man status wasn't because of his age, but more because he was always serious, rarely cracking a smile for anything these days.

Ash breathed a bit easier with the statement of their support and nodded, relief flooding through him. "I will. It could be a difficult case."

"And a difficult issue," Axel said, but he was starting to grin.

Ash turned to Xander, holding his brother's gaze. "She's a good friend of Autumn's as well." He wanted to give his older brother the warning and fought the urge to step backwards in case Xander exploded, which had been more often lately for some reason.

Xander immediately scowled and crossed his arms in the air. "You're going to need all of our help then," he said, implying that Autumn was the issue and not his client. "She only brings trouble."

Ash opened his mouth to say something, then looked at Axel and Ryker. Both men were thinking the same thing, but as their eyes connected, they all three decided to leave it alone.

"I've got to get back to her," he finally said. "I'll have Emma send each of you a brief on the evidence as soon as I get it from the prosecutor."

Back down on his own floor, he signaled to his investigator, Mark. "I need you to find out everything you can about these people," he said and handed him a list which contained the names of the assumed victim, the new fiancée and the very lovey Mia Paulson. "This is a rush issue. Get your team on it immediately and report back to me with whatever you can find," he ordered and Mark instantly nodded his head and moved back to his office.

Mark was one of those unassuming men who blended into all situations. But his powers of observation bordered on the supernatural and he had the best technical mind Ash had ever seen. The man could rig a camera to the most bizarre places, all to get evidence that would help their clients. He had a team of investigators that all had a scary expertise, having come from the intelligence communities or other investigative branches. Their combined expertise was worth their weight in gold because they continued to find evidence that exonerated their clients.

With the investigation starting, Ash looked towards his own office and wasn't surprised when he saw the pretty, dark head peek out of his office. He almost chuckled to himself if he hadn't felt that irritation start up again. There was just something about Mia Paulson that struck him in a way that no other female had ever done before. He couldn't define it, but he knew she had some powerful force that he wasn't going to ignore.

"Oh no, my little lady," he mumbled under his breath as he watched her pretty, grey eyes scan the room for an escape. "You aren't going anywhere."

He moved quickly and was in front of her before she even took two steps out of his office. Nudging her right back inside, he leaned against the doorway and looked down at her, amused when he saw her biting that full, pink lower lip. "Going somewhere?" he asked with a slight drawl.

Mia hid her hands behind her back. "I have to leave." At his raised eyebrow, she sighed. "Look, you're one of the best of the best," she said, pushing her hands into her pockets, unaware that the posture pulled the tee-shirt tight against her breasts, showing the hardened nipples and making his body harden as well. "I have no idea how much you charge per hour, but I simply can't afford you."

"Mia, you can't afford to walk out of this office," he said, ignoring her comment about his hourly rate.

She shook her head. "You probably charge two or three hundred dollars per hour, don't you?" she asked.

Ash shrugged one of his shoulders, her worried, grey eyes solidifying in his mind what he'd already decided earlier. "What's your point?" He didn't tell her that he charged closer to seven hundred to one thousand dollars an hour, depending on the complexity of the case. That was just his hourly rate and in her situation, it would be closer to the grand mark not to mention the hourly cost of all the investigators he'd just launched on the city as well as the support staff and the potential legal filings.

"I can't afford you. I can't raise nearly that amount of money," she explained, desperate now to get out of this office before more charges accumulated. She was so humiliated that she would even have to admit such a thing to a man like this who could probably afford anything his big heart desired.

"Mia, sit down," he commanded and walked over to his desk, indicating she should take a seat in one of the leather chairs in front of him. "Don't worry about the cost of your defense. Let's figure that out after everything is settled."

She stood there for a long moment, her mind battling with her instincts. She knew, deep down, that this man was trouble and her life would never be the same again.

He was sifting through some papers on his desk but when she continued to stand there by the door, he looked up at her. When he realized she was still worried, he walked back to stand in front of her. Taking one of her hands in his large one, he noted how cold her fingers were, and that they started trembling once again.

"I know that you're scared and not sure of what's going to happen next. But you're going to have to trust me. I'm very good at what I do, Mia. Just relax and let's take this one step at a time. You're no longer in jail, but I doubt you can work, so let's just take it slow and figure things out as they come along. Let me worry about the high level strategy and you worry about answering my questions. Does that work for you?" he asked softly, trying to reassure her but he was also fighting his instinct to pull her closer and kiss her. Instead of following on that instinct, he said, "So let's go through the issues," he suggested, trying to give her some sort of comfort but not sure how. "What was your fiancé like?" he asked, leading her over to his desk so she was sitting next to him.

Mia answered all of the man's questions, over and over again he found a detail in her story that she had to explain. People came into his office and handed him papers, which then shifted his interrogation. He was relentless in his questions, not letting her hide anything. Occasionally, someone interrupted about another case and Mia prayed that the man would give her a slight break from his interrogation, but he answered the person's question efficiently before coming right back to his questions to her. She told him about their dating relationship, the engagement, the ring, his reaction when she broke it off with him and all the small little gifts he'd sent to her, trying to convince her to come back to him.

By noon, she was exhausted. She'd been over and over the issue a million times, her fingers almost tearing her hair out. "I don't know!" she finally screamed at him. "I don't know where Jeff is! I told you, I haven't spoken to him in over a month. I threatened to put a restraining order on him because he wouldn't leave me alone!"

"And did you?"

"No!" she replied, exasperated and defeated.

"Why not?"

She sighed, shaking her head. "Because I didn't know how!" she snapped right back at him. She stood up and paced in front of the window in his office that looked out onto the Chicago skyline. "I know that sounds ridiculous to you, but normal people don't know what to do in these situations!" She was flustered that her stupidity was being brought up over and over again. "The only reason I know there's such a thing as a restraining order is because of television. But in those situations, the police are enforcing the restraining order that is already in place! The shows never explain how to actually go about putting one in place!"

She fell back down into the comfortable leather chair, bracing herself for his next question.

"Did you eat breakfast?" he asked.

Mia looked up, startled by the softer tone of his voice. When she could look at his eyes, she sighed. "No. They were too busy putting my wrists in handcuffs. They didn't give me a chance to grab my morning cereal," she replied sarcastically.

Ash thought that would be a very good look for her, but pushed that thought aside when his body instantly reacted to the visual that popped into his head. Of course, she wouldn't be clothed while the handcuffs were on. And he wouldn't be arresting her either. He cleared his throat which helped to dissipate the image a bit. "Wasn't there something offered at the jail?"

Mia looked startled by the gentleness in his voice now. "I guess so," she answered, but shrugged. "I wasn't really in the right frame of mind to grab food though."

"Come with me," Ash said, standing up and grabbing his jacket once again.

Mia stood also, but she wasn't sure she wanted to go anywhere with this man. "Where are we going?" she asked, her feet moving, but not as quickly as might be needed to keep up with his longer stride.

He looked down at her, a slight smile on his handsome face as he touched the dark circles under her eyes. "You need something to eat. And probably a few more hours of sleep, but unfortunately, that's not going to happen yet. Food, I can do. Rest is a luxury I can't offer you at this point."

Mia's shoulders drooped, but she knew he was right. "Food would be good. If you could drive me home, I can just grab a sandwich."

Ash hesitated and she looked up again. "What?" she asked, not sure if she wanted to hear what he might tell her. The look on his face promised that she wouldn't like anything he was about to say.

Ash wished he could drive her home and tuck her into her bed. He pictured her in a full sized bed with a handmade quilt draped over the top and hand embroidered pillows for decoration. She looked like the kind of woman who would embroider and quilt and he thought the idea was delightful. "You can't go home. Not yet, anyway."

Her whole body tensed with his words as well as the hard if wary look in his eyes. "Why not?"

He put a hand to the small of her back and led her out of his office. Several people handed him papers or notes and he grabbed all of them as he continued to walk out of the office. "Because your home is still being searched by the police," he said a moment before the elevator doors opened up. He nudged her inside, realizing that she was probably stunned by the news.

Mia thought about that for a moment, the news going over and over in her mind. And then it hit her. "They haven't found anything yet, have they?" she asked, her smile brightening. "That's a good thing, isn't it?"

Ash was impressed. When given that news, most people became either angry or defensive. Mia had found the bright side, which was usually what he told his clients when the police reached this point. "That's correct. It's good news."

"So they'll eventually drop the charges, right?"

He couldn't lie to her, even to give her a short period of hope. "Probably not. There is precedence where cases were tried, and the prosecution won, even when there wasn't a body. And that's what they're looking for in your yard. Apparently you have a lot of new shrubs, so the police are digging up those areas, thinking that you've buried the body in the garden."

Mia sighed, her shoulders drooping once more. She watched as his hand pressed the button to the parking garage and shook her head. "I wouldn't be so stupid as to bury anyone's body in my backyard. Not even my cats!" she grumbled.

Ash chuckled despite the seriousness of the situation. "Not even your cat's body? And why not your ex-fiancé? I thought everyone wanted their loved ones close by in the afterlife."

Mia shook her head while rolling her eyes. "Are you kidding me? Jeff bothered me enough over the past few months. If I killed him, which I didn't," she cautioned, "do you honest think I'd want him in my backyard? The obnoxious man would haunt me!"

Ash couldn't help but laugh at her logic. It might not be true, but it made sense. "You have a point," he said, his laughter subsiding to a chuckle as the doors to the elevator opened up.

He led her out of the building but, as the flashbulbs popped unexpectedly, he put his arm around Mia's shoulders protectively. His mind was frantically trying to pick up the pace and figure out what was going on.

CHAPTER 3

The crowd seemed to move in closer, blocking their way. The only reason they moved was because Ash was so much larger than they were and he was moving fast. Anyone not getting out of his way was libel to be crushed. "Has Ms. Paulson confessed to killing her fiancé?" one reporter shouted at them. "Are there any other suspects?" another called out. "She pleaded not-guilty, but why are the police digging up her yard? Do they think he's buried there?" someone else called out. All the while, the cameras were clicking away, catching Mia's stunned surprise.

Mia held onto Ash's hand, allowing him to guide her. She couldn't see a thing with all of the press gathered around them. He was more than a head taller than all of the other reporters so he could see over their heads. When he almost shoved her into a car, she didn't even care whose car it was, as long as it got her away from their cameras and questions.

Ash got into the car after her and drove away, his hands expertly handling the powerful vehicle.

After several moments, he said, "I'm sorry about that, Mia. I should have anticipated that happening."

"What was that all about?" she asked, still not sure why the press were so fired up about her case.

"You're a kindergarten teacher accused of killing your fiancé..."

"Ex-fiancé," she corrected quickly. She still didn't understand. "And don't people get accused of murder all the time? What's so special about this case?"

"The details seem to have caught the media's attention," he explained. He pressed a button on his steering wheel and a moment later, a voice came over the line. "Judy, make sure that security clears away the press in front of the building. Get a restraining order put in place for her home as well."

Mia's mouth formed a perfect "O" as she listened to him speak, ensuring that she had a clear path to her house whenever she was allowed to enter it again. "The media think I did it?" she asked weakly.

Ash didn't like the worry in her voice. She'd just started to stand up for herself a few moments ago. This was no time to get weak. "The press don't care if you did it or not. On a slow news day, anything is fair game for a story."

Mia looked out the window, shaking her head. "I teach kids," she said. "They're all young and impressionable. They won't understand what's going on, especially if the media start showing up at the school. It will scare them and be confusing. I'll lose my job over this."

Ash wasn't going to allow that. "We'll clear your name, Mia. Just hang in there."

She looked up at him, feeling his strength and power, but not sure she could trust it. "Even if you can clear my name of the criminal charges, there will always be some people out there who will think I did it."

She was right, he thought. "Then I'll just have to make sure there's no doubt in anyone's mind."

She sighed and slumped down into the soft, luxurious leather seat. "I'm not really hungry anymore. If you can just drop me off at my house," she asked.

"You can't go back there," he said again. His voice was hard and firm.

"Why not? Surely they won't be searching my house for the whole day, will they?" she asked.

"They might, depending on what they find or don't find." He considered his next words, "And even if they finish today, your house might not be habitable for a few days. Besides, we're not finished today. We have much more to do and we need your help. You're not off the hook."

He pulled into a sandwich shop and they got out. "Besides, you haven't eaten yet today. You have to grab something to eat. This is a long, tedious process and you're going to need your strength."

Mia started to follow him inside, but he waited at the front of the car for her and she felt that warm, squishy feeling in her tummy again. Darn him for being a gentleman! Why couldn't he just walk into the sandwich shop and wait for her to catch up to him like most guys? She was used to that. She could handle that. His gentlemanly manners combined with his gorgeousness were making her think and feel things that were completely inappropriate!

He even pulled out her chair for her while the waitress handed them the paper menus. She suddenly realized something and her whole face flamed with color.

"What's wrong?" he asked, instantly aware of something changing within her.

She shifted in her chair and put her menu off to the side. "Nothing," she replied nervously.

Ash's eyes narrowed towards her. "Something is wrong. Did you think of something relevant to the case?" he prompted, laying his menu down as well.

She couldn't even look at him, so horrified by her current predicament. "No. I just realized that I'm not very hungry after all."

Ash didn't believe her for a moment. "You're getting some food, Mia," he replied, his tone gentle but firm. "You haven't eaten all day and I'm going to need you alert tonight for more questions."

She sighed and closed her eyes briefly, but then her stomach betrayed her by making hunger noises. She placed her hand over her stomach and tried to play it off. "I'm just nervous that's all. It isn't every day a girl gets arrested," she said, pretending to laugh but the sound was more nervous than humorous.

Ash suspected what was wrong and tried not to smile. "How about a bowl of New England clam chowder and a Rueben sandwich?" he suggested. "Or a burger with extra cheese and onion rings?" he asked, watching her carefully. When her mouth dropped open slightly with the second option, he put his menu down with a satisfied nod. "Burger it is, then," he said and signaled to the waitress who had been standing by the counter waiting for him to be ready.

"No! Really. I'm fine."

Ash looked at the waitress and ordered their cheeseburgers with onion rings and an extra side of French fries. "Can you bring some vinegar with that as well?" he asked.

Of course the waitress nodded her ascent, eager to rush off and do his bidding as quickly as possible. Mia glared at the woman, wanting to spit when the hussy swayed her hips in an obvious invitation.

Mia looked back at the man, wanting to see if he was ogling the waitress. She needed something to calm these crazy feelings that were swimming through her mind. But the man wasn't watching the waitress! He was watching her watching the waitress. And was that amusement on those firm, sexy lips?

"I don't have my wallet," she finally admitted, needing to throw him off the scent of her jealousy over the waitress and onto new territory.

"I figured that out," he laughed. "Did you think I was going to make you buy your own meal?"

She glanced down at her fingers which were tangled tightly together on her lap, nervous with those blue eyes on her once again. "I'm not sure what I'm thinking today. It's been one of those crazy, unpredictable days that I hope never to experience again."

He chuckled softly. "And I'm here to make sure this one blows over quickly enough." He paused a moment, looking at her soft, worried and tired eyes. "Do you really save earthworms?" he asked, unable to stop the question once it popped into his mind.

She looked up at him, not sure what he was talking about. "Save earthworms?" she repeated, confused.

"Autumn was telling me what a stellar human being you were as she was pushing me out of my office to get to the courthouse faster. One of the things she said as a way to convince me of your innocence was your need to save earthworms from the heat of the sun."

Mia flushed and looked down again. She wasn't exactly sure what she could say, but she shrugged her shoulders slightly. "I don't like to see them suffering," she said in almost a whisper.

The possibility that earthworms had the ability to actually experience pain and suffering struck him and he threw back his head and laughed. He knew he was making her uncomfortable and he tried to hide his amusement, but every time he looked down at her from across the table, the laughter started up again. He couldn't help it. She was so cute and actually sincere about her need to save the same worms that he and his brothers speared onto hooks whenever they went fishing.

Thankfully, their burgers arrived at that moment and she was able to hide her flushed cheeks behind the burger which actually tasted fantastic, despite her worry over her current legal problems. He let her get halfway through her burger and fries before he started in on the questions again. This time, she wasn't sure why he was asking some of the questions, but she answered them as honestly as she could. But they were things like what her favorite color was, were her parents still alive and why she'd chosen teaching as opposed to a profession that might be more lucrative.

"We can't all be dynamo lawyers and billionaires, can we?" she asked with a smile, used to people wondering why she chose teaching. "It isn't a big secret," she explained, wiping her fingers on her napkin. "I love the kids. I love seeing them learn. When they enter my classroom at the beginning of the school year, most of them don't know how to read and can barely identify the alphabet. By the end of the year, they're excited to read me books, some have started math skills, and they are more confident and eager to please. It's just an exciting process," she said to him and then grabbed the last onion ring, not even sorry either.

He looked back at her with a blank look and she wondered what he was thinking. Most people thought she was crazy to be stuck in a room with twenty-five to thirty kids. They pictured a room filled with chaos and screams but that wasn't the way it was. She had fun with her students

They drove back to the office and Mia wearily followed him back to the elevator, grateful that all the reporters had left the area, but still nervous about whatever additional questions he might have for her. She'd never talked about herself as much as she had today and it made her uncomfortable.

Once inside the building, she shifted over to the other side of the elevator, feeling odd when she was too close to the man. She knew he didn't like her and it irritated her beyond anything to know that. There was something about this man that struck her deeply, made her feel….okay, this was cliché, but he made her feel weak in the knees. Him buying her a burger and fries didn't help either. Most men were horrified by how much she could eat but this guy, he just looked at her with admiration.

She just needed to keep telling herself that he didn't believe in her innocence. He was working this case because it was his job and he was getting paid an incredible amount of money to get her out of jail and keep her out. He didn't care about her innocence or guilt. He just cared about the next almighty dollar and how many hours he could bill against her poor, beleaguered bank account.

As she stepped out of the elevator, she turned so that he couldn't touch her back. Her body might think he was the sexiest man alive but her mind recoiled at the idea of any man who didn't think she was good and honest, and more importantly, not a murderess, to touch her.

Ash's eyebrow went up as she turned so as to ensure that he couldn't touch her. Fine, he thought with irritation. She wasn't even his type. He preferred blonds, he told himself. Tall, leggy blonds!

So what if he couldn't keep his eyes off of her adorable, sexy derriere? And he wasn't actually staring at her long legs, wondering what it would be like to slide his hand down her calf, see if the back of her knee was ticklish.

Ash shifted his belt buckle slightly as he led her into the conference room where everyone was already assembled. She started to take a seat over by the conference room wall but he grabbed her arm and forced her to sit next to him. Why the hell he cared where she sat was a mystery he wasn't going to think about. He just wanted the damn woman where he could see her. Call it suspicion or maybe even an instinct for survival. He was going with his gut this time around. To hell with logic.

"Okay everyone, settle down," he called out to the assembled group. He didn't want to stifle their thought processes, but he needed those thoughts organized and going in the same direction. "We have a new face in the group. If you haven't met her already, please introduce yourselves to Kiera Ward. If you haven't heard about the case she just won in California, well, then you're fired because you should be keeping up with all court cases no matter where they were tried," he said and the rest of the group laughed. "Don't let her age confuse you. She's a hard hitter who brings passion and a dedication to the team that is admirable. Her ability to win cases in several high profile trials recently will be an asset to our team. Don't be shy and make sure you include her in the progress of this trial." Obviously all of them had heard about the case so he moved on. "What do we have?"

Ash remained standing at the head of the table while the rest of his investigative and legal team briefed him on their progress of the morning.

Mark, the lead investigator, stood up and read from his notes. "First of all, there's the assumed victim's blood on a baseball trophy with Ms. Paulson's fingerprints all over it. The police have bagged it but I'm trying to get the placement of the fingerprints to determine hold."

Mia glanced up to see Ash's expression. He looked just as hard and tough as normal, no reaction to the fact that her fingerprints were on what everyone assumed was the murder weapon.

She spoke up, trying to offer help wherever possible. "I know that trophy. Jeff showed it to me when we were first dating," she interrupted and felt nervous now that all eyes were on her. "It was his pride and joy," she explained.

"That's a good explanation for how your fingerprints got onto the trophy. Mark will get more information on the placement."

She bit her lip, confused but afraid of speaking up again. She wasn't one who liked the spotlight and this was an intimidating group of men and women.

Ash noticed the change in her eyes and reacted to it. He wouldn't normally slow down to explain with so many people here, but he seemed to be doing everything differently with this woman. Including wanting her so badly he was tempted to order everyone out of the conference room so he could finally kiss her and taste those lips of hers that she kept biting. He wanted to bite them himself, see how soft they were and....

Getting off track, he reminded himself once again. "The placement of the fingerprints can show that you were holding it in a certain way. If you were to grab it at the top so that the heavy bottom side could strike the victim's head, that would be different than if your fingerprints were at the bottom of the trophy. That would indicate that you were holding it to look at it instead of using it as a weapon."

Mia smiled, grateful for his explanation but her mind instantly went back to the moment when she'd been holding it. She tried to picture it in her mind and she was relatively sure that she'd held it at both the top and the bottom, knowing how proud Jeff was about the trophy and not wanting to break it or drop it.

Ash was already onto the next problem with her defense. He turned back to Mark, nodding for him to continue with his discoveries. "The most obvious issue, the assumed victim has been missing for more than a week. He hasn't called in sick to work, none of his co-workers have heard from him, he just didn't show up. There's been no visible movement at his house, according to the neighbors I spoke with this morning, but that doesn't mean much since it doesn't appear that anyone really knew the guy much. The neighbors don't seem to be the type to socialize with each other."

Mia agreed with that. It had been one of the fights they'd gotten into during their relationship several times. She'd hated his neighborhood and he'd fought hard to keep her from buying her little cottage. But she'd fallen in love with both the house and the neighbors even before she'd moved in so she'd ignored his suggestion to save her money for something bigger.

Again, Ash didn't show any type of reaction to the news that Jeff was gone, missing and hadn't been seen. He didn't even look in her direction for her reaction.

Oooh! She really was starting to hate that man. But how could one like a guy who thought she'd killed her ex-fiancé?

"What else?" he prompted, writing something down on his notebook.

Mark signaled to another investigator. "A co-worker at Ms. Paulson's school gave a statement to the police that Ms. Paulson and the assumed victim were fighting on several occasions. No one heard what the conversations were about, but they explained that the arguments were heated."

Ash finally turned to Mia, one dark eyebrow arrogantly raised as if to declare that it was finally her turn to explain the circumstances. She sat up straighter in her chair, feeling nervous now that all of these confident and educated people were waiting for her to explain. "I can only think that the arguments were when I demanded that Jeff stop stalking me. I'd asked him repeatedly to leave me alone after our breakup but he was determined to try and convince me to give him another chance."

"What was the breakup about?" Ash demanded, turning to lean against the conference room table, his huge arms crossed over his chest, straining the material over those bulging biceps.

Mia shrugged. "I guess we, or perhaps just me, felt that the relationship wasn't going anywhere."

Again, without a word, he tilted his head, urging her to continue.

Mia sighed and slapped her thighs. "Jeff just became too demanding. He wanted…things, that I didn't feel we were ready for."

She felt as much as saw Ash's body stiffen. "You mean you…"

"Stop right there!" she snapped. She was glaring right back at the man. "My personal relationship with Jeff is not an issue here."

Ash shook his head and walked over to her. Without an explanation, he grabbed her arm and pulled her out of the conference room and into a smaller, empty conference room right across the hallway.

As soon as the door was closed, he turned to face her, looking stern and commanding. "Let's get something straight right now, Mia. Everything about your personal life is an issue now. Every detail is going to be dragged through the mud and through court. If this goes to trial, you can damn well expect that the prosecutor is going to ask it. He or she is going to try and make you squirm and if that means dragging your sex life through the mud, then that's going to happen."

He waited a moment to let that statement sink in before he continued. "So what was it that Jeff was asking you to do in the bedroom that you refused to do?"

"Nothing!" she gasped back, her hand covering her neck in shock.

Ash ran a hand through his hair. "What? Did he want you to dress up like a French maid and dust him off?"

"No!"

"Leather and chains?"

"No!"

"Whips? Bondage?"

"Absolutely not!"

"What the hell was it?"

"Nothing!" she snapped, disgusted by the idea of even considering doing any of those things with Jeff.

Ash rolled his eyes, his hands fisted on his hips and he glared down at her. "Mia, what was it that you wouldn't do in the bedroom with Jeff? I can tell that this is the pink elephant in the room."

"Nothing!" she yelled back at him, her hands pushing her hair out of her eyes. "Nothing okay? Nothing at all! I wouldn't sleep with him, I wouldn't have sex with him, I wouldn't do anything beyond kissing him and in the end, even that creeped me out. Okay? So nothing! The problem is that I wouldn't do anything with the jerk, okay?"

Ash looked down at her, trying to understand. "Wouldn't do what?" he asked again. He had an inkling, but it was so impossible, he couldn't conceive of it.

Mia crossed her arms over her chest, trying to suppress the anger and embarrassment she was feeling as this tall, gorgeous and obviously very sexually active man continued to stare down at her like she was some sort of weirdo.

"I wouldn't have sex!" she said, it again. "How else can I explain it? I didn't have sex with him! I know, I'm ridiculous. But I'm not a control freak. I just…" She shrugged, not sure how she could explain that she hadn't ever wanted to have sex, not even with a man who she'd agreed to marry.

"Not ever? Or just not with your ex?" he clarified. He told himself that it probably wasn't important for the case. But something inside of him knew it was extremely important to him.

Mia couldn't look at him. She turned slightly to the side and stared at the blank wall. "Not ever."

There was a long, painful silence while Mia waited for this terrifying man to start laughing at her. Her whole body tensed for that to happen which is exactly what Jeff had done when she'd told him. And once he'd stopped laughing, he wanted to know if she was mal-formed or if she was ashamed of her body.

She hated this. She wished she'd just gone ahead and had sex with one of her boyfriends in college. There had been ample opportunity. And it wasn't like she was opposed to sex. She just wanted it to mean something. She wanted to be swept away by the passion and desperate for the man to touch her. She didn't want it to be a strained, awkward activity. And she definitely didn't want to have sex with a man simply to prove to him that she was attracted to him, which was why she eventually broke things off with Jeff. He told her she had to have sex with him to prove that she loved him or he was walking away. So she let him walk.

But Ash didn't say a word. They stood facing each other, Mia looking straight at his chest while she waited tensely for his amusement and ridicule. "Okay then. Let's get back to the meeting," he said and walked back through the door, holding it open for her.

Mia couldn't believe it. Wasn't he going to laugh? Wasn't he going to question her further? Demand details? Tell her she was a freak?

She wasn't going to press it. She walked through the doorway and back into the conference room where the conversations automatically stopped. Everyone turned back to Ash, waiting for his next line of questioning.

Mia wanted to kiss him when he simply moved on to the next problem. He didn't bring up anything she'd just said or offer any sort of explanation. "Okay, Mark, you're in charge of the baseball trophy. I'll interview Mia's co-workers to see what they can give us. Ann," he called out to another investigator, "Go to the high school where Jeff worked and find out details of his work life." He looked around the room. "What else do we have?" he asked.

People started calling out various ideas and Ash nodded his head in approval or shifted their focus slightly. Mia listened, more in awe of his processes than she had been earlier in the day when he'd gotten her out of jail without any bail. The man was a powerhouse and she was pretty impressed. He commanded the room with fairness but complete authority. She could see that everyone who was working this case was impressed with how he worked. All were eager to shift their direction when he suggested a new course and proud when he approved of where they were already going.

They'd been brainstorming for about two hours and the afternoon was starting to shift towards evening when two other men came in and sat down towards the back of the room. A third man came in a few minutes later and she wiggled uncomfortably as they surveyed her while Ash and his team continued to throw out ideas. She answered everyone's questions, not really sure why they might be asking some of them, but she gave as much information as she could.

About an hour later, Mia was dragging even though everyone else in the room was still going strong. "That should be it," he called out to everyone.

People unhurriedly stood up, stretching after such a long meeting as they gathered up their things and slowly shuffled out the door. The three men towards the back remained and, when everyone else was gone, they stood up and moved towards Ash. The closer they came, the more nervous she became. And she could also see the resemblance between the four men, which meant they were the other

Thorpe brothers. Their reputations were fearsome and she could feel herself moving slightly closer to Ash, although she wasn't completely conscious of what she was doing. She only knew that she felt safer now that she was a few inches closer to his enormous body.

"What are the odds?" one of them asked as they came closer.

Ash shifted, subtly letting his brothers know that she was his. Staking his claim seemed like such a primitive action, but he felt primitive right now and he wasn't going to apologize for it. Nor was he going to delve into the reasons for that feeling right at the moment. She'd moved away from him before the meeting but she was shifting towards him now. And that was all the subtle signs he needed to go caveman with his brothers.

He put a hand to the small of her back, his body reacting when she moved even closer to him, almost leaning against his side unconsciously. "Mia, these ugly men are my brothers," he explained. "This is Ryker. He's the oldest and most boring," he said, referring to the one that looked the most serious. Mia shook his hand, but moved right back to Ash's side. "And this is Xander, the next oldest and most cynical," he waited while Mia shook Xander's hand carefully, "and Axel, the most irritating."

Mia shook each man's hand, hoping her smile appeared more sincere than it felt. It occurred to her that she didn't have the same reaction to their touch as she did when Ash touched her. When that happened, it felt like a lightning bolt shot through her body. She was left confused and disoriented not to mention her mind going in strange, embarrassing directions. All three men were staring at her as if trying to dissect her and she wanted to punch Ash's arm for being so rude. She felt he should say something like, "She's innocent." Or maybe "We're going to get the charges dropped soon." Instead, he just stood there discussing the case while silently telling his brothers some weird male message that she couldn't decipher.

"Sounds like a good strategy," Ryker said. "But you know she can't go home."

Mia looked from one to the other and they were all nodding.

Ash looked down at her to explain. "Your house and yard have been locked off as a potential crime scene. They claim they haven't finished looking for your ex's body yet so they won't allow you back in."

Her eyes widened. "They've been at it all day. What have they found that could possibly lead them to assume he still might be hidden in there somewhere? It's a pretty small house too. Only two bedrooms, one bathroom, a kitchen, and a family room. I don't even have a formal dining room!"

"It's an old house, from what I understand. You have a basement."

Mia waited, wondering where he was going with that. "And?" she prompted when he didn't continue.

"And there's fresh cement apparently."

She thought carefully, trying to remember what was in the basement. He was right, it was an old house but the basement had been stone before. The previous owners had cemented over the basement because of leaks during the spring rainy season. "But I didn't put the cement down," she exclaimed when she realized what they were thinking. "It was there before I moved in. I don't even know if it was the previous owners or the ones before that."

Ash leaned against the table again. "It doesn't matter. They can't tell the age of the cement. So they're trying to determine if anything is buried underneath."

She almost fell into the chair behind her. "So they have a jackhammer in my basement destroying the foundation. Great." She wasn't sure what she was going to do now. It sounded like her whole house was being completely destroyed brick by stone. "Okay, so I'll..." she thought quickly, trying to figure out what she was going to do. "I'll just stay in a hotel until this blows over. It won't be long, right?" she looked up at Ash, fighting tears and begging him to tell her that he would overcome this situation quickly. She didn't even care if it was a lie at this point. She just needed to hear him say it. If he said it, she could believe it. The man was too big and too strong for anyone to contradict him, right?

Ash saw the tears she was valiantly fighting and his gut twisted. "Yes. We'll get this all resolved quickly. But I doubt you can afford a hotel. So you'll stay with me."

Four sets of surprised eyes looked at Ash. He shifted uncomfortably, but he wasn't backing down. "She can stay in the spare bedroom. There's plenty of room." He said this as if it was the most obvious and common sense approach, but Mia was already shaking her head.

"I can watch out for myself," she said. "There's a hotel down the street from me."

Ash turned to face her, effectively blocking out his brothers. "Mia, two streets in any direction in your neighborhood and you're driving into gang violence or a highway. The hotels in your area might not be expensive, but they're probably filled with crawling characters you don't want to run into. And I'm not just talking about the eight legged kind either." He let that sink in a moment before he continued. "You can't stay in your house and you're not staying in a hotel that you can't afford or you might not come out of alive."

She still shook her head, refusing to budge on this issue. "I'm not staying with you."

"She can stay with me," Ryker offered.

Both Axel and Xander actually took a step backwards with that offer. But Ryker continued to stare back at his youngest brother, the offer still out there and amusement in his darker blue eyes.

"No way in hell," Ash growled, his hands fisting by his sides as he struggled to keep himself from punching his oldest brother. Ryker might be the serious and conservative member of the family, but that didn't stop him from enjoying the ladies. In fact, they swarmed to him, all of them eager to spend his money and ease his frustrations.

Someone cleared his throat with the rising tension. "I'm sure Autumn would let her stay with her," Axel piped up.

Ash turned to glare at his brothers, irritated that they were even butting in. Unfortunately, Autumn probably would be more than happy to offer her best friend a place to stay. It infuriated Ash that he couldn't easily refute that option.

"Autumn has book club tonight," Xander offered.

The three brothers all turned their attention to Xander, all of them wondering how the man knew Autumn's evening schedule so well but none were willing to ask the question. Each of them shook their heads and suppressed their curiosity. "She's staying with me," Ash countered. "Come on," he told her, grabbing her hand before anyone else could offer a solution that would actually work. He had no idea why it was so important to make sure that Mia was under his roof tonight. He just knew that it was and he was going to get out of here before anything changed.

"Get your purse," he grumbled. "Someone from the office went to your house and was able to get you some clothes, your purse, keys and wallet. They are in my office."

He reached inside the door and pulled out a duffle bag, slung it over his shoulder then continued to the elevators, keeping her hand in his the whole time.

The touch of his hands immediately sent her mind going in crazy directions and she couldn't focus for a moment. She'd never had this kind of a reaction when Jeff touched her, or any of her previous boyfriends. So why did this man's touch affect her so dramatically? Why was it that the one man who thought she might be a criminal was also the one that sent such a spark through her body?

Needing a break from his closeness, if only for one night, she thought to try one more argument so that she wasn't sleeping in his home tonight. "I'm pretty sure that Autumn won't be going to her book club tonight," Mia said, almost running to keep up with the man in the strange mood. "I'm in the same book club and all of the other members are friends of mine. They won't meet without me."

Ash pressed the elevator button and stared straight ahead. "Then she's probably there talking to your friends and getting their support, trying to figure out what happened to your ex. So she's working and we shouldn't disturb her."

Mia thought he might be right and bit her lower lip, trying to come up with a counter argument. "I should probably be there as well, to answer their questions. Then I can go home with Autumn afterwards."

"You'll come home with me and we'll go over the details one more time. Maybe something will come to you over dinner."

Mia sighed, knowing that he was right there. Every time someone had mentioned an issue the police had found, she'd been able to give them something to investigate, something to check into that might shed some light on why the police were pursuing her so vehemently.

Thankfully, the security guards had kept the press away so there weren't any cameras flashing in her eyes this time around. He tucked her into the passenger seat of his car and she was once again struck by how much money Ash must make to be able to afford a vehicle so amazingly luxurious.

Well, he defended criminals, charged them exorbitant rates and basically circumvented the justice system.

That probably wasn't a fair assessment of his skills. But he was so big and so intimidating, she didn't feel like being fair. She watched him walk around the front of his car, her eyes fascinated by his long legs and her mind trying to determine what was underneath his expensive suit. She couldn't believe her mind was going in that direction! It was so….naughty and she was never naughty!

She didn't like him one bit. And she continued to tell herself that the whole way home. She repeated the statement as he showed her through his gorgeous brownstone where he occupied all four floors of a beautiful townhouse in one of the older sections of Chicago. It was a quiet neighborhood with old, oak trees shading the sidewalks and elaborate, black bannisters leading up to a newly renovated home. Inside, the brick was still showing and he'd even pulled away the ceiling to show the raw wooden support beams, giving the place an edgy but comfortable feeling.

Ash watched her out of the corner of his eye as she entered his house, wanting to see her reaction. He loved this place. He had bought it several years ago and done most of the work himself. Of course, he could always count on his brothers to help when there was heavy lifting needed. Or when one of them wanted to burn off some stress from the office. For some reason he wasn't going to delve into too deeply, her reaction was extremely important to him.

When he noticed her eyes widen as she took in the main living area with the deep sofas and the rough looking floorboards, he wasn't sure if that was good or bad. But when she saw the large windows that looked out into the back yard with the deck and landscaping, she smiled and his shoulders relaxed somewhat.

"You can stay in here," he said, dumping the duffle bag inside the doorway of a comfortable looking bedroom that looked like a designer had created the space. "Why don't you freshen up and meet me out in the kitchen? I'll cook something for dinner and we can talk some more."

Mia was left alone for the first time since she'd been rudely woken up this morning. She just stood there for a moment, absorbing the silence. She didn't think about her own home or what she would or should be doing now. She refused to let her mind start worrying about her students and what they might be thinking about after hearing of her arrest. She focused only on relaxing her mind.

Focusing on the here and now, she looked around at the large, comfortable room. Someone obviously used the room because there were shirts and suits in the closet. Ash probably let his brothers crash at his place when they went out partying or something. She didn't really care. She was just grateful for the silence.

She went to the bathroom and washed her hands and face, feeling marginally better. When she looked into the duffel bag he'd dumped by the door for her, she found a pair of black slacks and a white blouse along with underwear. She hoped that Autumn had gone to her place and gotten these items because she couldn't imagine someone else going through her personal items. As she dug through her makeup, she was sure of it. Only Autumn would know which lipsticks were her favorite and how much she loved to brush her teeth. Whenever she was stressed, Mia brushed her teeth. The clean, minty feeling helped her feel more in control.

She did that now and felt even better but she knew what would relax her even more thoroughly. She didn't have her workout clothes, but she slipped her running shoes off along with her socks and centered herself in the middle of the room. Taking several deep breaths, she closed her eyes, then slowly leaned forward, letting her arms hang down to the floor with her knees straight. The stretch in her back muscles and on the back of her thighs was instant and relaxing. She let everything unwind from her waist upwards, or downwards since she was hanging down, her hands resting on the floor.

She moved from one yoga pose to the next, feeling the tension slowly seep out of her muscles. She went into cobra pose, her eyes closed and her face facing up to the ceiling, then shifting all of her weight back into downward dog.

Ash pulled out all the ingredients for dinner, opened a bottle of wine and got down the wine glasses. He normally drank beer when at home, but he didn't think Mia was the kind of woman who would appreciate a good lager. She struck him as more of a merlot kind of lady.

Several minutes later, when she still hadn't come downstairs, he started to worry about her. She'd been through a stressful, horrible day. Mia seemed too fragile to endure what she'd gone through today, but she'd rallied, answering all of his questions, enduring the arrest, the reporters, his staff shooting ideas and questions towards her. And she'd done it all with grace and patience. He'd never had a more cooperative client before. And she'd done it all while looking like the most desirable woman he'd ever seen.

What if she were upstairs, finally cracking under the pressure? She'd gone through so much, what if she were crying? What if she were struggling to get through the evening?

He didn't like where his thoughts were going. His mouth compressed into a grim line as he looked up the stairway to the opening above. When she still didn't emerge with her bright, happy smile like he wanted her to, he tossed the dish rag down onto the counter and strode across the combined kitchen and great room to the stairs. Taking them two at a time, Ash hurried to the room where he'd left her, his imagination making him increase the pace substantially. He hoped she wasn't the kind of woman who would do something stupid. Were there any sharp objects in his bathroom? He knew his brothers used the room when one of them stayed overnight, so there could be razors in the drawers. That thought had him almost sprinting down the hallway.

The sight that greeted him as he stood in the doorway was the farthest thing he could have imagined. Strike that! He couldn't have imagined this in any way.

Mia wasn't slitting her wrists or knotting bed sheets to hang herself from the rafters. She wasn't even sitting on the bed or in the middle of the floor sobbing her heart out. She was standing on the hardwood floor, doing possibly the most erotic moves he'd ever witnessed. In the back of his mind, he suspected she was doing yoga. But he wasn't in the right frame of mind to be rational about what she was doing. His whole body froze – except for one important part of him, and that was the part that was thinking right now. Okay, so thinking wasn't exactly the right term for what it was doing. Reacting was a better term.

She moved slowly. His eyes followed the curve of her neck, the arch of her spine and the way that arch pressed her breasts against her tee-shirt. Then she moved again, her body folding upwards, ending with her bottom in the air! Were her legs really that long? And damn if she didn't fold herself forward one more time, moving into yet another position.

"What the hell are you doing?" Ash demanded, desperately needing to either join in or stop her from going to another pose. He didn't think she would appreciate the positions he'd put her into if he joined her. But his feet wouldn't move so he could back away and give her some privacy, which is what he knew he should do if he were a gentleman. So the only option was to stop her from doing anything else.

Mia's body jerked out of downward dog and she tried to stop her fall, but couldn't quite manage it. She toppled gracelessly onto the floor with a loud "Hmph!" Seeing him standing there, his jacket and tie off, his tailored shirt unbuttoned down to the middle of his chest and his sleeves rolled up revealed the strong muscles on his forearms. What was a woman to do?

She pulled herself up and dusted her bottom, glaring up at him. "Yoga!" she snapped back at him. "What did it look like?"

"Torture," he calmly replied. Or the sexiest thing he'd ever seen in his life, he thought as he looked down at her indignant expression. "Feel better?" he asked, trying to suppress the laughter as she rubbed her cute, little bottom where she'd fallen on it a moment ago.

"I was. Until you rudely interrupted me." She took a deep breath and realized how rude she sounded. "I apologize. You're going out of your way to help me and I'm just being snarky. Thank you very much for putting me up for the night. I promise to be out of your house tomorrow. No matter what happens."

He didn't respond for a moment, just stared down at her. "We'll see," he finally replied. "Let's eat."

Ash walked back to the kitchen, painfully aware that she was following him. His body was already hard and ready for her, his jaw clenching with the need to touch her soft cheek, to see if those tender lips tasted as good as they looked. And he wanted to fill his hands up with her full, luscious breasts and test their weight, feel the hard points that he could see through her tee-shirt with his thumb and watch her reaction.

Damn! He was just making it worse.

But he'd probably help her relax a hell of a lot more than doing yoga! Or maybe it would just help him relax! He certainly wasn't relaxed watching her doing yoga. And he was fairly sure that men's bodies didn't move like she'd been moving, nor did he want to attempt any of those poses. Maybe he should just call up one of his brothers and tell him to meet him at the gym. A good boxing match would do the trick since he couldn't touch the lovely lady sitting primly across the counter from him.

He moved behind the island until he could get his body back under control. To occupy his mind, he poured her a glass of red wine. "I hope you like pasta," he said more gruffly than he'd intended as he lifted the glass to hand it to her. He cleared his throat, trying to get a grip on his raging lust. But every time he thought he might have it under control, he looked at her, saw her soft curls dancing around her pretty face and he pictured her in one of those damn yoga poses again!

"I love pasta," she said evenly, oblivious to his lust-filled state of mind, slipping onto one of the odd looking chairs warily. She was surprised when it was much more comfortable than it looked. "This is really nice," she said, taking a sip of the wine and looking around. "Who was your designer?" she asked, looking at the beams above her, the rough, brick wall and the enormous fireplace over in the corner that was so big, she suspected it would still be able to heat the kitchen area on a cold, winter's afternoon.

"I did it all myself," he replied, taking a plate and spooning an enormous pile of pasta onto the center. He then ladled rich, fragrant red sauce, topping it all with a handful of cheese. "Dig in."

Mia looked at the enormous amount of food he'd given her. It was about the same amount she would make whenever she cooked pasta, but she would also divide this up into four portions, freezing the other three for future dinners that she could easily heat up in the microwave. "Goodness, this is a lot of food." She tried not to laugh at his grim face, but she couldn't help a bit of the amusement she was feeling at his serving sizes. Amazingly, he served himself more than twice what he'd given her.

He took the chair next to her, ignoring her laughter as he pointed towards her plate, indicating she should eat up. "You've had a lot of stress today. You're going to need the energy to regroup."

She laughed softly. "That's sort of what yoga does," she replied back, but picked up her fork.

Ash mentally disagreed with her. Mia Paulson doing yoga definitely did not reduce his stress level. In fact, his stress level was pretty high right about now despite his attempts to calm down.

To help distract himself, he opened her file and read through the details. As they ate, he asked her questions. But when she answered, their conversation diverged and he asked her more personal questions than he would ask of his other clients. The conversation ended up being less about the case and more about him just learning about who she was as a person. And he was surprised to find her funny and intelligent.

Mia couldn't believe how relaxed she was just sitting here talking with him. Once there was a lull in his questions and she piped up, eager to gain her own insight into the man she'd been around for what seemed like days or even weeks although it was only hours. She sipped her wine and worked on whittling down the enormous pile of pasta he'd given her while she asked him questions about how he'd renovated this building on his own. She loved listening to him talk with his deep voice sending shivers along her skin with awareness. He seemed so competent in the legal areas, and yet he had this whole other side of him. She discovered that he liked cooking and working with his hands, explaining that it was the complete opposite of what he did all day long.

"It helps me work through the legal issues."

She thought about that for a moment, thinking that it made sense. "Sort of like occupying one side of your mind with the mundane while the other side is occupied with working through a problem," she suggested.

"I suppose that's one way to put it," he agreed.

She smiled. "I do that with my kids. After recess, I give them a craft project to work on. While their little hands are busy cutting and gluing pieces of a puzzle or a craft, I give them facts about history or science. I'm always amazed at how much they actually absorb during these periods. One would think that they were distracted with the craft materials and, to a point, they are. But our minds can process more than one thing if the distractions work together with the facts."

He was impressed. But then his eyes looked down at her lips one more time and he was once again lost in the idea of tasting those lips. Of feeling them tremble underneath his. He knew she would tremble too. He had no idea how he knew that. It was just a sense or maybe a vibe.

He was just about to lean forward and test his theory. But he stopped himself, suddenly realizing that she was his client. And she was terrified of what she was facing. He couldn't take advantage of her fragility right now. No matter how soft and sexy she looked, Mia Paulson was off limits.

"You must be tired," he said and stood up abruptly. He picked up both of their plates, noting absently that she'd eaten barely any of the pasta and only drank half a glass of wine. "Can I make you anything else?" he asked as he put the plates in the sink.

"Goodness, no!" Mia said, feeling awkward now. She'd been hoping that he would bend over and kiss her. But why on earth would she want that? This man didn't respect her at all! He thought she was a murderer.

He must have remembered that little issue and pulled back, repulsed by the idea of even touching her. "I will do the dishes," she offered, needing to pay him back in some small way for his hospitality.

"I have a housekeeper who comes in each morning and cleans up. She'll do the dishes," he countered. "Why don't you head to bed? I'll lock up." He was wiping his hands on a dishtowel, using it to keep his hands from reaching out and grabbing her, pulling her against him and kissing her until she was gasping for breath. He only stopped himself because he could see the dark circles under her eyes and her smile wasn't quite as bright as it had been this morning.

Then there was also that irritating little issue: he had to remind himself over and over how unethical it would be to kiss her!

Mia watched him for a long, painful moment, wishing he would wrap those big, strong arms around her and kiss her, make her forget all of the mess her life had become over the last eighteen hours. She shouldn't want him, and this crazy fluttering she kept experiencing was probably just because he looked so strong and capable. And she needed someone to reassure her today. No, it was probably nothing, but her emotions were teetering on the brink and she should just leave right now before she did something crazy. Like throw herself into his arms.

When she saw the distance in his eyes, she knew she should be relieved. She didn't like him. And he didn't like her. So why did she feel like crying simply because the man wouldn't kiss her?

She turned around and headed towards the bedroom he was loaning her for the night, but she paused. "Thank you very much," she said with one hand on the steel bar that acted as a railing for the architectural-like stairs, staring back at him from the distance for a long moment.

She walked slowly up the stairs and turned down the hallway, feeling like it was a march of shame. She should have just stayed away. Why had she silently begged him to kiss her? Was she slowly losing her mind? Today had been horrible, she thought as she brushed her teeth and slid into the bed. In fact, of all the bad days she'd experienced in her life, this one ranked just below the day her parents had died. She missed them terribly right now.

She pulled off her clothes, refusing to let the tears flow. She just had to get through this day one moment at a time. She should listen to Ash's advice because she knew he was the best. Financial issues aside, he was right. She should figure out how to save herself before she worried about how she was going to pay for him saving her.

With a sigh, she slunk down under the covers, impressed by how comfortable the bed was and how soft the sheets were. His housekeeper had good taste, she thought as she stared up at the ceiling. And he even knew how to cook! She smiled at his worried expression earlier when she was able to eat only a quarter of the enormous amount of food he'd given her. But she'd continued to sip the wine, downing a whole glass tonight. The alcohol had helped her relax and she definitely felt better with the extra carbs from the pasta.

CHAPTER 4

Ash heard the door click closed and was instantly awake. It was just after midnight! Where could the woman be going at this time of the night?

Several ideas occurred to him, one of which was to hide any evidence in her home that the police hadn't yet discovered. He probably should have been more concerned with her breaking the law to save herself. But the only thing he thought in that moment was to stop her from going home, because the police were surely there, waiting for her to come home. He couldn't let that happen!

Sitting up in bed, he listened carefully for a long moment but when he didn't hear anything else, he cursed under his breath and threw the covers off. Pulling on a pair of jeans and some old running shoes, he only took another second to grab a shirt, pulling it over his shoulders before sprinting down the hallway. He glanced in her bedroom and sure enough, the covers were pulled back and the bed was empty.

With another curse, he raced down the hallway, hoping he didn't break his ankle or trip over anything in the dark house. The building was only four stories so, instead of waiting for the elevator to come back up, he took the stairs down, hopping from level to level. If she was going out meeting with someone, trying to hide evidence or even out killing someone else, he was damn sure going to stop her. He dismissed from his mind the fact that he'd assumed she was innocent. He'd told people over and over again that looks could be deceiving and he wasn't going to let his libido control this situation. Just because he wanted to bed her didn't mean she was automatically innocent. No one was as innocent as Mia appeared to be. No one was that naïve either!

Damn her! She'd half convinced him that she was all that and a cupcake and here she was, sneaking out at midnight going who knows where. No one snuck out at midnight to do anything innocent which meant he was going to somehow stop her from committing whatever crime was on her mind now.

It only vaguely occurred to him that he was going to chase her down and stop her, only to drag her back to his place. A reasonable man would just leave her alone, let her fall down and make her mistakes, but something urged him forward, determined to save her, even if it was from herself.

He caught up with her just as she was exiting the building. Instead of announcing his presence and demanding that she march right back upstairs, and into his bed where he could keep an eye on her, he waited, watching to see where she might be going.

When she ducked into the convenience store on the corner, he blinked in surprise. Was she out of cash? Was she going to rob the place? He stood on the stoop, wondering what he should do. A sane lawyer would call the police and have her arrested but everything inside of him rebelled at the idea of Mia being in handcuffs again. No, he couldn't do that to her. Not again. His stomach clenched at the idea of anyone touching her with handcuffs. Well, except himself, he thought with a handful of lusty thoughts.

Shaking his head to clear out those images, he reminded himself that the police wouldn't be gentle if they arrived to arrest her again when it was their second arrest in less than twenty-four hours.

So when she appeared in his line of sight again, her arms loaded down with something he couldn't immediately identify, he went through what he knew of her. She didn't have a gun, at least not one that he could see. So how was she going to rob the store? He knew the store owner and wouldn't allow her to hurt any of Louey's employees. Louey was a good guy with five kids and ten grandkids. He needed every cent he could earn from the convenience store.

He was actually still standing there, debating what to do when the night shift employee laughed at something Mia said to him and started loading whatever she'd dumped onto the counter into a large, brown bag.

Was she stealing supplies for some heist? He saw her hand the guy a credit card and something in his chest eased somewhat. A true criminal wouldn't purchase items with a credit card. It was too easy to trace. Okay, that was yet another ridiculous thought. A true criminal wouldn't even have credit cards. Would they?

So what was she buying? What on earth could be so important that she had to go out in the middle of the night when she should be exhausted after the day she'd had.

When she came out of the store, he was still standing there, glaring down at her with his hands on his hips. "What was so important, Mia?" he asked.

He had a small sense of satisfaction to see her startled reaction to his presence. She looked up at him, worried and trying to hide the bag under her arm. "Ash! What on earth are you doing up at this time of the night?" she demanded.

Ash wasn't going to let her hide anything from him. "Remember what I said earlier today about full disclosure?" he asked, moving closer to her, invading her space before he wrenched the brown paper bag out of her hands. "What did you need that was so urgent that you had to sneak out at…?" He was looking into the bag and words failed him. He blinked once. Then again. Trying to focus on what he was seeing.

Impossible!

"Mia! What the hell were you doing sneaking out in the middle of the night to buy ice cream?" he demanded angrily.

Mia shifted on her feet, feeling embarrassed to be caught with her kryptonite. "Just give it back to me!" she demanded, holding out her hands and trying to get it back from him without actually touching him. She'd thought he looked nice in a suit and then he'd revealed a bit of that tanned, yummy looking skin over dinner. Now he was wearing jeans that molded to his muscular thighs and a tee shirt that was stretched taught over those bulging muscles in his arms and chest. That wasn't fair! He should be ugly or flabby or short and rude or…something! The man was just…damn him! He was hot!

Ash laughed as the relief surged through him. "You couldn't sleep so you had to sneak out and get…" he counted quickly, "six different flavors of ice cream?" he demanded.

"Give me back my bag!" she growled, reaching up and trying to take her ice cream bag back. But he was too tall and he held it over his head, way out of her reach. "You're being a jerk, Ash. Just give me back my bag!"

Ash wrapped his arm around her waist, laughing at her angry expression. "Don't you remember me telling you that everything you need is in my place?" he asked.

She sighed and glared up at him, pressing her palms against his chest, trying to put some room between their bodies, but he wasn't giving an inch and she was starting to react to his closeness. She needed that ice cream! "Ash, if you don't give me back my bag, I'm not going to be responsible for my actions!" She wished she could come up with something more specific, some dire threat that would make him reconsider holding her ice cream away from her. But she couldn't think about anything with his arm around her waist. And he smelled so good! Now that she was closer to him, she could smell his spicy, male scent that filled up her nostrils and made her ache to bury her nose in his chest or against his neck and just…inhale!

"Come with me," he said and grabbed her hand, pulling her back to his building.

"You're being a bully!" she said, following simply because she didn't have a choice. First of all, she wasn't going to be able to sleep until she'd had her ice cream which he didn't seem inclined to give back to her. And secondly, when Ash wanted her to move somewhere, he didn't really take no for an answer.

In the small elevator, she pressed her shoulders back against the paneled wall and crossed her arms over her chest. "You're a rude, insensitive jerk, you know that?"

Even words didn't hurt the big lug, she thought with resentment. He just laughed at her anger. When the front door opened up, he grabbed her hand again and pulled her all the way through to his stainless steel and brick kitchen. When the two of them were standing in front of the enormous freezer, he looked down at her a moment before opening the door.

And Mia just stared, not sure if she could believe her eyes.

Row after row on his freezer sat just about every different kind of ice cream she could imagine. There were maybe twenty different kinds and her mouth started drooling. "You're kidding!" she gasped with delight and surprise.

"I guess I should have told you that I love ice cream," he said. He turned to face her and a moment later, his hands were on her waist lifting her up. He lifted her easily and set her back down on the counter behind her. "My favorite is praline pecan, but feel free to try out each one and give it a try."

Mia thought she might have just died and gone to heaven. When Ash put a spoon in front of her face, she grabbed it, then twisted around, balancing herself on the counter while she grabbed the chocolate brownie ice cream. She didn't say a word but instead, dove into the ice cream, leaning against the counter behind her while she spooned the rich, creamy dessert into her mouth.

"I think I might have to marry you," she mumbled, then realized what she'd just said and looked up at him, startled and worried about his reaction.

He was reaching into the freezer himself and opened up the cherry vanilla ice cream, his own spoon already in his hand. "I accept. When's the wedding?"

Mia's mind froze and she looked up at him, suddenly realizing what she'd just said. When he only winked down at her as he dug into his own ice cream container, she sighed with relief. He was only taking the comment as a joke, which was how it was meant. Sort of.

Her mind froze again. Okay, she asked herself mentally, where had that "sort of" come from? Of course she'd been teasing! She shifted on the counter, tucking her feet underneath her and taking another large spoonful of the chocolate dessert. "Why couldn't you sleep?" she asked

He took a large spoonful of the cherry vanilla, then put the top back on the container and pulled out the rocky road. "I was sound asleep. I heard you sneak out and it woke me up."

She looked up at him sheepishly, feeling horrible for disturbing his slumber. "I'm sorry," she said and took another bite. "Whenever I have trouble sleeping, ice cream always makes me fall asleep faster. Probably the sugar and the milk, or something."

They talked a little about the case, more about their favorite ice creams and some about the different things they did to relax when they were stressed about work or life. By the time she was yawning, it was almost one o'clock in the morning.

"I think I can go to sleep now," she said with a sleepy smile and jumped off of the counter. She put the cartons of mostly melted ice cream back into the freezer, feeling self-conscious now that he was watching her in her bare feet, looking bedraggled after a long, difficult day.

She leaned against the counter slightly, smiling up at him. "Well...." She felt awkward and that painful awareness came raging back. "Good night," she said softly. "Again."

He chuckled, but moved closer, inexorably drawn to her softness. "Goodnight, Mia," he replied.

He wanted to touch her, to kiss her but it was late. She'd been up for almost twenty-four hours and he refused to take advantage of her.

Mia shifted on her feet, feeling a strange sort of power overtake her. It might have just been exhaustion, but she didn't care. Not at this point anyway.

She walked over to him and lifted up on her bare feet. She'd meant to just give him a soft, gentle kiss and then skitter away.

That was the plan anyway.

She lifted up but she lost her balance slightly and reached out to steady herself by placing her hand in the middle of his chest. She looked at her hand, felt his heartbeat underneath her fingers. She just stared, barely moving, barely breathing. For a long moment, they just stood there like that.

She felt her eyes move upwards as if in slow motion. She'd seen this in the movies so many times but it was surreal now. When her eyes looked into his, there was a complete awareness of him as a man.

Her hand moved higher, her fingers wrapping around his neck and she lifted her head to kiss him. She held her breath, needing so desperately to feel his lips against hers, to know what it was like to be kissed by this man. He hesitated for only a fraction of a second before lowering his head. She couldn't have kissed him without his help and she almost sobbed with relief when his lips finally touched hers.

She gasped at the heat that erupted with that barely-there touch. Mia pulled back, startled and looked into his eyes. He was looking right back at her. But his expression hardened, the heat flared to a roaring fire and his hands, which had been gripping the stone counter behind him, whipped around to hold her close, pulling her even more solidly against his hard body. One hand dove into her hair, holding her head in place while his lips ravished hers and the other arm wrapped round her waist, lifting her higher against his hard frame and making her whimper with need.

After that first touch, he wasn't gentle. But nor did Mia want gentleness. She might have cried against any kind of tenderness from this man. Right now, she desperately wanted only to be devoured. She wanted everything this hard, kind, generous and intelligent man had to give and he delivered without further hesitation. Over and over again he tilted his head, kissing her, his tongue diving into her mouth and demanding that hers mate with his. And when she complied, her whole body melted into his as he pulled her even closer.

She didn't feel him lift her up or spin her around. All she knew was that his heat was spreading to every portion of her body. Her mind was no longer in control. Only desire had control. Her hands were gripping his hair, holding him close so he couldn't get away. When he tore his mouth away from hers, she whimpered with need but the hand in her hair pulled her head backwards and she sighed with delight when his mouth nibbled on her neck and her earlobe, causing her to shudder with increased need. And then suddenly his mouth was back, he was demanding more, kissing her as if he were feeling everything she was feeling. She thrilled to that need in him even as it scared her a little.

And then it was over. He pulled back, their breathing heavy as they looked at each other. Realization slowly dawned on her and her mind started working once again. She looked around, getting her bearings. She was no longer standing on the floor but instead, she was sitting on his countertop, his hips between her legs and pressing against her core.

He pulled back just as she realized their position.

"I'm sorry, Mia. That won't happen again," he said softly. With strong, deft fingers, he lifted her off of the counter top. But then he walked stiffly away, taking the stairs two or three at a time as he put as much space between them as he could.

Mia stood there for several more minutes, wondering how a simple kiss had gotten so out of control. She'd never experienced anything like that before. And to experience it now, with a man she didn't even like? And who...

"Oh no," she sighed, the horrifying events of the day surging back to her mind.

"No," she told herself firmly. Shaking her head, she pulled herself together. With equal parts exhaustion and determination, she slowly made her way up the stairs and to the bedroom he'd loaned her. Sliding between the sheets, her last thought was if she would ever be able to fall asleep after that kiss.

Over the next three days, Ash worked like a demon. He was everywhere, arguing with the district attorney, examining evidence, going through all the documents the police had picked up and doing just about everything he could to get the charges dropped.

During the day, he kept Mia close by. Sometimes she would be working with Mark or his team. Other times, he might have her right next to him while his legal team went through the evidence.

The nights were the hardest though. He wouldn't let her go home, coming up with one reason after another why she should stay in his brownstone. He cooked dinner for her every night and talked with her about whatever came to mind while they drank wine or beer. He loved the fact that she enjoyed both.

And every night, he kissed her goodnight, enjoying the soft way she responded to his touch. She never failed to drive him crazy with her touch, but he was also careful not to let things get too out of control. It was hard because his body was aching to possess hers. But there was a line he wouldn't cross and making love to a client, especially one as vulnerable and kind as Mia, was something he simply wouldn't do no matter how much his body hurt.

CHAPTER 5

Ash gripped his cell phone in his hand, worry surpassing all other emotions right now. "Mia, where are you?" he demanded, knowing she'd left his place and she wasn't here in the office with him. That meant she wasn't where he could protect her and he didn't like that feeling.

He'd left his brownstone this morning after checking on her, watching her sleep for perhaps a bit longer than might be appropriate. But after their kiss last night, he'd had trouble tearing his eyes away from her. She'd looked so peaceful this morning – the exact opposite of how he felt right now.

"I'm just heading over to my place. I need some different clothes and I need to figure out what's going on with my house. I'm a little anxious after you mentioned the relatively fresh cement in my basement that was being torn up. It was put into the basement to stop the recurring flooding so now there's the added possibility that my house might flood with the next heavy rain."

Since Ash had just discussed the status of her little cottage with the police detective in charge of the investigation, his stomach clenched with worry over her reaction to what her house might look like. "Mia, if you need something, have Autumn go over and get it. If she's unavailable, I'll get someone else to do it or I'll do it myself," he said, quickly grabbing his coat off of the back of his chair and rushing out of the office. He might have known Mia for a little only a few days, but he was already starting to get to know this stubborn little woman and he was pretty sure she would ignore his suggestion.

She laughed and he gritted his teeth. She was certainly in a wonderful mood this morning. It was amazing what a good night's sleep had done for her. He wished he could say the same. That kiss had driven all possibility of sleep out of his mind last night. He'd lain awake, thinking of her soft, warm body in the bed just one room next to him and he'd ached to touch her again, hear her soft sighs when he touched her silky skin.

"Ash, don't worry about me. I'm tired of relying on everyone else, especially when I'm perfectly able to do things for myself."

Ash pressed the call button for the elevator several times, frantic to get to her before she saw what the police had done to her house. "Mia, just turn around and head back to my place," he said with what he hoped was a gentle voice but he wasn't sure. He was gritting his teeth as he spoke, too worried about her seeing her yard. "No one thinks you're relying on them too much. We're more than happy to help."

"I'm fine, Ash. Thank you for your help, but I'm just going to run home, take a shower with my own stuff and get my own clothes. I know the press might still be a problem so I'll be careful."

She wasn't listening to him and everything she said made perfect sense, but he knew the details! He had to stop her somehow! "Mia, don't you dare go back to your house," he commanded, relying on old instincts.

Mia pulled the cell phone back from her ear. "What just happened here?" she asked, her voice definitely colder. "You can't order me about, Ash."

He knew that was the truth but he didn't like it. Hell, he wished he had the right to simply tell her to turn around, or even better, he wished she trusted him enough to listen to him and trust him. That didn't make any difference now. She would be so upset if she saw her house. He just knew it!

"Mia, after the past few nights, I can damn well tell you what to do and I want you to tell the cab driver to turn around and head back to my place or to my office right now. If you don't want anyone else in your place, fine. I'll get your stuff for you later. Or even better, I'll bring you there myself." Really, he just didn't want her to see what had happened before he could fix everything. "Just turn around now," he said with as much authority as he could muster under the circumstances. "I'm getting in the elevator now. I'll meet you back at my place."

Mia was irritated with his tone and wasn't going to take orders from him or any man. Not after everything that had happened over the past week. "Goodbye Ash," she said and pressed the end button on her cell phone.

She dumped it right back into her purse, then fished it out again and pressed the silent mode. If she knew anything about Ash by now, it was that he didn't give up. He'd call her right back.

Ash stared at his phone for half a second before his anger exploded. He immediately hit redial even while he was rushing to his car. When her voice mail picked up, he was furious and worried all at the same time. "Damn it, Mia. Pick up the phone and call me back. Don't you dare go over to your house! I'm telling you now to just turn around. I'll take you over there myself tonight."

He dove into his car, tires screeching as he pulled out of the parking space. He ran three red lights in an attempt to get to her place faster. He didn't want her seeing what the police had done. After everything she'd gone through, this would be the final blow. He didn't know what she would do and he didn't want to take the chance that this would be the straw that broke her.

He pressed the call button on his steering wheel, cursing when he got her voice mail again. "Mia, call me back right now! I'm ordering you to stop doing this and call me!"

He drove three more miles and pressed the button again. When he only got her voice mail one more time, he shook his head and pressed the accelerator. "Mia, don't do this. I'm telling you," he said, changing from anger to coaxing, determined to stop her somehow, "just turn around and come back to my place."

She didn't even look at her cell phone again, feeling empowered now that she was finally heading home. She felt like she'd been gone for months instead of just days and she was eager to be around her own things, to sort through her mind and figure out what was going on.

Mia already had the money ready to pay the cab driver before they turned the corner on her street. But when the cab driver pulled up in front of her house, she couldn't believe her eyes. With a horrible, stabbing pain shooting through her entire body, she handed the cab driver the money and stepped out of the vehicle. Unfortunately, she couldn't go any further.

Her entire front yard was torn up. All her carefully planted hydrangeas, which had been lovely earlier in the summer, some pink, some blue and some with a creamy white, were just a wilted, scattered mess on the ground. Her roses and hostas, all were reduced to clumps of brown on top of the sidewalk. Even her grass had been torn up. There wasn't anything that wasn't destroyed. She could even see through her back gate that the backyard was worse than the front, if that was even possible.

She'd spent so many happy hours working on her garden, researching the plants that would grow easily in this area, making sure that they were well fertilized with organic compost, going around to the various coffee shops and getting extra coffee grounds, asking all of her neighbors to save their egg shells and banana peels just so her hostas were a deep, dark green and her roses could make it through the harsh winters and tough summers. And now everything was destroyed! It wasn't just that the yard had been dug up, it had been destroyed. She had no idea how to save these plants. If holes had been dug around them, she could help the plants survive. But these guys had been out of the soil for several days now. They hadn't had any water or food and their roots had dried up from the heat and no protection.

She just stood there, her heart breaking as the pain of her little house sunk in.

She didn't even hear the car skid to a halt behind her. But she felt Ash's presence as soon as he was next to her. She could feel his heat and that odd sense of security and sexual tension that she always felt when he was around her.

"Mia…" he started to say, not sure how to explain the disaster her home had become. He wasn't even looking at the house, only at her devastated expression and he ached to fix it somehow for her.

She didn't say anything, just looked up into his eyes. A moment later, she threw herself towards him and Ash closed his arms around her, holding her close and whispering in her ear how sorry he was for what the investigators had done to her house. It was the worst he'd ever seen. Never in his career had any search warrant gone this far but he suppressed his anger in order to help Mia through this devastation.

Mia had no idea how long she cried but when the sobbing slowed to an ebb, she remained in Ash's arms, drawing strength from him. With him holding her like this, she knew she could get through just about anything.

She pulled back slightly, noticing the wet area on his chest where her tears had dampened his shirt. He looked down at her, the kindness and anger obvious in his eyes. That anger was on her behalf and not directed at her and even that made her feel better, comforted somehow. "Come on, Mia. Let me get you out of here. I'm sorry you had to see this," he said gently.

Mia smiled up at him. "Is that why you were trying to order me around earlier?"

He chuckled softly despite his frustration over her stubbornness. "Yes. I knew what they'd done."

She felt better now. So he wasn't just trying to be a jerk. He was trying to be a sweet, kind man. "Thank you," she replied sincerely, taking a deep breath and turning back to her cottage. "Well, I guess I have a lot of work to do." She put her hands on her hips and looked around, mentally taking an inventory of all that needed to be done.

"I guess it's probably worse inside, isn't it?" she asked, not bothering to turn around and look up at him. She knew the answer. If they'd thought she'd buried him and torn up the yard, she suspected that they might have even considered that she'd chopped up the body and hid it inside her walls somehow. That was a gruesome thought so she pushed it aside, deciding not to borrow trouble until she knew the extent of the interior damage. Don't borrow trouble, she told herself firmly.

She walked up the path, bending down to examine some of the plants that were littered along the way. "They could have been a bit kinder on the roots," she said, almost to herself.

Ash walked behind her, not exactly sure what to do or how to help her through this. He was also confused as to what might be going through her mind. Only moments ago, she'd been sobbing out her anguish over her devastated home and now she was walking through the war-like zone as if this were just another chore.

"Mia?" he called out, reaching down to touch her shoulder.

Mia stood, looking up at him with a wilted hosta plant in each hand. "What's wrong?" she asked.

Ash didn't know what to say. "What's wrong?" he repeated, stunned that she would even ask. "Your house is destroyed, your plants all killed and you're still facing murder charges. That's what's wrong." He put his hands on her shoulders, trying to determine how upset she really was. If he were in her shoes, he'd be furious and launching a full out law suit against the city for the way they'd handled this search warrant.

Mia sighed, glanced around one more time, then smiled up at him. "Yes, that's all true. I can't do anything about the murder charges. I have to leave that up to you and just answer any questions that come up. You're the brilliant lawyer who has kept me out of jail so you're on top of that, as far as I'm concerned." She sighed as she continued. "I can't figure out what happened to Jeff. Something inside of me is telling me that he's fine, possibly on a warm, lush Caribbean island somewhere hanging out, not even aware that people are looking for him, but I can't believe that even he is that self-centered. Besides, I don't have my passport, so it isn't like I can fly off and search for him, can I?" She looked around at her yard, determination brightening her cheeks and stiffening her spine. "But I can do something about my yard. And you're going to get rid of the murder charges for me. Everything else is just noise."

It struck him how sensible her attitude was. And yes, he was definitely going to get her out of these ridiculous murder charges. The district attorney's office couldn't even find the body, but that didn't eliminate the possibility of a conviction, it just made it harder for the prosecution to prove their case. But circumstantial evidence could prove the case for them. It was dangerous to rely on reasonable thinking in these kinds of situations. Not everyone on a jury was reasonable.

"Mark and the rest of my team are slowly breaking down the prosecution's case, Mia. We'll get rid of these charges and figure out what really happened." He looked around the yard again, "But you can't stay here. Come on back to my place and I'll get someone out here to fix this for you."

Mia shook her head. "Goodness, I can't afford anyone to come clean up this mess for me," she replied.

After everything else, he couldn't let her deal with this. It was just too much. "Let me do this for you," he countered, determined to protect her however possible.

She smiled, grateful for the offer but shook her head. "I can't let you do that. You already feel bad enough." She sighed and looked around. "Besides, I enjoy gardening." She grimaced slightly and looked up at him. "Just make sure my freezer is stocked with ice cream tonight because I'm going to be pretty sore."

Ash wanted to curse but refrained, knowing that it would offend Mia. "I want to do this," he argued. "And you don't need this extra burden."

"Actually," she smiled and looked around, "fixing up all of this will give me something to do rather than worry about Jeff and the upcoming trial. I don't mind the work. Since I can't go to school until this is figured out, I might as well do something productive." She smiled up at him. "It will be just like your house renovations. You mentioned how easy it was to work through problems while you're working with wood or staining something. Well, I feel the same way about gardening. It makes me feel strong and powerful, somehow giving back to the earth a little bit." She shrugged her shoulders as she said, "Gardening is good for the soul."

Out of the corner of his eye, Ash caught a movement coming down the sidewalk. His first instinct was to shove her back into his car, not wanting her to have to deal with whatever some mean-spirited neighbor wanted to say to her.

They both turned at the same time to find an elderly couple approaching. Ash was just about to push Mia behind him, protecting her from what he expected would be a brutal verbal assault. Neighbors usually trusted the police, so when they arrested someone, the community automatically assumed that the person was guilty.

Ash was again stunned. The couple stopped right in front of her, their eyes gentle and concerned without even a hint of malice. "Mia, tell us where we can help," the man who looked to be about sixty or sixty-five, said while his wife nodded next to him. "We're here to fix up all this mess and get you back on your feet."

The woman reached out and gently touched Mia's hand, showing her support with the tender touch. "We couldn't believe what the police did to your beautiful yard, dear. We told them over and over again that you didn't kill that horrible man. We know you didn't do it. So just tell us what you need and we're here for you, honey."

Mia smiled warmly to the couple, reaching out to shake their hands. Instead, the couple reached out and gave her a bone crushing hug. "That's so generous of you," she said and Ash could hear the wobble in her tone again.

When she pulled back, she introduced Ash to the couple. "Arnie, Beth, this is my attorney, Ash Thorpe. Ash, these are the Corrinders. They live about three houses down and have four kids and ten grandkids."

Arnie Corrinder squinted at Ash and came a bit closer. "You're going to get our girl out of this mess, right? There's absolutely no way she could have murdered that slime, but if he ever turns up, you'd better believe I'm going to kill him for what he's put our girl through!"

Ash was so surprised that the man was confessing to murderous thoughts that he grinned. "I have a whole team of people who are working long hours to figure out who actually killed Mr. Meyers."

Beth shook her head. "I can't believe Jeff just disappeared, but I really don't like that new fiancée of his," she explained, latching onto Mia's arm protectively. "I'm sure she's up to something. When Jeff finally turns up, dead or alive, I'm putting my money on him being in her basement somehow." The woman tsked, shaking her head before she said, "Probably chained up and gagged just to keep his mouth shut," she said to her husband with a completely serious expression. "He tried to kick the Jameson's dog," she said as if that explained everything. "And when the Jameson's stopped him, that stupid man actually yelled at them. As if he had every right to stand out here and wake us up on a Saturday morning with his ridiculous wrath."

Mia nodded, remembering that day. "That was one of the times he'd shown up, unannounced, trying to get me to reconsider our engagement. It happened about two months ago."

Ash heard something behind him and spun around. There were about five more people coming from different directions, some had shovels and other gardening tools in their hands and all of them looked ready to either attack Mia as a mob or attack the dirt, he wasn't sure which.

"We saw ya coming!" one man said as he rounded the corner, pushing a wheelbarrow filled with gardening tools. "We're here to help! Just tell us what you need."

Mia's eyes turned misty and she bowed her head. Ash thought he might have spied her shoulders shake slightly, but she shook it off and lifted her head. He almost gasped at the glow of happiness that surrounded her at that moment. He was stunned by the beauty both inside of her and around her as her friends and neighbors surrounded her, dropping what they were doing so they could show up and help replant her devastated yard.

"They tore up the inside, too, Mia. Don't you dare go inside," a female voice said. Ash turned around and there were five women, all who had buckets, brooms and mops. "You just give us your house key and stay out here to direct the work. We'll be inside, cleaning up what those bastards did to your house."

Ash shook his head, never having witnessed anything so astonishing. One and all just took a corner of the yard and started raking or digging, ready to try and plant the wilted shrubs and rose bushes. One man even swore he could revive the hostas and piled all of them up into his arms as if they were his babies.

By the end of the day, the yard was back in order. He suspected it wasn't up to its previous glory, but it looked pretty good. He'd secretly called a gardening center and had several new bushes delivered. He had no idea what to order, but told them to bring stuff that was hardy as well as a load of mulch. He also ordered fifty pizzas to be delivered. The pizzas arrived at noon and someone brought out pitchers of lemonade and even some beer. No one stopped working though. The gardening center's truck pulled up after the pizza had been devoured and everyone simply took a bush or a bag of mulch and planted the bush, surrounding the roots with the mulch for protection from the upcoming winter. The nights were already cooler with cold starting to seep into the air. The fall was a strange time when one day could be hot, everyone walking around in short sleeves, while the next one everyone needed a coat.

No matter how many times her neighbors told her to stand back, Mia was right there in the thick of the repairs. She was covered in sweat and dirt, smiling at anyone who approached her to ask her where she wanted one plant or another. Even Ash drove home and changed into jeans and a tee-shirt. It took him less than an hour, but he was right back there, doing all the heavy lifting so the elderly people wouldn't hurt themselves. Anything that had to be moved or lifted, he tried to insert himself. Several times throughout the day, he looked over at her and winked or just absorbed her happiness. There wasn't much he could do, but the more he looked at her, the more he wanted her in his bed. He wanted to be the one to give her that contentment or excited expression.

If she would just stop this assertion that he was only trying to comfort her, they could curl up together, just the two of them tonight, and find bliss in each other's arms. And if he could just get this murder charge out of the way, he could show her how much he was starting to care for her. In just a few days, she'd gotten under his skin like no other woman ever had.

By the end of the day, just as the sun was setting over the horizon, he stood next to her as the last of her neighbors gave her a weak hug and walked down the sidewalk to their own homes. Every single one of them told him to call if he needed anything to get her out of this mess.

When the door closed on the last one, Mia looked across the room at Ash. "You stink," she teased.

Ash laughed and moved forward. "And you look sexy as hell," he replied. He'd enjoyed working with her today, laughing with her, watching her with her neighbors. She treated each of them as if they were special and, in turn, they treated her as if she were one of their children.

Mia rolled her eyes. "I probably smell worse than you."

"Where's your shower?" he asked.

Her eyes widened. "Shower?"

"Yes, the place where water comes down out of a faucet and there's generally soap?" He didn't wait for her to answer. Instead, he walked up the stairs to find it himself. "Never mind," he called back down the stairs. Then slammed the bathroom door closed.

She heard the water turn on and her mind couldn't stop picturing him in the shower. And she had an extremely good imagination. The hot water running down those muscles would be like a work of art, she thought. She could just imagine taking her washcloth and smoothing soap all over his chest, those powerful arms and all of that delicious skin on his back. On second thought, forget the washcloth. She wanted her hands on him. She didn't want anything between her fingers and his skin.

In less time than she would have liked, the water shut off again. It took him only moments before the door opened. He moved down the stairs, one hand holding a pink towel over his head as he rubbed his hair and another pink towel precariously wrapped around his lean hips. The towel was perfectly sized for her, but on him, the material barely went around his muscular legs, giving her an eyeful whenever he took a step.

She knew she was staring, but as he approached, she didn't think any woman in the world would blame her. The man was...shocking! Every part of his body was covered with muscles. She suspected that his body fat percentage was somewhere in the zero range. There wasn't a single part of the man that wasn't perfectly chiseled.

He was standing over her, looking down at her before he said, "Your turn," with that sexy, no-nonsense voice of his.

Mia wasn't sure what he was talking about. "My turn?" she asked, wondering if she was going to get her turn at touching all that wonderful, delicious, incredible...

"For a shower," he clarified.

Mia was stumped. A shower had been so far from her mind that it didn't even make sense. And then it struck her. "Shower!" she exclaimed and stood upright. "Yes, a shower!"

She stepped around him, moving up the stairs as quickly as possible. She was proud of herself for only stumbling on three of the steps but figured she earned extra credit for not turning around and gawking at him some more.

In the shower, she leaned against the door, smelling her own soap mingled with the maleness that was pure "Ash".

"You're in deep," she whispered to herself.

"Hurry up, Mia. I'll make some dinner."

That startled her away from the door and she reached in to turn on the shower. She didn't see where his clothes were, but she stripped off her own and threw them into the hamper. She stepped into the warm water, feeling a strong sense of intimacy, knowing that Ash had been in here only a few minutes ago. She loved how it felt to have the bathroom already warm from the steam of his shower.

She was so lost in the fantasy in her mind where Ash was still in the shower and he was helping her wash off...and she got to help him wash off, she didn't hear the knock on the door.

It wasn't until he poked his face behind the shower curtain that she realized he was in her bathroom and she yelped, trying to hide her nakedness with whatever she had. And the plastic scrunchie filled with soap really wasn't up to the task. His smile, and the dark glance down her body, told her that she was failing completely.

"You're too slow, babe. Hurry up. Dinner is ready."

With that, his face disappeared again and she heard the door close softly.

It still took her several minutes before she was able to move again. But after that, she rushed through her shower in record time, rinsing out the shampoo and conditioner faster than she thought possible.

In her bedroom, she tightened the towel around her chest, staring at her closet, trying to figure out what to wear.

"What's taking so long?" he asked, standing right behind her.

Mia spun around, her fingers once more grabbing the towel that was knotted just under her arms. "What are you doing in here?" she gasped. She looked him up and down, painfully disappointed that he'd lost the pink towel and was now wearing a clean pair of jeans and yet another one of those tee-shirts that made her drool as she took in the muscles straining the fabric to the limit.

"Trying to figure out why you're letting our dinner get cold." His eyes traveled up and down her damp figure with appreciation. "If you're trying to figure out if that works for you, let me be the first to say that I am in full agreement with you coming down exactly like that," he said with a sexy leer on his handsome face.

She grabbed a pair of yoga pants from her closet and a clean tee-shirt. "I'll be down in less than five minutes," she promised.

"Make it two," he told her, then disappeared again.

Mia didn't challenge him. She pulled on the yoga pants, a bra and tee shirt, then added a pair of socks, as if they could protect her against what she was feeling right now. Socks really weren't the best protection against throwing herself into Ash's arms, but she didn't have much else. Her thinking was, if she looked homely enough, it would keep her from wanting him as much.

As soon as she walked down the stairs, she knew that her thinking was painfully flawed. His hot eyes looked up from the plates that he'd already set up on the counter. Those eyes traveled from the top of her head where her hair was still wet, all the way down her body to her sock-clad toes peeking out from underneath her yoga pants.

"Is that what you wear to yoga class?" he asked, gripping the spatula in one hand and the handle of the pan in the other.

"Yes," she replied, smoothing her hands down her thighs self-consciously.

He nodded slowly, his eyes still moving along her petite figure. "I might just take up yoga so I can watch one day."

The idea of this big, strong, masculine man attending her yoga class, moving into all the various positions, somehow seemed hilariously funny to her. "I don't think that would be a good idea," she replied. "What did you make for dinner this time?" she asked, walking up to the counter and looking down at the plates.

"Pancakes. You need to get food other than diet meals," he growled and looked down, piling two more pancakes on her plate. "And what's with this veggie sausage?" he asked with obvious distrust. "I don't think anything that isn't meat should try and pass itself off as meat." But he plunked three of them on his plate and two on hers.

She laughed again, relieved by the slight dispersion in the sexual tension between them. "The sausages are delicious," she replied, shaking her head because she usually had only one of them for breakfast with a piece of fruit. She'd never be able to eat all that food, but Ash couldn't seem to grasp that she ate about a third of what he could go through during a meal.

"And you need real syrup," he snarled, plunking the sugar free syrup onto the middle of the table. "Sit," he said but softened the order by pulling out her chair, then sliding it in when she was seated. He then moved to the chair opposite her and she couldn't help but smile at how sexy he looked in her periwinkle kitchen surrounded by shabby chic curtains and pillows, not to mention the flowers on the window sill looking out from over her sink. The police hadn't done any permanent damage and even her inside plants and flowers were saved from their ruthless search, probably because they knew she couldn't hide a body in their small pots.

"What's so funny?" he asked as he cut up his enormous stack of pancakes, then poured her sugar-free syrup all over them.

"You."

He looked up, his dark eyebrows raised in question.

She couldn't help but laugh. He was just so tough looking – the complete antithesis of her entire household décor. "You just don't fit in with the pretty periwinkle kitchen," she said, laughing once again.

He rolled his eyes. "I should probably take offense at that, but I can't help but agree. My masculinity is at risk here."

She giggled but stuffed a bite of pancakes into her mouth, savoring the amazing taste. "What did you put into these?" she asked, closing her eyes in surprise.

"Vanilla and cinnamon," he came back, pouring her a glass of milk. "You need beer, too."

She sighed as if she were in heaven. "I have lemonade if you don't like milk."

He shook his head as if that were completely out of the question. "You're too wholesome. I need to do something about that."

Mia cringed. "Not totally wholesome," she said under her breath, thinking of her thoughts as he came out of the bathroom.

She was looking down at her plate when she said that but her eyes snapped up when she heard his knife and fork clatter onto the plate. "What do you mean by that?" he demanded, his eyes staring into hers with an intensity that caused all rational thinking to fly out the window.

"Um…I…just…"

"What unwholesome thoughts are you thinking, Mia?" he asked. His tone was soft, but it definitely wasn't gentle. Coaxing was a better term to describe the way he was speaking to her. As if he wanted her to reveal….

"I just…" she shrugged, blushing painfully and unable to maintain eye contact with him.

"Might you be having unwholesome thoughts about me?" he asked.

Mia looked up, startled that he could read her so easily. But then again, what else was he supposed to think. "I…"

He could see that she was embarrassed. But he could also see the truth in her eyes. "I can guarantee that almost none of my thoughts are very wholesome when you're around."

With that, her whole body heated up in flash so intense, she thought her chair might catch on fire. In fact, she wiggled slightly, uncomfortable now that she was on one side of the table and he was on the other. "You're my lawyer."

"I am. But I won't be soon."

"Because I'll be in jail?" she gasped.

"No. Because you'll be free. And you won't be my client any longer."

She fiddled with her fork, not sure what to do with her hands when she desperately wanted to run them over those shoulders like she had the last time he'd kissed her. "You're that far ahead on the case?" she asked, hoping that he would confirm that. She didn't even think about her being free. She just wanted him to want her, to believe in her innocence.

"I spoke to the prosecutor this morning before you decided to head over here to investigate. We discussed your case and every time he brought up an issue, I was able to slap it down. He doesn't have much to go on now. And he knows it."

Mia breathed a sigh of relief. "So the charges are going to be dropped, right?"

"I can't guarantee anything," he cautioned.

She smiled slightly, knowing deep down inside that he believed in her. That he knew she hadn't done this horrible thing they were accusing her of. "So that's it? It will all be over?"

"Don't get too excited," he said and leaned over to hold her hand. "I don't want you to get your hopes up about anything because I don't know what will happen tomorrow."

She looked down at his dark fingers tangling with her paler ones, her eyes entranced by the image. What would it be like to have more than her fingers tangled with more than his? What would it be like to have him kiss her and not stop? She'd never wanted this from any other man and she wanted this from him so desperately.

No more fears, she told herself firmly. So when his fingers tightened around hers, she went willingly into his arms, feeling his strong body against hers and reveling in the magic of his touch.

"What about dinner?" she asked, uncaring herself what happened to the food as long as she could continue to feel him touching her like this.

"That's not dinner," he groaned as he lifted her into his arms. "That's unreal sausage and unreal syrup."

She couldn't stop the laughter, but it quickly died when his mouth covered hers. A moment later, he lifted her into his arms and carried her back up the stairs, laying her gently on the bed. "Are you sure about this Mia?" he asked carefully, leaning over her but holding his weight away from hers.

Mia writhed under him, almost angry that he was holding his body away from hers. "I'm very sure," she gasped out. That was the last time she had a moment to talk. He didn't wait for her to change her mind or realize that this wasn't a good idea. If he were a better man, he would hold back until her name was cleared. But he couldn't and he wasn't. He wanted her and it felt like he'd wanted her for so long.

With gentle fingers, he lifted her tee-shirt up and over her head then took a moment to stare down at her soft, full breasts that were almost spilling out of her white, lace bra. "Not too wholesome here," he said with a gravelly voice while his fingers traced the line of her bra, just at the edge, teasing her ever so carefully.

"Ash!" she cried out when he didn't stop or move closer to where she wanted his fingers. "Please!" she gasped. And then he moved closer. Right where she wanted his fingers to be. When his thumb rubbed against the hard nubbin of her nipple, she jerked in reaction and pulled his hand away. But as soon as the sensation was gone, she needed it back again. With her hand holding his wrist, she brought his hand back to her breast, her hand forcing his to cover the whole area.

"Mia!" he groaned and then his head bent, his mouth covering hers while his fingers blindly explored her breast again. First one, then the other, his fingers and palms learned the way she liked to be touched. It seemed that there wasn't any wrong way to touch her, she was so responsive that it made him nearly mad with lust while her body pressed against his hand, her mouth becoming more ravenous as he discovered more secrets about those magnificent globes.

"No more," she gasped when his fingers moved again and she arched against him, almost whimpering with her need and the crazy way he made her feel.

"Much more," he countered and moved his mouth from hers, kissing along her neck, her shoulder and then hovering for a moment over her breast. He waited, wondering what she would do and he almost smiled when she froze, her whole body rigid as she waited for his mouth.

When he took her nipple in his mouth, she practically pushed him off of her but he was prepared for that, remembering her hand pulling his fingers away earlier. So when she tried to grab his head, he simply took her hands in his and had his wicked way with her, holding her still with his body. He didn't stop until she was arching against him once again and then he only stopped so he could move to the other breast, giving it equal attention.

"Ash!" she cried out, desperate for him to stop but not sure if she might be begging him to keep on going either. She wasn't sure about anything right now.

"I know," he said soothingly, but he didn't feel very soothed at all. Her reactions were making him even more crazy. He wanted to just bury himself inside of her heat. Instead, he moved his mouth lower, kissing her along her soft stomach.

Either she was stronger than she appeared or he was in a weak state, because she suddenly lifted up, pushing him backwards. He looked down at her, noting the dreamy look in her eyes and he smiled. Taking off his shirt, he ripped something but didn't look down. "You're mine," he growled as he tossed his jeans behind him. When he was fully naked, he moved closer to her, seeing the worry in her eyes as she took in his size. "It's okay," he crooned, knowing that this would be her first time. He grabbed the foil packet he'd been keeping in his wallet ever since the night of her ice cream adventure. Once he was fully sheathed, he moved down to cover her once again.

"Ash?" she gasped, feeling him against her leg.

"Don't worry," he told her and bent lower, catching her lips with his. Ever so carefully, he kissed her, bringing her back to that heated place where she was moving underneath him, her hips shifting frantically. He suspected she didn't know what she wanted, but he did. When he moved between her legs, he slid one finger inside of her. When she bowed her back, her legs instinctively moving wider for him, he knew she was right back with him.

He felt her slick heat and had to close his eyes to control himself. Every cell in his body wanted to just push into this heat but he wanted her to be with him every step of the way.

When she grabbed his wrist again, he smiled but it might have been more of a grimace. He wasn't sure at this point. "That didn't stop me last time," he said and bent to kiss her stomach, "and it isn't going to stop me this time either."

She quickly started shaking her head, but he didn't give her a chance to argue. He simply slipped another finger inside of her and her grip on his wrist when limp as her body experienced the next level. When her hips shifted, lifting to take his fingers deeper, he couldn't stop himself any longer. Moving over her, he quickly shifted his body into place and switched his fingers for his hard length, entering her hot core slowly so he wouldn't hurt her.

Mia grabbed onto his shoulders, her body no longer under her own control. She wanted this so desperately that she couldn't even form words. She wanted him deeper, but she also wanted him to stop and move away. If he did that though, she might just melt into a pool of desire and then evaporate with the heat.

"Please, now!" she gasped when she felt him move inside her, slightly deeper with each thrust. He was so slow, so gentle and she really didn't want that right now. She wasn't sure how to tell him so she slid her hands down his body. Tomorrow she might be embarrassed about grabbing his butt and pulling him inside her, but at that moment, when he was fully deep inside her, she couldn't be sorry. There was a slight bit of pain, but as she moved her hips, she became fully adjusted to his size and girth. And it felt so perfectly right!

Unfortunately, he started moving and the rightness no longer was present. It wasn't wrong, but could only be described as frantic. When he pulled out, she bit her lip and raised her hips to try and stop him. When he pushed inside her, ever so slowly, she thought she might just scream out or hit him. "Faster!" she cried, not sure what he would do but just instinctively knowing that she needed him to move inside of her, and not at this slow pace.

Ash laughed softly, thrilled that she was so demanding. It was such a turn-on, not to mention feeling her wrap her body around him so perfectly. He lifted her legs, wrapping each one around his waist so he could move deeper and he gave the little lady exactly what she wanted.

As he thrust back and forth, he watched her and could barely hold himself back because Mia in the throes of passion was sensuality personified. She closed her eyes, lifted her hips, her hands moving along his chest and scratching his arms when he moved at a particularly good angle.

In a shorter time than he would have liked, she exploded around him, her body climaxing in such a powerful, mind blowing manner that he almost stopped moving so he could watch her fall apart in his arms. But then his body realized what his mind was about to do and protested vehemently. He pounded into her after that, needing his own release. And when it came, he thought he was actually pouring his life into her slender, beautiful body. It was so complete, so intense that he couldn't even move for a long time afterwards.

Later that night, Ash stared up at the ceiling, holding Mia close against his side. He couldn't believe he had violated his personal code of ethics by sleeping with his client. It was a huge conflict, but as he listened to her deep, even breathing and felt her body snuggle closer to his side, he knew that he wouldn't have changed last night for anything.

He should at least feel guilty, he told himself. But as he examined his feelings, there was absolutely no guilt at all. If he had the chance, he would probably do it all over again. In fact, he would give her a few hours of sleep, and then he would do it all over again. Slowly, more thoroughly. And he would enjoy every single moment of the activity.

So there was really nothing else he could do except make sure that she was proven innocent. As he lay there in her bed surrounded by flowered sheets and flowered pillows, his mind went over every detail of her case. Something was missing besides the victim. He checked off every detail, went through various precedents that could be brought to the issues, ideas that could dismiss the evidence or refute each item when it was brought to court.

When he mentally had everything in place, knowing exactly how he could obliterate the prosecution's case even before it came to trial, he nodded his head. It wasn't good enough though. His ideas would only keep her out of court. They wouldn't prove that she hadn't murdered her ex-fiancé. He had to work harder, find that part that was missing, and bring it to light. He knew it was out there, he just wasn't sure exactly where to look to find it.

But he would.

With a nod of determination, he rolled over and nibbled on Mia's neck. He'd resisted her delectable body while working through everything, but he was finished with his mental checklist and he couldn't resist any longer. She was just too soft, too sweet and just too tempting. His hand smoothed down her body, slowly waking her up and he smiled with anticipation when he saw her smiling even before she opened her eyes.

CHAPTER 6

Ash walked into Mia's school building and looked around. He noted a very well-tended school with the children all laughing as they made their orderly way to their classes. The teachers chatted amongst themselves as they herded their pupils from one place to another, all keeping a watchful eye on the students. When the first bell rang, Ash couldn't help but be impressed by how quickly everything and everyone calmed down and moved to their assigned areas. Classroom doors were shut, the halls quieted down and there was an almost tangible feeling of energy everywhere.

He walked into the office and introduced himself. "I'm Ash Thorpe," he said, handing his card to the secretary.

"Oh, goodness!" she gasped and stood up after reading his card. She blushed as she took in his height, but Ash was used to that reaction. "You're the man defending our Mia, aren't you?" she gushed, clasping her hands together with excitement. "We're all thrilled that you've taken her case."

The others in the room all stopped their work and turned to see what was happening, their fingers halted in midair and papers stopped shuffling. He looked around, startled to have received such a reaction. Most of the time, people were wary of lawyers but this group only looked hopeful and eager. Excited?

Ash cleared his throat, his eyes taking in all the details. "I am. I was wondering if I could interview some of the staff. I know that some of Ms. Paulson's co-workers knew Jeff Richardson and might be able to give me some insight."

The other women looked at each other as if sending a silent message. Then they quickly gathered round, even the principal who came out of her office when she overheard the conversation, a very stern looking woman with a severe suit and no-nonsense attitude. All the women hurried to form a loose circle around him, more than eager to help him with any information. "Whatever you need," the principal replied with a nod of her head, her lips compressed as if she thought that were the only expression appropriate for this situation. "We need her back here as soon as possible."

That was news to him. Mia had stayed away from work for the past several days, always available to his team which was great, but he was now confused. "You mean you didn't put her on administrative leave?" he asked, trying to clarify the situation.

The principal waved her hand at her. "Goodness no, but I suppose the school board might have if she hadn't told me that she would need some personal time to sort this out. She's so sweet to be thinking about us at a time like this," the principal said, shaking her head grimly. "I'm Jeanie," she said, extending her hand. "And you just tell us who you need to speak with and we'll rotate that person out of their classroom for however long you need."

Ash couldn't believe this kind of reception. Normally, he had to threaten legal action to get people to take some time out of their day to help him with his work. That was one of the reasons he normally allowed Mark and his team to do these sorts of interviews and report back to him. Why he was here, Ash hadn't really figured out yet.

He mentally shook his head. That wasn't true at all, he accepted. He was here because he was determined to clear Mia's name. He'd made that decision last night while holding her in his arms and he wanted to be personally involved, to see the reactions of her co-workers and hear from others about Jeff and his relationship with Mia, the woman he now considered his.

Taking a piece of paper out of a file folder, he handed it to the principal. "Here's a list of the people Mia said knew of her relationship between Jeff and herself, and had met Jeff or socialized with them," he said, pulling out a neatly typed list of people.

The principal quickly scanned through the list and it was as if the entire office staff went into full-battle mode. "Eleanor," the principal said, handing the list to the secretary, "make a copy of this list and distribute it around to the other teachers. See if anyone is missing from the list that Mr. Thorpe might need to talk to." She turned to another woman. "Jane, could you get the first three people on this list down to the office? It's going to cause some disruption, but everyone will manage."

Two men walked into the office, obviously both staff members themselves. "I just heard that you need people to cover the classrooms to help Mia," they said. "Where do we go first?"

Within ten minutes, Ash was sitting in a conference room with three people, all of whom were telling him wonderful things about Mia and reviling her ex-fiancé. Apparently, no one liked Jeff Richardson and all were furious with him for the way he stalked her after their breakup. They gave him story after story about how Mia would slip out the back door of the school or a side door, parked her car on a side street or rode the bus, anything possible to slip by Jeff's notice so she could come and go from the school without his harassment. It had gotten so bad, one teacher talked about how she'd spoken to a police officer and asked how to get a restraining order.

"Did you follow through?" Ash asked, sitting up, his pen hovering over the notepaper.

The teacher shook her head, her eyes sad with regret. "Unfortunately, I only got the information last week and I was out sick with the flu. So I never got the chance to tell her what to do before all this happened last week. But I'm sure this is just another trick of Jeff's to get her back. He was a conniving snake," she said, anger brimming within her hazel eyes.

Ash left the school several hours later, chuckling at how protective all of the teachers were of Mia. She seemed to draw that out in several people. Including himself, he thought.

The little woman could take care of herself though. He thought of all the times he'd wanted to comfort her during this process, but she'd simply pulled herself up and worked it out. Of course, she'd tried to defend herself all alone initially which had been a huge mistake. There were too many intricacies within the law that she wouldn't know about. He shook his head, shuddering mentally at what would be happening to her right now if Autumn hadn't seen Mia's name on the docket list.

Mia thought she could do it all and in most cases, she was right. But he was damn well going to take on some of that burden. The woman needed to know her limits. Yoga and ice cream weren't going to solve her problems this time.

And then there was last night, he thought, castigating himself one more time. He'd broken one of his sacred rules. Never get involved with a client. Personal feelings and opinions had no place in his line of business. He was hired to keep people out of jail and he was extremely good at it. If he allowed emotions to muck up the process, it was always dangerous.

Once in his car, he dialed Mark who had gone over to Jeff's school to interview the victim's co-workers and subordinates. "What have you got?" Ash asked as he backed up and started driving back to the office.

"Interesting stuff," Mark replied, sounding confused and more than a little frustrated.

Ash knew the feeling. "All I've got over here are about thirty women who are ready to bake cakes with a steel saw inside and three or four men who are ready to marry Mia. Or at least worship at her feet." He didn't laugh at that though. It really pissed him off that those men were so devoted to Mia. Two of them were even married and the other was old enough to be her grandfather! Each one might argue that they were just concerned co-workers, but Ash knew the signs since he was suffering the same fate.

Mark's next comment broke through Ash's irritation with Mia's male co-workers. "I've discovered some interesting comments and opinions here. Meet me at the front of the school and I'll walk you to where I am. You can listen in on what I'm hearing and form your own opinion. I think there's more to the issue here, although I'm just not sure what it is."

This didn't sound good. "I'll be there in fifteen minutes," Ash replied and swung his steering wheel around so he could change directions.

He was at the school ten minutes later, not nearly as impressed with this school as he was with Mia's workplace. Even the outside wasn't as neat and tidy, but perhaps that was because this was a high school where the kids were a bit more rambunctious and harder to discipline than the elementary school kids.

The bell rang indicating that the students should change classes but many simply lingered in the hallways, not appearing to be in any hurry to move on to their next class. Administrators walked down the halls, ordering people to class, but as Ash watched, the kids only waited until the administrator was past them before they leaned right back against their lockers and continued their conversations.

Even one staff member was standing outside the doors to the building smoking a cigarette. Ash had no way of telling if the staff member was a teacher or administrator, but either way, he knew that smoking in and around school buildings was not permitted.

He saw Mark coming down the hallway towards him and headed in that direction. "What's up?" he asked when he was close enough.

Mark looked down at his notes. "Apparently, Mia borrowed several pieces of equipment from the physical education department for an event at her school and they haven't been returned. She also got Jeff to order some audio/visual equipment that was shipped directly to her."

None of that made any sense. Especially since he'd been in her house and her school and there wasn't any audio visual equipment anywhere to be seen. "Why would she order A/V equipment?"

Mark shrugged his shoulders in response. "That's the big question everyone here is asking. They want their stuff back."

His eyes narrowed on Mark's comments. "What do you mean, everyone?" he asked.

Mark scratched his head. "According to several other people, Jeff ordered equipment for the classrooms and gymnasium but Mia convinced him to send it through her so she could be a second accounting system. No one understands the new process, but apparently it started over a year ago and has been ongoing until Jeff disappeared last week."

Ash raised his eyebrows with this news. Mia hadn't said anything about doing any sort of accounting work for her ex-fiance, nor had she ever mentioned being particularly interested in numbers. "I guarantee that she doesn't have any A/V equipment at her house," Ash confirmed but he was looking down at his own notes so he didn't see Mark's surprised reaction to the news that his boss was familiar enough with the interior of their client's house to know about its contents. "So Jeff was ordering school supplies and pushing everything through Mia. How was she paying for the equipment to the vendors? More specifically, why weren't the supplies being ordered through the school board? I would think those things were done by the county's accounting department. I can't even imagine how Jeff had the ability to order supplies, much less dictate his own accounting procedures. Do you have an estimate on the total cost of all that was ordered this way?" Ash asked.

Mark went through his notes, calculating in his mind. "I would estimate about three hundred thousand, but that's just the stuff I've been able to find so far. I'm pretty sure there are more items purchased through Ms. Paulson for the school that haven't arrived yet."

Ash thought about that for a long moment, considering options. "This doesn't really look good for her," he said on a sigh.

Mark nodded his head. "I don't think the police have discovered this information yet. But when they do, it might actually revoke her bail."

Ash's jaw was tense. "I agree. So we have to figure out this latest twist before the police find out."

Mark crossed his arms over his chest and nodded in agreement. "And before the press. They were pretty brutal about her yesterday."

That caught his attention. "What do you mean?" He hadn't seen anything on the news, but then he hadn't watched the news last night either. Nor had he been into his office to get any information from his assistant.

Mark looked up, surprised. "Didn't you read the papers this morning?"

Ash shook his head. "No. I went directly over to Mia's school and started interviewing her co-workers." He looked around once again, seeing the school administrators in their office joking around about something. Not a very efficient work place, he thought with irritation. "What did the papers say?" he asked, still watching the administrators lounging around, drinking coffee and not appearing to be doing the business of the school in any way.

"The papers were talking about her relationship with Jeff. Apparently someone sent them information that she wanted to get back together with him but he wouldn't even talk to her. She became pretty angry with him and started hanging out in front of his school in an effort to get his attention."

Ash's eyebrows rose with that news. "What was the source?" he demanded, thinking of Mia and how soft she'd been earlier this morning. He completely discarded the idea that Mia was stalking her ex-fiancé. He'd heard too many stories about how Jeff was driving Mia crazy with his crazy antics for him to put any credibility towards the newspaper story. That was just another piece to the puzzle.

"The reporter claimed a confidential source so we don't have a name. But the story was pretty derogatory towards someone who teaches kindergarteners."

"Find out the name of that source," he practically snarled. He didn't like anyone maligning Mia's name any further and his mind was already heading towards filing a lawsuit against the reporter for unsubstantiated claims. He then headed into the office and spoke to the high school office staff, charming the ladies as best he could. Within thirty minutes, he had Mark's notes copied and was sitting with several other staff members in the teachers' lounge, talking to teachers on their breaks as well as the administrators who were just taking yet another break from their office responsibilities. "So what can you tell me about Jeff?" he asked, smiling despite his repugnance for their work ethic. He knew that teachers weren't paid nearly what they were worth, but the lack of energy in this group, the sense that none of them really cared about their jobs, made him angry on behalf of the students and parents who were entrusting their children to their care. It was yet another clue into the character of the victim. Jeff didn't appear to be a very motivating leader unlike Mia who inspired almost embarrassing levels of devotion from her supervisors and co-workers.

There was a long silence as each of the occupants looked at one another. No one wanted to speak up and say anything.

"Anyone know Mia Paulson personally?" he asked, taking a different approach.

People seemed more open to discussing his client. "I thought she was very sweet," one man said. "I didn't know she was such a good accountant until Jeff said all purchases should go through her. But I fixed it when I was ordering a new copier for the teacher's work room and made sure the order went through her. Jeff was pretty angry about that mix-up. I hope she's not angry with me as well," he said, leaning forward.

The man seemed almost fearful of his supervisor. And he didn't appear to be holding any ill will towards Mia. Ash continued to discuss the various items that had been purchased, supposedly through Mia so she could ensure that things were accounted for properly. But as the items that had been ordered through her, or sent to her house, or even the school property she'd borrowed from this school for whatever function and hadn't been returned, added up to a very large amount. Mark had found about three hundred thousand dollars but with all the additional items Ash was hearing about now, he suspected that the amount was closer to seven figures.

At the end of two hours and speaking with several other teachers who rotated through the teachers' lounge, he thought he had a good idea of what was happening. He just had to prove it now. Embezzlement was always a tough crime to prove, but he'd won harder cases than this.

"Mia, I need you over at my office," he said as soon as she picked up the phone. "We have a problem and need your help."

As soon as he walked into his office, he called a meeting to reveal the latest. He caught Mia's eye and wished she didn't look so nervous. But he couldn't stop to reassure her now. There was too much to do and he was racing against the clock as it was. As soon as the teachers realized that the press and the police didn't have this information, they would notify them. And he'd bet the police were going to show up here to arrest Mia. He had to get her out of this mess before that happened. And that meant he needed to get things figured out.

What a mess, he thought.

Mia looked across the busy office at Ash, wishing he would slow down and tell her what was going on. He had left her house early this morning before she'd woken. After the previous night, she'd wanted to wake up in his arms and feel that wonderful heat. But looking at him now, he looked so grim! Had she made a mistake? Why hadn't she gone with her intelligence last night instead of just letting her body rule her decisions? Over and over again, she'd told herself that Ash didn't believe in her. He thought she was a murderer but the last few days and especially last night, he'd been different. He'd been kind and gentle.

She thought about that night he'd followed her when she'd snuck out to get ice cream. He'd probably thought she was going to rob the convenience store! She'd disproved him that night and all the evidence the prosecuting attorney had against her was circumstantial. Ash had told her last night that he thought the charges would be dropped, so what was wrong now?

Why was he looking so angry?

She curled her arms around her, feeling scared and cold. He barely even looked at her. It was almost as if he couldn't bear to look at her, embarrassed that he'd slept with her last night.

Damn him! Why wouldn't he talk to her? He'd interrogated her over and over again during the past several days, why was he not talking to her now? If he'd discovered something new, something horrible, she should be the first one to hear it, shouldn't she?

She watched him walk across the room, talk something over with Mark and nod his head. He was so painfully handsome and strong. She sighed to herself, wishing she hadn't made such a fool of herself over him last night. She should have been more reserved. She should have stayed away from him.

So what if he'd been a sweetheart about her yard? She suspected he'd been the one to order all those pizzas for everyone. It suddenly occurred to her that a large truck had been pulling away from the curb when she'd come around from the backyard. That must have been where the mulch had come from! Had Ash ordered that as well?

If he had, she'd pay him back for every penny! She wasn't going to be beholden to a man who didn't believe in her innocence. This was ridiculous! The man was her lawyer. She should just maintain professional distance from him.

But even as she told herself that, her eyes hungrily watched him. He handed papers to one of the other lawyers, both of them discussing whatever information was on that paper.

She pulled her wallet out of her purse and wrote a check. When she was finished, she stormed over to him, her body shaking with her hurt and anger. "Here!" she snapped to him, holding out the check.

Ash looked down at her, seeing the vulnerability in her eyes. As much as he wanted to pull her into his arms and reassure her, he couldn't slow down. Jean had gotten a message from the district attorney, but he hadn't called back. It could only be bad news at this point. Good news would be the charges being dropped and that would most likely come in a formal notice as well as a call. Since it was only a phone call, he was fighting against the clock.

"What's this?" he asked, trying to focus on her, but he stopped to shout an order over to one of the investigators, "Get me a list of all the equipment." And then something else occurred to him so he put a hand on her shoulder, wincing when she stepped out of his reach. "Mark, look into storage units. And do another check on bank accounts. You know what we're looking for. We need to find it before the police to have better control over the information."

When Mark hurried off to his computers, his efficient fingers already flying over the keyboard, Ash turned back to Mia, looking down at her once again. "Sorry. What's this about?" he asked, waving the check in his hand.

"That's for the pizza and mulch yesterday. If that doesn't cover the expenses, please ask Jean to give me a revised amount. I'll pay it."

Someone handed him something else and he looked at it quickly. "This is good. Hand this to Mark. He's looking into stuff like this."

He sighed and looked back down at her. "Mia, why would you think I wanted a check for anything? And why do you think I paid for the pizza?"

"And the mulch," she said belligerently and moved even farther away from him. She couldn't be too close. She might just throw herself into his arms and beg him to save her. She didn't want to be saved. She could do this on her own.

"Mia, I'm not letting you pay for anything. Would you just hold on?" he asked, taking her arms before she could move even farther away from him. She kept inching away as if he were contaminated somehow. And after last night, it irritated him beyond words.

"You can't just..." she sniffed and shook her head. "Just stop. I'm not letting you do this," she said firmly and started to turn away. She had to get out of there. She would hire another lawyer. There had to be others in the Chicago area that were as good, or even better, than Ash Thorpe.

"You're not letting me do what?" he demanded, turning his full attention to her, hands on his hips as he glared down at her.

Mia refused to be intimidated by his angry attitude. He might be taller and stronger, but she wasn't bowing down to his glare. "All of this," she waved, indicating the numerous people around her who were rushing about, trying to solve this puzzle. "I want it to stop. I'll find someone else. Someone who believes in me and doesn't think I'm a criminal."

Ash stared at her, stunned. He wasn't sure what to say to get it through to her, but more importantly, he could almost feel the police and district attorney as they bore down on the details he'd discovered earlier today. "Mia..." he started to say, but shook his head. Instead, he grabbed her arm and pulled her into his office. Slamming the door, he pulled her into his arms, kissing her. She resisted for only a moment before he felt her arms go around his neck and his body relaxed somewhat.

The relaxation lasted only a moment before her soft body and the delicious taste of her hit him full force. He'd meant to just give her the most expedient reassurance he could, but that plan had backfired on him as soon as he'd taken her into his arms. As was always the case when he touched her, the intense heat of his desire inflamed his senses and it took every ounce of willpower to pull back. "You're not going anywhere," he told her firmly.

He took her hand and pulled her out of his office, smiling with the stunned and flustered look in her eyes which told him he hadn't been the only one who had been thrown by that kiss.

"Okay everyone! We need to get things in order. Bring whatever you have to the conference room," he called out.

When everyone was assembled, he looked around. "Mark, tell everyone what you discovered."

Mark swiveled in the leather chair so he was looking at more of the group. "We found that there was approximately one point two million dollars in school equipment and hardware that was ordered ostensibly through Ms. Paulson. That's not counting the equipment that everyone assumed Ms. Paulson had borrowed but hasn't yet been returned."

That captured Mia's attention and she leaned forward, obviously ready to argue her side of things but Ash held up his hand, silently asking her to hold off for the moment. Mia snapped her mouth closed, irritated that he wasn't even letting her defend herself! How rude! And arrogant, she thought, leaning back against the irritatingly comfortable leather chair and glaring at the man.

Ash ignored her irritation and continued to look at Mark. "Do you have a breakdown of what was borrowed versus which items were bought and never delivered?" he asked.

Mia shook her head. "I never…"

Ash stopped her yet again and Mia sat back in her chair with a huff. She glared at Ash, furious that he wouldn't let her talk.

After all they'd shared last night, she had thought that he was starting to care for her. She was so furious with herself for falling for his charm. Damn him! She'd believed in him! She'd believed they could share something together.

Okay, so they'd known each other for only a few days. And all of those days, he'd been defending her on murder charges. Add to that, she was a thief now.

Good grief, she didn't even know how to order some of these supplies, much less what they were. She was a kindergarten school teacher! What did she need with football equipment she thought mutinously as Mark read through the list of the items he'd discovered which had been borrowed? And why on earth would she tell Jeff that she needed that equipment for a field day at her school? They had their own equipment! High school sports equipment was too big for elementary aged children. Even the basketballs were smaller!

She crossed her arms over her chest, tapping her foot with impatience at how ludicrous this story was. Not to mention how betrayed she felt when she realized that Ash wasn't even arguing that she hadn't borrowed or stolen any of this equipment. He was being very clinical about the entire discussion while she sat here fuming with fury.

After last night, she would have thought that he trusted her more. But the way he was treating her, he was acting like she was a worse criminal than before. As if being a murderer versus a murderer as well as a thief….she stopped and thought about that. Okay, being a murderer versus a thief was worse. Taking a life was much more reprehensible than stealing material things. Not that she would do either, but still…she had to admit that murder ranked higher up on the "badness" scale than embezzlement and theft.

She crossed her legs, the top one swinging back and forth with impatience and anger. Her mind was whirling, trying to figure out why someone would even say that about her. She didn't really know the teachers and administrators over at Jeff's school. Of course, she'd met them at social functions. Jeff was the principal so as his girlfriend and fiancée, she'd had a few opportunities where she'd interacted with his staff.

She gasped. "That gives me motive!" she exclaimed, sitting up straight, her worried eyes moving to Ash's, begging him for reassurance.

Ash shook his head one more time and turned back to his team. "Kiera? It looks like you might have something."

The new lawyer on the team nodded her head, her eyes skimming over the report she'd pulled right before the meeting. Kiera's eyes were in a quandary. "I might. I started looking into Ms. Knightley's financials, like you asked," she explained.

That couldn't be good news, she thought, a lump forming in her throat and her stomach starting to twist into knots. "I didn't do this, Ash," she whispered up to him, begging him to believe her.

His only response was to place a firm hand on her shoulder, silently telling her to keep quiet.

She jerked her arm free and shook her head. "No! I won't shut up!" she cried out, furious with him and also with herself for putting herself into this kind of a position. She'd thought Jeff was nice and sweet. As soon as she'd figured him out, she'd tried hard to get out of his clutches but she'd been too naïve to do the right thing. Now the same thing was happening with Ash and she felt duped once again. She wasn't going to put up with it any longer.

She stood up and glared at Ash, desperately fighting for him to believe in her. To believe she wouldn't do these kinds of things. "I tried to get away from him," she explained to Ash, fighting back the tears and the panic. "And after..." she stopped herself, her body straining not to punch his arm because she did not believe in violence but there was a limit to a person's control. And right now, he was straining at her limits.

She couldn't say anything else without breaking down and she definitely didn't want to do that in front of all these people. "I have to get out of here," she said, realizing that everyone was staring at her, waiting for her to finish that sentence.

Before she embarrassed herself and broke down in tears, she rushed out of the conference room.

"Mia!" Ash called out, wanting to go after her, but his gut was telling him that whatever Kiera had to say was important.

He sighed, running a hand through his hair in frustration. He'd catch up with her once he'd figured this out. Everything inside of him was telling him to ignore the evidence against Mia. It just didn't jive with what he knew of her character. He was fully aware that people weren't always what they appeared to be, but he simply couldn't believe that she could so completely fool him.

Besides, she had an enormous army of people who were supporting her. Worst case scenario, he pulled in every single one of her co-workers and neighbors as character witnesses. Each one of them could give a story about what Mia had done to help them. Hell, she didn't have time to do any of the crap people were now saying about her because she was always baking a cake for someone, making soup for a sick person or helping someone in some other way.

No, Mia didn't embezzle over a million dollars from the school system. And she definitely didn't murder her ex-fiancé. He would bet his career on it. Hell, he was betting his life on it.

He smiled at the thought. Yes, he was going to have a pretty long, happy life. Filled with surprises and saved earthworms, but he could handle that. He wouldn't push the spiders out of the house though. Those things were road kill and she'd just have to get over it.

He looked back at the group with grim determination. "Okay, Kiera, whatcha got?" he prompted.

Kiera shifted in her chair. "This is just preliminary, mind you. I was looking through the data yesterday and found nothing, but something caught my attention this morning. Mia's finances are spotless. There's no evidence of any additional bank accounts, her expenses are miniscule except for the purchase of her house. All of her expenditures match the income of a school teacher with her level of experience. So I looked further into Jeff's finances. When I didn't find anything, I went on to his relatives and anyone who was close to him." She looked down at her papers and pulled one out. "Jeff's new fiancée is a nurse," she said carefully, passing the paper over to Ash. "Nurses make a good salary," she cautioned, "but I'm not sure they can afford a brand new, black BMW with all the bells and whistles."

Ash looked up sharply from the paper. "BMW?"

Kiera nodded confidently. "Bought the day after Ms. Paulson was arrested," she added.

Ash's face looked serious as he read through the details of the woman's purchase. But when his eyes fixed on the price, his eyes cleared. When he saw the date, he stood up and his face cleared of worry.

"Ladies and gentleman, I think we just found a new suspect in the murder of Jeff Richardson," he said.

Leslie, one of Mark's investigators rushed into the conference room, out of breath and obviously a bit frazzled. "Sir?"

Ash turned away from the conference room windows, trying to push his worry away from Mia. Focusing back on the group, he looked at Leslie, nodding his head for her to go ahead. "What did you find?"

Leslie pushed some pictures towards the center of the table. "You asked me to sit on the new fiancée," she said. With a grin, she pulled the most important one out of the pile.

Ash picked up the pictures she'd taken of the woman's house and looked at them, his smile growing when he realized what he was seeing. "And this is what you saw?" he asked, but it wasn't really a question since he was staring at the evidence.

Leslie nodded her head with a huge grin on her face. "I couldn't get a good shot," she cautioned, "but I'm pretty sure that's Jeff Richardson."

Ash was just about to laugh when a commotion outside the conference room caught his attention. Just as he'd anticipated, there were four police officers standing in the reception area.

Ash took the two pictures and walked out of the conference room.

Mia watched with growing terror as the police officers spotted her and moved in her direction. There were four of them! Did they really think she was going to run?

She held onto the desk behind her, her whole body feeling faint. This couldn't be happening! It was simply a nightmare and she was trapped in sleep, desperately fighting to wake up.

As the police officers came closer, she knew that it wasn't a dream. This was a nightmare, of course, but it was a real life nightmare in which she was about to be arrested, her bond revoked because everyone thought she had stolen over one million dollars from the school system and had the means to flee the country.

She didn't even have a passport!

And then Ash was there, his strong body placed between her and the police officers.

"Gentleman, you can't arrest Ms. Paulson for a murder that she didn't commit," Ash was saying.

"Mr. Thorpe," one of them, obviously the one in charge, had his hand on his gun. "I appreciate your efforts on behalf of your client, but we have a warrant for her arrest on suspicion of embezzlement. A judge signed the order just after lunchtime and her bail has been revoked."

Ash was shaking his head and holding up a picture. "You can't arrest someone for a crime that hasn't even been committed yet," he was saying.

Mia was completely confused. She tried to peer around Ash's shoulders, but his hand pushed her right back behind him. She should be irritated, but he was being protective and she kind of liked that. It might be old-fashioned, but in this one situation, she preferred being protected by a huge, heavy handed, supremely intelligent man who obviously had some sort of get-out-of-jail-free card. Because the police officers were staring at the photograph carefully.

"Is that...?" one of them started to ask.

"Yes, gentlemen, that is Jeff Richardson in the kitchen of his current fiancée." He pulled up another picture, one of a sleek, shiny new car. "And this is Ms. Knightley's new car, purchased, in cash, one day after Ms. Paulson was arrested."

Leslie came closer and handed him another photograph. "I know the first picture is a bit blurry, so here's a clearer picture of the two of them from their engagement photograph."

The police officers looked at the first, then the third picture, obviously confused.

"Where did you get that photograph?" a new voice chimed in.

Everyone turned to face a blond woman approaching the officers fearlessly. She snatched the photo out of the officer's hands and turned around. "Are you having me followed?" she demanded of Ryker Thorpe who was walking up behind her, a look of mild irritation on his handsome features.

"Why would you ask that?" he demanded. "Do you know the man in that photograph?"

Cricket glared up at the man, her irritation increasing as she lifted the photo up higher. "These two people are the heads of the charity my boss wants me to look into as a tax deduction. I was with them yesterday afternoon. Are you telling me you haven't had someone following me?"

Ash stepped in front of the blond beauty but his brother pushed him out of the way. Ash didn't have time to castigate his oldest brother right at the moment. He had to clarify this latest twist. "I don't know who you are…" he started to say.

Ryker interrupted him. "This is Cricket Fairchild. She's one of my clients."

The woman rolled her eyes. "Okay, so now that we've established who I am, would someone mind telling me why you are investigating the person I'm investigating?"

The police officer stepped in at that moment. "Ma'am, are you telling me that you were with this man yesterday afternoon?"

Cricket nodded her head, causing her blond curls to dance merrily around her stunning features. "I was with both of them. Isn't that what I just said? It was a lunch meeting at their request," she explained. "He ordered steak and she had some sort of disgusting fish meal."

"And you would be willing to testify to this?" the officer asked.

Cricket looked around, her green eyes trying to figure out why everyone was tense. "Of course. Why? Has someone bankrupted his charity or something? They're very passionate about saving the whales off the coast of Greenland."

Ash watched with amusement as his older brother rolled his eyes. "Cricket, the police believe this man was murdered last week."

She laughed and shook her head. "No. He wasn't murdered last week. He was giving me a pitch to help him fund the next ship they are trying to acquire."

Ryker looked over her head at his younger brother. "I think that sort of clinches things for you doesn't it?" he asked, a smile in his eyes as he glanced back to the brunette.

Ash was grinning broadly. "Pretty much," he said and turned to the officers. "Do you need anything else?" he asked them.

The officers shook their heads in amazement but they were all grinning. "We're all good here, Mr. Thorpe."

"Call me Ash," he said, slapping one of them on the arm jovially. "I think there are cupcakes in the break room," he offered. "Stop by and grab one. I've heard they're fantastic."

Mia bit her lip, her whole body waiting tensely. She only started to relax when one of the officers nodded politely to her. "I think we'd better skip the cupcake for now but we'll take a rain check. Can I have these two pictures?" he asked.

Ash quickly nodded. "Let me know if you need additional copies. We're more than happy to print more for you."

The police officer took the pictures, but hesitated in front of the blond woman. Ryker immediately understood what they were afraid to ask and stepped in to reassure all four of them. "Ms. Fairchild will make a statement if you need one," Ryker was offering.

"I will?" Cricket asked, looking up at the man she seemed to dislike intensely. "What will I be stating?"

"That you had lunch with a murder victim yesterday," he stated succinctly, not clearing up any of the woman's confusion before he took her arm and led her back down the hallway. "Come along. You and I have a lot to discuss."

Mia watched with fascination as the oldest of the Thorpe brothers dragged the beautiful woman down the hallway. She obviously didn't want to go, but she didn't fight him either.

Mia's smile started off small. But as the realization hit her, that grin expanded over her entire face, growing in intensity and she was almost light-headed with the relief that surged through her. And she was startled when the blond woman smiled brightly right back at her, waving her fingers in the air before she disappeared around the corner.

"In my office," Ash snapped at her.

Mia jumped and tore her eyes away from the disappearing blond woman and looked up at Ash. Gone was that feeling of freedom that had been starting to bubble up inside of her. All that anger she'd felt only moments ago surged right back to the front of her mind. "I'm not..." she started to say but Ash didn't wait for her to respond. He moved in closer, his face barely an inch from hers.

"Don't say another word, Mia. Just go right into my office. We have some things to discuss and I'm definitely not going to do them in front of my staff."

Mia pulled back slightly and looked around. Sure enough, just about every person in the area was frozen in place, waiting to see what she would do. No one disobeyed a direct command from Ash Thorpe. But some of them suspected that she might. She could see the hope in their eyes.

Unfortunately, she didn't have the courage to ignore him either. At least not this time.

She stepped back and marched into his office, just about to slam the door behind her when she felt it stop.

Swinging around, she glared at him, her hands on her hips defiantly while she watched him walk into his office behind her.

She waited a fraction of a second for his office door to slam closed before she started in on him. "Don't you dare ever speak to me like that!" she almost yelled. "I can't believe I slept with you last night!" she said, this time her voice definitely was louder. "I can't believe I let you into my house, that I thought I was in love with you and I slept with you!" Her hands went into her hair. "Good grief, there was almost no sleeping anyway! So I can't really say that, can I? No, I had to go sleep with the enemy! Not that you're really the enemy," she clarified for herself, pacing back and forth in his office, her fury rising higher as she contemplated all that she'd messed up in her life. "I was such a wimp! I can't believe it, every time you touched me, I thought you were feeling the same thing I felt! I thought that you cared for me! When all that time, you were just having a good old time, weren't you? And all that time, you thought I was not just a murderer, but a thief! And a thief who steals from the schools! The kids! I'm a horrible human being because I steal money that the kids need for their education. It isn't bad enough that some of them can't even afford clothes or food, but now there's a horrible woman who is stealing the equipment right out from under them."

She was really working herself up into a good lather now. "And I wasn't even smart about it! No! A smart thief would have used an alias to embezzle the funds. I had to use my own name." She gasped and turned around. "I can't believe you thought I was so stupid that I wouldn't know how to embezzle money!" She realized how ridiculous that sounded and shook her head. "Okay, so maybe I don't know how to embezzle money, but believe me, I'm not so stupid as to use my own name!"

"I know," Ash said softly, leaning against his door with his arms crossed over his chest, just watching her work herself up in anger.

She didn't listen to him, going on and on about how she'd been such a sap last night. "And believe it or not, I was actually hurt this morning when I woke up and found you no longer in bed." She slapped her forehead with exasperation at her naiveté. "I actually made excuses for you! I had this all worked out in my mind that you just figured something out in the middle of the night and left early, letting me sleep in because I was exhausted from the nightmare of the last few days. But all you were doing was finding more evidence of my crimes!"

The door opened and both of them turned to look at Ash's administrative assistant poke her head in. "I'm sorry to interrupt," she said, her face red for some reason, "but the DA is on the phone and wants to talk to you. He said it is urgent and he didn't sound happy."

Ash turned to look at Mia. "Stay here. We have more to discuss," he said and walked out the door, giving her privacy in the hopes that she would calm down.

As soon as he left, the middle aged woman stepped inside, carrying a cup of coffee. "I thought you might need this," she said softly. "I'm Jeanie," she said. "I think we'll be getting to know each other very well soon."

Mia took the cup gratefully and took a fortifying sip. "Thank you," she whispered, all of her energy gone now that her target was no longer in sight. "I appreciate the coffee, but I really need to get out of here."

Jeanie was quiet for a long moment, looking at the gorgeous brunette with understanding. "You're wrong about him," she said in a soothing tone of voice.

Mia halted her pacing and stopped to turn to the kind woman. "I'm sorry?" she asked.

Jeannie smiled gently. "You're wrong. About Mr. Thorpe."

Mia shook her head. "How do you…"

The kind woman smiled gently and took a step closer, as if she needed to emphasize her next words. "Mr. Thorpe never gets involved in investigations," she explained. "He manages at a high level, working on trial strategy, overseeing more than twenty different cases. He goes to court representing clients in only a small number of those cases." She let those words sink in before continuing. "Mr. Thorpe was at the school this morning interviewing your co-workers. He then went over to the high school after Mark called him about some odd issues."

That irritated her. "I know. That's where he started to think I was a thief as well."

Jeannie smiled and looked down, trying to figure out how to help this beautiful, young woman understand her point. "This case was different," she tried a different approach. "It wasn't that Mr. Thorpe was trying to get you acquitted."

Mia took a deep breath and tried to listen, tried to understand her point. "He always tries to get people acquitted. That's his job."

"Exactly. Mr. Thorpe wasn't trying to get you acquitted. He was trying to prove your innocence."

Mia knew the kind woman was trying to tell her something important but she just wasn't getting it. "I'm sorry, I'm just not getting your point."

Jeannie laughed. "Mr. Thorpe is a high level director. People hire him from all over the country because he's the best at getting people acquitted."

"That just means he doesn't care where he gets his money as long as he's still raking it in."

Jeannie once again shook her head. "You misunderstand. The man you're in love with has one of the highest codes of honor I've ever experienced in this business. Mr. Thorpe doesn't take cases when he's sure the defendant is guilty."

With those words, Jeannie turned and walked out of the office, leaving Mia to think about what had been revealed.

She was exhausted from a night of not sleeping well, plus the stress of the past several days. She wasn't sure what was going on and didn't completely understand what Ash's assistant had been trying to say.

Unfortunately, or maybe it was a good thing, because Autumn rushed into the office and grabbed Mia into a bear hug. "I just heard the news!" she screamed. "I'm so relieved. I told you Ash could get you out of this mess!" she said, rocking back and forth with her arms around Mia's shoulders.

Mia laughed and tried to nod her head, but Autumn's grip was too tight. "You were right. He got everything all cleared up. I can't believe it's actually over!"

Autumn laughed, delighted. "We have to go out and celebrate!" she exclaimed. "Let's go do Durango's!"

"Yes!" Mia agreed, knowing that a margarita was exactly what she needed right now. She needed to work her mind through Jeanie's comments, not completely understanding what she'd been trying to say. Perhaps she was too emotionally charged at this point. She needed to relax and wrap her mind around the fact that prison wasn't looming in her future. "I'm totally in!" She didn't tell her friend that she wanted to just drink herself free of the confusing man. Nor did she tell Autumn that her boss had told Mia to stay in his office. She wasn't going to listen to him, still feeling betrayed after last night.

It occurred to her that she should be more grateful to Ash. Without his help, she would be in a jail cell right now. His investigators had discovered the truth and he'd had the skills to put it all together. But staying here where he would come back and confuse her even more was not a good idea. She never thought clearly when Ash was around so it was better to figure things out far away from him.

She stopped when she was out in the open and looked around at all the smiling faces. "Thank you everyone," she said softly, but with sincerity. "Thank you so much for figuring this out. I'm so grateful to all of you for your efforts. All of you are amazing people!" she said. Everyone smiled right back at her, some raising their coffee cups in salute and she bowed her head in respect to their success.

Autumn pulled Mia out of the office, waving to the crowd as well, each of them celebrating for a moment before they moved on to the next case. She stopped at Jeannie's desk. "If Ash is looking for Mia, tell him I've kidnapped her and taken her to Durango's, okay?"

Jeannie's smile widened in approval. "Will do. Have one for me!"

Autumn hesitated and smiled right back. "Want to come along and celebrate?"

Jeannie waved her hand. "Thanks but I'm leaving early today so I can get my kids to a dentist appointment. Go ahead and have a great time. Make sure she relaxes," she told Autumn, referring to Mia who was obviously not as relaxed as she should be in the face of her absolution from the crimes she'd been accused of less than a week ago.

Autumn looked down at Mia, then back at Jeanie before saying, "Definitely."

At the elevator, Autumn and Mia were laughing, the realization that Mia was truly free slowly sinking in.

"Men!" the pretty, blond woman sighed as she pressed the elevator call button over and over. Mia and Autumn watched her touch the diamond ring on her finger reverently, then shake her head. Mia looked at Autumn and both women nodded at the same time, obviously having the exact same idea.

Mia smiled at the woman with genuine appreciation. "You're the woman who just helped me stay out of jail," Mia said. "Are you okay?"

Cricket spun around and noticed the two lovely women behind her. "I'm sorry," she said and took a deep breath while closing her eyes. "Nothing a good martini can't fix," she said, trying to calm down. "Men are just so confusing!" she snapped, the calming breath obviously not working too well.

Mia knew the feeling. "Why don't you come with us? I don't know about the martinis," she cautioned, "but the margaritas at Durango's are perfect for anything that ails you."

Cricket considered the option. She didn't know these two women, but she could definitely use a night on the town with some women her own age. "I'm not sure I should be around humanity right now," she came back.

Mia laughed. "That's exactly where I am. I'm Mia Paulson," she said. "And we're heading out to celebrate me not being in jail for the rest of my life."

Cricket smiled back, taking Mia's hand in hers. "That sounds like a perfect start to the weekend. I think I'll join you after all."

The three women walked out the door and headed down the sidewalk to the bar that was down the street from the office. They found a table in the back of the bar and settled down, ordering a huge pitcher of margaritas with three glasses.

When they were all poured with chips and salsa in the middle of the table, Autumn raised her glass in the air. "To avoiding jail time and men!" she said with emphatic conviction.

Mia was just about to raise her glass when she spotted another woman sitting alone at the bar. "Wait!" she called out, moments before they took a sip. "That woman, her name is Kira or Kiera, right?"

Autumn looked over at the bar and nodded. "Yes. She's the new lawyer on Ash's team. She started the day you were arrested."

Mia's grin grew wider as she watched the sad looking woman sitting off to the side at one of the darker tables. "She's the one who found the information about Jeff's current fiancée buying the new BMW."

Without another word, Autumn stood up and walked over to the woman who looked as sad and miserable as Mia felt at the moment.

Cricket and Mia watched as Autumn spoke softly to the other woman, gesturing in their direction. Mia knew instantly what was going on and she grabbed a chair from the next table, bringing it over to their own.

"Hi Kiera!" she called out, signaling to the waiter to bring another glass. "Looks like you're in the same boat as the rest of us so you might as well join us," she said and poured the woman a drink.

Kiera smiled gratefully and introduced herself to Cricket. "So back to where we were before," Cricket said, lifting her glass one more time. "To no jail time and no obnoxious men!"

The three other women laughed, but they all clinked glasses and took a long sip of the sweet and sour mixture, laughing about the men they'd dated in the past. Mia didn't bring up the fact that she was personally involved with Ash. She thought that would be a bit too revealing, but she thought it was interesting that Cricket reviled Ash's older brother Ryker. And Mia knew that Autumn was refusing to date any of the men she introduced her to but she was quite adamant that Xander Thorpe was the worst of the four Thorpe brothers. Which struck Mia as very interesting.

And it could just be the tequila finally hitting her system, but Mia thought it was fascinating that the lovely brunette lawyer looked down at her drink anytime one of the brothers was mentioned. Was the beautiful Kiera interested in another man? Or perhaps one that had already been mentioned? Mia watched her carefully and knew something was up when the slender woman held her breath at the mere mention of Axel Thorpe. Bingo, Mia thought and sat back, mentally congratulating herself on figuring out what was going on.

Two hours later, they were on their third pitcher of drinks and the four women were tight friends. "So what's up with the boss man?" Cricket asked, laughing as she grabbed another chip.

"You mean Ryker?" Autumn asked, taking a long gulp of her margarita despite the fact that the room was already swaying.

Cricket also took a long, satisfying swallow of her icy drink and nodded. "Or more appropriately referred to as the most obnoxious, irritating, domineering and arrogant man on the planet."

Autumn laughed and shook her head. "He's not so bad," she said. "You haven't met Xander yet if you think Ryker is bad. Xander's a jerk!"

"Oh crap!" Mia gasped, her drink frozen halfway to her lips.

Cricket looked over. "What's wrong?"

Her glass dropped to the table with a clink. "I just realized that I'm in love with the horrible man!"

Kiera smiled, having figured that one out about three drinks ago. "And? Sounds like we all have man troubles."

Mia, Autumn and Cricket all looked at their new best friend. "You too?" they gasped almost in unison.

Autumn's eyes narrowed. She looked around at counted. When she came to the right conclusion, she too gasped in horror. "No!"

Mia was having trouble keeping up. "What?" Were they talking about the Thorpe brothers still? She was a little fuzzy now.

Cricket laughed and shook her head. "Figures," she said and poured Kiera another glass.

"What?" Mia asked again, but took a sip while she looked over the rim of her glass.

Autumn threw back her head and laughed. "I can't believe it! You too?"

Kiera sighed and took a long sip of her drink as well.

Mia cringed she voiced the conclusion she'd come to a couple of hours ago. "Axel?" she asked, instantly feeling sorry for the poor woman.

Kiera's shoulders shrugged slightly. "Everyone has their albatross."

The four men standing behind the table listened with only slightly veiled amusement. Axel rolled his eyes when he was referred to as an albatross. "At least I wasn't referred to as obnoxious, irritating and domineering."

"Don't forget arrogant," Xander piped up, filling in the one adjective his brother had forgotten.

Ryker rolled his eyes. "You're the one that was most recently referred to as a jerk, if you recall."

Xander pushed away from the bar and put his half-drunk beer down on the bar behind him. "I think it's time to crash this party. Don't you gentlemen?"

Ryker completely agreed. "I'll get their tab. Who is going to be the first to break things up before we're tarred and feathered?"

He turned around and gestured to the ladies' waiter, handing him a credit card to cover their drinks for the night.

Ash was the first to step in, starting to move in behind Mia but Autumn's next words stopped him several feet from their table. He didn't move, just waited for more interesting information to be revealed.

"What were you saying 'crap' earlier? You and Ash are great together," Autumn commented, leaning back, completely oblivious to the four extremely large men warily approaching their table.

Mia shrugged and took another long sip of her drink. "Oh, nothing important. I just really don't want to be in love with my jerk."

The three women stopped drinking and stared hard. "Are you kidding?" Autumn asked, a huge grin on her face.

Mia's eyes narrowed as something occurred to her. She stared hard at her friend, her mind trying to work despite all the alcohol that was making everything fuzzy. "Did you have this planned already?" she asked.

Autumn laughed, delighted. "Not at all. When I saw your name on the docket, I didn't spare a moment to consider anything, but remember that last time you came by to pick me up for yoga?" she asked.

Mia nodded her head, already suspicious. "What about it?"

"You were late. You were supposed to come up and get me. And I was going to have you accidentally run into Ash."

Mia gasped. "You sneaky…! Why would you do that to me?"

Autumn smiled. "What's the problem? You're already in love with him."

"Yeah, but he's not in love with me. And besides, he doesn't trust me."

"Yes he does," Autumn contradicted.

"Yes, I do," A deep voice interrupted.

Mia spun around and groaned.

"What are you doing here?" she demanded, almost spilling her drink as her hand started shaking. "Go away. You don't trust me and I'm not going to be in love with a man who doesn't trust me."

Ash didn't even bother to reply to that. He simply took the glass out of her hand and bent down to lift her into his arms. Walking out of the restaurant, he nodded to his brothers who were starting to move in on what he suspected were their women. Or at least what he hoped were the women these men had been grouching over. He was at least relieved to see that Xander was moving in on Autumn's chair but didn't take the time to wonder what would happen between the two of them. He had too much to worry about with this one.

"Put me down," she grumbled. "I'm too heavy for you to carry me," she said and laid her head down on his broad shoulder.

Ash raised an eyebrow at that, but didn't slow down at all. He wanted her in his brownstone where he could strip off this ugly suit she'd chosen to wear and find all that lovely softness he knew was underneath. He was going to spend the rest of the evening and all of the night convincing her that he trusted her, had always trusted her and would always trust her in the future and she needed to marry him as soon as possible.

"I'm hiring a new lawyer," she said while he was tucking her into the passenger seat of his car.

"Of course you are," he said and strapped her seat belt on.

Her eyes narrowed on his amused face but she suspected the action might be diminished since she was having trouble focusing on him. "You might be big and gorgeous," she said with a sigh as she laughed when he tickled her, "but I can resist you easily."

"Think so?" he replied, not believing a word of it. Nice to hear that she thought he was gorgeous, he thought.

"Absolutely! You don't trust me. That's easy to resist."

"I trust you," he countered, but slammed the door so she couldn't argue with him any longer.

He chuckled as he walked around to the driver's seat. So the woman thought he was 'gorgeous'? He liked that.

Sliding into the car, he started it up and backed out of the parking space, glancing in her direction to see if she was okay. Her eyes were closed and she had a satisfied look on her lovely features, just like she had last night when he'd been making love to her.

"And you're not getting another lawyer," he said softly, thinking she'd fallen asleep after all the margaritas she'd imbibed.

He was wrong. Her widening smile indicated as much. "You can't stop me," she came right back, not bothering to open her eyes.

He chuckled as he drove through the streets of downtown Chicago. "Why would you need a new lawyer? Are you planning to let some earthworms die off on the sidewalk?"

That wiped her smile away and she turned to glare at him. "I'll have you know that earthworms are a very important part of our ecosystem. And because of that, they're one of the very best composters. You want gorgeous plants and flowers, get a bunch of worms."

He laughed and shook his head. "Are we talking about our relationship or worm dung?" he asked, confidently maneuvering through the streets.

"We don't have a relationship. So let's talk about worm..." she hesitated to use the other term so she just said, "poop."

"We definitely have a relationship. And I'll make sure you don't get a new lawyer."

She laughed as if his statement as well as his confidence were outrageous. "How do you think you're going to stop me?" she asked, snuggling down into the soft leather seat. "And stop being charming. I don't like you." Worry lines appeared on her forehead and she turned to look up at him. "I can't remember why at the moment, but it will come to me."

"You think I don't trust you," he told her with a wink.

"Right!" she said, trying to snap her fingers but they wouldn't connect properly for some reason. After several failed attempts, she simply waved her hands and then let them fall onto her lap.

"Autumn is in love with Xander, isn't she?" Mia asked, squinting through the darkened windshield.

"That's our theory. But no one will touch it and question either party to find out why they won't do anything about it."

Mia mulled that over in her mind. "I don't think I have the courage either."

Ash laughed, shaking his head. "Mia, you're one of the bravest women I know."

She blinked, not sure she'd heard him correctly. "That was possibly the sweetest thing anyone has ever said to me."

He braked for a red light and looked down at her. "We're getting married, you know."

Mia rolled her eyes. "And there goes the sweetness and charm." She shrugged philosophically. "I figured as much. Only an ogre would ask a woman to marry her in such an outrageous manner."

He chuckled again. "You've already told me I'm gorgeous and charming."

"I never said charming," she came right back. "And I didn't say gorgeous."

"I heard gorgeous," he countered.

"I never will admit to saying gorgeous." With that she sighed and leaned back in the leather seat one more time. "And where are you taking me?" she demanded, trying to figure out where they were. "I'm not going back to your brownstone," she told him firmly. "I need to go home."

"You're going to have to sell your pretty house, Mia. I can't live in a house with a blue kitchen. We've already discussed that."

"I'm not selling my house, I'm not living with you and so your masculinity is safe from my kitchen, which is periwinkle. Not blue."

He couldn't believe she was arguing about the color of her kitchen when he'd just proposed to her. Albeit in a rather unromantic manner. Even he had to admit that telling someone they were going to get married was rather unromantic. But hell, she was talking about getting a new lawyer! What was a man supposed to do?

Not that he was threatened at all. The woman was too wholesome for words. He couldn't imagine another bizarre situation where she would need a lawyer. So the point was mute anyway. "You're coming to my house, and I'll try to be more romantic once the alcohol has worn off. How's that?"

She immediately shook her head. "I'm not going back to your house," she stated firmly once again. "I'm going to my house and I'm going to have breakfast in my periwinkle kitchen and I'll sleep in my flowered sheets and you can't do anything to stop me."

Since they were already parked in his garage, he'd like to know how she was going to get home. But he didn't point that out to her. He simply got out of the car and walked around to her side, intending to lift her out of the seat again and carry her into his house where she belonged.

Instead, she was standing, rather unsteadily, beside his car and looking at him with triumph. "What are you so proud of?" he asked, taking her hand and leading her into his house.

"Just being firm about everything!" she said, then ruined her triumphant moment by tripping and falling into his arms. She gasped with the contact and Ash didn't even move his hand once he realized that it was on her breast.

She straightened up again and took a step backwards. "You are not a gentleman."

Ash laughed softly and looked down at her. "And you're drunk. How about some coffee?" he suggested.

She shook her head. "I'm not drunk and I can't drink coffee this late at night. I'll never get to sleep," she said.

He fixed two cups of coffee anyway and handed her one as she wandered about his home. She didn't even argue with him, just started sipping the coffee as she poked and prodded at the various books on his bookshelf. "Have you read all of these?" she asked, glad that her eyes were actually starting to focus more easily now.

"Yes."

She was impressed. "You're pretty smart then." She turned to grin at him. "But I guess you already proved that, haven't you?"

Ash was sitting in his big leather chair and he'd already turned on the fireplace which was now crackling with the gas logs licking at the top of the firebox. "I kept you out of jail."

She turned to face him, her smile bright and luminous once again. "You did, didn't you?"

"And you left my office when I told you to stay put."

She laughed and nodded her head. "If you want someone to stay put, get a dog."

"But I want you."

"No you don't. You want a dog."

He threw back his head and laughed. "I guarantee that I'm not marrying a dog, Mia. You'll have to get over that and just accept your fate."

She took another sip of the coffee, impressed with how quickly it really was sobering her up. "You'll have to find someone else. I won't marry a man who doesn't trust me."

He sighed and stood up, coming over to loom over her with the fire lighting her features with a soft glow. "Mia, let's get this out in the open and hopefully you'll remember this so we won't ever have this conversation again. I might not have trusted you that first morning, but we were going through a lot of issues then. By the time I took you out to lunch and you wouldn't eat anything because you didn't have your wallet with you, that pretty much clinched it for me."

"What are you talking about?" she demanded, embarrassed by that lunch event all over again.

He pulled her close, taking her coffee cup out of her hand. "A true criminal wouldn't have tried to pay for her own meal. Real criminals do everything they can to get someone else to pay for their lives in one way or another. So from that moment on, I was sure of your innocence."

She pulled back slightly, not sure if she should trust him. She'd done so before and where had that landed her? In a bar drinking margaritas with friends. Not exactly where she'd planned to be tonight.

But at least she wasn't in jail!

"What about all those times you pulled back? All the times you looked at me with horror on your face? As if you'd just done something horrible?"

He pulled her closer, his hands smoothing up her back. "I had done something horrible! You were my client! I was taking advantage of your worried state and that wasn't fair."

She bit her lip. "Was that illegal?" she asked, worried for him now.

He sighed but wouldn't let her move away from him. "Not illegal, but it violated my personal code of ethics and probably all other lawyers' as well."

She cringed. "Okay, so all that backing away after kissing me or touching me, that was just....guilt?"

"Hell yes!"

"So...what does that mean now?"

He lifted her into his arms and carried her back over to where he'd been sitting several minutes ago. "It means that we're getting married now. You love me."

"How do you know that?' she asked, but her arms went around his neck. Could she trust what he was saying?

"Because you gave yourself to me last night. And you said it with the ladies earlier in the evening."

She gasped and pulled back, trying to push against his chest but he wouldn't let her off of his lap. "I did not!" she denied vehemently.

"You did. I have several witnesses. And what's more, I'm in love with you. I probably was in love with you from the moment Autumn told me you saved earthworms," he told her.

She laughed but rolled her eyes. "You're going to have to forget that." Then she hesitated. "Wait a minute, Autumn told you that even before you'd met me. You couldn't have been in love with me then."

He shrugged. "Okay, so maybe love is too strong of a word. But I was fascinated by anyone who would be so worried about a species that has a brain only large enough to survive and can't really experience pain or anxiety over drying out in the hot sun."

She was already shaking her head. "You can't know that. And just put yourself in their position."

He kissed her to stop her argument. And when she was soft and compliant in his arms again, he lifted his head and looked down at her. "I'm still not going to argue about worms," he told her, sliding his hand up her back and causing her to wiggle deliciously.

She grabbed his hand to stop him and refocused on his statement. "So if you were so convinced of my innocence, why did you leave my bed this morning?"

"A combination of my guilt over sleeping with a client, even when I knew I was going to marry said client, and an aching need to protect you, keep you from going back to jail and a sixth sense that something was going to pop up this morning. I knew something was wrong and was racing against the clock."

"Is that why you ignored me in the office? Because you were trying to work?"

"Did I hurt your feelings?" he asked, using his other hand to touch her cheek gently.

"Yes. I thought you were angry with yourself for giving in and making love to me."

"I was furious with myself for violating my code of ethics and determined to fix it so I could still be in your bed tonight without the guilt."

She smiled brightly. "So today was all about making sure I would be in your bed?"

"Exactly. And that you would agree to marry me," he said, moving his head closer to her neck and nuzzling the sensitive skin.

"I haven't said I'll marry you," she contradicted, but she tilted her head, letting her own hand slide up his chest.

"You will," he said and bit her earlobe gently but with enough pressure to make her gasp.

"I might not," she countered.

He slid his hand underneath her sweater. "I have ways of convincing you."

She laughed and grabbed his wrist again. But he wasn't going to allow that. In one swift move, he lifted her up into his arms and carried her over to the sofa where the soft throw blanket was already draped over the back. He pulled it down and set her on top of it, then covered her body with his own. "You're mine, Mia Paulson. And the sooner you accept that, the better because I'm not letting you out of this house until you agree to marry me."

With that threat looming over her, she smiled and snuggled up to his chest. She was more than happy to have him keep her here. Maybe if she refused him over and over again, he would make love to her over and over again. She definitely wouldn't mind that scenario.

"If you insist," she said with a huge grin.

"I love you," he said as he bent to kiss her.

She sighed, wrapping her arms around his neck. "I love you too, you gorgeous man."

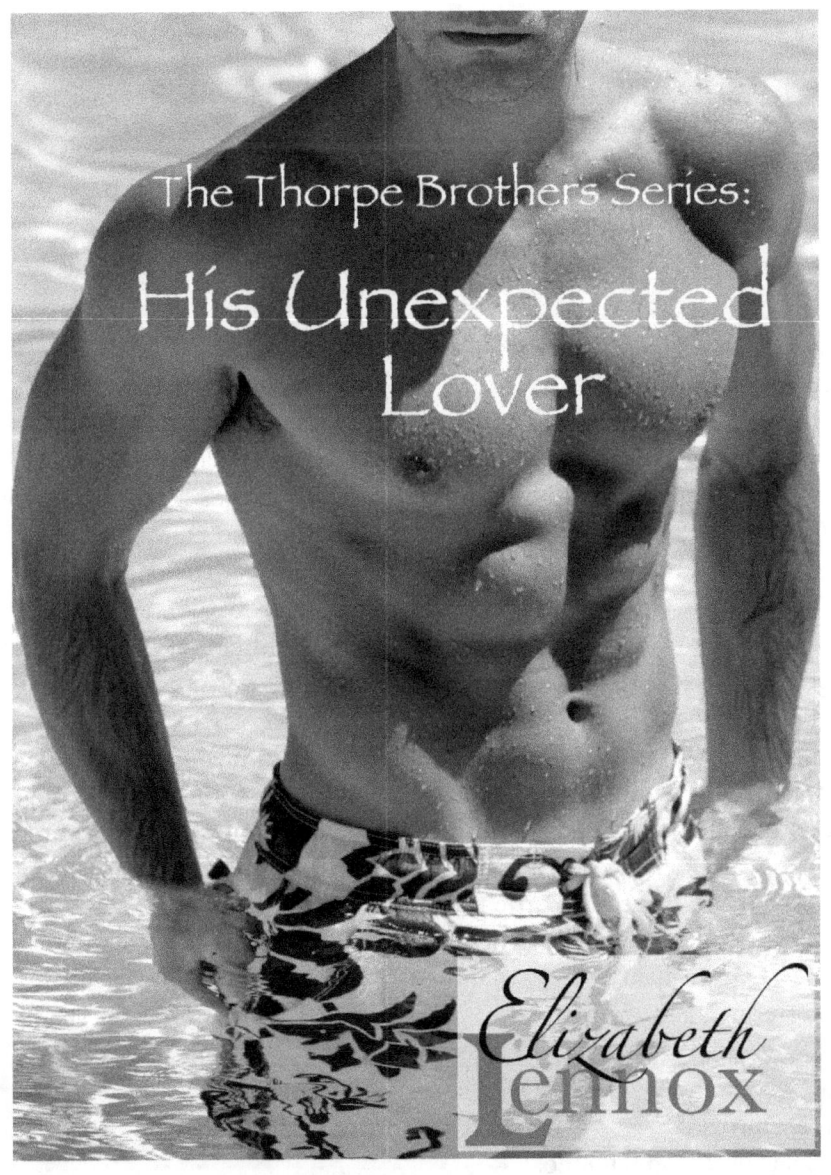

The Thorpe Brothers Series:

His Unexpected Lover

Elizabeth Lennox

Book 2:
His Unexpected Lover

INTRODUCTION

Axel's Story…

"Hey! Axel, you coming?"

Axel glanced over to the left and groaned when he saw his friends. Turning back to Lorrie, he said, "I'll be right back, okay?" It was a gorgeous spring day and all he wanted to do was enjoy the warmth after the painfully cold, Chicago winter and get to know Lorrie a little better. She seemed like a nice person, a huge change from his last girlfriend.

Lorrie smiled shyly at him and nodded a moment before Axel trotted over to the group of guys. "Hey, I know I said I'd hit the party with you tonight, but something's come up."

Darren peered around Axel's shoulders and grinned. "Come up, huh? I guess mine would too if I got to head down to the park with Lorrie Dumphries."

Axel punched his friend's arm, irritated that Darren would be so crude about the girl he was interested in. "Don't be disgusting. Lorrie is a nice girl." He turned around and waved to Lorrie to indicate that things were okay.

Joe snorted. "Why would you date a nice girl when you could be going out with Janey Smithers?"

Axel cringed at the reminder. "Janey and I broke up. I'm seeing Lorrie now."

Joe's eyes turned wary. "Does Janey know that?"

Axel shrugged. "As far as I'm concerned, she doesn't need to know. Besides, she broke up with me."

Darren laughed and shook his head. "I don't think she sees it that way."

Joe laughed as well. "I think it was all a ploy, because she's going around school saying that you're taking her to the dance next week."

Axel shook his head, dumbfounded by his ex-girlfriend's antics. "I have no idea why she's saying that," he replied. But deep down, he suspected the answer. Janey was trying to make him jealous, but he just wasn't into her enough anymore to care. She'd tried to manipulate him one too many times. He was through with her. It had been a relief last week when she'd dumped him. It had given him the "out" he'd needed without hurting her feelings – although why he even cared at this point, he couldn't answer.

He was walking back to Lorrie when he stopped and turned back to his friends. "Hey, don't mention I won't be at the party, okay? If Janey hears, she'll just try and find me and I'd rather have a drama-free night tonight. Okay?"

Joe and Darren both shrugged with their non-backpack shoulders. "Sure. Whatever you say. But if you're not at the party by ten o'clock, you know she'll come looking for you. She's already done it several times."

Axel knew that all too well. "I know. And I'm not asking you to lie to her. Just tell her the truth. That you don't know where I am."

Joe grinned with his quirky laugh. "I can do that," he said and punched his friend on the upper arm. "Go get her!"

Axel laughed and jogged back to where Lorrie was standing. "All set," he said and led her down the sidewalk. As he walked her home that afternoon, he found out more about Lorrie and discovered they had a lot in common. They both liked the same football team, both had no idea what they wanted to be when they grew up, both loved history and hated geometry. "So I'll pick you up at six?" he asked when they were both standing awkwardly on the walkway up to her house.

She smiled and glanced up into his eyes. "That would be great," she said.

"Okay. Until tonight," he replied and touched her lightly on her shoulder. He actually wanted to kiss her, but thought it was too soon. Tonight though…yes, he would be able to kiss her tonight after they'd had a burger at the diner down the street and caught a movie at the theatre. Lorrie was cute and kind although she was a bit more timid than he would have liked. But that was okay.

Janey, the head of the cheerleading squad, was brash and forward. He'd liked that initially. He'd even been flattered when she'd gone out of her way to catch his eye. Not that anyone wouldn't know about Janey Smithers – she was the prettiest girl in their class. But once he'd gotten to know her, he realized that she wasn't a very nice person. She was mean and vindictive and, when she'd pulled a stunt to hurt her science partner during an experiment last week, he'd become angry with her. Her partner had been burned by a chemical they'd been working on and Janey had deliberately caused the "accident". He didn't know how, but she'd bragged about it with him later that afternoon, chuckling at how stupid the other girl had been.

When he'd questioned why she'd done it, Janey had shrugged and said, "We got a bad grade on our exam and lab last week. So I got back at her."

Axel couldn't believe that she'd been so vicious, but there wasn't anything he could do about it. He had no proof, other than her statement, but he'd pulled back after that day, not wanting to even hang out with his friends when she was around.

As soon as Janey realized that he was no longer devoted to her, she'd become furious. She'd challenged him that day, saying that if he didn't stop his "pouting", she would break up with him. He'd urged her to go find someone new and hadn't even minded when she'd spread the word that she'd broken up with him. All he'd felt was relief that things were over.

Apparently, she didn't agree with her foiled battle strategy, but he wasn't going to worry about Janey Smithers any longer. He had plans for the night. Thankfully, football season was over so he didn't have to worry about Friday night games.

Rushing into his house, he dumped his books on his bed, called out to his mother that he was home, then scurried out to the backyard to do his chores and avoid his brothers. Ryker was a senior in high school this year and getting ready to go off to college. He was going away with his parents tonight to spend a weekend visiting colleges, even though he already knew which one he was going to. Xander was in charge for the weekend, but Axel knew that Xander had a date tonight as well, so there wouldn't be any problems tonight.

Unfortunately, even though his parents were heading out of town, he still had to get his chores done before he could go out. So instead of opening up his computer and surfing the Internet, he sprinted down the stairs and out the back door, heading to the shed. He pulled the lawnmower out, checked the fluids and primed the pump. Then he spent the next fifteen minutes cursing the stubborn machine, trying to get it to start. When it finally roared to life, he whipped through mowing the grass as quickly as possible, ignoring the turns around the trees so he could finish faster. He figured he still had about an hour to shower and change before walking back to pick up Lorrie for their date.

He was just pushing the ancient machine back into the shed when he felt the hairs on the back of his neck prickle in warning. He looked around and Janey was sauntering through the gate towards him, a "come-hither" smile on her pretty face. Axel looked towards the house and actually thought about making a run for it, but knew he had to face her now, get it over with. He finally understood that Janey was more like a spider, lying in wait for her prey to fall into her trap before she spun her evil web and trapped her victim.

"What's up?" he asked.

She grinned up into his face, her blue eyes twinkling merrily. "You look hot mowing the grass like that," she said, putting her hands on his waist and giving him that special look that promised so much to a guy.

Axel was actually repulsed by her now. He pulled her fingers out from under his tee-shirt and took a step back. "I thought we broke up. Why are you here?"

Her smile never faltered. "Oh, that was just a tiff. We're still together. And we should go to the party tonight. I heard that Jonas' parents weren't going to be at his house tonight. Maybe we could sneak upstairs and discover what the master bedroom looks like."

Axel knew exactly what she was talking about. And most guys would jump at the opportunity to be alone in a bed with Janey Smithers but she just made his skin crawl now. "I'm not sure what my plans are for tonight."

She laughed and swung her long, blond hair over her shoulder. "Well, of course you're going to the party tonight. Everyone is going to be there."

"Joe and Darren mentioned it earlier today."

"So how about if you pick me up? You can steal your dad's car for the night, right?"

He shook his head. "You know I don't do things like that."

She giggled and moved closer. "Even if it means a nice, big back seat? With me right there with you?"

Axel pulled her hands away from his waist and stepped backwards. "Like I said, I'm not sure what's going to happen tonight." It wasn't exactly a lie. He knew he was taking Lorrie to the diner for a burger then to a movie, but there were a lot of details that he hadn't planned out. Although, he knew with certainty that he wasn't going to steal his dad's car and pick up this black widow.

Janey didn't seem to be getting the hint. She backed up slightly and shook her head. "Axel, you're such a goody goody. If you weren't so big and gorgeous, I might just tease you about that." He had no response to her compliment about his physical attributes. He was just a guy with long legs. Since all of his brothers were about the same height and breadth, he didn't think he was very special. "I gotta go take a shower," he said and turned away from her, not even offering her a drink like he normally would have.

She moved closer, ignoring all the signs that he wasn't interested simply because she didn't believe that any man wouldn't be interested. "Hey, when we get to Jonas' party tonight," she twisted slightly and reached into her purse, pulling out a plastic bag, "I have plans to make it even more interesting."

Axel looked at the bag of marijuana, stunned that she would be so blatant. "What are you going to do with that?" he asked, even more disgusted with her. He didn't do drugs, nor did any of his brothers or friends.

She snorted delicately. "We're going to smoke it, silly!" she replied as if that were the most obvious answer. "We can share with the others, or we can hide out behind the pool house and have our own little party," she said, moving closer, snuggling up against his big, wide chest.

Axel stepped back and headed towards his house, not wanting her anywhere near him. "I'll see you around, okay?"

Janey watched with narrowed, angry eyes as the biggest and sexiest guy in the school walked away from her. He walked away from her! How dare he!

She stood in the middle of his backyard, plotting her next move. Axel had better figure out where his priorities should be. She stuffed the bag of weed back into her purse and stomped out of his backyard, her mind working the different angles, trying to figure out how she was going to manipulate the situation tonight so that he was paying attention to her, devoting himself to making her happy.

Four hours later, Axel whistled as he walked home from Lorrie's house. Her father had told her to be home by ten o'clock and it was now five minutes before that hour. What's better, he'd even gotten a kiss, which had been sweet. Lorrie was nice, he thought as he cut through his neighbor's yard and went in through the back door.

His youngest brother, Ash, was sitting on the couch with four of his friends, chowing down on popcorn and soda.

"You're home early," Ash teased, glancing over the back of the couch at his brother. "Why's that?"

Axel put a hand to the back of the couch then swung his legs over, landing with a thud on the cushion with a smile of victory. He'd never do that if his mom was around but his parents had left several hours ago with Ryker. "I just dropped Lorrie off at home. Her dad wanted her in early tonight."

"I heard Janey earlier today telling everyone that you guys were back together."

Axel snorted and shook his head while grabbing a handful of popcorn. "Not on a dare," he replied. "What are you watching?"

"Nightmare on Elm Street," Ash replied.

Axel rolled his eyes. "You guys were watching this last week."

"Yeah, but we didn't catch all the mistakes."

Axel threw a piece of popcorn at the screen when the wrong lamp exploded. The main character, Nancy, had rigged another one and all four of the guys sitting in the living room booed and threw more popcorn at the screen.

By midnight, Ash's friends were all gone and the popcorn was vacuumed up. Xander walked through the front door and, a second later, the phone rang. "Hi mom," Xander said, grinning from ear to ear because their parents were calling to make sure all three of their boys were safe and sound inside the house at the required time.

When all three had spoken to both parents, they were off to sleep. The following morning, Axel couldn't believe the rumors on his cell phone. Joe and Darren had been arrested for drug possession? He knew those guys would never do drugs! The three of them had been offered drugs before but none had ever been tempted.

The phone rang and Ash grabbed it while Axel read through the text messages, astonished that only his two friends had been arrested although the police had broken up the party at Jonas' house. Several people texted that the drugs that the police found weren't even out in the open. They'd found the stash stuffed into Darren's jacket, which had been dropped down over one of the patio chairs along with several other coats.

"Can they even do that?" he asked to no one in particular. "I mean, don't they need a search warrant to look in someone's pocket?"

Xander was looking at his own text messages as he simultaneously flipped the eggs he was making for breakfast. "I don't think that's right. It seems like an invasion of privacy, but maybe there was something about exigent circumstances."

Axel was furious. "Don't the police need to think that someone's life is in danger for that to apply? And why would they need to search someone's coat pocket?"

Xander's response was only a shoulder shrug. "Maybe they thought there was a gun in the pocket."

Ash shook his head and tossed his napkin at Xander. "That doesn't fall under exigent circumstances."

"How do you even know what that is?" Xander demanded, taking the napkin and lighting it on fire with the gas grill. He turned on the range hood which quickly dispelled the smoke.

Ash and Axel both ignored the fire that would have caused his mother to be livid if she'd been here. "We had a debate about it in civics class last month. Someone's life has to be in danger for the police to be able to enter a building. I don't think it applies to searching someone's pockets while breaking up a teenage party."

Axel listened to his brothers as they bantered back and forth, fascinated by the possibilities. "So what would allow the police to search Darren's coat pocket?"

Ash and Xander looked at each other and shook their heads, neither aware of any reason. "What are we? Lawyers?" Ash scoffed. "Go to the library and find out for yourself," he said, leaning back in his chair with his feet up on the table, a pose his mother would never allow were she here with the three of them.

"I'm calling dad," Axel said and walked out of the kitchen.

The doorbell rang just as he was passing by. He swung around, hoping it might be one of his other friends who had more information.

But when he opened the front door, it was to find Janey standing there, looking smug and self-righteous.

"What's up?" he asked, trying to be polite.

She stepped into the foyer without waiting for an invitation. "You didn't show up at the party last night," she said, looking up at him and moving closer than he wanted her to be.

"You're right," he said and took a step back, putting a hand to her shoulder to stop her when she moved closer.

Janey stopped but only because Axel was so much bigger and stronger. She couldn't break his hold. "Your friends were there though. Why weren't you?"

Axel was tired of the woman and wanted her out of his life. "Janey, I have more important things to deal with than you. Get out."

Axel was taking the stairs two at a time when she called up to him, "Like getting your friends out of juvenile detention?"

He froze and turned around. Looking down at her, he suddenly realized that she was the one who set up Joe and Darren. He walked back down the stairs, amazed at her vindictiveness. "Did you set them up? Those were your drugs! Weren't they?" he demanded.

She sauntered closer once again. "Answer my question first."

He glared down at her. "No."

Her eyes widened at the unprecedented rejection. "No? No, you're not going to answer my question or…just no?"

Axel leaned down, furious with the evil woman. "No. I'm not going to have anything to do with you. No, we're not getting back together. No, I'm not answering your question."

He saw the fury light up her previously pretty blue eyes. "Then you're friends are going down for drug possession. And when the police weigh that bag, I'm pretty sure they'll charge your friends with intent to distribute because there's too much marijuana in that bag for just personal use." She was snapping the words at him, furious that any man wouldn't bow down to her powers. It had never happened before and she wasn't going to be thwarted now.

Axel was amazed that anyone could be so vicious. "Are you implying that you set up my friends simply because I didn't show up at the party last night?"

She moved closer, unafraid of him despite his size and the power behind his anger. "I'm saying, if you start acting appropriately, I'll go to the police and tell them that I saw the drugs put into your friends' pockets by someone else. If you don't behave, then I'll let them fry."

He was stunned, truly shocked by how far she would go. "So…you're using extortion to get a boyfriend."

She shrugged her shoulders delicately. "I thought the term was blackmail, but whatever. I don't care what you call it. I just want results."

"You're only fifteen, Janey. How can you be so manipulative?"

She laughed and tossed her hair behind her shoulders. "You've never met my mother, have you?"

It suddenly occurred to Axel that he hadn't actually met her parents. He'd been to her house a few times, but neither of her parents had been there. "No, now that you mention it, I haven't."

Janey shrugged. "She's taught me everything I know."

Axel felt bad for Mr. Smithers. "Regardless, I'll figure out how to get Joe and Darren out without giving you what you want."

"I'll help too," Xander said, stepping out of the living room so he was now visible.

Ash came into the foyer from the opposite side. "I'm in too. I don't think we can let an extortionist go unpunished, can we?"

Janey looked up at the two other young men, both of whom were almost identical in size but with differences to their features. All four of the Thorpe boys were handsome, but Janey only wanted Axel. "Do whatever you want," she said, her chin going up. "Axel, I'll expect you at my house tonight. We're going out to dinner."

She didn't wait for a reply but simply stepped out of the house and sashayed down the street.

The three boys stared after her. "We're not letting her get away with that, are we?" Ash asked, shutting off the almost continuous stream of text messages from his friends to his cell phone. This was much more important.

"She won't stop until someone makes her," Xander pointed out.

Axel turned to face his older brother. "We should call mom and dad."

Xander nodded his agreement. "We should head to the police station while we're doing it too."

The three boys climbed into his mother's giant SUV, which had been left for their use but only in emergency situations. All three boys considered this to be an emergency. While Xander drove, Ash and Axel called their parents and explained the situation.

At the police station, they told the story several more times, first to the reception officer, next to another uniformed police officer, and then one more time to two detectives, all with their parents conferenced in on the line.

It took several hours, multiple phone calls, bringing the parents of Joe and Darren into the situation, and even the assistant district attorney, but by dinner time, Joe and Darren were free and relieved that the nightmare was over. The Thorpe boys' parents had aborted their tour of the college, but it was worth it to be there to protect and support their children.

In the end, the bag of drugs was fingerprinted and neither Joe nor Darren had touched it. So there was no way the police could accept that they'd been using or intending to distribute the drugs when they hadn't even handled them.

The best part came when they were all walking out. Janey and her mother were walking into the police station, ready to make a statement. Their expressions were smug until Janey saw Axel walking out at the same time. Then her face showed her surprise and a hint of concern.

Kiera's Story….

Kiera stood up when her name was called, wiping her sweaty palms on the sides of her dress. But she refused to allow anyone to know how nervous she was as she stepped onto the stage. She was only fourteen years old, the youngest ever to be on the varsity debate team and she was terrified. But she was also ready to take on the challenge!

"The topic is…" Kiera held her breath, praying that she would be prepared for this. But as the host paused, Kiera couldn't help but feel her chest tightening, the muscles in her stomach contracting with anxiety. "Do you believe school uniforms are beneficial?"

Kiera's breath caught in her throat. Was she kidding? She turned to the speaker and stared. School uniforms? That was her topic?

"You are pro," the narrator said in Kiera's direction then turned to her opponent, "and you are opposed." She took a moment to organize her papers. "You have ten minutes to form your argument."

Kiera used her pen and paper to scribble out thoughts, but her mind was whirling about the simplicity of the topic. She was hoping for something harder, like global warming or capital punishment. Those were hot topics and she could really get to the meat of those arguments. But school uniforms? How ridiculous!

Regardless, she tackled the problem with the same intensity that she would have with any other subject. While making her notes, she didn't even look at her opponent, focusing only on what she thought the main issues were, both the pros, which she would argue, and the cons, which she would need to counter after her opponent raised them.

Thirty minutes later, the debate was over and she was smiling hugely as she accepted the certificate for winning with the most points. Stepping down off of the platform, she humbly accepted the congratulations of her teammates, all of whom were part of the success, while the stress slowly seeped out of her body. "Let's get a burger!" someone called out.

Chaperones and team members shifted en masse, everyone eager to grab something to eat. Kiera was suddenly starving, having skipped breakfast as well as lunch in her nervousness. Since it was almost dinner time now, she wanted food and lots of it.

Kevin Lewis moved closer to her, smiling at Kiera as he said, "Those were some good points you made. I never would have thought about community spirit as a benefit to school uniforms."

Kiera laughed, looking down at her shoes. "That was something I read a while ago. I don't know if it's true."

"I think it makes a lot of sense," he replied, moving closer to her. Kiera glanced up at him, not sure she understood his body language.

"We should catch up with the others," she said nervously. It wasn't that she didn't like Kevin, it was just that she didn't want to hurt his feelings because she only liked him as a friend. And if she was grasping his body language properly, he was about to ask her something, or do something, that would make both of them uncomfortable.

Kevin looked over at the rest of the group who were all heading towards the parking lot and the bus that had driven them to the debate site across town. "It's just that…well," he shifted on his feet nervously. "I was just wondering…"

Kiera stepped in at that point. "Kevin, do you think Lauren is pretty?" she asked, changing the subject towards her friend.

Kevin looked back at their group, seeing the tall brunette looking back at them. "Yeah, Lauren is nice enough."

Kiera turned and started walking towards the bus, looking back at Kevin when he didn't immediately follow. "She thinks you're very cute," she explained, shifting the focus away from herself and on to her friend. Kiera knew that Lauren had been mooning over Kevin for several weeks now. That was a record for her friend, who usually flitted from one boy-crush to another whenever someone new caught her eye.

"She's nice. But I was wondering…"

"She says she liked your argument about classroom size last week. She didn't agree with you, but she said it sounded like you really knew what you were talking about. She likes that in a guy."

Kevin looked confused and they were getting closer to the others. He was missing his chance. But then Lauren caught his eye again and he smiled in her direction. When she smiled right back at him, then quickly looked away, he chuckled. "You're trying to get me and Lauren together, aren't you?" he asked.

Kiera smothered her giggle but nodded her head. "She really likes you but you'll have to be quick about it. Lauren has a tendency to be fickle if the object of her affection doesn't return those feelings. She's not the most confident girl around, but that's probably normal and isn't going to waste her time."

Kevin looked up again at the other girl, then back at Kiera. "You definitely have a way of adjusting the world so that it suits your plans, don't you?"

Kiera thought that was the sweetest thing he'd ever said to her. "Well, I do have a plan for my life," she came right back. "And so far, I've been able to stay on track. That doesn't mean everything will fit into my plan."

He really liked Kiera, but he was starting to understand that she wasn't interested in him. Maybe Kiera was more driven than he preferred in a girl. He wanted someone he could talk with and who would challenge his mind about issues but he also knew that Kiera was much smarter than he was. He didn't really enjoy that feeling. It made him feel insecure and he knew he would grow to resent that after a while.

There was also the inkling he was starting to understand about her that was probably more bothersome. Kiera didn't want anything in her life that didn't coincide with her plans for life. "I guess since I'm planning to attend the University of California next year, you're not interested in attending the dance with me next Friday night?"

Kiera was exasperated at the idea of wasting her time on Kevin. He was nice enough for a friend but a long term relationship with him wasn't in the future. He needed to accept that. "I'm going to Georgetown University," she came right back.

His eyes widened as he took in her completely serious statement. "But that's in three years. We might have some good times in between."

She shook her head sadly. "Kevin, you're a senior. I'm a freshman. Wouldn't it be embarrassing to be dating me?"

He looked at her beautiful face and knockout figure and laughed. "Are you kidding me? Half the guys on the debate team are in love with you."

She rolled her eyes. "You're exaggerating."

Kevin didn't think he'd ever known another female who was as oblivious to her beauty as this woman standing in front of him. "You really don't know, do you?"

"What? That guys are silly? Of course I know that," she said and stood up on her tip toes and kissed his cheek. "Now go ask Lauren to next Friday's dance. I'll bet by the time we drive back to school, she'll have told you all about her rock collection."

He was about to walk away but that last statement stopped him. "Rock collection?" he asked warily. "Are you kidding?"

Kiera laughed again, delighted that her friend was going to the dance and she'd maintained her friendship with a very smart guy. "Go!" she urged. "And be nice!"

Kiera could actually feel the sigh of relief that Lauren released as her crush came closer. Within five minutes, Lauren was smiling excitedly up at Kevin. It was sweet and romantic, but Kiera was ravenous for a burger and fries, and all this chit-chatting was getting in the way of her devouring those carbs. It still took more than twenty minutes to get everyone on board the bus, but thankfully, they were quickly on their way – first for some tasty fast food, and then home.

CHAPTER 1

"I can't do this," she whispered to herself. "I thought I could, but it's simply too painful."

Kiera's shoulders slumped and she tried to find the answers within the depths of her martini. Unfortunately, the liquid only mocked her, small circles forming on the top and quickly dissipating as if to say, "You never should have come here."

Or maybe the glass was only telling her that a heavy-footed person was walking by.

She held her head up with her forehead, trying to figure out what to do. She'd only been at her new job for a less than a week and already she loved it. The people were fun, hard-working, extremely smart...that all added up to an ideal workplace where she was challenged to excel and stand out, but what was even better, she respected her peers. Instinctively, she knew that The Thorpe Group encouraged competition but, unlike other law firms, didn't condone the backstabbing and win-or-get-out pressure on cases. Oh, they won cases! Clients came to The Thorpe Group for legal advice from all over the country, all over the world even, because they knew that The Thorpe Group would deliver. The difference was that their success was due to a brilliant legal team versus barely ethical legal tactics.

There were other law firms out there with a similar reputation, although none as glamorous as The Thorpe Group. Gaining a few years at this firm on her resume would set her up perfectly for success wherever she wanted to go as a next step.

No, the work and the workers weren't the problem.

Even the location was great. Chicago was a fabulous city with excellent museums, a thriving art community, tons of shopping and a wide range of people with which to interact.

Nope, all of her issues were personal. She'd foolishly convinced herself that she would be able to deal with this problem but, after only a few days, she knew that the issue was bigger than she could handle.

Axel Thorpe.

She'd seen the gorgeous, huge male in the hallway earlier today. And that one sighting, just the short glimpse of the man as he walked into a conference room, was why she was here, trying to drown her problems in a martini.

Unfortunately, she realized after ordering the potent cocktail that she didn't like martinis.

She also didn't like her body's reaction to seeing Axel Thorpe again. She'd almost embarrassed herself when she'd seen him. Thankfully, she didn't think he'd seen her trip. Nor had any of her co-workers, which was at least something. She'd had to catch herself by grabbing onto a chair, which probably looked ridiculous, but mercifully, she hadn't fallen on the floor. She might have passed off the accident as just a fluke, but she'd almost fallen over the conference room table. Not something most people trip over because of its size and obvious placement in the room. But then again, most people hadn't just seen the love of their life after so many years.

Kiera sighed and took another sip of her martini. Maybe she just needed to plow through the drink. Keep forcing it down. Hopefully, the alcohol would keep her mind from replaying the scene. She would eventually feel nothing. Maybe that was the way she should handle Axel too. Just keep running into him until her body was numb from the reaction.

Perhaps today's sighting and the humiliating aftermath was just a fluke. Maybe if she just went up and spoke to him, greeted him and asked him how his day was going, she wouldn't be so flustered when she accidentally saw him. Sort of like taking an allergy shot every week to build up one's immune system.

She sighed and took another sip of her martini, her face squinching up ridiculously as she tried to swallow the foul stuff. And she had to acknowledge the stupidity of her idea. Being around him six years ago hadn't diminished his appeal or the impact he'd had on her when she was in college. Every time she'd seen him, she'd been floored. Just like today. Her knees went weak, she had trouble breathing, her whole body started shaking and she was unable to speak coherently.

Maybe it was just an allergy!

She almost giggled to herself and looked down at her drink. Was she reaching the giggle stage after only a few sips of the martini?

She pulled a file folder out of her leather bag, intending to get some work done. She wouldn't think about Axel. She would simply push him from her mind every time he entered. And if she saw him in the hallways at work? Well, she'd known that would happen when she'd accepted the position at The Thorpe Group.

The man was one of the co-owners, for goodness sake. She would have been a fool to think she'd never see him.

But after so many years, she'd hoped that she was over him.

She shook her head with derision. Did one ever get over someone like Axel? He really was one in a million. She remembered the first time she'd seen him, laughing in a bar just like this one. She'd been a sophomore at Georgetown University in Washington, D.C. and he'd been clerking for a Supreme Court justice.

He'd been magnificent, she thought with a smile. So tall, so handsome and one could just see the charm and charisma oozing from the man's smile...

Six Years Earlier....

"This place is too crowded," Kiera pointed out, peering through the windows of the upscale bar in Georgetown. "Why don't we go back to our usual hangout?"

Debbie just grabbed Kiera's hand and pulled her deeper into the crowd, obviously eager to be here for some reason. "Because Brian will be there," Debbie replied, referring to her ex-boyfriend, almost yelling over the noise of the bar. "And I really don't want to run into him again. He's still angry about our breakup last week."

She quickly shifted out of the way of someone who almost spilled beer on her. "This place is a bit rowdier than the places we usually hang out," Kiera cautioned.

Debbie looked around and smiled. "It's nice! I like trying out new places and meeting new people."

Except that Debbie had invited all of their old friends here so they probably wouldn't meet anyone they didn't already know. "I'm not sure I'm feeling all that adventurous tonight, Debbie," Kiera cautioned. It wasn't so much that she wasn't into trying new things, but she preferred less crowded conditions. This bar was wall to wall people.

"Just pretend for one night," Debbie laughed back, pulling Kiera up to the bar and ordered two beers.

Kiera shook her head, but followed her friend, not sure this was such a good idea. "Fine," she agreed and tried to hide the weird feeling that had come over her suddenly. Midterms had just finished, and she had a bit of breathing room before her next paper was due, so it wouldn't be a bad thing to relax for a few hours. "We're not staying late."

Was she being too cautious? Probably, she told herself as she slipped between a couple that was heavy into a debate on the latest political wranglings. It was hard to avoid those kinds of discussions in a Georgetown bar. Not only were they mere miles from the heart of the federal buildings where real estate was so expensive, the area was teeming with history. The streets were mostly cobblestones from the colonial period and even a small townhouse would cost well over one million dollars. The cobblestones were ballast from the rum trade, but the political debates were due to the proximity of the federal government. She suspected that many of the people here were either international studies students, political science majors, or were interning for a senator or representative.

"This is awesome," Debbie called back to her, grinning from ear to ear, obviously excited to be in a new setting instead of their normal haunts. The bar was darker, probably proud of the bare bricks and heavy, wooden beams overhead that might or might not date back to the colonial period. If they weren't, Kiera doubted the owner would 'fess up to having new beams. Many of the establishments promoted the "old time" feel of their buildings by refurbishing so that the décor was reminiscent of colonial times, but with all the bells and whistles of modern conveniences. Of course, there was the one trendy bar she knew of that bragged about having bullet holes in the walls. Not that they claimed the bullets were colonial, but every bar had to have its quirks, she supposed.

She took the beer Debbie handed her and then turned around, trying to find a place to sit down. The odds of finding a chair or stool in a place this crowded would be pretty slim, she thought while her eyes surveyed the room.

Kiera noticed him the moment Debbie's back was turned. He was in a group of four or five other men, all of them laughing about something. But not him. He was staring right back at her. His eyes seemed to capture hers. That look was so powerful, his gaze so strong that it jolted her all the way down to her toes. More than just her eyes were captured. Her whole body was frozen in place, the noise and crowds, the damp smell of beer and other drinks…all of it just disappeared from her consciousness as she stared right back at him. She couldn't breathe and she couldn't pull her eyes away. She couldn't even move.

She hadn't even realized that Debbie had turned around and was trying engage her in conversation until Debbie breathed, "Who is that?"

Kiera struggled, but she was finally able to pull her eyes away and glanced at her friend. To her horror, Debbie was staring at the man! Her man! And there was a great deal of interest on Debbie's lovely features. Jealousy, hot and powerful stabbed through Kiera's body. She didn't like her friend even looking at a man she already considered to be hers.

Okay, so that was ridiculous. She couldn't claim ownership of a human being simply because they were looking at each other from across the room. But there was no way to suppress the furious feelings that surged through Kiera as her friend surveyed the tall, handsome stranger. Kiera tried to be rational about this. She had no claim on the man. But regardless, she was suddenly incensed that Debbie had dared to look at the guy. It was a sudden and all-consuming jealousy, something Kiera had never experienced before, so she wasn't sure how to handle that level of intensity. Men had never affected her in the past. To her, they were simply other human beings she could study with or joke with during non-study hours.

It was completely different with this man. And completely irrational.

Instead of revealing her jealousy, Kiera took a sip of her beer and pulled Debbie through the crowd until they couldn't see the man anymore, although Debbie's blond head kept craning at different angles to try and take another gander at him.

Debbie wasn't shy about letting a guy know she was interested. But didn't she need a bit of time to get over Brian? Debbie had just broken up with her boyfriend earlier this week! What was she doing ogling another man so quickly? It was ridiculous and disrespectful of Brian's feelings not to mention the three years they'd been together.

Kiera tried hard to ignore her jealousy, pushing Debbie to talk about classes and their friends in an effort to distract her from the gorgeous man. When a couple more friends showed up, Kiera was relieved to finally have support distracting Debbie from the man Kiera had already claimed, at least mentally. Not that she would do anything about her gnawing desire to find out more about the tall, intensely handsome man with the piercing, ice blue eyes.

Unfortunately, Kiera wasn't like Debbie. Where Kiera was shy and introverted, Debbie was the party girl, the one that pushed Kiera to get out and have more fun. Debbie also didn't hide her interest in the opposite sex. When Debbie wanted a man, she walked right up to him and started talking to him. Kiera hadn't ever felt this way, but she knew that she wouldn't go up to that man tonight. She wasn't that brave. Besides, the look he was giving her sent some scary feelings right through her body. And he hadn't even touched her! No, she couldn't handle him, so it was better to just stay away from that kind of…whatever it was.

An hour later, Kiera desperately needed to use the ladies' room. Unfortunately, the man she'd spotted earlier had been positioned right next to the hallway where the bathrooms were located. She wiggled in her chair, determined to ignore the need. But when Debbie popped up with the same intention, Kiera wasn't going to allow her to go alone. "I'll come with you," she said, determined to keep Debbie and the stranger from seeing each other again. Kiera knew she couldn't have the man. She wasn't glamorous or rich or any of those adjectives that would apply to the woman on that kind of man's arm. She was passably pretty with curly brown hair that tended to get out of control. She had a good enough figure but she wasn't any lingerie model.

In short, Kiera knew she was just an average kind of gal.

Debbie, on the other hand, was not only blond and beautiful, she had a way about her that seemed to draw men into her realm. She was fun and nice, not to mention extremely intelligent. And over the past year, they'd been good friends and study partners. But at this moment, Kiera could honestly say that she hated Debbie. Because Kiera knew that Debbie was going to talk to the stranger. Kiera could see it in Debbie's eyes and was helpless to stop the action. Kiera felt helpless, desperate to keep Debbie from acquiring yet another conquest, but unable to come up with any ideas on how to stop her from working her magic.

Kiera had no doubt that Debbie was going to approach the man. It was in her eyes and Kiera glanced over at the man, her eyes worried as she gauged the distance between Debbie and the man.

But as soon as she found him through the crowd, she realized that he was looking at her!

Debbie was even primping, doing her best to get noticed. Kiera looked from Debbie to the stranger, wondering when he would notice the blond beauty standing next to her.

The stranger's eyes never wavered and Kiera's stomach did flip flops at the realization.

They made their way down the hallway to the ladies' room and Kiera breathed a sigh of relief. One gauntlet down, one more to go. Maybe she could get Debbie out of the bar. Maybe if they just left, Debbie wouldn't have time to set her sights on…

"Did you see him again?" Debbie gushed as they both washed their hands.

Kiera's throat constricted when she noticed the light of intent in Debbie's eyes. "I'm going to talk to him," she declared. Kiera sighed with resignation. When Debbie went on the prowl, men tended to fall to their knees and worship her.

She fluffed her blond hair one more time and Kiera wished she had done something more interesting with her out-of-control curls. They floated around her like some sort of bohemian gypsy instead of being smooth and glossy-straight like Debbie's blond hair. Debbie even had those pretty blue eyes that she could bat at any man and have him desperate to do her bidding. Kiera stared at her boring brown eyes, wishing for the first time that her face could be more interesting, more devastatingly beautiful. Her lashes might be long, but her mouth was too wide and too full, her nose too small to be anything other than cute instead of sophisticated and interesting. Her cheeks weren't gaunt, which was so hip lately. She even had a sprinkling of freckles over the bridge of her nose and her cheeks that she normally covered up with makeup but hadn't bothered tonight, much to her irritation now.

With a sigh, Kiera looked behind her at Debbie's luscious figure, wondering how long it would be before Debbie had the stranger wrapped around her pinky finger.

They stepped out of the hallway, Kiera holding her head down, not wanting to watch Debbie snag yet another man. Why couldn't her friend leave this one alone? Why couldn't she just let one, this special one, go about his business and not make him fall under her spell?

Suddenly, her path was blocked and someone was holding a beer towards her. She looked up, but all she saw was a denim clad chest. It was an extraordinarily muscular chest, she noticed. Her heartbeat picked up rapidly because she knew exactly who this man was. Her eyes continued to climb and she couldn't believe it when her light brown eyes captured the ice blue ones of her stranger.

The man was smiling down at her, not even noticing her blond friend beside her. Of course, Kiera had no idea if Debbie was still there or if she'd moved on. It was just this man, herself and her racing heart.

"I wish I could come up with some witty line to get your attention, but I'll admit, I'm stumped," he said with a deep voice that reminded her of spicy chocolate.

Kiera tried to smile. She tried to catch her breath. But with this man standing so close to her, his body heat and that incredible male scent wafting towards her, she just couldn't think. "I believe I'm in the same situation," she replied nervously.

He looked down at her hands and smiled. "I noticed you were drinking beer. I got you another one," he said, referring to the second beer he still had in his hands. "I know that was forward of me, but…"

Kiera straightened quickly, not wanting him to think she was rejecting the offer. "No, that's very kind of you," she replied, taking the beer. But her hand accidentally touched his and she felt some sort of…spark? She pulled back quickly, unsure of what was going on. Unfortunately, at the same time, he was releasing the beer. The result was both of them grabbing for the beer again, fumbling and beer spilled out, landing on her hand.

"I'm so sorry!" she gasped, horrified at how clumsy she was acting.

"My fault," his deep, sexy voice replied.

"No, really, I was the clumsy one," she countered, looking up into those blue eyes once again. And she couldn't move. Not even to take a breath. They looked into each other's eyes and it was as if the noise of the bar once again faded away leaving only the noise of her heartbeat. Time was frozen as she stood in front of this large man standing in front of her and the cold beer in her hand.

"I'm Axel Thorpe," he said softly, that deep baritone soothing over her skin like a balm.

"I'm Kiera Ward," she replied. As his large, strong hand took hers, she prayed hard that her knees wouldn't give out on her and she wouldn't throw up because she was suddenly feeling like something had just exploded inside of her stomach.

She had no idea how long they stood there like that. It could have been only a moment or it might have been a half hour. At that point in her life, she honestly could have looked into his ice blue eyes for the rest of her life.

"What are you doing here?" he asked, grabbing a napkin off of the bar and wiping down her hand.

She was struck by the strength in those hands. His denim sleeves were rolled up slightly and she could see the muscles in his forearms. She smiled, thinking the man had more than just good bones. She could tell by the controlled way he moved that there were muscles underneath that shirt to back up the height and breadth of those incredible shoulders.

She shivered and tried to pretend that she wasn't so affected by his closeness, not wanting this sophisticated man to realize how nervous she was. "I'm a student over at Georgetown."

He smiled and they discussed the various bars they'd frequented. That conversation led to their hobbies and jobs. She found out that he was one of four brothers, all of whom were in the legal profession. Kiera couldn't help but be impressed that he was clerking for a Supreme Court justice at the moment and she smiled, telling him of her goal to go to law school at Georgetown.

Kiera had no idea how long they'd talked, but one of the waitresses was wiping down tables when she finally looked around. "I think I'd better head home," she said, suddenly realizing that the bar had cleared out at some point while they were talking. She looked around for Debbie but all of her friends had left.

"I'll walk you home," Axel stated firmly and stood up himself.

She smiled up at him, relieved that their night wasn't going to end just yet. "That would be nice," she replied.

They walked through the now-quiet streets of Georgetown, the uneven brick sidewalks and centuries old townhomes adding charm and intimacy to their conversation. But too quickly, she was standing in front of the tiny townhome she shared with four other women and she silently wished that she was still living in the college dorms. Because then she'd have more time with this fascinating man since the dorms were farther away.

"Something inside of me is telling me not to kiss you," he stated as he moved closer to her. Kiera's heartbeat increased as she smiled up at him.

"But you're going to ignore that voice, aren't you?" she whispered, shocked that she could be so bold. She'd never been this way with another man before, always preferring to hold off and get to know a guy before becoming physical in any way. But there was just something about Axel that made it feel like she knew everything she needed to know about him.

"I believe I am," he replied.

She saw his eyes light up despite the darkness of the night. When his lips touched hers, Kiera pulled back, shocked by the touch. But when she saw the same reaction on his face, it warmed her, giving her a secure feeling that she wasn't alone with this strange, new feeling.

He kissed her again, his lips barely brushing hers, over and over again, just touching. Until she reached up and touched his cheek, signaling her desperate need for more. And he gave it to her. The next kiss obliterated everything she'd ever known about kissing a man. This was new, different...both terrifying and amazing. She never wanted to stop kissing this man. So when he lifted his head, she was embarrassed by how ragged her breathing was. It felt like she'd just run a marathon.

"Have breakfast with me tomorrow morning," he sort of asked and demanded at the same time.

Kiera smiled up at him. "I'd love it," she said, her fingers floating over his shoulders and arms. She wasn't sure she wanted him to kiss her again. But she was pretty sure she didn't want to stop touching him.

"I can't leave if you're going to keep doing that," he told her, his hands on her waist flexing against her skin.

Kiera's hands stopped. She bit her lip, feeling an almost physical ache at the idea of pulling her hands away.

But she did it. She took a step back and smiled up at him. "I'll see you tomorrow," she whispered, then turned and ran into the house, closing the door quietly so she didn't wake up her housemates.

She had breakfast with him the next morning, and dinner that same day. In fact, they spent almost the entire weekend together, parting on Sunday night only because he had to work and she had classes. But they also had dinner every night that week. By Friday night, when he came to pick her up at her townhouse, she jumped into his arms, wrapping her legs around his waist and kissing him with everything she had inside of her, showing him in the only way she knew how what she wanted.

Axel had caught her that evening and hadn't let her go. They drove to his apartment and Kiera didn't even see the décor until the following morning when they both realized that they hadn't taken time to eat dinner the previous night. He'd taken her into his arms in the parking lot of his apartment complex and started kissing her and they'd fallen into bed together.

He had been her first lover and he was the most tender, caring and sweet man she'd ever met.

It took her less than twenty-four hours to know that she was in love with Axel Thorpe. And every time they were together, she found him more fascinating, more amazing. They had their fights, arguments over silly things. But it was one of those relationships that was so overpowering, by the time they realized they were fighting, they were already laughing and pulling the other closer to make up and apologize.

It was all so perfect until that fateful day when he picked her up with a huge grin on his handsome face. She smiled as she slipped into his powerful, low-slung car. "What's up?" she asked, excited for whatever was making him smile. She had just finished her finals but had decided to take summer courses so she could be closer to Axel over the summer months. They'd even discussed the possibility of renting a house on the beach for the long, Labor Day weekend after her summer classes finished and the fall semester started.

He kissed her gently before starting up the engine. "I'll tell you when we get to dinner."

"Where are we going for dinner?" she asked, uncaring, as long as she could be with him. They always had stimulating conversations until he kissed her and carried her to his bed. She loved this man and couldn't believe how wonderful life was with him.

"My place," he responded. "I want you all to myself when I tell you this news."

She grinned, eager to be alone with him. They had better, livelier conversations when it was just the two of them and they didn't need to worry about interrupting people at the next table with their heated debates or the waiter arriving to interrupt them. She also loved it because she didn't have to hide her need to touch him, to kiss him. And she didn't need to hide her desire for him to take her to his bed.

She was in full agreement with his plan. "Sounds perfect to me."

It took only a few minutes to arrive at his apartment complex. And when she walked through the door of his apartment, she knew exactly what to expect. Dinner was never first on the menu. It had been the same ever since they'd met that first night in the bar. At the first touch, they were on fire for each other and Axel lifted her into his arms and carried her into his bedroom. It wasn't much to look at, just a bed and dresser. Everything about the man was utilitarian. Until he was in the bedroom. Then he was anything but.

And when it was all over, she sighed with happiness as he held her in his arms. "So what's your big exciting news?" she asked once her breathing was back to normal.

He swatted her bottom and pulled her out of bed. "Come with me," he said and pulled her out the door, refusing to let her carry the sheet with her.

Kiera grabbed his shirt just as he pulled her out the door and slipped her arms into the warm material. No matter how many times he'd encouraged her to be more casual around him, she couldn't walk around his place naked. He had no qualms though.

"Here," he said, placing several pamphlets in her hands.

She looked down at the brochures, not sure what these had to do with him. "Are you going back to school?" she asked. Her heart lurched at the possibility since these brochures were for schools in Illinois.

He pulled her closer, his hands resting lightly on her back as he kissed the top of her head. "I was hoping you might transfer to the University of Chicago."

She smiled up at him, but her smile wasn't as bright as it had been a moment ago. "Why would I do that?" she asked.

"Because I'm going back to start up the mergers and acquisitions division at The Thorpe Group, the law firm my brothers own."

She pulled back slightly. "You're leaving Washington, D.C.?" she asked, a sharp, stabbing pain shooting through her stomach and chest at the idea. "I thought you loved your job at the Supreme Court? It's such a coup to have that opportunity."

"It is, but it's also just a stepping stone. The ultimate goal all along was to figure out which type of law I wanted to practice, so I could start up and build that division in my brothers' law firm. It's a great opportunity. And when you finish school, I'm sure there would be a job there for you as well."

Kiera pulled back, appalled by the idea. "I can get my own jobs, thank you very much." She was offended that he would suggest that he get her a job somewhere. She was going to be a great lawyer! She definitely didn't need handouts!

Axel pulled her back into his arms. "Of course you can. But why would you when you could have a ready-made job waiting for you?"

She didn't like his answer one little bit. "Because I need to prove myself on my own?" she suggested sarcastically, unable to hide the hurt in her voice with his idea. Did he think she couldn't cut it on her own merits?

He laughed again, shaking his head. "I have complete faith in your abilities, Kiera. That was never a question. But if you transferred to U of Chicago, we could still be together."

She pulled back, irritated for some reason. "And what about Georgetown University?" she challenged. "It has a better reputation than the University of Chicago. I had to work very hard to get into Georgetown."

He pulled back slightly, looking down at her with eyes that were hurt at her quick rejection. "I thought you wanted to go to law school?" he asked, his shoulders straightening in the face of her resistance. It all seemed like a great plan in his mind. Why couldn't she see how perfect this was?

"I do!"

"So what's wrong with law school in Chicago?"

She couldn't believe what he was actually suggesting. "What's wrong with working in a law firm right here in Washington, D.C.? It's the center of legal activity."

He shook his head, dismissing her idea completely. "This is all politics and lobbyists. It isn't the type of law I want to practice."

Words failed her. "Are you suggesting that I give up a great school, one that I've wanted to attend since I was ten years old, just because you have a cushy job with your brother's law firm?"

Axel stood there looking down at her, confused. "I'm not sure I understand. There is no downside to this for you. Hell, Kiera, you don't even need to work if you don't want to."

Kiera stood there staring at him, not sure how to react. "I don't think I understand what you're suggesting." Her body was going numb.

Axel pulled her closer, feeling her tense muscles underneath his fingers. "I want you to marry me. I would love it if you would come back to Chicago with me and be my wife."

Her mouth fell open and her chest felt about the same but with additional pain shooting throughout her whole body. "Are you suggesting that I give up going to law school, drop out of college and just follow you so I can be your wife?"

"You don't have to give up anything. But if you wanted to, I'm just saying that's okay. You can do anything you want. I intend on making enough money to support both of us."

Kiera knew he thought this was a good deal. But to her ears, she was giving up everything and he was getting the life he always wanted. "So let me get this straight. You want me to drop out of one of the best schools in the country, follow you to Chicago so you can pursue your dream career. You're not willing to get a job here in Washington, D.C., not even look for one here that might fit your desired legal area, because you want to go back to Chicago. You want me to give up everything while you gain everything. Is that it?"

He ran a hand through his hair, frustrated with the way she was interpreting his offer. "It isn't like you have to give up everything. Just transfer schools! And we can still be together! I know you love me and I feel exactly the same for you! What's the problem here?"

"The problem is that you're not sacrificing anything and yet you're asking me to sacrifice all of my dreams!"

They stood there in his small living area, glaring at each other.

If he thought that was who she was, he didn't know her at all.

"I have to go," she whispered, hurt beyond anything by his attitude and assumptions.

"No you don't," he said, trying to calm her down. "Just stay and talk about this," he tried to coax her.

She slipped back into the bedroom and grabbed her clothes, refusing to even look at him. When she was dressed, she walked back out to his barren living room and something occurred to her. "You've never really made this into a home because you always knew you'd be going back to Chicago, right?"

He'd grabbed his jeans as well, his frustration obvious. Axel looked around his apartment, not sure what she was talking about. "What do you mean?"

"This apartment…" she said, waving her hand around to encompass the sofa and books but no television, no coffee table. There was nothing that would make one sit back and relax. "It isn't just a bachelor pad. You've never really moved in here."

"Of course I have. All of my stuff is in the closet. What would you expect me to do?"

Kiera closed her mouth, so many things falling into place. "Well, I guess I should at least be flattered that you wanted me to come with you."

He grabbed his shirt, buttoning it up partway but his frustration was obvious. "We're not finished talking about this," he said and started looking for his keys. "Let's just go out to dinner." He stopped looking for them when he noticed her chin wobbling, a sure sign that she was closer to breaking down than he thought. He sighed heavily and moved towards her, intending to take her into his arms and reassure her that they could make this work.

She pulled back when he started to touch her, not sure what she might do if she felt his hands on her back. Kiera was so hurt by his suggestion that she didn't need to work. But she was also feeling a great deal of pain caused by the fact that he wouldn't even consider finding a job here in Washington, D.C., at least until she finished school herself. He wasn't willing to sacrifice anything for her. She'd been such a fool! She'd thought he genuinely cared for her, that they had something special, but his offer explained it all to her. She was a convenience. He didn't see her as an equal partner at all, but just a good lay that he wanted to transport to his home town.

She was holding on to her emotions with all the control she had at the moment and she didn't want to break down into tears now. He already thought of her as the kind of woman who went to college to get an MRS degree, what would he think of her if she started weeping all over him, begging him to stay here with her? He'd lose even more respect for her.

She couldn't handle that. If there was nothing else, she wanted him to at least respect her.

"I'm not really hungry any more. I'll just make my own way home."

That infuriated Axel. "There's no way I'm letting you take the bus or catch a cab, Kiera. I'll drive you home. And we need to talk about this. There has to be some way to make this work."

"No!" she snapped at him, not sure if she was saying 'no' about making it work or him driving her home. "I'll get home on my own."

"Don't be ridiculous," he practically growled. "Hold on. I think my keys are in the bedroom."

As soon as he disappeared in search of his car keys, she slipped out the door. Thankfully, a cab was at the curb letting someone else off so she was able to dive into the back just as Axel was rushing out the door. Her last image of him was his furious face as the cab driver pulled away and she knew that the tears were already streaming down her cheeks.

CHAPTER 2

Current Day....

Kiera pushed the martini out of her line of sight. She wasn't going to drink it. She looked up to try and find a waitress, wanting something a bit less lethal. She was just about to raise her hand when the office manager for The Thorpe Group spotted her from another table. Kiera wanted to just slide under the table and pretend like she wasn't here, but Autumn – a stunning brunette woman – walked gracefully to Kiera's table.

"What are you doing here all alone?" she asked, smiling sincerely at Kiera. "Why don't you join us? We're about to celebrate Mia's newfound freedom, and I heard that you were instrumental in figuring out what was really going on with that sleezebag ex-fiancé of hers."

Kiera was already shaking her head when Mia Paulson herself appeared at the edge of the table. "It's you!" she gasped and bent low, hugging Kiera tightly. "I didn't have a chance to thank you for what you did earlier today! You are my hero!"

Kiera laughed, feeling painfully self-conscious, when a blond woman appeared next. Of the three new arrivals, Autumn was the tallest, but only because she was wearing three inch, spike heels that must kill her feet every day. Mia was a bit shorter, but only because her sleek black slacks and neat white shirt weren't in a style that could handle three inch heels. The latest arrival was about an inch shorter, which meant that Autumn and Mia were about Kiera's own height of five feet, six inches.

"This is our former client, Mia Paulson, but of course you already knew that," Autumn was explaining, "and this is Cricket Fairchild, who we found cursing out our beloved leader. So we kidnapped her into joining us as well, thinking she would be a perfect addition to our party." Cricket was a vivacious blond woman with startlingly intelligent eyes. She was shorter by a couple of inches, but what she lacked in height, she made up for in energy. It practically sizzled throughout her body and her blond curls bounced around her beautiful face.

The three women didn't wait for an invitation. They hustled Kiera over to their table, an empty chair already pulled over from another table. Autumn even pulled Kiera's work folder away and stuffed it back into Kiera's leather bag before turning to raise her hand, getting the attention of the waitress. "We'll have a pitcher of margaritas and four glasses please," she said with a smile to soften the request.

Kiera sat uncomfortably by the three, gorgeous women, feeling insecure and inadequate while she slowly sipped her drink. The women chatted on about Ash Thorpe and how Mia was furious with him for being so arrogant and domineering. A few "stupids" and "jerks" were thrown in there for good measure.

But as they talked, Kiera realized that, although these ladies were shockingly beautiful, they were all down to earth, funny, and more laid-back than they'd initially appeared.

"Sounds like we all have man troubles," Kiera observed, taking another sip. These women weren't intimidating. They were just like her, all in love with men who were just as irritating and obnoxious as Axel.

Of course, she wasn't in love with Axel. At least, not any more. There had been a time…

No, not going there, she told herself firmly and took another long sip of her margarita. She felt the other women's eyes on her and silently cursed herself for revealing her feelings.

"Axel?" Mia asked carefully, her eyes narrowed as she considered the woman's predicament.

Kiera was proud of herself for not cringing. "Everyone has their albatross," she replied wistfully, wishing she honestly felt nothing for Axel Thorpe.

There was a bit more chatter back and forth but Kiera suddenly stopped, feeling something strange…she wasn't sure what. She'd had too much to drink to figure it out, so she ignored the strange, oddly familiar feeling and took another long sip of her drink, still trying to get Axel out of her mind. She shook her head and set her glass down on the table. Unfortunately, the weird sensation wouldn't go away. It was almost the same feeling she'd gotten that first time…No!

"Ladies," she started to say, trying to give them a warning about…well, she wasn't sure for what. Her head was spinning and she was feeling too relaxed to feel truly threatened.

Kiera smiled wistfully as Mia admitted that she was in love with Ash. It was so sweet that she stopped thinking about Axel for a few moments and welcomed the relief.

"But he doesn't trust me," Mia was saying before sighing with frustration.

Mia almost spilled her drink when the man snuck up behind her. "Yes I do," Kiera's new boss was saying, probably in reference to trusting Mia but none of the women were completely sure. Kiera swallowed painfully, her mind still too murky to figure out the rest. But she shifted in her seat and...yep, sure enough. All four Thorpe men were standing behind them, partially hidden by the décor of Durangos, but it was obvious that they had all heard their conversation.

Her eyes lifted slowly, her heart racing in that horrible way that it always did when Axel moved around the table. And he was definitely coming nearer to their table. Or was it more grammatically correct to say closer? She wasn't sure about the appropriate grammar at the moment because her margarita-fuzzy mind was spinning with both the alcohol and his proximity.

"What are you doing here?" she whispered when he stopped right next to her. She wasn't worried. The alcohol had taken care of any nervousness for her. But there was still that zinging chemistry that was always present whenever he was around. She'd thought the years would diminish the impact of his body so close to hers, but the truth was, the years had only made the affect more acute. She should have realized that when she'd almost tripped earlier today after just a glimpse of him in the hallway.

Axel looked down at the obviously inebriated but still shockingly beautiful woman that had haunted him for years. Damn, he'd missed looking at those freckles. She looked so sophisticated and untouchable with her lush curls flying everywhere and her brown eyes drawing him closer, as if she could read his soul.

She was a bit thinner now than she'd been in college. Definitely more sophisticated with her power suits and her killer heels. But he knew what was underneath those suits and it drove him nuts that he couldn't strip away all those layers and get to the real woman underneath. He wanted to see the woman who writhed in his arms or laughed at his jokes, challenged his arguments.

He wasn't sure if he was angry with her or thrilled that she was finally here in Chicago. "I'm going to drive you home," he explained, picking up her leather bag and her purse and tucking both under his arm as he took her hand and pulled her out of her chair.

"I don't want to go home," she shot back, her voice breathy and nervous. She stumbled slightly, not sure if that was because she'd had too much to drink or because her legs were always wobbly whenever she was close to Axel, but his arm immediately wrapped around her waist, pulling her hard against his muscular body. "Don't hold me like that," she commanded, but even that order was said without much force.

He turned slightly so he was holding her against his chest, enjoying the view of her cleavage from this angle. He took in her unfocused gaze and the soft curls that had escaped the clasp at the back of her neck. She looked so soft and sexy, and she had no idea how gorgeous she was. Men stopped and stared at her and she was oblivious. From a distance, she looked like some sort of sexual siren, luring men closer but once they saw her, many pulled back, struck by how lovely she was. Those adorable freckles only confused the issue. Years ago, he'd been thrilled to know that he was the only man who knew that the freckles were only on her face.

He hated the idea that another man, possibly more than one, had held her incredible body, experienced her passion, and discovered that the rest of her lush body was covered in milk white skin without a blemish anywhere.

Right now, her hands were resting against his chest and he didn't say a word. There was a point when he'd thought he'd never have her soft, gentle hands on him again but here she was, holding onto him like a lifeline. "Are you going to fall over?" he asked, looking down into her expressive brown eyes with amusement, enjoying her dependence on him, even if it only lasted until she sobered up.

Kiera narrowed her eyes and her adorable tongue poked out of her mouth, as if she were trying to evaluate the possibility of falling over. "I haven't decided," she told him honestly, then berated herself for that honesty. "But I don't need your arm around me either way." Unfortunately, she didn't have the will or the ability to move out of his arms. He was stronger than she was by a significant margin, but there was also his warmth seeping into her body that she'd desperately missed since she'd walked out of his apartment all those years ago. Standing here with his arms around her, she realized that she hadn't been warm since the last time he'd held her. And that warmth had absolutely nothing to do with the air temperature and everything to do with how he made her feel inside.

He didn't let go of her but, instead, turned her around so they were walking out of the bar. "Let's get you some coffee," he said.

"I don't want coffee either," she grumbled. She wanted to stand there in his arms, revel in just being close to him and how wonderful it felt. But there wasn't much to do about it since he was walking her out the door. Thankfully, she wasn't so far gone that she said anything to him about how much she liked his arms around her. Yes, at least she'd held that back, not wanting to make a fool of herself.

"Tough," Axel replied, chuckling to himself because this was the first time he'd ever seen Kiera drunk. He liked it actually. He was enjoying the soft feel of her body against his, her gentle curves that he remembered so vividly. This woman had appeared in his dreams over the years so often, he'd actually cursed her when he'd woken up. "You probably need some food too, don't you?"

"Not at all," she countered, proud that she could say that she wasn't the least bit hungry.

"What have you eaten tonight?" he asked, evaluating how far gone she really was. She was leaning against him but she wasn't stumbling. That was a good sign.

Damn he'd missed her! He hadn't let himself admit it all these years, but having her here, in his arms tonight, he knew that a part of him had never felt alive after she'd walked out of his life. And he'd let her! That was the worst part.

But now she was here. He'd known that Ash was hiring her. The four brothers discussed all hiring decisions before they were finalized, except for the support people who Autumn managed. But when Kiera's name had come up, her brothers had instantly been impressed, eager even to bring her on board. She had outstanding credentials and had more trial expertise under her belt than all the other candidates, several of whom were older than she was. What could he have told his brothers? No, you can't hire the best trial lawyer to come out of law school in the past five years because I might just toss her in bed and never let her out again? Axel didn't think that would go over too well with his brothers.

Unfortunately, when he'd seen her earlier this afternoon, even after he'd known to be expecting her in the hallways, he'd still felt like someone had punched him in the gut. Over the years, she'd grown even more beautiful than she'd been while in college. Back then, she'd had a sort of innocent-bohemian quality to her. She'd been casual and laid back but in an oddly intense sort of way.

Now she was all polished and sexy – with those professional suits that he wanted to just peel away and find out what she wore underneath.

He tucked her into his car, almost groaning as she crossed her legs with those damnable heels that made her legs look even sexier. He stared at her legs, unaware of what he was doing until he heard a noise behind him. He'd just drive her home, make sure she was safe and then head home himself.

"Where do you live?" he asked when he slipped into the leather seat beside her.

When he got no response, he looked over at her and was surprised to find that she'd fallen asleep.

"Well, hell," he thought with a chuckle. "I guess I'll just have to drive you to my place," he told the sleeping beauty. The idea didn't bother him one little bit. In fact, he preferred it this way.

He drove through the night, his body on fire for the woman in the passenger seat but, more importantly, he was more relaxed now than he had been in...years. He had his Kiera right where he wanted her.

Well, not exactly, he thought. He might put her in his bed to let her sleep off the tequila, but unfortunately, he couldn't share that bed with her.

As he carried her into his house, he thought about the conversation the four women had been having before he and his brothers interrupted. Kiera had said, "We all have man troubles." But did that mean that she was as attracted to him as Autumn was to Xander? Or did that mean she had another man she was interested in? Was she seeing someone? She'd only been in town for a few days, having moved here from San Francisco, where she'd taken a job right out of college. She'd graduated from Georgetown Law School with honors and had been a hot commodity, he knew. He'd watched her career, followed her through his acquaintances and knew that she'd excelled at criminal law.

He thought back again to the conversation at the bar earlier tonight and smiled at the thought of the cute woman who had just gotten free of a murder charge. She was sweet in a fluffy kind of way. He was pretty sure that Ash's problems were over tonight. The four of them had been discussing Ash's upcoming nuptials in Ryker's office before they'd found out that all four women had gone to Durango's to celebrate Mia's freedom.

Axel laid the still sleeping Kiera on his bed and contemplated Ash's reaction tonight about the conversation between the women. Ash was going to propose to Mia, Axel thought. Well, maybe he'll wait until the morning. Axel wasn't sure that Mia would understand anything Ash asked her tonight.

Axel considered his woman, laying curled up on his bed, exactly as he'd pictured her so many times over the years. Well, not quite exactly as he'd imagined her. She'd been naked in his dreams.

He bent down and took off her shoes, smiling slightly when her toes curled up as if they'd been scrunched into the shoes for too long and were now aching to be free of all restrictions. He held the shoe in his hand, looking from the shoe to her foot with fascination. In college, she'd worn sneakers or flats and he'd been turned on every time she'd come near him. Now he had to contend with these sexy heels that made her legs look several feet longer? He was a gonner!

He smiled, enjoying the possibility of getting lost in Kiera's newest form of sexy. He wouldn't mind having that kind of trouble one little bit.

She needed to be comfortable, he thought as he took in her dark lashes against her pale, white skin. And as a gentleman, wasn't it his duty to help her sleep off the alcohol in comfort? Besides, this dress had probably cost her couple hundred dollars at least. She would ruin it if she slept in it. And Axel really didn't want her to blame him if she ruined her dress. It would get all wrinkled because he knew that she snuggled up in her sleep in a way that would bunch the tailored material up around her waist.

It was such a lovely dress too!

His fingers moved carefully down her back, letting the zipper slide through the material, itching to touch the skin slowly revealed to his hungry eyes. But he kept his fingers on the fabric and not on her soft, silken skin. He peeled the dress down over her shoulders and legs, almost groaning when she shifted her body to make the process easier. He almost suspected she was awake and tormenting him, but then she sighed in her sleep. He knew from past experience how she slept. He'd stayed awake several nights just watching her, enjoying the way she curled up next to him. He remembered how her warm breasts pressed against his chest.

He remembered many nights when he'd felt those breasts, felt the way she'd rubbed against him in her sleep. It didn't matter if they'd just made love throughout the night, every time she'd done that, he'd wanted to roll her over and make love to her again. In his mind, her breasts had been absolutely perfect and he'd never gotten tired of exploring their sensitive, pink peaks or the soft, white mounds.

Well, to be honest, he'd thought everything about her was perfect. He'd enjoyed hours in bed with her, exploring every part of her body. She'd protested at times, even fighting him back in an effort to get the upper hand sexually but even back then he'd been stronger and he'd always won their tussles. He'd pin her to the bed and have his way with her, taking his time tasting, kissing and enjoying every inch of her delicate skin despite her screams of frustration and need. It had only turned him on more when she'd done that.

Damn! His body was hard and aching for her and he hadn't even touched her. No woman had ever had this kind of power over his body. Not before he met her and certainly not after.

He carefully hung the dress up in his closet, enjoying the sight of her dress mixed in with his suits and tailored shirts before moving back to the bed, pulling the soft blanket from the bottom of the bed up to cover her. He refused to let his eyes wander over that pretty black bra. Nor would he allow his eyes to explore that black, lace thong! Why the hell was she wearing a thong?

Hell, now he was going to picture her every day, in every one of her professional suits wearing some color of thong!

This was not fair!

He almost slammed his bedroom door as he stormed out of the room. After a pointless cold shower, he flopped onto the bed in one of his spare bedrooms. He'd always loved this house with the extra bedrooms and lots of space. He lived further out of the city than his brothers, but that allowed him much more privacy. He had ten acres of land and his house sat right in the middle of it. He had a couple of horses that he enjoyed riding and even a vegetable garden that he tended on the weekends. Unlike Ash who enjoyed working with wood and Xander who worked out at the gym like a fiend, he'd found gardening to be a great stress reliever. He had no idea what Ryker did to relieve the stress of work related issues. He wasn't even sure if Ryker acknowledged stress. In fact, now that he thought about it, he suspected that his oldest brother worked to relieve the stress of work. All four of them regularly showed up at the gym for sparring in the boxing ring so perhaps that was what Ryker did to let off steam.

He stared up at the ceiling, wondering what Kiera did for relaxation now. Did she live in one of the apartments closer in to the city? Or did she prefer being in the outer suburbs, wanting more fresh air and space?

The distance from the city tended to be a hassle sometimes. The traffic could be bad, but since he worked long hours, most of his drives into or back from work were during off hours, often early in the morning before most people were coming into the city for work or later in the evening when they were already at home and eating dinner. When he had to stay in the city late at night for a social event or because of work, he would simply crash at one of his brothers' places for the night. They reciprocated by coming out to his place on the weekends to ride his horses or just hang out and eat his fresh produce.

Thinking of Kiera in the other room made him smile with satisfaction. He'd wanted her here for so long. All the years, all the changes to this house, he knew now that he'd always had her preferences in the back of his mind. He wasn't sure about all of them, and he hadn't even been aware of doing it, but he'd built this house with her in mind based solely off of the conversations they'd had during their short time together six years ago.

He'd worked hard to renovate this old house and the barn behind it. He'd done some of the work himself but Ash had helped him with a lot of the more complicated issues of restoring an old house. Ash was much better at woodwork but between the four of them, they'd gotten this place in shape and he loved it. It might still look old, but there were modern conveniences all over.

In fact, it reminded him of that bar where he'd first seen Kiera. The late evening sunshine had been lighting her hair on fire. In normal light, she looked like a gorgeous brunette. But that day, with the sun behind her, the light had sparked diamonds all through her curls, turning some of them to red and auburn mixed in with the darker colors. He'd been fascinated by her hair even before he'd looked into her soft, chocolate eyes.

Rolling over, he punched his pillow, forcing thoughts of his former lover out of his mind. Or at least trying. He couldn't completely obliterate her from his thoughts because she was only one wall away from him. He didn't get much sleep that night, thinking about Kiera back in his bed after all these years. So when the sun woke him up, he gave up on trying to get back to sleep. He checked on Kiera and found her to be still sleeping. He quietly grabbed a pair of jeans, showered and went downstairs to his favorite place in the house. The kitchen.

The kitchen was a large, brick and stone room with a huge stove off to one side, a double oven and even an inside grill for those days when it was too cold to get outside and grill steaks, chicken or whatever he wanted. There were lots of windows and light coming in with roughhewn rafters and a cabin feel to the room. It was huge and spacious and designed around how he liked to cook. All of his brothers enjoyed cooking, but none of his brothers had his gardening talents. Not that they would know it since they all lived in the city with no place to even try their hand at gardening. Which meant that they were constantly nagging him for tomatoes, cucumbers and whatever else he'd planted in the spring.

This year, he was having a bumper crop of peppers. There were banana peppers, green, red and yellow peppers and, his favorite, jalapeno peppers. Grabbing a bowl, he walked outside barefoot and snagged a fresh, red tomato off the vine, some jalapenos and banana peppers and then bent down to dig out an onion and a potato from his potato barrel. He felt like a Spanish omelet, he thought as he came back inside and started coffee.

He smiled at the thought of Kiera waking up. He wished he could be there to watch it but he stayed downstairs, making coffee and reading the newspaper while he waited for her to stir.

When he finally heard her move upstairs, he poured a cup of coffee for her, adding in a touch of sugar, then brought it up the stairs.

"Good morning," he said, leaning against the doorway as he watched her look around, trying to get her bearings.

Kiera pushed her out-of-control hair back from her eyes and looked around, not recognizing anything but the man standing in the doorway. She blamed her dry mouth on the drink last night and not on the fact that the man wasn't wearing a shirt and those jeans hung low on his slim hips. Her reaction had absolutely nothing to do with those muscles rippling along his lower abdomen, or the amazingly ripped shoulders and biceps the man had developed.

This definitely wasn't fair, she thought with increasing resentment as she tried to hold the soft blanket in front of her. "Where am I?" she asked, her voice hoarse. She was already embarrassed that she was wearing only her favorite black, lace underwear but now she was self-conscious that she was so affected by the man standing in the doorway looking like some sort of Greek god and she had no idea where she was or what happened last night after getting into his car. The leather seats had been so comfortable and she'd been so tired. It had been a long, first week at her new job, punctuated at the end with the traumatic sight of the man she…not loved anymore, but of the man she'd loved at one time in her life. A time long ago.

"At my house," Axel replied, moving into the room and handing her the cup of steaming hot coffee. "You look like hell," he commented.

Kiera didn't bother to argue with him. She knew she looked awful but her highest priority right at the moment was caffeine. He could say just about anything right now but until she had coffee, she wasn't going to argue with him.

She sat back against the pillows, feeling painfully self-conscious as she gripped her coffee in both hands while desperately trying to hold onto the blanket as well. She honestly wasn't sure which was the more important task, getting caffeine into her system or hiding her body from his too-knowing eyes. "Why am I at your house?" she asked.

One sardonic eyebrow went up and he smiled slightly. "Because you were too drunk last night to tell me where you lived."

Her eyebrows went up with that bland statement. "You didn't bother to read my driver's license?" she asked with rising anger.

He tilted his head. "Hm...I didn't think of that," he replied. He hadn't thought about it because he'd wanted her here. Case closed.

She bit her lip and looked around, her fingers trying to bring the blanket higher but that uncovered her toes. She curled her legs underneath her, not wanting any additional skin to show. She remembered too vividly what he liked to do when he saw skin and mentally she wasn't able to fight him off. Not that he would try anything, she told herself. They'd finished together long ago. There was no reason he might want her now. "Did we...?" she asked, leaving the statement hanging.

He knew exactly what she was asking and decided to have a bit of fun with her. "Did we make love?" he asked, and enjoyed the fire that sparked into her eyes. "Did you scream out with your release the way you used to whenever I touched you?" He waited for his words to sink in. "Did we spend the whole night in each other's arms, satisfying the craving that obviously hasn't died out even after years of being apart?"

"Stop it," she whispered, her tongue darting out and licking her lips, feeling the need start to throb once again inside of her. She didn't want to feel this way about Axel. He'd broken her heart once and it had taken her a long time to start living again. She might have walked out on him that night, but he'd pushed her out the door with his assumptions that she'd drop everything to follow him when he wouldn't sacrifice anything for her. She'd been devastated that semester, not even able to take summer classes because she'd been so upset about his betrayal.

"Stop what?" he asked, his eyes looking down at hers with that heat, that intensity she'd never been able to ignore. "Stop saying what we both want?" he suggested. He didn't move into the room, staying right there in the doorway but it didn't matter. His presence was more powerful than movement or space. "Or stop offering what you so desperately need?"

"Just stop talking," she said and slid her legs to the left, getting up off the bed. It was difficult since she wouldn't relinquish either the blanket or the coffee cup.

Axel watched her, shaking his head. "You never were able to walk around naked with me, were you?" he teased.

Her head snapped around and she blushed. "Where are my clothes?" she demanded, trying for dignity but knowing that she was losing that battle. Especially when he was watching her so closely, those ice blue eyes never leaving her body even though the blanket covered most of her skin.

"In the closet," he said, leaning back and watching her, enjoying the way she walked and held herself. She was grace personified and he wished she'd just give in and accept that what they'd had all those years ago hadn't died out from lack of communication. If anything, his need for her was stronger. He couldn't believe how intensely he wanted to grab her and make love to her, to touch every part of her delectable body.

He pushed away from the door and turned around, trying to shift slightly to accommodate his reaction to her in his bedroom once again. "I hope you're hungry," he called out as he made his way down the hallway. "I'm making Spanish omelets." He wasn't giving her mercy from his watchful gaze so much as he was giving himself a bit of mercy by moving away from her. A man could only take so much enticement, he told himself.

Kiera watched as he walked out, wishing she could tear her eyes away and remain immune to his physique. But then, what woman wouldn't watch? The man was a god!

When he was gone, she sighed and clasped the blanket around her more securely and took another fortifying sip of coffee.

"Spanish omelets?" she repeated suddenly.

Her stomach growled and she realized that she hadn't eaten anything since she'd had some yogurt yesterday morning for breakfast. She'd seen Axel just before she was going to grab lunch and hadn't had the stomach for anything after that. And then she'd been drinking with the ladies last night and...she thought carefully...nope, no food for dinner either. There had been chips and salsa, but Kiera knew she'd been too busy trying to drown out the memory of Axel's presence on her mind and body to worry about anything nutritious.

She opened several doors, finding a bathroom that was made of white and grey wood. Very rustic, she thought with envy. There were skylights overhead and the shower was more like a large room enclosed with glass but with big, smooth stones as the outer walls and matching tiles on the floor. She blushed, thinking of Axel in that space, the hot water rushing over those muscles and...

She shook her head and looked around. After freshening up, she finally found the closet that had been hiding her dress and pulled it back on. But she didn't put her shoes on, carrying them downstairs instead. She felt a bit silly walking barefoot through Axel's domain. But she couldn't deny that she was fascinated by all that she was seeing. His large, spacious house was a far cry from the undecorated apartment he'd lived in before. This house even had plants! She loved indoor plants, thinking they gave an area a sense of vibrancy and health. She'd always had plants in her living areas until she'd moved to San Francisco. At that point, she knew she wasn't going to be living there forever so she hadn't wanted to have plants that might not get the attention they needed with her long hours of work.

After searching through the other rooms and not feeling guilty in the slightest, she found Axel in the kitchen and almost swooned with the space and light not to mention the ultra-sleek kitchen equipment. She stared at the convection ovens and the shiny stove with six burners and all the newest gadgets that made cooking so much fun.

And then there was Axel cooking. Still without a darn shirt and looking so delicious that her mouth almost fell open. She should have been prepared for that. He'd shown up in the bedroom doorway without a shirt, why would he stop and put one on now? It was Saturday, he was obviously relaxed in his home and wanting to be comfortable. It didn't matter that his bare chest was making her very, very uncomfortable.

Looking around, she was stunned by how homey and yet still spacious this kitchen felt. The stone and brick should normally be one or the other, but the two seemed to mesh together perfectly, reminding one that this was an older home, a place that had protected generations of families over the years. The hardwood floors were probably original to the house, but had been sanded and stained to a glossy finish, adding warmth to the whole atmosphere.

She turned and faced the man, a thought occurring to her. "Are you married?" she asked, furious and hurt, feeling horribly betrayed. Deep down inside, she knew she had no right to feel that way, but she waited tensely for him to answer her question, ignoring the painful hurt at the possibility.

Axel stood at the stove, the omelet finished but frozen in mid-air. "Married?" he asked, noting the fury in her beautiful eyes. "Why do you think I'm married?" he asked, slicing the omelet in half and sliding it expertly onto two plates.

The idea of Axel being married hurt more than she could handle. And the way he hadn't answered immediately terrified her right down to her soul. "Answer the question!" she demanded, storming over to the island, taking in more of the homey details and feeling sick suddenly. Had a woman actually been in here and made it look so warm and comfortable? Had Axel married at some point over the past six years? It wasn't an impossibility, she told herself but she desperately didn't want it to be true.

"No. I'm not married. Now tell me why you would ask me something like that."

He refilled her coffee cup, then carried the two plates over to the table that was doused in sunshine from the large windows that looked out over pastures and gardens.

She pushed the dizzying relief away to examine at another, more private, moment. "Because of all this," she said, gesturing widely at all the warmth in his kitchen with her shoes still dangling from her fingertips.

"This?" he asked, looking around. "What's wrong with this?" He'd always loved this room. He'd thought she would like it as well.

"Your house!" she came back with confusion, sure that he was lying about his marital status. "This isn't like your other place. This is…" she looked around, shaking with her anger and betrayal, "nice!" she finally finished.

Axel watched her for another moment, then burst out laughing. He set the two plates down on the table, adding a generous portion of browned, seasoned potatoes. "Well, I'm glad you like my home," he replied, then poured her some fresh squeezed orange juice. "But I'm not married."

His words instantly settled her stomach and she relaxed, almost light-headed from relief. "You did all this yourself?" she asked, her eyes wide with hope and fear.

"Sit," he told her, smothering his laughter at her disbelief. "Eat something."

Kiera looked at the omelet and her stomach growled. So instead of ignoring him or even arguing with him any longer, she took a seat at his sunny breakfast table, setting her shoes down next to her on the wide-plank floor. When she took her first bite, she closed her eyes in bliss. "This is incredible!" she gasped, forking another bite into her mouth. "Who made these?" she asked, looking for the box from the restaurant.

Since she'd watched him slide the omelet onto the plate, he rolled his eyes at her question. "I made them. Obviously," he told her, refilling her cup of coffee.

Her eyes widened. He'd cooked for her in the past, but nothing this good. It had been mostly sandwiches or a quick burger. More often they'd gone out to restaurants. Cheap ones if she were buying and more expensive ones when he could convince her to let him pay for the meal.

"When did you learn to cook?" she asked, taking another bite of the fluffy, cheesy, vegetable filled omelet. "This is incredible!" she exclaimed.

"Thanks," Axel said, taking a long sip of his cold orange juice. "As for when I learned to cook, I picked it up here and there. All my brothers cook so I guess I learned from them. And once I got into it, I liked looking up new recipes although most of what I cook is pretty simple."

She sighed as if she were in heaven. She couldn't remember ever tasting anything so flavorful. "Is that a jalapeno in the mixture?" she asked, not believing that he would be creative enough to think about putting a spicy vegetable into an egg mix.

"Yes. I grow them myself. Sometimes they aren't very spicy but this year was a good crop."

Her hand froze as she looked across the table at him. "You grow your own jalapenos?" she asked, stunned and somewhat disbelieving.

"And tomatoes and other vegetables. I grew all the stuff in your meal except for the eggs and the cheese," he said and winked at her. He knew exactly what she was thinking and loved that he'd surprised her. Kiera was one of those down to earth women who wasn't easily surprised so this was one for the books.

"I don't believe you," she came back and took another bite. "And even if you have a vegetable garden, you probably hire someone to do all the growing for you, don't you?"

He laughed, shaking his head at her disbelief. "Of course not. In fact, I'll take you out to my garden after breakfast." He looked down at the floor where her dressy shoes were laying next to her bare feet. "Of course, you'll have to borrow a pair of my boots."

She peered over the table as well but looked at his feet instead of hers. "I don't think they'll fit."

He shrugged his shoulders. "Suit yourself. But you're looking at my garden. I can't have you thinking I'm a liar."

She laughed, still disbelieving but impressed that he would even have a garden.

Kiera shook her head again, then turned back to her plate, starving for more food and the omelet was exactly what her body needed, lots of protein and veggies.

"Okay, let's go," he said when she was finished.

She blinked and looked up at him. "You're taking me home? I can just…"

"I'm taking you out to my garden. And then perhaps I'll drive you home. Don't you dare tell me that you're catching a cab because you'll be severely punished if you think about doing that again."

Kiera knew that both of them were thinking about the last time they'd seen each other which had been through the window of a cab as Kiera ran away from him.

Instead of answering him, he lifted a pair of boots he'd pulled out of his mudroom. "Put these on."

Kiera couldn't help it. She burst out laughing, never having seen this side of Axel before. She'd spent hours arguing with him about various legal issues, political topics, preferences on food and the best hamburgers. He was the ultimate intellectual in her mind. But at this moment in time, he actually looked eager to show her the garden he apparently was proud of working.

She looked down at the boots, not sure what to think. Taking them out of his hands, she slipped her heels off her feet and gestured to the door. "Lead the way. I'm fascinated by the mighty Axel's vegetable garden." She quickly slipped her feet into his huge boots, unconcerned about how silly she looked in them.

He raised one eyebrow at her cynical tone. "You still don't believe me, do you?" he asked as he opened the door and stepped back so she could precede him out doors.

She stepped onto the cement stoop and shrugged her shoulders. "Let's just say I'm ready to be convinced."

As soon as she looked around, she stopped in stunned amazement. "Axel, it is gorgeous out here!" she gasped, seeing all the amazing hues of bright orange and red, yellow and even a bit more green as the last gasp of summer held onto the leaves.

"Thanks," he said, picking up a water bucket that had fallen over, placing it back against the wall.

The way he was handling the bucket made her suspect something she wasn't prepared for. "Axel, did you plant all of this as well?" she asked, not sure what to believe now.

"Yes," he said simply, looking around at the bushes that were staggered along the pathway, interspersed with perennial flowers.

She stared up at him, seeing the pride on his face and knew that he wasn't teasing her. "I'm impressed," she said softly, her admiration for all that he'd achieved showing through in her eyes.

He took her on a tour not just of his vegetable garden but also of the entire back yard. There was a small pond at the corner of his property where the horses could drink from but he'd also built a small sitting area, complete with a wisteria covered pergola. "This is beautiful," she gasped as she stepped onto the stone patio, looking up at the changing leaves. "Did you build this as well?"

"Yes. With Ash's help. Xander and Ryker helped a bit but Ash is the one who designed it."

She stared up in wonder at all the details, impressed with the curly corners and the way the wisteria plant twisted over the top. She could easily imagine the wisteria flowers flowing down through the wood in the springtime, creating a lovely, purple cover draping down. "I love this!" and she smiled up at him.

"The garden is over here," he said, smiling because he'd been thinking of her reading in a big, comfortable chair underneath that wisteria. Take it slow, he told himself. They'd probably taken things too quickly the last time and he'd blown it. Now that she was here, he suddenly knew how much he wanted her to stay.

He led her through more bushes that grew up high, forming a wall where he'd set up a stone pathway. At the end of the path, there was an open area with raised beds filled with plants that looked pretty rough except for the deep red tomatoes, the dangling cucumbers that seemed to be greener than normal. In fact, all the vegetables in his garden looked to be much more vibrant and colorful than what she normally saw in the grocery store.

She stared, still not believing that he actually did all this but she could easily tell that this was not a professional garden. It wasn't messy so much as just…well used.

"Okay, I'm convinced," she laughed.

"So next time I tell you something, you're going to believe it, right?"

Kiera looked up and realized that he was closer than she'd thought. Her breath caught in her throat and she tried to take a step backwards, but the garden fence was behind her. "I think…" She felt trapped but didn't really want to remove herself from the trap. For so long, she'd remembered the strength and power of Axel's body, the way his arms would wrap around her or the way his hands would touch her, as if she were his woman and she'd never wanted any other man to touch her like that.

"I think you should come back up to the house and let me make love to you." He stared at her, his ice blue eyes demanding that she follow through with his suggestion.

She thought about it long and hard. There was no question that that intense chemistry was still there between them. Her body wouldn't mind experiencing the mind-blowing release that only Axel could give her.

But in the end, she simply couldn't risk it. She'd been so hurt the last time and she'd trusted him completely six years ago only to have him turn around and break her heart because he hadn't been willing to make any sacrifices for their relationship. He'd wanted her to do it all. In her mind, that only proved that she'd been more invested in their love than he had been. Or maybe not, because she hadn't been willing to drop everything and follow him. Or maybe he hadn't loved her enough to sacrifice. Maybe they had both been too young and stubborn.

Either way, she'd been too hurt and she couldn't go through it again.

"I need to go home," she said softly and looked away. She didn't bother to wait for him but trudged through the yard back to his house. Inside his mudroom, she took off the boots and placed them carefully to the side while she slipped her own feet inside her shoes.

"I'll call a cab," she said.

Axel was furious at the suggestion. It was just like it had been that last time, both of them angry and hurt and all she wanted to do was run away. Not this time. "I'll drive you," he snapped at her.

Slow down, he told himself. He had to be practical about this. Kiera was here, he had to show her that they could work together. He had to show her that they could build upon their past and make this time work out.

Unfortunately, he didn't want to be practical and he was having a damn hard time slowing down. He had been watching her walk through his garden, enjoying her being there but also knowing what was underneath that dress. His mind could vividly picture her body in that black lace and he wanted to strip off the clothes and show her exactly what they could be like together.

Instead, he grabbed his keys and headed out the door to his garage. He wouldn't let her even turn towards the front door and slammed the passenger seat closed once she was seated inside.

When he was sitting in the driver's seat, he took a deep breath and calmed down. "I'm sorry, Kiera. I know that was out of line. But I remember what it was like with you, how good we were be together." He turned to look at her, his blue eyes intense and unrelenting. "We will be together again, Kiera. Count on it," he said.

Without another word, he started up the car and backed out of his garage. It took barely twenty minutes to reach her apartment building and the only words spoken between the two of them were her directions. When she reached her building, she jumped out but just before she was about to slam the door and race inside, she bent down and stopped. "Thank you for your help last night. I appreciate the breakfast too. And the tour of your garden."

With that, she closed the door and walked into her building with as much dignity as possible even though she knew that he was staring at her the whole time.

CHAPTER 3

"Are you ready?" Autumn asked, popping into Kiera's office just before five o'clock.

Kiera looked up, then quickly back at her computer. "Just one more thing," she said and typed in several more words to the brief she was working on. "Okay," and she pressed the save button. "Let's go!" She grabbed her duffel bag and followed Autumn into the ladies' room. "So who else is on the team?" she asked as she dove into one of the stalls to change from her business suit to shorts and her newly minted softball shirt Autumn had given her just that morning.

"There are ten of us. You'll replace Samantha who left for her honeymoon last week. We're in first place so far, but Ash's team is not far behind us." Kiera was putting her jacket on the hook of the bathroom stall when she heard the next few words. "Axel is pretty good at keeping everyone motivated but we're all competitive."

"Axel?" Kiera squeaked out, her heart racing just at the man's name. She'd impulsively agreed to be on the law firm's softball team yesterday, simply as a way to get more involved socially with her co-workers as well as to stop thinking about Axel. She held her breath as she silently prayed that her plan hadn't just backfired on her.

"Sure. He's the captain," Autumn explained, although her voice was muffled as she pulled a shirt over her head. "But don't worry. He's a great coach and will help you through your turn up to bat."

Kiera leaned her forehead against the cool metal of the bathroom stall, closing her eyes and trying to figure out a way to get out of this game. For all of her efforts at staying away from the man, she was failing miserably. After seeing his home last weekend and knowing that he still wanted her, the man was constantly on her mind. She'd tried to be strong, but every time she saw him in the hallway or if he happened to walk by a conference room when she was inside, her mind was devoid of focus for several minutes. And those were the good moments because she was sitting down in the conference meetings. When she passed him in the hallway, her balance was actually affected because she wanted him so badly. When was his impact on her going to dull?

She stared at her softball outfit, wishing she'd brought something else to wear. Unfortunately, she hadn't completely unpacked so she'd just reached into the box of clothes that contained her summer outfits and grabbed a pair of shorts, knowing it was going to be one of those hot, fall days. Since the shorts were all she had, she pulled them on, then the softball shirt and hat, making sure her hair was tucked up and tied back so it wouldn't get in her eyes. Taking a deep breath, she stepped out of the bathroom stall, mentally giving herself a pep talk.

She could deal with this, she told herself as she turned on the cold water and ran it over her wrists. She just had to be casual about this, show him that she could handle the two of them working together and playing together on the firm's softball team. She was a lawyer in his firm now which meant there would be other social situations in which they would need to interact with each other. She'd have to figure out a way to handle them better. So far, no one had picked up on her blank moments, or if they had, they hadn't made any connection with Axel's presence. She'd hate to think her co-workers might know about how she felt about the man.

Well, to be perfectly honest, Axel was a big topic of conversation in the kitchens so a lot of women were pretty obsessed with him. All four of the Thorpe brothers were subjects of conversations. The ladies in the office were constantly talking, speculating, eyeing their bosses whenever possible. Who wouldn't? The Thorpe brothers as a group were gorgeous and sexy, charming and brilliant. There really wasn't a better catch for a single woman. But there was a down side to all of this speculation, she knew. Xander's dating habits were legendary, apparently. There were bets going about how long his current lady love would last. The record was four weeks so word was out that Xander Thorpe was a player. A charming and very sweet player, but his reputation was cause for a betting pool to be constantly be under way.

Ash was the one brother Kiera didn't hear much about, except when she was out with Mia lately. After their drinking-fest last week, the four of them had gotten together for dinner on Sunday night. It was interesting how cute Mia was now that it was out that she was engaged to Ash Thorpe. She was even sporting a huge diamond ring that was definitely drool worthy.

Ryker Thorpe was the only one that no one speculated about in the office. Oh, the women definitely had the hots for him. Kiera didn't understand that because she thought Axel was the most handsome of the four brothers. Ryker was more intimidating than anything else. As the oldest, he also appeared to be the most stern which basically translated into terrifying. Generally, he always had a scowl on his handsome features.

"Ready?" Autumn asked, stepping out in a pair of cute shorts which made her long legs appear a mile long. "You look great!" she exclaimed.

Kiera looked at her own shorts, thinking they hadn't been this short the previous summer. She peered at her bottom as inconspicuously as possible and cringed. Nope, these definitely had not been this short last year. They covered her bottom but only about an inch below that.

"Come on, let's go kick some Thorpe butt!" Autumn called out and grabbed her duffel bag.

Kiera followed reluctantly, wishing she could go back to her office and hide out for a while longer. Her breakfast last weekend with Axel was sticking in her mind though. He'd been so clear about his desire, she was nervous about being around him again.

And then there were the few times recently he'd walked by her office and caught her at odd hours. He'd walked by just last night around ten o'clock and paused in his stunning tuxedo, the bow tie hanging down around his neck as if he'd just come from some glamorous function near the office, which was probably the case since the Thorpe brothers worked the social circuit just like any other business owner would. But that day he'd shaken his head when he'd seen her. He'd also caught her here early in the morning and several more times late at night. His expression indicated that he thought she didn't do anything other than work. As she remembered his disapproving face that night, she squared her shoulders and followed Autumn. She'd show him!

Fifteen minutes later, the sun was beating down on her hat and the two teams were trash talking as Axel and Ash flipped a coin to see who would be up to bat first. Unfortunately, Axel lost the coin toss. He came over to the team and started calling out field assignments. When he was done, she stood alone while everyone else ran out to their positions.

"What about me?" she asked, standing up to Axel as her anger increased.

Axel looked out at the field and she couldn't see his eyes at all because of his dark sunglasses. "Why don't you sit this inning out?" he suggested. "I'll get you out there soon." He watched her pale skin suffuse with pink which he knew wasn't a blush but a sure sign that she was angry with him. Unfortunately, he was thinking about how cute she looked in those short shorts and the way her freckles stood out a bit more when she was angry. He also didn't want her pale skin to get burned out here in the abnormally hot sun. It might be fall here and the weather cooling down, but skin like hers would probably burn at the first touch of sunshine.

Besides, he didn't want the other guys on the team, or the men in the stands, to see her butt in those shorts. They were too short, he thought. His imagination was going wild, wondering what kind of underwear she was wearing underneath those shorts. He never should have taken off that dress last weekend, he told himself. He wouldn't be able to handle her bending over when she was up to bat. Nor would he be able to tear his eyes away from her if she were out on the field.

There was also the possibility that she would embarrass herself by missing the ball or striking out. He liked playing ball, but Kiera probably didn't even know how to hold the bat much less hit or catch the ball when it came at her.

Kiera thought about arguing with him, but he obviously knew the other players, their strengths and weaknesses better so she walked stiffly over to the bench and sat down with a thunk. If they'd had a few practices, she might have been able to show him that she wasn't a novice at softball. She loved the sport and had played in high school. Admittedly, she hadn't done much in the past few years but she'd caught a few games with friends in San Francisco. Crossing her arms over her chest and leaning back against the dugout wall, she watched through her own sunglasses, feeling smug since she got to watch Axel as he walked around, coaching the other players. It gave her a nice view of his very tempting butt and deliciously broad shoulders.

After the first inning, she had to accept that he was a pretty good coach. He didn't step in when he wasn't needed and he simply laughed when someone got out. He recognized that this was a competition, but not a win or die game. It was just a fun, social game that everyone pushed to win, but they weren't going to lose anything if they lost.

The only thing that really infuriated her was that he didn't put her in any of the field positions and he didn't let her go up to bat. She kept telling herself to be patient, that he didn't know she could actually play softball. It had never come up in their conversations all those years ago, so he had no clue that she was actually a pretty good hitter.

When the sixth inning arrived and left, she'd had enough. "Put me up to bat, Axel," she demanded, glaring up at him through her sunglasses. He didn't need to see her eyes to know she was angry.

Axel stared down at her, worried about embarrassing her. He mentally debated back and forth with himself. All of her co-workers were out there and if she messed up or struck out, she'd be hearing about it for the next week. He'd known she was on the team and he should have brought her out here to the park earlier in the week to see what she could do, but he'd been tied up in court. And he hadn't been sure he could keep his hands off of her, to be perfectly honest. Even now, looking at her long, sexy legs in those shorts was driving him more than a little nuts. She might be wearing a sports bra under the softball shirt, but that didn't help him a lot in dealing with the need to pull that shirt up over her head and free her perfect breasts from the confines of the merciless bra.

Focus, man! He'd told himself that over and over this past week. He'd seen her so often in the office and he'd been trying to figure out a reason to get her alone, but she was always working.

He sighed and looked around at the other players. Some were watching him, wondering what he was going to do. He had to put her in or everyone would be talking about her lack of game time tomorrow as well. He was dammed if he did and dammed if he didn't. "Are you sure you want to do this?" he asked gently.

Kiera refrained from rolling her eyes. Instead, she just stood there, staring at him and waiting for him to come to his senses.

Axel sighed, pushed his hat back on his head and shook his head. "Look Kiera, I know Autumn roped you into joining the team while you were out to dinner with the ladies last weekend. You don't have to do this," he said calmly.

Again, she didn't say a word, just waited angrily for him to agree to her demand.

"Fine!" he relented, recognizing the stubbornness that made her such a good lawyer. He bent down and picked up a bat. "Stand with your feet apart, bracing just so. Don't choke the bat. Keep your hands like this," he said and showed her how to hold the aluminum bat.

Kiera's irritation grew exponentially as he patronized her. Grabbing the bat, she flipped it around easily so she was holding it at the grip end. Then she poked him in the middle of the chest with the other end. "Back off, buddy!" she snapped. "Just stand there and watch."

There were several yelps from the other team and from the rest of the crowd who had shown up to watch. She didn't look back to gauge Axel's reaction to her prodding but took up her position at home base and signaled to the pitcher that she was ready.

The pitcher, another lawyer in Ryker's group, nodded his head and smiled, thinking this was going to be an easy out. Kiera didn't mind. Let them assume the worst. It would just lower their guard and she'd be able to show them more easily that she wasn't some hothouse flower that needed to be coddled. She hadn't joined the team just to show up and warm the bench. She was a good player, darn him!

She watched carefully, painfully aware of Axel standing right behind her and the length of her shorts. She was pretty sure he was watching her butt instead of her stance, but she pushed that thought out of her mind. She was on a mission and she wasn't going to let his lascivious thoughts impair her....

"Strike one!" the referee called out behind her.

Kiera blinked and looked around. When had the pitcher thrown the ball?

Shoot! Focus girl, she told herself firmly.

She was just about to take up her position again but Axel called a time out.

She turned around and looked at him, silently questioning why he'd stopped the game.

He walked over to her and leaned down. "Just take your time. Watch the ball and when it passes over that point," he explained, pointing to a space a few feet out from home base, "Start your swing. Okay?"

Kiera shook her head. "Axel, I really can do this."

He smiled slightly and she had a moment of panic when it looked like he was going to bend down and kiss her. "I know, honey. Just…" he was at a loss for words and she felt her knees melting with his endearment.

"I promise I know what I'm doing, Axel," she shook her head, saying that more to herself than to him. "Just stand back," she said, looking up at him, almost pleading with him through her eyes that he couldn't see because of her sunglasses. "I can do this. I promise. Have a little faith."

Axel's jaw tightened and he hesitated for only a moment. "Fine," he said and stepped back again.

Axel watched as she stepped back into position and signaled to the pitcher to go ahead. His whole body was tense and worried. He didn't want her to be embarrassed by another strike but…. "Strike two!" the referee called out again.

He bit the inside of his mouth, wishing he'd never put her into the game. It had nothing to do with winning even though they were down by three points and they had three players on base. This was all about making sure she wasn't hurt. The teasing in the office tomorrow could be brutal!

He tried hard to focus on the pitcher, wishing he could give Kiera some sort of signal on when to swing, but he couldn't look at her. His eyes weren't paying attention to the pitcher or even the ball. Not with her adorable, round butt poking back at him.

And then he heard the thwack! He swung back to see what had happened and sure enough, the softball was flying through the air! It wasn't just flying either, it was arching way out and several outfielders on the opposing team were racing to try and intersect with the ball.

He looked at the field and one, two and then three people came over home base! The ball went far and no one was able to connect fast enough so it dropped to the ground. He looked out and his breath caught in his chest as he watched Kiera's gorgeous, long legs racing from first base, then second base. He looked at the ball and suddenly realized that he was supposed to be giving her direction based on where the ball was. "Go to third," he called out, racing over to third base. His eyes flashed from the ball that was now being thrown from one player to the next and then to Kiera who was flying past third base. "Stay there!" he called out.

But did the stubborn woman listen to him? No!

Damn her, she was racing the ball now! The other team was getting the ball and Kiera was flying fast, but was she fast enough? Halfway to home base, the pitcher caught the ball then swung around, throwing as fast as he could to the catcher.

He watched as Kiera caught the other team member pass the ball out of the corner of her eye and, he couldn't believe it, but the woman found a burst of speed and flew by him.

It was close! But Kiera slid through the sand and dirt and Axel watched with amazement as Kiera and the ball flew over the base. Dust was flying everywhere, blocking his view and his heart jumped to his throat as his eyes leapt to watch the referee. When he saw the ref's arms swing outward, indicating that she was "safe", he threw back his head and laughed with the release of tension.

Damn! He walked over to where everyone else on the team had already assembled. Everyone was patting her on the back but Axel was watching her face, seeing the dust settle not just on her but on everyone else around her, all of whom were almost dancing with amazement and glee. Then he noticed something else. Something not good. Someone patted her on the back but the crowd accidentally pushed the person into Kiera's side. It was fast, only a flash, but he caught the cringe when the person bumped against her and he quickly pushed his way through the crowd. Bending low, he saw the scrapes on her leg and the blood that was starting to seep through the thick layer of dust.

"You're hurt!" he growled, ignoring the whoops and hollers of congratulations that were being thrown about.

"I'm fine," she said, grinning from ear to ear, trying to dismiss the concern in his voice. "And I told ya so!" She was too elated to worry about a few scrapes or bruises. She might be in pain later tonight, but for now, she was just reveling in her wonderful I-told-ya-so moment.

Axel was stunned for a long moment, looking down into her gorgeous eyes and shook his head. "Yes, you did," he replied, smiling back at her.

Conscious of everyone in the office congratulating her, he stepped back, not wanting anyone to see how concerned he really was for her but still stunned at the pride swelling up in his chest. She'd won the game for them, he acknowledged with a shake of his head. She'd actually won the game.

"Beers at Durango's!" he called out and everyone cheered and started heading towards the bar that was one block away from the park where they'd played.

A movement to his right caught his eye. He shook his head as he watched Autumn and Xander argue about something. Then to his left, he spotted Ryker and Ash looking smug, both with their arms crossed over their chests as they watched him with an irritating smile.

He thought about going over to demand an explanation, but then saw Kiera again and his brothers were forgotten. Everyone had cleared out quickly with the promise of beer but Kiera was one of the last to grab her bag. And she was limping!

He glanced down at her leg and cursed under his breath. Marching over to her, he was suddenly furious with her for lying to him. "You're hurt!" he growled when he finally reached her.

He bent down and examined the scraps and knew that they were deeper and more painful than she was letting on. "Damn it, Kiera! Why didn't you tell me?"

"Because I knew this would be your reaction!" she yelled right back at him. "Besides, I'm perfectly fine!" Or she would be if he would take his hands off of her leg. Those large, gentle hands were making her stomach flip flop. Not to mention, his brother, her boss, was looking in this direction and she didn't like appearing weak when her boss was around. She had to be sharp and on top of her game. She'd just brought in three players in a game that they could have easily lost, couldn't he stand back and let her have her moment?

On the plus side, she wasn't thinking about the pain in her leg when he was touching her. On the down side, she was thinking about too many other things which were completely taboo when he was touching her.

Axel was having none of that. She could be strong and confident in court. He wasn't going to let her walk on a damaged leg outside of the office. "You're not fine!" he countered and lifted her up into his arms. He ignored her protests and carried her back into the dugout, setting her down gently on the bench.

"I'm fine," she exclaimed when she realized what he was about to do. She tried to wiggle away, to stop his large hand from touching her leg but he simply moved his hand higher up onto her hip so she couldn't move. "Really, I'm fine. It was just a small scratch and I'll put some ice on it when I get home tonight."

Axel was having none of that. "Shut up and let me clean up your leg." He walked over to his bag which contained a first aid kit and grabbed the towel out of his duffel bag. Dunking the towel into the cooler, he came back over and started cleaning her leg.

The towel was now freezing and she cringed at the first touch. "Axel! That's cold!" she said, her breath hissing through her teeth as she tried to pull away. But he just put a hand on her thigh, holding her in place.

"This needs to get cleaned up," he said, focusing only on her leg that was quickly bruising although the bleeding was slowing down. He refused to think about her warm thigh or the way the muscles in her leg flinched under his palm. And he definitely wasn't going to think about how her whole body used to flinch when he would touch her before. Or the way those flinches were usually followed by "Please Axel" or "Hurry Axel!" or she might gasp when she would touch him back, making him flinch and growl with need.

"Fine, but hurry up," she grumbled. She closed her eyes, not wanting to see his dark hand against the lighter skin of her thigh. But a fraction of a second later, her eyes flew open again but she wouldn't look down. Closing her eyes caused her mind to flash several images that were better left un-flashed. Mentally, she couldn't handle those flashes along with his gentle touch right now. He was too close and too big. And it had been way too long since he'd touched her like this.

Axel looked up and caught the blush staining her cheeks. She was remembering those same moments, he realized.

He looked back down at her leg, carefully cleaning the scrapes from all the dirt that had been ground in by her slide into home plate. "You should have stayed on third base," he told her, his voice deeper than normal.

"I made it home and I scored," she countered with a grin. But then he touched a tender spot and she hissed again, her body stiffening with the pain.

Axel's eyes narrowed in frustration over her stubbornness. "I'm taking you to the hospital," Axel said with grim determination.

Kiera quickly shook her head. "You can't take me to the hospital for a cut on my thigh!" she replied, almost laughing except that her leg really was throbbing. The idea of going to the hospital was outrageous though. Doctors in the emergency room had to deal with gunshot wounds, broken limbs and heart attacks. A bruised and scraped thigh didn't even rate on the emergency room 'badness' scale.

"I can and I will," he said, grabbing her duffel and his own a moment before he picked her up in his arms once again.

She grabbed his shoulders only because that was the only thing available to hold onto. "Axel, going to the hospital for a few scrapes and a bruise is silly. I'll just head home and take a warm shower."

"Fine," he said but deposited her in his own luxury car instead of her more practical sedan.

"I can drive myself," she said as she started to get out of the car.

He stopped her by simply putting his hands on her legs and shifting her right back into the passenger seat. "Either I take you home and make sure you take care of this, or I take you to the emergency room and a doctor takes care of it. I don't care which, it's your decision."

Kiera grumbled but knew he wouldn't relent. "Fine, but I can take care of it myself."

Axel slammed her door shut and walked around, calling Ryker on his cell phone. "You're going to have to pick up the tab at the bar. I'm taking Kiera home. Her leg is pretty banged up." He'd ignored the smug expressions on his brothers' faces right after the game and he didn't care if he and Kiera were the only ones not at the bar with the other players. Let them think anything they wanted. He was going to take care of Kiera!

He listened for another moment, then shook his head. "You're an ass," he replied to whatever his oldest brother replied and ended the call.

Slipping into his car, Axel started up the engine and backed out. Five minutes later, he was pulling up at her apartment building and coming around to her side to help her out. They hadn't spoken a word since he'd gotten into the car, Kiera too nervous about being alone with Axel again. It was just like last weekend, but this time, Kiera knew she wouldn't be able to gracefully and confidently walk away from him.

She was too nervous to look him in the eye so she focused only on placing her feet on the asphalt so she didn't fall on her face in front of him. "I can take it from here," she said and stepped out, smothering the grimace when she accidentally banged her leg on the side of his car because she was trying to move too quickly, needing to be away from him.

She was just reaching for her duffel bag when he plucked it out of her hand. In one swift movement, he lifted her into his arms one more time and kicked the car door closed with his foot then walked effortlessly towards the elevators,.

She breathed in slowly, trying to calm her racing heart. "I can walk, you know." And she ignored the other issues that were happening in her body because his arms were around her like this. It felt too wonderful, the memories of other times she'd snuggled in his arms, against his chest just like this racing through her mind.

Axel ignored her and pressed the call button.

"I'm not an invalid, Axel," she said more assertively, wanting desperately to get down from his arms.

Again, he just ignored her.

"You might have congratulated me on winning the game. I helped score four points."

Still, nothing.

When he was standing in front of her apartment door, not sure what to do, she smiled. "Now you're going to have to put me down. My keys are in my purse, which is in my duffel back which is over your shoulder."

Axel contemplated her comment for a moment but in the end, he lowered her feet to the floor and handed her the bag.

Kiera smiled triumphantly and pulled her purse out of her bag, dug in and found her keys. She'd just unlocked her apartment door and was turned around to tell him goodbye when he picked her up in his arms once again and carried her through the doorway.

"Axel put me down!" she commanded, grabbing onto her purse and her bag so it didn't scatter all over the floor.

He ignored her, carrying her through to her bathroom, looking around at her apartment. "You haven't decorated your place," he commented as he put her down on the bathroom counter. When she tried to slip off, he put a hand to her leg, holding her where he wanted her.

"I haven't had a chance yet," she replied, irritated that her body started shivering once again with his touch. She wished she could control her reaction whenever he was around but there wasn't anything she could do to temper her trembling. When he was near, and especially when he was touching her, she was jelly. And trembling, googly-eyed jelly at that.

He went through her bathroom cabinets and Kiera blushed painfully when he discovered all of her feminine products under the bathroom sinks.

"If you tell me what you're looking for, I can tell you where it is," she told him, her face blushing painfully. She hated it when she blushed because her freckles stood out more, making her look ridiculous.

But the man simply closed that one and opened the next, not even blinking an eye at such an obviously personal item. When he found the washcloths, he pulled several out, laying them on the counter before he turned on the bathroom faucet, waiting for the warm water to flow. When it did, he picked up one of the washcloths and wet it before carefully cleaning the rest of her scrapes and scratches.

Kiera had thought that the cold water was difficult to endure, but she was finding she'd been very, very wrong. The warm water against her skin was almost sensuous. Paired with his strong, hot hand and she gasped, looking into his icy, blue eyes. He looked up at her at the same moment and she knew he was feeling it too.

"I'm fine," she whispered, praying that he would just leave and she wouldn't need to find the willpower to resist him. Because she was seriously doubting her ability to do so.

His eyes looked back down at her thigh, but his hands changed, his touch seemed softer somehow. He was still cleaning all the dirt off, but it was more of a caress than anything else. His hand smoothed over her skin, cleaning and exploring, tenderly touching the tortured areas of her skin, his fingertips a light touch, which was even more beguiling.

"You have beautiful skin, Kiera," he said softly, his voice deeper, huskier.

She took a deep breath, wishing it didn't sound so shaky. "I'm too white," she argued, trying to think of anything to get herself out of this, to make him go away before she begged him to stay.

"Tell me you miss what we had together," he demanded, his eyes capturing hers while his fingers continued to trail fire down her leg.

Kiera wished she could deny his command, but the way he was touching her had eliminated all her defenses to him. "I miss it," she replied, trembling now as his fingers moved down to her knee, then her calf.

With those words, he stood up and Kiera was painfully disappointed that he was no longer touching her. But she'd been mistaken in his intentions. He didn't hesitate a moment before he took her head between both of his hands and kissed her, deeply. His kiss caused her to moan with the contact. Her mouth didn't stop him in any way. In fact, she encouraged him in the only way she knew how. She kissed him right back, forgetting that she was supposed to resist him. Forgetting that this job was only a stepping stone and he'd hurt her terribly the last time their careers had diverged.

It was only Axel now. His hands, his mouth, his tongue invading hers and she kissed him right back with every ounce of desire that had been stored up over the past six years for this man. She wanted him and all the remembered pain was hidden at the moment. It was only the desire, sure and strong, that was on her mind now.

His hands pulled her forward on the countertop and Kiera's hands fisted on his shirt, trying to hold on even though her world was tilting precariously. If he were to stop right now, she might just fizzle out in a spark of heat so intense there would be nothing left of her afterwards.

Of course, if he continued, there was the possibility that the same thing could happen. Her only option was to pull herself closer, to mold her body against his. But that didn't help her in any way either. She needed him so desperately she was in pain with that desire. She couldn't wait. Her hands slipped underneath his shirt, feeling the velvet steel of his chest and stomach covered by a light dusting of hair. He was stronger, she realized. Her fingers explored the angles under his shirt, needing to discover all the changes that had occurred over the years but he was pulling at her. She didn't understand and she almost growled when he did something to pull her hands away. But she realized that he was only taking his shirt off, giving her better access and her hands immediately jumped right back to his chest, her eyes following so she could see the changes as well as feel them. Her fingers moved over his skin, finding all those spots she remembered so well that drove him crazy. When they weren't making love, those spots were only ticklish but as soon as their touch heated up, those spots were an instant erogenous zone and she loved every one of them, touching them all and wishing she could send him as far over the edge as she already was.

He growled himself and lifted her up, carrying her into her bedroom and placing her on her bed. "My turn," he said and swiftly, efficiently, pulled the softball shirt up and over her head. He didn't even hesitate, give her time to understand what he was doing before his hands had even released the clasp behind her back to free her breasts. The ugly but effective sports bra was tossed away and his eyes were hot as he looked down at her bare breasts.

"You're beautiful," he groaned before his head bent, lowered to kiss the tip of her breast. Her nipple pebbled underneath his lips and she arched against him, needing his body against hers. She was frantic now, needing him inside her more than she needed oxygen. She wanted him so painfully, felt empty and terrified that he might leave her before he moved inside of her.

Her hands reached down for the snap of his shorts, wanting to feel his erection in her hands, to guide him to her so he could fill her up. Axel was just as desperate and with swift fingers, her shorts and underwear were gone. He lifted himself up and stripped off his clothes before grabbing a condom out of his wallet. He sheathed himself with the protection a moment before he lowered himself down to her again. Just to be certain, he pushed his hips between her knees, his finger sliding inside her heat. The wetness he discovered there almost made him lose control but he closed his eyes and took a moment before grabbing her hands and holding them over her head while he pushed her legs farther apart, sliding into her welcome heat. "Damn you feel good, Kiera," he groaned while he pushed himself deeper, watching her face to make sure he wasn't hurting her in any way.

"Don't stop," she begged when she thought he might be about to pull out of her. He was larger than she remembered him, but he was still filling her up and making her feel whole again. She hadn't felt this since she'd left that day and she couldn't believe how wonderful it felt to be so intimately connected to this man once more.

And then he started moving. His body surged into hers and she lifted her hips, eager to match his passion. Over and over again he slammed into her, both of them panting in a desperate need to fulfill the ache that had been inside each of them for so long.

When Kiera thought she couldn't take anymore, she started to push his hips away but he knew all her tricks and wouldn't let her. He shifted ever so slightly and that was all it took. Kiera flew over the edge into one of the most mind-blowing climaxes she'd ever experienced. She wasn't even aware of Axel finding his own release because she was still throbbing, still seeing stars.

When he finally stopped and pulled her close, she sighed with happiness. "I remember," she whispered, her hand reaching out and touching his shoulders, his back, anything that was part of Axel.

Axel chuckled and nuzzled her hair out of his way with his nose, kissing her neck and that spot behind her ear that never failed to elicit a giggle of delight. It worked even now and he smiled at the memory as well as the present.

He stood up and went to the bathroom and Kiera heard the water running for a moment but she was too content to try and figure out what he was doing. She pulled the sheet over her as her eyes drifted slightly closed.

"Still shy?" he asked, laughing as he slid back into the bed behind her, pulling the sheet away so that his hands could smooth over her skin.

Kiera gasped, but she wasn't sure if it was because he took away the sheet or because he was touching her again and her body, so recently satisfied, was no longer content. She reveled in the fact that just a simple touch from this man had her whole body tensing with renewed desire. Never before had any man ever had this kind of effect on her. Tomorrow, she might regret his ability to control her so easily. But right now, she couldn't do anything but enjoy the whole process over again, but this time at a much slower pace.

CHAPTER 4

Kiera woke up and instantly knew something was wrong. She looked around, feeling the sheets for Axel and finding his side of the bed empty.

She sighed and thought about that for a moment before she opened her eyes, pulling his pillow close but knowing it would be a cold substitute for the man himself. It was probably for the best. She shouldn't have fallen into bed with him again last night. It was wrong and nothing could come of it. They wanted different things in life and she would move on to the next job while he was settled in here in Chicago.

Then she heard a noise in her kitchen and she jerked around, just in time to see Axel coming back into the bedroom.

His eyes quickly moved over her body silhouetted by the sheet she continued to hide herself under. "You never answered my question last night, Kiera," he said, standing at the bottom of her bed and looking down at her.

Kiera looked at him curiously, pushing her curls out of her eyes and sitting up, making sure to keep the sheet over her nakedness. She ignored his raised eyebrow and focused on what he was asking her. Something about a question? She didn't remember any questions. All she remembered was the incredible, wonderful heat of him as he held her close throughout the night. Even though he'd woken her up several times during the night, she hadn't slept so well since....well, for six years.

"What was the question again?" she asked, not fully awake. But even if she were, she wasn't sure she would be able to concentrate. Not with Axel standing there at the end of her bed in only the pair of shorts he'd worn last night to the game and nothing else. All those rippling muscles and broad shoulders were very distracting.

"Why haven't you decorated this place?" he challenged, his hands fisted on his hips.

Kiera leaned back against the pillows, trying to determine what time it was. "Decorating?" She glanced at the clock across the room from her bed. "It's before six o'clock in the morning and you're asking why I haven't decorated my apartment?" She tried to remember what day it was but everything was off kilter at the moment.

He looked across the room as well and smiled slightly. "I guess your inability to wake up to an alarm clock hasn't changed, eh?" he shook his head. "Still need to put it across the room so you'll get up out of bed?"

She blushed, remembering how he would wake her up when she was trying to shut off the alarm clock. He used to laugh and tickle her, then make love to her until they were both panting and wide awake.

She shrugged about her trouble waking up in the morning as if it were normal. "It works for me," she said softly and shifted uncomfortably. "What are you doing?"

He glared at her. "You thought I'd left, hadn't you?" Her blush was all the answer he needed. "Kiera, why haven't you decorated this apartment?" he demanded.

Kiera sighed and looked down at the comforter, pretending like she didn't want him to come right back to bed with her and make love to her one more time. "I just haven't gotten around to it yet."

There was a long silence while she waited tensely for him to respond. She wasn't sure what to say to him, how to explain the barrenness of her living area.

"You're not staying, are you?" he guessed. But it wasn't a question. "You're only here for a little while, just enough time to get The Thorpe Group on your resume before you move on to another job." He watched her carefully and, by the guilty look in her face, knew that he'd guessed accurately.

She looked around, trying to think of some comment that would appease him. But he was right. And she knew she looked guilty.

"How long were you willing to stick it out, Kiera?" he demanded, becoming angry with her lack of forthrightness. "A year? Two years?"

She shrugged slightly. "Why do you care?" She slipped out of bed and grabbed her robe. "And how can you judge me when you were doing the same thing years ago? When we first met, you didn't bother to even unpack some of your things," she countered, referring to the boxes he'd kept in his closet that contained all the things he hadn't needed and so he hadn't bothered to find a place for in his apartment. "Don't judge me for doing the same thing you did."

He was livid with her refusal to understand what they had together. She was purposely being obtuse. "Except the position with the Supreme Court was just that, a temporary position. I went into it knowing that I wouldn't be staying with them."

"So what's wrong with me doing the same thing?" she yelled back at him, feeling defensive at being caught. She wished this conversation hadn't happened, but she wasn't going to lie to him. Besides, of all the people she knew, Axel was the one person she thought would understand.

Axel's hand went through his hair, messing it up with his frustration. "The difference is that my position in Washington, D.C. started out only being a temporary position. A job with The Thorpe Group isn't temporary. Nor do we offer positions to people who think we're just a stepping stone."

That wasn't fair. She had no idea what could happen in the future but he was purposely being stubborn about admitting that anything could happen. "But you have people coming and going all the time. It isn't like The Thorpe Group is a be all and end all for employment."

"It could be for you!" he came right back, furious with her for not investing more in their relationship even though it had only started up again the previous night. "You can't tell me that you thought The Thorpe Group was offering you employment only for a limited time."

She shifted uncomfortably, wishing he weren't so perceptive. But that was one of the reasons she'd fallen in love with him. He was amazingly astute and intelligent and he'd seen things in her that even she hadn't known existed. He thought she was pretty, he liked her freckles and he'd made her laugh at the ridiculous things in life. That didn't help her now though. "No, but that isn't the point."

"What is the point?" He was so furious with her he could barely think straight. She'd come back, but not to him. He'd thought last night...but everything he'd hoped for as he'd made love to her, as he'd held her in his arms last night had been a lie. "Am I just a stepping stone?" he asked with an emotionless tone of voice.

Kiera's neck snapped around, shocked that he would ask that kind of question.

"What's that supposed to mean?"

"Am I only your next lover in a long line of stepping stone lovers?"

She gasped. "I haven't ever..." she stopped herself and closed her mouth. "Don't..." she was so hurt that he would think that of her, especially when she hadn't been with any other man besides Axel. All these years she'd dated, but no man had ever made her feel the same kind of intensity that Axel could do to her with just a look. "Get out!" she snapped. She wasn't going to admit that to him. Ever! Let him think the worst of her. He meant nothing. He was just a jerk who thought the worst of everyone!

"Gladly!" he growled back, grabbing his softball shirt and snapping it over his shoulders. He didn't even bother straightening it, just grabbed his shoes and socks and walked out of her apartment.

Kiera watched him leave, furious and hurt and aching, wishing she had the courage to call him back. But what could she explain? He was right. She had accepted this offer and considered it just a stepping stone. All lawyers worked their way from one law firm to another, gaining experience until they had the ability and reputation to open their own law firm or made partner in a firm that was prestigious enough to keep them. The Thorpe Group was the cream of the crop of legal firms in the United States, but that didn't mean something might not come along that would serve her future better. Only a stupid person would go into a job thinking they were there to stay. Things happened, the world changed, opinions shifted and companies were bought and sold.

He was wrong about the way she thought of him though. She never would have thought of him as a temporary lover much less a man who was one in a long line of lovers. She whipped her robe off and marched to the shower, trying to scrub off the touch of him, his scent. But no matter how hard she scrubbed, she couldn't get the incredibly alluring scent of Axel out of her mind.

She hurried to get ready for work, needing something to take her mind off of his hurtful words.

Her thigh ached and she took some ibuprofen, stuffing the bottle into her purse, knowing she would need more later. It was a work day and she didn't have time to waste pining away about a man who had unrealistic expectations of her. And unfair ones!

She was fully dressed once again, feeling protected in her business suit and heels. She had a full day of client meetings today along with strategy meetings. She had several briefings to type up and so many things to do that didn't have anything to do with considering where she would be in a year or two. She definitely didn't have time to mess around with Axel Thorpe and all of his obnoxious assumptions.

At the last minute, she remembered that she'd agreed to meet Autumn, Mia and Cricket after work for a workout. So she ran back and grabbed her yoga gear, slinging the duffel bag over her shoulder before storming out of her apartment. Adding to her irritation this morning, she had to take a cab back to the softball field because of Axel's overly protective actions of the night before. Since he'd insisted on driving her back to her place, she didn't have her car.

She could ask Autumn, Mia and Cricket what she should do, she thought. After their workout, they would go out for dinner and she could explain the situation to them. She thought about Autumn's position in the Thorpe Group and bit her lip in indecision. It might not be a good idea to tell the office manager about this. But then shook her head. Autumn was her friend. They'd shared other things and this would just be one more. She trusted Autumn's advice and knew that her friend could separate herself from the situation and give her an unbiased opinion. Besides, Mia was engaged to one of the other partners and Kiera suspected that there was something going on with Cricket and Ryker. So they were all connected somehow to the owners of the law firm.

As she stepped into the cab and gave the driver directions back to the softball field, she considered her options again from their perspective. Maybe it wasn't such a good idea, she thought as the cab made its way through rush hour traffic. She didn't want to put her friends into an awkward position.

The day was tough but she plowed through her work, getting kudos from several senior lawyers on the briefs she helped them with. But she was relieved when it was finally six o'clock and she could get out of the office. She'd tried to stay in her office and out of sight as much as possible, not wanting to run into Axel today. Her feelings were a bit too raw to see him so she avoided as much contact with her co-workers as possible.

When she walked out with Autumn, she breathed a sigh of relief that she'd successfully avoided Axel all day. As she drove with Autumn to their yoga class, she found out that Axel had been out of the office all day in court. Kiera was so relieved that she took several deep breaths, feeling instantly better.

The four of them changed in the locker rooms of the gym, laughing and joking about the day. Autumn and Mia had been friends for a long time, but Kiera already felt like these three women were her sisters. They'd laughed and dined together and she felt a kinship with them that she'd never felt with her other friends in the past.

Axel had endured a miserable day, irritated with everything. His client hadn't followed his advice so there had been a potential lawsuit over some problems with materials coming into the country. He'd fixed that, but it had required him to drive down to the waterfront, then to the courts again so he could defend his client in front of a judge.

At least the day was over, he thought, rubbing the back of his neck to try and relieve the stress. It might not have been such a horrible day, but the beginning had left him furious with the world in general and one lovely, irritating and stubborn woman in particular.

Axel drove through the evening rush hour, still furious over Kiera's responses this morning. Or her lack of the response he wanted to hear. He couldn't believe she'd curled up against him all night, knowing that she wouldn't be here in a year or two.

How could she react to him like that and all the while, know that she was going to move out of his life? Didn't she realize how precious this thing they shared was? He'd dated other women, of course. But none had ever touched him like she had. Oh, they might have touched him physically but Kiera struck something deeper, more elemental and he knew that she felt it too.

He hated the idea of her moving on, of another man touching her like he wanted to touch her. He'd had her at his house, in his bed and he was right back to trying to figure out a way to make her want to stay, to live with him forever.

His phone rang and he glanced at the caller. Since it was his brother Ash, he pressed a button on his steering wheel to answer the call. "What's up?" he asked, wondering what Ash might need now that he had Mia in his life. The man was besotted with her. Axel was happy for his brother, but he couldn't deny that there was a large chunk of jealousy that his youngest brother had found the love of his life.

Well, truth be told, Axel had found the love of his life as well. He just hadn't figured out how to convince that stubborn woman to love him back.

"Hey, are you coming back to the office tonight?" Ash asked.

"I'll be there in about thirty minutes," he replied, still distracted by his situation with Kiera. It didn't help that Ash was disgustingly happy with his new fiancée and he was still livid with Kiera.

"Mia's car isn't working properly. I just had someone pick it up and tow it to the shop but can you pick her up from yoga class? It's right on the way from where you probably are right now and the office."

"Sure. Send me the address and I'll bring her to you."

"Thanks bro!" Ash said and hung up.

A moment later, a text came onto his screen and he plugged it into his GPS. It was right on the way, so he didn't even need to alter his route.

Ten minutes later, after parking and walking into the yoga center his brother had sent him to, he was even more furious than he had been when he'd taken his brother's call. He definitely didn't mind picking Mia up. She was sweet and made his brother happy so, as far as he was concerned, Mia was family already. He'd protect her just like he would his brothers.

No, he wasn't angry at the issue of picking up Mia. It was that Mia was in a yoga class with none other than Kiera. And the way Kiera was moving was nothing short of….erotic. He hated using that term to describe a form of physical fitness but the downward dog had Kiera's adorable but going straight up into the air. Axel swallowed painfully as his mind conjured up all the things he wanted to do to Kiera while she was in that position.

Position after position, Axel watched with rapt attention, fixated on Kiera's long legs and round, amazing butt, her strong arms and her slender body. After each movement, he wanted to yell at her for making him hard as a rock but he couldn't speak, could only stare in rapt fascination.

And that was before she arched her back with her legs flat on the floor. She looked like some sort of snake with her face up towards the ceiling.

Axel remembered the expressions on Ash's face as well as Ryker's last night after the softball game. Had his youngest brother set him up? They'd both known, just from the way he was treating Kiera, that she was significant to him. When Kiera moved into yet another yoga pose, he had to tear his eyes away.

Either that, or storm into the room, grab her delectable body and carry her off to some place private so he could ravish her.

He stepped away so his voice couldn't be overheard and dialed Ash's number. When his brother answered, the tone in his voice confirmed his suspicions. "You did this on purpose didn't you?" he demanded.

Ash's only response was to laugh through the phone lines. "I don't know what you're talking about. But isn't Kiera in that class as well? I saw her walking out with Autumn earlier and they both looked determined to get out of the office in a hurry."

"You'll pay for this," Axel groaned, watching with fascination as the group stood up, then hung down from the hips with their fingers to the floor. Yet another perfect position for him to observe Kiera's derriere. He turned away. "Why don't you do your matchmaking with Autumn and Xander!" he snapped. "Lord knows something needs to be done about those two before they kill each other."

"What, do I suddenly have a death wish?" Ash asked with amusement.

"Leave me out of this," he barked in the lowest tone his aching body could handle.

He heard a chorus of "Namaste" and snapped his phone off. Turning, he tried to appear casual, but the wary expression of the four women when they saw him told him that his casualness wasn't working.

"What are you doing here?" Kiera demanded, her eyes scowling at him as she confronted him on behalf of her friends.

He looked down into Kiera's eyes, trying to get his body back under control. She stood in front of him with pink cheeks and sweat glistening on every inch of her perfect, pale skin. He took a deep breath, but that didn't help since all he could smell was Kiera's sweet scent and it made him ache even more.

"I'm here to pick up Mia. Ash said he towed your car in for repairs." He spoke to Mia, but his eyes remained on Kiera, noting the sweat glistening on her chest and shoulders where the yoga outfit didn't cover her skin. "Are you ready to go?"

Kiera stepped in front of Mia, shaking her head. "Mia didn't do anything to make you angry. I'll drive her anywhere she needs to go."

Axel was having a hard enough time not pulling her into his arms and kissing her until she didn't have the strength to argue, so her belligerence only sparked his anger hotter. "Kiera, so help me, after this morning, I'm likely to toss you over my shoulder and finish our argument. So just let me get Mia and get out of your way, or prepare for a battle you won't be able to win."

Kiera considered his words, not really sure how to handle him like this. She'd never seen him so furious but she wasn't going to let her friend get into his car. "I'll take…"

"It's okay," Mia said behind her, laying a calming hand on Kiera's shoulder. "If Ash sent him, I'm sure everything is okay."

Kiera thought about that for a moment. "Are you going to behave?" she demanded of Axel, getting angry herself, nervous that he was too angry to drive.

His eyebrows went up at her challenge and he was intrigued that she would even dare him in such a way. "What are you going to do to stop me if I don't?" he challenged, actually stepping closer to her and glaring down at her.

She told herself that she wasn't afraid of him, and fervently hoped that she was faking it well. "I'm not going to let you take Mia."

He almost chuckled at her brave words, noticing the rapid pulse throbbing at the base of her throat. "And you think you're big enough to stop me?" he asked, his voice silky soft and smooth now.

"I think I could take you down," she replied, but the words didn't have any force to them now.

"Everything okay?" a new voice called out to everyone.

The new voice was the instructor who was busy gathering up the next class. Kiera looked over at the kind woman and smiled. "Everything is just great," she said and looked up at Axel. "Isn't it?"

"Great," he replied back at her. "Ready to go Mia?" he asked, still watching Kiera.

Mia smiled and nodded brightly, understanding the underlying tension between these two people. "Very ready," she replied, trying to stifle her laughter as she watched the two combatants try and intimidate each other. Axel was so similar to Ash in this way that she wasn't worried in the least. She knew that Axel wouldn't harm anyone and Mia also knew that Kiera was pining for this man quite urgently herself.

Axel turned and looked at Mia, forcing a smile to his face. "Let's hit it then," he said and put a gentle hand on her arm to lead her out the door.

Mia's smile broadened and she started walking, but right before they reached the door, she turned around and winked at Kiera before running ahead and pushing the doors open to precede Axel.

Kiera watched, furious for some unexplainable reason. When the two of them were out of sight, she turned around with a low growl and started stuffing her towel and yoga matt into her gym bag, trying to ease the anger out of her body. She'd felt so good after her yoga class, then she saw the man who only infuriated her further. Every time she saw him her emotions became extreme! Why couldn't she just remain calm and unaffected?

Autumn and Cricket had remained back about a foot during the entire confrontation. Even now, they glanced at each other then back at Kiera as she furiously stuffed clothes, yoga mat and water bottle into her gym bag.

"Are you thinking what I'm thinking?" Cricket asked Autumn.

Autumn nodded her head, her eyes wide with surprise. "Pizza?" she suggested to Cricket who immediately agreed. "And ice cream," she added in, just in case.

"Maybe even chocolate," Cricket sighed, completely understanding what Kiera was going through.

Kiera didn't hear the others, but was totally in agreement when they pulled up to a pizza place instead of going back to the office. She ate two pieces before she could   even   see   straight.

CHAPTER 5

Kiera looked outside, sighing as she realized that she was still in the office later than anticipated. But why should she care? It wasn't like she had anything special to do tonight. Mia was going out to dinner with Ash, Autumn had a repair person coming to her townhouse to fix something and Cricket had some mysterious dinner to attend. Kiera was slightly concerned about Cricket since her friend didn't seem to be looking forward to the event, but there wasn't much she could do about it at this point but maybe call her later and make sure she was okay.

She saved her document and shut down her computer, clearing off her desk as best she could so she could start up again first thing in the morning. She sighed miserably, knowing the only thing she had to look forward to was a lonely, depressing apartment and a microwavable dinner or a bowl of cereal.

With a sigh of resignation, she packed up her bag, intending to work on her brief once she got home and could snuggle up into a pair of yoga pants and a soft sweatshirt. The nights were cooler now and she could open her balcony doors and let the night air in. It was a welcome relief from the painfully hot summer heat they'd been experiencing over the past few weeks. It was a sign that the fall really was finally coming and she loved the anticipation of the cooler temperatures.

She'd heard several people talking about a boxing gym that was down the block. She smiled at the idea of learning to box. Yoga was good at relieving stress, but perhaps she could add boxing to the weekly agenda. It was different, probably good cardio and she could work out her aggressions. Maybe she could pretend that her partner or punching bag was Axel!

She grabbed her gym bag and walked out of the building, turning right down the street instead of left to head to the parking garage. She felt better now that she had a new purpose to the evening. There was a skip to her step as she anticipated learning a new skill and getting rid of some of this tension caused by worry over seeing Axel in the hallways.

When she entered the gym, she was surprised at how many people were still there working out. It was noisy with music and lots of people doing their best to kick or punch large, black bags that looked to be painfully heavy. Most of the people there were men, but she saw several females working out as well which was a relief.

"Hi," she said to the clerk. "I wanted to ask about a trial membership."

The man was more than eager to sign her up for a free week of classes. He showed her around, introducing her to the kickboxing instructor and the boxing instructors that were on hand. The gym even had the normal exercise equipment which was an added bonus. She went through to the women's locker room and changed, getting ready for the next kickboxing class which was scheduled to start in ten minutes. She walked out feeling very proud and brave, selected a pair of boxing gloves and stood by, watching the end of the current class.

She was looking around, noting the different boxers in the rings. Over in the far corner, there were two men in particular that looked especially buff and amazingly determined to knock each other out. She didn't realize her feet were taking her closer, but something about the way one of the men was moving or shifting on his feet drew her closer. Peering through the elastic bands that enclosed the boxing ring, she squinted at the two men, one in particular.

As she got closer, she started trembling as her suspicions grew. And sure enough, when she was closer, she recognized Axel. Her mouth dropped open, stunned at the strength behind each punch and jab. The other man was grinning like an idiot and taunting him and she recognized Xander as Axel's opponent. Their heads were almost completely covered by a safety helmet, but she'd recognize Axel anywhere and she couldn't believe how glorious he looked as he and Xander boxed and danced around each other. Their shots were well placed and determined, both men working hard to win.

Kiera didn't realize that others were now watching her as she stared, open mouthed, at the two combatants in the ring. Her hand touched the bands while her eyes remained transfixed on Axel's amazing, bulging and sweaty muscles. Although Xander was no slouch, in her mind, no man had ever compared to Axel in both strength and perfection. He was like a Roman statue, all perfectly toned and tall, looking even more fascinating by the sweat making all that glorious skin glisten in the overhead lights.

What happened next was completely her fault. She was still watching but she must have moved slightly because Axel was suddenly distracted. Just as he looked over in her direction and their eyes caught, Xander's left fist swung out, catching Axel's jaw. Kiera watched in horror as Axel's head snapped to the right, then his body fell, almost in slow motion, to the mat.

Kiera had no idea how she'd gotten through the ropes so quickly, but by the time she reached him, her own boxing gloves were torn off and thrown to the side in her effort to get to her man.

"No!" she screamed, running towards him, bending down to take his beaten face between her hands. "Are you okay?" she cried, feeling like her stomach was going to toss out everything she'd eaten earlier today. "Speak to me, Axel," she begged, her fingers shaking as she tried to get the helmet off of his head. "Just say something. Anything!"

"I'm okay," she heard him groan. She couldn't believe it, but his groan almost sounded like laughter but that was impossible!

Kiera sobbed out her relief. "Where are you hurt?" she asked, running her hands over his body and his skull in an effort to find out if anything was broken.

"Only my pride, honey," he said, lifting his hand and touching her face gently but his fingers were still wrapped up in the boxing glove so it wasn't a very effective caress. "I'm sorry if you were worried," he said so only she could hear him.

She laughed, shaking her head. "You took a pretty hard fall. I think you should see a doctor."

Axel laughed as well, putting his arm around her shoulder. "No need but you can help me up," he offered.

She wrapped her arm around his waist and lifted, feeling his enormous weight produced from all that height and those muscles. "Let me take you to the emergency room, just to make sure your head is okay."

She heard several chuckles behind him and Axel smiled lightly. "Really, I'm fine except for my pride. I got distracted and Xander took a good swing. It's happened before."

She tilted her head as she looked up at him. "And it really doesn't hurt?" she asked.

He smiled down to her, genuinely touched by her concern. Hell, he'd take several more hits if it got her running to him like she'd just done. "No. There's enough safety equipment. I'm fine, really."

He stood up, but kept his arm around her shoulders. It felt too wonderful having her close again and he forgot, for the moment, all of his anger at her perception of her job, and him, as temporary.

She watched him walk, noting that he wasn't limping and didn't have any trouble weaving or falling into her. "Well, I guess that's a good thing," she grinned, even smiling at Xander as he approached, taking off his helmet. "If it doesn't hurt, that gives me a bit more confidence that I can handle boxing."

"Why is that?" Axel asked, unsnapping his own helmet.

"Because I got a week long pass to try out the gym. I thought it would be fun to try boxing," she explained.

The two men stared at her for a long, suspended moment. When Xander actually took a step back, Kiera looked up and caught Axel's furious expression.

"What?" she asked, glancing back and forth between the two men.

"You will NOT be doing any boxing," Axel almost yelled, thinking he would take apart any man who stepped into the ring with her. He would not allow her to be beaten and punched by anyone.

Kiera stepped back, looking at him strangely. "But you just said that there's a lot of safety equipment and you didn't get hurt. You even went down, almost knocked out, by Xander's last punch."

Xander chuckled as he walked away quickly. Axel, on the other hand, moved so he was standing right in front of her. "Kiera, listen carefully, I will not allow you to take up boxing. It is too dangerous."

She squared her shoulders, not intimidated by him at all. "Oh, so you're saying it's a good enough sport for you, but when a little woman gets into the picture, it's too dangerous?" Her voice was low and ominous.

"It's not too dangerous for me because I've been training for years."

"And yet you still almost got knocked out."

He threw up his hands in frustration. "Will you stop saying that?" he growled, irritated that she kept bringing that up. "I told you. I was distracted."

"By what?"

"By you!" he came right back. He looked around and noticed the other men who were watching, amused by their argument. "Let's get out of here. We don't need to continue being a spectacle for the rest of the gym."

Kiera glanced around as well and saw the other men. She pulled back and stepped out of the boxing ring. "Don't worry," she snapped at him. "I'm in the other class."

"What other class?" he demanded, right behind her.

"Kickboxing," she replied and stepped into the area where there were fifteen or twenty black punching bags hanging down from the ceiling.

The instructor was calling out instructions already and Kiera took up her position, refusing to look at Axel as he glared at her from the sidelines. In the end, he turned and headed towards the men's locker rooms and Kiera took out all of her frustration on the punching bag, irritated that she'd let her feelings for him show. Again!

CHAPTER 6

Axel stormed into her office and closed the door. He'd made up his mind and wasn't in the mood to be interrupted. "We have to talk," he told her, leaning against the doorway.

Kiera looked up at him, not sure she wanted to hear what he had to say to her. "Why?"

"Because I can't keep going on like this."

"Can't?" she asked, confused by what the subject might be. Although she could give it a pretty good guess.

He sighed and ran a hand through his dark hair. "Okay, I don't want to keep on going this way." He started pacing back and forth in her small office while Kiera leaned back in her chair and watched him nervously.

She definitely didn't like where this was going. "What do we have to talk about?" she asked, her stomach tightening with dread because she knew exactly what they should be talking about. Mia, Cricket and Autumn had all told her to do the same thing, but she'd ignored their advice, too afraid to face the possible outcomes of the conversation.

"Our relationship."

She looked down at her desk, not able to maintain eye contact with him. "We can't have a relationship."

"I know you think so, because you're hell bent on getting work experience then getting out of Dodge. But hear me out," he offered. "We're both attracted to each other," he said, bracing his arms on her desk and leaning towards her, daring her to contradict that bold statement.

"I don't..."

"No, don't even try to deny it, Kiera. That wasn't a question. The way we react around each other makes it pretty obvious that the attraction we had for each other is still there no matter how much we want to pretend otherwise."

Kiera could accept that, but she still wasn't sure what his point was. "And you're suggesting...?" She swallowed, too afraid to finish the thought.

When she didn't continue, Axel finished for her. "I'm proposing that we stop ignoring this attraction we have for each other. Why don't we just let it out, ride the wave? We haven't been successful at ignoring it, why not try and let it burn itself out?"

She blinked, surprised at his suggestion. "Burn out?"

"Exactly. Starving the fire hasn't helped. Let's just be together until you feel that you have to move on. When that happens, we'll part ways as friends."

"Friends." She tested the word out, not really liking the idea. She didn't want to be friends with him. She wanted to… "I don't think we would be very good friends." She'd been too hurt the last time they'd parted. How was she going to do it again?

He stood up and shrugged those huge, broad shoulders. "Well, we're obviously not very good at pretending we're not lovers. So something has got to give." He sighed. "People are starting to talk."

That was news to her, but she'd been trying to fly under the radar her first few weeks on the job. "Who is?" she asked, sitting up straight in her chair. Gossip was vicious and could ruin people's careers if it wasn't nipped in the bud.

"I don't know specifically who is gossiping, but people are starting to speculate about our relationship. They saw us at the softball game, then again at the gym."

Her eyes widened with horror. "They can't!"

"They are. And the only way to stop it is to not give them anything to discuss. I figure if we stop trying to ignore each other, then maybe we can work this attraction out of our system and it will burn itself out. The fire between us is too hot. Every time we're together, we're singed from the heat so I suggest we let it flare up. Just like all fires, they eventually run out of fuel. I'm guessing this will be the same between the two of us."

She licked her lips, considering his proposition. "You mean, we intentionally become lovers, just with no hope of any future?" she asked, trying to clarify what he wanted.

Axel hated the sound of that. He definitely wanted a future. With Kiera. But he'd been thinking about it and he couldn't figure out how to avoid running into her in the hallways and office events. Their cases would even be connected at times so they had to do something. "Here's the way I see it," he said. "We both want each other. You have future plans that don't necessarily include Chicago. How am I doing so far?"

Kiera wanted to deny everything but she couldn't. So she remained silent.

His jaw tightened furiously when her silence re-confirmed what he'd already guessed. "That's what I thought. So let's just enjoy each other until one of us decides it is over or you move on. Sound good?"

She started to shake her head.

"So I'll pick you up for dinner tonight and we'll discuss the details." He pushed off of her desk and headed towards the doorway.

Kiera bit her lip, her body shaking with the possibility of becoming Axel's lover once again.

He walked out of her office and disappeared down the hallway. She wasn't sure what to do or think and so she stared at her computer screen for a long time.

She wasn't sure how long she remained frozen there, but she knew she had to get her work done. Ash was expecting this to be finished by the end of the day so it could be filed with the courts. That meant she had to hurry up and meet the five o'clock deadline.

Pushing herself hard, mainly to meet the deadline but with a side benefit of not thinking about Axel's suggestion, she worked mercilessly throughout the rest of the afternoon. By the time she sent the brief off to Ash, her fingers were numb. Whether that was due to the speed and duration at which she had been typing or the sheer terror of facing an evening with Axel, she wasn't sure.

Her phone rang by her elbow and she felt her stomach drop out of her body. She knew that it was Axel calling her even before she looked over at the caller ID. Sure enough, Axel's name showed up and her hand shook as she tried to answer the phone.

Unfortunately, it took her too long to answer it so by the time she picked up the receiver, he had already hung up.

A part of her was relieved that she had a slight reprieve but then her cell phone started ringing and she scrambled to answer that before he hung up and thought she was trying to avoid him. She fumbled with the buttons, her thumbs initially unable to press the answer button but she finally did it and was able to bring the contraption to her ear. "Hello?" she answered.

"You're not avoiding me, are you?" Axel's deep voice asked.

Kiera wasn't sure how to answer. "I'm not sure," she finally replied.

His rumbling chuckle told her that he appreciated her honesty. "Good enough. I'll be down in a moment," he replied.

"Wait!" she gasped, sitting up and looking around to see if anyone else had noticed her outburst. "Can I...maybe we should meet at my place. I'll cook something."

There was silence for a long moment until he finally said, "Meet me at my place. Yours is boring."

Kiera immediately sensed that he wasn't thrilled with her suggestion but she wasn't sure why. There was only one way to find out, she told herself and packed up for the night. She hurried through the lobby and down the stairs, hoping to get out of the building before Axel. Her intent was for others in the office to not see them together. If Axel was right and the other lawyers and office staff were noticing them together, she didn't want to add any fuel to that fire. She had enough fires to deal with.

She exited the building and crossed the parking garage and knew instantly that Axel was there as well. She could feel his eyes on her as she walked to her tiny car. She refused to look at him though. If there was anyone else in the parking lot right now, they would see them looking and speculation would increase. She wasn't sure what she wanted from Axel, or even what he wanted, but her primary goal was to not let others know that they were seeing each other. Why that was the case, she wasn't exactly sure.

She drove out of the parking garage, a shiver running through her as she caught Axel staring at her the whole time. She ignored him and drove out, getting onto the highway that would take her to his place. When she spotted him zoom past her in his sporty car, she sighed and accepted that he really was angry with her. He got in front of her and led the way through the streets. Thankfully the traffic wasn't too heavy by this point and they made it to his place without much incident. It would have been easier to go to her apartment which was closer, but she understood that her place represented something he didn't want to acknowledge.

She pulled in right behind him and got out, leaving her work bag in her car, just bringing in her purse. Again it occurred to her that she wasn't completely sure what Axel wanted of their relationship.

"Glad you could make it," he said as she approached.

Kiera looked up at him, hearing the sarcasm in his voice. "What's going on?" she asked carefully, not wanting to irritate him further, but needing to get in sync with his mindset before going forward with anything.

Axel looked down at the woman that he wanted so badly it was now a constant, physical ache. Perhaps if he hadn't had that one night with her. Or maybe if they'd never met so many years ago, he could have met someone else, someone who might be willing to spend her life with him, share her future and her hopes and dreams.

But none of that had happened. And here he was, wanting to pull her into his arms and carry her up to his bed and never let her out of it. He wanted to show her all that they could be together, know all of her dreams and make them come true.

Unfortunately, all she wanted was a temporary lover. Axel had to accept he was a stepping stone.

Instead of answering her and causing words to get in the way, he moved closer, his hands reaching up to hold her head while he bent low and kissed her, showing her what he wanted. He wanted her. Exclusively, for the rest of his life. He wanted to love her unconditionally and have lots of babies with her, to watch those children grow up and for the two of them to grow old together. He wanted to know what it would be like to see her beautiful skin age with time and her soft, brown hair turn silver as their grandchildren laughed around them.

Instead, he had this one night with her. And perhaps a few more.

He would take it. He would take anything she would give him and savor every moment, every kiss and touch and take those memories out in his mind when he was old and alone to keep him warm on those cold nights that he knew were coming.

When he lifted his head, he felt her soft hands gripping his arms, her lush body pressed against him and he felt an odd sort of victory. At least she couldn't deny that they had this between them. "Come inside," he answered her.

"Are you sure?" she asked.

His only response was to raise his eyebrows and pull her hips closer to his.

She laughed softly, blushing at the obvious answer pressing against her belly. "I guess you're sure."

He pulled back and took her hand, leading her through the house. "Are you hungry?" he asked.

Kiera felt the quiet all around her, but there was also the tension that she remembered from years ago. It never quite left whenever they were together. "I'm starving," she answered, holding his hand tightly and hoping he got the message.

He smiled slightly and led her to his bedroom, kissing her as soon as they reached the top of the landing, pushing her backwards as he slowly eased her to his bed.

Kiera didn't need words any longer. When he kissed her, he communicated extremely well. She followed his lead, demanding right along with him. Touching him everywhere, re-learning his touch and his scent, the way he touched her as well, feeling glorious as they spun out of control. And when he entered her, she knew that she would never feel as whole as she did at this moment. With Axel, the world always seemed perfect. No matter what was going on outside the world, Axel and the way he looked at her or touched her, or just smiled in her direction, made everything right and she was happy.

CHAPTER 7

Kiera rested her chin on her palm as the conversation swirled around her. She didn't even realize that she had a goofy grin on her face as Mia, Cricket and Autumn discussed wedding plans. Mia was throwing a big wedding with all of her neighbors and co-workers invited. They'd all helped her when she was arrested and she wanted to thank them, to show them all how much their loyalty and support meant to her.

Autumn had suggested to Mia that she should get married on the same day that her ex-fiancé was to be sentenced for his fraud and embezzlement charges. But Mia only smiled and waved that idea away. Jeff wasn't in her life any longer. Ash was the only man that was important to her. She didn't care what happened to Jeff. They'd broken up long before he tried to frame her for stealing all that money and then his faked murder. They'd all been disgusted when they'd learned how he'd gotten his blood drawn over several months in order to have enough to fake his own death. That was just repulsive not to mention a waste since there were so many people who needed blood as a life saver. Jeff had been selfish on so many levels, it was hard to figure out which was worse.

Her wedding was three months away now and they were frantically getting things organized. A wedding this size normally took at least a year to pull together but Ash refused to wait that long to marry her. So the wedding would be sooner and he gave Mia an enormous budget to make things happen more quickly.

"What about you?" Mia asked.

Kiera looked around and suddenly realized that all three women were now staring at her. "I'm sorry, I didn't get much sleep last night," she replied, smothering yet another yawn. "What was the question?"

The three other women shared a look which Kiera missed because she was nervously adjusting her napkin on her lap.

Autumn spoke up. "Mia was asking what our ideal wedding would be. She's looking for ideas."

Kiera instantly knew that she wanted to get married in the field behind Axel's house, right at dusk with white lights sparkling underneath the huge, oak tree. She didn't want a large group of people. In fact, she would be perfectly happy with just these three women, a few of her college friends she still kept in touch with and…

She was about to think of Axel's brothers but that would mean that Axel was the groom.

She sighed and shook her head. "Yes, um…I don't know exactly what kind of wedding. But probably…"

"Something in the country?" Cricket suggested with a kind, understanding look.

Kiera smiled and nodded her head. "Yes. Definitely something simple and countryish."

Autumn cleared her throat, all of them knowing what was happening. But until Kiera was ready to discuss it, the other women were trying to be mute on the subject and respect her privacy. "What kind of flowers are you getting Mia?"

Mia looked away from Kiera's longing look and focused on her water. "I haven't really picked out the flowers."

Three women stared at her. "The flowers have to be ordered, honey," Autumn said with a slight sense of urgency. "You have the church and the groom, we have our dresses and you have yours. The reception place, the food, the cake and flowers are all that's left."

"I know," she sighed. "That's why I'm asking you guys. I don't really have a favorite flower. I don't want roses because they are too expensive although I love the way they smell and their elegance. And I don't like orchids."

"Daisies," Kiera stated, then looked up, surprised that she'd even said the word.

Mia's eyes lit up. "I like daisies," she said, considering the idea.

Cricket watched as Kiera's eyes turned worried. She shook her head. "I don't think daisies would go with the dress you chose. Daisies aren't formal enough."

Mia considered that for a moment, then nodded her head. "You're right. I guess I should just head to a florist and ask for advice, but they always seem to just get dollar signs in their heads whenever I tell them who I'm marrying. I hate the way all these vendors act like Ash is their lottery ticket. I don't like it so I was hoping to go in with an idea first, tell them to keep it as simple as possible."

Cricket smiled when Kiera relaxed slightly. "What about if we head to the flower market this Saturday?"

Mia cringed. "Ash is taking me out of town this weekend."

Kiera realized this was a good excuse to get out of Axel's proximity this weekend. They'd been spending a lot of time together lately, laughing and cooking, riding his horses. She was starting to have trouble keeping things uncomplicated. She was falling in love again.

Or had she ever been out of love? Was it possible that she'd only learned to deal with the loneliness of being without Axel after they'd left each other during her college years? Had she been in love with him all this time and just suppressing the emotion?

It was possible. She hadn't been with any other man. All of her dates had left her cold and unmoved. She'd even been irritated that they would dare to touch her.

She sighed, unaware that her friends were staring at her once again.

"Did you hear about Linda coming back last week from vacation?" Autumn asked, changing the subject since it appeared that the previous topic was too painful for Kiera at the moment. She turned to Cricket and Mia, explaining that Linda was one of the lawyers in Ryker's group.

"Was she not supposed to come back?" Cricket asked, trying to pretend disinterest.

"It wasn't that she came back early," Autumn said, rolling her eyes. "It was how she came back. She used to have a pretty nice figure, but now she's a bit more...voluptuous."

Kiera and Cricket both looked down at their modest breasts. It wasn't that their breasts were small, they were just...in proportion to their figures. Autumn and Mia were a bit more endowed.

Mia laughed. "If I were to change anything on me, I'd go for bigger lips. I'd love to be able to pout just like those fashion models."

Autumn chuckled. "I'd like to be taller. But I don't think there's any plastic surgery for that kind of wish."

Kiera was fascinated. "Why on earth would you want to be taller?" she asked, leaning back as their lunch plates were taken away. She'd barely eaten any of her salad, but had pushed it around on the plate as thoughts of Axel swirled through her mind.

Autumn leaned back in her chair and grimaced. "I'd just like to be as tall or taller than one obnoxious, irritating lawyer who seems to think he can boss me around."

Kiera laughed, delighted with her friend's desires, even though they were unrealistic. "I hate to break it to you, but Xander can boss you around." If only those two could figure out that they were hopelessly in love with one another, they would be so happy, Kiera thought.

Autumn's eyes flashed. "I know. And he knows it. But if I were taller, I wouldn't be so..." she thought about it for a moment. "I don't know what it is about him that drives me so crazy but he just irritates me. If I were taller, I don't think he would intimidate me as much."

Kiera recognized the signs in Autumn and Xander's arguing because she and Axel argued just like that whenever they weren't talking about things. Like now, for instance. Axel's temper flared at the slightest issue lately. Until she kissed him each night, they always felt like they were on the verge of a huge argument. And Kiera had no idea how to address the issue since she didn't know what was bothering him.

"What about you?" Cricket asked Kiera.

"What would I change if I could do any plastic surgery?" she laughed. "I don't know. Probably go with Linda's idea and get bigger breasts. It might be nice to be considered bodacious," she said, one hand subconsciously going to her chest. "And you?" she asked Cricket.

Cricket laughed right back. "Oh, it would be no contest. I'd definitely become a brunette. These blond curls make everyone think I'm a complete ditz when they first meet me. Including the head honcho over at your firm. He's the worst! I'm pretty sure he's convinced I'm a complete idiot."

The four women were just about to say something when they were interrupted by a very angry, very large Axel who was bearing down on their table.

"Several things," he growled to the four women who were now staring at him with wide, stunned expressions as he leaned over their table. "First," he turned to Cricket, "Ryker feels many things for you, but I guarantee that he doesn't think of you as an idiot. And I daresay he would be furious with you if you dyed your hair." He turned to Mia and started to say something, but stopped himself and just shook his head. "As for being taller," he said to Autumn, "I can guarantee that topping him in height won't solve the problem." He glared down at Kiera and all of his anger seemed to explode in her direction. "And if I ever hear you say you're going to change anything on your incredibly gorgeous, sexy figure, I think I might have to put you over my knee and..." he stopped himself, his lips compressed as he tried to regain control of his fury. "Just don't even think about changing your breasts, or your legs or lips or your hair!" he growled. "Don't change a damn thing!"

With that, he walked away, dropping several large bills on the leather bill carrier that the waiter was bringing to their table before storming out of the restaurant.

The four women stared at the man's retreating back in stunned silence for a long moment before they turned back to each other. A moment later, they all burst out in shocked laughter.

Axel stormed out of the restaurant and back to the office, so livid he didn't even see his brothers who were walking into the building together.

"Axel?" Ash called out when Axel just walked by them, looking like a thunder cloud.

Axel spun around, more than ready to hit anyone who stopped him. When he realized it was his brothers, his fists relaxed, but not completely. "What's up?" he asked, running a hand through his hair in an effort to calm down.

"Are you okay?" Ryker asked.

Axel took a deep breath, trying to get hold of himself. He nodded, but deep down, he wasn't sure he was okay.

Xander wasn't convinced. "How about if we head over to the gym and you can punch my lights out?" he suggested, knowing that something had been bothering Axel for a couple of weeks now.

Axel thought about it, but shook his head. "I don't think that's a good idea," he came back, fisting his hands on his hips. "Why are you three all out here?" he asked.

Ash laughed and rolled his eyes. "We were trying to find you."

"What's wrong?"

His three brothers looked at each other, then back at Axel. "How about if we all head over to my place and we can discuss it?" Ash suggested.

Axel thought about the work he had piled up on his desk, then remembered Kiera suggesting that she get a breast augmentation and he knew he wouldn't get anything else done today. "Fine," he replied and followed them back out to the parking garage. He let Ash drive him to his house, leaving his car in the parking garage. Once there, he slumped down in Ash's plush leather sofa and took the offered beer, downing almost the whole thing in one swish.

Once he put the bottle down and grabbed another, he looked up, only to realize all three of his brothers were waiting.

"What?" he asked, surprised that they were almost ganging up on him.

"What's going on between you and Kiera?" Ryker asked, taking a swig of his own beer.

Axel rubbed his hand over his face, trying to figure it out for himself. "I don't know."

"Why don't you start from the beginning? How long have you two been seeing each other?" Ash asked.

Axel smiled, realizing that Ash wasn't asking just as a brother but as a boss. He considered all of his employees to be part of a team. Not quite family. They all had enough family, they said. But their teams were close, all of them working together, working together as a cohesive unit. A team couldn't do that without some family-like closeness among peers.

In other words, each of his brothers, himself included, watched out for their workers, stepping in when things were getting tough and ensuring everyone had as much of a work/life balance as possible in their stressful environment.

Seeing Ash standing up for Kiera made him feel better. But only a little. He wanted to have the right to stick up for Kiera but she was pulling away, becoming more and more distant even while the sex between them was getting better, more explosive and addictive. He couldn't imagine a time when she wasn't sleeping next to him. In fact, the nights she insisted on sleeping at her own apartment were the nights he barely slept at all.

"We knew each other over six years ago," Axel finally said. His head was leaning back against the leather sofa and his eyes were closed, so he didn't see the surprise in his brothers' faces, but he could feel it. "Stop looking at me like that," he said, still with his eyes closed.

His brothers all chuckled because they knew each other so well. "Why didn't you say something when I presented her to be hired," Ash asked.

Axel felt one of his brother sit down at the opposite end of the sofa and he peeked out. "What was I supposed to say? 'Don't hire her. She's the woman who broke my heart.'?"

Ryker was leaning against the mantle but Axel caught his eyes widen at that confession. "So she's the one?" he asked, just to clarify. All three of them remembered when Axel had come back from Washington, D.C. He'd been driven, mindlessly pushing harder than necessary to get his division up and running. He'd been a bear to be around and had worked eighteen and twenty hours every day no matter how fast his business was growing.

Axel sighed as he nodded his head. "Yep."

Xander shrugged his shoulders. "So what's the problem?"

Axel leaned forward, holding the cold beer in both his hands. "We met in Washington, D.C. when she was in school and I was finishing up my time clerking at the Supreme Court. By the time I'd met her, more than half the pieces were already in place for me to come back here and start my section of the law firm."

"That was a tough time in your life," Xander said, concern on his face as he watched his brother struggle with the story.

"I was pretty angry with her. And coming on board with you guys, I saw it as if I were starting my own law firm. I didn't want to lean on you two for clients or any other support." He turned to Ash and smiled. "You were doing your own clerkship for a federal judge out in California at the time so you weren't around yet."

Ash nodded, then swung his beer out, indicating Axel should continue the story.

Xander interrupted before he could go on. "Why didn't you just bring her back here with you?" he asked.

Ash laughed and the other three brothers looked at him as if he'd lost his mind. "What's wrong with that suggestion?" Ryker asked.

That made Ash laugh even harder. "You wanted her to give up everything so she could come back here and hang out with you?" Ash asked. He reached out and punched his older brother on the arm.

Axel glared at his brother, but didn't retaliate as he normally would. He was too interested to figure out why Ash had said those words. "That's almost exactly what she said. But I still don't get it. I wanted to marry her."

That surprised all of them but they quickly recovered. "And now?"

"I'd marry her in a heartbeat if she'd have me. But she's only here until the next big assignment comes along."

Ash definitely didn't like that. "Has she said this to you?"

Axel finished off his beer. "Not in so many words, but it's true. So I'm only her boyfriend out of convenience."

There was a long silence before Xander spoke up. "I don't believe that for a minute."

Axel stood up and walked over to the fridge, pulling out four more beers and popping the tops before he came back, handing them out to his brothers but keeping one for himself. "What makes you say that?" he asked when he was sitting down again.

Xander shifted on the huge leather club chair so he could see Axel better. "I've seen the way she looks at you. She's hooked. And if you're too stupid to realize it, then you don't deserve her."

Axel's eyes looked at his older brother, then at Ryker and Ash, both of whom were obviously thinking the same thing. Xander was saying that about Axel and Kiera when he was obviously in love with Autumn? Really?

Axel laughed along with Ryker and Ash, all three of them catching the irony in Xander's statement.

"Okay, fair enough. I've got to figure out how to keep her on my own. But if you've got any advice, please let me know. I've been trying to figure this out for a couple of weeks and so far, it seems that my strategy has only backfired."

The men changed the subject after that and the four men proceeded to get drunk in an effort to lose their problems. Only Ash was sober by the time each of them were finding a bed in his house somewhere. He smiled when the doorbell rang, knowing that his newcomer would be Mia. He didn't let her sleep alone these days and she'd been out to dinner with friends.

"Hello, Handsome," she said as soon as he opened the door.

"Why didn't you use your key?" he asked, pulling her into his arms and kissing her so she couldn't answer him.

"I don't know," she laughed when he'd pulled back slightly. "I guess I'm just not used to it."

"You'd better get used to it," he growled and pulled her into his room. "All my brothers are here, by the way," he warned before he slammed the door to what he now considered their bedroom.

"All of them?" she asked, her eyes wide with surprise.

He answered her while his fingers started taking off her clothes. "All three of them. They're in the other bedrooms. Are you okay with them being here?" he asked before he lifted her up and placed her on the bed.

She laughed but snuggled up to him, not the least bit surprised that he'd taken off all of her clothes as soon as they were alone. She was used to it now. "Just wondering," she said mysteriously.

"Forget about my brothers," Ash said as he bent his head to kiss her. "I have other things to discuss."

Mia was in complete agreement with his agenda and smiled as she wrapped her arms around his neck.

CHAPTER 8

"Axel Thorpe," Axel snapped as he answered the phone.

"Having a bad day, old man?" a familiar voice came back with a chuckle.

"Brett?" Axel asked, thinking this might be his old college buddy.

"At your service," Brett Hanson responded with another jovial laugh.

Axel leaned back in his big leather chair, his frustration with his current situation with Kiera forgotten for a moment. "It's been a while. How have you been?" he asked.

The two men talked for several minutes, catching up on their respective lives. Axel was only slightly jealous that his old friend already had two kids and was madly in love with his wife. He thought about what it would be like to say that about himself and Kiera with their kids entering school. And then he thought about Kiera pregnant with their children and he had a hard time breathing for a moment. Kiera pregnant would possibly be the most beautiful thing in the world. As long as he had sons. He couldn't imagine raising a daughter that might look like Kiera. He had enough problems already. Adding a beautiful teenage daughter and he thought he might just lose it. He pushed that out of his mind, refusing to get caught up in that dream. Kiera didn't want that, he knew. She wanted the career.

Maybe at some point in the future, they could work things out and she would be ready to start a family. If he could hold onto her for that long, he thought. He hadn't talked to her about the issue for a while. Maybe it was time to broach the subject. He wanted her and he was willing to do just about anything to keep her.

Axel re-focused on Brett's voice, hearing about all the strange and wonderful things his wife and children were up to. He made a mental note to try and get back to Washington, D.C. to visit him and his family. Brett was a good guy, having gone into business while Axel studied law. They'd done some crazy things throughout their college years together.

"So what's the call for? Surely you didn't just call me to catch up," Axel asked. "You always have an angle."

Brett laughed. "You've caught me. I heard through the grapevine that someone in your group hired a woman named Kiera Ward. She graduated from Georgetown and I've been hearing that she's just the person I need."

Axel hesitated, not wanting to confirm or deny that Kiera was on staff. "What about her?" As far as he was concerned, Kiera was his. Brett needed to keep his paws off of her. It took Axel several minutes to remember that Brett was madly in love with his wife and Antonia was just as infatuated with him. It still took several more minutes to tamp down the jealousy that rose up.

Brett continued, unaware that his friend was having homicidal thoughts. "I have a position that I think she would be perfect for. It's in Paris, which I know she's fluent in French and she also did some work with an international client I stole out from under Watson and Watson three days ago. They're asking for her to join them in Paris and work through some legal issues they're having." Axel listened as Brett continued to describe the role and the criminal problems the client was having.

Axel felt like his old friend had just slugged him. "Why would you need her on your team?" he asked, gripping the phone so hard he was amazed it didn't break into little pieces. "Kiera is more of a trial lawyer than an organizational lawyer. She's pretty amazing in the courtroom."

"That's what I've heard. And exactly the person I need for the job. Ms. Ward has a reputation for being able to see the small details and make them into big ones that a jury can understand. She's quite the litigator even at such a young age."

"You're right. She's pretty amazing," Axel agreed. But that didn't mean he wanted Brett even within a ten mile radius of his woman.

Brett laughed, trying to keep things jovial. "It's an incredible opportunity for her." Brett went on to give Axel more of the details of the position. As Axel listened, his gut tightened. This was an incredible opportunity for Kiera. She would be a fool to turn it down.

"So what do you say? Any chance you could help me convert her to the dark side?" he teased.

Axel sighed and rubbed his forehead. He wasn't sure how to handle this. If he convinced Kiera to take the job, it would be the end of their relationship. If he didn't bring this to her, he wouldn't ever feel right about them being together. This was the nightmare he'd been dreading but it had come significantly sooner than he'd expected. Hell, she hadn't even been working here for a month!

It was still an awesome opportunity. A part of him was thrilled for her, excited that her work and reputation have paid off. The other part of him wanted to hide her away so no one else would ever discover what a fantastic lawyer she was. "I'll talk to her about it," was all he would commit to at this point.

"Sounds great, buddy!" Brett came back. "I'll talk to you later. And thanks for your help. This would be a huge coup for her career."

Axel hung up and just about slammed his fist against his desk. Standing up, he walked over to the windows, staring out into the gloomy afternoon weather but not really seeing anything. His mind was remembering Kiera as she was last night, in his arms and smiling up at him as she touched different parts of his body, making him want her as much as she wanted him. Every moment in her company was an exploration either of her mind or her body and he wasn't sure which he liked more, making her scream out in passion or arguing with her about legal issues. Both fired his mind like no other woman ever had.

He was pacing back and forth, a plan forming in his mind. He wasn't sure it would work but he had to at least give it a try. He walked up the stairs, for the first time ignoring his staff when they called out to him. He had a mission and he had to work out the details as fast as possible. He didn't want Brett calling Kiera before he had a chance to talk to her first.

There was so much he needed to do before this could actually work, but this was not an opportunity that he would relinquish. Hell, he wasn't even sure if Kiera would go through with the plan. He didn't even know if she would want him to come to Paris with her. There was no doubt in his mind that Kiera would take the job. It was too good of an opportunity for her not to take it. This job was a career maker. Once she'd finished working through this issue in Paris, which he suspected might take two or three years from what Brett had explained, she could basically write her own ticket.

Ash was going to be furious about losing her after such a short period of time. He'd already been singing her praises and her clients, even in the short period she'd been here, had come to rely on her more than anyone had expected. Everything everyone said about Kiera was true. She was a fabulous lawyer. But he'd known she would get there six years ago.

He went up to Ryker's office and paused by his assistant's desk. "Is he in?" he asked Joan who was always cheerful despite Ryker's reputation for being a grump most of the time.

Joan looked up and smiled. "He's just reviewing some files. Go on in."

Axel walked in and stopped in the middle of his brother's office, pacing back and forth while he continued to work the issue through in his mind. He didn't even notice when Ryker put down his papers and watched while Axel paced, his mind figuring out the problems that might come up and solutions to overcome or even circumvent them before they happened.

When Axel didn't say anything for several minutes, Ryker picked up the phone and called Xander. "Better come up. Something is going on. Get Ash on your way, okay?" He listened for a moment, then glanced up at Axel and said, "Yes." The pacing continued and Ryker waited patiently while Axel worked through whatever was going on in his mind. Ryker trusted his brothers so if Axel was in here pacing, this was monumental.

A few minutes later, Ash and Xander stepped into Ryker's office, only to see the same thing Ryker had been witnessing for several minutes. They came inside and closed the door, assuming correctly that this was probably a conversation that was better left to just the four of them. All of them glanced at each other, their eyes communicating their suspicion that it had to do with the issue they'd been discussing a few nights ago.

"What's going on?" Xander asked, always the first one to step into any confrontation or issue. Except in one area, that is. And all three of Xander's brothers wished he would face up to his romantic issues with Autumn but none were brave enough to demand it.

"No clue," Ryker replied, leaning his head back against his large, leather chair, waiting for Axel to explain.

Axel turned at the noise and looked around, relieved that his other brothers were here now. "I have a problem," he said. He turned to face Ash. "I'm still in love with Kiera and I can't let her get away from me for another six years."

Ash grinned. "And what are you going to do about Kiera?"

Axel wasn't surprised. Ash would know that this wasn't an arbitrary liaison that would cause problems later on with the proximity of one worker being involved, even formerly, with another staff member. "Thanks. I know we discussed this the other night but now I'm going to do something, or at least I hope she'll let me do something, to make our relationship permanent."

Xander shook his head, relieved that his brother was going to finally do something about the woman he obviously loved. "It's about time!" he teased.

"That's rich," Ash said under his breath. But when Xander turned to face his brother, Ryker stepped in and brought them back to the original issue before things got out of hand. They weren't at the gym with an open space and he didn't relish his furniture being turned into toothpicks by one of his brothers' epic fights. "Are you announcing your engagement?" he asked.

Axel ran a frustrated hand over his face and shook his head. "I'd like to but I doubt she'd accept. Like I mentioned the other night, she's not here for long," he explained. "And what's worse, I just got a call from an old college buddy. He has a fantastic position he wants to offer Kiera."

Ash was already shaking his head. "He can't have her. She just got here and she's already one of the best lawyers I've had on my team. She's smart and funny and the clients love her. It doesn't hurt that she's nice to look at either."

Axel almost leapt across the room at Ash but Xander knew exactly what was about to happen and stepped in at just the right moment to stop the beating. "Not now!" he commanded, holding Axel's shoulders while Ryker stood up and came around to the other side of his desk.

"Ash is right," Ryker said. "Even I've been impressed with Kiera's work. Question is, what are you going to do to keep her on the team?"

Axel turned away and started his pacing. "I can't stop her," he said and all of his brothers heard the pained emotion in Axel's voice. "This really is a great opportunity. She can't turn it down." He took a deep breath and closed his eyes. "This is the same thing that happened in Washington, D.C. but in reverse. Back then, I had the great job I was moving off to and she had to stay put. Now she's got the great opportunity and I'm here in Chicago."

None of them pointed out that he shouldn't consider himself "stuck" when he was one of the managing partners in one of the most reputable law firms in the country. "That was years ago."

Axel nodded. "I know. And I'm not going to make the same mistake I made last time. I lost her back then because I was being a selfish jerk. I didn't understand back then, but I do now and I can't lose her this time."

All three brothers stood shoulder to shoulder, bracing for whatever Axel was about to tell them.

Axel took a long breath, steadying himself for what he was about to say. He didn't want to leave Chicago and his brothers. But Kiera was more important now. Besides, he could fly back and forth to see his brothers. Not having Kiera in his life would be like severing a limb. She was that essential to him now. She had been six years ago, but he hadn't understood all of it then. He wouldn't be so stupid as to lose her this time around. "I'd like to start up a branch of The Thorpe Group in Paris."

"France?" Ash clarified, stunned into saying something obviously stupid.

Axel nodded even while Xander smacked him on the back of the head for being so dense. "Of course Paris, France, you idiot."

That reminded Axel of the conversation he'd overheard recently. Turning to Ryker he said, "Cricket Fairchild is planning to dye her hair brown," he said and waited for the explosion.

"What?" Ryker demanded, his whole body tensing with fury at the idea. "Why the hell would she do that?"

Axel grinned, feeling relief for a moment now that someone else had problems other than him. They'd come back to him, but at least for a few moments, someone else was confused. "Because she thinks that you think she's an idiot. She says that being a brunette would help her disperse that perception."

Ryker rolled his eyes. "Of all the ridiculous…" he stopped himself and took a deep breath. "I'll deal with Cricket. What about Paris?"

Axel wasn't finished. "Oh, and Mia wants roses at her wedding but she doesn't want you to have to pay for them. She's trying to keep the cost of her wedding down since she can't pay for it and you've already offered to do that."

The four brothers stared at each other before bursting out with laughter. When they'd calmed down, Ash nodded his head. "Thanks for the head's up. I'll talk to her."

Axel was about to say something to Xander, but stopped. "Never mind," he said and turned away.

"What?" Xander demanded, stepping in front of Ryker and Ash.

Axel wished he hadn't said anything. But since it was out there, he took a deep breath and said, "Autumn wants to be taller so she can take you down and won't be intimidated when you and she fight. Which seems to be all the time lately."

Xander just stared for a long moment, unaware of the tension that statement had unleashed in the room. Ryker and Ash slowly moved back, knowing that Xander tended to lash out whenever Autumn's name came up lately.

Shockingly, Xander didn't say a word. He didn't get angry or explode in any way. He simply nodded his head and crossed his arms over his chest. "I'll take care of it," he said softly but with vehemence. "Anything else?"

Axel turned back to Ash and chuckled. "Mia said something about wanting fatter lips. I have no clue what that was about."

Ash laughed again. "I'll make sure her lips look..." he stopped and grinned. "Never mind."

The other brothers turned back to Axel, all silently asking him if there was anything else they should know about.

"That's it," Axel confirmed. "Oh, wait," he said, remembering one more thing. "Apparently Linda Sanders got a boob job to try and catch your attention," he told Ryker with an evil grin. "Cricket doesn't approve of Linda's efforts to turn you eye."

Ryker looked confused for a moment. "Linda Sanders? She just came back from sick leave, didn't she?"

Axel chuckled. "Apparently, she had cosmetic surgery."

Ryker still didn't understand. "She looks the same to me." He shrugged his shoulders.

"How did you hear all of this?" Ash asked.

Axel smiled as he remembered the lunch he'd overheard. "I was eavesdropping during my lunch meeting with Phil Matthews last week. They were at a table nearby. The subject of Linda's boob job came up and they all started considering cosmetic or physical changes they would make to themselves. It was interesting to say the least."

"What would Kiera do?" Xander asked, laughing at the idea. He wished he could do a bit of eavesdropping himself.

"Boob job again."

The three other men were surprised. "I know!" Axel said, shaking his head as if he couldn't figure out why she would consider something like that. Then he glared at his brothers because he's just realized that they also considered her figure pretty awesome, which meant they'd been looking at her.

"We're guys!" Xander said in reaction as if that were explanation enough.

"Don't let it happen again!" he growled and all three of his brothers laughed.

As usual, Ryker was the first to get them back to business. "In any case, what are your plans for Paris?"

Axel sighed and started pacing again. "I'm not sure of all the details yet. The only thing I know about is that I'm in love with Kiera Ward and I believe she's in love with me. But she loved me before and she wasn't going to give up her career to be with me. I won't give up my career, but I'll definitely give up my office if it means I get to keep her in my life."

"So you're going to give up your department for her?" Xander asked, not completely understanding but he was starting to get an inkling of what was going on.

Axel didn't hesitate to answer. "I won't lose her again," he replied. "I left her before to start up my department. If it means giving it up and moving with her, I'm going to do it."

Ryker stared at his younger brother for a long moment. "I have several clients in Paris. I'm sure expanding internationally will help me with my group as well."

Xander spoke up with his own input. "And I had a potential client I just turned down yesterday because we don't have a presence in Europe. If you set up a branch there, we could keep some of those clients as well."

"It's tricky," Ash added, "but doable."

Axel's shoulders relaxed. He should have known that his brothers would support him. The four of them always had each other's backs. There was just the four of them, and now Mia. And hopefully Kiera.

"I guess I'd better go try and convince her to take this job then," he said. He didn't want to go to Paris. He loved his house and he loved being with his brothers. But he loved Kiera more. He'd let her go the last time but he didn't think he would survive losing her again. There was so much more to her and he wanted to know every aspect of her.

"You'd better brush up on your French," Xander said, slapping Axel's back.

Ash shook his head. "It's only a twelve hour flight from here to Paris. We'll see each other often. So you'd better get a big place in Paris. Mia will be shopping there all the time. I'll make sure of it."

Axel laughed, truly grateful for such amazing brothers. "Deal!"

He walked out of Ryker's office, feeling better than he had in weeks. He had a plan and he was damn well going to convince Kiera that it would work out this time. He knew she loved him. It was just a matter of getting her to admit it to him. And probably to herself as well, and then working through all the little details that living together created. They could make it though. They had a lot more going for them than many other couples.

Axel walked down the stairs once again, stopping on Ash's floor instead of heading down yet another flight of stairs to his own domain. Now that he'd made the decision and gotten the support of his brothers, he didn't want to wait until later tonight to get her thinking about his idea. He made his way through the chaos that was always present when a team of lawyers worked together on a case. In some cases, when the stress levels were high or a deadline was imminent, lawyers and investigators shouted ideas to each other or rushed papers from one person to another or to one drop off point in a rush to a judge's chambers. He heard it all but ignored the noise, moved around the people rushing through the hallways, stopping only when he reached Kiera's door.

He found her staring out her window, just as he'd been doing about an hour ago. "Got a minute?" he asked, stepping inside and closing her door, leaning against it so he could watch her carefully. He caught the surprised look in her pretty, brown eyes and wished he knew what she was thinking. When she was happy or excited, he could see that clearly but all other times, she hid her emotions well. Maybe, if she gave him the chance, he'd be able to read her in fifty or sixty years.

Kiera spun around, drinking in the sight of Axel with all of his commanding presence and incredible shoulders that she'd come to know so intimately over the past couple of weeks. She couldn't believe that she'd actually thought she could ignore this man. He was just too domineering and handsome for that to have been a realistic plan. What hope could she have had? When the man wanted something, he went after it with a single minded purpose. And he'd told her what he wanted from her that very first weekend when she'd woken up in his bed.

She smiled, thinking of how terrified she'd been that morning, worried about being in his arms and what it might imply for the future. Now she knew, Kiera thought.

With a sigh, she accepted the truth about her feelings for this man. No, she hadn't fallen out of love with him. She'd just learned to smother the pain of not being with him. And six years ago, she'd convinced herself that not following him had been the right thing to do.

Oh, she'd been so so wrong! Falling in love with Axel Thorpe had been the beginning of the end of her independence. She might still be going after the dream, but Kiera knew that the dream wouldn't be complete without Axel Thorpe in it, holding hands with her, laughing and arguing with her and just generally being the man of her dreams.

She loved him so much it almost overwhelmed her.

"Here's the deal," he said and pushed away from the doorway to come into her office, making everything seem smaller somehow. It was only a fraction of the size of his own office, but she didn't mind. It kept her close to him. "I got a call from a guy named Brett that I know from college. He told me about a job in Paris that he thinks would be perfect for you," he explained, his stomach clenching with the smile that appeared on her beautiful face. "I think you should take the job." He ignored her surprise. "But here's the deal." He waited a moment, wondering what her reaction to his "deal" might be. Would she laugh and tell him he couldn't come with her? Or would she kindly accept his presence? Then he shook his head, remembering waking up with her arms wrapped around him this morning. He dove right into it by saying, "I'm coming with you. I've already spoken to my brothers and we've all agreed that it would be a good idea to open up a branch of The Thorpe Group in Europe. Paris could be the first stop and I'll head it up." He crossed his arms over his chest and looked down at her. "We already have ideas for potential clients. And Ash says Mia will be over to shop in the stores as soon as we're settled."

Kiera was shaking her head. "You'll hate Paris," she said softly. She stood up and came around her desk so she was right in front of him and, more importantly, closer to him. She stopped when they were face to face, or more accurately, face to chest since he was so much taller than she was. With a sigh of happiness, she reached up and kissed him lightly. "Your brothers will hate you not being here in Chicago."

Axel's eyes darkened. "Kiera, you're not getting this. I love you," he said with absolute conviction. "And you love me. We're not going through the same thing we did years ago." He put his hands on her shoulders, shaking her slightly to emphasize his point.

"I agree," she said, her smile broadening.

The relief he felt at her words loosened up the band that had been squeezing his chest. "Then call this guy," he said and pulled a piece of paper out of his shirt pocket, "and ask him about the job in Paris. It's a perfect opportunity."

Kiera glanced at the paper, then tossed it onto her desk without interest.

Axel looked down at the paper that had floated off of her desk to the floor, then down at her. "You'll call him later?" he asked, trying to figure her out. She wasn't making any sense. Why wasn't she running around her desk and eagerly dialing the number he'd just given her? It wasn't like her to procrastinate about anything. She dove right into every situation, handling the problems with finesse and class.

She laughed at his confusion. "Nope."

He wasn't sure what was going on. "Kiera, why are you being so vague?"

She laughed softly and reached up again, kissing him one more time. "I've already turned down the job."

That was unexpected. "You've already spoken to him?"

"About an hour ago."

Axel cursed Brett under his breath. "That lying, conniving…" He shook his head and pulled her closer. "You're going to accept the job. It's a great job."

She grabbed onto his tie and pulled, bringing his head lower. She lifted up one more time and kissed him gently, but with more feeling this time. "I'm not taking the job," she whispered against his lips. "And we're not moving out of Chicago."

Axel would have argued further, but he couldn't speak while he was kissing her. "I love you," he told her several minutes later when they came up for air.

Her smile widened and she looked up at him with all the love she had for this man in her eyes. "I love you too!" she laughed, delighted that things were working out so well. Her life might not be what she'd hoped, but thankfully, it was turning out to be even better!

He turned serious all of a sudden and Kiera's smile faded. "What's wrong?" she asked, unaware that her hands were gripping his arms more tightly.

He sighed and ran his hand up her back as if he needed to make sure she was still here with him. "I don't want this to be temporary."

"I don't either," she replied, not sure why he would think anything like that.

"I want to marry you, Kiera. I want to know that every day, you're going to be there by my side. I don't want to worry that you're going to get another job offer and I might lose you."

Was that all he was worried about? She moved closer, snuggling against his broad, muscular chest, reveling in his strength. "Hopefully I'll have a place here at The Thorpe Group for at least a few years. Until we decide to…."

"To what?" Axel demanded, pulling back slightly but not letting her get away from him. "I mean it. I want the whole thing. I want you forever."

She laughed and kissed the middle of his chest. "Until we decide to have kids," she explained shyly. And then something occurred to her. "You do want to have kids, don't you?" she asked, suddenly worried.

Axel let his breath out in a whoosh, relieved that she wasn't thinking of leaving him in a few years. "Of course I want to have kids. With you! Lots of them. And I want to practice making kids a whole lot more right at the moment," he told her, lifting her up onto her desk and pushing her back so she had to hang onto his shoulders to steady herself. "I want you completely at my mercy as well," he said, nibbling at her neck and enjoying her laughter.

There was a knock on her door and, before Axel could give the person permission to enter, they were already coming into the office.

Axel turned to snap at whoever had been so rude but stopped when he saw his frowning brother Ash standing there in the doorway.

"What do you want?" Axel demanded, keeping Kiera in his arms even while she struggled to sit up. She was more than a little embarrassed to have her boss see her in this kind of a compromising position.

"So it's going to happen?" Ash asked, his eyes taking in his best lawyer in his brother's arms. "You're off to Paris?"

Kiera was trying to stand up and look professional in front of her boss, but Axel was making it very difficult. "Um…no…we're uh…" She couldn't get his hands off of her waist to pull her suit jacket down properly no matter how many times she batted his hands away.

"Yes. She's taking the job."

"No. We're staying here."

Axel turned to glare down at her. "You're taking the job. I'm opening up a branch of the firm in Paris. We can be there next month and I can start laying the ground work."

She smiled up at him, already shaking her head. "We're staying here and I'm going to become your brother's most brilliant lawyer," she countered.

"I'm all for that," Ash stated firmly, crossing his arms over his large chest.

Axel sighed. "You're taking the job. It is a fantastic opportunity and you'll regret it later on. You'll resent me for not getting you to Paris. You can be back here in two or three years and we can work through the issues later."

She grinned up at him, thinking she had the trump cards. "I was kind of hoping to be pregnant in two or three years. Maybe even with our second child."

The picture of Kiera pregnant caused a lump to form in his throat and he had to swallow, several times, to be able to even speak. And even then, he wasn't very coherent.

While Axel tried to think of a response, she turned to her boss. "Did you need me for something?" she asked.

Ash was grinning like an idiot but at her question, he snapped out of it and remembered what he'd come in here for. "Yes." He jerked up again and handed her a small piece of paper. "Here," he said. "I'm marrying Mia next weekend. She says you already have the dress to be one of her bridesmaids."

Axel finally found his voice. He pulled Kiera back so his arm was around her waist protectively. "I thought you were getting married in three months. What happened to that plan?"

Ash shook his head as if he still couldn't believe what he'd found out. "I realized that Mia was delaying the wedding so she could get better prices on the food and cake and such. So I called up all of the people she'd worked with and told them to get everything done in one week versus three months and I'd double the amount already agreed upon."

Kiera gasped, her hand flying over her mouth in shock. "Does Mia know about this?" she asked.

Ash laughed. "She does now. We fought about it on the phone but I won." He winked at Kiera. "Mostly because she wants to be married as well anyway so she was only uncomfortable about the money."

Axel chuckled at the idea of his almost sister-in-law being so frugal. It made him feel even better about her joining the family. "At least she isn't after you for your money."

Ash grinned right back at him. "Just my body," he said before he turned and left. He was just about to close the door again but he stopped and said, "By the way, stop molesting my team members during work hours."

"Get out of here," Axel ordered, looking around to throw something at his brother who simply pulled the door closed while laughing uproariously.

"He's right," Kiera said, trying to pull out of his arms.

Axel was having none of that. He'd waited six years for this woman to be his and he wasn't going to listen to anyone telling him he couldn't touch her whenever he wanted to. "We'll fix everyone's perception quickly," he said and took her hand, pulling her out the door.

"Where are we going?" she asked, almost running to try and keep up with him.

"You'll see," he said and stopped in front of the elevator. She pulled her hand out of his since there were so many people waiting there as well.

No matter how many times she asked, he wouldn't tell her where they were going but simply pulled her out of the building and down the street. When they were in front of one of the most exclusive jewelry store in Chicago, she pulled back, shaking her head. "We can't go in there!" she gasped, horrified at what he was thinking.

"Of course we can. I want a ring on your finger so there isn't any confusion. We can't make out in the hallways if people think we're just having an affair," he told her, pulling her close and biting her earlobe.

She laughed and tried to pull out of his arms, but he wouldn't let her and the effort was only halfhearted anyway. "I will definitely marry you, but I don't need a diamond ring to show everyone that. Let's just get married," she said earnestly.

He looked down at her and shook his head. "We're getting married in my backyard, in the field with my brothers and your friends around us. We'll have the wedding reception under that old oak tree with lights going throughout all the branches and champagne to toast our new life together. And there will be daisies everywhere."

Kiera's mind was whirling with shock and surprise. "How did you..."

"I heard you talk about it that day over lunch," he said, his hand moving up to caress her cheek gently. "I want it all, Kiera. I want you, the wedding under the tree, the celebration and the kids."

She didn't realize that a tear had escaped her eyes until he caught the tear with his finger. "I screwed up royally the last time. It caused us to lose six years together. So would you please allow me to do it right this time?" he asked softly but with feeling.

She couldn't believe what a wonderful man he was. "Okay," she whispered back, not able to speak too loudly over the rapid beating of her heart.

"Good. Come on," he said and pulled her into the jewelry store. Ten minutes later, they were walking out again and Axel stopped her right on the street and kissed her, showing her and everyone around how much he loved her. "Now I'm going to call your boss and tell him that you're playing hookie today so I can take you to your apartment and move every box out to my place."

She grinned. "Should be pretty easy since I've barely unpacked."

He rolled his eyes. "There are some advantages to your crazy mindset," he told her and pulled her closer.

EPILOGUE

"Are you…" Axel stopped a few steps into their bedroom, his eyes surveying Kiera in stunned silence.

Kiera turned around nervously, smoothing the satin dress over her curves. "Does it look okay?" she asked, her fingers twitching with the low neckline. "It isn't too…"

Axel suddenly found his voice and looked down at her. "It isn't 'too' anything," he replied, a grin forming on his handsome features. "In fact, I think I might just have to miss my own brother's wedding!"

Kiera laughed, relieved that she didn't look horrible in the dress. It was a lovely shade of blue but the neckline plunged, not so low that it was indecent, but it showed a great deal of cleavage. The rest of the satin hugged her body, cinching around the waistline and hugging her hips and bottom.

Axel came over and reached for her.

"No! You can't touch me," she said and took a step back. "You might stain the dress!"

Axel laughed and grabbed her anyway. "Who chose this dress?" he asked as his hands smoothed over Kiera's hips and bottom before sliding upwards.

Kiera closed her eyes, sighing with the desire now surging through her. "Mia of course. She said she saw the dresses and instantly knew they were perfect."

Axel bent low to nuzzle her neck, enjoying the way her curls tickled his nose. "I fully approve," he commented as his fingers moved up higher, tracing the neckline. He suddenly stopped and lifted his head. "Are Cricket and Autumn wearing the same dress?" he asked sharply.

Kiera had been intent on his fingers and the way his mouth felt against her neck so she didn't understand the question at first. She had to blink several times before she could figure out what he'd just said. "Similar, but slightly different. Why?"

Axel wasn't able to answer immediately because he was too busy laughing. He was laughing so hard he was bent over, holding himself against the dresser, half of which was now hers since she'd moved in.

Kiera stood there, arms crossed over her stomach as she waited for him to regain control of himself. In the meantime, she surveyed his fabulous physique in the tailored tuxedo, reveling in how amazing he looked in the elegant attire. The man wore clothes exceptionally well, she thought. No matter what he pulled on, or off, she was always amazed at how hot he looked.

When his laughter slowed to a chuckle, she raised her eyebrows at him in silent question.

"I think my almost-sister-in-law is doing some matchmaking. And boy am I glad that I was already smart enough to get you before you showed up in that dress," he explained, chuckling again as he imagined his brothers when they got their first look at Cricket and Autumn in this dress. "Xander in particular is going to be furious."

Kiera immediately understood and was amused. "You think Mia chose this dress to spur Xander to do something about his attraction to Autumn?"

Axel nodded, his eyes alight with suppressed laughter. "And I think there's something going on between Cricket and Ryker as well." He led her down the stairs and out to the garage.

Kiera agreed with him. "I think Cricket is great. She and Ryker will make a fantastic couple if they can ever work things out. Although I can't completely figure out what's going on with them. There's definitely some strange vibes happening."

"What kind of strange vibes?" Axel asked, holding her hand while she stepped carefully into his black sports car.

Kiera shrugged. "I can't really put a finger on it," she said.

Axel moved around the car, slipping into the driver's seat. "I'm glad I'm not in his shoes today," he said as his eyes moved up and down Kiera's curves in the figure hugging dress. "I like knowing that I get to peel that dress off of you at the end of the night," he said and took her hands, his thumb rubbing over the beautiful diamond ring he'd put on her finger so recently. "I wouldn't like to figure out how to keep my hands off of you," he said and kissed her gently so he didn't mess up her lipstick.

"Are you ready for some fun?" he asked, looking down at her with pride in his eyes.

She laughed softly. "Now that we get more than a wedding, I'm more than ready. This should be an interesting day," she said and linked her fingers through his.

He suddenly stopped and turned to her, his eyes serious as he said, "I haven't told you that I love you today," he said, his voice warm and husky as he bent to kiss her gently.

She sighed with happiness. "Yes you did," she said. "Not in words, but in all the small, wonderful things you did this morning."

Axel thought about their morning and raised an eyebrow. "Small?" he asked suggestively.

Kiera rolled her eyes, trying not to laugh. "Not all things were small," she clarified, understanding that he was thinking about the way he woke her up this morning with soft, feather-light kisses on her back. All of which turned to not-very-light kisses once she was fully awake. However, she was thinking of the coffee he brought to her in the shower, or the warm towel he wrapped around her after their shower, the delicious eggs he made her with the last of his summer vegetables or the quiet silence as he held her hand while they read the morning paper. "But I love you too," she whispered with all the happiness she was feeling.

Book 3:
His Secretive Lover

INTRODUCTION

Cricket's Story...

Cricket Fairchild pulled the books more tightly against her chest, her green eyes huge and anxious. Another school, another set of strangers. Biting her lip, she walked into the classroom filled with new faces and took the only empty seat. She tried not to feel self-conscious, but she was painfully aware of all the eyes that watched her as she sat down. She prayed she wouldn't trip on the legs of the desk or chair.

"Bonjour class!" the teacher started off. Cricket glanced down at her class schedule. French? She was in Beginner's French? She was fluent in French! She'd just moved from Paris last week! Why had her father signed her up for Beginner's French?

She slumped down into the chair, keeping her mouth shut as she watched the other students. Everyone was struggling with pronunciation so she pretended to not know how to say the most basic words, even though she could speak not only French, but also Spanish and Italian. German was a bit harder, but she could even get through a conversation in that language as well.

She wasn't in Paris anymore, she reminded herself a half hour later when she lifted her books once again and glanced down at her schedule to find her next class. History. She had to chuckle at her father's sense of humor. With the emphasis her father placed on learning about the countries where they had lived, she probably knew more than the teacher. Her father not only pressed Cricket to learn about their histories and governments, but even the history and significance of the artworks he stole.

She doodled on her notebook in history class, wondering what "project" her father was working on now. What was in San Francisco that had lured her parents here? What amazing piece of art was he going to pilfer and sell on the black market? Or maybe he already had a buyer ready. Who knew with her father. Theft wasn't just his job, it was his passion. A passion she hated, she thought as she crouched lower in her chair, trying to blend in.

The teacher called on her and she jerked up in her seat, spewing out the correct answer before she could stop herself. She then looked around, worried that the other students would think she was weird. Only a few stray glances came her way, and she sighed with relief when they didn't look too hostile.

"Very good, Ms. Fairchild," the teacher beamed, proud of the newest student in her classroom. "Anthony," she called out, moving on to the next question and the next student. Cricket was able to slump back down into her chair, trying to appear inconspicuous. Avoid attention, she reminded herself. Blend in. Standing out caused the other students to not trust her. Blending in was the key to survival.

She pulled her hands up inside of the sleeves of her turtleneck sweater, wishing she could just curl up into an invisible ball. Unconsciously, her eyes scanned the room, her mind easily figuring out how to pick the lock on the classroom door, the deadbolt on the teacher's locker and, even more effortlessly, the teacher's desk. Cricket smiled, wondering what the teacher kept inside of her desk to need it locked up all the time.

As she wandered out of the classroom after the bell, she didn't realize that she was counting the ceiling blocks so she would know exactly how many squares inside the walls she'd need to climb in order to be directly over the cabinets or the desk. Her father was always proud of her casing abilities, calling her a natural thief. She shuddered at the thought, hating what her parents did while she was either at school or sleeping.

She made her way to the library instead of the cafeteria during lunch. Cricket didn't want to sit all by herself, feeling gauche and awkward. So she carried her books to the back of the library, pulled her partially demolished sandwich out of her backpack, and nibbled while she completed the homework she'd been assigned so far.

Looking around, she saw several other girls and a couple of boys doing the same thing and she smiled to one of the girls with straight, brown hair and thick, black glasses. The girl smiled back when the bell rang, indicating that the lunch period was over.

"I'm Halley," the girl said as she hurried to catch up to Cricket in the hallway.

Cricket looked carefully at the other girl, immediately mimicking the way she walked and the slant of her shoulders. It was a trick she'd learned over the years to help her blend in and act like the students around her. "I'm Cricket," she replied, wishing for the millionth time that her parents had named her something classic like Ann or Julie. The name Cricket was simply too weird. In the past, she'd tried to pretend that her name was something else, but "Cricket" always caught up with her.

"That's a cool name," Halley said, her intelligent eyes looking over Cricket carefully. "Where are you from?" she asked.

Ah yes, Cricket thought, yet another mine field. "I lived in Virginia," she replied, which technically wasn't a lie. She had lived in Virginia. And New York, and Paris, London, a small city just outside of Rome and a dozen other cities around the world. Her home followed her parents' "projects". When one stole the most valuable art work and jewelry in the world, one tended to have to move around a great deal.

"How long have you lived here?" Cricket asked, pushing the focus off of her so she didn't have to lie any longer

"All my life," Halley replied, rolling her eyes. "I've never been anywhere but San Francisco. And maybe over to Yosemite for camping, but my parents don't like to travel very much."

That sounded like heaven to Cricket who had never had a permanent home in her life. She was a freshman in high school and she'd been in more than fifteen different schools over her lifetime. And that didn't include the periods when her mother or father had taught her themselves because they had a "project" in an area without good schools.

The two walked down the hallways that rapidly filled up with the other students, all of whom were rushing to their next class. "If you're not doing anything after school, want to meet in the library to study again?" Halley asked, her eyes filled with eager hope.

Cricket latched onto the offer of friendship with both hands. "That would be great," she replied, her heart filling with happiness that she wasn't alone any longer. First days of school were always terrifying until she'd found a kindred spirit. Not someone in the "business," of course, but someone else who was in desperate need of a kind and compassionate smile.

Cricket didn't concern herself with being popular or having a crush on the cutest boy in school. Her ambitions were much lower, just wanting not to be alone. She hated that painful feeling of others' staring as the lone student walked silently and awkwardly down the hallway, wondering if others were whispering about the new girl.

As she walked happily down the hallway, she asked Halley questions, steering the conversation away from herself, since there were so many questions she couldn't answer truthfully. Besides, it was always interesting to find out about "normal" people, to live vicariously through their routines and traditions.

Someday, she promised herself, she would own her own house and a big yard with a dog running through the leaves in the fall and jumping through the sprinkler in the summer. She'd have a kitchen where she could bake cookies, and storage units filled up with junk she didn't know what to do with. As she listened to Halley talk about her Christmas plans, Cricket promised herself she would have a real home in the future!

Ryker's Story...

Thwak! The ball bounced perfectly against the brick wall of the school gymnasium, then onto the asphalt and back to Ryker's opponent. He smiled even as his eyes watched the ball, his mind instantly calculating the angle while his feet moved into position to take the next shot. Another thwak! And the ball bounced high out of reach, but still inside the chalked up boundaries. One more point in his favor!

"Good job!" a chorus of girls exclaimed as they sat primly on the low, brick retaining wall of the school playground.

He gave them a small nod of acknowledgement, then moved quickly into place, determined to win the wall-ball game before the teacher called them in from recess.

Rick "Iceman" Gable smiled with grim determination, shaking his head and rolling his eyes at the girls. Ryker agreed with him, but the ladies were the farthest thing from his mind at the moment. He wanted to win the game! Not that he was competitive or anything, but he didn't like to fail at anything. Second place was not allowed in his mind. This might just be a recess wall-ball game, but he played everything as if it were an Olympic sport.

The ball flew out of Rick's hand and Ryker moved into position. But in the next moment, something caught his eye off to the left of the playground. He knew that Xander, his younger brother by one year, was out on the playground as well, although their recess times were slightly different. Xander was in fifth grade while Ryker was in sixth. The fifth graders normally didn't rate any attention from the sixth graders but Ryker sensed something was wrong.

Ryker stood up, completely ignoring the ball as it whizzed by his head. Looking towards the basketball courts, he noticed that several boys were ganging up on Xander.

"Not going to happen!" he growled and his feet were eliminating the distance between himself and his younger brother quickly.

"What's going on?" he demanded as he stood shoulder to shoulder with his brother. He felt, more than heard, his two other brothers, both of them younger as well, standing beside himself and Xander. How all four of the Thorpe brothers were out on the playground at the same time was a mystery, but here they were, protecting each other.

"Xander cheated!" one of his classmates was saying. The five boys who were trying to gang up on Xander backed down quickly with Ryker there now. Ryker was the oldest, but all four of the brothers were unusually big for their age. Xander was the tallest in their fifth grade class by more than a head and Ryker was just over that. Ash, at seven years old and youngest of the four, focused on looking mean since he didn't yet have the height while Axel, the third in line, was almost as tall as his two older brothers, but still not willing to let any family member be beaten up for any reason.

"Xander never cheats," Ryker asserted firmly. "If you're losing, then lose like a man!" he snapped.

Ash and Axel nodded their heads in agreement, but all of them knew that Xander wasn't so pristine. He didn't cheat because he didn't have to. Xander was an outstanding athlete, as were all the Thorpe brothers, but sometimes Xander tended to stretch the rules a wee bit. Soccer in the Thorpe backyard could be more taxing than a full marathon, and Monopoly in their house was a blood sport at times. A babysitter coming to watch the four boys was a thing of the past, since no sitter would venture into the Thorpe household without a shield and an escape plan. But the Thorpe brothers watched out for their own, forming a united front when someone tried to hurt one of them.

The accusing boys backed down, none of them willing to take on all four of the brothers at once. But Ryker knew this wouldn't be the end of it. "How about if we play ball to settle this?" he offered, not wanting Xander to be cornered later on because of the disagreement.

"What did you have in mind?" one of the other boys asked cautiously.

Ryker easily assessed the skills of the other boys simply by the way they were standing or holding the ball. "The four of us against the five of you."

The five boys all smiled confidently and bumped shoulders, thinking this would be easy. "You're on," one of them replied.

Ryker bent low, looking at each of his brothers. Ash and Axel might be young, but the four of them played ball on the driveway at home. All of them were merciless competitors, none of them coming away without several bruises during any match. But they also knew how to play as a team against an enemy. "Okay, guys, you know what to do." He turned to Xander. "None of that funny stuff," he cautioned. "You saw it on the globetrotters, but we have no idea if it is legal or not."

Xander rolled his eyes, looked like he was about to argue, then just smiled and nodded his head. Looking at Ash and Axel, Ryker noted the determination in their eyes. "Good. Let's do it!"

Turning back, the five boys immediately tossed the ball to one another. They were able to maintain control of the ball for perhaps sixty seconds before each of the Thorpe brothers kicked in their speed and agility. The five boys didn't have a chance after that, especially with Ryker calling out strategy. There were a few times one of the other boys scored a point, but they didn't do it legally, and several of the baskets were sheer luck.

When the teachers started calling their classes in for the next part of the day, Ryker grabbed the ball and tossed it to the other team. "We're square now, right?"

The other boys were bent over, gasping for breath while Ryker and his brothers walked away, barely even breathing hard.

The younger three separated quickly, going to their own class lines, where their teachers were trying to get the class under control. Ryker groaned as he moved closer to line up with his teacher, seeing the girls on the sidelines, waiting for him.

Rick laughed and joined him at that point, patting him on the shoulder in sympathy. "They're all hot for you, dude. All girls love a hero and you just defended your brother."

Ryker shook his head, not understanding girls at all. "They're silly," he said and stood in line, trying to figure out how to get through the day without Nancy and Emma trying to convince him to walk them home.

He glanced one more time back at the playground, ensuring that Xander and his other two brothers were okay. He was fiercely protective of his family, no matter what kind of trouble they got into.

Five years later....

Ryker stood outside the doorway to Emma's last class of the day, eager for the bell to ring so he could walk her home. When the bell finally sounded, he waited, leaning against the wall on the opposite side for her to come out. When she finally did, he smiled, thinking she looked pretty cute in her new jeans and leather boots. Ah, leather boots, he thought with appreciation. Was there really anything better on a woman?

"Ready to go home?" he asked.

Emma smiled up at him, blushing because Ryker was the handsomest boy in the school – not to mention the best basketball player the district had ever seen. "Of course," she replied, leaning against him as his strong arm moved around her shoulders.

"Did you finally get your SAT scores?" she asked, referring to the college entrance exams.

"Yeah," he replied. "Are you finished with your math homework?" he asked, trying to change the subject.

"Yes," she answered then looked up at him, seeing the tense jaw. "Ryker, what's wrong? Did you do poorly on the exam?" Emma hadn't ever heard of Ryker doing poorly at anything so this would be a huge downfall.

They turned the corner, heading towards her house. "No. I did okay. What are you studying in biology?"

Ryker had taken biology during summer school after his freshman year so he was already in the advanced chemistry class. Emma had no idea how Ryker dealt with the pressure of all of his courses. He was relentless, and wouldn't settle for anything less than an A in all of his subjects, yet he still had the time to play basketball and football. All that intelligence and gorgeous too!

Emma huffed and came to a stop, pulling Ryker to a halt beside her. "Okay, what's going on?" she asked. Emma had no idea if she was in love with Ryker or just in awe of him. He was so smart, it was almost scary!

"Nothing. Did Linda contact you about the dance next Friday? We're all going together."

Emma watched him carefully, then the reason for his resistance hit her. "You got a perfect score, didn't you?"

Ryker shrugged. "Sort of," he said, looking away from her. He'd already dismissed the college entrance exams from his mind, focusing on his next goal.

Emma laughed and took his arm, hugging it against her chest. "You're amazing," she said, shaking her head. "You do realize that less than five hundred people nationally are able to pull off a perfect score on that brutal exam, right?"

Ryker shrugged. "It's all cool."

Emma smiled wistfully, wondering how she could keep this guy in her life after high school. He was so gorgeous and so smart, she just knew that he would make her the perfect husband. "So where are you applying to college?" she asked, determined to apply to a school as close as possible.

Ryker frowned again. "I've been accepted to Harvard," he told her.

Emma didn't like that at all. Harvard wasn't close to any of the lower level schools. She bit her lip, her mind already spinning with plans. "Well, we'll figure it all out."

Ryker had no idea what Emma needed to "figure out" but he was delighted to pull her around to the side of her house. He remembered all those times in fifth and sixth grade when she'd tried to get him to kiss her. How he'd wasted time! Not that this was the love of his life, he thought. But she was certainly soft and pretty and he was just the man to enjoy her slender arms around his neck while he kissed her.

After dropping Emma off, Ryker slipped through the neighborhood and through the back door of his house. He breathed a sigh of relief when he was able to make it to his bedroom without getting caught. He knew he had chores to do, but he needed to get his homework done and he seriously didn't want to deal with his three younger brothers today.

He was just opening up his lab book when Ash burst into his room. "Ryker, you've got to help me!" he exclaimed. He reached down and punched his oldest brother in the arm to ensure that Ryker would follow.

Ryker glared at his younger brother's retreating back, wondering what could be so important. In the end, it didn't matter. Ash has issued a challenge with that punch and Ryker wasn't one to let a challenge go. When he went downstairs, he noticed Xander and his other brothers sitting around the kitchen table with several of their friends, a big pile of pretzels in the middle and all of them with playing cards clutched in their hands. "Mom's going to be home in a half hour," he cautioned. "You know she hates gambling." But that didn't stop him from taking the only available seat next to Ash.

"Yeah, yeah," Ash griped, then handed Ryker his cards. "Here, play these," he said.

Xander and Axel both started arguing. "No way! You can't just toss your cards to another player!"

Ryker shifted back in the chair, rearranging the cards, ignoring the outbursts. He then pushed all of his brother's remaining pretzels into the center of the pot. "He's all in, guys."

Xander and Axel looked at Ryker's face, didn't notice a single "tell", looked back down at their own cards, then immediately tossed their cards into the pot, giving up on even trying to bet against their oldest brother. Ryker could out-bet a professional, they suspected. They had never won against him and had no clue what his secret was when bluffing or playing it cool.

The other guys looked at the Thorpe brothers nervously, then down at their own pile of pretzels. As if in unison, all of them tossed their cards in, folding quickly.

Ryker handed the cards back to Ash who was immediately pulling all the pretzels to him and into a bag. "Come to papa!" he grinned with relish.

"Deal me in," he announced and leaned back, watching the others carefully. Within two hands, he had figured out everyone's way of bluffing and started winning.

"I'm out," Xander stated with disgust. He stood up and punched Ash on the arm. The youngest of the brothers didn't even flinch, knowing that he deserved the punishment for bringing Ryker into the game.

"Sorry," he grumbled, then tossed his own cards onto the table.

Ryker didn't even blink as he pulled the rest of the pretzels over towards his pile. He looked around at the miniscule piles in front of the other boys and realized that he didn't have time to clean out the rest. "Gotta go," he claimed and scooped his pile into a bag and quickly disappeared up the stairs. A fraction of a second later the front door to their house opened up and their mother stepped into the house. "What's going on?" She surveyed the cards and the pretzels in front of each of her sons and pursed her lips. "Boys…?"

Xander, Axel and Ash all let their heads fall backwards, staring up at the ceiling. "How did he know?" Ash asked, referring to Ryker's ability to know exactly when they were about to get into trouble. Not to mention his astounding capability to extricate himself before that happened!

"Ryker was here too, Mom," Xander asserted. "It wasn't just us."

The look on her face told the remaining boys that she didn't believe them for a moment. "Go get ready for dinner," she commanded firmly. "We'll discuss this later."

She watched as her boys said goodbye to their friends, then morosely walked to the kitchen to start their dinner chores.

"Don't worry," Xander said, his mind already working a mile a minute. "We'll get him back."

Ash and Axel both looked at Xander and their expressions changed from grim to eager. If the three of them put their minds to it, they could surely figure out a way to get back at Ryker. It was only a matter of time.

CHAPTER 1

The dark figure stopped in her tracks, listening carefully, not even allowing herself to breathe. The silence was thick, but something was wrong. The carpeting had suppressed her steps, but she knew that, in the night, every sound, every moment was louder than during the daytime hours.

She closed her eyes and relaxed her mind, letting all the sounds become louder and the movements almost a physical vibration. Relaxing helped her focus all her other senses, her mind working hard to grasp if there was a real threat or if she'd just imagined something. She'd been trained from childhood and knew what to do, how to react and had contingency plans in place. Her training had been thorough.

Total silence. She kept her eyes closed, her body still. Listening.

There it was, she thought with a cheeky, secret smile, her body still frozen in place. The shuffling sound was barely there, but someone was trying to creep up on her.

She would have laughed with delight, but she knew that would give her presence as well as her location away. Silence was the most important aspect of this night. Without silence, she would be caught.

With stealth built up over years of practice, she grabbed the last object in the middle of the desk, then climbed the rope right back up into the ceiling. She suppressed an inner giggle and watched through the air conditioning vent as the large, awkward figure moved into the office. Overhead lights were turned on and the dark head moved to the right and left. As much as she'd like to watch, she knew better than to remain still at this point in the mission. She slowly turned, her body slithering down through the vents. She didn't wait around to see if the inept, power-hungry security guard would spot her through the metal slats.

Gliding lithely through the air system, she made her way back to her starting point. At the last moment, she hesitated, feeling the hairs on the back of her neck rise up. Those little hairs had saved her neck on more than one occasion so she'd learned to listen to their silent warning.

Pausing, she lifted herself higher, using all her upper body strength to pull up another three inches. With that, she knew she was basically invisible to the cameras that she'd already put on a loop. But her position also meant she was invisible to anyone coming out the door directly beneath her. If she hadn't done all those workouts recently, she never would have made it to this point before the guard burst through the door for his nightly, if off schedule and unsanctioned, cigarette and whiskey break.

In that moment, her heart rate accelerated to triple time and she felt a renewed shot of adrenaline spike through her body. She bit her lip and looked around, trying to determine if her back-up escape plan was still viable. She saw the door and the window above it and knew she could do it.

With grim determination, she lifted herself higher up, swung her leg over the ledge and looked down. It was higher than she was used to, but a glance behind her showed that she couldn't go back the other way. With a grin, she sprang forward and caught the opposite ledge just in time. Her gloved hands gripped the edge with just enough strength to pull herself forward once again. With a grunt, she swung her body left, then right, then left again, gaining enough momentum and, at the last moment, swung her whole body over the ledge. With that, she was home free. She got to her feet, maintaining a crouch as she sprinted across the rooftop. The ladder was in sight and she scanned the area. Sure enough, the guards were still focused on the opposite side of the building.

She pulled the harness over her head, then strapped it around her waist and thighs. This was the good part, she thought with relish. Hmmm…maybe the theft part was the best. Or perhaps it was the planning. She really loved planning things out, figuring out all the details. Or maybe, the best part was when she slipped by the guards without them even knowing something had happened.

She smiled in remembrance of the job and the incomparable excitement. It was all good, she thought as she snapped the last of the hooks into place and tightened the harness. With careful eyes, she checked all of her equipment one last time. This was not the time to be careless. She'd already gone over everything four times, but this equipment check would be just as important as the first.

Once she was confident that everything was in place and all the connectors were secure, she moved over to the side of the building, taking a moment to look out over the fabulous city. Chicago really was a beautiful town. Thankfully, she hadn't planned this adventure during the winter months but even now as the October wind blew over the lake and through all the tall buildings there was a definite bite to the air. It was getting colder. This might be the last time she could take this route until springtime, she thought with regret.

With a shrug of her shoulders and an eager smile on her face, she took one more breath, grasped the rope, and threw herself over the ledge with barely a sound.

Down she went! With a whoosh, she flew down the side of the building. She dropped fifty stories down in just seconds, feeling the cold air swish around her. When she was about two thirds of the way down, she clamped the brake that slowed her fall. She was only three inches from the ground before she came to a full and silent stop. It took two more snaps and her thumb flicked the release. The rope zipped up into its carrier, the carrier was stuffed into her leather bag and the harness was stashed into a pocket. Only fifteen seconds after placing her feet on the sidewalk, there was no evidence that she had been here.

She stuffed everything into her bag, turned her hoodie inside out so the pink part was showing instead of the black and slung her bag over her shoulder. She'd done it, she thought with increasing excitement. Maybe this was the best part. Walking away, feeling the thrill of success and the adrenaline pumping through her system. She'd gotten into the office, accomplished her goal and gotten out of the building without anyone knowing she'd even been there.

She almost skipped down the sidewalk but she suppressed the urge, knowing she was supposed to be inconspicuous.

CHAPTER 2

Ryker smiled inwardly as he pulled into his parking spot, but not a hint of that personal satisfaction showed on his handsome features. Ryker was known to be reserved, cool and in control. He rarely put his emotions on display unless he was alone with his brothers. And even then, he was the eldest, needing to be the calming influence. He knew his responsibilities and took them very seriously.

That didn't mean he couldn't appreciate life, he thought as his eyes looked around for the woman.

To the casual observer, he knew that he generally looked serious and intent, but he didn't really care. The opinions of others were of no consequence; he had more important things to worry about than whether someone perceived him as likable. Ryker didn't mind that his staff was intimidated by him. It enabled him to run The Thorpe Group more effectively. He not only had his entire division to run, he was also responsible for the whole company not to mention his three younger brothers who tended to lean towards the boisterous side of life. Thankfully, they didn't fight as much as they used to.

Well, Xander did, but that was because of…Ryker sighed as he thought about that situation. Xander was the second oldest and in charge of the family law division of The Thorpe Group. Ryker thought about the cynicism he'd seen recently in his younger brother. It wasn't healthy, and Xander was definitely becoming more jaded. Maybe that's why the arguments between he and their office manager, Autumn, were getting more…pointed.

Stepping out of his black Tesla sedan, he lifted his briefcase and walked efficiently towards the building's entrance. He timed it perfectly every day and, sure enough, there she was. The exquisite woman with curly blond hair was hurrying into the building on the opposite side of the courtyard. She was lovely and had the sexiest walk, even when she was rushing.

He waited until she was through the doors, watching her for as long as possible before he proceeded into his building. It was a morning ritual that he intended to stop, as soon as he could figure out how to get her to agree to dinner with him. She was painfully shy, he knew. On previous occasions he'd tried to get her attention, but she'd just scurried away after a brief glimpse in his direction.

They played this game every morning, staring at each other across the courtyard, both of them obviously interested but she was too timid and ran away before he could figure out how to interact with her. He'd tried to speak with her once when they ran into each other at the deli. She'd been even more beautiful up close but she'd blushed and hurried out the door, not even getting her lunch in her rush to get away from him. He'd watched her blond curls and extraordinary figure hurry out the door as quickly as her heels could carry her but he'd caught her blush as well as the small gasp that escaped from her lush mouth as soon as she saw him.

A weaker man might be discouraged but not him. That woman was worth the effort, he told himself as he pressed the elevator button for his floor. He would have her sitting across a restaurant table from him very soon. He walked into his office, his assistant, Joan, meeting him at the doorway to the lobby as she did every single morning, following behind him as she read through his early morning messages.

"And lastly, Jason Moran left a message last night, wanting to speak with you urgently. This is his third message in two weeks," she told him without any kind of expression on her face. Joan knew not to be judgmental about any of the issues that came through this office. If her boss hadn't called the man back, there was a reason.

Ryker's eyes slashed over to Joan's. "Jason?" he repeated, his irritation at the man's persistence annoying. "I gave Jason to Martha as a client," he explained, referring to one of the other lawyers in his group. "I know she called him back the last time he called. What does he need to speak with me about?"

Ryker knew that Jason Moran worked in the building across the courtyard. The same building in which his introverted stranger worked. That was a promising development, he thought as he took that message and glanced down at the writing. Perhaps Jason could give him more information about the lovely mystery woman.

Making the decision quickly, he handed the pink square paper back to Joan and continued into his office. "Tell Jason I can see him this afternoon. Give him whatever opening is available on my calendar after my lunch meeting."

Joan nodded and made a note, then turned and walked out of his office to follow his instructions.

CHAPTER 3

Cricket leaned against the back of her office door, breathing deeply of the cool air and trying to slow down her frantic heart rate. She couldn't believe that she felt so exhilarated just because that man watched her walk into the building. Even from a distance, the look was so hot, so intense she felt like she was going to burn up as she walked from the parking garage to the door and then into the building.

Often, on her drive into the office, she tried to talk herself into actually looking at the man, maybe acknowledging him. She'd seen him up close once and he was...amazing! She'd been such a wimp that day. She'd seen his intention to talk to her, to actually communicate, but she'd run away. It was one thing to have a secret infatuation with a man, to build up stories about him and wonder what it would be like to actually talk to him and meet him. She imagined herself sitting down with him in a fancy, elegant restaurant, enjoying witty repartee while he laughed at her quick wit and pithy observations.

Alas, she wasn't quick witted and she rarely had profound reflections about people other than whether they had adequate security or if their jewelry was real or fake. Other than that, her normal, some might say tedious and boring, life revolved around numbers and finding the stories in the numbers. She might be able to sneak into a high security building without being noticed or find variances down to the penny in a multi-million dollar project, but conversing with a gorgeous man? Nope, she was too shy. Especially around her tall, terrifyingly huge and intimidating morning-man.

She really needed to change her schedule so she wasn't showing up at the exact same moment he was arriving each day. But then she smiled inside her tiny office where no one else could see, her body's reaction slowing down. As long as he continued to arrive at the same time, she'd probably keep the same schedule that had her driving up at the same moment. Her mind relished the zing that she got from his look each morning which was better than a double shot of espresso. It might be silly, looking forward to simply seeing a man every morning, but she loved her morning excitement. If she changed her schedule, she'd miss that man terribly.

She should be brave and just talk to the guy. Every morning, she set her alarm clock so her morning was timed to park at the exact right time, skipped breakfast if she was running late, went around the block a few times if she was early...all so she could get a glimpse of him each morning. It was more than a little pathetic, she told herself.

But the idea of actually talking to him, of meeting him face to face instead of across the courtyard set her whole body to shivering in fear. What would she say to him? What could they possibly have in common? He looked like some sort of executive while she was a lowly accountant. She'd probably trip on her own feet if she got any closer to him. He made her so nervous just with a look!

With a sigh, she sat down behind her dull, brown laminate desk and pulled her chair in close, turning on her computer and pulling the large stack of messy and poorly written expense reports closer, forcing her mind away from one dazzling, sexy and scary man. Now that she'd had her morning jolt it was time to start her day. Cricket smiled as she sifted through the stack of papers. She might be a boring, cautious accountant but that didn't mean she wasn't also a secret adrenaline junkie.

Speaking of which, she thought silently...

With an inward giggle, she went back to her office door and opened it once again. She definitely didn't want to miss this morning's excitement. Last night's adventure had been more fun than all the rest because she'd almost gotten caught by that security guard. Well, not almost. She'd been pretty stealthy last night but she'd enjoyed the extra challenge when she'd seen him through the ventilation screen.

And now it was show time. Her boss would walk into his office, see what she'd done and the show would begin. She couldn't wait to hear the outcry when her boss walked into his office.

Last night's escapade was yet another reason she probably shouldn't even think about the elegant stranger. Most likely, he confronted the people who irritated him head on. Cricket had a knack for being creative, but it was a silly, passive aggressive creativity. Her antics might be amusing, but still...she should just get a new job instead of dealing with Jason Moran's petty ways.

She smiled and sat back down at her desk, working diligently at the tiresome expense reports that had been piling up over the past few days, scowling at the mostly handwritten notes and trying to interpret the scribbles. Why couldn't this company automate these reports? She'd submitted a proposal to do just that last month, had even included the cost of a relatively simple software program that would expedite the whole process and help employees get their reimbursement checks more quickly. Unfortunately, she hadn't heard a word from Jason Moran.

His silence told her that there was no way he was going to spend any money on something like a basic software package, even if it saved him more money in the long run.

When she finished one expense report and set it up to be processed for payment, she pulled the next one forward, reminding herself that she'd chosen to become an accountant. She could have gotten a degree in any subject but accounting had suited her needs perfectly. And she was pretty good at it too. One had to have the ability to pay attention to small details to get this job done well which meant that the skills her mother and father had taught her growing up were perfectly suited to being an accountant.

So what if she hated every moment of her day? It paid well and gave her the sense of security that she needed. That feeling was more important than loving one's job. She'd hated the insecurity growing up, wishing desperately that her parents hadn't been so good at their chosen profession. So no matter how much she loathed this job, she reveled in that sense of peace.

This job might be mind-numbingly boring and tedious but it kept her out of prison, which is something her parent's occupation couldn't guarantee.

Her mind was focusing on the expense reports but, once she got into a rhythm, she was able to whip through the stack in record time. There were a few that had messy handwriting and nonsensical amounts but most were pretty straightforward. Those were so easy she could almost do them in her sleep.

"Hey Cricket," Debbie, one of the other accountants poked her head into her office. "How about lunch today?" she asked.

Cricket looked up and smiled. "I'd love it," she replied, relieved to have an excuse for a break from entering numbers into spreadsheets and software programs for an hour. But then her eyes turned wary. "What about Mr. Moran?" she asked in almost a whisper.

Debbie's smile brightened and her hand waved away the concern about their boss. "I've already checked with Dorothy," Debbie replied, referring to their boss's assistant, "and he has a lunch scheduled. So there won't be any flak from trying to take a break today."

"Excellent!" Cricket exclaimed, relieved and excited about just getting some fresh air not to mention talking about something that didn't have to do with numbers.

Jason Moran was possibly the worst boss in the world, Cricket thought. But he paid well and provided excellent benefits to his employees, probably because he was such a horrible human being and the salary and perks he provided were the only way he could keep people on staff. Otherwise, Jason Moran walked around the office yelling at people to work harder, stop taking breaks, belittling some of the more junior staff members and just generally being a jerk. Interns rarely lasted more than a week or two because he used their free labor to accomplish the tedious administrative work he was too cheap to pay someone a good salary to do.

The man didn't even like people leaving the office for their lunch breaks. Legally, he couldn't stop employees from taking an hour for lunch, but he made snide comments when he noticed someone actually leaving for their break. He preferred having people eat their meals at their desk or in the kitchen where he could find someone if he needed them. And he made a point of interrupting lunches when too many people congregated in the kitchen so the team had learned ways to…

"Where the hell are all my pens?" someone yelled down the hallway.

Cricket heard the bellow and had to work hard to keep herself from bursting out with laughter. Debbie was still standing in her doorway but, thankfully, was looking in the direction of the yelling so Cricket had time to compose her features into an expression of concern and confusion.

"What?" Debbie whispered as she squinted in the direction from which the bellow had come. "Not again!" she giggled then quickly covered her face with her hands to keep their boss from seeing her laughter at his expense. Debbie turned back to Cricket, a huge grin on her pixie-like features. "Oh, this is too good! After yesterday afternoon's staff meeting, he deserves much more than someone stealing all of his…"

"And how the hell did all of my pictures get turned upside down?" the man yelled again to no one in particular.

Debbie stepped inside Cricket's office so their boss didn't see her laughing. "This is perfect," she laughed, covering her mouth with one hand while the other held her stomach as both women laughed at the latest joke at their boss' expense. "Who would think to turn the man's pictures upside down?" she burst out.

Cricket felt that it was now safe to release her laughter and went right along with Debbie as they both laughed while their boss, Jason Moran, stomped through the hallways on his rampage, trying to figure out who could have done something like this to his office. The man had accused several employees of disturbing his office over the past several months but since normally only his pens were stolen, the police wouldn't even get involved. "This is not funny!" he growled when he stomped passed Cricket's doorway and caught the two of them, as well as several other people, laughing in the hallways.

"Whoever did this," he called out to everyone in general, "you're fired! You hear me? You're fired!"

He walked into his office and slammed the door while the rest of the staff scurried away, still snickering at the mischief maker's bravery and creativity. Of course, that was before their boss let loose his wrath on everyone over the next few hours. He dumped the contents of the coffee pot down the drain and refused to let anyone make another pot or leave the office to grab their caffeine jolt at the deli in the lobby of the stairs. He also tossed papers across the conference room table when someone was trying to make a proposal about how to resolve an issue in the office, he stormed through the office stealing everyone else's pens and dumped them into their garbage cans. It was a highly ineffective retaliation since everyone simply picked their pens out of their trashcans again after he left their office but it was still demoralizing.

By the time he left for his lunch meeting, Cricket was feeling bad about what she'd done. Normally, Jason simply yelled and growled about her antics. He'd never actually made people more miserable as he had today. But apparently he was on a rampage to find out who was stealing his ball point pens and turning his cheap artwork upside down.

Cricket frowned throughout the morning while doing the data entry that was her job. She was on her last expense report when Debbie and two other co-workers stepped into her office.

"Coast clear?" Cricket asked with relish, more than ready to get out of this horrible environment.

"All clear. He left five minutes ago. We're actually one of the last to leave for lunch so grab your purse and let's go," Debbie urged.

"Did you hear that Mona and Jeff both quit this morning?" Debbie announced, shaking her head because probably the entire staff felt the same way.

Josie rolled her eyes at the loss. "We're more insulated from his wrath because he doesn't believe anyone here in the accounting department has any kind of imagination. We're just boring data entry clerks in his mind."

Cricket listened to their comments but didn't hesitate to log out of her computer for a break. She grabbed her purse and the four women were out the door, eagerly rushing towards the elevators. "Where are we going?" Cricket asked, thinking just a simple sandwich would suffice. She preferred to be back before Jason returned, not wanting to hear him growl about how his staff went out to lunch right after he did. In his mind, he's paying everyone so, therefore, his staff should work harder than he does.

Josie clapped her hands as an idea occurred to her. "Let's spoil ourselves and hit Antoine's for lunch. Anyone up for something decadent and fattening?"

"I'm all for that. Why don't we only order appetizers and desserts so we're all slow this afternoon with a sugar coma?" Debbie suggested.

Cricket smiled, more than ready to eat just about anything. She'd had to rush this morning in order to make it to the parking garage in time. She'd woken up fifteen minutes late and, instead of just arriving a few minutes late for work or, more specifically, late to see her mystery man, she'd skipped breakfast.

She smiled while she stood behind the three other women as she remembered the thrill she'd experienced when she'd arrived just in time to walk to the building while the stranger watched her. Then it occurred to her how crazy her life had become since the first time she'd seen the handsome man. Was she really cutting out food so she could arrive in time to get her adrenaline rush now?

She bit her lip and nodded to herself. Yes, she really was.

But who could blame her? The man was hot! She could berate herself all she wanted in her mind, but the truth was, his gaze across the courtyard was definitely the thrill of her day.

"Let's go," Josie called out as soon as the elevator doors opened. "I'm starving." Debbie, Josie and Allyson all chatted among themselves, trying to include Cricket in their conversation but since they were discussing husbands, children and babies, Cricket couldn't really contribute much since she didn't know anything about that aspect of life. The elegant restaurant was only a block and a half away from their office, but it was one of those exclusive places which meant it wasn't normally in the price range of four lowly accountants. So this was a real treat and much better than a deli sandwich or the burgers at Durango's where they normally grabbed lunch.

The four women were seated immediately since Allyson, the fourth member of their group, was dating one of the waiters at the restaurant. She might be divorced with two kids, but she still had an active eye for the men. The four women smiled excitedly as they took their seats among Chicago's elite. These were the power brokers, the wealthy patrons of the arts and the controllers of money. Bankers, successful entrepreneurs, wealthy tourists and anyone who wanted to be seen showed up at Antoine's for lunch. In another two hours, the powerful wives of Chicago would arrive in droves for their afternoon tea and brandy and two hours after that, the martini crowd would press together in the bar, eager to be seen mingling among the other patrons at the exclusive restaurant.

As the four of them were seated, Allyson's boyfriend came by and told them what to order since there weren't any prices on the menu. He handed each of them water with cucumber slices, then walked away to let them decide on their meals and to help his other tables.

The ladies sipped their water, excited to be a part of this daily spectacle. Well, three of them were, at least. Cricket sipped her water, but she didn't ooh and ahh at the people around them. She knew several of them by reputation, but her mind was also doing an inventory of their assets. Not their bank accounts, but their art and jewelry collections.

Other people might not have that kind of knowledge, but Cricket hadn't come from a normal family. Her father was one of the best art thieves in the world, and her mother was one of three thieves internationally who could relieve owners of just about any piece of jewelry she wanted, any time she wanted.

Of course, neither her mother nor her father ever kept their stolen pieces. At least, Cricket didn't think they kept any of it.

She shook her head as she contemplated the possibility. No, the absolute rule with thieves was to never hold onto anything one didn't want to lose. There was always someone coming up through the ranks who was more daring, more skillful with the latest technology, or more stealthy at removing others' possessions. Why would a thief trust a security system that they easily knew how to circumvent?

The other never-break rule was…Don't Get Caught.

So far, neither parent had ever been caught, thankfully. But Cricket lived in fear of her father attempting a "project" (his term, not hers) that would be more of a trap than a heist. The police knew of her father, but they'd never been able to pin anything to him. He was more of a ghost or a legend in the art thieves' community than anyone else. The police still didn't understand how he'd done many of the heists he'd accomplished and he took pride in no one knowing how or, even sometimes, when he'd done a job. He only pulled the riskiest jobs and only if he knew he could get rid of the loot quickly. If a thief was caught, it was harder for the authorities to prove guilt if the evidence was no longer in their possession.

So although Cricket didn't actually steal anything, she'd grown up in a family that lived for the next job, thrived on the exhilaration of an anticipated heist. And she'd been taught all the tricks of the trade in the hopes of her joining the family business once she was old enough.

She hated stealing though. Just the idea of stealing something of value made her stomach turn over. She wasn't afraid of the risk. In fact, she loved the risk, the thrill of the challenge and the adventure, not to mention the incredible self-discipline needed to learn the intricate skills of the art of thievery. The planning was always fascinating too, but she'd limited her missions to the more mundane pen-stealing or office altering achievements.

No, the stress of getting caught as well as the guilt over taking something that wasn't hers definitely wasn't worth it. She only wanted the thrill, not the risk.

"Oh my goodness!" Josie gasped. "Isn't that the President of the United States over there?" she asked, pointing towards a table in the corner that was surrounded by stern looking men and women, all wearing sunglasses with what looked to be ear pieces for surreptitious communication.

Cricket turned to look, as did the two other women. There was a communal gasp when they realized that it was indeed the president. Cricket even groaned when she realized that the president was lunching with none other than her handsome mystery man. How was that possible? The man worked here in Chicago, what business would the president have with anyone here?

Okay, so Antoine's was the best restaurant in the city. And it was close to their office, just down the block in fact.

But really, the President? That just put her mystery man further out of her league. And a dangerous person for her to associate with. Her family history and a powerful, well connected man were not a mixture that worked well for any kind of long term relationship.

Not that she had any chance of a relationship with a man like that anyway. He probably dated more glamorous women. She'd most likely been mistaken when she'd thought he was going to talk to her in the deli that day. A man like that did not approach a woman like her. She was too mousy, too boring. She was an accountant, for goodness sake! He probably dated models or society women!

She turned around, feeling despondent all of a sudden, and faced her menu. "I think I'm going to order a burger and horrify the chef," she said, trying to throw off her sadness.

Thankfully, the other three turned back to the table, knowing that this was as close as they would get to the lofty man. It was pointless to ogle.

Unfortunately, that didn't stop her from gawking. The man wasn't directly in her line of vision, but if she turned her head just slightly to the right, she saw him. Everyone in the restaurant saw him because he was with the president, but she had eyes only for him.

It seemed like every time she looked in that direction, he was looking directly back at her. It was more than a little disconcerting and she actually had no idea what they ate for lunch. She went through the motions, but by the time Allyson's boyfriend was taking their plates away, she couldn't have named a single thing that had been in front of her for almost the past hour.

Her heart was pounding and she looked up again, her eyes colliding with his. He looked to almost be ignoring the president as he stared right back at her.

"You're awfully quiet," Josie said and Cricket's attention snapped right back to her co-workers. They'd all relished the meal that had apparently been above and beyond their expectations.

"Is the president really that fascinating?" Debbie asked. All of them had noticed her lack of attention during the meal. "And are you okay? You look flushed. Maybe you're coming down with something?"

Josie smiled and wiggled her eyebrows. "It isn't our illustrious leader that has Cricket so distracted."

Debbie and Allyson both turned their heads and caught the president walking out while he said something to a taller man. "Oh…!" Debbie said with a sigh as she realized who Cricket had been looking at. "That's the dreamy guy who works in the building across the courtyard, isn't it?" she asked, sighing with happiness as the man disappeared out of the restaurant.

Josie and Debbie both turned their heads, trying to see him one more time, but by then he was already out the door, only the last few secret service agents scanning the room giving any indication that it hadn't been their imagination about the president being in the same dining room with them.

"Come to think of it," Josie said, "I think I've seen him too."

"He's just the guy that works in the other building," Cricket said again. "I'm sure he's very nice but I didn't get a good look at him." She wasn't really lying, even though she'd been sneaking peeks at him all through the meal.

Allyson looked at her watch. "We'd better head back and forget about the tall, dark and handsome stranger Cricket is drooling over," she teased. "Mr. Moran is bound to be back and furious with his staff for taking a legally allotted lunch period."

The four women nodded their concurrence and started taking out their wallets. But before anyone could pull out cash or credit card, their waiter arrived magically at their table. He put a hand to Allyson's shoulder affectionately as he said, "You're check has been taken care of, ladies."

All four of them stared at him with their mouths open. "Excuse me?" Cricket asked, confused.

"A man took care of your check already," he repeated. "I don't know by whom, but my boss took your bill and told me to tell all of you that it was paid." He shrugged and winked at Allyson before moving off to his next table, eager to earn tips from the lunch crowd.

They sat there in stunned silence for a long moment, each of them processing the news. Then one by one, they turned to look at Cricket and smiled as the realization came upon them. "It was him!" Allyson hissed excitedly. "You somehow got that hottie to pay for your meal and we all benefitted!"

Josie and Debbie were all grinning from ear to ear, laughing when Cricket blushed painfully. "I doubt he would do that for us. I don't even know who he is."

"Why not?" Josie asked. "You and he were exchanging those heated glances all during the meal. Good grief, you barely ate anything because you were too focused on him!"

The three of them laughed as she blushed painfully but Cricket simply shook her head. "It was probably Allyson's boyfriend being nice."

"Uh huh," they each said almost in unison, none of them actually believing it. But they knew they had a limited amount of time before their boss came back and they had to be at their desks, looking busy before that happened. So they all grabbed their purses and coats, rushed out of the restaurant, and hurried down the sidewalk. The afternoon wind had turned colder over the past hour, typical of this time of the year in Chicago. With the lake just a block away, the wind could pick up unexpectedly and bring along with it a painful chill. It was also why Chicago got more snow than many parts of the country, but not nearly as much snow as Buffalo or central New York areas.

They all hurried into the building, bundling into the elevator and laughing at how quickly the weather changed. By the time they reached their floor, their faces were grim, all traces of relaxation from their break gone as they once again faced the work on their respective desks.

"I'm going job hunting," Josie whispered as they walked down the depressing hallways. "Jason might pay higher salaries, but nothing is worth this much irritation."

"I'm with you," Allyson said as she ducked into her office.

"Count me in," Debbie called back as she went into her office as well.

None of them realized that Cricket was silent. She definitely wanted a new job, but if she didn't work here, she would miss her morning "meeting".

How ridiculous was that? She sat down at her desk and told herself firmly that she was definitely going to have to find a new job. She'd start the search tonight. The man might be tempting, but her friends were right. This was not a good work environment. She needed something new. With any luck, she'd find a fabulous job right here in the building and she'd still get to see her mystery man every day.

CHAPTER 4

Ryker watched the blond woman across the restaurant, more convinced than ever that he was going to meet the lovely lady from across the courtyard. She was sitting primly at her table during lunch, looking serenely beautiful. Her friends were giggling about something, but Ryker noticed that his lovely lady only smiled weakly at whatever they were discussing. Probably because she was more focused on peering in his direction than she was in paying attention to the lunch conversation. Even Ryker was distracted from his conversation with the President because he kept trying to catch her eye.

Thankfully, the President knew exactly what was going on. "I can see that global politics and the national legal system are poor competition compared to the blond beauty across the room."

Ryker laughed even though he'd been caught being rude. The President wasn't one to hold a grudge though and he even approved. "What's her name?" he asked, changing the subject since there was little chance he could get Ryker to focus on accepting a federal judgeship.

"I don't know yet," Ryker replied, a possessive feeling coming to him at that moment. "Is it that obvious?" Ryker asked, cringing inside at how unfocused he'd been. He prided himself on his discipline but there was something about that woman that just got to him.

"Just a bit. But only because I've known you for so long."

After that, they discussed personal issues which were easier to follow, allowing Ryker to use most of his brain power to think of ways to meet his lovely lady. Unfortunately, he had a meeting right after lunch that he had to hurry back to the office for. He walked out with the President, shaking hands with him before the man ducked into his armored limousine and sped away out of sight.

Ryker was about to go back to the office, but he had a thought and went back into the restaurant. Whispering something to the waiter, he pointed to the table where his lady was sitting, giving him instructions to take care of their lunch tab.

Walking back to his office, he smiled to himself. She might not have been sitting across the table from him, but at least he got to pay for her lunch. That was something, he told himself. It was odd, but he wasn't normally attracted to women who were shy. He typically preferred the more aggressive, confident women. That was probably because he didn't normally have time to waste on chasing women. Besides, they generally seemed to do the chasing and he either accepted their offers or passed, not really bothered either way.

This woman was different. There was just something about her that made him place her in a distinctive category. He probably should have gone over to her table and offered his business card, asked her to give him a call when it was convenient.

On second thought, she probably wouldn't have called him. He knew that she was interested, but she wouldn't even look him in the eye except when it was by accident. So he would have to get her information first, figure out what she liked and pursue her with a bit more flair and patience.

Back at his desk, he was going through several reports when Joan interrupted him to announce his next appointment had arrived. Ryker looked at the name and sighed, wishing he'd canceled the meeting. He didn't want to deal with this man today, he thought as the door to his office burst open and a short, rotund man with a badly receding hairline came into view.

"Good afternoon, Jason," Ryker said, standing up and moving around to the other side of the desk to shake the shorter man's hand. Ryker wasn't a huge fan of Jason Moran, but he was a client. At least for now. The man was a blowhard who originally thought he could order Ryker around. The first time Jason had done this, Ryker had politely walked him out of the office, shaking his hand at the elevator door and told him that he didn't think The Thorpe Group was the kind of law firm that would be of service to Jason's company.

The man quickly realized his mistake and it hadn't ever happened again. Since that day, Jason Moran had been charm personified around this office. But Ryker knew that the man abused his staff, and he didn't like that. He was tempted to tell the man to find another lawyer, but he hadn't yet made up his mind. Perhaps this visit would tilt the decision one way or another. Ryker found that he didn't have the patience to deal with clients he didn't respect. And since he didn't need to deal with the little man, he had no qualms about either eliminating the man from their client list, or pushing him off to one of his junior associates.

"Thanks for seeing me on such short notice. I know you're extremely busy." Jason took the liberty of sitting down before Ryker even offered him a seat.

Ryker remained standing, telling the shorter man in no uncertain terms what Ryker thought of Jason's manners. "My assistant mentioned you need some help urgently."

Jason flushed, knowing that Ryker Thorpe was one of those powerful men in Chicago a business owner didn't want to mess with. The man might be a lawyer who was probably always on the lookout for clients, but Ryker Thorpe had many powerful friends. One didn't want to insult him. Jason knew he'd done that during his first appointment and had worked hard to maintain a polite demeanor ever since. But it was hard. As far as Jason was concerned, Ryker Thorpe was paid by Jason, therefore the man should act like an employee.

That wasn't the way things worked, at least not where The Thorpe Brothers were concerned. Having Ryker Thorpe, or any Thorpe brother, as one's lawyer, pretty much pushed away most legal issues. Their reputation for winning just about any case they took on was legendary. The Thorpe Group's rates might be twice as high as other lawyers, maybe even three times the going rate, but they also eliminated most legal issues from even happening. Either by their reputation, or by offering sound, legal advice in advance so one didn't get into legal messes in the first place.

Unfortunately, this wasn't one of those situations that might have been avoided with legal advice. This was almost personal now. "I have a huge problem," Jason started out, wishing he could stand up, but also knowing that it wouldn't do any good since Ryker Thorpe was almost a foot taller. Jason knew he would still feel small and inferior so he remained seated. At least he could enjoy the ultra-soft sofa while feeling small!

"And that would be?' Ryker prompted, smothering his impatience. He glanced at his watch, knowing that he had another appointment in ten minutes. He'd only squeezed Moran in now so he wouldn't have to endure his presence for a longer period of time later on.

Jason rubbed his forehead, almost embarrassed now to discuss the issue. But he had no clue how to stop the problem. "I have someone breaking into my office on a regular basis. I need help catching the thief."

Ryker tried to keep his facial expression blank, but he was having a hard time hiding his surprise. This wasn't really a legal issue. Was the man wasting his time in addition to being an irritation? "Have you spoken to the police?" Ryker asked, wondering how he could help. "If you catch the person, I can represent your interests. But until then, I'm not sure how I can assist you."

Jason grimaced, his irritation getting the better of him now that he was thinking back to his problem instead of focusing on being polite. "You have investigators, don't you?" Jason snapped. Then calmed down when he caught Ryker's dark scowl. "Sorry. This has been plaguing me for a while. The police won't help me because they say nothing of value has been stolen and I can't even prove that it wasn't an employee playing a prank on me. They said it was an internal issue and if I wanted to stop the thefts, I'd have to discuss the issue with my employees. I don't know who else to turn to. I've hired a private investigator, but they haven't been able to stop the guy for the past four break-ins."

That was a surprise. And confusing. What kind of pranks would be played in an office environment? He knew that his staff had some office betting going on. In fact, even he had some private bets on the problem between his brother and their office manager. But he didn't really consider an office betting pool to be a prank. And no one stole anything. At least nothing that had been reported. Office pencils, pens, paper clips, envelopes and small items were obtained for personal use all the time, but that wasn't really theft in his mind. He considered it more along the lines of "the cost of doing business" and not a crime. "What is this person stealing?" Ryker asked, intrigued despite the arrogant man.

Jason sighed and rubbed the back of his neck. "Pens," he said, smothering his mouth with his hand.

Ryker stood still, deciphering the man's words. "I'm sorry, Jason, but did you just tell me that the thief is stealing pens?"

Jason nodded, looking down at the floor.

Ryker watched carefully, wondering if Jason was going to offer any additional information. "Are they expensive pens?" he prompted when the exasperating man remained silent.

"No!" Jason almost yelled, standing up and starting to pace through the office that was more than twice the size of his own. "In fact, that's what's so infuriating about the issue. There was a two hundred dollar pen on my desk last night but whoever broke into my office only stole all my cheap, ball point pens. About ten of them!"

Ryker stared, shocked and amused. "So this is more of a practical joke?" he offered, trying to get to the heart of the issue.

"It's a pain in my ass!" Jason came back. Then rubbed his face and neck once more. "I just want to find the bastard who is doing this and make it stop!" He paced back and forth then threw his hands up in the air in exasperation. "And last night, all of my paintings were…" he hesitated.

Ryker stood up straighter, starting to realize that there was more of a crime here when artwork was involved. "Stolen?" he suggested.

Jason shook his head, his face turning beet red with embarrassment. "They were pinned upside down."

Ryker almost laughed, both at the idea of someone messing with the man's head like this, and the obnoxious man's irritation at the culprit's antics. "Well, that's…." Ryker hesitated, not sure how to diplomatically describe Jason's issue. "Problematic," he finally finished.

Jason was too angry to notice Ryker's amusement. "You're damn right it is! But here's the thing," he finally said, putting his hands on his hips, mimicking Ryker's pose. "You have a great team of investigators. I've heard you've deployed them for your clients on numerous occasions. I'm asking for your help with this issue now."

Ryker leaned against the back of the chair, considering the man's request. He finally said, "I think the police are right in this case. It sounds more like a personnel issue than a legal issue, Jason. If these antics are going on in your office, have you questioned your staff? Are they happy and ready to work or are they angry at some benefit that is being eliminated from their package? Or are salaries down?" Ryker knew that many times people got back at their employers in creative ways. But stealing pens? "These kinds of things sound like someone who is just working late and snuck into your office."

"It can't be an employee," he grumbled, looking like he was at his wits end because of this situation. "Since this started, I've put in a new security system, installed new measures, put in cameras, electrical monitoring devices, badging equipment. Every time there is a break-in, I call my security firm and demand them to fix my security so the break-ins will stop but this guy is able to circumvent everything my security people put in. And there's no trace of anything. The police dusted for fingerprints but found nothing. And they said the same thing you did so they aren't willing to investigate any further." Jason took a deep breath. "Look, I know this isn't really your area, but I also know your investigator, Mark, and his team are great at finding out things. I don't want to know how they do it. I just want to find out who is pulling these pranks or thefts or whatever you want to call them and make it all stop." The man took a deep breath and rubbed his hand over his face. "I'm looking like a fool and I don't like that. Not one little bit!"

Ryker considered the man's request and actually started to feel sorry for him. He was right. These kinds of things did make a boss look foolish and disrespected. It would eventually create fallout in decreased business and he'd have to lay people off. So in the end, Ryker agreed to help out not so much for Jason's sake but to keep all those people employed. "How about if I speak with Mark and ask him how he can help? If there is anything he can do, I'll have him get in contact with you. Will that work?"

Jason breathed a sigh of relief. At least there was hope, he thought.

"That sounds fair," he replied and puffed up, relieved that he was getting some help. Shaking Ryker's hand, Jason wished he could walk down the hallway to this mysterious Mark's office and demand a consultation. But Jason also knew that wasn't the way The Thorpe Group operated. Jason would wait around and this Mark fellow would give him a call.

At least the company was customer oriented so it wouldn't be a long wait. But any sort of wait, in Jason's mind, was irritating. He wasn't a patient kind of man. When he wanted something, he wanted it done yesterday.

Walking out, he crossed the courtyard slowly, wishing he could think of another way to deal with the situation. In the end, he knew he'd just have to wait for Mark's call.

Ryker walked down the hallway to Mark's office as soon as Jason Moran left. "Do you have a moment?" Ryker asked.

Mark turned to face his boss, forcing his mind away from the six computer screens that were mounted in a row and on top of each other for easier viewing. "Sure, boss. What's up?"

Ryker quickly explained Jason's problem, smiling as soon as Mark laughed out loud. In the end Mark said, "I'll give him a call as soon as I get this report down to Axel. Maybe there's something I can do."

"That's all I can ask," he said and walked out, heading out of the building and to his lunch appointment.

Later that evening, he left the office in a hurry to get to a business dinner that he was not looking forward to. He'd agreed to take Xander's place tonight because Xander got caught up in a meeting. But all he wanted to do now was head home and relax with the football game on.

Then he saw her. She was leaving the office with her coat wrapped around her tightly to ward off the cold wind that had picked up earlier in the day. The sun had already set but the lights of the courtyard as well as the headlights of the other vehicles that were exiting the parking garage made it easy to see everything around.

He watched for only a moment before he made a decision. Ryker hadn't made it this far by letting any opportunity slip out of his grasp.

Walking towards her at a perfect intercept angle, he made for his target. He also knew the exact moment when she realized he was coming towards her. It was fairly evident that she recognized him. It was in her eyes, in the way her body tensed and her cheeks turned a lovely shade of pink.

"Good evening," he said, smoothly adjusting their positions so they were out of the line of employee traffic heading towards the parking garage, eager to get home to their families. "I'm Ryker Thorpe," he said, extending his hand, taking her smaller one in his. "I've seen you over at the other building in the mornings. Since we've seen each other so often, I thought it was past time to introduce ourselves. Maybe you'd even let me buy you a cup of coffee? Or dinner sometime?" he asked.

Cricket couldn't stop the trembling. It was one thing to see this man across the courtyard. It was a completely different issue to see him up close and personal like this. He was taller than she'd anticipated. And bigger! The man had muscles upon muscles underneath that suit. Her mother had been an excellent teacher at being able to spot faux anything and this man's shoulders were not padded with fluff. Only muscle.

"Um…" she stammered, feeling ridiculous. Her mother would be outraged by her lack of finesse. "I'm Cricket Fairchild," she finally was able to say, looking down and wishing she could extricate her hand from his. "I really have to go," she said. "I need to get home to…." she couldn't think of a valid reason why she needed to hurry home other than to escape this man's enigmatic and terrifying closeness that had her knees wobbling and her heart fluttering like she was experiencing her first eighth grade crush.

Ryker smiled, tucking her arm onto his elbow. "We're heading in the same direction so I'll walk you to your car. That will give you time to tell me how you got the name Cricket."

Cricket couldn't help but smile. Most people made some irritating reference to a bug. His comment was close, but it was much nicer. So was his smile. Those icy blue eyes were more than a little intimidating, but if she just looked at his chin or his nose, she could think a bit more coherently.

"My parents are a bit unorthodox. Apparently, a picnic was involved."

They were out on the street, walking down the sidewalk by this point. She saw her friends turn the corner, all of them rushing to get home to their families. Cricket didn't blame them. If she had this man to rush home to, she'd be scurrying along as well. After such a trying day, everyone in the office felt a strong need to head home and hug their children or their husbands before settling down to a nice, relaxing glass of wine.

"I thought ants were the main irritant at a picnic," he commented.

Cricket laughed. "My parents really don't do anything in the normal manner."

"What do they do?" he asked, instantly curious and enjoying the walk more than he thought he would. He had that business dinner that started in less than thirty minutes but for the first time in his life, he wanted to relax with a female instead of hurrying off to resolve some legal or business issue.

When her hand went up, waving about in the cool, autumn air, Ryker knew that she was going to try and either lie, or pass off the question. "Oh, they don't have any particular profession that they talk about," she said.

Her comment instantly raised his curiosity. "What kind of profession do they not talk about?" he asked.

Cricket couldn't believe how perceptive the man was. Normally her comment made people think that her parents were ultra-rich, or dirt poor. Either they didn't discuss their business interests because it was considered crass to do so, or they didn't have any business interests to discuss.

With this man's comment, she couldn't help but laugh. "You don't allow any ambiguity, do you?" she asked carefully.

He smiled, charmed by her smile and fascinated by the glint in her clear, green eyes. "And you are still avoiding the question. Which means that your parents are either very naughty, or embarrassingly wealthy. Which is it?"

Cricket didn't know that her green eyes were sparkling as she considered ways to answer his question without giving anything away. "That only tells me that you are a very cynical man. Does everyone have to have a secret? Or hide their parents away? Why can't I just be one of those women who don't have parents any longer? Or maybe I had a tough upbringing and I just don't talk about my parents in any way?"

They'd reached the courtyard already and Ryker was even more intrigued. Never had any woman so effectively avoided answering his questions before. Most of the women of his acquaintance were more than eager to brag about their familial associations, thinking he cared about that kind of thing. He didn't, but something about the way this lovely woman with the honey glints of her hair sparkling in the overhead lights made him think that the woman had more secrets than the FBI. And he intended to find out all of them.

"Have dinner with me tonight," he commanded, keeping her hand tucked on his elbow even while she tried to pull it away. He didn't care about the business dinner he was supposed to attend. The hell with them, he thought. He'd never missed a business meeting before, but if this woman would agree to dinner with him, he'd blow it all off in order to unravel her mysteries.

Cricket smiled, instantly flattered, but still not willing to agree to dinner tonight. "Give me your card and I'll call you." It was the best way she'd learned to push men away when she didn't want any further communication with them. Unfortunately, she didn't want to get to know this man. She preferred the fantasy because the reality was terrifying!

Ryker considered her request for all of a fraction of a second. "No you won't," he said with a shake of his head. "You'll walk away from me and won't call me. Then I'll have to stalk you out here in the courtyard every day. But you'll probably shift your schedule now that we've met."

Her green eyes widened at his accurate assessment of her plans. "If I promise to call?" she laughed, caught in her own trap. He was right. She wouldn't have called him back. The man was completely charming, amazingly sexy and totally out of her league. She knew she would be much more comfortable feeling the zing of his gaze from afar.

Ryker shook his head. He reached into his breast pocket and extracted a leather case, pulling a white business card out. "You won't. But here's my card anyway. I dare you to call me," he teased. "And if you don't, I'm not worried. I have my ways of finding people," he promised ominously.

Cricket's nervousness increased tenfold with his words. She took the card and spun around on her heel, almost running into the parking garage in a sudden, desperate need to get away from this strange, shockingly direct and amazingly sexy man.

She walked to her car and slipped in behind the wheel, feeling a little like Alice in Wonderland. The world was definitely topsy-turvy when she was walked out of work with a man who dined with the President of the United States!

Goodness, her father would break down with a stroke if he ever found out about Ryker Thorpe's interest!

CHAPTER 5

Cricket's whole body stiffened at the sound of the doorbell ringing. She looked up from her mystery novel, her eyes staring at the door as if she could somehow see through the wood. She had only one deadbolt on the door, knowing that it was too easy to break through elaborate security systems so why bother?

But now, hearing the doorbell ring and thinking of the stranger's ice blue eyes, she wished she had something that could more effectively lock him out of her house.

It had taken her over an hour to calm down after their brief conversation earlier tonight. She'd been so excited and flustered, she'd almost taken the wrong roads home!

Maybe it wasn't him. Maybe she'd just been thinking about him so much lately that he was on her mind. So when the doorbell rang, she'd just assumed it was the man. Maybe it was one of her neighbors. Maybe Jennie next door needed a babysitter because her husband was late coming home from work and she needed to go out for some reason. Or perhaps it was Leandra across the street coming to return the baking dish she'd borrowed last week.

Cricket continued to stare at the door, flinching when the doorbell rang once again because she hadn't opened it.

With growing trepidation, she walked over to the doorway. She knew with absolute certainty that she wasn't going to see her baking dish tonight, nor was she going to get to play Candyland with toddlers.. No, the person on the other side of that slab of wood was her stranger, the man with the strange, scary eyes. The man she skipped breakfast in order to see in the morning.

The man who terrified her as no one else ever could.

Her fingers trembled as she laid her hand down on the craftsman style door knob, taking a deep breath before she twisted the cold metal. Every part of her mind listened to the door opening. The slight squeak as the deadbolt was released, the scrape as the door tumblers retracted and the swish while the air shifted with the door opening.

"I thought you'd never answer the door," Ryker Thorpe's deep, hypnotic voice said.

Cricket shivered with the sound, her mind saying the words over and over again. "I knew it would be you," she whispered, her breath caught in her throat and her eyes wide with fascination at the handsome, amazingly virile man standing on her doorstep.

"Were you expecting someone else?" he asked, smiling at how cute she looked as she peered out of her doorway. She looked warm and cozy, like she'd been under a blanket reading a book.

Cricket didn't want him to think that and she quickly shook her head. "Not at all!"

"Good. Then I'm not interrupting anything?"

She grinned despite her nervousness. "Can I help you?" she asked. She held her breath, hoping anxiously he wasn't here to just sell her a magazine subscription or something similarly tedious.

"You can open the door and let me in," the man's voice replied. He was leaning against the door jamb, looking smooth and ultra-sophisticated with the expensive suit loose around his flat stomach, his five-hundred dollar tie gone and the top buttons of his Indian cotton shirt opened at the his neck.

Good grief, she even thought his neck was sexy!

She sighed with exasperation at herself, wondering why she was so wary of this man. She met men all the time. She avoided bars because men hit on her constantly. So it was almost annoying that this man didn't irritate her like the other men. She had a defense set up for when the men hit on her but she knew that she was defenseless around this man. Her face turned embarrassingly pink and her nerves did something she didn't want to even try to describe.

She bit her lip, wondering how she was going to get out of this mess. "I don't know."

Ryker smiled, relaxing since she hadn't slammed the door in his face. "Aren't you interested to know why I'm here?" he asked.

Cricket bit her lower lip, trying to decide how much she feared this man, and how much of her fear was unrealistic.

"I don't think I should care why you are here," she replied with complete honesty and the hint of a shy smile.

He chuckled, the deep sound making her heart flicker more quickly.

"That's an honest answer, at least." He straightened his shoulders and stood up; Cricket suddenly realized how small she really was compared to Ryker Thorpe. "How about if I come bearing gifts?" he offered and raised the bottle of wine he'd brought from his wine cellar. He'd called Xander and discussed the business dinner he'd agreed to go to earlier. But when Xander told him the whole story, they both agreed that it wasn't absolutely necessary for a representative of

The Thorpe Group show up at this particular function so here he was, hoping to have a quiet evening with the lovely Cricket Fairchild.

Cricket inhaled sharply when she read the wine label, her eyes snapping back up into his ice blue eyes, wishing he'd brought something other than wine. Wine was her kryptonite! And when she dared to glance downward, she gasped audibly as she read the label. "That's cheating!" she said with her eyebrows low over her eyes. Palmer 2009 Margaux was one of the great wines of that year. And she loved wine! She rarely drank wine because she couldn't afford the good stuff on her salary but her mother had taught her to truly appreciate the thrilling intensity and burst of flavors in a good wine.

Ryker put his palm to the door and gently pushed. "I'm coming in, Cricket," he said softly, his ice blue eyes never leaving her worried, green ones, watching for any sign of resistance. But she couldn't push him out. And it had nothing to do with the fabulous bottle of wine he held in his hand.

It had everything to do with the magical feeling she was experiencing as the man pushed his way into her house. She'd thought he was exceptionally handsome from across the courtyard. And today in the courtyard as he'd walked her to her car, he'd been shockingly forward, a character trait she generally didn't like. But in this man, it seemed to fit. Now, with him standing here, his height and broad shoulders making her feel small and feminine, she couldn't deny him entry. There was something about him that called to her like no other man ever had.

"Wine glasses?" he prompted when she just stood there in her foyer.

Cricket jumped, embarrassed that she'd just been standing there staring at the man's shoulders, and pulled her eyes away. "Yes! Wine glasses!" She spun around, surprised that she'd actually forgotten about the wine, his entire entry strategy. She never forgot about wine!

She moved off to the kitchen, trying to get her mind back in gear. "How did you know where I lived?" she asked as she reached up and pulled down two wine glasses from the cabinet over her fridge. They were dusty from lack of use so she cleaned them both in the sink, afraid to look into the window in front of her. It was dark outside which made the window like a mirror and she'd probably drop her wine glasses if he caught her eye in the window right at this moment.

Ryker watched with growing interest as the woman stretched up, her soft, pink sweater moving along with her arms to reveal pale skin on her back and allowing him an unlimited view of her adorable backside. It was round and firm, pressing against the black slacks she'd worn to work that morning. Her pink sweater was still on, but it wasn't pulled over her slacks any longer. He suspected she didn't even realize how adorable she looked, all frazzled and rumpled. He was used to seeing her looking perfectly coifed and walking with professional determination. He liked this look. She was much more appealing. And definitely sexier.

She spun around with the now-sparkling glasses, her eyes sliding reluctantly up to his and he wanted to kiss her. He wanted to see what she would feel like with those soft, full breasts pressed against his chest, her warm sighs blowing against his neck. And his body reacted instantly to the image.

She waited expectantly, glancing from his eyes to the bottle. When she realized what he was thinking, her heart sped up and she felt her cheeks heat. "Oh," she sighed and almost forgot about the glasses in her hand.

Ryker knew he was making her even more nervous. That hadn't been his intention but the woman was incredibly sexy standing there looking confused. He smiled and relented slightly. "Bottle opener?" he asked.

Again, her whole body jerked with the question and the realization that she was still staring at his mouth, almost begging the man to kiss her.

She shook her head and placed the glasses on the countertop behind her, almost smacking one of the stems off when she missed the counter because of her nervousness. Her fingers were clumsy as she rummaged around in her kitchen drawers. When she finally found her bottle opener, she swung around, holding the tool up victoriously.

"You found it," he said, amusement apparent in his eyes. "I take it you don't drink wine very often?" he asked as he opened the bottle with expertise.

She smiled and leaned against the counter, relieved that she finally had a break from trying to think for a few moments. "Not often, no."

"Are you a beer drinker?" he asked, pouring some wine into both glasses before handing her one.

"I enjoy the occasional beer," she said, accepting the glass with growing excitement. "But I'll admit, I'm a sucker for a good bottle of wine. Hence your presence in my kitchen," she grinned.

"Ouch!" he laughed and clinked her glass. "To finally meeting," he offered as a toast.

Cricket thought about that, then smiled and brought the glass to her nose. She took a long moment to enjoy the bouquet, letting the fruity scent fill her nostrils and enjoyment sensors. When she took the first sip, she let the wine slip slowly into her mouth, feeling the burst of flavor on her tongue, amazed by the incredible taste. "Oh my!" she sighed happily, her eyes still closed as she savored her first taste. "This is truly amazing."

Ryker watched as the woman he'd thought was the sexiest human being alive just blew him away with the most sensual image he'd ever seen in his life. He enjoyed wine just like the rest of the world. But watching Cricket Fairchild take her first sip of the Palmer Margaux had him aching to possess her. He wanted all of that passion, that erotic sensitivity, to be directed at him, or with him as he took her over the peak into sexual bliss.

He was standing about a foot away from her in the little periwinkle kitchen, his eyes looking at her strangely. The wine bottle was in one hand and his glass of wine in the other, but he was just standing there staring at her. "Aren't you going to try it?" she asked, looking up at him curiously.

Ryker blinked and glanced down at his glass. "I'm not sure I need to. Your enjoyment is much more interesting than anything I've ever seen," he said and watched with fascination as she blushed once again. He wondered if she sunburned or tanned. Probably the former with her fair skin, he thought, noting the platinum highlights in her hair. "So what do you do?" he asked, trying to change the subject so that she was more comfortable around him. He instinctively knew that he'd have to get her used to him before he could make a move on her and since he was aching to take her into his arms, he had to speed the "comfort" process along more quickly or he might just go up in flames with wanting her.

She led him out of the kitchen so they could be more comfortable in her little den. "I'm an accountant for Jason Moran's office."

That surprised him, knowing how Jason treated his staff. This woman didn't look like someone who would take a lot of verbal abuse. "And how do you like that work?" he asked, thinking that she didn't strike him as an accounting type. She looked more like a ballet dancer or a gourmet chef, someone with hidden passions and secrets that he wanted to discover.

Cricket shrugged her shoulder. "It pays the mortgage," she said and looked around at her tiny house. "It's small, but I love this house," she explained. There was only a family room and kitchen with a half bath downstairs and two small bedrooms upstairs, but it was hers. She paid the mortgage on it faithfully every month and kept meticulous records of her income and expenditures. She'd been taught as a kid that thieves could never own property; they had to be ready to leave at a moment's notice. She'd lived all over the world and could speak French, Italian and Spanish fluently, German well enough to get by, and a tad of Portuguese. But only because her mother and father had dragged her all over the world, following their next "project". Cricket had learned to adapt, to blend in and understand the culture of each city quickly, including absorbing the dialect and accents so people wouldn't think she was a stranger. Strangers were dangerous. Someone who "spoke the language" was a safer bet as a friend.

Ryker looked around as well, impressed with how cozy the room looked. It was as if there were a fire in the fireplace, but it was really just the warm hues and the soft lighting. She'd done a great job of decorating to make the area inviting and comfortable. "How long have you lived here?" he asked. And the conversation went on for hours. She curled up in her big chair with him across from her, relaxing as the wine crept into her bloodstream, making her more talkative than she normally would have been. He was a fascinating man, having visited almost all of the cities she'd been to and spoke several languages as well. By the end of the evening, she felt like she knew him a bit more thoroughly, but she never accepted that she might actually know his mind. This man was not like the one dimensional, easy going gentlemen she'd casually dated in the past. .

As they talked about art and history, college and their favorite foods, Cricket came to realize that Ryker Thorpe had so many facets to his complex personality. He was a fascinating man. She could honestly say she'd never met anyone more intelligent and well-educated than Ryker Thorpe, including her father which was saying a lot. Her father might not have attended college or a university, but he could argue right along with the best of them about any subject. He prided himself on reading as much as he could get his hands on, but the man sitting in her family room was much more well-read, able to converse on just about any subject. He even knew about art, which wasn't a topic most people excelled at.

Of course, she didn't go into much detail about her knowledge of art and art history, and she didn't even touch on her ability to spot real versus fake diamonds, much less pick out the most flawless diamond in any room at a glance. No, all the skills that had been passed on by her mother and father would only lead to questions. Questions she couldn't answer. Or at least shouldn't answer. The answers would raise too many other questions.

They'd finished the bottle of wine and Cricket smothered a yawn, not wanting him to see it because he'd probably get up and leave. But this time, she couldn't suppress it and he quickly glanced at his watch, realizing how late it had gotten. "I'd better let you get some sleep," Ryker said, standing up.

Cricket rose as well, feeling painfully disappointed that their time together was coming to an end. She wished she could think of something to make him stay, keep him talking to her. But now that they were closer, her mind just fizzled out.

"Well," she started off, hiding her hands behind her back, feeling as nervous and awkward as a sixteen year old on her first date all of a sudden. "Um…thank you for bringing the wine. It was exceptionally wonderful." There! That was a good way to clear the air and say goodbye. If she could just stay on this side of the coffee table, then she might not throw herself into his arms and beg him to kiss her goodnight.

Ryker could see right through her attempts and he wasn't going to allow her the chance. He'd wanted to kiss her the moment he walked into this house and he wasn't going to be able to do that if she stayed over there with the furniture in the way. "Walk me to the door," he commanded, not waiting for her to respond but reaching out and easily taking her hand, leading her towards her front door.

When they were standing there in the tiny foyer, Cricket's hands still held in his, she stared straight ahead, looking only at his chest. She couldn't look at his eyes, nor his mouth. If she looked at either, he would know how desperately she wanted to kiss him. How much she wanted him to just pull her into his arms and ravish her.

And how desperately she wished she were anyone else's daughter. Earlier today, she'd seen this man with The President of the United States. She now knew he was a lawyer, which meant he was an officer of the courts – just one step away from the police. A lawyer and a thief did not mix under any formula, she told herself firmly.

"Goodnight," she whispered, trying to hide the nervousness and sadness from her voice and her eyes.

Ryker wasn't going to be dismissed so easily. He knew that they both needed what was to come. Bending lower, he put a finger under her chin, lifting her face so she was looking at him. There in her eyes, he saw what he was looking for. The same need that was filling him.

And that was all the permission he needed. Bending lower, he took her lips in his, kissing her gently, slowly, teasing her into participating with the kiss. Cricket's breath came out in a low, shocked hiss as she looked up at him. But that only lasted for a fraction of a second before she lifted her mouth up again, silently asking him to continue kissing her. She knew it was wrong, that this could never go anywhere, but for this one moment, this one kiss, she was going to enjoy the feelings, the surprise and the amazement of how lovely and crazy she felt in this man's arms.

She didn't realize that her own arms had moved up his shoulders and were now wrapped around his neck or that her fingers were in his hair, feeling the surprisingly soft texture. There was a moment's spinning but then she felt the door on her back and realized that he'd spun them around so that she was pressed against the door with his body pressing against hers. She loved the way he felt, pressed her softness against him, gasping in shock and thrilling with the knowledge that she could do this to this strong, virile man. His hands had been on her waist but she shivered when she felt those hands move upwards, wrapping around her rib cage and she silently begged him to move higher.

Ryker had to mentally shake himself. This woman was so soft and sexy, all he wanted to do was continue kissing her just like this. He tried to stop, but then her hand touched his cheek and he was lost once again. Lifting her up, his hands moved down to her hips, pulling her legs so they were wrapped around his waist.

Cricket couldn't believe what was happening. Surely she wasn't doing this, she thought when he lifted his head up. Then the urge to touch his skin was overwhelming so she moved her hand out of his hair. Her fingers touched his hard jawline, riveted with the texture. It was rougher than she'd expected, more fascinating and hot to the touch. She didn't realize she was gasping for air or that her chest was heaving against his. All she knew was that her fingertips were on fire from the simple gesture against his skin. And then she really got lost. His hands were rough as he lifted her higher, his mouth ravaging hers and she needed more! It wasn't enough and she shifted her body, her head falling backwards when she felt that hardness...no, it wasn't on her stomach any longer it was...just....perfect! She thought that her eyes might be rolling back in her head with the waves of pleasure washing over her again and again but even that wasn't enough. Everything felt so good, every time he moved his hand, every place his hard, demanding lips touched just made her ache a little bit more. She'd never experienced anything like his touch or his kiss and she wanted so much more.

Ryker pulled his head back and stared down into her eyes. "Cricket, if we don't stop right now, I'm going to carry you up those stairs behind me and make love to you." He watched, so turned on just by the look in her eyes that he was having trouble forming the words. "Do you understand me?" he demanded when she continued to look back up at him with that sultry look in her pretty, green eyes. Damn! He wanted this woman with an almost painful need. He couldn't believe things had gotten so out of hand so quickly. He'd meant to gently kiss her goodnight and then head out. How had it reached the point where he was rock hard and silently begging her to give him permission to continue?

His words slowly broke through her haze of desire and Cricket gasped when she realized the position she was in. "Oh goodness!" she exclaimed and disentangled herself from him.

"Wait! Cricket don't..." and he groaned as her hips shifted against him. Cricket knew exactly what he was dealing with because she felt it too. That crazy, almost painful desire when she moved against his erection shot through her as well. She froze, her body not wanting to do anything that would cause that feeling to happen again. And yet....maybe if she....

"Cricket!" he groaned, closing his eyes and shaking his head. "You know exactly what you're doing, don't you?" he asked, a slight smile on those lips that Cricket now knew could deliver so much pleasure. How could a man that looked this stern and serious know how to kiss like that?

"Sorry," she whispered, her fingers gripping his shoulders so she wouldn't move like that again. "How do I get down without..." she couldn't say the words and knew her face was flaming red now.

"Hold onto me," he told her and moved closer, his hands grabbing onto her hips. With great finesse, he lifted her up and set her down onto the floor once again. "There," he growled, but his hands didn't move away from her and his body pressed against her one more time. "I've got to go," he said with that sexy, husky voice. He didn't leave. His body pressed hers against the door again, his lips finding hers and kissing her again. It was slower this time, sensuous but still got her a little higher on the crazy-for-Ryker scale.

She moaned and her arms moved back up around his neck and she arched into his body, wanting that pleasure back, needing more.

"I have to go," he said again, but his mouth moved against her neck, making her shiver with delight when he found a spot at the base where seemingly all of her nerve endings zipped to attention, sparking that need even higher.

She pulled back slightly, surprised. "You have to go," she whispered, but her fingers remained in his hair and her body was still moving against his

"I'm going to leave now," he said and gritted his teeth. He actually did it this time, pulling back and bracing his arms against the wooden door behind her. "Thank you for tonight," he said and touched her cheek with his rough finger.

She sighed, practically melting against the door behind her. Her fingers were clumsy, barely able to function but she finally was able to find the doorknob. She twisted, didn't get it the first time and tried again. This time, she was able to turn the knob and open the door. She almost forgot to stop leaning against it but, as she practically tripped over her feet when the door pushed her body out of the way, she figured out that she needed to move.

"Goodnight, Cricket," he said again and walked out into the cold night.

Cricket hurried around the room, turning out all the lights as quickly as possible. Then she rushed to the back of her den – just in time to watch him step into his car. When he had the door open and one foot inside, he hesitated and looked back at her house. Cricket stared, biting her lip and praying that he would come back inside and finish what he'd started. She didn't have the courage to ask him herself, but every cell in her body was aching to find out what it would be like to make love with Ryker Thorpe.

In the end, he shook his head and got into the driver's seat. A moment later, his powerful car drove down the street and Cricket sagged against the wall, so disappointed she thought she might actually cry.

Instead, she picked up the two wine glasses and the empty bottle of wine, tossing the bottle into the recycling bin and placing the glasses into the sink before she moved upstairs. Preparing for bed, she drug out her flannel nightgown and pulled it over her head, wishing that she was doing the complete opposite. She actually blushed at all the thoughts that were racing through her mind as she brushed her teeth and washed her face. She didn't really want Ryker to come back. She'd just met the guy today!

She had to remind herself over and over again that this was the kind of man who dined with important people. He wasn't the man for her!

CHAPTER 6

Cricket woke the following morning feeling fresh and alive, and more excited to get to work than she had in a long time. She hurried through her morning routine, eager to get to the office. It had nothing at all to do with her job and everything to do with the idea of seeing Ryker as he walked into the building across the courtyard.

She was ready for her early morning system shock.

Cricket showered and dressed, putting extra effort into her appearance that morning. She even chose a shorter than normal skirt and extra high heels, thinking it wouldn't hurt to be a bit sexier. The man was a genuine hottie, after all.

All her admonishments of the night before were banished from her mind. What harm could come from seeing the man? She was just going to work and, hopefully, he was going to work on his normal schedule. So if they happened to see each other, that didn't mean anything, she told herself. It wasn't a commitment, just an early morning adrenaline rush.

She was grabbing her car keys and purse, checking her lipstick in the mirror one more time when her cell phone rang.

Cricket's whole body cringed and she shook her head when she recognized the ring tone. It wasn't important, she told herself, determined to ignore it. After several rings, it stopped, automatically going to voice mail. When it finally stopped, she took a deep breath and was just about to step out into the crisp, morning air when the ringing started up once more.

She looked at the phone, then shook her head. No one would be calling her at this time of the morning other that those horrible political action calls for surveys. Or it could be her father. Either way, there was no way she was going to answer that call.

Feeling free again, she grabbed her coat, tightening the belt around her waist and rushed out the door. The cool morning air felt fresh and invigorating on her face and she smiled to the sunshine that was just starting to peek over the horizon. Yes, it was going to be a good…

Her phone started ringing again!

"Darn him!" She stopped on her tiny front porch and grabbed the phone out of her purse, flipping it open and answering it with an irritated, "Good morning, Father!"

The answering chuckle only set her nerves on edge.

"Good morning, my beautiful daughter. You're looking exceptionally lovely this fine morning. Is that an excited glow I see on your face or are you just thrilled to hear your old man's voice?"

Cricket looked around, trying to find out where her father was hiding. But she saw nothing and she should have known better. If her father didn't want to be seen, he wouldn't be seen. "Why are you up so early this morning?" she asked, glancing into the trees and the park across the street, anywhere he might be hiding. The man worked nights, was sometimes up all night so how was he still awake this early in the morning?

Her father chuckled softly at her question, obviously enjoying teasing his one and only daughter. "Who says I'm up early? Perhaps I'm up late?"

Her steps froze as she walked to her car and she held her breath as she asked, "You didn't do anything here in Chicago, did you Dad?" She waited several seconds, bracing for his answer. They had an agreement! "You promised," she whispered, anxiety lacing her voice as she waited for him to either confirm or deny whether he had accomplished, or was about to tackle, a project within the metropolitan area of Chicago. He might have agreed to leave this area free of his efforts while she lived here, but that was never a guarantee that he would follow through on his promise.

He was a thief. He obviously had a problem with ethics. She might love him dearly, but she was completely aware of his limitations. If he were tempted by something here in Chicago, a silly promise to his daughter wouldn't stop him.

She walked to her car, unlocking the driver's side door, all the while, looking out the corner of her eye to see if she could spot him somehow.

"I haven't touched a thing in the area in years, my dear. How little faith you have in my promises," he tut-tutted. "But you still haven't answered my question about why you are looking so spiffy. Eager to get to your cold, boring office so you can type in numbers for the rest of the day?" he suggested with the touch of sarcasm that always accompanied his words about her chosen occupation. "Or could that twinkle in your eye have something to do with the man who was in your house last night?" he demanded, his voice no longer as friendly as it was a moment ago.

Cricket was about to start up her car but she stopped, worried now. "You were here last night? You saw…" she had been about to say Ryker's name but stopped herself in time. If her father didn't know who the man was, Cricket wasn't going to give him any hints.

"I know what's going on and you'd better steer clear of Ryker Thorpe," he warned. "The man isn't stupid. He's one of the best lawyers in the country, Cricket. He might not be law enforcement, but don't cross him. He's one of them," he said firmly, saying "them" as if were a four letter word that left a bad taste in his mouth. Her father was very protective, had barely allowed her to date when she'd been younger. No matter where they were in the world, her father had been against her dating. It was only her mother's calming influence that had enabled Cricket to go on dates as a teen. Until she'd gone to college, she'd had very little freedom in the dating area.

Which was ironic. Her mother and father had taught her all these illegal skills, showing her how to break into buildings, steal priceless pieces owned by another human being, but when it came to someone dating his little girl, her father was as protective as a momma bear.

She was shaking her head at this latest invasion of her privacy, wanting to argue with her father, but she couldn't find the words. Possibly because he was right. Ryker was dangerous. She'd found out that Ryker was a lawyer yesterday and it had sent a dangerous thrill throughout her whole body. "If you don't do any jobs in Chicago, there's no reason to be concerned," she pointed out with what she considered irrefutable logic. If the man didn't do anything illegal, he shouldn't be concerned about his daughter dating someone associated with the law.

She could already sense that her father didn't agree. She could feel his anger and frustration coming through the atmosphere to her phone.

"The man's an expert at international law," he stated as if she were being ridiculously stubborn and obtuse. "That means his contacts aren't just in Chicago, Cricket. They're everywhere. The man travels half the year. So not only does that mean he has connections at Interpol, but he wouldn't be good husband material for you. You should be looking for a man who will be home with my grandbabies, helping you raise them. Not off in some foreign country while you stay at home doing diaper duty."

Cricket rolled her eyes. "Dad! I just had a casual night with him. He brought over wine."

There was a long pause before her father finally said, "Cricket, I don't know if you're lying to yourself or to me, but either way, ditch him. He's dangerous."

With those words, he ended the call and Cricket leaned her head against the steering wheel, wishing that her parents were normal and that their chosen career path wasn't so dangerous. And that it didn't interfere with her own life.

She started her car, thinking to ignore his command. She liked Ryker. He was different from the other men she'd either dated or come into contact with over the years. He was kind and sensitive without being wimpy, but also scary smart.

And he made her laugh at some of his observations. Even better, he laughed with her! Most men hadn't understood her sense of humor. She knew she was a little off to the left about some things. But Ryker "got" her. Last night, he'd chuckled when she'd told him stories about one thing or another and she'd enjoyed everything about him. Even that scary, almost terrifying attraction she had towards the man.

Goodness, and when he touched her! She'd never experienced anything like that before! She shivered just at the memory and she'd dreamed about him last night in the most erotic, embarrassing way!

Unfortunately, as she drove through the streets of Chicago that were quickly filling up with other commuters, she knew that her father was right. Besides, why waste time enjoying the man's company only to discover that he's a real jerk later on? It would just put her parents in jeopardy. Men always put on a good front initially but once the newness of a relationship wore off, the real person came out. She couldn't risk her parents' future incarceration simply because she thought a man was sexy and funny.

That thought caused another to pop into her head and she used the voice activated phone on her steering wheel to call her father back. When her father picked up, she asked, "Dad, if you're nervous about getting caught, does that mean there's evidence against you?" she asked, suddenly worried.

"Of course not," he growled, his pride in his work wounded. "You know me and your mother better than that." The man considered himself a professional and she had to admit that there hadn't ever been any evidence the police in any country which could connect him to a theft.

So his comments didn't make sense. "So why are you so worried about me seeing a lawyer socially?" she asked, still not convinced.

There was a hesitation on the other end of the line before her father said, "You know that this man is more than a social acquaintance, Cricket. Don't insult me like that."

She shook her head and tried to steer the conversation back to the original subject. "Well, why are you so afraid of this man?"

"Because I don't know everything Interpol has on me or your mother, my dear," he said with strained patience. "They might have our faces, although I doubt it. Or they might know we are connected. You know how it is, Cricket. We've been extremely successful in our careers," he said, that inappropriate pride coming through in his voice once again. "And I doubt your mother or I have made any mistakes, but we're not perfect."

Despite the seriousness of the topic, she had to laugh. "Okay, Dad." She pressed the button on her steering wheel that would disconnect the call and worked her way through the traffic but instead of going straight to the office, which would put her on an intercept course with Ryker at the time they normally walked into the office each morning, she pulled into a coffee shop. Since she couldn't get her daily zing with Ryker's ice blue eyes, she'd treat herself to a special cup of coffee.

Ten minutes later, as she strolled out of the café once again, she knew that the coffee definitely didn't have the same impact on her senses as knowing that Ryker Thorpe was watching her walk into her building. She set her newly acquired and over-priced coffee in the cup holder and meandered her way through traffic to her office, depressed and irritated, the ever present desire to have a normal life creeping up on her.

She couldn't believe how depressed she felt at the idea of not seeing the man. But she told herself over and over that she was being ridiculous. She had spent one night in the man's company. It wasn't like she'd fallen in love with him!

All throughout her childhood, she'd just wanted to be normal, to have friends she knew she could see each day in school. But because of her parents' careers, there were years when she hadn't even been in an official school. Thankfully, her parents pushed her harder than any teacher might. Besides all the skills they'd acquired over the years, they also taught her math, reading and writing. The science part came naturally to her because of all the skills she'd been taught by her parents. She understood chemistry because she'd learned to break into buildings. She had in-depth computer skills because she'd been taught to hack into any computer system or security system.

She sighed and pulled into the parking lot, angry with her parents for such a crazy upbringing. She might have seen the world, but she'd hated every moment of it. When she'd finally gone off to college and formed friendships with her college buddies, she'd thought she'd died and gone to heaven. That had been her first taste at normalcy. Her first freedom from the constant worry about her parents getting caught. It had been wonderful.

And now their chosen occupation was interfering in her life once again. But this felt more harsh than all the other times.

She went through the motions of work, but she didn't really put much effort into it. She might not like her work, but at least before she would take pride in doing the data entry exceptionally well. Today, and for the next three days when she wouldn't allow herself to see Ryker, she thought she genuinely hated her job. If she stared longingly out the window in the hopes of getting a peek at the strong, tall man striding out the office doors towards the parking garage, that certainly couldn't be a crime in her father's world, could it?

It had been bad when she'd had to leave her friends, but for some reason she didn't quite understand, not seeing Ryker every morning felt significantly worse.

By Friday evening, she was exhausted and depressed, feeling angry and resentful at her father for…everything. She walked into her tiny but wonderfully, legally obtained and owned house, dumping her purse and walking straight up the stairs to her bedroom where she flopped backwards onto her bed, staring up at the ceiling.

She didn't even look at the large, glass vase filled to the brim with ball point pens, not wanting to be tempted to get her fix with another early morning nose-snubbing at the expense of her boss. It wouldn't help anyway, she told herself. An adrenaline rush probably wouldn't help her solve her blues this time.

With a sigh, she pulled herself together. Did she really want to jeopardize her parent's security over an exciting fling? She actually hesitated over that answer but realized what she was thinking and shook her head. Of course not! Her parents might be career criminals who just had the luck and intelligence to have not gotten caught, but, except for moving all over the world, they'd been excellent parents. They were kind and caring, giving her experiences other kids couldn't even dream of. So what if she'd been to twenty different countries but her official passport only had two? She knew the languages and, in her mind, she had the memories of all of those adventures. And if it made her stomach churn at the idea of what they did, or the fear of one of them getting caught, it was a small price to pay. They would not be safe with her dating someone as well connected and powerful as Ryker Thorpe.

It wouldn't have worked anyway. Ryker might set her nerve endings on fire with just a touch, but she had to remind herself that he was way out of her league. And besides, what hope did she have of keeping him interested in her long term? She was just an accountant!

She stood up and stripped off her business suit, pulling on a pair of soft, well-worn jeans. One leg had a ragged hem and a back pocket was missing, but these were her favorite jeans, softened by years of washing. Adding a tee-shirt and grabbing a scrunchy to pull her hair off of her neck, she started to feel slightly better. With her work clothes carefully put away, she padded barefoot back downstairs to find something to eat for dinner.

Unfortunately, nothing in her pantry looked appetizing. Her options were limited since she despised going grocery shopping so there wasn't much left. She hadn't been to the grocery store in about two weeks so her choices were a can of tomato soup or a frozen meal, neither of which were particularly appealing.

She probably should have gone out to happy hour with her friends. Unfortunately, she was finding that she didn't have very much to talk about with Josie, Allyson and Debbie. They were wonderful women, but their lives revolved around their kids and their husbands or ex-husbands. It was hard to relate since she was single without kids.

She picked up the can of soup with a grimace. If she'd gone with them, she might have relaxed somewhat or maybe even had something more appetizing to eat than...she opened her freezer and surveyed the stacks of frozen meals...chicken and broccoli. Yuck! Why had she even chosen this one? She hated broccoli!

Then she sighed. Dad! He'd snuck into her house and filled her freezer with healthier choices.

She thought of something else. Closing the freezer, she braced herself to open her fridge and...yep! Filled with fruits and vegetables. She knew they hadn't been there two days ago because she'd grabbed a yogurt yesterday morning for breakfast. But she couldn't guess if he'd filled up her fridge yesterday or today because she'd skipped breakfast this morning and had bought a yogurt at the deli in the building for lunch today.

When the doorbell rang, she actually hoped it was her mother or father. She would love to see them, maybe even cry on their shoulder. Her mother would be better, she thought. At least her mother would understand what she was going through. Her father would just pat her shoulder and tell her that Ryker wasn't the man for her. That she should get over him and find a nice, reliable, non-lawyerly type of man to fall in love with and give him grandchildren.

Tossing the frozen meal back into the freezer, she almost skipped to the front door.

Just as she was opening the door, suddenly realizing that she hadn't looked through her peep hole to see who was there, it occurred to her that her parents wouldn't ring the doorbell. They wouldn't even knock. In fact, if it were her parents, they would be sitting in her den, reading the newspaper or a book.

By the time all those thoughts raced through her mind, the door was open and she was staring at a very handsome, very tall and very muscular Ryker Thorpe.

"You've been avoiding me," he said as he stepped into her miniscule foyer. "And you didn't call me." He stepped closer to her, taking the door out of her hand and slamming it shut behind him. "So I stopped waiting," he said and took her into his arms.

Cricket was stiff for perhaps one, maybe two seconds before the heat of his arms and the deliberate, commanding feel of his lips snapped her out of it and she was curling into his embrace, kissing him back with all the feeling she'd denied herself by not seeing him each morning. Her arms wrapped around his neck and her body plastered against his, feeling all those delicious hard planes that were so completely different from her body and sent breathtaking zings all throughout her system.

When he deepened the kiss, she heard herself whimper, but couldn't stop her arms from reaching up and wrapping around his neck, her leg shifting so his...was that...? Yes, she pressed her tummy closer, feeling his erection against her belly and her whole body melted even more. She felt the wall behind her back and was relieved, using it to press herself more fully against him, stretching up on her toes to feel him in more places. When she felt his hand under her sweater, she almost sobbed out with the excitement that she couldn't control. And didn't want to.

She'd never felt anything like this before and she didn't want it to stop. This was ten times better than sneaking through some security system! No adrenaline rush could make her feel this…exhilarated!

Cricket felt her body lifted, her back pressing harder against the wall and she instinctively lifted her legs, wrapping them around his waist while his body pressed against her own. She felt his hands underneath her shirt and gasped at the contact, her eyes opening wide to look into his. Slowly, ever so slowly, his hand moved against her bare skin. Cricket wasn't aware of her mouth falling open, or her eyes almost closing while her hips shifted along with his hand.

She heard him growl for some reason, but all she cared about was his hands on her skin, wanting more. Needing more! "Please don't stop," she begged when his hands moved away from her skin.

"I don't intend to," he growled right back, lifting her higher into his arms.

Cricket had no idea what was happening, only that he'd moved her hips so she wasn't feeling that delicious pressure anymore and she squirmed in his arms, trying to bring back that feeling, to appease the ache that was building in her body.

"Ryker! You're not…"

"I will be," he came back, his voice still barely above a growl.

She sighed with happiness when she felt the softness at her back but she couldn't stop touching him long enough to realize that it was her bed. She didn't care that he'd brought her up to her bedroom, not even sure how he'd accomplished something so effortlessly. All she cared about was feeling his strong fingers against her skin again. She took his hand and placed it against her stomach, then moved her own hands up to the buttons on his shirt, almost ripping the buttons open in her desperate need to discover what lay beneath those expensive shirts.

She wasn't disappointed, her fingers roaming over his heated skin, feeling his muscles flinch wherever she touched. She was so fascinated, that she lifted her head, her tongue darting out to taste that amazing skin and all the enthralling muscles that flexed and shifted under her fingers.

Cricket was only vaguely aware of Ryker pulling her sweater over her head and tossing it somewhere. She didn't want to think any longer. It had been a week of worrying and denial but she couldn't deny herself anything any longer. She'd wanted this man three nights ago. She'd denied herself then and every morning after. No more!

She arched against him, whimpering when he pulled her white, lace bra off of her shoulder so he could kiss the peak of her breast. Her leg rose up, pressing against his thigh and her hips pressed, seeking that special pressure she'd discovered the last time he'd been here. She wanted it, needed it!

"Please!" she begged him when he moved his mouth away from her breast but just about sighed with happiness when he pulled the strap down on the other side, taking her nipple in his mouth and sucking. Then it wasn't a sigh. She screamed out with the new feelings that jolted her. She pressed her hips against him harder, still trying to find that special place on his body that felt so perfect.

His mouth moved lower and she felt his fingers expertly open the button on her jeans. A moment later, her jeans were gone along with her white, lace underwear. She was completely naked underneath him but she needed to touch him as well. He was too far down her body now for her to do anything. When his mouth kissed her stomach, she wiggled, smiling as he tickled her.

When his mouth found that special place, she just about screamed again. But his arm was heavy over her hips, holding her down. She had no intention of pulling away but she couldn't deal with that kind of pleasure. It was so powerful and then he started sucking, one finger moving inside of her and she simply couldn't hold back any longer. That ache that had been building to unbearable heights exploded. Her whole body exploded. She closed her eyes as she screamed out, her climax shooting waves of intense pleasure throughout her whole being.

And when it was over, she lay on the bed, panting with her eyes closed, not sure how to even open them and look at him after that kind of experience.

Ryker stood up and tore his clothes off. When he was finally naked, he looked down at the woman on her bed, surrounded by flowered sheets and flowered pillows and still reeling in the haze of her climax. Damn, he'd never been this impatient before. He felt like a teenager again but he couldn't deny that Cricket was the sexiest, most sensuous woman he'd ever seen. Tasting her orgasm had made him almost lose control. The only thing that held him back was the incredible pleasure of seeing her fall apart at his touch.

He pulled the condom out of his wallet, and put it on, all the while watching as she slid against the sheets in the aftermath of her climax. Bending lower, he nuzzled her neck, finding that magic spot on her neck he'd discovered only moments ago. Sure enough, she gasped and reacted instantly. Her arms moved to his shoulders, a little slower this time, but when his fingers slid inside of her, he knew that she was right back with him.

"Hold onto me, Cricket," he said and lifted her arms so they were around his neck once again. "Look at me," he said and moved her legs wider so they could accommodate his hips. With the slightest movement, he slid inside her just an inch. When her eyes widened, he moved a bit deeper. Inch by inch, he pressed into her heat, then out again, watching her face for signs that he was doing something she liked or didn't like. He felt the sweat break out on his back and forehead as he worked hard to keep control. He wanted this first time with her to be incredible, but it was using everything inside of him to slow down, to make sure she was enjoying this as much as he was. But as her tight heat gripped him, he pressed deeper.

When he saw the flinch on her face and her eyes closed briefly, he stopped and looked down at her. "Cricket?" he asked. "Are you okay?"

She wiggled her hips slightly, trying to get used to his size. Biting her lip, she shifted again, not seeing the almost pained look in his eyes until she opened her own again and looked up at him. When she saw what was going on with him, her hand moved to his cheek. "What's wrong?" she whispered, worried that she'd done something wrong. "Did I hurt you?" she asked.

"Damn no!" he groaned. "But I think I just hurt you," he said. He tried not to move, suspecting that this was her first time; he didn't want her to be hurt any more than was needed. He cursed himself for moving so fast. He should have been more patient. He should have gotten to know her better. If he had gone slower, if he'd just talked to her like he'd planned tonight, then he might have known that she was a virgin. Or had been.

"I'm sorry, Cricket," he growled, berating himself for being so obtuse. "I didn't know."

She moved her hips again, the pain completely gone and the need to move, to feel him inside of her was more overpowering than she could have imagined. "I'm good," she said, then gasped when he moved just slightly.

"Are you sure?" he asked, freezing once again.

She wiggled her hips and placed her hands on his chest, the need to move becoming more urgent. "Ryker, please don't stop," she gasped out and then closed her eyes once again when he did just that, shifting his weight which caused him to shift inside of her, delicious, amazing and overwhelming pleasure zipped through her whole body and she closed her eyes, arching into him to feel it again.

That was all the encouragement he needed. Ryker pulled slightly out of her heat, then pressed right back into her. Over and over again, faster and faster, he watched her climb up that pleasure cliff with him and it was such a turn-on to see her like this, to know that he was the only man who had done this to her. When she screamed out with her second orgasm, the tightness of her brought him right along with her. He'd wanted to watch her, but the way she writhed underneath him pulled him over to his own climax.

Cricket felt like she was showered in waves of pleasure so intense, she saw spots and lights and stars. When it was all over, she fell back against her quilt, feeling boneless. She felt him move, but she couldn't figure out why or what he might be doing. He came back from the bathroom and curled up behind her, pulling her close while he kissed her shoulder and neck.

She sighed with happiness as Ryker's fingers skimmed along her hip, tickling her waist. She laughed when he started to move higher, grabbing his fingers and looked over her shoulder at him. He was propped up on his elbow, looking down at her and she blushed at the look in his eyes.

"You think that's going to stop me?" he asked, his hand moving around to her stomach and pulling her more tightly against his chest, her bottom snuggled against his groin.

"No," she smiled and wiggled her derriere.

She felt a sharp sting when his hand smacked her bottom lightly. It wasn't hard enough to hurt, but it was surprising and she looked over her shoulder at him inquiringly.

"You're trying to tempt me into doing everything once more but I need nourishment if you want to ravish me again."

She laughed happily, but her body was tingling from that touch and the look in his eyes. "I think we need to determine who ravished whom tonight," she said, feeling cold when he stood up from her bed. She pulled the soft comforter over her nakedness, but fully admired his own muscular body as he walked into her bathroom.

"I have frozen dinners in the freezer if you're hungry," she said, pushing the pillows behind her so she could sit up and have a better view.

He came back into her bedroom, amused with her modesty. "I actually brought Chinese food with me," he said.

She was surprised. And tempted! "You did?" she asked. "Where is it?"

Ryker put his hands on his hips and shook his head, apparently just as confused as she was. "I believe it's still on your foyer floor. I think I dropped it when you attacked me as I entered your house a few hours ago."

"I attacked you?" she gasped, holding the blanket over her breasts but her hunger suddenly resurfaced. Then she leaned back against her pillow again, a twinkle entering her eyes. "I hope my dog didn't eat the food," she teased.

Ryker froze and looked back at her, surprised. "You have a dog?" He was immediately moving towards the door and stairs but he glanced back, saw the mischief in her eyes and stopped.

Cricket couldn't stop the laughter at his surprised, confused expression. "No. But I had you fooled for a moment, didn't I?"

Ryker wasn't going to take that. He might have chuckled, but he also stormed right back to her bed and pulled the blanket off of her. "You're going to pay for that," he said a moment before his hand grabbed her ankle as she tried to laughingly get away from him. It was no contest and a moment later, she was right back in his arms, his mouth covering hers and that now familiar but still shocking tidal wave of desire came over her, swamping her senses. She lifted her arms, wrapping them around his neck as she gave in to the storm.

Another hour and an invigorating shower later, and they were sitting at her kitchen table eating re-heated Chinese food directly out of the containers, arguing about one thing after another. She pushed the chicken and broccoli away from her, wrinkling her nose when he stabbed a broccoli stalk and offered it to her. He laughed and caught her foot with both of his as she tried to push his chair farther away.

"So you don't like broccoli," he said and popped the vegetable into his mouth with a wink in her direction. "And you've never had sex before today. You're still embarrassed to be naked around me," he teased as he snuck a peek down the loose neck of the robe she'd pulled on after their shower, "and you don't have a dog. What else don't I know about you?" he asked.

Cricket thought about her parents but then pushed them out of her mind. Ryker didn't want to know her whole history. "I hate grocery stores, I hate to cook and I'm afraid of spiders. What more do you want to know?"

He pulled her onto his lap and wrapped his arms around her, feeding himself from behind her while she rested her back against his chest, feeding herself except for the times when he stole whatever chunk she was about to eat herself. All the while, they talked about themselves, learning all those things that should have been discussed before they'd had sex. It was sweet and wonderful, even if Cricket sometimes worried that her father might be outside watching her.

And when they'd filled themselves with Chinese food, he picked her up into his arms and carried her back to her bedroom to make love to her throughout the night.

A long time later, when they were snuggled underneath her flowered quilt and their bodies barely able to move any more, she heard him say, "Come to Paris with me."

She'd been half asleep but had woken when he had a moment ago although she still felt like snuggling into her pillow with him curled up behind her. She opened one eye, trying to determine if he was serious. The look in those blue eyes told her that he was completely serious and she rolled over, completely awake now. "I can't go to Paris with you," she answered, surprised but feeling wonderful that he'd asked.

Ryker shifted their positions so she was underneath him. "Of course you can. Just call your boss and tell him you need some personal days," he said, kissing her shoulder, her arm. When his mouth took her finger and started sucking, the jolt went straight to her core and she gasped.

"No Paris," she struggled to say, all the while shifting her body underneath his better so she could get what she wanted, which was him, inside her and moving in that magical way that destroyed her control and made her feel like she was floating among the stars.

"Why not?" he asked, sliding into her heat and watching her face, his body actually becoming harder when her mouth fell open and her eyes closed, sheer bliss on her beautiful, makeup free face. Her blond curls were spread out on the pillow and her body was gorgeously naked and moving against his instinctively. Ryker could honestly say that he'd never had a more incredibly sexual experience with another woman. And he didn't want it to stop despite the fact that he had an important meeting in Paris the next day. "It will be for just three days and we can be together."

"Sounds perfect," she replied, her hands clenching his shoulders. "But if you could just...concentrate on the here and now," she said, lifting her hips, silently begging him to move faster, press deeper.

After hours of making love to this woman, he knew exactly what she wanted but he didn't give it to her. He held back even though his own body was clamoring for him to give in and just enjoy the incredible feel of her, he wanted this to go on longer. Forever possibly.

"Agree to come to Paris then."

Cricket was ready to scream, needing him to just... "Paris is too far away."

"I can get you there in six hours," he said, shifting just the way she liked him to move.

"Can't!" she groaned and moved herself, knowing that he liked that...yep, just like that, she smiled when he groaned himself.

"You can," he whispered back.

In response, she moved her hand down his back, her fingers trailing against his skin and she almost laughed out loud when she won the argument and he gave both of them what they desperately needed.

CHAPTER 7

Cricket smiled as she let herself into her house, thinking about Ryker's request this morning for her to travel with him to Paris. What a romantic!

It was quiet now that he was gone and she lugged her groceries into the kitchen. She knew her father had stocked her fridge, but he hadn't loaded it with appropriate levels of carbs and fats. She'd bought ice cream and potato chips along with some chicken breasts and a few things that would make a good dinner. In her mind, she was planning a romantic meal with Ryker when he returned from Paris in three days. He said he would call and let her know when he was landing and she'd loved the way he'd said goodbye to her this morning.

"Wipe that silly smile off of your face!"

Cricket yelped and jumped at least a foot in the air, dropping both bags of groceries onto the floor which then scattered their contents everywhere, including the ice cream which exploded in every direction on impact.

Cricket looked at the mess, then glanced up, her face still shocked. "Dad! What are you doing in my house!" she exclaimed angrily.

Her father was one of those extremely handsome, dangerously charming and irritatingly good thieves. To date, there wasn't a lock he couldn't pick or a safe he couldn't open. In his mind, security systems were more of an amusement to him than a hindrance.

"Do I need an excuse to come visit my favorite daughter?" he joked.

Cricket wasn't in the mood to be teased. "I'm your only daughter! And yes, you should wait for an invitation before letting yourself in." She grabbed the broom and started sweeping up the spilled cereal and broken cookies. "Did you at least use the key I gave you or did you pick my lock?"

"Of course I didn't use a key!" he scoffed. He stood there while she swept up the mess, shaking his head as if he were shocked by her groceries. "Why did you even need to go shopping? I bought you everything you need just the other day."

She dumped the first load into the trashcan. "You know I don't like broccoli, Dad," she said and picked up what remained of her ice cream, sighing when she accepted that it was a total loss before dumping it too into the trash can. "Why couldn't you have let me know you were here at least?"

He crossed his arms over his chest, glaring at her with admonishment. "I didn't want to run into anyone I wasn't supposed to run into."

Cricket looked up at him, suddenly wary. "About that," she started to say.

"You're still seeing him!" her father roared, throwing his arms up in the air with profound exasperation. "Even after I told you to stop seeing him, he was in this house, wasn't he?"

Cricket refused to be intimidated by her father's anger. This was her house and he had no business trying to tell her who could and couldn't come into her own home. "How do you know I'm still seeing him?" she yelled right back at him, undaunted since she knew that his bark was much worse than his bite. The man was a pussy cat, actually. Some people might be frightened of him, but she knew he wouldn't hurt her in any way. Except to drive her crazy sometimes. And continue in a career that scared the bejeezus out of her for fear of losing him to prison.

"Are you kidding me?" he demanded, standing over her and trying to make her feel his wrath. "The man was here all last night! He even came downstairs with..."

"Don't say it!" she told him, covering his mouth with her open palm. "Don't you dare say it because then I'll know you were spying on me last night and I would consider that a huge violation of the trust I thought we shared together."

Edward Fairchild grabbed her wrist and pulled her hand away from his mouth. "All trust issues are null and void when you start sleeping with the enemy," he told her.

She couldn't believe he was saying things like that! "Ryker Thorpe is not the enemy. He is a very nice man."

Edward waited for her to continue, but when she hesitated, he rolled his eyes. "Do not tell me that you're falling in love with a lawyer. You know what that would do to your mother!"

Cricket pulled back, horrified at what might happen. "What's wrong with Mom?" she asked, instantly worried.

Her father continued to glower at her, but seeing the worry in her eyes, he relented slightly. "Nothing. Yet. But if she found out that you were sleeping around, she'd be very, very upset!"

Cricket swallowed painfully, trying not to let her father know how much that hurt. "Is Mom here?" she asked, hiding her face from his view.

Edward stared down at the back of his daughter's head, knowing she was close to tears. "She's in Rome right now, shopping I think."

Cricket's whole body froze and she looked up at her father, anxiety showing in the green depths. "Shopping-shopping? Or shopping for something…in particular that might not be…"

"She's just spending money, honey. Nothing nefarious." He pushed away from the counter and took her hands, lifting her up and giving her a gentle hug. "Don't worry about your Momma," he told her softly. "But don't put her in jeopardy by continuing to see this man. He's bad news. I can feel it in my bones."

Cricket felt like her heart was breaking. She wanted so desperately to tell her father that she would continue to see Ryker. She wanted him to understand that the man made her feel special and pretty, feminine. And the way he touched her! She'd never felt anything like this with another man. Even beyond the physical side of their relationship, she loved just talking to him.

But how could she be happy when that very happiness put her parents in danger? "He's a very nice man, Dad," she said with hope that he would understand.

His face was implacable. "He's part of the system. We've already had this conversation."

"You could stop stealing stuff," she offered hopefully. "Then it wouldn't be a problem for me to see Ryker." She would love it if her parents would change their occupation, or even just retire! What would be the harm in them stopping their projects?

Her dad pulled back and shook his head. "Gotta go, my love. I'll see you soon, okay?"

Cricket watched with growing resentment as her father walked out of her house. At least he unlocked the door this time. That was something. That's what she told herself anyway but it didn't soothe her aching heart at the thought of not seeing Ryker again.

She bent down to clean up the rest of the trashed groceries from the floor, salvaging what she could. And then, because she was so depressed about her father's demands, she took the saved box of Oreo cookies, plunked herself down in her favorite chair and ate cookies for lunch, ignoring all the healthy fruit and vegetables he'd provided for her. It was a petty, childish backlash, but it made her feel somewhat in control of her life.

When a whole line of Oreos were gone and she still didn't feel better, she knew there was only one thing she could do. It would help her get out of her doldrums and would clear her mind. With a smile of anticipation, she hurried up the stairs to her room and pulled on her "going out" clothes, then her jeans and sweatshirt over top of that. It was a cool evening and it would be an even colder night. Perfect for going out.

This was one reason she didn't condemn her parents so completely for their lifestyle. She knew the thrill of success and the excitement of planning. She stopped at the hardware store and got all of the equipment she would need, then hit the dollar store to get wrapping paper. The cashier looked at her somewhat strangely when she came up to the cash register with twenty rolls of various wrapping paper, but when she said, "It's a surprise for my boss," the cashier just smiled and rung up the various items.

She ran from store to store, gathering the other items she would need, careful to only spend cash and also to not buy too much in one place. The dollar store was the only exception and she knew that would be okay since people bought strange things from that place all the time for projects and parties and such.

She was humming as she strolled down the street, feeling like a normal person and hoping she looked like one. But inside, her mind was going through all the minute details, anticipating whatever new security Jason might have installed and going over the information she knew about the security guards' routines. She almost giggled out loud in anticipation!

It was finally dark enough for her exploration. She worked her way up the building, coming in from a different route this time. She looked around, her eyes surveying the equipment in place. There was a heat sensor installed now. That was pretty good, she thought. Heat sensors were very difficult to even perceive, much less circumvent, since their alarm was triggered when the heat in the room rose in any way. Normally, they were set to adjust for the thermostat's inability to keep the area at a constant temperature.

With shining eyes, she disabled the sensor and patched in a software program that would keep the alarm system from realizing that the sensors were down. Scooting forward, she disabled two more issues, and then looked around for any other issues.

When she felt safe enough, she went to work. It took her over an hour to accomplish everything but by the time she was slithering out, again on a different route from her entrance, and re-enabling all of the security systems, she felt enormously better.

CHAPTER 8

Cricket sighed as she got out of her car several days later. She wouldn't see Ryker today even though she knew he'd returned from Paris yesterday afternoon. He'd left her a message on her cell phone letting her know and asking her to meeting him for dinner.

She hadn't returned his phone call and this morning she was completely off schedule in order to avoid running into him. She should be brave and just call him back, explain that she couldn't see him anymore. But she knew what would happen when she heard his voice. She'd completely cave in and try to figure out a way to be with him without her father knowing.

It was pointless, she told herself. She needed to be firm, mostly with her own mind and body, both of which were craving just the sight of him. She'd love to curl up in his arms and feel those wonderful, tingling sensations that only he could give her. But she had to stay away from him.

Now if she could just stop thinking about him!

Rounding the corner to her office, she had come in the back way just to guarantee that she wouldn't….

She gasped as someone grabbed her arm and pulled her into one of the lobby hallways. She was just about to fight, her natural instincts rising up, when she realized that it was Ryker's hand and Ryker's body that was pressing her against the wall. And then she sighed with happiness when Ryker's mouth descended to hers and smothered whatever protest she was going to make. She kissed him back with all the emotions she'd been bottling up inside of her, eager to taste and feel him once again.

He lifted his head briefly to look down at her and she smiled up at him. "You're back!" she sighed, shifting her body against his and wishing desperately that it was still summer and she wasn't wearing this bulky coat. "I can't see you," she whispered, but her head tilted back, begging him to kiss her.

He must have felt the same way since his fingers moved away from her waist and deftly unbuttoned her coat, slipping his body closer and Cricket sighed with desire as she felt more of his hard angles and planes. "You feel wonderful," she whispered, her fingers clenching at his shoulders as if he might get away from her.

"Why didn't you call me back?" he said while his head dipped lower to kiss her neck.

She tilted her head to the side, enjoying the frizzle of excitement that shot down her body. "Because," was all she would say for an explanation. In her mind, she was trying to come up with a solution that would work with her father, but when he was touching her in this way, she wasn't able to think about anything other than his touch.

He bit her neck hard enough to make her gasp and jerk away, but not hard enough to hurt. "Give me a better reason," he growled in her ear.

"Because I can't see you," she said with a groan while her hands smoothed down his body from his shoulders to his stomach, teasing him in the same way he was doing to her on her neck.

He grabbed her hands before they could move any lower. "That's not really an explanation. Nor is it even going to work. We will be seeing each other."

She sighed and laid her head against the wall behind her. "We can't."

He chuckled. "You're going to have to give me a better explanation than that," he said and pressed his knee between her legs, causing her whole body to jerk in reaction. Her eyes closed. He pressed her hips against his leg, shifting ever so slightly until he caught her shudder in his arms. "What's going on Cricket?" he asked, holding her hips so she couldn't move away from him.

She bit her lip, trying to control her body's reaction but it was pointless. They'd spent only one night together but he already knew her body well enough, knew what she wanted and how to make her body hum with need.

"You're not playing fair," she whispered through clenched teeth.

"I don't ever play fair. Tell me what's going on."

"My father doesn't want us seeing each other."

His hands moved higher along the silk of her blouse, easily finding her nipples underneath the smooth material. His thumb was merciless as he flicked the peak to hardness. She tried to grab his hands and pull them away, but she was his sexual prisoner for the moment. "Your father can't control us, Cricket. You're an adult."

"You don't understand," she said, begging him with her eyes to stop torturing her like this.

Ryker sighed with frustration and need. He hadn't planned on seducing her in the hallway of her office building so he'd completely messed this up. But she hadn't called and she hadn't arrived at work at her normal time so he'd been frustrated and determined to know what had happened in the past three days. It hadn't ever occurred to him that her parents would interfere.

Unfortunately, he had a meeting and he knew she had to get to work. "Meet me for dinner tonight and we'll discuss it," he said, shifting his leg ever so slightly in the hopes that she would agree.

"I can't," she argued, but her body shifted again.

Ryker knew exactly what she was doing and if sex was the only way he could get to her, he'd use it. He wanted this woman, but he wanted more than just sex. He pulled his leg away and almost laughed with the frustrated look on her face. "Meet me for dinner and we'll continue this afterwards," he coaxed, bending down and going straight for that spot on her neck.

Cricket whimpered, her hands both holding him in place one moment, then wanting to push him away. Her fingers gripped his hair, unsure of which need was more overpowering, the one to make him stop or the one to make him finish what he'd started.

"I can't."

His fingers moved up to cup her breast once again, his thumb hovering over her nipple. "Just dinner, Cricket. No harm in meeting me for dinner."

Cricket held her breath, her whole body primed to feel his thumb on her nipple. But he didn't touch her, just hovered, driving her crazier than she'd ever thought possible.

"Dinner. Fine!" she screamed and was rewarded by his thumb flicking over her nipple again. It was both sweet and painful since there was no way to culminate this liaison and her need for him was making her crazy.

Ryker stepped back, his eyes hot with his own need shining through. "I'll pick you up," he said.

"No!" she gasped, not wanting her father to see Ryker arrive. "I'll meet you somewhere," she countered. "Just give me an address."

Ryker didn't like that suggestion. He wanted to pick her up and talk to her in the privacy of her house where they wouldn't be disturbed. He fully intended to take her out for dinner, but he wanted answers first. He could see in her eyes that she wasn't going to give in on this issue so he relented, wanting her company too much to argue. "Fine. Meet me at Simpson's at seven. Does that work for you?" he asked gently, wanting to grab her back into his arms and find a more private place to finish what he'd started, but that was impossible.

"Simpson's," she repeated and nodded her head to reinforce it. "Yes. Seven o'clock, I'll be there."

He watched her closely, seeing something in her eyes that worried him. "If you're not there, Cricket, I'll come to your house and wait until you arrive. I'm not giving up on you. And whatever is going on, we'll work through it."

She nodded numbly, but brushed past him as she hurried back to the main lobby area. She pressed the elevator call button with shaking fingers, eager to get up to her office and pull herself together again. Good grief, the man knew what he was doing!

Once she had the door to her office closed behind her, she took several deep breaths. Running her hand over the stacks of invoices and reports, she grounded herself in reality. Ryker was fantasy. This was real. This was what was important. Normalcy. Her parents. Ryker was a fling that could destroy her family. Her job and her parents, they would be with her forever.

Yes, she told herself firmly as she turned on her computer and logged into her e-mails, this was what she should be focusing on. She shouldn't have let him kiss her. She shouldn't have even spoken to him. If he did that again, she'd just press her hand against his chest to keep him away.

The image of his broad, muscular chest came to mind. And all the ways she'd touched that chest a few nights ago. He tasted so good. And he had that sexy indentation right under his breast plate. She'd run her finger over that place several times, fascinated with the area. He'd even shuddered when she'd kissed his flat nipples. She smiled at the memory and her body reacted.

"Who is he?" Josie asked, leaning against the door to her office.

Cricket jumped about a foot in the air, almost falling off of her chair at Josie's voice. She'd thought she was alone!

"Who's who?" she asked, grabbing onto the chair and pulling herself back into place. She smoothed her hair and laid her hands over the papers on her desk.

"Who is the guy you're thinking about?" she clarified, her eyes excited at the prospect.

"Is Jason in? Shouldn't we be working?" she asked.

"Jason is out of town this week so we have a quiet few days ahead of us," she explained with relish. She moved away from the doorway and came to sit down in her chair. "So spill it. Who's the guy?"

Cricket shrugged. "What guy?"

Josie laughed and shook her head. "The fact that you keep repeating that phrase only makes me more positive that you have a new guy in your life. So who is he?" she demanded. "Come on, give us a hint. I've been married for fifteen years and I have four kids. I have to live through your escapades and this is the first time I've heard of you doing anything other than working. So tell me!" she teased.

Cricket shook her head. "I'm not seeing anyone," she told Josie. And it was only partially a lie. She wasn't supposed to be seeing Ryker. And just because she'd agreed to meet him for dinner, that didn't mean she actually would get to the restaurant.

Besides, had she really seen him this morning? Only briefly, which technically counted, she guessed. But most of the time her eyes had been closed so she didn't feel like she was genuinely lying to her friend.

"If it wasn't a guy, what put that dreamy, star gazing look on your face?" she asked, not believing Cricket for a moment.

Cricket felt the blush coming up her neck and tried to stop it, but since she'd never felt this way about a man, she'd had no idea if it was even possible.

"You are! You're seeing someone!" she laughed, pointing at Cricket's now-pink cheeks. "Who is he?" she demanded, on the edge of her chair now. "Is he someone in this building?"

"No!" Cricket exclaimed, worried that Josie would follow her around and find out the truth. "Seriously, I'm not dating anyone." She made the assertion with a strong voice and prayed that Josie would believe her this time. She couldn't imagine how embarrassing it would be if anyone caught her doing what she and Ryker had been doing earlier this morning.

Josie clapped her hands excitedly. "Is he hot? Is he absolutely gorgeous? Or is he one of those geeky, cerebral types that make one think of dark, desperate poetry?"

Cricket stared at Josie for a long, pregnant moment before the woman's words sunk in. She laughed and leaned back in her chair, wondering how Josie ever came up with these ideas. "Josie, you read way too many romance novels."

"I know. Now stop changing the subject and tell me what he does for a living. Is he rich?" Her eyes narrowed as she watched for any reaction on Cricket's face. "No, he's probably one of those desperately poor men who are more earthy and yummy."

"Why do you think that?" she couldn't help but ask.

Josie grinned and bounced a little in her chair. "Because you're one of those extremely nice women who don't hurt any sort of living thing. So it would be natural for you to be attracted to someone who needs your sort of compassion and understanding."

Cricket blinked, wondering where Josie had gotten the idea that she was a nice person. She hadn't ever thought about that before, always striving just to be perceived as normal. "You think I'm nice?" she asked, feeling a startling sense of warmth seep through her body at the idea. She also had to laugh at the idea of Ryker Thorpe needing anyone's compassion or understanding. She didn't know him very well, but what she did know of him, she could tell that he wasn't the kind of man who would need anyone, much less their compassion. And understanding? He went his own way, forging his own path. People came to him for his understanding, not the other way around.

"Of course you're nice," Josie replied, rolling her eyes. "Probably too nice which is why you need to 'fess up and let me stalk your man for a little while, find out if he's good enough for you. I wouldn't want some creepy guy trying to spin you up into a frazzle and then dump you later on."

Cricket thought about Ryker's hands and mouth this morning. Yes, he'd definitely worked her up into a "frazzle" this morning. She blinked and refocused on Josie, shaking her head at the ridiculous thoughts she was having about Ryker. "I'm fine. And I'm just as boring as I was yesterday and the day before." That was a perfectly honest statement if she'd ever heard one. "And there's no guy in my life. I have a very obnoxious father who steps in whenever he thinks I'm dating someone so it's too hard right now. Maybe later," she told Josie, feeling her heart clench at the idea of never seeing Ryker again. But that was how it had to be.

Cricket's phone rang at that moment and their work day started. Just because their boss was out of the office didn't mean there wasn't work to be done. Cricket worked through the stacks of invoices on her desk, diligently ensuring they were all accurate and in the system to be paid. When she finished that stack, she pulled the second one forward, refusing to give in to the feeling of being a gerbil running around on an exercise wheel but never making any progress. This was what she wanted, she told herself. There wasn't anything more normal than accounting.

As she worked through her tasks that afternoon, her mind was frantically working out what she was going to do about dinner tonight. She'd told him that she was going to meet him, but that had been this morning. At that point, she'd had every intention of calling him up and canceling, then figuring out how to be away from her house so he couldn't find her there either. It was a cowardly instinct, but she hadn't figured out a better plan.

She sat in her office, contemplating her options. What she should do was just send him a message telling him that she wouldn't be able to meet him for dinner. No explanations, no apologies. She should simply break off all communications with him.

But she knew that she couldn't just leave him hanging like that. He deserved better treatment than that. She wasn't just attracted to him like crazy now. She respected him. She'd listened to him while they'd conversed and she suspected that he really was a brilliant, powerful lawyer and a good man. Those didn't come around very often.

It took her forty-five minutes to reach the restaurant, but only because she had to go around and backtrack. She suspected that she saw her father at one point, but she wasn't certain. By the time she arrived at the restaurant, she was flustered from walking so much and she was later than she'd anticipated. She stopped in the lobby, hurriedly slipping her running shoes off and putting her heels back on so Ryker wouldn't notice that she'd walked most of the way. She suspected that he would be furious with her about that and she didn't want to argue with him.

She was just turning around to speak to the hostess when Ryker stepped forward. One eyebrow was raised as he watched her shove her running shoes into her black bag.

"I just needed some exercise," she told him.

Ryker's eyebrow actually went a little higher and she bit her lip, hoping he wouldn't question her explanation. Because it didn't really make a lot of sense. Especially since he could have driven both of them, or she could have. They were right across the courtyard from each other.

No, this wasn't going to work, she told herself as she followed Ryker and the hostess to their table. When the waiter had taken their orders and disappeared once again, Cricket leaned back in her chair, knowing she had to end this but not sure how. She was becoming a yoyo, she thought miserably. One moment, she wanted to jump into his arms, the next moment she was so flustered at the idea of her father catching them, she was trying to figure out how to end the relationship that had barely started. She was a mess! She'd never been this pathetic before! Her father was driving her nuts!

She took a deep breath, ready to start the discussion but at the same moment, the wine steward arrived with the wine Ryker had ordered. She snapped her mouth shut and waited as patiently as possible while he went through the whole wine pouring process. When he was gone and they were once again alone, she took a long sip of the excellent wine. When she set it down again, he was already waiting for her, obviously knowing she had something to discuss.

"We can't see each other anymore," she finally said and then closed her eyes at how horrible that statement came out. She opened them again, trying to gauge his reaction. Oddly, he didn't look upset or irritated.

"Why is that?" he asked, leaning forward and looking at her across the linen covered tablecloth. The candlelight made his face look more angular, but softened those angles at the same time. Even his ice blue eyes looked lighter somehow.

Cricket tried to come up with a reason that would make sense, but how does one tell a magnificent, sexy, confident man that her father wouldn't approve of him? In Ryker's case, the idea was ludicrous.

"It's complicated," she finally blurted out.

"So un-complicate it and give me your reasons." He took a sip of wine. "It obviously isn't that we're not attracted to each other."

She flushed red with that comment since he was right. It was very hard for her to deny that she was attracted to him when she couldn't seem to stay out of his arms. And every time he held her, she was ravenous for him. "No. I think you're right about that being obvious."

"So what's the problem?"

Cricket held her wine glass as if it were a lifesaver. "I don't really have a traditional background," she said, knowing that wasn't enough of an explanation, but she wasn't sure what to say next without revealing something that would put him in an awkward situation and her parents in prison.

"Tell me about it," he encouraged patiently. When she still hesitated, he started to tell her stories about growing up as the oldest of four boys. Cricket was so captivated by his stories, she forgot to get him to understand why she couldn't see him any longer.

"So when your parents died, all of your brothers were already in college?" she asked, fascinated.

"Yes. At various levels and all over the country."

"And you flew out to each of them to tell them the news in person." She'd already figured that out from some of the other things he'd said.

"Yes. And brought them all back for the funeral."

"That must have been hard since they were in the four corners of the country. How did you do it in time?"

Ryker smiled slightly. "Despite our growing years and the antics the three younger ones got into during high school, they're all pretty responsible."

"So they just got on the plane with you and came back?"

"Basically, yes."

She nodded her head, more impressed with him every time she spoke to him. "And you were dealing with your own grief the whole time."

"Getting my brothers back home helped a lot."

"And now you all work together. How did the four of you end up becoming lawyers?"

He smiled, remembering some of the arguments in their household about the subject. "We might all be lawyers, but we specialize in different kinds of law. For instance, Xander does family law, which basically translates into him being a damn fine divorce attorney."

She cringed, thinking of what kind of an impact that would have psychologically on a single man. "So he sees the worst in most relationships, doesn't he?"

"Yes. I didn't want him going into that area. I knew it would be hard on him."

"What kind of impact has it had on him now? He's a year younger than you, right?"

"Yes. But he's twenty years more cynical about marriage and relationships. And he's in love with someone but won't go near her because he's afraid it will turn out like the marriages he's hired to help end."

"I guess some of his cases become pretty bitter, don't they?"

Ryker nodded sagely. "Some of them, yes. There have been physical battles he's had to break up when the husband and wife start tearing into each other."

She cringed, picturing the problems that would create. "Why did he choose to go into that area anyway?"

"He dated a lot of girls in high school and college, several of whom weren't…" he hesitated, trying to come up with the right way to express Xander's female problems.

"Moral?" she offered, starting to see the issue. "Honest? Ethical? Are you trying to beat around the bush and tell me that he dated women who cheated on their boyfriends?"

"Not intentionally. At least not at first. Xander was the kind of guy who is charming and laughs a lot. Women are drawn to him like flies to honey. And he loves them all right back. But when he discovered that some of them had promised themselves to another guy, he was devastated that he'd broken up their relationship. He had a sort of….reputation for being…"

Cricket smiled, realizing he was trying to be honest but still keep his brother's confidences. "Good in bed?" she offered again. "Like you?"

Ryker winked at her but nodded. "My dating habits would be pathetic when compared to Xander's previous lifestyle."

She nodded, knowing that would be a hard place to be. "But your other brothers are okay, right?"

Ryker smiled. "None of us wanted Ash to get into criminal law. But he's just as stubborn. He wanted to help the underdog."

"And what happened to him?" she asked.

"He got his eyes opened. He's still an excellent criminal defense attorney but he doesn't have that doe eyed idealism he once had. He takes a lot of pro-bono cases though. Especially when he hears that someone is being beaten down by the legal system and can't afford a good attorney."

"And does that cause friction among the four of you?" she asked, already knowing the answer.

"Not at all. We all take pro bono cases. More than we're required to take but we back each other up. Especially when there's a personal issue involved."

The waiter took their dinner plates away and she felt slightly bereft, not sure what to do with her hands now. Eating the meal had acted as a sort of buffer. And Ryker had carried the conversation while trying to demonstrate that he'd also had a non-traditional upbringing. But he had no idea what he was getting into with her family. Now she fiddled with her wine glass, wondering how to completely break things off with him.

"Anyway…" she started to say. The waiter interrupted her once again with the largest, most decadent piece of chocolate cake she'd ever seen. And it wasn't just a chocolate cake. There was fudge, chocolate whip cream, more fudge and dark, chocolate cake that looked so moist it might as well have been fudge or pudding. "You didn't," she breathed, her mouth already watering just at the sight of the dessert in between the two of them.

"I did," he teased and handed her one of the forks the waiter had placed next to the plate. "You looked stressed about pretending you don't want to see me anymore. I thought this might help break through the tension."

Cricket couldn't believe how rich and amazing the dessert tasted. With her first bite, she closed her eyes as if she were in heaven. "Oh my," she sighed. "This is amazing!"

He took a bite as well, chuckling at her glazed over eyes. "I'm glad you like it."

They sat there and ate the dessert and Cricket loved every decadent, fattening moment of it. "I'm going to have to run a few extra miles tomorrow to work this off," she said as she leaned back in her chair and wiped her mouth delicately with her linen napkin.

Ryker signed the check the waiter had brought. "I'll make sure you don't have to run those extra miles," he said and took her hand, lifting her out of her chair easily.

Cricket grabbed her purse and followed, not sure what he meant by that statement. But as soon as they were in the lobby and he'd handed the valet his ticket, he took her into his arms and kissed her. This one wasn't anything like the other two they'd shared this morning. It felt more powerful, more deliberate. And she melted just like the chocolate, clinging to him as if he were the only normal part of her world.

The valet cleared his throat, standing awkwardly behind the two of them.

Ryker pulled away, a satisfied look in his eyes when he noticed that her eyes were glazed over once again, this time from his kiss and not the chocolate cake. "Let's go," he said and took her hand, handing her into his luxurious car.

They were already driving away by the time Cricket could think properly. "Where are we going?" she asked, nervous all of a sudden.

"We're heading to my place," he said and took her hand, bringing it over so that their fingers were intertwined, but the part that made her mind go blank was the way he laid their hands on his thigh. She could feel the muscles move every time he switched from the accelerator to the brake. She didn't realize she was doing it, but she stared at their hands, or at his thigh, the entire way out to his place. Since he lived relatively close by, it was a fast trip. The next thing she knew, he was pulling into a garage, and then she was in his arms. She didn't even hesitate when he lifted her out of her seat, his expert hands already dispensing with her seat belt so she could land on his lap.

The moment he touched her in private, she was out of control. She couldn't worry about her father or possible prison issues when Ryker touched her. The differences in their backgrounds faded to nothing. She'd wanted this all day long.

From the first moment he'd touched her this morning, she'd been craving his touch. All those sensors that had been suppressed after her father's visit woke up fully now, more demanding than they'd ever been.

The first time they'd come together, it had been frantic and demanding. This time, there was an urgency that she couldn't slow down. In the back of her mind, there was the possibility that this might be the last time she saw him. She needed him. All of him. Now!

He tore his mouth away, looking down at her in the dim light of the garage light but she could see that he was feeling the same urgency that she was. "Get out of the car, Cricket," he ordered her.

He left her a fraction of a second after that but by the time she realized what was going on, he was already on her side of the vehicle. He reached in and lifted her out of her seat. He didn't stop there. With demanding hands that only turned her on more, he lifted her against him, and then pressed her back against the side of the car. She didn't wait around to figure out what he might do. With shaking fingers, she ripped his tie out of the way then worked on the buttons of his dress shirt. When she finally got several buttons undone, she sighed with happiness as her fingers were able to touch his heated skin. But at that same moment, he freed her breasts from her bra. Her arms were still tangled up in both her shirt and her bra, but she didn't care. His mouth was already latching onto her nipple and she screamed out with the intense heat of his mouth there combined with the cool, night air that was in the garage.

His hand reached down and pushed her skirt up, ripping her underwear off. When she felt his finger inside her, she couldn't believe how perfect it felt. "Yes!" she sighed, closing her eyes and leaning her head back once again against the top of the car. But it wasn't enough. "More," she demanded. "Please, Ryker. Don't stop," she gasped and shifted her hips, trying to move in the way that she'd learned just a few days ago that caused so much pleasure.

And then his finger was gone! She opened her eyes, almost growling with the need to have him back there, moving inside her. She heard the foil wrapper and wanted to help him, but her arms were trapped in her blouse and bra. All she could do was hold on to his waist with her legs while his hands pushed the condom onto his erection. A moment later, his large hands were back on her hips and he didn't hesitate to fill her up. Completely!

She gasped, moving against him. The urgency only intensified as he moved deeper inside her. "More," she begged of him. And he delivered. She was already splintering apart by his third or fourth stroke. It didn't take much more before he was also pounding into her with his own climax. It was so intense, so mind-blowing, that Cricket was sure she was going to pass out from pleasure.

When her breathing had finally returned to a somewhat normal pace, she opened her eyes and looked around. Her arms were still around his neck and she thought she might be strangling him. But then she felt his feather-light kisses along her shoulders and neck and smiled because he wasn't about to asphyxiate.

"Sorry," she choked out and released the stranglehold she had on his neck.

She relaxed when she heard his chuckle. "Please don't apologize for anything, Cricket. In fact," he lifted his head and kissed her gently, "I think we might be able to do that again, but better, once we're inside."

She smiled, unable to hide her happiness after that kind of release. "I don't think I want to do it any better," she countered. "I thought I'd killed you that last time."

He threw back his head and laughed, continuing to hold her in his strong arms. "Please. I'd love to be killed like that over and over again."

He pulled back and they straightened their clothing, but he took her hand and led her through his house, straight up to his bedroom. There, he undressed her slowly, kissing every part of her gently until she was writhing underneath him once again. He took her slower this time, pulling out of her almost all the way until she begged him to come back to her. Over and over again, he took her just to the edge, but wouldn't let her fall. She was almost crying with her need before he allowed her to climax in his arms. And he was right along with her. Cricket felt him come with her and thought he was the most incredible man she'd ever met in her life.

As she lay in his arms that night, feeling his fingers stroke her gently, she worked out in her mind a plan that might allow her to enjoy his company for a little while longer. It would be difficult, but if she were extremely creative and careful, maybe she could pull it off.

For the next three weeks, she snuck around in an effort to be with Ryker without her father becoming aware. She was with him every evening and all weekend when possible but she'd never spend the night, always leaving his warm, comfortable bed about ten o'clock so she could get home at what might be a reasonable hour. She knew he was exasperated with her but she couldn't shake the feeling that her father was still around and would intervene if he found out who she was with.

CHAPTER 9

By Saturday night of that week, Ryker was fed up with her nervousness and he was irritated that she insisted on sleeping alone. The only time she wasn't looking behind her or jumping when he came up on her too quietly was when she was in his bed. He also suspected that she wasn't in this relationship for the long term. He'd never been able to discuss the future because every time he'd brought it up, she'd changed the subject quickly.

But that was going to end. He wanted this woman in his life forever. Whatever was holding her back, he was going to fix it and eliminate the issue.

"Okay, what's going on?" Ryker demanded as soon as they stepped into his house after dinner that night.

Cricket turned away from the window where she'd been trying to determine if they'd been followed. At his angry outburst, she blinked and looked up at him. "What do you mean?" she asked, already worried that she'd been too obvious.

Ryker took her hand and led her deeper into the house, setting her purse to the side of the couch while he pulled her down next to him. "Cricket, we've been sneaking around the streets of Chicago for too long. Anytime I want to talk to you, I have a new phone number to call. We always meet at out of the way places first instead of just going to your place or coming here to mine. And there isn't a moment when you aren't looking behind the cab or in my rear view mirror, as if you're trying to find out if someone is following us." He paused before he continued with, "Are you in some sort of trouble?"

Cricket actually laughed at that idea. "No. I can honestly say that I have committed no crimes for which I am running from the law," she said with a smile. She scooted closer to him, feeling his heat and enjoying the way his arms automatically wrapped around her shoulders protectively.

"So why all this cloak and dagger stuff?" he asked, relaxing back against the cushions of the deep sofa. Instinctively, he knew that something was seriously wrong, something that was keeping her from committing to him completely. But for the life of him, he couldn't figure out what it was. She was jumpy and nervous and he was damn well going to fix anything that might harm her. He'd never felt protective towards any of the women he'd dated in the past. But Cricket was different. He'd known that from the first moment he'd laid eyes on her and he wasn't going to let anything happen to her.

For the moment, he relaxed though. She was in his arms and she was safe. He had a security system in his house that was state of the art. So if anyone were trying to break in, he'd know about it before they got too close.

"What's cloak and dagger about what we've been doing?" she asked, running her hand along his thigh to distract him. She knew he was becoming impatient with her, which meant she only had a little longer to be with him before he called it quits. No one could put up with her kind of behavior for long. He'd move on to a woman who didn't have her complications.

She knew it had only been a short time, but she also knew that she was head over heels in love with Ryker Thorpe. She'd known from the start that she needed to protect herself from just this sort of occurrence, but the man was just too wonderful to not fall in love with. Every moment with him she considered a gift. Something to be cherished and stored as a memory of their time together. In too short a time, he would find someone new and she'd need all the memories to keep her warm. Because she knew she'd never find anyone as wonderful, sexy, intelligent and funny as Ryker.

Ryker sighed. "The burner phones," he started off and felt her stiffen in his arms which told him he was right on target, "the meandering drives through streets where we double back to make sure someone isn't following us, the out of the way restaurants where you're less likely to be recognized…they all add up to a person who is trying to hide something." He waited a moment then said, "What are you hiding, Cricket? I can help you if you'll just trust me."

She moved over so she was sitting on his lap. "There are some things you just can't fix," she said, then bent to kiss him tenderly. It was the first time she'd ever initiated any kind of touch. Normally, he was the one who kissed her, pulled her into his arms or even just held her hand while they were walking somewhere. It startled him initially, but she knew him well enough, knew his body and how to distract him. He'd done it often enough to her lately, although she didn't think he'd done it as deliberately as she was now doing to him. She had a small pang of guilt over her actions, but then his hands came up to cup her breasts and she wasn't able to think any more than he could.

A long time later, Ryker leaned over her. "You did that on purpose, didn't you?" he asked. He might have been angry about it another time, but she just felt too good in his arms right now.

"Did what?" she asked, running her fingers over his arms, then down his chest. If it had worked once, surely it could work again.

Unfortunately, this time he wasn't playing her game. Grabbing her fingers, he rolled over so that he had her trapped underneath him, pressing his knee between her legs so she was thoroughly under his control. To further tease her, he pulled the sheet down from her chest – not allowing her to cover up. "Now that you are subdued…" he reached over to his bedside table and pulled something out of the drawer.

She knew what he normally pulled out from that drawer and she smiled in anticipation. But what he was holding definitely wasn't what she'd been expecting. "I know we've known each other for only a short time, but…" he opened the square, black box and Cricket gasped at the stunning diamond ring that was revealed. "Will you marry me?" he asked softly, watching her to try and gauge her reaction.

Her fingers shook as she reached out, barely touching the diamond ring. It was possibly the most beautiful diamond she'd ever seen in her life, and that was saying a lot due to her mother's past.

She didn't say anything for a long time, just stared, unaware that her mouth was open and there were tears forming on her lashes.

"Should I take the absence of a rejection as an acceptance?" he teased, taking the ring out of the box and sliding it down her finger. "I love you, Cricket. I know you have secrets, but I'll eventually get you to trust me enough and we'll figure them out together."

Cricket shook her head, her eyes never leaving the gorgeous diamond that was now on her finger. She couldn't believe it. He wanted to marry her?

"You can't mean this," she said, reaching out to touch the ring with her other hand. Shaking her head, she turned to face him. She could barely see him through her tears, but since he was less than a foot away, his face was only a little bit fuzzy.

"I do mean it. I want you to marry me. I want to have kids with you and grow old with you and I want to live and laugh with you."

She shook her head. "You don't know me. You don't know my family," and she cringed with those words. They were too close to the real problem. "And don't you need someone who is a bit more…" she couldn't figure out how to say it.

"I don't want anyone more anything, Cricket. I've wanted you ever since I first saw you."

"No," she denied. She grasped onto the one reason they wouldn't work that she could openly discuss. "You need a more social person. I'm not. I don't like going out and attending parties. I don't like the social whirl that you need in your business. I like staying home and being with close friends. I can barely form words when I'm around someone who intimidates me. You should know. I was like that with you the first time we met. In fact, I think I ran away."

Ryker laughed. "That you did," he confirmed. "But I thought you were cute. And yes, I have to socialize for my business, but not nearly as much as you might think. Besides, I have three other brothers who can do that for a while. We can stay home and practice making babies," he said with a lascivious grin. Then he moved his hand moved down her waist to her hip. And then lower.

A long time later, Cricket lay in his arms, listening to his deep, even breathing as he slept, his arms wrapped around her as if he couldn't release her, even in his sleep. She knew exactly how he felt, she thought, running her fingers down his arm, reveling in the rough feeling of the hair on his forearm and the muscles on his shoulder that were bulging even in his sleep.

Cricket knew she couldn't accept his proposal. She looked down at the ring on her finger, twinkling even in the darkness. It was more beautiful because it wasn't just a ring. It had meaning. It was an important message he wanted to convey to her. And because of that, it was more precious than anything she'd ever owned.

Cricket pulled on her clothes, ignoring the tears streaming down her cheeks as she looked down at the man sleeping on the bed right next to where she'd been a moment ago. This would have to be the last time she saw him. It would even be better to find a new job just so she wouldn't be tempted to spy on him while he walked from his office building to his car.

She wiped her cheeks mercilessly as she picked up her purse. She went directly to his security system and plugged in the code, then re-armed it before slipping out the door. She might be leaving him, but she also wanted him safe in his house. Not that the alarm would keep out a serious intruder, but she doubted anyone like that was lurking about at this point in the pre-dawn morning.

She didn't call a cab until she'd walked several blocks down the street, getting strange looks from several others who were driving by. This wasn't the kind of neighborhood where a person walked places. At least not unless they were wearing exercise clothes. The people of this neighborhood walked only for cardiovascular health, otherwise driving cars worth six figures to and from their destinations.

Ryker heard the door close and rolled over, sighing as he tried to figure out what was going on with Cricket. Damn her! She had him tied up in knots worrying about her safety and what she was going to do or say next.

He looked around and breathed a sigh of relief that at least she was still wearing his ring. That was something, at least. Of course, it was no guarantee that she wouldn't hand it back to him as soon as he got into the office today.

As he stared up at the ceiling, he decided then and there that it was time to be a bit more proactive about the lovely lady. He knew she wasn't a criminal, which only meant that she was running away or trying to hide from someone who was less than savory in their daily dealings with the law.

Tossing the covers aside, he decided to go ahead and get ready for the day. He was too angry to sleep any longer and his mind was already plotting to corner his lovely new fiancée and get the information he needed. He suspected she was trying to leave him, but there was no way he was going to allow that. As he showered and dressed, he formed a plan, one that would hopefully result in Mark helping him protect the little lady until he could get her down the aisle.

He also thought about calling an old friend. Mitch Hamilton ran one of the best security firms in the world. They'd been college buddies a long time ago and had kept up with each other over the years. He'd recently married a woman named Claire, he remembered. Maybe Mitch could get together for drinks and offer some advice. Ryker decided to give Mitch a call as soon as he got into the office. He could fly down this afternoon for drinks with him and be back in time to be back in bed with Cricket before she fell asleep for the night. Or even better, maybe he could wake her up!

In the meantime, Ryker knew he had a lot to get in place before the stubborn woman got to work. He'd have to tell his brothers, he supposed. That would be an irritating conversation under the circumstances. He smiled as he thought about the expressions on their faces, almost laughing at how stunned he knew they would all be.

Well, maybe not. Ash had mentioned that his work defending Mia Paulson was important. Although, last time he checked, Ash hadn't figured out how important. Ryker realized that he'd been so caught up in what was happening with Cricket, he hadn't really checked in with his brothers lately. They'd all been going separate ways.

Something occurred to him suddenly. Autumn and Xander hadn't been sniping at each other as often as normal lately. He wondered if something had finally happened between the two of them. And Axle, come to think of it, had been acting strangely yesterday. Yes, something was definitely going on.

He finished showering and grabbed a towel, wrapping one around his waist and using another to dry his hair as he walked to his closet and considered the possibility that perhaps his brother had finally ignored his irritating resistance to being with Autumn and might have done something about it.

He certainly hoped so.

CHAPTER 10

Unfortunately, Ryker's plan was foiled by a very adept woman. He'd gone into the office, only to find that Cricket wasn't there. He called her cell phone several times, left messages but she never called him back. When he called the receptionist's desk at her company, he was told that Cricket had called in sick to work.

She didn't answer her home phone, so he continued to leave messages on her cell phone and her work phone. But by the end of the day, he hadn't heard from her.

As he was driving to her house, he received a text message that just about blew his mind. "I love you. But we can't be together," was all she said. No explanation for why they couldn't be together, no final goodbye. Nothing!

Ryker read the message but continued on to her house. There was no way he was going to allow her to get away with something like that.

But when he pulled up outside of her house, it was dark. He knocked on her door, but there was no answer. It was as if she'd simply disappeared. If it weren't for that text message, he would be worried.

As it was, he drove back to his place and poured himself a tumbler of scotch, pacing back and forth in his living room and bedroom, becoming even more furious that she'd pulled this stunt. The pacing continued until nearly midnight when he fell asleep on his couch, unable to sleep in his bed without her with him. But as his eyes faded closed, his mind went over all the things he was going to do to punish her for putting him through this kind of hell.

Never, not even in the darkest part of the night, did he allow the possibility that she would get away from him. No, that wasn't even an option.

By the end of the week, he was still fuming, but he'd taken on a different tactic. He still called her each day, but only to tell her how much he loved her as well. And to explain that he wasn't giving up on their relationship. When he flew out to Barcelona Wednesday, he called her and told her he'd be gone for two days but that he loved her. When he left Barcelona and made a stop for one of his clients in London, he called her up and told her what was going on, and that he still loved her, that he was waiting for her to come tell him what the problem was.

During that whole time, Cricket sent him one more message. "I love you, but it's just impossible," was all she texted.

Ryker smiled at the message as he walked into a meeting with his London client, shaking his head at how naïve she was.

"Twelve more hours, Love" he texted right back to her, then sat down and discussed the issue that had brought him here, all the while, thinking of what he was going to do to her when he got back to Chicago.

Cricket read the words and just about broke down in tears. She'd called in sick for the past two days but when she heard that Ryker would be out of the country, she pulled herself out from under her covers, showered and forced herself to go into the office. She knew she looked horrible, with red rimmed eyes from crying, her face looked gaunt because she'd barely eaten anything more than a glass of milk or cookies for the past three days. But the idea of food made her stomach turn over.

She wanted Ryker's arms around her so badly, her body actually ached.

If only she could figure out how to protect her parents while still seeing Ryker, she would do it. But she couldn't come up with a plan, or even an explanation for what her parents do for a living, that Ryker could believe. Well, she could if she were willing to lie to him. But she simply couldn't do that. She loved him so much and she couldn't sully those feelings with a lie. So the only alternative was for her to simply break things off with him.

Josie stopped by her office Wednesday. "How are you..." she stopped midsentence when she caught sight of Cricket's pale face and sad eyes. "You're still sick, aren't you?"

Cricket took a deep breath and nodded her head. She was sick from missing Ryker and that definitely counted in her mind. She couldn't respond verbally because her throat was raw from crying.

Josie shook her head and sat down in front of Cricket's desk. "You probably shouldn't be here," she said. "Why don't you go home and rest for another few days?"

Cricket picked up a tissue and pretended to blow her nose. "I can work," she finally said, hiding her teary eyes behind the tissue until she had herself under control. She didn't want to go home because all she did was think about Ryker and how much she missed him. At least here, she could think about something other than how much she wanted to be with him.

Josie shook her head. "I don't think you should be here. But Jason's been out of town for a while so at least you don't have to deal with his wrath." She stood up and looked down at the younger woman. "If you need anything, just give me a ring, okay?"

Cricket nodded her head and pulled a stack of invoices closer, blinking rapidly to control the next bout of tears. Damn her father! He could do anything and she'd be able to be with Ryker without any concern of her father or mother being imprisoned.

She picked up her phone and thought about calling her mother. If there was ever a time when she needed her mother's shoulder to cry on, it was now. But in the end, she put the phone down again and forced herself to work through the invoices that needed to be paid. Her mother would rush out here and pat her on the back, but Cricket's father was right. There really wasn't any way that they could continue to do what they did and for her to marry Ryker. The two words were opposite. Something had to give.

But why was she always the one that had to make the adjustments, she thought angrily as she pounded the keyboard, entering data into the accounting system. She'd grown up adjusting to their lifestyle! Wasn't it about time they started adjusting to hers? Her fingers clutched at the ring dangling from the chain around her neck, feeling the beautiful diamond as if it were the most precious thing in the world to her. She even rubbed her finger where she'd been wearing it for the past three days. Her finger felt bare, naked, without the ring. She wanted so badly to put it back on her finger, but she shook her head and forced herself to focus on her work.

She had to get over Ryker, she told herself firmly. She'd have to mail his ring back to him but the thought of not having it either on her finger or close to her heart brought up a new bout of tears and she mercilessly pushed them away.

She was exhausted by the end of the day. She thought about calling in sick the following day, but since Ryker was still in Spain, she knew she should push through and get work done. But that night, sitting at home in her tiny den, she tearfully composed a letter of resignation. She'd have to quit. She accepted that now. She'd immediately start looking for a new job, but she'd leave her current position even if she didn't have another one lined up.

She had the resignation letter in her purse for the next several days, but didn't turn it in. She kept finding excuses to not submit it, feeling a strange sense of relief at the end of each day when her supervisor walked out and the opportunity to hand in her resignation was gone.

CHAPTER 11

Walking into the building the following week, Mark caught Ryker at the door to his office. "What's up?" Ryker asked, sitting down behind his desk. His mind was flipping through all the cell phone numbers Cricket had given him over the past few weeks, trying to guess which one he was going to try this time. On the flight back from Europe, his mind had changed from anger, to one of anticipation. Cricket's text messages told him loud and clear that she loved him. There was no ambiguity there. The only question was why she felt they couldn't be together. So until he heard her explanation, he wasn't going to give up. He'd come up with a plan and he was going to get through to her, solve whatever problem she thought might be hindering their relationship and get her down the aisle.

Mark smiled eagerly. "Remember that Jason Moran fellow who was getting pranked sporadically?"

Ryker smiled at the memory, immediately picturing Cricket in his mind since she worked for the ass. "Yes. I seem to recall the visit." That was another problem he was going to resolve. Cricket hated her job. He'd help her figure out what she wanted to do, other than accounting.

"Well, I went through his security and computer systems and he seemed to just keep on adding on new high tech gadgets to try and slow this person down." Mark put his laptop down on Ryker's desk. "So a few weeks ago, I added in a few new things but also went low tech as well. And here's what I caught on what's basically a nanny-cam. Those are just small video cameras that parents put into teddy bears to catch the babysitter doing something wrong," he clarified. When Ryker nodded, he pressed a button on his computer. "I put the small camera into a picture frame that was already on his desk and here's what I caught on camera. I'm not sure when this occurred since I was only monitoring the high tech stuff. I picked up the camera last night and was looking at it at home."

Ryker watched the black and white screen carefully, not really interested in catching the person but wanting to clear the issue out of his schedule so he could pass Jason off to someone else in his department. Everything was still for several seconds, but then a movement caught his eye. Something was happening in the ceiling. It was very slow, very subtle, as if the culprit were checking things out before moving anything too quickly. But once the culprit realized that everything was okay, the ceiling tile was pushed out of place and a sexy, very feminine, black-clad body appeared to lithely drop from the ceiling to the floor. Unfortunately, as soon as the figure dropped down, Ryker's gut clenched. And it just got worse the more he watched.

The person in the video was completely masked and dressed all in black, but the form-fitting clothes showed off the culprit's figure. And it was a body he knew extremely well. In fact, he had been holding that body against his only a week ago.

Mark chuckled when the figure wrapped up several pieces of the client's office furniture in wrapping paper, thinking it was a hilarious joke, but Ryker didn't find any of it very amusing. In fact, the more he watched, the angrier he became.

So his little fiancée was a cat burglar? In this instance, she hadn't stolen anything, but what about the other times?

When the woman easily lifted herself back through the ceiling, Mark shut down the video and stood up straight, a huge grin on his face. "This still doesn't give us the person, or even a face. Whoever is doing this is smart. Brilliant, actually."

Sitting back in his leather chair, Ryker considered all aspects of the issue. If Cricket were ever discovered, he could argue that she hadn't actually done any breaking and entering since she was an employee of the company. Jason had issued badges to his employees that would give them access to the building at all times of the day and night. Ryker knew he could argue that those badges gave his employees the ability to enter. Cricket just chose a less conventional method of entry. And she hadn't stolen anything of value.

Just at that moment, an image struck him of something he'd seen in her bedroom a while ago. He'd asked her about the glass vase filled with pens that she kept on the floor of her bedroom. At the time, Cricket had said she just hated to be without pens but he now suspected that those pens were stolen property of Jason's firm.

Were they of significant value? He didn't think so. And if Jason took her to court, Ryker knew he could put the issue of the stolen items in front of the jury and Jason would be laughed out of court. He suspected there wasn't a person in the country who hadn't purposely or inadvertently stolen a pen from a hotel, office or business at least once in their life. Hell, he even had a drawer filled with pens from various places despite the fact that he kept a very good writing device in his jacket pocket.

"Have you shown this to Jason yet?" Ryker asked, his mind working, the wheels spinning.

"Not yet. I was going to call him this morning." Mark picked up his laptop, feeling pretty proud of himself.

Ryker moved his hands so they were forming a pyramid, his eyes looking over the top into nothing in particular. As he thought through all the ramifications, his index fingers tapped together. "Hold off on that for a while. We might have a conflict of interest on this issue," he said. He was already picking up his phone and dialing a number. He just hoped she'd pick up when he called this time.

Mark didn't argue, already experienced enough with the Thorpe brothers that he knew there often was more to the issue than he understood. He simply nodded his head and picked up his laptop, heading out of Ryker's office.

Cricket picked up the phone without thinking about it, feeling morose after a long, horrible weekend where she'd sat on her bed, ate popcorn and watched romantic movies by herself. Her father had called five or six times, but she was too angry with him to pick up the phone. And what was worse, Ryker had stopped calling as well.

She was miserable and irritated by her job in particular and life in general. So she forgot to look at the caller ID before answering the phone this time. "Cricket Fairchild," she said with as much enthusiasm as she could muster, which wasn't very much.

Ryker's jaw clenched. "I thought you'd lost this phone?" he challenged, wishing she were here in front of him so he could see her pretty green eyes as she lied to him.

Cricket's heard jumped into her throat as she heard his deep, sexy voice. She could also picture his angry, blue eyes and had a bit of trouble breathing for several moments. "I found it," she quickly fabricated. "What's going on?" It sounded so good to hear his voice. Her fingers clenched the phone desperately.

"Besides the fact that you snuck out of my house last week before five in the morning without saying goodbye, disappeared from my life, tried to push me away and have ignored my phone calls and every voice mail for the past seven days?"

There was a slight hesitation before she said, "I..." she started to say something, then stopped, her mind drawing a blank on what she could possibly explain. The only thought that popped into her mind was how much she loved him and missed him. Not seeing him over the past week had been painful but she closed her eyes, trying to be strong. She couldn't give in to the temptation to see him again. She was in too deep already.

"Don't even try to lie to me," he said with that smooth, silky voice that forewarned her that he wasn't fooling around. "I'll get to the truth eventually. And we will be together. Don't doubt that for a moment."

Cricket sighed, rubbing her forehead as a headache slowly inched up the back of her neck. Traffic was painful today and everyone seemed to be trying to get into her lane. She wished she could just turn to the right and drive to his house, but she couldn't take any more time off of work. Besides, she had to submit her letter of resignation and start getting over Ryker. As if that were possible, she thought with dread. "Ryker, you don't understand," she replied, trying to calm him down.

He took a deep breath, trying to regain his famous control. But the idea of her not telling him something, something that seemed to have the power to scare her, infuriated him because he felt powerless to help her, protect her. And it made him even angrier that she wouldn't confide in him. "You're right. I don't understand. But you're going to explain it to me as soon as you get into the office today. No more avoiding me or ignoring my messages. We're going to talk, Cricket." He looked at his watch to see the time. "I'm guessing you'll be here in about five minutes?" he suggested, assuming she was on her normal schedule.

She heard the strange undertones in his voice and reacted to that, her stomach clenching in fear. "Yes. I'm almost there, but what's going on?" Had he discovered what her parents did for a living? Did he have some information that could hurt them in some way? She went through all she knew of their projects but she was drawing a blank since she didn't talk to her parents about their "work" any longer, not wanting to hear about it.

"Come to my office instead of going to yours," he told her firmly. "We need to talk."

Cricket hung up the phone, her mind whirling in an attempt to figure out how she was going to get through this conversation with Ryker. She realized suddenly that she'd just stopped talking to him as a way to break things off, because a formal conversation where she stood in front of him and told him she couldn't see him any longer would be too painful. She might not have even gotten the words out.

Also, not having that conversation kept up the pretense that she was still with him, that she might be able to go back to him. It was a silly dream, but she'd kept it secretly burning in her heart. Maybe that was why she'd told him that she loved him. Maybe she'd been subconsciously hoping she could figure out a way to make her relationship with her parents and her lover work out.

That had been an epic failure, she realized.

She pulled into the parking garage and sat in her car, her whole body shaking with tension.

She bit her lip and tried to stifle the sob that almost burst out of her. Looking down at her hand, she gently touched the beautiful diamond he'd given her last week. She put it on her finger when she was alone, but slipped it onto the chain around her neck whenever she was around others. She'd already determined that she had to give it back to him. She just liked the idea of being his woman for a little while, pretending that she was still his when she was alone and the darkness surrounded her, when she couldn't stop the tears any longer and there was no one to witness them anyway.

She slipped the ring up and down her finger an inch, the metal now warm from her body heat. She tried to take it off, but her fingers just couldn't do the job. It wasn't that it didn't fit and was now too tight. It was only that she wanted to keep it on her finger.

She'd wear it until she got to his office, then take it off once she was there. Just so she didn't lose it, she told herself. It was a beautiful diamond, outstanding quality and color. But more than that, it was special to her.

She stepped out of her car and was about to walk across the courtyard and into Ryker's building but a flash of something caught her eye. She looked to the left where the flash had come from, but she didn't see anything out of the ordinary. Trying to look casual, she took several steps, still trying to determine what had flashed or what was causing her instincts to flare up with concern. She'd been taught by her father always to trust her instincts and right now, her instincts were screaming for her to run.

Had someone followed her? She didn't want Ryker involved in anything her father or mother might have done so if they'd angered someone, Ryker could be in danger. And that someone might be following her in order to get to her parents. Especially since her father seemed to be hanging around her house and office too often lately. How he knew what she was doing all the time, Cricket had no idea, but it had to stop. Especially if his activities were putting Ryker in danger!

The hairs on the back of her neck were standing up in protest. Something was definitely wrong! Instead of going to his office, she adjusted her path and headed to the deli instead. She grabbed a cup of coffee, then went directly to her own building and up into her office. Generally, she never came to the deli to purchase a cup of coffee since the coffee wasn't exceptionally good and, except when Jason was on a rampage, there was always a pot of free coffee in the office kitchen. Also not very good, but it was caffeinated which is all most people needed. In this instance, however, she was using her detour as a way to scope out the courtyard. Maybe, if someone thought she was otherwise occupied, they would be less cautious. She might catch a glimpse of who or what might be causing her instincts to be going crazy in warning.

Unfortunately, she didn't see anything out of the ordinary. At this early hour, and because of the chill that had settled over the city, there weren't even any casual walkers in the courtyard. Everyone was hurrying to or from the building with a purpose.

She left the deli, her hands at least getting warmth from the coffee she had no intention of drinking, and headed into her own building, not even glancing across the courtyard to Ryker's. She didn't want anyone associating her with someone in that building if at all possible.

When she was in her office, worriedly sitting behind her desk, she called Ryker.

"Where are you?" he demanded as soon as he picked up the phone.

"Something came up," she said, standing up and peering through the blinds in her windows to see if she could spot the person who might be following her from higher up. Still nothing, she thought with frustration. "Can I meet you later?" she asked.

There was a long sigh and Cricket could imagine Ryker's strong hand running through his thick, dark hair. Just like she'd done last night. "Cricket, what's going on?" he asked, his voice softer now. "First you avoid me for a week and now I can hear in your voice that something is seriously wrong." He paused, waiting for her to tell him what was happening but when there was still silence, he said, "I promise I can help you with whatever is going on, Cricket. You agreed to be my wife," he said even more softly. "That means sharing one's problems and concerns."

Cricket closed her eyes to try and stop the tears. "I don't think…" she started to say but because he was so wonderful and she loved him so much, she just couldn't say anything more. She needed to tell him that she couldn't marry him, but that wasn't a conversation one could have over the phone. "I love you. I truly do, but I can't talk now," she said, angry that her voice broke while she spoke, revealing how deeply she was upset. "I'll call you later," she said and hung up the phone.

She sat down at her desk again, grabbing a tissue to sop up the tears and try to repair her makeup.

Taking deep, calming breaths, she refused to let her mind even think of Ryker. It took her several minutes, but she finally got the tears under control. She had to simply put him out of her mind…

The door to her office opened causing her to spin around in surprise. "What's going on?" a deep voice demanded.

Cricket looked up from her desk, her mouth falling open in astonishment as Ryker himself stood in her office looking awesome and terrifying.

It had felt like a century since she'd feasted her eyes on him and he looked…magnificent! She had no idea how long she stood there staring at him, but she felt all warm and wonderful as she drank in his tall, strong appearance.

And then the reality of his presence reached her and she jumped up. "What are you doing here?" she demanded in a whisper, her heart in her throat as she worried about someone following him. She almost tripped over her desk in her rush to get to the windows so she could close the blinds. She then hurried behind him, ignoring the confused expression on his handsome face when she closed the door as well, leaning against it and taking deep breaths, trying not to hyperventilate in her panic.

Ryker watched her carefully, looking for any clue that would tell him what was going on. "I'm here because you didn't come to me this morning."

"I told you," she said, glancing up into his eyes and then down again, unable to hold his gaze when she was lying. "Something came up."

"What?" he demanded, sliding his hands into his pockets and waiting for her answer as if he had all the time in the world.

She bit her lip and looked around, frantically searching for something to distract him. "Don't you have meetings this morning?" she asked, trying to think of some reason to get him out of her office and away from her. Until she knew if he was in danger, she didn't want him close by.

"At least you're still wearing my ring," he said grimly.

Cricket's right hand came up to cover her left hand protectively. She'd forgotten to take it off and hang it around her neck. "I...we..." she glanced down at the gorgeous ring on her finger, angry that the tears were threatening again. She had to be strong. She had to protect him! "I don't think..." she started to slip the ring off of her finger but his sharp tone stopped her.

"Don't even think about it!" he growled at her, placing both hands on hers, stopping her from removing the ring as he loomed over her. "There are obviously things that we need to work out, honesty being one of them, but you're not leaving me. We're getting married, Cricket. And you're going to tell me what's going on. But in the meantime, look at this," he said and dropped a flash drive onto her desk.

Cricket felt the muscles in her neck ease up somewhat now that she didn't have to take off the ring immediately. It would have to come off eventually, but at least she had time now to savor the feeling of being engaged. Just a few more hours, she told herself. She sat down at her desk, almost falling into her chair because her knees were about to give out on her.

Picking up the drive, she looked at him curiously. "What's this?"

He crossed his arms over his chest and stood up straight. "Watch it, Cricket," he said with that commanding, deep voice that never failed to create shivers throughout her entire body.

She looked up at him, then blindly took the flash drive and plugged it into her computer. As soon as she clicked on the only file, the image of Jason Moran's office appeared but nothing was happening. It didn't matter though. As soon as she saw that office, Cricket knew exactly what was going to happen on the screen.

Sure enough, a few seconds later, she watched her digital image as she dropped from the ceiling onto the floor, crouched and ready to spring away, just as her mother and father had taught her all those years ago.

Her face and hair were covered by the mask and there wasn't really anything that one could absolutely pinpoint as evidence of Cricket's identity.

Unfortunately, when she glanced up into his ice blue eyes, she knew that he knew that the person on the screen was her.

She swallowed painfully, those neck muscles tensing up once again. She pulled her eyes away from his again and looked at the screen, cringing when she watched herself wrap up Jason's chairs, computer monitor, pictures…everything in his office. Even his pens were wrapped up with pretty, pink paper with flowers on it, a design perfect for a baby shower. Exactly what his staff thought of his latest round of temper tantrums.

There was a noise outside of her office and someone knocked on her door. Cricket's eyes snapped from the computer screen to the doorway, then up to Ryker, the panic written all over her face. She quickly clicked the "stop" button, afraid of anyone seeing her on the screen even in her disguise.

With a sigh, he leaned over and said, "What are we going to do about this, Cricket?" he asked very softly.

She swallowed and there was another knock on her door. "I…um…"

The door to her office swung open and Josie jumped back. "Oh! I'm sorry to interrupt, Cricket. It's just that…" she noticed the extremely tall man standing up and looking down at her and her voice simply trailed off as Ryker's normally terrifying presence worked it's magic.

"She'll be out in a moment," he said very smoothly, almost softly.

Josie's wide eyes just stared for a full five seconds before she realized she was supposed to respond. "Um…Yes, well, okay." And Josie slowly, carefully backed out of the office, closing the door behind her.

Cricket was pretty sure that Josie was already speeding down the hallway to talk to their friends, spreading the news that Cricket had a large, overwhelming male in her office with the door closed.

Forgetting about Josie for the moment, she swallowed as she turned back, cringing as she watched the screen. Cricket was almost finished with Jason's office. A moment later, she sprung upwards and pulled herself through the ceiling tiles, exactly how she'd entered several minutes earlier. "What are you going to do about this?" she asked, her mind frantically trying to figure out a way to resolve this without her losing her job.

"What would you like me to do about it?" he asked softly, crossing his arms over his massive chest and looking down at her.

Cricket didn't like feeling this small so she stood up from her desk and took several steps backwards. "Um…If I had my preference, I'd like you to lose that file." Her mother and father would be ashamed to know that she'd left evidence. But even worse, she didn't know what Ryker thought about her midnight escapade. Was he angry? Of course he was angry! Why wouldn't he be angry?

Ryker watched her carefully, noting that she placed her back to a solid wall instead of a window, making herself feel more secure.

He moved closer to her. When he was less than an inch away, his arm came up to brace himself against the wall behind her and his mind filled with her feminine scent, he said, "What are you willing to do to make that happen?" he asked.

She bit her lip, wondering if he was really asking that of her. Not Ryker! Please not this! She didn't like this side of Ryker. She didn't like that he seemed to be asking her to sell herself. Her eyes narrowed and she pushed against his shoulders. "Get away from me," she growled, saddened by his suggestion.

Of course he didn't move.

Ryker breathed a huge sigh of relief when she didn't go down the most obvious path. It confirmed all of his suspicions of her. She was sweet and kind, playing a simple prank on her boss but she wasn't morally corrupt. She could have sold secrets from her boss' business to his competitors but instead, she'd turned his pictures upside down, rearranged his furniture, stole his cheap, ball point pens and wrapped his office up in ridiculous wrapping paper. She wasn't malicious. She was funny and creative.

An idea suddenly occurred to him and he wondered if she might be honest enough with him to make it work.

"Give me a dollar," he said, his eyes lighting up with the feelings he had for this woman. His woman! And he protected what was his. Damn! He loved her even more now! And now that he knew she wasn't completely lying to him, he could admit that she'd looked pretty hot in that stealth outfit. He wouldn't mind seeing her in it again. Alone. In his bedroom where he could explore all those curves underneath the thin, black material.

She was completely confused. He'd gone from trying to get her to prostitute herself to asking for money? She would have sworn the look that crossed those blue eyes was relief. But why would he be relieved? That didn't make sense. And why would he need a dollar? The man was shockingly wealthy! She'd seen his house. Every room in that place had been custom designed by some fabulous architect.

Cricket blinked, not sure why he would ask something like that of her. "Excuse me?" she asked.

"Give me a dollar," he repeated softly and with pride in his voice. "Quickly Cricket," he said to add urgency to the moment. He was aware of the other employees moving about in the hallway. The work day was starting and he knew he had to get this issue resolved fast or this could blow up around both of them.

Cricket ducked under his arm and reached for her wallet. She extracted a dollar and was about to give it to him, still confused, but she pulled back when he was about to take it from her. "Why do you need a dollar?" she asked.

"Do you trust me?" he asked. He almost laughed at the wary expression that came into her eyes.

Cricket eyed him for a long moment, about to shake her head no when she heard the word, "Yes," instead. She was so surprised by her response because she never trusted anyone. She had friends and acquaintances, but never had she allowed her personal feelings to reach the level of trust. Until him. She was literally putting her life in this man's hands. He had the power to get her fired and she didn't like that. Not one little bit.

But as she looked up at him, she realized that she really did trust him. She actually trusted him completely. She knew that he'd never do anything to hurt her, not even turn her in to her boss as the culprit for the latest office splash, which Jason didn't even known about since he'd been out of town last week.

She loved him and this new sensation of loving as well as trusting someone was completely new.

"Good," he said, hiding his relief from this surprisingly complicated woman. "Then give me the dollar," he commanded her once again.

Cricket slowly handed him the dollar, her mind frantically trying to figure out what he was going to do.

Ryker took the dollar and shoved it into his pocket. "Good. Now that you've paid me a retainer, I'm your lawyer. Will you promise me never to illegally break into anyone's business, home, building or any other type of edifice that assumes security for a person?"

Cricket had to smile at the way the man covered more than a person's home or office. "I promise," she replied with a chuckle.

His ice blue eyes told her how much he loved her and she almost melted with that realization. "Good. Now here's what's going to happen," he told her, moving closer once again. He put his hands on her hips and pulled her closer. "First of all, you will never sneak out of my bed and my home again. Is that understood?"

"I understand," she replied, not agreeing, but assuring him that she grasped the meaning of his words. Perhaps a technicality, but she wasn't guaranteeing that she might not get mad at him and want to get out of his bed. Since stealth was her training, he might perceive it as sneaking.

His eyes narrowed because he knew what she was doing. "You're never going to avoid my phone calls again, never going to ignore me for any reason. When you're mad at me or have a problem, we'll work it out together." He waited for his words to sink in before he continued, "And you're going to meet me for dinner tonight. At Antoine's and we're not going to sneak out of the building and go several blocks out of our way to find out who might be tailing you or me or both of us, agreed?"

Cricket wanted to agree to this, but she simply couldn't. "Um…could we go to maybe…?"

"No," he interrupted her resolutely. "We're going to Antoine's and you're going to listen to what I have to say. And anyone who might be trying to find us will have to make a reservation there as well."

She cringed at the idea, knowing that her father was extremely creative at getting into and out of places. "I'll be there."

"Good," he said, knowing that she hadn't agreed to the route of getting to the restaurant, only that she would arrive there and possibly eat dinner with him. He was going to understand what's going on in her life, even if it drove him crazy trying to figure it out. "I'll see you at seven then."

With that, he released her and moved away, but at the last moment, he came right back and pulled her into his arms, bent down and kissed her so completely that she was clinging to him by the time he lifted his head again. She almost whimpered when he stepped backwards and she had to hold onto the desk to keep her balance.

Just as she suspected, as soon as the door was opened, Josie, Debbie and Allyson were standing at the door, obviously trying to hear what was going on. Their mouths literally dropped open when they first saw Ryker walk through the doorway. He nodded politely to them, saying a charming, "Ladies," before he moved on down the hallway and out of her line of sight.

The three women crowded into Cricket's office, all of them demanding information in very loud, very adamant voices.

Cricket stared at the three women for a long moment, her eyes bouncing from one woman to the next as they popped one question after another at her.

After several minutes of this, she raised her hands in an attempt to halt, or just slow their barrage of questions, but she stopped when she heard a gasp from Allyson.

"What's that!" she demanded, grabbing Cricket's hand while all three women bent over to view the gorgeous, large diamond on her finger.

"Did he give this to you?" they demanded. "Is he the reason you looked so horrible last week?" "Is he the reason you've ditched us so often over the past few weeks?" "I would have chosen him over us as well!" They were saying over the top of each other, oohing and ahhing over the ring. "Who is he?"

Cricket pulled her hand away, curling her fingers up so that the ring couldn't slip off of her finger. She'd completely forgotten about the ring because of Ryker's kiss or she never would have been so forgetful.

Before she could explain anything to her friends, they heard their boss's voice down the hallway, yelling for someone to bring him one thing or another. With a sigh of irritation, the three ladies rolled their eyes and filed out of Cricket's office, ready to start the work day and get the commanded items for their boss. Obviously, her boss hadn't entered his office yet or he'd be yelling for a whole other reason.

Any other day, she'd be anticipating his wrath but not today. She had too many other issues on her mind.

Cricket sat down behind her desk and immediately pulled a stack of invoices forward. She had to input all of them, ensure that they were accurate, and then get them paid. She let her fingers fly over the keyboard and was finished with the stack in record time, ignoring Jason's bellow of outrage as he tore the wrapping paper off of his office furniture. All the while, her mind was frantically trying to come up with an answer for Ryker, an explanation that he might believe and would be as close to the truth as possible without him hating her in the end.

She didn't release any of the invoices, knowing that she wasn't focusing enough which would make her accuracy plummet, but she pulled another stack of invoices forward, needing the mindless task so the other part of her brain could work through the earlier conversation with Ryker. He didn't seem to be angry but he also didn't know the whole story. And truthfully, the video didn't reveal anything of her identity, so how could Ryker know it was her who had fallen through the ceiling?

She considered all sorts of explanations throughout the day. She even forgot about grabbing something for lunch but a sandwich arrived on her desk, delivered by the receptionist at two o'clock that afternoon. "What's this?" she asked.

Sally, the receptionist, smiled at Cricket. "It was just delivered by messenger. Which is odd because a female called about an hour ago asking if you'd gone out for lunch."

Cricket stared at the sandwich and smiled. "Thanks," she said, unable to tear her eyes away from the sweet, considerate gesture. Ryker! The man was trying to soften her up, she thought as she unwrapped the sandwich. And it was even a turkey on rye with the special mustard she liked so much! They'd only gone out for lunch once, but he'd remembered exactly what she liked.

She ate up her sandwich and then sighed with the feeling of fullness and happiness that surrounded her. She didn't even realize what she was doing until she was standing in the lobby of Ryker's law firm. "Is there any chance I could speak with Ryker Thorpe?" she asked nervously.

The receptionist smiled and picked up the phone. "Do you have an appointment?" she asked.

Cricket shook her head, biting her lip. "I don't. But just tell him Cricket is here to see him if he has a moment. It isn't important so if he's…"

The door to the lobby opened up and a very sophisticated middle aged woman stepped out. "Ms. Fairchild?" she asked, extending her hand. "I'm Joan, Mr. Thorpe's assistant. Would you like to come this way?" she asked, holding the door open for Cricket.

Cricket had already shaken the woman's hand but her mind was still reeling from the efficiency of her sudden appearance in the lobby. She stepped towards the woman's hand, looking back at the receptionist. "How did you…"

The woman laughed softly. "No, I don't have any superpowers," she replied. "I was passing by and Diane, the receptionist typed in your name. I just received it a moment ago and was passing by the lobby. It was just good timing that you arrived at the same time."

Cricket sighed, relieved that the woman wasn't that fast and efficient. That was spooky! "Is Ryker busy? I don't want to interrupt him."

"He just stepped into a meeting, but I don't think he'll mind if I pull him out for you. In fact, I'm guessing that he would be very upset if you stopped by and I didn't let him know," she said with a smile, opening a door to Ryker's large, luxurious office. "You can wait in here. Would you like some tea or coffee?" she asked.

Cricket quickly shook her head. "No, but really, you don't need to pull him out of his meeting. I don't…" Cricket wasn't really even sure what she was going to say to him. Yesterday, she'd been desolate that she couldn't see him anymore, today she'd been caught and they hadn't resolved a single thing.

"It's no problem," Joan smiled. She was already typing on her cell phone and a moment later, the door to the conference room across the hallway opened up and Ryker stepped through the doorway. The man literally took her breath away as he approached her. She couldn't tear her eyes off of him and she didn't realize that she was smiling as he walked towards her.

"Thanks Joan," he said as he passed by her. But he closed the door a moment before he took her into his arms and kissed her.

Once again, he didn't stop until Cricket's arms were wrapped around those enormous shoulders, pressing her body against his, demonstrating her need for him to continue with his attentions.

"You came here on your own," he growled low and husky when he lifted his head finally.

"You sent me a sandwich," she replied with a growing smile and an expanding feeling that this was right. Surely there was some way to work Ryker into her life without jeopardizing her parent's freedom!

His eyes turned serious. "I suspected you would be too worried about the file and dinner tonight to remember to have some lunch. And I doubt you had any breakfast, did you?" he asked.

She smiled shyly up at him, her mind frantically trying to come to terms with the problems they were facing together. But that was for later. Right now, she just enjoyed being in his arms again. "No. You're right. And you're very sweet to have thought about me. I know you're extremely busy. Did I break up an important meeting?" she asked, not even bothering to peer around his shoulders because they were too broad.

"They can wait."

She laughed, feeling giddy with his arms around her. In fact, his touch and being in his arms felt so perfectly "right", she made a snap decision right there. She'd work it out with her mother and father. Somehow, she'd make this work. "I'll tell you everything tonight," she assured him. With that decision made, she felt a huge weight lifted from her shoulders and she reached up to kiss him. He wasn't going to let her get away with the simple peck she'd intended and bent lower, deepening the kiss. He groaned and finally lifted his head. "I'll walk you out," he said to her. "Maybe I can introduce you to one or more of your future brothers-in-law."

Cricket didn't like the sound of that, but she figured if she was going to tell him about her past and her family, she might as well at least meet his brothers.

He put a hand to the small of her back as he led her through the office. They went down an elegant staircase and into a room filled with people bustling about in some sort of hurried fashion. "That's Ash over there," he said, pointing to a man who was, shockingly, taller than Ryker.

"That's your brother?" she demanded, her eyes gawking at the huge man.

Ryker looked at Ash, then back down at Cricket's astonished gaze. "Yes. Why?"

She shook her head. "I didn't think they made them any bigger than you." She laughed when she looked up and noticed Ryker's half smile. "Are all of your brothers your size?" she asked.

"Yes. You have a lot to look forward to," he said and winked down at her.

She was just about to greet Ryker's brother when a picture in the man's hand caught her eye. "Are you having me followed?" she demanded of Ryker who was walking right behind her, a look of mild irritation on his handsome features with her question.

Ryker looked back at her sharply. "Why would you ask that?" he demanded. He looked over at the file Ash was holding and something clicked in his mind. "Do you know the man in that photograph?" he asked, taking the file folder from his youngest brother and handing it to her so she could see the pictures more clearly.

Cricket glared up at Ryker, wondering if all of her tension this morning had been for nothing. She looked back at the smiling couple in the picture that was paper-clipped to a heavy file folder, thinking about how much she'd disliked them the previous day, her irritation increasing as she lifted the photo up higher. "These two people are the heads of the charity my boss wants me to look into as a tax deduction. I was with them yesterday afternoon. Are you telling me you haven't had someone following me?"

Ash stepped in front of the blond beauty but his brother pushed him out of the way and put his arm around her protectively. Ash didn't have time to castigate his oldest brother right at the moment. He had to clarify this latest twist. "I don't know who you are…" he started to say.

Ryker interrupted him, not willing to let his youngest brother be rude to his fiancée, but also suspecting that Cricket wouldn't want their relationship broadcast just yet. Even that suspicion irritated him because he wanted to shout it out to everyone that this was his woman, partly because he wanted to claim her as his own but also so she couldn't get away from him like she had over the past week. Instead, he said, "This is Cricket Fairchild. She's one of my clients."

Cricket smothered a secret smile. "Okay, so now that we've established who I am," she said, relieved that Ryker hadn't announced their relationship to everyone, especially since they needed to talk about that video and he needed to hear everything she had to tell him tonight over dinner before he announced anything to his brothers, "would someone mind telling me why you are investigating the person that I'm investigating?"

Cricket hadn't noticed before because of all the confusion, but there were four police officers and a very nervous, very pretty brunette standing behind Ash Thorpe, all of whom were shifting forward, and they all seemed inordinately interested in the two people in the picture. The police officer stepped in at that moment, taking charge of the problem. "Ma'am, are you telling me that you were with this man yesterday afternoon?"

Cricket nodded her head, causing her blond curls to dance merrily around her stunning features and the police officer blushed slightly under her direct, green gaze. "Isn't that what I just said? It was a lunch meeting at their request," she explained. "He ordered steak and she had some sort of disgusting fish meal."

Several pairs of stunned eyes were looking back at her. "And you would be willing to testify to this?" the officer asked.

Cricket looked around, her green eyes trying to figure out why everyone was tense, as if her next words were of miraculous import. "Of course. Why? Has someone bankrupted his charity or something? They're very passionate about saving the whales off the coast of Greenland." Cricket had thought they were a bit too passionate but she'd taken their information, agreeing to pass it along to Jason.

Ash watched with increasing relief as Ash's eyes started to clear, a grin beginning to form on his features. "Cricket, this man was murdered recently," Ryker was explaining calmly.

She was surprised for a moment, but then laughed and shook her head. "No. He isn't dead. He was giving me a pitch to help him fund the next ship they are trying to acquire."

Cricket watched in amazement as the mood of the entire area changed. The tension was immediately gone and the pretty woman who had been standing behind the giant was almost bouncing in excitement. Cricket wasn't sure why, but she suspected that the police had been about to arrest her.

"You're the hero of the hour," Ryker said to her ear and led her out of the area after shaking his brother's hand. "Go for it," she heard him say to his brother, Ash, and then Ryker was nudging her out of the room. She peered back and saw the elation on everyone's face and knew she must have given them some incredible information.

"What's going on?" she asked when they were in the hallway.

"The woman behind my brother had been arrested for murdering her ex-fiancé. The supposed victim was the same man in the picture, the one who you met with yesterday over lunch. Which means that he wasn't murdered and he is alive and well, pulling another scam. So you not only saved the woman – whom I suspect is very important to my brother based on his activities recently – you also potentially saved several, possibly many, people from being scammed by the man in the picture. Hopefully, the police are going to turn their investigation away from murder to fraud."

Cricket's face was beaming with excitement. "That's incredible! Wow! I'm glad I was walking by at the right time," she added.

"Me too," Ryker replied, taking her into his arms, uncaring of the rest of the world as he bent down to kiss her in his very own lobby.

"I'll see you tonight," he said when he lifted his head. "And we're going to talk. You're going to tell me everything and we're going to get all of it straightened out."

She stepped out of his arms and tried to hide the worry. "Until tonight," she replied with a nervous nod. She might have mentally agreed to give him the information, but that still made her anxious. She'd never revealed any of her family history to anyone so this was a huge step for her.

She was in the hallway waiting for the elevator when the beautiful brunette appeared through the doors accompanied by another taller, stunning brunette. Both women were gorgeous but in different ways. The shorter one seemed friendlier but the taller one was willowy, like one of those top fashion models, but not that tall. And she didn't look mean. Nor did she look like she starved herself. She had a softness to her that was much more attractive than the anorexic skeletons that strolled down the runways with zero body fat and missing wisdom teeth so their cheekbones looked more pronounced.

She pressed the elevator button more harshly than was needed since she felt pale and washed out next to these two stunning women. Where was a plant to hide behind when one needed it?

"You're the woman who just helped me stay out of jail," the shorter woman said with a huge grin on her lovely face. "Are you okay?"

Cricket's thumb once again touched the ring on her finger, needing to feel it to make sure it was real. That he'd really given her such a significant symbol of the way he felt about her. He would most likely want it back by the time she finished dinner with him, but it was hers for now and she wasn't going to hide it on the chain around her neck.

"I'm okay," she said, wishing things were different and that her life wasn't so complicated. "Nothing a good martini can't fix," she replied with a self-deprecating smile. She thought about her father and Ryker, still not sure how to make everything work out for the men in her life that she loved. "Men are just so confusing!"

"Why don't you come with us? I don't know about the martinis," she cautioned, "but the margaritas at Durango's are perfect for anything that ails you."

Cricket considered the option. She didn't know these two women, but she could definitely use a night on the town with some women her own age. "I'm not sure I should be around humanity right now," she came back, thinking about the enormous issue weighing her down. Her lover or the father who loved her…what a monumental issue to overcome.

Mia laughed. "That's exactly where I am. I'm Mia Paulson," she said. "And we're heading out to celebrate me not being in jail for the rest of my life."

The willowy beauty stepped forward at that moment, extending her hand in a warm, friendly greeting. "I'm Autumn. I work as the office manager at The Thorpe Group so I really know how frustrating those men can be!"

Cricket smiled back, taking Mia's hand in hers and shaking it with more confidence than she felt. It had been a long time since she'd had friends her own age. She remembered Jason's furious rantings about his newly wrapped office and decided to take the afternoon off. She already had her resignation letter typed up, so why not? "That sounds like a perfect start to the weekend. I think I'll join you after all."

Fifteen minutes later, they were settled at one of the back tables of the local hangout, a pitcher of margaritas in front of them with three glasses, already filled. "To avoiding jail time and men!" Autumn said.

"Wait!" Autumn called out mid-toast. A moment later, Autumn jumped up and walked to another table where a woman was sitting all alone, looking like her martini might be the enemy. She had curly, bohemian hair that she tried to contain, but Cricket suspected that it didn't always cooperate. When Autumn and the new woman walked back to their table, Autumn immediately introduced her. "This is Kiera and she's one of the newest team members at The Thorpe Group."

Mia was almost dancing in her chair, so excited to meet the new woman to the group. "She's the one who found the information about Jeff's current fiancée buying the new BMW," she explained to Cricket with a huge grin. "If it weren't for the two of you, I would be in jail right now being charged with embezzlement as well as murder."

When all four of them were sitting down once again, Kiera with a full margarita as well, they proceeded to drink, eat salty chips and tear up the male population, laughing at their foibles and their challenges.

Cricket liked Ryker's office manager instantly. She might look like a stunning model, but she was much more friendly and down to earth. And apparently, Autumn had men problems just like the rest of them did.

Cricket laughed and joined in the conversation, enjoying herself immensely, feeling a connection with these women that she hadn't felt in a long, long time. Josie, Allyson and Debbie were wonderful, but they were at a different stage in their lives than Cricket. She couldn't connect with her office friends. Not the way she felt like she could talk to these three women.

She actually groaned when she saw Ryker move forward. When she saw three other men looking almost exactly like him, she glanced down at her margarita glass, wondering if she might have had more to drink than she thought. She looked back up to find that Ryker was standing behind her, taking her glass and downing the rest himself.

"What are you doing?" she asked, irritated that he would steal her drink.

"I'm saving you from yourself," he explained with a wink.

"Why are there so many of you?" she asked, turning to grin up at him, forgetting for the moment how nervous she was at having to explain her family to him. Well, and the fact that he was going to run for the hills as soon as he heard. She was just going to enjoy these last few minutes with him, her fuzzy mind told herself.

He lifted her out of her chair gently, almost laughing when she sagged against his side. "There's only one of me, my love. The rest are my brothers."

Her eyes widened. "Really? I might have been their sister-in-law!" she sighed, wishing things could end differently.

"You are going to be their sister-in-law," he countered, pulling her out of the bar. She didn't see him wave to his brothers but nor were his brothers paying much attention to him either. He noticed that each of them were coaxing, arguing and teasing their respective women out of their chairs as well. He and his brothers had been sitting at the bar listening to the four lovely women berate each of them in particular and men in general. He suspected that Cricket wasn't drunk, but she was feeling very relaxed.

At the door, he glanced back and realized that each of his brothers looked like they were feeling the exact same way he felt right at the moment. Possessive. Interesting, he thought, but he didn't have time to analyze that at this point. He wanted Cricket all alone and she was relaxed enough now with the tequila to hopefully tell him all her secrets. He should be a gentleman and just bring her home so she could sleep it off, but he wanted information. Once he knew what was wrong, he could more easily protect her. And he was damn well going to protect his woman! She wasn't going to run away from him either, which is what he suspected she wanted to do.

Cricket shivered as the cool, night air hit her. She was about to complain and pull away from Ryker but before she had a chance, a heavy coat was put around her shoulders. She looked up and Ryker was walking right next to her, wearing only his shirt because he'd taken off his jacket which was now around her, keeping her warm from his body heat.

She smiled up at him, automatically moving closer as his arm wrapped around her shoulders. "Everything turn out okay after we left?" she asked happily, enjoying the warmth of his coat as well as his arm around her like this.

He chuckled as he thought back to the scene in Durango's. "I think everything is going to be better than all right. Mia Paulson is probably right now in Ash's arms," he came back. He wasn't sure about Autumn and Xander. That could be explosive. But when he thought back to their interaction, they didn't appear to be at each other's throats tonight. Odd, he thought. And Axel was looking strangely confident of Kiera's status.

"That's great," she replied, sighing with relief that her new friend was out of danger and Ryker's arms were still around her. When they entered the exclusive restaurant, the hostess perked up as soon as she saw Ryker. "Your table is ready, Mr. Thorpe," she said and took two menus, leading them through the mostly-filled tables.

When they were seated, Cricket used her menu to cover her face while she looked around, feeling more than a little warm. She probably shouldn't have had that second margarita, she thought, trying to focus on the menu. She had no idea what she wanted to eat, having eaten too many salty chips. But she'd order something, just to satisfy Ryker.

Suddenly, that crazy feeling, as if something were very, very wrong came roaring back to life. She hadn't felt it at the bar, but she just knew that someone was here, someone trying to watch her. She looked around as inconspicuously as possible, trying to see if anyone were hiding behind a menu or looking in her direction.

When she didn't spy anyone watching her, she relaxed slightly and lowered her menu. Looking up, she knew she'd been caught once again. Ryker was watching her, his eyebrows raised in question.

Darn it! She definitely shouldn't have had that last drink! She carefully put the menu down beside her and took a deep breath, ready to tell him everything.

But at that moment, the waiter arrived. "Can I take your order?" he asked with a bit more force than she expected.

Cricket looked up at the cryptic waiter, surprise initially in her eyes but they widened in horror when she took in the crazy looking waiter standing beside their table. "Dad?" she gasped, letting the word slip out before she could stop it. Yep! Those were strong margaritas!

Her father's eyes narrowed and she suspected that his eyebrows would show his anger, if she could actually see his eyebrows. The man was wearing a wig that was so fuzzy that it covered his ears and his forehead. He was even wearing a mustache that, if one squinted and looked through several windows, might appear real.

"You look ridiculous, Dad," she told him brazenly She should be nervous and anxious that he was interfering once again, spying on her and driving her nuts. But she was only angry – and for all of the same reasons. The man was interfering and wouldn't leave her alone. "Take that horrible disguise off and get out of here. I'm talking to Ryker and I'll deal with you later."

She couldn't believe she'd just spoken to her father like that, but then again, neither could he. For the first time in her life, she was really irritated that his past was interfering in her future. She'd always protected the "family business" and all of the secrets that came along with their nefarious activities. But for some reason, probably her afternoon of drinking and getting to know the three women whom she admired greatly, she wasn't going to put up with it anymore. All the lies, the secrets, the illegal activities and the strange code of ethics, they were no longer hers. And she wasn't going to live with them any longer.

"Dad…" she started to say.

But he interrupted her. "Before you say another word, you need to know that your mother is in town as well and she's…"

"She can speak for herself," her mother interrupted imperiously from behind him, her elegant figure coming around the corner to stand beside the table.

Cricket had always admired her mother for her sophistication and fashion sense. Tonight was no exception. Her mother was wearing a lovely, pale blue Versace suit that hugged her figure in all the right places. Her hair was perfectly coiffed and pulled back off of her face to show off those famous cheekbones that had gotten her into more high society parties than any other thief in the world. Possibly because of the alcohol she'd imbibed, Cricket actually giggled at the enormous diamond necklace that graced her mother's neck. Which was completely fake!

With a haughty wave of her hand, Lydia Fairchild silently told one of the waiters to bring two more chairs to the table. Within moments, her directions had been completed. Ryker was already standing, taking her mother's hand.

"Ryker, this is my mother, Lydia Fairchild," Cricket explained with a sigh of resignation. "All of the best laid plans of mice and men often go astray…" she quoted Robert Burns and leaned back in her chair.

"It is a pleasure to meet you, Mr. Thorpe," her mother said with sincerity and a wide, gracious smile. "I'm assuming you are the gentleman who put that beautiful ring on my daughter's finger recently?" she asked.

"I am," Ryker responded calmly despite his dinner plans going so awry.

Cricket caught her father's eyes as they snapped towards her hand and his anger actually increased. She could feel his anger but she wasn't afraid of it any longer.

"Sit down, Mother," Cricket said. "Father, you too," she told him, ignoring his glare in her direction.

She was relieved when they both sat down, Ryker following as well. "Now that we're all here," she said and looked at her mother and father with irritation, "I want you to know that Ryker has asked me to marry him," she explained.

Lydia smiled, her eyes brightening with happiness. "I'm so glad for you dear. I was starting to worry that you wouldn't ever find the same exhilaration your father and I have shared throughout our lives." She looked over at Ryker, then back at her daughter. "I can tell that you have. And he is a good man," she confirmed, looking down at the diamond on her finger.

Cricket rolled her eyes. "Mother, Ryker is a good man because he is smart and sensitive and makes me laugh. Not because he has excellent taste in jewelry."

"It's always a good sign though, my love." Her mother winked at Ryker who only chuckled at the conversation.

Cricket turned to face her father, confronting his glare head on instead of avoiding the reason behind it. "Father, I know that you're worried about Mother, but I don't think…"

"Wait just a moment, dear," she interrupted and leaned forward. "Edward," she glared across the table at him. "How long have you known about Cricket's romance?" she asked carefully.

Cricket's eyes widened when her father actually squirmed in his chair. "Well, dear…"

"Don't you dare 'dear' me, Edward. What have you done?" She demanded angrily.

The waiter arrived at that moment, the real waiter, and was startled to find a guest sitting at the table in the restaurant's uniform. "Don't ask," Ryker stepped in for the benefit of the confused waiter. "Can you bring us a bottle of Hiedsieck Diamont Bleu, please?"

The waiter immediately bowed and stepped backwards, eager to bring the requested champagne quickly. But Ryker called him back, "And some coffee."

Cricket didn't even blush when Ryker looked at her overly flushed cheeks. She only smiled back at him, silently thanking him because she really didn't want to mix alcohols.

With the waiter gone, Ryker turned back to Cricket, silently asking her to proceed.

Cricket took a deep breath and looked back to her father. "Dad, I know that you are worried about Mom's reaction, but…"

"She's thrilled!" Lydia interrupted, speaking for herself and looking at her husband as if to say, "You're in trouble if you say another word."

Cricket stared at her mother, then at her father. "So what was all this stuff earlier about not worrying mom?" she demanded of her father.

Edward leaned forward, trying to smooth things over. "Your mother was shopping…"

"And she can still speak for herself," she interrupted again. "I'm thrilled dear. I'm very excited that you've finally found someone to love. And I wish you all the best." She leaned over and kissed Cricket's cheek, then sat back and glared at her husband once again.

Cricket watched the interplay between her mother and father, wishing both of them could understand what she was about to do. "I'm telling Ryker everything."

Her mother smiled gently. "Dear, there isn't really anything to tell."

Cricket blinked, then shook her head. "What does that mean?"

Lydia smiled gently. "Darling, we haven't had any special projects since you were about eight or nine years old."

"When we knew how much it bothered you," her father grumbled, crossing his arms over his chest despite the fact that the action looked uncomfortable in the ridiculous and ill-fitting waiter's jacket.

She couldn't believe what they were saying. They didn't steal? They didn't pick up "baubles" when they needed some excitement? They were the best in the business! "But, you trained me in all the ways." Could they really have retired so long ago?

"Honey, we taught you everything we know. That's what parents do," Lydia explained with a dramatic wave of her hands.

Cricket shook her head, stunned by this latest revelation. "No mother. Parents teach their children to read and turn in their homework on time, to avoid horrible men and not get drunk while at college."

Edward grunted. "You taught yourself all that stuff," he grumbled. "We taught you what you didn't know. We gave you a legacy."

Cricket didn't understand. "So all these years, what have you been living off of? How have you been able to afford your lifestyle?"

Edward smiled proudly and sat up straighter in his chair. "Just because we aren't in the business any longer doesn't mean we didn't invest our…profits well over the years." Edward glanced at Ryker, trying to gauge the new man's understanding of the conversation and all that it implied.

"Your father is very good at investing, dear," her mother said with pride.

She glanced between her beautiful, elegant mother and her normally handsome father, stunned. "So neither of you do...anything?"

"Well, we keep our skills up," she explained with an indignant tone. "But no, we haven't profited from our endeavors in any way. We didn't want you to feel uncomfortable any longer."

Her mind was spinning with the news that her parents hadn't stolen anything in years. Decades almost! "Why didn't you tell me?" she asked.

Both her mother and father shrugged. "We thought you knew."

Cricket fell backwards, shaking her head. "So what was all that about last week, Dad?" she demanded.

Her father sighed. "I just..."

Lydia watched her husband carefully, her heart melting for the man who had loved their daughter so deeply over the years. "He didn't want you to find a man to replace him," she said, staring pointedly at her husband. "Apologize to your daughter, Edward."

Edward shifted uncomfortably. "I didn't think you would be happy with this guy," he mumbled.

Cricket shook her head. "This is like a really bad movie!" she stated with anger rising inside of her. "Do you know what you've done to me? I was trying to protect Ryker! I thought someone was following me! But it was you all the time, wasn't it?" she asked.

The waiter arrived, startled by the rising tension from the participants at a table who, in his mind, should be celebrating. Nevertheless, he poured the sparkling wine, set the silver pot of coffee and china cup on the edge of the table, then backed away as quickly as possible, leaving the bottle in the ice bucket.

Ryker looked around the table, amazed that so much had happened in such a short period of time. "So let me get this straight, just to make sure I understand everything that has been said over the past few minutes." He looked at Edward. "You and you're wife," he glanced at Lydia, "are thieves, am I correct?" He watched them carefully, looking for signs that he was way off base.

"Retired collectors," Edward corrected firmly. "I enjoyed art collecting and my wife, she was more into the sparkly things. She collected beautiful diamonds."

Ryker's mind worked quickly. "And both of you retired as soon as you realized that Cricket didn't like the lifestyle, but you taught her all the tricks of the trade, just in case she grew up and realized that she enjoyed doing that sort of thing." Everything was clicking into place: her aversion to stealing, her midnight video where she wrapped things up, and her collection of pens in her bedroom.

"And because she had the talent for it," Edward confirmed, proud of his daughter's accomplishments.

"She's exceptionally good at it," Lydia agreed, smiling at her daughter with delight. "If only she could stomach the details." She sighed dramatically as if the details included filing papers or folding laundry versus fencing stolen articles on the black market, relieving rightful owners of their property, etcetera.

Ryker was finally getting a good picture of what was going on. "Cricket enjoys breaking into offices and pulling pranks and, up until last week, she hadn't ever gotten caught." He paused for a moment. "Am I missing anything?" he asked.

All three people shook their heads, Cricket smiling at how good he was at reading between the not-so-subtle lines. And what was even better? He didn't appear to be upset by any of what he'd heard.

Or perhaps he wasn't as calm as she thought. His next words didn't leave any room for doubt. "As Cricket's lawyer, I have to inform you that, anything you tell me is privileged information, but if I ever become aware of a crime that is about to be committed, I am required by law to inform the police."

Edward huffed and puffed a bit, irritated that someone would dare to give him orders. "So we won't talk about any of our activities with you around," Edward stated firmly as if that were the most obvious conclusion to come to.

Cricket laughed and shook her head. "That means he won't be doing anything wrong," she translated, looking directly at her father until he harrumphed and crossed his arms over his chest in a different direction.

When she'd gotten his grudging acceptance, she turned to Ryker, lifting her coffee cup in a celebratory toast. "That's all settled then," she said, her mood just as bubbly as the wine. "To the future," she said with joy.

They all raised their glass and clinked each other's, but there was something in Ryker's eyes that caused her to hesitate. She sipped her coffee, but it was hard to swallow. She was worried, wondering if perhaps he was already having second thoughts about marrying her. She had a crazy family and he didn't even know the half of it despite her father's insane disguise right at the moment.

Ryker knew exactly where her mind was going. "Don't even think it, Cricket. We're getting married. The sooner the better."

She turned to look at him more directly, wanting to understand him. That understanding probably should come before the engagement, but she hadn't done anything normal in her life so far, why start now? "So what's on your mind now?"

"That's for later tonight," he said. "Let's have some dinner."

She smiled slightly, but was still nervous about whatever he wanted to discuss with her. She picked at her meal, unable to swallow anything with her muscles clenching in fear that she was about to lose the one man who really knew how to talk to her, not to mention all the other things he did so well. She actually blushed at that thought and the man sitting across from her saw the blush. Those dark, sexy eyebrows that could silently speak so eloquently, went up in question. But when she shook her head slightly, he smiled right back at her with a wink.

Darn it! He knew exactly what she'd been thinking!

Well, she didn't really mind when it came right down to it. As long as he was going to actually act on those activities that made her blush. And just thinking of that made her whole body heat up and she looked down at her plate. She didn't want to know if he was watching her this time. It was too embarrassing how easily he could read her body language.

A few hours later, once they'd dropped her parents off at their hotel, Cricket turned slightly in her seat so she could face Ryker while he drove. He handled the powerful car expertly, not needing to weave in and out of traffic to prove his masculinity which made her much more comfortable. She was impressed with his control and his ability to be so self-assured. He wasn't cocky or arrogant but there was an aura about him that just gave one a sense of confidence.

Realizing that, she sat back and relaxed, enjoying both the ride as well as the anticipation of him taking her into his arms. At least, she hoped he was going to take her into his arms. That thought had her stiffening and looking over at him.

"What just popped into your head?" he asked as he turned down his driveway.

She considered not answering him, afraid she might sound too seductive if she said the words out loud. But then she remembered that she was trying hard to be honest with him and took a deep breath. "I was just wondering what was going to happen when we get inside your house."

He chuckled. "At this point, there shouldn't be any doubt in your mind about what is going to happen," he replied. "I've been without you for over a week. You do the math."

Her face brightened and she relaxed back against the leather seat while he drove into his garage. He didn't even wait for the garage door to close before he was out of the driver's seat and coming around the front of the car. She thought perhaps she should wait until he reached her and opened the door for her, but she couldn't wait, wanting him too desperately. After the day she'd had, she needed his touch to reassure her that they were still okay, that he hadn't changed his mind after everything he'd learned about her crazy, abnormal family.

When he reached her, he did exactly that, lifting her up into his arms and pressing her back against the car while his body pinned her there, his mouth kissing her deeply until she was trembling against him. She didn't even realize that her legs were now wrapped around his waist until he growled, "You should always wear skirts!"

"Why?" and she gasped when his teeth nibbled along her neck and shoulder.

He didn't answer. He didn't have to speak, but the way his hips pressed against hers, his arousal extremely evident, she smiled against his mouth.

She gasped when he lifted her into his arms and carried her into his house, not even pausing to turn on lights as he strode up the stairs to his bedroom. When he was finally there, he let her feet drop to the floor and he expeditiously stripped off her clothes before taking her back into his arms and kissing her silly once again. "Not fair," she gasped when her hands only encountered fabric.

"If you're not going to take advantage of a situation, then don't blame me," he teased her as he laid her in the middle of the bed. He then stood up and looked down at her, his eyes on fire as he took in her naked beauty.

She laughed but wasn't going to take that lying down. "You're a magnificent man, Ryker," she whispered.

With that, he stripped off his own clothes and took her back into his arms. With one thrust, he was inside her and she sighed with the happiness she felt as he took her higher than she ever thought possible.

CHAPTER 12

Cricket sighed as she snuggled her back up against him, enjoying his deep laughter as his large hand smoothed up her stomach, pulling her more closely against his chest. "Do that again and we'll have to start all over."

She didn't disagree with that idea, but smiled as she hugged his arm that was wrapped around her waist. "Why do you want to marry me?" she asked after a long silence. She thought that he might be asleep, but his instant response contradicted that possibility.

She could feel him smile at her question in the darkness a moment before he kissed her hair. "For the past month, each morning I would see you across the courtyard and my day would be better." His hand stroked down her hip, resting against her bottom. "And I would see you smile and everything looked more colorful. Now that I know you and feel you, I can't get enough of you. I want to spend every waking moment being with you, making you smile and protecting you."

Her smile widened and she had to close her eyes so he couldn't see the tears of happiness that welled up in them. "Is that all?" she laughed softly, but it came out as more of a hiccup than a laugh and she felt his arm come back up to hug her closely.

"Well, there's also the fact that I love you. I love your laugh and your smile. I love talking to you and laughing with you." His hand moved up to cup her breast and she gasped with the intensity of desire that streaked through her whole body. "And every time we make love, I need to do it again and again. I can't seem to get enough of your lovely, sexy body."

She turned her head, looking over her shoulder at him in the dark. "What if I get fat? Or if I get pregnant?"

He chuckled. "I'm going to work very hard at ensuring that the second one happens because I want a big family." He kissed her shoulder and said, "Only girls though, please."

Cricket giggled at his reference to his three younger brothers. "But what about my family?"

He sighed and lifted himself up onto his elbow so she was laying on her back staring up at him. "I wanted to talk to you about that until you distracted me tonight."

She laughed and playfully punched his shoulder. "I distracted you? I was innocently sitting in the passenger seat and…"

"And you got out," he stated firmly, as if all she had to do was stand up and he was ready for her.

"I don't think that actually counts as a seduction method," she argued, but her hands slid up his muscular arms, enjoying the different texture of his skin under her fingertips.

"The way you do it, it counts." And he kissed her to stop her from arguing.

Cricket was really starting to get into the kiss when he pinned her hands over her head. "We have to talk about something important though."

Her leg lifted against his thigh and she shifted slightly. "I think this is very important," she said, gasping when his hips shifted so they were right where she wanted him to be. Well…almost.

"The video file," he said and those three words were all that were needed before she was still once again, her eyes wide with fear as she looked up into his serious face.

"The file," she sighed.

"You are just like your mother and father, aren't you?"

She tried to pull away, not liking that question at all. "I'm not like them in any way," she countered, trying to pull her arms out of his but he held them gently and she wasn't able to break his hold.

"You are. You might not steal things, but I saw the look in your eyes on that video. You enjoy breaking into places, don't you?"

Cricket glared up at him, refusing to answer his question.

Ryker laughed at her attempt at being angry when she was naked under his body. "Admit it. You enjoy the adrenaline rush, don't you?"

Cricket shrugged her shoulder slightly. "Yes. Okay? I admit it! I like breaking into people's offices and houses just to see if I can. I like the thrill of not getting caught and escaping without anyone even knowing I was there. Does that mean you're out? Are you running for the hills?"

He laughed and bent lower to kiss her but when she moved her face to the side, he simply bit her ear lobe as punishment. Not hard, but enough to show her that he was still in command of her body and she shouldn't even try to hide from him.

"I think you should quit your job," he said softly, nibbling on her neck once again. "I have a friend in Virginia, just outside of Washington, D.C. who owns a security firm. I spoke to him earlier today, told him all about you. He has a division that tests companies' security systems."

She was more than a little intrigued and turned her face so she could see him in the dim light of the bedroom. "What do you mean? How does he do that?" But she knew! And her whole body was vibrating with excitement at the possibility.

Ryker laughed and shifted again, causing her to gasp. "He has a team that breaks in to buildings and figures out what the company can do better to secure their intellectual or physical property. They are a mix of ex-military and intelligence personnel, all of whom enjoy the challenge of overcoming any security system and figuring out how to make it better."

With all of her strength, she shifted and rolled on top of him. "And?" she asked, moving so she was sitting on top of him.

Ryker took her hips in both of his large hands and moved her where he wanted her to be. He loved watching her in the throes of passion. And when he filled her up, her head tilted backwards while her body adjusted to his invasion. "And…" he said as he put on a condom a moment before he shifted her hips, lifting her against him, then slowly letting her move back down, "You have an interview with him the day after tomorrow. He's interested in hiring you."

"Ryker!" she whispered with all the love and excitement she was feeling.

Those were the last words she was able to speak until she fell against his chest, her whole body draped against him as she slowly came down from her climax. "I love you," she breathed as she fell into a deep sleep, a smile on her face and her world now perfect since she was in his arms. With his job offer, she knew that he accepted all of her, quirks and craziness and everything in between.

CHAPTER 13

Cricket raced through the airport, her mind frantically trying to make a list of everything she needed to do. She was getting married in…well, soon, she thought because she wasn't really sure what day it was. But she couldn't believe her new job and even her first assignment! Mitch Hamilton had hired her during the interview, which wasn't really an interview but more of a test to challenge her skills. When she'd passed all of his tests, the man as well as several of the team members who she would be working with, stood by the "secure" building with their mouths hanging open in astonishment when she'd walked around from the back. She had to giggle at the memory of the four men, all of them huge and brawny, two with weapons strapped to their thighs cowboy style but dressed more like SWAT team members with their black cargo pants and black, knit shirts that stretched across their muscles.

All four of them were staring up at the building, waiting for her to exit from the top. So when she came around from the back, actually sneaking up on all four of them with the file folder in her hand, they swung around, prepared to do battle but froze at the sight of her smiling up at them.

The only words spoken were, "You're hired," by Mitch himself as the grins slowly evolved on the other men's faces.

The rest of the afternoon was spent going through her first assignment. She had the blueprints of the building tucked into her purse although she hadn't fully worked out how she was going to get in. Each assignment required her, or the team of personnel from Hamilton Securities, to break through a company's security system and place a note on a specific person's desk. If they were able to do that, getting in and out without anyone knowing, the mission was complete. An after-action report and security recommendations were written up and delivered to the client.

Mitch charged a crazy fee for this service but he also paid his team extremely well. He'd quoted a salary that was three times what she was earning from her accounting job. She had to give Jason Moran her notice and he was going to be furious when she wasn't able to give him the normal two week's warning. But how was a woman supposed to give two weeks notice when she had to put her house on the market, get all of her personal items moved over to her fiancée's house, plan a wedding and figure out how to break into a Fort Knox-like museum all at the same time? Something had to go and the first one was to get out of one job so she could start her new one.

Oh, and she needed to ask her new friends to be in her wedding. Yes, that would be a pretty high priority too. She sighed as she stepped out of Chicago's O'Hare Airport, about to hail a taxi to get her back to Ryker's house. She thought that maybe she could cook for him as well. Dinner…

"Need a ride, gorgeous?" a deep voice said from behind her.

Cricket dropped her arm and grinned as she spun around and threw herself into Ryker's arms. "I got the job!" she exclaimed, so excited she could barely think about anything except marrying this man and making him as happy as he made her. "I love you!" she said before standing on tip toe to kiss him.

Ryker smiled down at her, thrilled with her enthusiasm. Of course, he'd known that she'd gotten the job since Mitch had called him back earlier this morning, asking him where he'd found her. When he'd explained that Cricket was his fiancée, Mitch laughed and Ryker could even see his friend shaking his head. "You're in for a long, interesting life, my friend," he'd said.

Ryker wrapped his arm around his lovely fiancée as he walked her to his car. He certainly hoped so!

EPILOGUE

"Any chance we could announce our engagement to my brothers after the wedding?" Ryker asked, adjusting his tuxedo tie in the mirror.

Cricket had disappeared into the closet several minutes ago and he had no idea what was going on. "Cricket?" he called out, picking up the gold cufflinks Ash had given him as a groomsman gift.

Cricket emerged from the closet and Ryker's eyebrows dropped low over his eyes as he angrily looked at her figure hugging, blue satin dress. "What the hell are you wearing?" he demanded, looking at her gorgeous, lush figure wrapped up in the blue satin.

Cricket smiled warmly, spinning around for him. "I'm wearing a bridesmaid dress, silly!" She smoothed the satin down over her hips and Ryker's mouth went dry. "What do you think?"

He stared at her hard, thinking he wanted to peel that dress off of her, not take her out in it. "I think you should find something else to wear," he told her grimly.

Cricket looked up at him, surprised. She walked over to him with a huge grin on her face. "I think Mia might be trying to spur you into action," she explained as she smoothed her hands over his silk tuxedo shirt.

Ryker's hands gripped her hips firmly. "Mission accomplished," he told her as his voice became huskier while his fingers explored her curves under the satin dress. His hands stilled and he looked down at her with surprise.

"What's wrong?" she asked, nervous about the look in his eyes.

"Are all the bridesmaids wearing this dress?" he asked, thinking of one person in particular he was hoping would be wearing the same dress.

"Similar, yes," she replied, confused. "Why?"

Ryker grinned and kissed her behind her ear. "Because that means Xander is going to see Autumn in this dress."

Cricket's eyes were blank for a long moment, then she realized what he was saying and her grin matched his. "Why yes, he is!" she said and lifted up onto her toes to hug him. "Do you think it will work?" she asked, almost bouncing with anticipation and excitement.

Ryker shrugged his broad shoulders. "Nothing else has snapped those two out of their habit of fighting with each other." He'd thought they had worked out a détente recently because they'd stopped fighting but their animosity towards each other was right back, at an even higher level than before.

"I don't know why Autumn doesn't just grab Xander and kiss him," Cricket said, stepping away from Ryker to put on a pair of fake pearl earrings.

Ryker watched her, his eyebrows drawn low. "You need real pearls," he stated firmly. "And Autumn won't because Xander's been such an ass to her." He pulled a box from behind him and handed it to her.

Cricket looked at the box, afraid to touch it. "What's that?" she asked, putting her hands behind her back so she couldn't take whatever was inside.

"Why don't you open it and find out?" he suggested with an almost evil twinkle to his eyes.

Cricket shook her head. "No. It's jewelry and I'm not going to accept anything else from you. You've already spent too much with this ring," she told him, covering her engagement ring with her other hand as she often did because she loved it so much.

"Take the box, Cricket."

She shook her head. "Ryker, put it away and take it back to the store."

"Take the box," he repeated, the glint in his eyes turning into a challenge.

Cricket crossed her arms and shook her head once again. "You can't order me around," she stated firmly.

He didn't answer, but just raised one eyebrow.

She huffed. "Okay, so you can order me around in bed. Sometimes."

He chuckled and set the box down behind him. But that wasn't the end of it. He opened the box himself and pulled out a stunning diamond necklace, the icy rocks draping over his fingers like a shining waterfall.

Cricket gasped and stared hard, her whole body in shock that he would purchase something so extravagant. "No!" she whispered with reverence and indignation.

He smiled at the look and whispered back, "Yes," while kissing her neck. His hands were deft as they reached around her, fixing the clasp in place. He looked at her in their mirror, his hand smoothing out the diamonds that formed a perfect circle around her delicate neck. "That looks better," he said.

Cricket's hand went up, touching the diamonds in amazement. "This is too much," she said softly, her worried eyes catching his in the mirror. "I can't accept this."

"You don't have a choice," he replied, then reached around her and lifted the black box once again.

She almost jerked backwards when she saw the matching diamond earrings nestled in the black velvet, right in the center of where the necklace had been.

"Ryker!" she gasped but he caught her jerk against his body, his arms wrapping around her waist to hold her steady. "This is outrageous," she exclaimed.

"I now have the right to shower you with gifts," he told her, holding the earrings out in front of her. "And you'd better get used to this. I have a lot of money stored up and haven't had someone to spend it on. So deal with it. Take out the pearls, Cricket," he told her, his fingers teasing the skin on her ears.

"No. Take them back," she begged.

"I can't take them back," he laughed softly at her. "And it makes me feel good to see you in the jewels I gave you. Would you please wear them?" he asked.

When he put it that way, she couldn't really deny him. She quickly changed out her earrings and replaced them with the diamonds, then turned to face him. "You're going to spoil me," she said, grinning up into his handsome face.

"That's the plan, my love," he said and kissed her gently. "Now let's get out of here and go see how Xander deals with Autumn in that dress." He grabbed her hand and led her out the door. "Besides, the faster we get there, the sooner I can have you back here. Minus that dress."

"You're horrible," she laughed, but followed just as eagerly.

Book 4:
His Challenging Lover

INTRODUCTION

Autumn's Story...

"He's hot," Stephanie exclaimed after Joey Rider was a safe distance beyond their lunch table. Both girls smiled, trying to get the young athlete's attention. Unfortunately, Joey only had eyes for Autumn, who was too busy reading her book. She was oblivious to his attention.

Julia, who was sitting next to Autumn, nudged her friend, trying to give her a signal to look up and take an interest. But Autumn simply glanced at Julia before turning back to her book. The story was a murder mystery, and the killer was stalking the man in the red shirt. She had to find out why in the next ten minutes or the bell would ring and Auutmn wouldn't know who the killer was until after school.

"Autumn!" Stephanie glowered, Stephanie couldn't understand what was going on – why her friend wasn't drooling over the guy who never had given any of them the time of day before.

Autumn glanced up again, looking around and blinking. But at thirteen, she hadn't yet developed anything she might consider interesting to boys. She was tall, gangly, had zero fashion sense and there was even less to notice in the boob area. Her idea of getting ready for school was to pull on a pair of jeans, a tee-shirt and her sneakers. Anything else seemed like a waste of reading time.

"What did he want?" she asked, flipping the page and only partially listening to her friends. She really wanted to find out the whodunit ending.

Stephanie and Julia rolled their eyes at their friend, not sure how Autumn could be so oblivious to the boys' attention lately. In the past year, their friend had grown from a nervous, anxious girl into a slender, budding beauty. They could see it, obviously Joey Rider could see it, why couldn't she?

Stephanie placed her hand on top of the book, forcing their friend to pay attention for a moment. "Autumn, you're going to have to take your nose out of that book sooner or later. Don't forget, the winter dance is coming up."

Autumn nibbled on a carrot, nodding her head as if she were paying attention, but really, she was wrapped up in the story, trying to read between Stephanie's fingers. Finally, Stephanie gave up and took her hand away, looking to Julia who only shrugged her shoulders.

Julia wasn't giving up. "The purple elephant behind you is trying to eat your hair," Julia said, and both of them waited with mischievous smiles to see if Autumn would react. The only response was a thoughtless wave of her hand in the general vicinity of the fat braid holding back Autumn's hair.

The two friends just sighed and turned back to talk between themselves, leaving Autumn to her reading. The bell rang and the three of them stood up, carrying their lunch trays to the garbage can.

"Autumn," someone called from her right.

Autumn looked around, her mind still focused on the plot in her book. "Yes?" she answered and her eyes finally focused on the tall, handsome boy standing in front of her. "Hi Joey," she answered, suddenly feeling awkward. Joey was, hands down, the cutest boy in school. Not just the cutest in her class, but in the entire school. With him standing here in front of her, she felt painfully self-conscious, as if everyone around her was also looking, wondering why Joey would be talking to someone like her.

"Hi," he said, leaning forward slightly. "I was wondering if you were going to the dance tomorrow night."

Stephanie, realizing exactly where her friend's mind was going, instantly stepped up and answered for Autumn. "She hasn't decided," she offered, knowing the words would prompt him to either show his hand and ask Autumn to the dance, or move off.

Joey glanced at Stephanie, then back at Autumn. "Well, if you aren't going with anyone, why don't we go together?" he offered, shifting back and forth on his feet as if he were nervous. Autumn thought that idea was impossible because, well duh! This was Joey Rider! Why in the world would he be nervous while talking to her? She was the boring, studious type that liked to organize her mother's closets and cabinets!

Stephanie looked back up at Autumn, then at Joey. Before Autumn could say a word, Stephanie piped up and answered for her. "She'd love to. It would be perfect. What time?"

Joey laughed slightly, running his hand over his head as if trying to smooth down his hair. "Um…how about I pick you up at seven o'clock?" he offered.

Again, Stephanie waited a moment, then shook her head and turned back to Joey. "That's perfect. Thanks Joey."

Joey moved off, smiling at Autumn who simply stood there looking confused.

When they were alone again, Stephanie and Julia both grinned right back at Autumn who was still staring at the empty space where Joey had just been with wide, bewildered eyes. "What just happened here?" she asked.

Julia giggled, enjoying the entire scene. "Joey just asked you out to the school dance tomorrow night."

Autumn blinked and shook her head as if to clear the fog. "Why?"

Stephanie and Julia looked at Autumn, then at each other, then back at Autumn. "Are you kidding me?" When Autumn just shrugged her shoulders, they said simultaneously, "Because you're gorgeous!"

Autumn caused another giggle when she looked down at her jeans and tee-shirt, realizing that there was a scuff on her Converse sneakers. "I'm pretty plain," she replied back.

Stephanie and Julia linked arms on either side of their friend, dragging her along to their geometry class. "We've got some news for you, girl," Julia sighed. "You know all those stories about the ugly duckling?"

Autumn sighed. "I know. I'm the ugly duckling."

Stephanie rolled her eyes as they slipped into their desks. "No silly. You're the swan!" When Autumn shook her head, dismissing the idea as preposterous, Julia piped in. "You've blossomed!" she explained with emphasis. Both of them leaned closer, whispering, "And you've got boobs!"

When Autumn's mouth fell open, she looked down at her chest. Sure enough, something had happened! She'd always worn a bra, simply because she was old enough and all the other girls were wearing one. But she'd never really needed one. Until now!

Stephanie giggled, watching out of the corner of her eye as the teacher said something to a student, preparing to start class. "You've got to stop reading those books and take a look at the world. And yourself. You're gorgeous and you've got all the right features. You should consider becoming a model," she urged.

That finally broke through Autumn's confusion and she threw back her head laughing, holding her stomach at how hilarious her friend's assertion was. "A model?" she asked, taking a deep breath to calm herself down since the teacher was glaring at her now. "Be real!"

Stephanie and Julia couldn't continue to argue their point since class started, but they were both shaking their heads in amazement that their friend had no idea how stunningly beautiful she had become in the past year.

By the following day, Autumn was standing in front of the mirror, worrying about what to wear while Julia and Stephanie sat on her bed, giving her advice.

They'd all come home with her after school and she'd tried on several outfits already, but none of them made her feel very pretty.

"Wear the denim skirt and my flowered shirt," Julia commanded. "And wear your hair down for once!"

Autumn obediently pulled on her denim skirt, the one her mother had bought her several months ago but she'd never worn because she'd always thought her legs were too skinny. She ran her hands down her thighs, wishing she weren't so pale. And that her hair wasn't so straight. Why couldn't she have glorious curly hair? Or even hair with a tiny bit of body?!

She sighed and flopped back onto the bed, ignoring Julia and Stephanie who were peering down at her. "This is useless! I should just call him up and tell him I'm a dumpy fool who prefers to sit on a pile of pillows and read. I can't go out with a guy like Joey!"

Stephanie looked down at her friend with amusement. "You're going to the dance!' she said firmly. "Get up and I'll do your hair. You'll look amazing," she assured Autumn.

"And I'll do your makeup. I've been dying to put some mascara on those gorgeous brown eyes of yours for ages!" Julia scrambled off of the bed and burrowed in her bag. "Here. Wear these," she commanded, holding up a pair of sandals with a kitten heel. "These will make your legs look sexy instead of skinny."

Autumn took the proffered sandals, staring at them dubiously. "Seriously? A pair of sandals are going to transform my knobby knees into something extraordinary?" she asked, thinking her friends were reading too many fashion magazines.

Stephanie handed Autumn the flowered shirt. "Put them on," she said forcefully.

Autumn closed her eyes, feeling cornered and useless. "Fine. But if this is all some sort of sick joke and Joey is just luring me into the trap so everyone will laugh at me, then I'm blaming this all on you two!"

With that, she sat up and let them work their magic, but she didn't really believe that they could do anything that would dramatically change her appearance. She supposed she should just accept that she was the ugly duckling that never really un-uglied.

Forty-five minutes later, Stephanie and Julia pulled her over to the mirror and forced her to take a look at what they'd done. Autumn stared back at the image, not sure who she was looking at. "Is that me?" she asked.

Julia and Stephanie high-fived behind Autumn's head but she ignored them, still staring at her reflection. Her skin was no longer pale, but looked to be creamy with just a hint of rose on her cheeks, softening her entire face. Her eyes, which had always seemed to be a boring brown, now looked huge! Her lashes actually touched the tops of her eyelids and she blinked, realizing there was a very light dusting of gold eye shadow and a thin line of eyeliner that made her eyes look….exotic!

"What did you guys do?" she whispered. Even her hair, which had always fallen straight down her back, now looked fuller, almost glowing. There was movement when she shook her head!

"Do you like it?" Julia asked, worried now that Autumn hadn't said anything.

Autumn continued to stare at her reflection but heard the worry in her friend's voice. She tore her eyes away and grabbed both of them in a big hug. "I love it! I can't believe you did it but I absolutely love it!"

"Good! Now put on the sandals!" Julia ordered.

Autumn accepted the shoes and slipped them onto her feet, surprised that they fit her. But she was even more surprised at how long her legs looked with the slight angle of her calves! The heel wasn't high, but it was just enough to transform her skinny legs to sexy legs! "Wow!"

The girls giggled and laughed, and continued to give her advice. Autumn listened while she picked her clothes up off of the floor and hung them carefully in the closet, ensuring that the colors and seasons were in the right place. She tended to organize things when she was nervous or anxious. Getting chaos into order was her way of controlling her world and keeping her anxiety at bay.

When the doorbell rang, Julia and Stephanie both pushed Autumn out the bedroom door, encouraging her to smile and be interesting while on her date with Joey.

Four hours later, Autumn accepted that her miraculous date with the cutest boy in school was a total bust. She was bored out of her mind. Joey might be cute and a total babe in the muscles department, but he was dull as dirt...and not much smarter. "So what kinds of books do you like to read?" she asked as they sat in a booth at the corner coffee shop. She'd ordered herbal tea while Joey sat across from her with his big hands wrapped around a double espresso.

He shook his head, laughing. "I hate reading. It seems like such a waste of time. I'd rather be out in the world, experiencing life."

Autumn thought about that for a moment. "You have a point," she said. "I guess I read so much and don't actually go out and do anything."

Joey puffed up with pride at saying something right. "See? You've gotta come out to the driving range with me tomorrow," he enthused. "You'll love playing golf."

Autumn forced a smile, not sure what a driving range was or why anyone would go to one. "That sounds like fun," she lied, not sure if she really wanted to do it, but pretty sure she shouldn't turn him down.

"Great, I'll pick you up about ten?" he suggested.

Autumn thought about her Saturday schedule and nodded. "That should be okay. I still need to ask my parents," she cautioned.

"No sweat," he replied.

She glanced at her watch and realized her curfew was approaching. "I'd better get home," she said, standing up and sliding her chair under the table.

Joey stood up as well, but just walked away from the table, leaving his empty, plastic coffee cup sitting on the table and his chair askew. Autumn picked it up and threw both of them away and adjusted the chairs, thinking of the tired waitress who would have to clean up pretty soon. Her mind instantly thought that the act of leaving trash was inconsiderate and lazy, but she pushed the thought away, trying not to judge too harshly.

When he pulled up to her house, he turned off the car and shifted to face her. "I had a really nice time tonight," he said. "And I like the way you did your hair. Very pretty."

Autumn beamed with pride and her heart was racing, pounding so hard with excitement and nervousness because she knew that Joey was going to try and kiss her goodnight.

"I had fun too," she lied once again, but told herself it was for a good cause. It was a first date, she told herself. Everyone is slightly different from who they really are on a first date. At least she suspected that was the case. She didn't have a wide range of experience on the subject since this was her first, first date.

With that small bit of encouragement, Joey leaned closer, put a hand on the back of her neck and pulled her forward.

Autumn had been waiting for this for so long and here it was! Her first kiss!

Joey's lips moved over hers and they were soft and….then his tongue was pushing into her mouth. Autumn tried to pull back but Joey only deepened the kiss. It wasn't bad, she thought, trying to get into the spirit of the moment. But she definitely didn't like the way his tongue just sort of laid in her mouth.

She pulled back, looking at him quizzically. Meanwhile, Joey looked like he'd just accomplished some major feat and she almost laughed. "Well, thanks for tonight." She turned and opened the car door.

"Don't forget about tomorrow," he said, leaning slightly forward. "I'll pick you up at ten tomorrow morning and teach you how to play golf." His grin widened. "You're gonna love it!"

Autumn could only nod her head and take a deep breath to try and prevent her eyes from rolling upwards. Joey played just about every sport there was. He was the quarterback on the football team and had helped the team almost reach the state championship. He played baseball, golf and even a touch of basketball, but he hadn't tried out for the high school team since the football and basketball seasons overlapped.

As she walked inside her house, she wondered if that was all Joey was about. They'd barely been able to converse tonight because they simply didn't have enough things in common. So why had he asked her out again? What was the point? They couldn't talk which meant they couldn't connect with each other.

And his kiss! Blech! How annoying was that?!

"How was your date, dear?" her mother asked as soon as she walked into the house. Her mother was ready for bed, sipping a cup of tea while Autumn's father snored on the couch beside her. They were obviously waiting up for her since they normally were in bed by nine-thirty. Ten o'clock was shockingly late for her parents to be awake and here it was, eleven!

"It was fine," she said and flopped onto the overstuffed chair that faced the sofa and her parents. "Joey is nice enough, but…"

Her mother smiled kindly. "He seemed like a very handsome boy."

Autumn laughed. "He's a year older than I am and the most popular guy in the school. I have no idea why he asked me out. Especially since we have nothing in common. Not even any classes together."

Her father snorted awake at that point. "I know why," he grumbled. "And he's not getting it!" With those words of wisdom, he hefted himself off the sofa, kissed Autumn on the top of her head and moved off to bed. "Goodnight, my beauties," he said as he headed up the stairs.

Autumn giggled at her father, not believing for a moment that she was truly a beauty. She accepted that she might look better with makeup on, but he was only referring to Autumn's beautiful mother when he thought of "beauty". Autumn's mother was exceptionally pretty, even without any makeup like right now. And what was even more important, her mother was beautiful inside. She rarely had a bad thing to say about anyone, never gossiped and always smiled her way through life. The only time Autumn had seen her mother cry was after her grandparents had passed away. Otherwise, she loved life and thought every day was an adventure. Autumn wanted to live just like that!

"So tell me what happened. Did he kiss you goodnight?"

Autumn's nose wrinkled with distaste. "Yes."

"And?" her mother prompted when Autumn didn't elaborate.

Autumn sighed. "It wasn't the stars and lightning I was expecting."

Her mother smiled gently. "I don't really believe that there's one woman for every man, but I do believe there's a special chemistry between two people that is either there, or it isn't. And there's nothing anyone can do to create that special energy if it is missing."

She thought about that for a moment. "What happens if you have chemistry with someone and they don't feel the same towards you?" she asked, worrying about this whole male and female relationship thing. "Or what if you feel it and you don't like the person?"

Her mother laughed. "Dear, you're worrying about things that might not ever happen. Just relax and enjoy dating for a while," she advised gently.

Autumn leaned her head back against the chair's cushion and thought about those words. She didn't like not knowing. She preferred her life to be ordered and consistent. Mysteries were annoying unless she was reading one. She didn't want to live one!

"I definitely don't have any chemistry with Joey. But he's going to teach me how to play golf tomorrow." She cringed as if the idea were boring.

Autumn's mother laughed softly. "Good luck with that. Your father tried to teach me to play golf. He now forbids me to even drive into the parking lot when he's there. He says I'm worse than a water hazard, whatever that means."

Autumn laughed as well. "Mom, it means that you hit the ball towards people instead of the hole."

"Phsht!" was her mother's only response. "So did you like him?" she asked.

Autumn thought about that for a moment. "He was nice enough. Much nicer than I thought he would be. I thought jocks were generally rude, obnoxious people."

"What have I told you about stereotypes?" her mother admonished.

"I know," she sighed. "But the stereotypes form from something."

"True," her mother replied. She stood up and came over to her daughter. "I'm sorry the chemistry wasn't there for you, my love."

Autumn stood up as well, hugging her mother. "It wasn't too bad," she said as she followed her mother into the kitchen. After her mother's cup was put into the dishwasher, they made their way up the stairs, laughing about the silly things men did to impress girls.

But as Autumn slipped into bed, she wondered if she would ever find that chemistry with a man. She'd read about it in her books, craved the idea of how wonderful it would be to instantly melt when a man touched her. But so far, none of the guys in her school had even sparked a tiny bit of excitement inside of her.

She stared up at the ceiling, thinking about how exciting it would be to find a man who could make her weak in the knees from just a look across the room.

Someday, she told herself. It would happen to her too. She just knew it would!

Xander's Story...

Xander watched warily, but with ample appreciation, as Jessica Meyers walked cautiously through the construction site.

It wasn't so much that she walked, he thought, wiping the sweat off of his forehead with a rag. Jessica Meyers glided. He'd never thought about a woman's walk before, but Jessica had walking down to an art form, ensuring that every man between the ages of eight and eighty stopped and admired.

Five minutes ago, there had been drilling and banging, power tools whirling and men calling out instructions to one another. But as Jessica crossed through the debris and construction equipment littering the yard, every man around stopped and stared, gawking at the female teen with long legs and perfect breasts, all displayed to perfection in the short shorts and skin tight, low cut tee-shirt.

"Hi Xander," she said with an I-know-you-want-me smile. "How's it going?"

Xander wiped his forehead again, not sure if the sweat was completely due to working in the hot sun or from Jessica's attention. It seemed like her curves were pulling all the liquid from his body and pouring it out through his pores, making his mouth dry.

Well, not all liquid, he thought uncomfortably.

"What's up Jessica?" he asked, wishing he could bring saliva back to his mouth. He was eternally grateful for whoever invented sunglasses because he simply couldn't pull his eyes upward long enough to focus on her face when there were so many other, more interesting, places on which his eyes preferred to focus.

"We've all been wondering why you haven't been to the pool this summer." She smiled and her eyes wandered down his body, completely unembarrassed by her perusal. He was naked from the chest up, his teenage muscles protruding in all the right places while his jeans rode low on his hips, showing off the perfect contours of his abdomen…and lower. "I made it my mission to find out where you were."

Someone to his right coughed, an obvious effort to cover up his laughter.

"I thought it might be time to earn a few bucks this summer," he told her. He bent down low and lifted the next bag of cement. Since he was only sixteen, he couldn't actually do any of the construction work, but he'd gotten a job as one of the manual laborers, which basically meant he hauled all the heavy stuff from one place to another so the carpenters or bricklayers could do their jobs more efficiently. It was hard work, but paid better than most of the other jobs his friends had been able to land for the summer. They hadn't been big enough or strong enough to qualify, while Xander had been hired on the spot because of his height and brawn.

"What's been happening lately?" he asked, but he already knew since he was in touch with his friends. He just asked to humor her until she was ready to explain the real reason for her visit.

Jessica followed Xander, picking her way through the debris like a fairy princess. Xander simply tromped over the wood and piles of equipment, his work boots protecting his feet from the nails and other sharp objects.

"Well, I broke up with Lionel yesterday," she said, obviously an opening she hoped he would take.

"That's too bad," he said. "You and Lionel seemed made for each other."

Jessica scoffed. "I didn't think so," she replied with derision. "I realized quickly that Lionel wasn't going anywhere fast."

That was news to Xander. He dumped the bag of cement onto the pile he'd already carried across the yard, vaguely noting that the construction noise had slowly resumed to previous levels. "So why are you here?"

Jessica laughed, twirling a lock of hair around her fingertip while her voluptuous body posed carefully for his titillation. "I told you. I wanted to know what you've been up to."

Xander walked back to his starting point and hauled another bag onto his shoulder, wishing the woman would just go away. "Listen, Lionel is my friend. I know what you're getting at and I'm not getting in the way."

She huffed for a moment, then traipsed behind him. "I'm not his personal property," she hissed. "I can go out with anyone I want!"

Xander gritted his teeth, and not from the exertion from the fifty pound bag of cement. The thought of those curves in his hands made his body tighten. He was a healthy male teenager and he might not like her intellectually, but the teenage male body didn't need that in order to be interested. Xander was quickly discovering the male body didn't need anything more than a willing female for his interest to be captivated.

"What's everyone else doing this summer?" he asked, even though he already knew what most of his friends were up to. They got together occasionally for pool parties and such, although he hadn't heard that Lionel and Jessica had broken up.

Jessica stared at the hard back of the man she wanted, her mind working quickly. There was no way she was going to let this guy out of her sights. Xander was bigger, stronger and more handsome than Lionel. Not to mention, Xander was more charming. She liked that. She wanted to have him on her arm and had been working towards this goal all year. She'd just kept Lionel on the sidelines as someone to keep her company while she worked on Xander.

When he was about to pick up one of the other bags, she pushed it slightly off balance. He was glaring up at her when she pressed herself against his chest, her hands diving into his hair so he had no doubt about what she was going to offer. "Look Xander. I've wanted you for a while now. I don't care if you see other women, but I want to be considered your girlfriend. So you let me have what I want," and she hesitated, licking her lips and pressing herself against him more tightly, ensuring that she got her message across, "and I'll let you have what you want. Do we understand each other?"

Xander wasn't sure exactly how to reply, but he hated the way his body reacted. Seeing her knowing smile, he knew that she was fully aware of his reaction too.

"I can tell that we understand each other perfectly." She stepped backwards, her hands sliding down his sweat-soaked chest and stomach. "So pick me up when you get off from work today and I'll let you take me out to dinner."

With that, she walked away. Xander and everyone else on the work site watched her tight little bottom as she practically skipped through the obstacle-laden yard to her car. When she finally roared off down the street, the construction noise increased once again. But after that afternoon, Xander earned the respect of every man on that work site, many of them patting him on the back when he passed by and telling him they would jump onto that offer in a heartbeat. All of them fully expecting Xander to take what was being offered by the delectable Jessica Meyers.

Back home that evening, Xander jumped off his motorcycle. He and Ryker had bought it for less than a hundred bucks and repaired it the previous summer. It ran, but it was loud and bumpy, since he and his brother hadn't been able to afford new shock absorbers or a muffler yet. Those were luxuries they were planning to install later in the bike's lifecycle.

He walked into the kitchen, the delicious scents of his mother's cooking reaching him as soon as he walked through the door. "What's for dinner?" he asked, kissing her on the cheek.

The scent of her son's sweat-soaked body hit her full force and she cringed, laughing at his rascally expression. "Uh! Go take a shower before dinner!" she admonished him, but kissed him back before pointing towards the stairs to reinforce her command. She was focused on pulling the cheese biscuits out of the oven, dumping them onto the cooling rack before turning once again towards the stove to stir the chili they would be having for their evening meal.

Xander stole one of the biscuits and took a huge bite; it didn't even start to ease the gnawing hunger in his belly but he was used to that. He could never get enough food, especially now that he worked construction.

When his mother called out to him, he realized he might get caught with his purloined biscuit and thought quickly. "Hey Axel!" he called out to his younger brother. As soon as Axel looked up from the magazine he was reading, Xander tossed the biscuit in his direction. Axel's automatic reflexes kicked in and he caught the missile a moment before Xander turned the corner that would hide him from his mother's laser-sharp eyes.

"Axel Thorpe!" his mother cried out when she saw the pilfered food in her son's hand. "Those are for dinner!"

Xander covered his mouth so his burst of laughter wasn't heard while he stared at Axel's confused face. An expression that quickly changed to anger when he realized what his older brother had done.

"It wasn't me, Mom," Axel said, but took a bite himself.

Xander didn't hear the rest of the explanation since he raced up the stairs and turned on the shower, just in case. The water from the shower would cover the shout from his mother when he was caught.

He was drying off after his shower when Ash banged on his door. Without waiting for a response, his youngest brother opened the door and tossed the phone in. "Phone call for you," he snapped, then disappeared before any missile could head back at him.

Xander picked up the phone and answered. "Hello?"

"Hi Xander, this is Diana."

Xander flopped back onto his bed, a smile forming on his face. "What's up?"

"I was wondering what you were up to. I don't have anything to do tonight and thought maybe we could hang out together."

Xander's smile widened. "Hanging out" was hopefully a euphemism for something more interesting than literally hanging out and talking. But something cautioned him. Diane had been dating his buddy Mark back at the end of the school year. "What's Mark doing? Aren't you and he still going out?" The image of Jessica's calculating eyes came to his mind and he shuddered with revulsion. Diane was pretty and he'd always thought she was sweet and kind.

Diane laughed through the phone lines. "He's out at the lake this week with his parents."

That caused every excited thought in his mind to freeze to a painful, screeching halt. "Did you guys break up or something?" he asked, trying to clarify, not sure he believed what he was hearing.

"Of course not," she laughed again. "He's a great guy. But he's also not here at the moment. And I was trying to drum up something exciting to do for the night."

"And I came to mind, eh?" Xander pulled on a pair of boxers and shorts, grabbing a tee-shirt before heading out of his room towards the kitchen once again.

Her tinkling giggle this time just made his skin crawl.

"You got it," she replied. "So what do you say? Want to meet over at the ball field in say…an hour?"

Xander thought about Jessica and Diane, not sure he liked the trend he was picking up on. "I'm going to have to pass," he answered. "I just got off of work and I'm pretty beat."

"Oh, poor baby." She paused for a moment and Xander could picture her pretty blue eyes trying to come up with some idea while her cute, pink tongue slipped out between her inviting, full lips. He shook his head to dispel the image, not liking what was beneath the imagined invitation.

"Listen, Diane, I gotta go. My mom is calling all of us to dinner. I'll talk to you later, okay?"

"Okay. But if you change your mind, just give me a call back. Mark is out of town all week."

Xander didn't respond, too amazed by the blatant disregard for Mark's feelings on the subject. He picked up his cell phone and texted Mark. "Hey Dude! How's the lake this summer?"

As he was walking down the stairs to dinner, pulling a clean shirt over his head, his cell phone pinged back, indicating he had a message. Looking down, he couldn't believe the words he read. Mark had already replied, "Gorgeous women here at the lake. Met girl named Missy. Hot!"

He sat down at the dinner table, not hearing his father's deep voice as he blessed the food or his mother's admonishment for the men in her life to slow down. All he thought about was the disparity between what he'd always thought of relationships between men and women and the reality he was discovering. His eyes looked from one end of the table where his father joked with Ryker about something while Ash and Axel chimed in, causing everyone to laugh. Then he glanced to the other end of the table while his mother rolled her eyes, shaking her head at the antics of the five men surrounding her.

He'd always thought that male and female relationships would be like his parents' marriage, both of whom were dedicated to each other and their family. His mother went out of her way to do small things to help his father and Xander knew that his dad worshiped his mom. But several of his friends' parents were already divorced. He didn't mind if the couples of his group broke up and found other girlfriends or boyfriends, but he'd always thought that there would at least be fidelity within the relationship while it lasted. Hell, he'd even had several girlfriends since he'd discovered how fascinating the female population could be. But he'd never even thought of cheating on his girlfriend. He now wondered if any of his girlfriends had been with other guys.

Shaking his head, he looked down at his bowl, not sure what he'd eaten for dinner, but his bowl was empty. "May I be excused?" he asked politely.

His mother looked at him with a concerned expression in her eyes. "Is everything okay, dear?" she asked, placing a gentle hand on his arm.

"I'm good," he replied, not moving his hand. He liked his mother's soft touch, felt reassured by her hand on his arm. "I'm just beat from work today."

His mother excused him and, thankfully, it wasn't his turn to do the dishes so he was able to get away quickly. He picked up a book and tried to read, but as the summer sun started to set over the horizon and the evening turned to night, he hadn't turned the page. He remembered his co-workers at the site today. Most of them were married but almost every one of them had smacked him on the back and said they'd have pursued Jessica's offer if she ever made it to one of them. He knew there were honest, faithful partners in the world. But he was quickly discovering that many were not. A concept he'd never even contemplated before..

CHAPTER 1

Autumn stood by the side of the receptionist's desk, praying the woman wouldn't say the words that would once again break her heart. Just ask for any other name, she silently prayed. Any name, even someone who didn't work here would make her feel better.

Unfortunately, fate wasn't playing nice today.

"I'm here to see Xander Thorpe," the blond woman with the almost dripping red lips said while flicking her thick, blond hair back over her shoulder.

Autumn knew that the hair flip was only to show off her impressive bosom, perfectly displayed by the deep V of her red dress.

Diane, the receptionist, acted professionally, exactly as Autumn had trained her. She turned to her computer with a gracious smile, her fingers poised over the keyboard as she said, "Do you have an appointment?" Diane knew that her boss, the amazingly lovely brunette with the deep brown eyes, was standing beside her stiffly, watching to see how this exchange played out. And everyone knew that there was something going on between Autumn and the gorgeous Xander Thorpe, although none were entirely sure what that "something" was.

The blond bimbo, as Autumn now thought of the latest female intrusion, laughed and waved her hand. "I don't, but I'm pretty sure he'll see me," she said and smoothed her hands down her hips. "Just tell him Jessica is here to speak with him."

Diane knew the process. She typed the information into the computer, then sent off the notice to Xander's assistant, a new woman by the name of Tilly. She was a temporary employee, brought in yesterday when his last one quit without any notice. Xander had a bad habit of going through assistants at a horrible rate. With gritted teeth, Autumn slapped the file folder down onto the table and walked quickly out of the area. Her feet pushed her faster, desperate to not see…

Unfortunately, Autumn didn't make her escape fast enough. When the woman in red entered Xander's office and closed the door, the jokes and money from the other staff members quickly started exchanging hands.

"How much did you win?" James, one of the third year lawyers asked another associate just as Autumn hurried past his desk.

Autumn gritted her teeth and shook her head, walking quickly by him but trying to paste a calm-looking smile on her face. As usual, wagers were being settled now that the previous girlfriend, a lovely brunette, had been replaced by the gorgeous blond. Autumn desperately didn't want anyone in the office to know how painful she found the betting. Xander's love life served as entertainment for the rest of the office, but it hurt her more than it should. Every time a new woman came into his life, Autumn hated Xander just a little bit more. Why should she even care who he dates? He could date anyone he wanted! She just wished he would keep his personal life outside the office.

Maybe that's what bothered her so much about his philandering ways. She hurried down the hallway, ignoring the laughter and money changing hands. It looked like a new pool was being set up. If Xander would keep his private life more private, it wouldn't bother her so much. She preferred efficiency and order, trained her support staff to work hard, look and act professionally and be exceptionally helpful and competent.effective. The bets about how long the current flavor-of-the-moment would last reduced everyone's productivity.

Autumn knew that the betting on Xander's love live occurred but she never participated. Everyone thought she was just being polite and trying to ignore her boss's dalliances. But she knew better why she wasn't delving into the bitter world of Xander's girlfriend office pool.

Axel and Ash were walking towards her and she quickly looked down. But Axel wasn't having any of that. He caught the flash of pain in her eyes and touched her arm gently, obviously concerned.

"What's going on, Autumn? You look like you've just lost your best friend."

Autumn laughed bitterly. "Oh, goodness, nothing so dramatic as that," she came back, her shoulders squared off against the pain ripping through her silly, vulnerable heart. "It's just the changing of the guard." At their blank looks, she sighed and said, "Xander's old girlfriend is out and a new one is in. Everyone in the cubicles is paying up on their bets and placing new wagers on this next woman." She was looking downwards, wishing she could just race to her own office and hide away until the pain abated, but then she caught the twenty dollar bill exchange from Axel to Ash. "That was thirty-one days, right?" he asked.

She nodded numbly, unaware that her mouth was hanging open in shock that even Xander's two younger brothers would be involved in the betting.

When those dratted tears threatened to spill over her lashes, she took a deep, frantic breath and started moving around the two extremely large men. "If you'll excuse me," she said, but didn't bother finishing the sentence as she raced down the hallway and into her office.

She wasn't aware of the two men staring after her, both of them frozen into stunned silence. "Well I'll be…" Axel said, watching until she slammed the door to her office.

Ash stopped staring at the now-closed door and grinned towards his brother. "I think that's another twenty you owe me," he said.

Axel looked at his brother, then back at the closed door one more time. "I would have sworn…" he started to say, then shook his head. "You were right." And he handed Ash another twenty. "At least it was just around us."

Ash nodded his head as well, his mouth grim with irritation over his older brother's insensitivity. "Yeah. She's usually more in control."

Axel grinned as they both turned to continue their walk down the hallway. "Want to bet on when he'll crack and admit it to her?"

Ash was already shaking his head. "Hell no! Big Brother Xander realizing what's going on?"

Both men laughed as they continued towards their destination, unaware of the woman leaning against the doorway fighting back the tears. Thankfully, Autumn didn't hear their conversation or she would have been even more humiliated. As it was, she just had to deal with the pain of seeing Xander with yet another beautiful woman. She hated this, she told herself, brutally wiping the tears from her cheeks. He was such a jerk! Why did he have to bring those women here? It was an insult to everyone's professionalism and productivity.

He should be more inconspicuous about his personal life during business hours, and he should never have his girlfriends trot around here like that! It was unprincipled and inappropriate!

And it hurt! Damn the man!

She sat down behind her desk and dropped her head onto her hands, trying to control the painful emotions that were threatening to choke her. She should find another job, she told herself firmly. She shouldn't put herself through the pain of watching him come and go with those women.

The idea of not being here, of not seeing…all the Thorpe brothers, caused another sharp stab of pain. She liked her job, except when there was a changing of the guard. She really shouldn't let it bother her so much. She should just look the other way and leave him to his philandering ways.

Or maybe she should talk to him, try and convince him to keep his lady loves outside the office. Too many staff members watched them come and go. Not to mention the younger men on the staff seeing ridiculous antics like that. Xander was a role model! He was teaching the younger men that women were disposable, that they weren't worth the effort to invest in a real relationship.

When the meeting notification pinged, she looked at her computer and sighed. She wouldn't have time to consider the option of finding a new job right at the moment. She had yet another meeting to attend. Thankfully this one was just with her own staff so she wouldn't have to sit at the conference table and feel Xander's presence. Or even worse, fight the growing anger whenever he prodded her temper. The man was ingenious about getting a rise out of her and no matter how hard she tried to stay calm, she inevitably ended up firing one or two pointed jibes his way just to get back at him. He changed her, she thought resentfully. He made her act in a petty manner and she hated it. She wanted to remain calm and unemotional, to appear professional at all times. But he just kept on pushing her buttons, making her angry and forcing her temper out into the open.

She took a deep breath and grabbed a tissue out of her drawer, patting down her cheeks. With efficient movements, she pulled a mirror out of another drawer and repaired her makeup, furious that he'd reduced her to tears this time. When her face looked calm once again, she stood up and walked to the window in her office, taking several deep breaths.

From the other side of the office, Xander watched with rising fury and frustration as Autumn Hallman walked into her office, closing the door. Closing everyone out. He saw his brothers turn the corner and he made a mental note to ask them later if they knew what had upset her. He would do it now, but he had to get rid of Jessica Lilsedale. The irritating woman had attached herself to his arm last night at some charity function and he hadn't been able to get rid of her. Why had she shown up here? He'd given her absolutely no encouragement last night. And now she wanted a private word with him?

He'd gotten into the office early this morning, needing time to get work done because he had a busy schedule. Normally, the fall was a slower than normal period in his division, but not this year for some reason. Business was thriving and he was going to have to bring on a few more lawyers if this pace kept up.

He ran the family law practice in The Thorpe Group, which included all family issues, but mostly it came down to the divorce division. He had a thriving practice with people almost lining up at the door wanting to tear apart the spouse that, only a few years earlier, they'd promised to love, honor and cherish. It always astounded him that people who had once claimed to love each other so much that they wanted to dedicate their lives together, could reduce their entire world down to money and a desire to hurt someone as painfully as possible, in any way available.

Jessica was rattling on and on about some inane issue. All the while, he was looking down the hallway towards Autumn's office door, willing her to come out and show her face just so he could see that she was okay. Had someone hurt her feelings? Was she overwhelmed with her work load? He'd go directly to his brothers if they were laying too much on her slender shoulders. She was just one woman, but she continued to accept more and more responsibility within the firm.

Good grief, what was Jessica prattling on about now?

"So what do you think?" she asked, tilting her head and twirling her bleached blond hair with her talon-tipped fingers.

Xander hadn't heard a word she'd said. "I'm sorry, what was the question?"

Jessica laughed and playfully punched his shoulder. "Tonight! The party? Are you up for some fun?"

Attending any social function with this annoying female was definitely not going to happen. With as much patience as he could muster, he walked the irritating woman to the elevators, ignoring her obnoxious chatter. "I'm sure you'll have a much better time without me," he said and took her hand, effectively releasing her grip on his arm. He lifted her hand to his lips and, as graciously as possible, kissed her fingers in an effort to send her off into the descending elevators.

As soon as she was gone, he breathed a sigh of relief. Unfortunately, the cloying cloud of perfume she left in her wake almost made him gag. Why did women insist on bathing in the rancid stuff? His mind instantly thought of the way Autumn smelled. She was always fresh and clean. He couldn't think of a single time that she'd worn perfume. But she always smelled…incredible.

Back in the office, he stood at the end of the hallway, contemplating Autumn's closed door. She was upset and he had no idea why but it tore him apart.

He had no right to feel this way. She was an employee, and an exceptional one at that. He was one of the owners, so he should remain distant and treat her just like he would any other employee. He and his three other brothers owned equal shares in The Thorpe Group and, between the four of them, they could cover about every area of law possible.

What he couldn't cover was his need to hold Autumn Hallman in his arms. Seeing her like this, her beautiful, brown eyes filled with tears, tore him apart. He hated seeing her in pain.

What could be wrong?

She'd been with the firm for five years, working here as a receptionist while still in college, and she'd become even more valuable as she'd matured. And more beautiful. He'd been aching for her ever since she'd first walked through the doors looking for a job, and that need had only intensified as he'd gotten to know her.

He knew that she thought of him as a royal pain in the ass. At times, he annoyed her just to see her brown eyes sparkle with anger and those pretty, pale cheeks bloom with color. And other times, he was in so much pain to possess her, to be with her and be near her that he snapped at the world. His administrative assistants bore the brunt of his irritation, but he couldn't deny the pleasure of working with Autumn every time he had to replace the previous assistant who had quit.

Of course, it helped that the last several assistants were completely inept. He wasn't one to pressure someone into quitting, just so he could have one-on-one time with Autumn. No, he'd never do that to his staff. The ones that had left over the past two years had genuinely been under skilled and possessed of a bad attitude.

The last one had quit just yesterday, but he didn't mind since he'd been about to fire her anyway. The client files were a complete mess and the woman had lost track of all of his appointments, triple scheduling clients and leaving large gaps in between.

But now he felt like someone was tearing off his arm – all because Autumn was upset about something. And she had to be genuinely upset because, unless she was snapping at him, she never let her emotions interrupt business. This was extremely unusual.

"Ms. Davenport is here to see you," his temporary assistant said, handing him the file.

Xander took the file with resignation. He wanted to toss the file into his office and storm down to Autumn's office so he could fix whatever had hurt her. Instead, he focused on his next client, reading through the file and skimming through the details. "She has coffee already?" Xander asked, distracted by the file and thinking about Autumn, worried that someone in the office might have hurt her feelings.

No, that was impossible. Besides him and his brothers, there wasn't anyone with as much authority in the office as Autumn. She ruled the schedules and the case loads with military precision. If anyone dared to irritate her, she quickly and efficiently put them in their place.

He loved hearing that too. When one of the other lawyers tried to get uppity, she'd simply give them a piece of her mind. Anyone who came up against the mighty Autumn Hallman went away with their tail between their legs.

Except him. He loved going head to head with her.

Unfortunately, he knew that Autumn wasn't interested in him. She had her own life, her own hobbies and plans for the future.

But he couldn't stop his eyes from looking at Autumn's closed door before he sighed and made his way into his own office. Ms. Davenport awaited. She was on her third marriage and each one made her wealthier than the last. With his help, of course.

CHAPTER 2

Autumn came into the office early the next day, needing to get some work done in the quiet time before the rest of the staff came into work. She couldn't believe the week she was having. First, her best friend gets arrested for murder and next, yet another assistant quits on Xander. That was the third one in six months! What does that man do that annoys them so much?

Okay, so the last one wasn't up to scratch. She was embarrassed to say it, but she'd known from the beginning that that one wasn't going to work out.

But in her defense, she had to work closely with Xander each time they hired a personal assistant for him. During that last round, she'd just short circuited the interview process because it was getting harder and harder to be around him. Keeping her distance was the most important way she kept her sanity while working so closely with him. Unfortunately, doing interviews for his assistant meant sitting next to him, feeling the man's heat emanating from his body even from the distance she maintained from him. She couldn't handle that for more than a few days so she'd convinced him that the last woman was good enough.

Now she had to pay the price for cutting the interview process short. She had to go through the whole process over again: sit next to him, listen to his teasing comments, and argue with him about one candidate or another.

It was an exhausting process.

She couldn't understand why even her office had to be so close to his. It was like the man invented ways to torture her.

But of course, he couldn't know how she felt about him. To the rest of the office, she and Xander were combatants with brief periods of peaceful coexistence. Lately though, those peaceful periods were few and far between. They had been snapping at each other more often lately and, although at times it was exhilarating, she had to admit that it sometimes became exhausting.

Especially when one of his lady loves came to pick him up for their date.

She truly hated the man during those periods. It wasn't even that the man had a type! He dated redheads, blonds, brunettes. He escorted celebrities, famous actresses, social butterflies and power-hungry career women.

With a sigh, she wiped her eyes and shook her head. "Enough!" she told herself firmly. "The day marches on!" And so would she.

She turned around and looked at her computer. She had numerous issues to deal with and not much time to finish them. She was worried about her friend Mia who was battling murder charges, but every time she asked Ash about her, he just told her that he had everything under control. She had to trust him on that. And if anyone could get Mia out of that mess, it would be Ash. He was brilliant.

Mia would be in the office again today, answering more questions from Ash and his team. Maybe the two of them could catch a movie tonight, escape from the pressure of Mia's murder charges and Autumn's irritating boss.

She sighed and slid her chair under her desk, losing herself in the latest plans to make the law firm more efficient. Once again, she lost track of time as one issue after another cropped up during the morning. She loved her job, loved the way people relied on her to smooth out the troubles. Fixing things was her forte and she thrived on finding good solutions to every problem and keeping The Thorpe Group organized.

When she finally realized how hungry she was, it was past the normal lunch period. She grabbed her wallet and headed outside, raising her face up to the warm sunshine. There wouldn't be too many more days like this, she thought. The days were already shorter and there was a definite bite to the night time air. Winter was coming quickly.

Despite the later hour, the lunch crowd at the building deli was heavy and Autumn sighed as she waited at the end of the line. This deli was always crowded but it also had the best sandwiches at a reasonable price for several miles. They made some sort of sauce that added a zing and a zip, making the whole experience much more enjoyable. No one knew what that sauce was, but several people had tried. Occasionally there were recipes in the office kitchen where someone thought they might have figured out the recipe. No one had discovered the formula exactly though so the mystery remained.

Normally, she would have called in her order and had it waiting at the checkout line, a great service the deli provided. But it had been too busy today in the office. And because she'd had trouble falling asleep last night, worrying about Mia and Xander and wondering what he might be doing, she'd woken up too late to grab something for breakfast. So here she was, waiting impatiently for her chance to order a sandwich.

She glanced across the street, considering just grabbing a yogurt at the small convenience store. It would certainly be faster, but at that moment, the line moved forward and she stuck with her desire for a filling, spicy sandwich.

"Hey!" a voice called out from somewhere to the left of her. She glanced in that direction, but she was too hungry to give it much thought.

Suddenly, the crowd parted and she saw what was happening. And couldn't believe her eyes!

"Get the hell out of the way, lady!" a brutish, bullish man was saying to an elderly woman wearing sensible shoes and a warm cardigan even on the warmish October day. Her grey hair looked frazzled and her eyes nervous as she watched the man with the fuzzy mustache warily.

Another man, this one thinner and taller, shook his head. "She was in line first," the stranger said in a placating tone, but even he didn't want to confront the portly blowhard.

"Oh yea?" the man taunted, his eyes narrowing and his hands balling into fists. "Well, prove it!" he snapped and started forward. His intent was clear and everyone around scattered, pushing backwards to avoid getting caught in the fight.

The horrible man swung out, his hand missing the thin gentleman but side striking the elderly lady who went down with the initial bump. Her cry of fright was heard by one and all but no one stepped forward to intervene.

A small part of Autumn's mind was still functioning properly and told her to stay out of it. But the other part of her brain, the part that wasn't functioning rationally and was outraged that someone would hit an elderly person, was in control and she was livid that this man had hurt someone who was just standing, waiting for lunch. Instead of pushing back into the crowd, she stepped forward, her instincts made her grab onto the fat man's arm. Unfortunately, she realized too late that the arm wasn't just lard, but packed with muscles. But by the time she realized that, he was already turning around to confront his newest threat.

Autumn dropped the man's arm and stood with her feet braced apart, her hands at the ready, trying to anticipate what the burly man might do next. "Call the police," she ordered to the crowd. Not to anyone in particular, and she knew that the police wouldn't be able to get here in time to save her but she threw that out as a threat anyway, hoping the man would stop and think. It might even give her a tiny reprieve, enough to slow him down.

No such luck. The call for the police only enraged the man further. That rational part of her mind, the part that wasn't blanking out with the anger over what this man had done, noticed all the other men and women standing back, their mouths open and their eyes wide with amazement of all that was unfolding. It flashed through her mind that, if everyone put their efforts together, they could stop this man simply by grabbing his arms and pinning him to the ground.

But obviously no one was thinking clearly. Not even her. And the man rushed her, his fist swinging out and clipping her under her jaw while his other hand swung out and aimed for her ribs. She gasped at the pain, twisted slightly and used the man's momentum to throw him off balance. He came back at her in only seconds, not giving her enough time to regroup. As she stared at the bloodlust in his eyes, she knew that the previous tackle was only a precursor to this one but she spun around and braced herself, prepared to do whatever it took to stop this man.

All she saw was him coming towards her one moment and the next, he was gone, slammed up against the wall of the deli with his arm twisted behind his back and his right cheek smashed so he wasn't able to look anywhere but up at the ceiling.

"So, you like taking swings at women half your size, eh?" Xander was saying, twisting the man's arm slightly and causing him to flinch again. "How about if you take on someone a bit bigger and see how you fare?" he asked.

There was applause all around but Autumn only saw Xander's enormous, magnificent body as he glared down at the portly man. She knew she should hide her appreciation for his tall, muscular form, but it was simply too impressive.

There was another commotion over by the doors as the police belatedly arrived, hands on their pistols as they quickly surveyed the situation. When they saw who was holding the man, both police officers' jaw dropped.

"Are you okay, Mr. Thorpe?" one of them asked, rushing over with his handcuffs in his hand, efficiently taking over the man being restrained.

"I'm fine. But this man assaulted the lady on the floor and Autumn Hallman, my office manager."

The police officer was more than a little overwhelmed by the idea of talking to Xander Thorpe. He was sort of a legend in the boxing ring as well as the legal community. But the officer squared his shoulders, eager to look good in front of the man most officers revered. "We'll book him for assault and battery as well as disorderly conduct," the other officer said. He went over to the elderly woman, helping her stand up and checking her to see if she needed an ambulance. Meanwhile, Xander spun around to glare at Autumn and she cringed at the furious look in his indigo blue eyes. Why was he angry with her?

Okay, so that was a silly question. Xander was always angry with her for one reason or another. And normally, she would spit the fire right back at him, giving as good as she got. But she'd never seen him this furious. Normally, he reserved his anger to sarcastic, pithy comments in a meeting or biting remarks when she didn't find him a staff addition or replacement quickly enough.

This was a whole new level of fury.

With the police officers trying to organize the witnesses, get statements and haul the brute away, Xander walked slowly towards her. Actually, it wasn't so much walking as it was stalking. There were only about five steps separating both of them, but it seemed like a lifetime for him to reach her. When he was less than an inch away from her, she looked up into his blue eyes, her neck craning back because she couldn't move backwards and he wasn't relenting.

He didn't say a word. He simply grabbed her arm in a vicelike grip and hauled her out of the deli.

"We're going to need Ms. Hallman to give us a statement," one of the officers was saying as Xander dragged her to the doorway.

Autumn scrambled to keep up but it was hard because the Xander was so much taller than she was. Well, and she was wearing three inch heels. She knew they made her legs look awesome, but they didn't make running too easy.

"I'll bring her to you later," Xander replied to the officer as politely as his anger would allow.

Autumn was about to demand an explanation but he didn't stop long enough for her to even get a breath. This man had tormented her for years with his anger and she was sick of it! It was going to end today! She was just about to pull her arm free and confront the man when he pulled her to the side of the building.

Xander didn't even try to get control of his anger. He'd never been so terrified in his life as when he saw Autumn confront that ridiculous excuse for a human being. And when the man had actually hit her, marred her perfect, beautiful skin, he'd seen red. There had been no conscious thought after that. It was pure instinct. With a rage surging through his blood, he'd grabbed the man before he could harm Autumn again, moments before he was about to make contact in his second charge, and slammed the man against the wall. With a vicious twist, Xander had pulled the man's arm behind his back, wanting desperately to snap the arm off of him. He'd glanced back, catching sight of Autumn again. Seeing her, knowing that she was once again safe, was the only thing that gave him back some measure of control.

When the police arrived, he was more than happy to release the dung heap to them but he still couldn't rid himself of the fury and fear. With a growl and a determination to ensure that Autumn, his Autumn, his beautiful, delicate, sweet and overly brave Autumn, was okay, he grabbed her arm. He wasn't sure what he was going to do. All he knew was that he had to ensure that she was okay. That she was still whole.

When he saw the side of the building, out of the way of other people passing by, he hauled her there. He'd thought he was only going to confront her, demand an explanation as to why she'd taken such ridiculous risks with her life and her body. But instead, he found himself kissing her. But this wasn't just a kiss. This was a life affirming, knee bracing, stomach clenching demonstration of all that he felt for this woman.

Autumn was so surprised when his mouth covered hers that she was stunned motionless for all of about one eighth of a second. And then her mind realized that Xander was kissing her. No, not just kissing her. His body was pressing against hers, his hips were grinding into hers, his hands were sliding up against her body…underneath her silk blouse no less…and she couldn't stop the immediate and overwhelming lust that surged through her. She wasn't just going to take this kiss. She gave back, demanding more, her hands sliding up his arms, feeling those bulging muscles underneath the deceptively tame dress shirt until she felt the heat of his skin on his neck. Pausing, she reveled in that heat, her fingers absorbing the texture before they moved higher, her fingers discovering that his hair was so soft, so silky. It was probably the only part of this man that was soft and she couldn't believe how good he felt, how incredible he tasted. She wanted this man like nothing she'd ever experienced in her life. She wanted him more than she'd ever thought possible.

And then he pulled back!

Her eyes looked up at him, surprised and confused. Her lips were aching for more, to feel Xander's firm lips against hers, taking and tasting and giving.

Why did he stop? Why was he doing this to her? Didn't he realize what he'd stirred inside of her?

When the wonderful, tantalizing heat of him pulled slightly away and her mind wasn't occupied by his mind-blowing kiss, her ribs suddenly started hurting. She tried not to cringe, but she must have failed because his eyes narrowed and he pulled away so he could look down at her.

"You're hurt!" he snapped, his breath hissing through his teeth as he bent lower, examining her cheek and jawline which were just starting to show signs of the blow she took.

"I'm fine," she whispered but his hands shifted slightly and she let out a small cry of pain.

His lips compressed as he looked down at her, that same fury breaking through the thick haze of lust. "You aren't fine," he contradicted, his fingers deftly feeling her ribs. When she cringed again, he shook his head. "I'm taking you to the hospital," he told her.

She shook her head. "No! No hospital!" she told him firmly. Her mother had died in a hospital and, in her mind, they were intricately, irrationally, woven into her psyche as buildings of death.

"You need to see a doctor," he told her firmly. "And probably an x-ray for your ribs."

"My ribs are fine," she stated emphatically, her fingers grabbing onto his forearm to keep him from doing something cruel, like taking his warm hand away from her skin that suddenly knew what his touch was like. "Just bruised. I'll be fine." To prove it, she held her breath, wondering if his fingers would move that small, fraction of an inch higher. Her breasts wanted that movement so badly, her mind shattering at the idea of his thumb, which was resting just below her breast, to move higher. Her nipple was already pebbled in anticipation but she couldn't say anything, couldn't beg him to finish what he'd just started.

They stared at each other for a long moment, the air crackling between them with the electricity sparking between their bodies. She couldn't breathe, she couldn't move. Nothing in the world made sense except for this man's hand to slide higher, to cover her breast and show her what his heat would feel like.

When he shifted his hand just slightly, she couldn't hide the pain that shot through her.

Xander said something under his breath that was unrepeatable then stepped back. "You're going to the hospital."

He started to take her hand and pull her towards his car, but she pulled right back. "Please," she begged, her eyes revealing the fear she felt towards hospitals. "I'll soak in a hot bath and everything will be fine," she promised. "Just no hospital."

"You need to see a doctor," he argued right back.

A doctor was better, but she'd rather just stay away from all of it. Her philosophy about sickness in the past had been to ignore everything. So far, it had worked out well enough. "If I don't feel better tomorrow, I promise to see my doctor."

Xander knew she'd be better off if she saw a doctor now, but he couldn't ignore the pleading look in those lustrous, brown eyes. He'd seen that stubbornness before and knew she wouldn't budge on the subject. Leaning down, his arms braced on the building behind her on either side of her head, he said, "Fine, you'll soak in a hot tub and relax for the rest of the afternoon. Otherwise, I'm taking you to the hospital and I'll tie you down to the x-ray machine if I have to. And I'll do that anyway if the hot bath doesn't help." He relented slightly, his hand reaching out and gently touching her cheek, cradling her head in his large, strong hand. "I promise I won't let anything happen to you at the hospital if it comes to that," he said with a deep, husky voice.

When he turned all sweet and gentle on her, Autumn's heart swelled with something she refused to identify. She didn't know how to deal with a kind Xander. She was so used to going head to head with him on every issue that this new Xander was a mystery. And so were the feelings that threatened tears to well up in her eyes. She blinked rapidly, trying to hide her vulnerability from him. She didn't understand what she was feeling and it scared her.

"Come along," he said, still with that soft, gentle voice. He took her hand and led her through the back of the building to the parking garage. With a click, he unarmed his black, sleek sedan and opened the passenger side door for her.

"I can drive…"

"Get in, Autumn," he interrupted. It was firm, but still with that gentle, coaxing, you're-not-getting-out-of-this tone.

With a sigh, she slipped into the soft leather seat, amazed at how luxurious the car felt as it hugged her body. She didn't have time to think more about that though because a second later, Xander was getting in next to her, his long legs coming precariously close to her thighs. The car might be a luxury sedan, but Xander was an extremely large man and there rarely was a space big enough to contain him. Whatever room he was in, it always felt small to her. His shoulders were huge, his muscles bulged everywhere on his body and his legs were so long they ate up the distance between point A and point B. It was awesome when point A was her office door and point B was her desk. Every time he entered her office, her eyes were drawn to his legs, her mouth going dry as she watched those muscles bulge underneath his hand-tailored slacks.

"Where are we going?" she asked, swallowing the nervousness that suddenly sprang up with his nearness.

"I'm taking you home," he told her, his long, lean fingers deftly handling the steering wheel and Autumn was mesmerized by those fingers, her mind imagining what they looked like when they were examining her ribs, wondering what they would look like against her pale skin.

She took a deep breath and tore her eyes away, looking out the window instead. "Thank you for your help," she said.

Xander heard the wobble in her voice and realized that reaction was slowly setting in. The adrenaline was ebbing away and she would start to become exhausted pretty quickly.

"You're welcome," he said, then had to shake his head at the memory of her standing in front of that little lady, protecting her while confronting the furious man. "Why did you do it?" he asked, turning left and then right.

She might be looking out the window but she wasn't watching the landscape. She was thinking back to the point in the deli when the man had become belligerent, her mind starting to go over everything that happened. "I don't know. No one else was going to help those two. Someone had to do it."

He glanced down at her slender legs, demurely crossed at the ankles and her hands clenched in her lap. "So you stepped up and showed him who was boss." He chuckled at the way she'd stood, those sexy, three inch heels braced shoulder width apart in perfect fighting stance and her arms held out from her body, fists raised as if her hundred and twenty pound figure could stop a two hundred and fifty pound raging bull.

Autumn blushed at the memory. "Okay, so you were the one who showed him who the boss was. It was pretty amazing of you, how you stepped in and stopped him cold."

"My brothers and I spar in the ring." He looked down at her briefly, but she got the message. He was clearly stating that he was trained to step in and do something like that. She wasn't.

She bit her lip and looked out the window, feeling teary eyed and embarrassed by it. "I wasn't going to let that woman be hurt by that man."

"Admirable. Brave," he said with a nod, "but also stupid. You could have been seriously hurt."

"But I wasn't," she said simply, ignoring the pain that was starting to throb in her jaw and her ribs. She'd never admit to him how hard the man had punched her. She could deal with this, she told herself silently.

He took a deep breath as the anger started to well up inside him again. "This time. Promise me that you won't ever do something like that again."

She bit her lip and looked to the right, out the window. "I promise I won't do anything that I think is stupid."

He cursed under his breath, fighting to control his anger again. "Which leaves open a great deal of what I think might be stupid," he said, completely understanding what she was telling him.

He pulled into a parking garage and swung immediately into a space. "Come on," he said and turned off the engine.

Autumn was already out of the car before she realized that this wasn't her house. This wasn't even her neighborhood. Even if she'd saved her entire salary for the rest of her life, she'd never be able to afford just the smallest apartment in this neighborhood. "Where are we?" she asked.

"My place. I'm going to make sure you take care of yourself," he said and put a hand to the small of her back to guide her over to the elevators.

Autumn's heartbeat picked up, going triple time at the idea of entering Xander's space. She didn't even enter his office, standing in the doorway when she needed to talk to him about any subject. There was no way she was going into his private dwelling space. If his office was too personal, she couldn't even imagine what she would feel entering his apartment.

"I should just go home," she said quickly, starting to turn around. She intended to get a cab that would take her to her house so she could hide away, fearful about being alone in Xander's home. The alone part was the main worry, but there was also the idea of being surrounded by things that were all "Xander". It was hard enough being around him.

But Xander wasn't having that at all. "Come along," he countered and wrapped his arm around her waist, careful not to touch the bruise on her ribs. "You'll be fine. I won't let anything harm you."

She went, but only because her knees were shaking so badly that she couldn't stop their momentum towards the elevators. She stepped into the elevator and moved away from Xander, but he was still too close and too big. Just like in a conference room or back in his car, the man took up the space, filling every air particle with his maleness.

When the doors opened, he put that strong arm around her waist again, leading her into the apartment. She didn't even get a chance to look around, he nudged her right into a fabulous bedroom and then into a large, marble bathroom with steel and chrome everywhere. And a giant, soaking tub complete with jets. Her eyes bulged at such luxury and she couldn't stop the enormous sigh at the idea of soaking in that giant marble tub.

He heard her sigh and chuckled softly. "I'm glad there's finally something about me that you approve of."

She kept her mouth shut while he bent over and turned on the water, thinking that she definitely approved of his butt. It was a very nice butt, outlined by the stretched fabric of those slacks and her mouth went dry once again. Her eyes couldn't pull away and she wasn't aware that he added something to the water, causing bubbles to rise up as the water quickly filled the tub.

He turned around and caught her blushing, but didn't understand it. "I'll get you something for the pain. Get in the tub and relax."

She thought she might have nodded, but she wasn't completely sure. She was too stunned, frightened and her mind was frozen. She couldn't react, unable to believe that she was actually standing in Xander's luxurious bathroom.

The door clicked closed behind her but she still stared at the tub that was quickly filling up with bubbles and water. The lure was too much for her aching body to resist. With shaking fingers and quick looks behind her, she slipped her clothes off, folding them quickly and hiding her lacy underwear. Her eyes watched the inviting water, her body now desperate for the relief that hot water might offer.

There were steps getting up to the raised tub and even steps descending down the other side. It was huge! And amazing! It was set in the corner of the bathroom and the windows overlooked the city, revealing the Chicago River and all the skyscrapers and highways as people moved about the city.

She slid into the hot, scented water, closing her eyes as the heat spread through her whole body, making the aches quickly disappear, at least for the moment. Leaning back, she was amazed at how wonderful the marble contoured to her body, relaxing her back and her legs. It was possibly the most comfortable tub she'd ever lain in, but that wasn't really saying much since the only types of tubs she'd had the privilege to luxuriate in were the regular hardware store tubs that were more suitable to washing little kids than soaking an adult body. Her own townhouse was nice, perfect for her needs, except for the utilitarian bathrooms.

With a sigh, she allowed her body to relax, her eyes closed and her mind drifted back to that kiss on the side of the building. For the moment, she didn't try and figure out why she'd allowed Xander to kiss her, or why she'd even reacted to his kiss. She'd seen the women who paraded into the office to meet him. The man escorted a different woman every month around town to the fabulous, glamorous parties and social functions. The lucky ones lasted maybe five weeks, the boring ones perhaps only three. One lucky woman had been able to hang onto his interest for a record six weeks.

Not that she noticed how long each of them was able to last in Xander's arms. It wasn't that she was trying to measure how long each of them lasted, but it was hard not to when they were so frequent.

Besides, the other people in the office had bets going on how long each would last so it was hard to miss the office talk or the office pool that was taped to the freezer door in the office kitchen.

She shivered involuntarily at the thought of her co-workers betting on how long she could keep his interest. Not that she would even try. The man was an absolute jerk!

She couldn't blame him though. He saw the worst in relationships. In a very basic sense, his job was to tear up a marriage, dissect it to pieces and get the most from the relationship for one or the other person. He saw not only the worst part of a marriage; he saw the evilness and maliciousness of each person. Not only his client, either the wife or the husband, but sitting across the table, he also witnessed the worst in the opposite party. The fights that erupted occasionally were vicious as the hurt feelings poured out in every way possible.

Perhaps she should be nicer to him, more considerate. The man saw the bad in so many people; he shouldn't have to see it in the people he worked with.

Maybe she should move her office to another floor. She didn't need to be on his floor, she thought as she mentally reviewed the four floors and their layouts. Whenever they'd expanded their presence in the building, it was her job to assign office space to all the lawyers and support personnel. She'd always, for some inexplicable reason, kept her own office on the same floor as Xander.

Well, one time after a particularly frustrating week, she'd shuffled things around and was going to move her office to Ryker's area. But that move had been vetoed. She didn't understand all the details, but she hadn't fought the change at the time.

Maybe it was now time to move to a new area, get away from him a bit more. The man could probably use her office to hire another lawyer. He had more than seventy divorce attorneys under his domain across the country with more than thirty of them here in the Chicago office. It always amazed her how many people were dissolving their marriage but his business was thriving.

She turned off the water, reveling in the silence as the ache in her ribs slowly receded even more. Xander had been right. A hot bath was exactly what she'd needed. And she probably would have ignored the idea if she'd gone home. She most likely would have pulled out her computer and worked on the millions of issues that required her attention every day.

Yes, this was perfect, she thought with a thrill. Autumn had to keep reminding herself that she wasn't excited because it was Xander's bathroom. It was simply because she was relaxed for the first time in….months.

Not really relaxed. No, what she was feeling wasn't in any way relaxed. Rejuvenated. Yes, that was the word. She felt rejuvenated by the water and the bubbles. It was probably the lavender scented bubbles he'd provided for her.

It suddenly occurred to her – why did Xander have lavender scented bath bubbles? He hadn't even needed to search for them. That feeling of happiness quickly dissipated and something new and angry emerged within her even as the bubbles popped and deflated.

Suddenly, the door to the bathroom opened up and Xander stood there, his indigo blue eyes glared at her. "You kissed me back!" he growled.

Gone were the thoughts about who had brought the bubbles into his place and her mouth went dry at the memory of that kiss. That one, incredible, passionate and mind blowing kiss.

She started to shake her head but he strode over to the edge of the bathroom, his hands fisted on his hips and he barely stopped when he was right next to the bathtub. "Yes, you kissed me right back."

With that, he reached down and lifted her up, the water streaming down her body, bubbles floating around in non-strategic places. "Why did you respond to me?" he said, but he didn't wait for an answer.

His kiss made her toes curl. She didn't have time to be embarrassed that she was completely naked, nor did she have time to caution him that she was dripping wet. It barely even registered that he'd taken off his suit jacket and tie at some point. All she knew was that his strong arms were wrapping around her and he was once again kissing her. Those shocking feelings of desire, which had been suppressed on the short drive from the office to his apartment building fired right back to life and she was shivering in reaction.

She wasn't aware of her arms wrapping around his neck but she shivered with need when his own hands moved from her arms down her back, cupping her bottom and pulling her hips against his own. She couldn't seem to get enough of the man, her body pressing closely, her mind not even trying to understand what was happening as everything in her dealt with the surging, pounding, unrelenting need that was centered down low in her belly.

When he tore his mouth away, she cried out in protest but he ignored that and lifted her into his arms, straight up into the air. She looked down and just about melted when his mouth covered her nipple. She didn't realize that her legs wrapped around his waist or anything else. Time, business, responsibility…they were all suspended as she let her head fall backwards, the ache increasing as his mouth sucked hard on her breast, teasing then gentling before increasing the pressure again. When he moved his mouth to the other breast, she thought she might just melt into a puddle of desire.

He wasn't giving her any time to process, to even reciprocate. His arms lowered her back down and she kissed him back, her whole body trying to figure out what to do and how to manage what he was making her feel. But it was pointless. His hands were everywhere, finding places on her body she didn't even know had nerve endings. It seemed that everywhere he touched just made that horrible and wonderful ache intensify.

The cold on her back was her only moment of sanity but that was obliterated when she felt him slide into her heat. She had no memory of her fingers pulling, practically ripping his clothes off or of him grabbing his wallet and sheathing himself with protection. She only knew that, for a fraction of a second when he was finally naked and their bodies could touch without the hindrance of clothing, she felt satisfied. That moment in time disappeared the moment he moved against her, her skin firing in so many places and the need was driving her out of her mind. When his body shifted, she cried out. The ache soothed slightly and she shifted to take in more of him. She didn't know that her nails were digging into the skin on his shoulders. All she knew was that she wanted this feeling to continue, and she wanted to find something to soothe that ache.

When she felt the slight pain, she ignored it and moved her hands lower against his back to pull him deeper. When he was fully embedded inside of her, she smiled with exhilaration.

But then he started moving and that ache was almost painful. She couldn't handle this and her head slashed back and forth, her hips moving up to meet his thrust while her hands shifted downwards, her fingers pushing against his hips, encouraging him to move faster.

When her world splintered apart, she gasped and screamed out, clinging to Xander, not exactly sure how to deal with the wave after wave of pleasure his body was creating within her but enjoying the ride regardless.

Xander felt her climax and watched with fascination. He controlled his own release, wanting her to enjoy this to the fullest. But as her body writhed underneath him, he couldn't hold back any longer and he poured himself out, gritting his teeth with the most intense, most amazing climax he'd ever experienced.

He almost collapsed on top of her, but at the last moment, remembered her tender ribs and he rolled over. The cold tiles underneath his back startled him but then his fingers found her hair and he played with the soft tendrils, reveling for a long moment in the thrill that Autumn was here and he had just made love to the most perfect female he'd ever met.

Autumn gasped when she felt him shift their positions but she couldn't work up enough energy to protest. So when she found herself draped over his muscular chest instead of underneath him, she could only lay there, trying desperately hard to catch her breath.

She shivered when she felt his hands move down her back and smiled while her own fingers tangled in the light dusting of hair on his chest. But then she felt something lower and her eyes widened. She lifted her head slightly, looking up at him and almost laughed at his tight jaw.

She shifted slightly, feeling him fill her up once again and she gasped, shifting her hips slightly.

"Don't do that!" he growled and tried to hold her hips still.

Autumn closed her eyes and pushed against his chest. "Why not?" she asked, her body trembling all over again.

Xander's hands slid up her body, cupping her breasts from this vantage point. "Because if you don't, we're going to start all over again," he said with a husky growl.

She was fascinated. Shifting slightly, she gasped when she felt those quivers all over her body. "Wow,' she sighed and closed her eyes. Her head fell back slightly and she braced her hands on his stomach, shifting one more time. She definitely liked this position, having heard about it from others and read about it in books. Although she needed a much more detailed analysis of this position versus the last one to fully gauge which one was better.

She inhaled sharply when she felt his hands on her hips, bringing her down hard on his erection. Her mouth formed an "O" of surprise, not sure how anything so invasive could feel so…amazing!

"Do that again," he growled.

Autumn lifted her hips again, feeling the friction and shuddering at all the tingles that centered right down there on her body and radiated outwards. "Yes," she sighed.

"Damn it, Autum," he groaned. "You've got to move, honey."

She bit her lip, continuing the slow pace so she could feel all of him, absorb every sensation. She liked this. A lot! Ignoring him, she moved however she wanted, grabbing his hands away from her hips when he tried to make her move the way he wanted her to. She looked down at him, her eyes dilated, her body undulating against his and Xander laid his head back against the bathroom tiles and let her have her way. He enjoyed the view even though he thought he might die a slow death at the way she was moving, so slowly and her body trembling so beautifully.

With each press of her hips, she took him higher and higher. Xander tried very hard to restrain himself, finding a thrill in watching her discover her body, but after several minutes of this slow torture, he couldn't take it any longer. Lifting himself up so she was basically sitting in his lap, his mouth latched onto her nipple, sucking hard, then laving it with his tongue before doing it again and moving to the other one. Her cries egged him on and he grabbed her hips with his hands and took control of the pace. Lifting her up and pressing into her, he kissed her breasts at the same time that her climax caused her to scream out, her body both writhing to get away from him and demanding that he continue until she sagged against him. It took him only a few more strokes before he found his own climax and he fell backwards onto the bathroom tiles, once more replete as he held this incredible woman in his arms.

CHAPTER 3

Autumn looked around, stunned by the dim light starting to come through the windows. Xander hadn't bothered to close the blinds to his bedroom last night but she hadn't really given him a chance. She sighed and tried to bury her face in the pillow beside her. She might be alone in the bed, but she could still feel his heat all over her body. Even as exhausted as she was right at the moment, she still wanted to find him and kiss him, feel his hands all over her once again. She'd never experienced anything like that before. The way she felt when he touched her was nothing short of....electric.

She heard the shower running and knew she should get out of here. She wasn't sure what his reaction would be in the daylight, but she was a coward and didn't want to face him. Not after everything they'd done last night.

She sat up, holding the sheet in front of her. She bit her lip when she looked over and saw her clothes draped against one of the chairs. She'd been so careful to fold them up with her underwear hidden away. But now her lacy underwear and bra were dramatically draped on top of her clothes.

Autumn knew that her face was blushing even though he wasn't here to see it. She slid out of bed, in a panic now to get out of his bedroom before he finished with his shower. She didn't really understand why she didn't want to face him. They probably should talk about what had occurred, but she simply couldn't do it right now.

She pulled on her clothes in record time, then cursed when she realized that she didn't have her wallet. She must have lost it in the deli yesterday when the fight had broken out. She was about to burst into tears at the thought of seeing Xander this morning but then she spotted his wallet.

As she carried her shoes, she walked over to the wallet. Good grief, the man carried about three hundred dollars in his wallet. Who did that? Well, obviously the uber-wealthy did that. Xander clearly fell into that category.

She didn't have time to think about that. She grabbed a ten, wrote him a quick note telling him that she owed him the money, and then scampered out of the gorgeous place. When she stepped out of his apartment and there was only one apartment and the elevator door, she wondered about that, but didn't have time. She had to get out of there, panic setting in at the idea of seeing Xander this morning. She'd have to face him later, surely he'd be at the office, but that would give her an hour or two to figure things out without him close by, filling her nostrils with his spicy, male scent that was so incredibly tempting.

Damn! She rushed out of the building and raised her hand high, relieved a cab was just letting someone off. Thankfully, Xander lived right in the heart of the city which had a surplus of cabs available.

She jumped into the back of the cab and gave her address, then realized she didn't have keys or anything so she changed her mind and asked the driver to take her to the office. He didn't like that as much since it was a much shorter fare, but she didn't have time to worry about the feelings of the driver.

At the office, she ignored the curious stares of the receptionist and a few other early bird lawyers and hurried to her office. There she grabbed her keys and purse, still not sure where her wallet was. But she didn't care either. She raced home, fighting tears of confusion, bewilderment. How could she have fallen into bed so easily with Xander? They'd been duking it out about every issue ever since she'd started here.

Actually, that wasn't true really. The first year she'd been here, she'd taken the receptionist job while in college, thinking it would just be a temporary position until she found something in her field of business administration. Xander had stopped by the front desk on numerous occasions, flirting with her outrageously, giving her small gifts for Christmas or her birthday, making sure she got all the vacation time she requested. He'd been very sweet that first year.

It had been when she'd gotten promoted to administrative assistant to Axel that he'd started to change. Even then, it hadn't been mean, just a bit more standoffish. She hadn't understood it at first, but it had hurt. She'd missed his smiles and those funny conversations. They were never about anything in particular but he'd always been very kind and sweet. And when she'd bought her condo, he'd made sure that Axel had taken care of all the legal issues for free.

She didn't understand it at first, his distance. But she'd slowly pulled back as well. Their flirty friendship had slowly gone from friendship to acquaintances and then to outright battles at times.

As she stepped into her shower, she had to be perfectly honest with herself. It hadn't always been his fault. She'd been hurt when he'd showed up with his girlfriends at work. So maybe she had been the first one to pull away.

But he had become nasty when she'd stopped by one night with a date to grab her coat after a spontaneous dinner. Ever since then, they'd been battling each other over every issue possible.

With a sigh, she stepped out of the shower and stood in front of her mirror. She'd have to hurry in order to make it to work on time but the sight of her chin, looking definitely purplish blue, was quit hideous! How could he have made love to her when she'd looked like this? How crazy! The lights must have been even dimmer than she'd realized.

She quickly applied a thick coat of makeup, not wanting to draw attention to her bruise. Her ribs were also a bit blue, but they could be covered up by her silk shirt and suit jacket. She'd just wear her jacket all day, not wanting to answer the numerous questions about yesterday's deli incident.

After skillful application, she was able to hide most of the bruise. If one knew to look, they could see the color but otherwise, it just looked like she was wearing a lot of makeup. That was unusual, but couldn't be helped. She had enough work to do to stay in her office most of the day and avoid people so that should cut down on the questions and curiosity a bit.

She made it to the office and pretended like nothing earth shattering had just happened the previous night.

"Xander Thorpe is looking for you," Diane said as soon as she walked through the entrance.

Autumn stopped, frozen in place. "Why?" she asked after a prolonged, odd look.

Diane was startled by Autumn's question. She struggled for an answer but in the end, she simply said, "I'm not sure. He didn't say but he's called me three times in the last half hour to see if you've arrived. Should I call and tell him that you're on your way to his office?" she asked, lifting the phone and looking at Autumn.

"No," she snapped, then shook her head, putting her hand to her forehead and telling herself to calm down. "No," she said again, but not in a panicked voice. "I'll go to his office as soon as I get settled in."

Diane put the phone down and Autumn raced to her own office. She closed the door, taking deep breaths as she leaned against the wood. She'd have to face him at some point. Better to just get it over with.

She put her purse down and tried to gather her strength. But the knock on the door had her spinning around, her eyes wide with fright.

Sure enough, Xander stood in the doorway looking huge and delicious. At the first sight of him, all she could think about doing was throwing herself into his arms again, asking him to kiss her like he'd done last night, make her feel those strange and amazing feelings once again.

But he looked wary, not exactly in the catching-a-woman mindset.

"You okay?" he asked, his dark blue eyes looking at her from the top of her head to her black, pointed heels. She wasn't positive, but she thought he might have paused as his eyes moved over her breasts. Please don't let him be wondering what her current underwear looked like, she thought feverishly.

"I'm fine," she said but couldn't hold his gaze.

"You left this morning," he came back after a long silence.

She bit her lip. "Yes. I'm sorry. I wasn't sure…what to…what you might think…what might…" she couldn't finish her statement. She wasn't really sure what she was thinking anyway.

"You weren't sure what I might say when I saw you in my bed? Or perhaps if you'd cared to join me in the shower?" he asked, his voice deep and sexy.

She looked into his eyes, unaware of the heat, the longing that was there for him to see. "Well, I wouldn't have put it that way," she finally said.

He rubbed his jaw, shaking his head. "Should I just put last night up to the adrenaline in your system after the fight?" he asked.

Her eyes widened and she initially thought about denying it, but then she stopped herself just in time. That was a perfect excuse. And maybe it was true.

No, she thought with honesty, it wasn't true. But it would do for an explanation.

"I guess that's probably what it was," she finally said but didn't want to state it as the complete truth. She couldn't outright lie to Xander.

"I'm sorry I took advantage of you last night then," he said as he stepped around her to look out the window. "I wanted to assure you that it won't happen again. I know I was out of line. I took you back to my place to take care of you, to make sure that you were okay and I…" he stopped, sighing. "I'm sorry," he said again.

Turning around, he looked down into her eyes, willing her to tell him that it had nothing to do with the adrenaline. That it had everything to do with wanting him as a man. But those pretty brown eyes couldn't meet his. And he felt like more of an ass than before.

Damn, why couldn't he just leave her alone? Why was he so drawn to this one woman? She didn't feel the same and never had. Now, he'd just compounded their problem by taking advantage of her. He'd acted like a cheap, horrible suit by being all over her last night. Every time she'd moved, he'd been turned on, his mind and control obliterated by the fact that she was finally in his bed, in his arms and kissing him back like she had in so many of his dreams over the past several years.

But even now, being so close to her, smelling her soft shampoo and the strawberry shower gel she used, he wanted to pull her into his arms, sweep everything off of the desk behind her and make love to her until she couldn't speak any longer.

If only he hadn't gotten out of bed this morning. But he'd had to. He'd made love to her so many times last night; all he'd wanted to do was bury himself inside her again. He'd woken up with her soft body wrapped around him, her slender arms holding him close and his body had hardened like a teenage boy on his first date.

Only Autumn had this effect on him. He wanted her so painfully and all she wanted from him was distance.

He had no choice now. He'd had his shot last night. He'd have to back off, give her the space she wanted. He wouldn't even manipulate the office space again when she tried to move off of his floor. Maybe if he didn't see her every day, didn't smell her soft, feminine scent or see her in those sexy, high heels she preferred, he would get over her. And maybe, if she wasn't on his floor, he wouldn't picture her in those lacy nothings he'd picked up last night.

"Well, I just wanted to make sure we were okay," he said, trying to fill that awkward silence once again.

She forced a smile. "Thank you very much for your concern. I'm really okay," she said, looking down, embarrassed by the need she felt when he was this close.

And then he did something completely unexpected. He stepped forward, so close she could just lean forward and they would be touching again, his fingers sliding down her jaw right where the bruise was. His fingers were so light on her skin she could barely feel him. "Does it hurt?" he asked softly.

"No," she said, because in truth, she wasn't feeling anything right now. She couldn't even tell him what day it was or if the sun was out. Her whole world was focused on this one man and his gentle touch. "I thought I'd covered it up well enough."

He smiled slightly, that half smile that made him look sexier than James Bond. "You did. If I hadn't seen it develop last night, I wouldn't know it was there."

She blushed, thinking he'd definitely seen it all last night, including the ugly bruise on her ribs.

"I'll take you down to the police station today so you can make a statement."

She thought about that, about being in his presence more than necessary. She knew it wouldn't be a good idea for her. "I can do that," she told him. "Thank you though."

Xander took the hint and stepped back. "Okay then," he said and turned towards the doorway. "You look beautiful," he finally said before walking out of her office.

Autumn stood there for a long time, her mind going over those words again and again. She'd dressed with him in mind for so long and he'd finally seen her. And now everything was so wrong!

She slumped down into her chair, burying her face in her hands and praying that she wouldn't burst into tears. After several more minutes, she told herself to pull it together. She took a deep breath and lifted herself up. Looking at her computer, she realized that she had over fifty e-mail messages and knew from experience that most of them would be action items. There was nothing slow or plodding about the daily tasks at The Thorpe Group. Everything seemed to happen at warp speed. So no time to feel sorry for the mess she'd just made of her life. She had to get back to work.

She was fine all that day, but had to work hard to avoid Xander. He seemed to be everywhere. She saw him in the copy room, in the office kitchen and even when she was heading to the elevator to leave for lunch. When she saw that, she simply turned around, acting like she was heading for the stairway instead of the elevator. It didn't matter that she had her purse over her shoulder and her coat on her arm. She might look ridiculous walking down the stairs, and it might even be obvious to him that she was avoiding him. But she didn't care. There was no way she was getting into that elevator with Xander. The space was too small, he was too big and her need for him to touch her like he'd done last night was too intense. She'd make a fool of herself and she was tired of doing that.

By the middle of the next day, she was exhausted and hiding out in her office. She slumped down in her chair, idly scrolling through her e-mail messages, trying to find an issue that could be taken care of without her needing to leave the confines of her office.

"What are you going to do about finding me an administrative assistant?" Xander asked, stepping into her office.

Autumn jerked upright, her hungry eyes taking in his tall, handsome frame despite the furious look in his eyes and his hands fisted on his hips.

"Um…" she blinked. She'd been avoiding that issue for the past several days, not sure how to work with him without actually talking to him, seeing him or getting close to him in any way.

"I need someone, Autumn. The last three haven't worked out at all. So the next one has to be pretty exceptional."

She knew that. She'd found fabulous assistants for all three of his brothers, plus all of the other lawyers. She'd just had miserable luck trying to find someone to handle Xander.

"Yes. You're right," she said, digging deep within herself to find the last vestiges of her professionalism. "I'll get right on that. And I'm sorry that…"

His voice was almost gentle but still firm when he interrupted her. "No more sorries, Autumn. Just find me someone who can dig me out of this administrative mess the last one created. I know you have a slew of resumes that you keep on hand of potential candidates. Go through them and bring me the best ones by four o'clock. We'll start the interviews again in two days." With that, he walked out of her office.

She sighed and slumped right back down into her chair, her head dropping into her hands in defeat.

"Are you okay?" Mary asked, walking into Autumn's office.

Autumn grimaced. "I guess so." Her fingers flicked over her keyboard. "Know of any good assistants who are looking for a job?" she asked. Xander was right. She had an archive of support personnel, but he'd already rejected the good ones that she had on file.

Mary shrugged. "I know a couple of people. They aren't legal assistants though."

Autumn could just imagine Xander's reaction to that. "Probably not good," she replied. "I guess I'd better call around to the agencies, see what they can give me."

"I thought that approach was more expensive."

"It is," Autumn explained, mentally irritated that Xander was putting her to that level of effort just because he was so demanding. He'd rejected several, very good candidates because he had such specific needs for his administrative support staff. "But I've got to get someone really good this time. Someone who can fix all the issues that the previous three messed up."

"I can help," Mary said. "Maybe if the two of us worked on the files, we could get things cleaned up."

Autumn thought about that for a moment. She knew she could get the files fixed relatively quickly, but that would mean being close to Xander all day long. She needed to avoid that if possible. "I'll keep that offer in mind. But let me see what I can dig up before we go that route."

Mary disappeared and Autumn picked up the phone. For the next two hours, she called the employment agencies, review resumes and created a chart with the various possibilities and their skills, the pros and cons of each candidate. She also generated a comment sheet to prepare for the interview process, a system she'd developed over the years as a good way to write up notes on a candidate while the ideas and impressions were fresh in the interviewer's mind.

At four o'clock, she nervously brought all her materials into the conference room, set up the copies for Xander and set hers on the other side so she was facing him. In the past, he'd sat down next to her and it had always made her nervous. This way, she could at least have some space and maybe she wouldn't get so angry by his rejections.

Of course, if he rejected candidates without any reason, she'd fight him on the issue. She hated it when he rejected a candidate, simply saying, "I don't like him," or "She struck me wrong." It wasn't fair to the candidates to not have a fair shake at the job simply because they formatted their resume differently than he preferred.

Xander walked into the conference room and saw the stack of resumes placed on the opposite side of the table. He knew exactly what she was doing. For a moment, he thought about letting her get away with it, but in the end, he wasn't that nice of a guy.

He grabbed the papers from across the table and slid them in front of the chair right next to hers, ignoring the look of horror in her eyes. "So who are we going to look at today?" he asked, stretching his legs out so they were close to hers.

For the next two hours, they argued over the candidates' resumes. Back and forth, Autumn pointed out the benefits of one person over another while he chose other candidates that he thought looked better, at least on paper.

"You can't reject someone simply because they 'sound' too young," Autumn snapped at him.

"Yes I can," he countered coolly. "He doesn't have enough experience. Next?"

"Stop! That's ridiculous. What part of your requirements does he not have?" she demanded, sliding the job description towards him.

He actually had the audacity to sit there and point out that the resume didn't spell out a person's organizational skills. "That's a big deal to me after the last person you brought in."

"You agreed that Rosa was a good candidate!" she cried back, defending their joint decision.

"Only after you argued that she would work out. You convinced me. I took your advice. Rosa was nice, but she was an idiot. I need someone who can think."

"You need someone who can follow orders blindly!" she snapped right back. "You don't want a human being," she said, exasperated by all of his demands. "You want a robot."

"Do you have one?" he came right back.

She tossed her arms up in the air, defeated. "So none of these candidates meet your requirements?" she asked, totally dumbfounded.

"Not a single one," he said and leaned forward, ostensibly to look through all the dozen or so resumes she'd brought with her. But in reality, he just wanted to smell her hair, feel her soft skin one more time. He didn't touch her, not getting any signals that she would be receptive to any touch from him. But that didn't mean he couldn't dream.

He stood up, needing to get away from her before he took her into his arms and kissed her senseless. "Have some more resumes for me by tomorrow morning." Without another word, he walked out of the conference room, leaving her glaring at his back while her eyes shot arrows at his head.

The following morning was exactly the same. By the end of the hour, he'd rejected all of the candidates and Autumn was flabbergasted. "You're being unreasonable!" she yelled at him and then looked at him with a horrified expression.

"I'm sorry!" she gasped. She'd never yelled at anyone before but she was too nervous around him to be able to control her temper. She could smell his cologne and his soap and she ached to just curl up in his lap and feel his strong arms wrap around her, make her feel better.

Xander stared back at her for a long moment, then burst out laughing. "Don't be sorry," he said and put a hand on her back. She flinched away and he pulled back immediately, but he wanted so badly to…well, to do everything to her.

"How about if we go out to lunch today to discuss options?" he suggested, leaning against the conference room table.

Autumn took a deep breath, trying to calm herself down. "Perhaps we should just meet and discuss your requirements again." And maybe get two people in to help him out since no one candidate seemed to meet all of his needs. "We don't need to go out to lunch."

Xander looked down at his watch, shaking his head. "I didn't think it would take this long to get some candidates lined up for interviews. The only time I have available is lunch time."

Autumn sighed, resigned to having lunch with him. "Fine," she said, thinking she could just run down to the deli and grab both of them something so they could eat while they discussed new resumes. Although how she was going to find even more resumes in just a couple of hours she had no clue. Not to mention, her stomach always acted weird around him so eating might be difficult. Maybe if he would finally sit across the table from her instead of next to her!

He walked out of the conference room at that point and she slumped down in the soft, leather chair, feeling defeated. She'd gone through all of her resources to find this second set of resumes. She couldn't figure out where else to go for a new batch. Maybe if she were honest with him, told him that she was stumped, he would relent a bit.

Then she thought about his irritated expression when she'd passed by his office earlier today. Tilly must have been looking for some file and Xander was standing behind her impatiently. Normally, she required her support staff to know exactly where things were, to have files pulled before they were needed. If Xander had a meeting with a client, he'd need the files for that client pulled the night before so he could take them home to review at night if he'd wanted. The fact that Tilly was just pulling a file while Xander stood waiting must mean she wasn't doing an adequate job.

Par for the course, she thought as she gathered up all of the resumes and charts she'd created. Perhaps someone had come into one of the agencies this morning that would be the ideal candidate. And maybe, if all the planets aligned and the stars were shining down on her today, the candidate could come in for an interview this afternoon. Then she'd be free from any further discussions with the man she was growing to hate.

She walked slowly back to her office, wondering where all of his charm had gone. Xander used to be one of those men who could make women go gaga with just his smile. How had he ended up with such horrible employees lately?

Okay, the last one was her fault. But what about the ones before? The previous two had been wonderful. Until the day they'd walked out in fury over Xander's continuous demands. She'd spoken to them as they'd cried out their frustration with their jobs. Nothing they had told her seemed unreasonable. Perhaps she'd been with The Thorpe Group for so long she didn't realize the pressure new people had to endure to get up to speed. Things probably worked faster here. People definitely looked busy non-stop throughout the day.

She passed by Xander's office again on her way back and she cringed when she caught Xander once again leaning against the wall, impatiently waiting for Tilly to find something for him.

She hugged her files closer to her and walked on by, head down and ashamed that she hadn't been able to fix this problem. It had been going on for much too long and Xander was right. He should have someone that can do the job properly. He had too much to worry about and the lack of a good support team was an enormous burden.

Hurrying back to her office, she dumped the rejected resumes and picked up her phone. She would get him the perfect candidate, even if it killed her. Ninety minutes later, she had five more resumes to show Xander. She walked nervously down the hallway with her notebook and pencil, clutching the resumes in her hand.

She hesitated before she knocked though. Looking at him, her heart did something weird inside her chest. He looked so serious as he sat behind his huge desk, reviewing something that looked complicated and important. She stared at his tanned, sexy hands and long fingers that could touch her so gently she went wild. Currently, though, they held a red pen; she wanted to lean over his shoulder and see what he was scribbling in the margins. He had his suit jacket off so she could better see the muscles in his arms and shoulders, muscles she remembered touching so well that her fingertips ached to feel them again.

"Ready to go?" he asked, tossing his pen down onto his desk and standing up.

"Go?" she repeated blankly, still standing in his doorway. "I was just going to run downstairs to the deli and grab a sandwich for us," she replied, her pen hovering over her notebook, ready to take his order so she could escape quickly. "We can just eat our meal in one of the conference rooms."

He shook his head and grabbed his suit jacket, sliding those long, strong arms into the sleeves. "We're getting out of here. A change of scenery is probably going to help."

Autumn was shaking her head even as he walked out of his office, coming closer to her so quickly she had trouble telling her feet to move out of the way. She stood beside his door, awkwardly trying to argue with him, but he just ignored her stammers and spoke directly to his temporary assistant. "Tilly, could you call Mary and have her grab Autumn's coat? We'll meet her in the lobby."

Autumn didn't like this one little bit. She didn't want to leave the office with him. She felt safer here, more secure and able to keep her mind on business. Going out of the office meant dangerous territory. Unknown territory. She didn't like unknown and dangerous. And Xander scared her on so many levels. So much more now than before she'd been in his house and in his bed.

"You really don't…"

"I really do," he countered and put a hand to the small of her back, nudging her out of his area.

The ever efficient Mary was already standing in the lobby with Autumn's coat and purse. Xander handed Mary the notebook and pen Autumn had been holding, then held her coat up for her.

Autumn stared up at him, her stomach clenching at the idea of putting her arms into her coat because then his hands would be on her shoulders. It would almost feel like he was hugging her. Her knees started wobbling at that idea and she took a deep, painful breath. There was nothing to do but put her coat on, and move out of the way as quickly as possible. Her hands dove into the sleeves but the rest was a blur. She felt his hands on her shoulders and froze. Then he did something equally crazy. His fingers moved carefully under her hair, sliding against her neck and sparking more shivers to shoot down her spine.

She had no idea what he was doing. All she knew was that his hands were touching her. She'd dreamed about him doing this again so often over the past few days and now it was happening. His fingers tangled in her hair, running through the tresses. To a casual observer, it probably looked like he was just pulling her hair out from under her coat, but it was so much more than that. It was a caress. A sensual, titillating touch of his fingers that almost knocked her flat.

Their eyes met. She looked over her shoulder at his handsome face and time froze. She could smell his aftershave, feel the heat of his body against her back which had nothing to do with the light wool of her fall coat. She couldn't breathe, couldn't hear anything but the racing of her heart.

And then the sound of the elevator chimed, bringing her back from the fantasy she was having about him turning her around and kissing her. Voices broke through and the almost constantly ringing phones started to come back. She jerked away, taking several steps to put some distance between them. She looked at the floor as her trembling fingers buttoned up her coat.

"Thank you," she whispered, taking her purse from his hands as well.

"My pleasure," he came right back.

Then that hand was back! Right there in the center of her back. She thought that perhaps her entire nervous system started and ended in that exact spot where his hand was resting on her back because every cell in her body tingled, acutely aware of his touch.

"Where are we going?" she asked when they were out of the building and in the October sunshine. It was warmer than expected so she slipped her coat off of her shoulders, turning her face up to the sun.

"Would you rather eat at Antoine's or Durango's?" he asked, watching her as she absorbed the heat on her lovely face. "Or we could just jet off to Aruba so you could get more sunshine," he teased.

Autumn's eyes popped open and she looked up into his amused face. "Sorry," she blushed. "I love October and the cooler temperatures but it's still warm enough to enjoy the outdoors."

"What's your favorite season?" he asked, putting a hand on her back to guide her towards Antoine's, one of the city's most exclusive restaurants.

She realized immediately where they were heading and pulled back. "Would you mind if we went to Durango's instead?"

"Sure. Why?" he asked, but they headed in the opposite direction for the more casual restaurant.

She bit her lip and admitted, "I've just wanted a burger for a long time."

He laughed but they went inside the darker bar and restaurant. The owner immediately recognized them and seated them at one of the windows. "I have five new…"

"We can talk about those later. Let's just relax and have lunch," he suggested. And with that, they talked about everything but work and resumes. During the entire lunch while they downed greasy burgers and cheese topped fries, they talked like they had so long ago, as friends and people instead of combatants.

It was probably the nicest lunch she'd had in years, Autumn thought as she walked back to the office that afternoon.

CHAPTER 4

Autumn glared at the man's back, so angry she couldn't even speak. She'd had fights with Xander before, but this was above and beyond. She couldn't believe he was being this stubborn! Every one of these resumes would be an ideal candidate for his assistant. How could he have rejected all of them? Impossible!

Now she knew he was simply being unreasonable and that infuriated her even more than if he simply disagreed. He'd be wrong in this case. And in many cases, but that was different.

Oh! That man just....infuriated her!

How could he justify being so arbitrary?

Autumn walked back to her office and practically threw her stack of resumes onto her desk, uncaring that several other reports fell off the other side because of the force of her throw.

Mary came in behind her, eyes wide and her body language wary. "I guess your meeting didn't go well?" she asked carefully.

"That's an understatement!" she exclaimed, then tried to calm down by taking several deep breaths.

Mary tried to suppress a smile, but she was glad her boss had her back turned towards her because she didn't think she was very successful. "So your meeting was with Xander, I take it?" she suggested, then took an involuntary step backwards when Autumn spun around, her eyes on fire.

"Sorry, I shouldn't have asked."

Autumn closed her eyes and took several deep breaths. "No, I'm sorry, Mary. I've been acting horribly lately and none of this is your fault. What's worse, I'm taking it out on you and that's not fair." Autumn tried to calm down, but every time she pictured Xander in that conference room demanding more resumes. He wouldn't even talk to some of these candidates and they were the best of the best!

"So what are you going to do next?"

Autumn was stumped. She'd gone to all of her sources three different times. There weren't any other candidates out there! "I have no idea," she said and fell backwards into her chair. "The man really is impossible."

Mary put her hand over her mouth. "I think you said that already."

Autumn chuckled but then glared teasingly at her assistant. "If you're going to point out the obvious, I'm going to assign you as his assistant."

Mary's eyes widened and she backed up, her palms held outwards as if she were being held up at gunpoint. "Not that!" she begged. "Anything but that! Xander Thorpe is a hottie, but he's also mean and irascible. I'd rather not have to deal with him on a daily basis."

Autumn knew exactly what she meant. And it was an odd thing too because Xander hadn't ever been this exacting before. She remembered him at lunch yesterday and she couldn't believe he was the same man. She simply didn't understand what had happened with all of his assistants. Why had they left so quickly and why was it so hard to find someone to take over? She couldn't even promote someone into that position because no one wanted it.

Not that Xander would agree to have anyone already employed, she thought.

"If you have any suggestions, please let me know."

Mary's lips compressed for a long moment before she finally took a breath and suggested, "I think it's time for a shopping trip. You haven't gotten any new shoes in a long time. Why don't you go out and treat yourself."

Autumn's eyes dropped down to her feet and she examined her black shoes. They were still a good pair of shoes, but they could stand to be replaced. The edges were worn away a bit and the heel was starting to wear down.

Besides, shoe shopping really did make her feel much better. It was completely superficial, but she truly felt better when she was wearing a good pair of shoes. A pair that went with her outfit, but even better, a pair of shoes that brought her entire outfit together so it was perfect.

Autumn smiled and stood up. "I think that's a great idea," she said. "And you're right. Shoe shopping really does make me feel better."

"That's the spirit!" she said, clapping her hands together, relieved that her boss was going to go out and get some fresh air. The tension in the office because of the war between these two had become so thick it could be cut with a dull knife. "Go have some fun. And don't come back until you feel better. I'll take care of everything around here."

Autumn grabbed her purse but left her coat. It was a beautiful, sunny day and it had warmed up enough so a coat wasn't necessary. She loved these gorgeous fall afternoons when the sun was shining, the skies were crystal blue and the humidity was so low that her hair didn't go flat. In other words, a perfect shopping day!

"I'll see you a bit later," she said, checking to make sure her phone was on in case an emergency came up and she needed to rush back.

Autumn walked out of the office, feeling better than she had in a long time. There was something about buying a good pair of shoes, or even the anticipation of finding the perfect pair, that made her breathe a little easier, feel much more free.

Xander watched with clenched jaw as Autumn walked out of the office. She had a spring in her step and a smile on her face. Since they'd both been yelling at each other, that could only mean one thing. She was going out with a guy.

He wanted to slam his fist into something and actually had to restrain himself when his brother Ash walked up to him. "Hey, I need your help on something."

Xander turned to face Ash – who took one look at his older brother and stopped, actually taking a step backwards and holding out his hands. "What did I do?" he asked, trying to understand his brother's current mood.

Xander took a breath and shook his head. "Nothing. Sorry. What do you need?" he asked.

"This woman, I think…" and the two of them walked into Xander's office to discuss a legal matter. When they were finished, Ash stood up and pounded his brother on his back. "Was that Autumn heading out, looking so happy?" he asked.

Xander's mood took a dive once again. "What of it?" he demanded.

"Just that she's been looking pretty miserable lately. Any idea what's going on?"

Xander's stomach twisted. If other people were noticing that Autumn was upset, he must have been really tough on her. He rubbed his forehead, wishing he could do something to clear the air between the two of them. It was a constant battle to keep his hands off of her. But the only way he knew to keep her talking to him was to reject all of her candidates. He was being an ass though. He had to relent.

He picked up the stack of resumes one more time and looked through the candidates. "She's trying to find me a new assistant," Xander explained.

Ash nodded his head, but he didn't really understand. "So you pissed her off?"

Xander pulled three resumes out of the stack of twenty that he and Autumn had reviewed in the past two days. "Yes. I've been pretty annoying." And then he thought of her bright, shining face when she'd left a moment ago and he felt that gut-punch again.

"So she must be off shoe shopping again, eh?"

Xander's eyes snapped up to his youngest brother's, confusion in his eyes. "Shoe shopping?" he repeated.

Ash shrugged. "Sure. Anytime she's really upset, or you've just annoyed her to the point where she's reached the limit of her patience, she goes shoe shopping.

By the time she gets back to the office, everything is all better and she's smiling again." Ash punched Xander on the arm as he walked quickly out the door. "At least until she has to deal with you again, that is."

Xander stood there in the middle of his office, almost light-headed from the relief he was feeling. Ash was right. That smile and the hop in her step were more likely due to her going out and hitting the shops. It probably didn't have anything to do with her having a date with anyone!

He threw back his head and laughed, feeling awesome all of a sudden.

But when his relief was finished, he was still grinning, but he also knew he'd have to make things right again. He'd been pretty horrible to her this morning. And most likely, very unreasonable.

Grabbing his suit coat, he walked quickly out of his office. "I'll be back in a while, Tilly," he said to the woman who jerked in fright now every time he spoke to her. He might have some areas to patch up with her as well. She wasn't the brightest bulb in the package, but she wasn't as bad as how he'd been treating her. Or maybe she was just nervous because he was always arguing with Autumn, her boss while she was working here.

Once he was out on the street, he walked quickly, his eyes scanning the people walking on the sidewalk and looking into the various stores, trying to find Autumn. He caught her just as she was walking into the big department store on the next block. He picked up his pace and caught up with her as she was entering the shoe department.

He watched with a mixture of amusement and interest as she walked by several shoes, picking them up, examining one, flexing another, sticking her finger inside and doing something. A salesperson approached her and she looked longingly at two different pairs of shoes, one black and one red. But she walked over to the discount shoe rack and picked up a pair of sexy, black heels. They weren't as hot as the ones she had looked at a moment ago, but they were nice enough. He stayed in the background, but worked his way over to the sales desk, ensuring that he kept out of her line of sight. When the sales clerk was coming back with the shoes she'd selected in her size, Xander pulled him over. "Bring her the shoes in her size she'd been looking at several minutes ago, okay?" he asked.

The salesperson looked him up and down, then smiled, acknowledging the hand-tailored suit and Indian cotton shirts. Salespeople the world over knew how to pick up the signals of a wealthy customer and cater to them. This one was no exception.

He quickly delivered the originally requested shoes, but then went back to get the other pairs in Autumn's size. While Xander waited, he picked up several other shoes that he thought she might like, plus a few others that he personally liked.

Handing all of them to the salesclerk, he piled the man high with the shoes, telling him to bring all of them in her size as well.

Then Xander sat down in one of the chairs and watched as Autumn tried on each pair of shoes. He could tell by the expression on her face which ones she liked and which she didn't like. The salesperson was perfect, telling her that he didn't have anything else to do so he didn't mind getting her shoes in the various sizes "just for fun" was what he said.

Each time Autumn tried on a new pair, if she liked it, Xander would signal to the salesperson to put them in one pile. If she didn't like the shoe, the clerk put them in another pile. It was the best lunchtime break he'd had in a long, long time. Well, besides the lunch he'd spent with her at Durango's yesterday. She'd been so fun and free, talking about everything and anything. He'd enjoyed just looking at her smiling face.

In the end, she purchased her discounted, black shoes and walked out of the store, still feeling pretty good. When she was out of sight, Xander walked up to the salesclerk and handed him his credit card. Put all the others in the 'like' pile on this credit card and have them sent to this address," he told the man who looked like he had just about won the lottery today due to the commission he'd earn on this shoe extravaganza.

On the way out, he picked up a box of pretty chocolates, thinking they might go a ways towards soothing Tilly's panic every time he asked her for something. As the cashier was ringing up that purchase, he saw another box of chocolates. This one was bigger, more elaborate and he immediately thought of Autumn. "Can you wrap that box up," he said to the cashier. "Have them sent to this address?" he told her, handing him another business card. On the back, he wrote Autumn's name and her extension, just in case.

"Thanks," and he smiled, walking out of the store with the smaller box of chocolates, feeling much better. Autumn loved shoes, but she was a huge fan of chocolates too.

Back in her office, Autumn pulled her old shoes off and slid her feet into the new ones, loving the way the supple leather enclosed her foot. She stood up and walked around her office, making sure that they still felt good while she was on the carpeting. Smiling, she walked down the hallway, a definite perk in her step. She wasn't even going to tackle the problem of trying to find new candidates for Xander today. She felt too good and she didn't want to spoil the mood. She'd figure something out tomorrow, she told herself as she slowly whittled down her workload that had been piling up over the past few days since she'd spent so much time trying to find Xander a new assistant.

She sighed as the tension left her body with each step and felt wonderful. She stayed on the opposite end of the hallway from Xander, not wanting to ruin this good mood by running into him and having him demand more resumes. Resumes which she didn't have right now, since she was purposely ignoring his problem.

When she came back to her office an hour later, she noticed a strange look on Mary's face. "What's up?" Autumn asked, her hand resting on the doorknob to her office. "And why is my office door closed?"

Mary smiled weakly, then shrugged. "I didn't know what to do with all of them, so I just stacked them in your office," she explained.

"Stacked what up?" Autumn asked, confused.

"All the boxes."

Autumn still didn't understand. "Did an order come in that didn't fit in the storage room?" she asked, pushing open the door. And then she just stopped.

Her office wasn't filled, but there were definitely a lot of boxes on her desk. Bags with about ten different boxes. Shoe boxes! And a huge box of chocolates sat on the corner of her desk.

"What's all this?" Autumn asked, wondering what kind of mistake had been made. "Where did all of these come from?"

She opened one box and saw the red, suede shoes she'd absolutely loved earlier this afternoon. "Oh my!" she gasped. Opening the next one, she saw the black ones with the zipper on the size. Box after box revealed all the beautiful shoes that she'd tried on earlier. "I didn't buy these," she whispered, her voice completely gone as her heart beat frantically. "At least, I don't think I did," she said. She pulled her receipt out of the smaller bag and looked. Sure enough, there was only one pair of shoes on that receipt.

"There's definitely been a mistake," she said. "Some of these shoes are way out of my price range. I can't spend this much money on shoes!"

Mary was sighing as she held up a pair of lime green, leather shoes with a gold bow on the side. "Can you keep them for a day or two? I just like holding them," she said with awe in her eyes.

Autumn didn't even answer her, too busy looking up the phone number of the department store. It took her several tries, but she eventually was connected to the shoe department. And miracle of miracles, the salesclerk who had helped her earlier was actually still there.

"Hi there," she said with as friendly a tone of voice as she could. "I was there earlier today and you helped me try on several pairs of shoes."

"Yes ma'am," the clerk replied with a friendly, deferential tone. "Did you receive the delivery?" he asked politely.

"Um," Autumn stared around at all the boxes of shoes. "Well, yes. I got more than ten pairs of shoes, but there's been some mistake. I didn't buy all of these," she explained. "I need to return them."

"No mistake ma'am. You won a sort of lottery this afternoon. All those shoes are bought and paid for. I hope you enjoy them!" he said with enthusiasm running through his voice.

She didn't say anything for a long moment. "Are you sure?" she asked.

"Absolutely. Please come back and visit us soon! And let me know if I can be of any future assistance."

Autumn thanked the man before she hung up, her eyes still staring at all the shoes around her office. Mary had pulled out several more shoes, trying on all of them in the vain hope that they might be a different size, several sizes larger, so she could steal one or two of them. No such luck, she accepted when the last of the boxes of shoes was opened.

"What did the guy say?" Mary asked, running her finger down the side of a black, patent leather shoe with a gold tipped heel that almost looked lethal.

Autumn picked up a grey flannel pair. She'd thought they were like slippers but they had a slightly higher heel. "He said I won the afternoon shopping lottery." She'd loved these so much but they were way too expensive. Oh, she knew that some people spent two or three thousand dollars on one pair of shoes and these were only in the two or three hundred dollar range, but still! Her price range was more along the lines of fifty to one hundred dollars, a bit more when it was a high quality pair or something she simply had to have.

And she'd never bought this many pairs of shoes at one time!

Something just didn't sound right about the whole thing. Windfalls like this simply didn't happen to her. She'd never won anything in her life.

"I wish I'd gone with you," Mary said and put the last pair of shoes back in the box, carefully pushing the tissue back in place. "Well, better get back to work. Since no shoe fairy is going to hand me twelve pairs of shoes, I need to earn more money so I can buy my own."

Mary laughed at her silly joke as she walked back out to her desk.

Autumn stacked the boxes of shoes back up, pushing them into the bags while her mind whirled through the possibilities. The shoe lottery didn't make any sense!

Then she looked at her desk and spotted the box of chocolates. Chocolates? She never got chocolates because she ate them all! She couldn't have chocolates around or she'd gain ten pounds!

Ignoring the chocolates, she continued to work, even pulled up a few more resumes but rejected them since they didn't look better than the ones she'd already discussed with Xander. She didn't realize the passing of time, but by the time she looked up, it was past eight o'clock at night.

Autumn leaned back in her chair and stared at the stack of shoes. If it didn't make sense, she couldn't accept it. Maybe if she spoke to the store manager tomorrow, she would feel a little better about the windfall. But right now, she didn't understand it, so she didn't get excited about all the shoes.

"Autumn I was wondering…" Ash stood in the doorway, his eyes frozen as he took in the stack of shoes in their bags. "Man he must have really pissed you off," Ash said as he counted the number of shoe boxes. "Twelve pairs of shoes?" he exclaimed. "What did that ass do to you that you needed to buy twelve pairs?" he asked, becoming angry on her behalf.

Autumn was completely confused. "What are you talking about and who made me angry?"

Ash shrugged. "Xander of course. He's pretty much the only one you fight with. Did he do this to you?" Ash demanded.

Her mind worked quickly through his comments, trying to interpret what he was saying. "Did Xander make me so angry that I bought twelve pairs of shoes? Is that what you're asking me?"

Ash shook his head. "I'll talk to him Autumn. I know that something is wrong, but I promise, I'll get him to apologize." He glanced at the stack of shoes once more.

"What are you talking about?" she demanded, standing up and looked up at him. "How is Xander involved in the shoe issue?"

Ash looked at her, then at the shoes. "This afternoon, when you were leaving I could tell that you were in a better mood."

"And?" she prompted when he didn't go on.

"And," he laughed, "Xander was right next to me and I mentioned you looked happy because you were going shoe shopping."

Autumn simply stared at him, trying to connect the dots.

Ash was starting to look uncomfortable. "Isn't that what you do when he pisses you off?" he asked, obviously still confused by the intricacies of the female mind.

"He's been…" she searched her mind for an appropriate word, careful since Ash was Xander's younger brother. They were the closest siblings she'd ever met so she didn't want to insult anyone.

"Xander's been an ass, Autumn. I don't know what's going on, but I'll talk with him."

Ash turned and walked out of her office, forgetting whatever it was he was going to ask of her. She looked at the stack of shoes, her mind whirling with the possibilities. She pulled out a black and white polka dotted pair, her finger smoothing over the fabulous material.

And then it hit her. She hadn't won any ridiculous lottery! Somehow, Xander had paid for these shoes!

She grabbed the polka dotted shoes and stormed out of her office, straight down the hallway. Everyone else was pretty much gone for the night but she saw the light in his office and was thrilled that her prey was still available.

"You bastard!" she called out, completely ignoring all office protocols as her anger took over. She wasn't thinking, just reacting to the fact that Xander had bought her all of these shoes as a way to placate her!

Xander had been sitting behind his desk, the papers he was working on illuminated by just his desk light so when he looked up to watch her storm into his office, she couldn't see his face very well. She didn't care. Not one little bit. He'd tried to buy her! "You're a horrible, evil, ridiculous scoundrel!" she said and threw the shoe across the room at him.

Xander was never so glad that he'd played football in high school and college. And that his instincts hadn't diminished over time. His boxing workouts probably helped here as well. He was easily able to duck the flying shoe-missile. When he looked up again, he saw that she had another shoe primed and ready to fire and he went into survival mode, his face breaking out in a huge grin as he took on the challenge of a furious Autumn. Damn, she looked hot in her new shoes!

He rounded his desk, his hands open in a placating gesture. "Autumn, I have no idea what you're thinking, but let's talk about this," he said. No sooner had the words left his mouth that he had to duck when she threw the second shoe right at his head. Thankfully, he was pretty good at dodging fists in the ring, which lent itself well to dodging shoes.

"You bought all these shoes, didn't you?"

Xander realized he was caught but he was too busy trying to figure out how to avoid getting bashed in the head to come up with a good lie. She was so angry, she reached down and whipped off the shoe she was wearing, firing it just as hard.

Xander knew he had to hurry up and tackle her before he was impaled on those shoes. And he also had to stop thinking she looked incredibly sexy when she was threatening him with bodily harm.

"Let's talk, Autumn."

"NO! We've been talking for the last three days and all you do is drive me crazy! I'm done talking with you. And just when I have things worked out in my mind, you go out and buy me shoes! How crazy is that?" And there flew the last shoe.

He didn't take any chances. Going in low, before she could grab the books on the bookshelf, he dove for her middle. With both grace and gentleness, he plowed into her and pinned her back against the wall. She struggled for all she was worth but he wasn't letting up. His hands held her arms above her head and his body pinned the rest of her. He just watched, fascinated while she struggled, writhing against him. In the end, his pinning her didn't stop her. It was her realization that she was turning him on that froze her movements.

When she was finally still but out of breath, he smiled down at her. "So how about you tell me why you are so angry with me," he said, but his mind was on the way her breasts were now flattened against his chest. He didn't really give a damn about her anger. Well, he did, but that was for later. After he…

Autumn groaned when he bent low and nibbled on her earlobe.

"Tell me what I did wrong," he said, sincerely confused.

Autumn looked up at him, her body on pins and needles, wishing he would kiss her, make love to her just like he had that one night. And then she remembered all the other women in his life and she burst into tears.

All sexual need dissipated with Autumn's first tears. He loved her anger and her passion, thought she was sexy as all get out when she was on a mission to fix something in the office. But tears unmanned him. He couldn't handle tears, not from her! Which was ironic since women had used tears on him all the time and he was always completely unmoved. But when she looked up at him with those sparkling tears in her eyes, he felt like the biggest jerk in the world.

"Autumn, talk to me. How can I fix this?" he asked her gently, holding her close to him as he hugged her against him. When she sagged against his chest, the tears came stronger. He lifted her into his arms and carried her over to his sofa, sitting down with her in his lap, rocking her gently while she cried out her sorrow. He couldn't believe he'd done this to her and he felt worse the longer her tears lasted.

When the tears finally subsided, he pulled back and looked down at her, his arms still around her waist. "Can you talk to me?" he asked gently. "I still don't understand what I did wrong. I thought you loved new shoes."

She sniffed, lifting her face out of his neck, almost bursting into tears again when she saw her makeup smeared against his collar. He probably paid a couple hundred dollars for those shirts of his and she'd just gone and stained one of them. "I'm sorry," she whispered, embarrassed by her outburst. He handed her a tissue and she used it to try and wipe away the mess on his collar.

"That's for you, Autumn," he said and tried to stop her from cleaning his collar.

"But I messed up your shirt."

"Don't worry about that. Tell me what I did wrong."

She sniffed once again and looked away from the mess on his shirt, trying to get off of his lap.

"You're not leaving until you help me understand," he said, his hands tightening around her waist.

She laughed slightly, but it sounded more like a hiccup. "You bought me the shoes, didn't you?" she asked, but she could already see the answer in his eyes.

"What difference does it make if I bought you the shoes or not?"

She took a deep breath, trying to calm down. "It matters because of why you did it. And the cost of all those shoes."

"The cost is nothing," he said, dismissing the expense with a wave of his hand. "Why do you think I bought them for you?"

"Because you made me angry."

"Yes. That's part of it," he said.

She slipped off his lap, needing to put some space between them now that her emotional outburst was finished. "You shouldn't have done that," she said, feeling sad both because he'd bought her shoes to appease his guilt and because she knew she'd have to take back all of those lovely shoes. She shouldn't have, but she'd fallen in love with some of those shoes this afternoon. Just looking at them in their boxes had been a painful temptation. She already had outfits picked out for some of them. "I know you were just trying to make me feel better. And appease your guilt. But I'm okay."

Xander stood up as well, towering over her as only Xander could. Ryker and Axel were about the same height as him and Ash was even taller, but those men didn't seem to do it the same way Xander did. He didn't just stand there. He loomed. He intimidated. He….turned her on when he stood there looking so powerful and dominating. Some people needed oysters or asparagus. Autumn only needed Xander. He was a sexy and enticing aphrodisiac all by himself.

He bent down and picked up one of her shoes, then lifted her up unexpectedly, setting her back onto his desk. "I can't really say that I bought you these shoes to appease my guilt. Although I do apologize for being such an obnoxious, irritating person lately."

She swallowed, barely hearing his words because his fingers were holding her leg, his hand smoothing down the skin of her calf. It was almost as if she weren't wearing stockings at all. When his hand lifted her foot while his other hand put her shoe back on, he said, "What about if you just accept that I like seeing you in these shoes? I like it when you walk down the hallway and you have these sexy heels on, you're sexy skirts and you're sexy makeup, looking like some sort of goddess of business or something."

She couldn't help it. The laugh just sort of escaped. "Goddess of business?" she repeated.

He nodded his head, his hand sliding back up her leg, sneaking under her skirt sensuously. "A goddess anyway." He chuckled as well. "Maybe of more than just business."

She smiled, feeling pretty sexy at that moment. "I really don't want to be a goddess of business," she laughed. She realized where this was going, what her head was thinking and she pulled back. Taking her foot out of his hand, she shook her head. "I'd better get home," she told him and slipped off his desk. "It's been a pretty long and horrible day. I have a feeling Tilly is about to quit on you too."

Xander leaned back against his desk, watching with appreciation as she bent down low to pick up her other shoe and slip it onto her foot. "Don't worry about Tilly," he said as she bent to pick up the other two missiles she'd fired at his head earlier tonight. "I bought her a box of chocolates as an apology."

Autumn was crushed. The shoes and the chocolates. He had a lot to apologize for, she thought warily. "Well, I'd better get out of here."

She turned around and walked to his door. But she stopped and turned around. "I'm sorry for throwing my shoes at you," she said.

Xander laughed softly. "Please feel free to throw any clothing you'd like to take off," he said. Then he got to enjoy the blush that burst into her cheeks before she turned away again and walked down the hallway.

CHAPTER 5

Ash watched Autumn walk down the hallway and he instantly knew something was wrong. He watched her face, noted the dark circles under her eyes and his eyes narrowed. And then it hit him. When he realized what was wrong, his temper almost exploded.

Storming down the hallway, he didn't even bother to knock before he walked into Xander's office. He did hesitate, ensuring that his brother wasn't with a client before he demanded. "What did you do to her?"

Xander turned around, sliding the book back onto the bookshelf that he'd been reading. "Do to who?" he asked, not sure what his brother was talking about. He was exhausted from lack of sleep, frustrated because he couldn't figure out how to get Autumn back into his bed and everything he did seemed to backfire on him. So he definitely wasn't in the mood to deal with his youngest brother right at the moment.

"Autumn!" Ash growled, his hands fisted at his sides.

Xander's eyes narrowed. "What do you mean? What's wrong with her?" he demanded, his body ready to head down the hallway to make sure she was okay.

"That's what I'm asking you!" Ash countered, taking a step forward. "What did you do to her? How did you upset her this time?"

"Why do you think she's upset?"

Ash didn't have time to answer before Axel burst into Xander's office, pushing Ash out of the way in order to confront Xander. "What did you do to her?"

Xander looked from one to the other of his younger brothers, completely befuddled. "What the hell are you two talking about?" He was starting to get angry himself now. He didn't like the idea of Autumn being upset, but more to the point, he didn't like anyone else caring as much about his woman being upset.

"Autumn!" Axel almost yelled. "She's upset about something and you have to be the reason. You've been driving her crazy with all your ridiculous demands and now you've broken her!"

Xander's heart just about stopped with those words. "Tell me what you know!" he growled.

Again, no one could answer because Ryker walked in at that moment. He wasn't as abrasive as his two youngest brothers, but the concern was written all over his features. "Xander, do you know anything about why Autumn is so upset?" he asked, his eyebrows drawn low over his eyes, a strong indicator of how upset he really was. Ryker didn't yell. One had to look into his eyes to know what was going on. He held everything very controlled and close to himself.

Xander threw up his hands with exasperation. "What are you guys all talking about? I spoke to her last night and she was perfectly fine!" Well, at the end she was fine, he thought silently. He wouldn't tell them about her crying. That was between the two of them and he wasn't about to discuss it with his nosy brothers.

"She's obviously upset about something," Ryker said, stepping to the side.

Xander glared at the wall of brothers, wishing, not for the first time, that he'd had only sisters. "If someone doesn't explain this to me, we're going to experience a whole lot more than just words and accusations!" he threatened to all three of them in general. It might be three against one, but he was protecting his woman now and that made him stronger.

"She's wearing flats!" Ash spat out as if shoes without heels were illegal and offensive.

Xander looked at the other two, both of which were nodding their heads in agreement. "She's wearing flats?" he asked, not sure what they meant.

"Yes!" Axel yelled. "So what did you do to her?"

Xander was worried now. What they were saying didn't make any sense at all. "Get out of my way," he growled, trying to push past the three of them.

Axel crossed his arms over his huge chest, glaring intently at his brother. "You're not going near her if you're going to hurt her feelings again."

"And you've got to figure out how to fix this!" Ash told him.

Ryker was in the process of nodding while Xander was considering which one to punch out first. He was frantic to get to Autumn and find out what they were talking about. But a moment before he was going to take a swing, a soft, feminine voice interrupted and broke through his haze of fury.

"What's going on in here?" Autumn asked, stepping around Ryker, Ash and Axel. She looked up at Xander, trying to get an answer. But she felt the blush stain her cheeks when all four men looked down at her feet.

Xander was the first to recover. He looked at her shoes, saw the cheetah print flats that went perfectly with her chocolate brown pants and burst out laughing. Autumn smiled at his amusement, shaking her head as she looked up at the other three Thorpe brothers.

"Can anyone explain this to me?" she asked while Xander leaned over his desk, bracing himself as his laughter took over his common sense and manners.

Ryker stepped forward and touched her forearm gently. "Are you okay?" he asked, his eyes concerned.

Autumn looked at Xander, still laughing and rolled her eyes. "I had a hard day yesterday, but by the end of it, things were back into perspective."

Ash and Axel relaxed somewhat, but they still looked like they wouldn't mind punching their brother.

"Six o'clock at the gym," Ash told Xander, smacking him on the back before leaving.

"I'll be there too," Axel said and walked out, not bothering to even acknowledge his older brother.

Ryker shook his head, glanced down at Autumn's flat shoes once more, then walked out. "I'll be there too," he told Xander.

Autumn watched three of her four bosses walk out of Xander's office, not sure what was going on. "Would you mind telling me what just happened here?" she asked, speaking over the still-laughing Xander.

When he continued to laugh, she huffed and started to walk out of his office, determined to get things done instead of stand here awkwardly. But he stopped her by grabbing her wrist and pulling her back. He was still laughing, but at least he was somewhat in control now.

She took a deep breath and waited, feeling tiny and silly in her flats, especially next to Xander. He was so darn tall!

"Why are you wearing flats?" he asked, still chuckling. "Is it because of our conversation last night?"

She shifted uncomfortably. "Yes. I didn't want you to think I was trying to lure you into my web."

He lifted a hand to touch her cheek in a feather-like caress. "And what if I want to be lured into your web?"

Her mouth fell open and her body softened. She glanced down at his mouth, then back to his eyes. "You can't do this here," she whispered.

"Where can I do it?"

She was just about to respond when Tilly interrupted them. "Mr. Thorpe, your…" she stopped when she saw the way the two of them were standing. "Oh, I'm sorry," she gasped and tried to back out of the office. "I didn't mean to interrupt."

Autumn looked behind her and pulled out of Xander's grip. "You're not interrupting anything," she said and quickly walked out of Xander's office. She didn't bother to look back at him, cursing herself for falling under that famous spell of his. She couldn't believe how close she'd been to telling him to come over to her house and fall into her web. Thank goodness for Tilly's interruption. She'd been about to make a complete fool of herself.

The next few days, she worked harder than normal. She stayed late so she wouldn't run into Xander leaving with any of his latest lady loves and she came in early. The thought of running into him on the way into the office, perhaps seeing him with a grin on his face which she would automatically think was because he "got lucky" the previous night, would hurt too much to bear. So she assiduously avoided seeing the man, even in the hallways. She knew his routine and worked hard to avoid him.

She was successful until their normal Friday morning staff meeting. Her luck wore out but she was braced for it. The other three Thorpe brothers came in and took their seats but Xander rushed in right before the meeting was to start. Unfortunately, that meant he was sitting right next to her. On the up side, it allowed her to avoid looking at him. Even when he spoke, she could pretend to be writing something. On the down side, she thought she could actually feel the heat of his body even from one chair away. That was impossible, she told herself, feeling ridiculous for even thinking it. But she wasn't aware of her body moving towards that source of incredible heat. Her legs crossed and uncrossed until half of her body was practically facing his.

When the meeting finally adjourned, Autumn looked around, surprised that everyone was getting up and moving out the door. Had she missed the entire meeting? She looked down at her note pad, wondering what she'd written. But the page was basically blank. There were a few doodles, but she'd written nothing else.

Normally, these meetings caused her to take several pages of notes, but not today.

"I'll be there in just a moment," she heard Xander say and her whole body froze.

And then she heard what she'd been dreading she might hear. The door closed.

Slowly, as if her neck muscles were refusing to cooperate, she lifted her head, looking up at Xander as he stood leaning against the door.

"What's going on?" he demanded as he crossed his arms over his massive chest.

Her heart was beating so loudly, she was afraid he might be able to hear it from across the room. "I don't know what you mean," she replied and stood up, straightening all of the papers that had been handed out during the meeting. Some had actually been her handouts. How had they been distributed? She didn't remember any of it.

"Something is obviously wrong," he said and moved so he was standing over her with the back of her thighs pressing against the edge of the conference room table.

She couldn't look at him in the eye so she stared at his chest, afraid of what he might see. And afraid of what she might see in his eyes as well. "I don't know what you mean, Xander. Everything is perfectly fine. Nothing at all is wrong," she stammered nervously. She was lying through her teeth and he probably knew it, but she was going to brave through it as long as possible. The alternative, being honest with Xander, wasn't a possibility.

"Then why did you tell the others that we needed an office change?" he asked softly, his indigo blue eyes looking at her features slowly, as if he were savoring the moment alone with her.

She pulled back slightly, her brain not functioning properly with him so close to her. They always kept their distance especially when they were fighting each other. Except for that... well, that one afternoon.

She hadn't remembered saying anything about an office change so this was all news to her. She'd thought it, especially this week while trying to avoid running into Xander in the hallways.

Trying to keep herself from looking like a complete idiot, she ran with the question as best she could. "What's wrong with an office change?" she whispered, her soft, brown eyes dropping down to look at his mouth. She didn't know that her body language had softened and she was instinctively turning towards him, her fingers fluttering by her side because she wanted to reach out and touch him so badly. She wondered what it would be like to be able to touch him whenever she wanted, to stretch up onto her tip toes and kiss him, to ask him to take her into his arms and make love to her.

She sighed and bowed her head slightly, knowing she didn't have those rights and never would. Xander was every lady's man, not just hers.

Xander's entire body reacted to the way she was looking at him. She was always so standoffish, yelling at him whenever he pressed her buttons. Granted, he pressed them as often as he could, loving the way her face turned all soft pink and flushed when she got angry. But she hadn't snapped at him once today, hadn't risen to any of his verbal jibes during the staff meeting, and she'd even agreed with him on a few issues he'd brought up.

"Nothing is wrong with an office change, Autumn," he said, moving slightly closer to her, filling his nostrils with that pretty, feminine scent he remembered from their one time together. Damn, she smelled so good! And she tasted....

Nope, not thinking of that, he told himself firmly. That boat has already sailed. She didn't want him that way anymore or she wouldn't have run out of his place while he showered. She'd spoken loud and clear that morning.

But what was she telling him now? She wasn't moving away from him, he realized.

"Change is good," she said, barely a whisper this time. She didn't have the strength to raise her voice above a whisper. Not when Xander was this close. Not when she could feel every particle of heat he was emanating from his incredible body. And she was so cold. She'd been so cold for so very long. It wasn't right that he had all this heat and she had…none. It felt like her entire body was aching, desperate for Xander's heat, for him to wrap his arms around her and…yes, to do what he'd done with her that one afternoon.

"We can't be like this," she said, trying to move backwards, willing herself to give up this sudden fascination with…all of him.

"We're in a conference room, discussing business," he replied, but he shifted his body so no one could see them if the door were to open accidentally.

Autumn sighed with relief when he said that. She looked up and around, realizing that her vision was obstructed by his extremely large chest. Had he actually moved closer? Was he bending his head and…oh please don't let him kiss her! Oh please don't let him stop if that was what he planned!

She lifted her head at the same moment his mouth captured hers, wrapping her arms around his neck and pulling him closer. When he deepened the kiss, she opened her mouth, reveling in the hot waves that washed over her as he put his hands on her waist and lifted her up against him.

The force of that kiss made her mind whirl with need and desire. She'd never kissed a man and felt like this before. She couldn't get enough of him, rising up on her tip toes so she could feel more of him against her body, press herself closer and know that, for this instant, this moment in time, he was all hers. She had the freedom and the right to touch him and her fingers moved over his neck, his shoulders then back up to tangle in his hair.

Xander couldn't believe how incredible she felt in his arms. She was all softness and light, heat and energy. He hadn't imagined how it felt to hold her, to feel that incredible power surge through him, making him feel even more powerful simply because she was letting him hold her.

Suddenly, there was a noise outside of the conference room and Autumn broke away. She quickly put several feet between their bodies, just in time actually since a second later, several people opened up the conference room door and were piling in for their scheduled meeting, coming to an abrupt stop when they saw who was already in the room.

Autumn glanced at Xander, then at the group of lawyers who were standing there, mouths open as they tried to figure out what was going on and if they should just back out. Thankfully, Xander's eyes looked furious which was too normal of an occurrence, especially when she was around. The fights between the two of them were becoming legendary around the office.

She quickly gathered up her papers and walked out of the conference room, pretending like nothing unusual had just occurred, that the tension the newcomers felt was simply the normal anger that blew up whenever she and Xander were in a room for more than thirty seconds.

It probably didn't help that her face was red or that she couldn't regain control of her breathing. Her fingers were shaking and her knees not very steady, but they couldn't see that. And if they did, hopefully they would simply attribute those symptoms to a fight as well.

She made her way through the hallways, ignoring anyone who tried to call to her for a question or to let her know whatever it was that they felt she needed to know. She didn't stop until she was in her office alone with the door slammed shut, blocking out the rest of the world and all the craziness that had occurred since she'd been in Xander's arms. She closed her eyes and took several deep breaths, trying very hard to regain her semblance of normalcy.

Had she really just kissed Xander? In a conference room?! Where anyone could, and did, interrupt them! She shook her head and practically fell into her chair, her whole body shaking from the impact of him. Well, actually, she was shaking from her reaction to him and not the man himself.

Okay, so it was most likely a combination of both the man and the way he touched her and the way she reacted to him.

Stop! She closed her eyes and leaned back in her chair.

"Are you okay?" a female voice asked.

Autumn's eyes popped open and she looked back up at her assistant. "Yes. I'm fine," she said and sat forward, placing her hands over her keyboard. She tried to look as if she were working but knew she was failing miserably. It was probably the guilty look in her eyes that gave her away so she looked down at her keyboard. "Why do you ask?"

Mary looked at her curiously. "You rushed in here like the hounds of hell were chasing after you. I guess you've been acting a bit strangely this week so I shouldn't think anything of it, but it just feels like something more is going on." She hesitated for a moment, looking curiously at her boss from the doorway. "And your cheeks are all pink, like you might have a fever or something." Mary walked over to Autumn's desk and handed her a sheaf of papers. "Are you not feeling well? Maybe you're coming down with something. This crazy fall weather, cold in the morning, hot in the afternoon, can do that to a person's system. Our bodies don't know whether to produce heat or find air conditioning. Do you need to go home? I can cover for you. It's Friday so most people are already heading out."

Autumn thought longingly of her home and the solace it would provide. Her comfortable townhouse was exactly what she needed right now. She could skip out of here and hide her head under a pillow, pretend like she never had to come out again.

But what would Xander say if he found out she'd left early. He'd probably show up at her door, just to make sure she was okay. He'd been fairly protective of her lately.

Well one day did not make a protector, she corrected herself. She smiled back to the memory of the three other Thorpe brothers confronting Xander when she'd worn her flat shoes. That made her feel good, all of them ganging up on him to make sure she was okay. She almost chuckled at the confused expression in his eyes, and all because she'd worn a pair of flats. Boy, she'd really thrown everyone off that day!

She shook her head, banishing the memory and all those warm fuzzy feelings Xander tended to generate inside of her whenever he did the he-man-my-woman routine for her benefit. He was probably like that with all the women. He definitely did it to all of his female clients, making sure they were financially protected when their husbands finalized a divorce. She actually liked that about him. Unless he was doing it to the women he dated. She wouldn't like that at all.

Mary was still waiting for a response and she focused on the work she had to get done today. "I'm fine," she smiled wearily. "Just tired. It's been a hectic week."

Mary smiled back and handed her the other reports Autumn had asked for earlier. "The client system is up and running now. All the cases are fully loaded from prior years and can be cross-referenced for any issue or keyword. Several people have already stopped by my desk to compliment you on fighting for that system," Mary commented as she walked out of Autumn's office.

Autumn smiled, feeling a huge sense of victory wash over her with those words. She'd fought hard for that system, arguing with Xander mostly. He'd said they hadn't needed something like that because there were already research databases that were online and the firm subscribed to them. What was the point, he'd asked over and over again. She'd given him several arguments, fighting with him about productivity, the statistics she'd gathered about the various resources, the capability of the support staff to gather data and market more effectively for new clients. The Thorpe Group didn't need more clients, he'd argued. They were turning clients away all the time because they couldn't hire and train new lawyers fast enough.

She'd fought him tooth and nail on every last penny spent on the system so it was a huge relief that it had been easy to implement and that staff members were actually using it. A point for her, she thought.

But somehow, the idea of scoring one more point in their ongoing office battle just didn't make her feel as victorious as it used to. Another problem with sleeping with the enemy, she berated herself one more time. Even winning a point didn't excite her as much.

She sighed and looked around at her office. She'd spent so much time here lately; the space was starting to feel a bit closed in. More like a prison than a sanctuary. Maybe she should head out after all. She wasn't doing much here anyway. Why log the hours when she wasn't being productive? She suspected that, if she left the office for a little while, she might get more done at home. It was worth a try anyway. At least it would get her away from Xander. She simply couldn't run into him again after that kiss! She had no idea how to explain her reaction, or even why she'd let it happen.

She stuffed her bag with work she might do over the weekend, then shut down her laptop and stuffed that into her bag as well.

"Mary, I've changed my mind. I'm going to head out. If anyone asks, just tell them I'm fine but working from home this afternoon."

"Sure thing," Mary replied, barely pausing in her typing.

Autumn walked out of the office, but instead of taking a right to head towards the elevator, she turned left instead and walked to the stairs. She didn't care that they were so many floors up and her heels were not meant to take that kind of abuse. She just didn't want to risk running into Xander one more time today. She'd embarrassed herself enough for one week.

When she got home, she changed into a pair of soft, well-worn jeans, thick, fuzzy socks, poured herself a glass of wine and carried all of her work onto the back patio. Today was warm enough, but by the time night arrived, it would most likely be too cold to sit out here. So she took advantage of the sunshine while she could.

She curled up on her extra-large chair and pulled her laptop out. But that was as far as she made it in her quest to finish up the project she'd been working on earlier today. Instead of focusing on the report about employee productivity Ryker had asked for, she stared into space, not even remembering the wine she'd poured that was warming by her elbow.

"I thought you said you were working at home," a deep voice said from her doorway.

Autumn's head whipped around and her mouth fell open when she spotted Xander standing in her doorway. "What are you doing here?" she asked, standing up quickly but she forgot about all the papers that she'd spread out around her and the computer she'd had balanced on her knees. The papers slipped down from the cushions but she couldn't stop them since she was trying so hard not to let the expensive laptop hit the stone patio.

Before she knew what was happening, Xander was there on his knee as well, grabbing papers and computer. She looked up, right into his eyes and realized that he was closer than she'd thought.

There was a long, tense moment when her eyes went from his and then down to his mouth. And then she remembered what had happened earlier today when she'd done that and she took a deep breath and pulled back. "What are you doing here?" she asked again.

He smiled that charming grin that always made her stomach flutter. "I knew you'd need help catching all of these papers," he explained, "so I rushed over as quickly as I could." She used to love that smile, she thought. Initially, she'd thought he reserved that smile just for her. He'd tease her in the lobby or when they accidentally run into each other in the hallways. But then she'd seen him use it on one of the women that showed up in the office to collect him. And that smile, directed towards another woman, had shown her that he spread that smile around to everyone and anyone.

She stepped back and sat down on the chair again, wishing he would stop doing this to her. "And the real reason?" she snapped at him, stuffing her papers into her bag again. She wasn't getting any work done today, why even pretend?

"Because Mary said you went home early and I wanted to check on you, make sure you were okay."

"I'm fine," she said and lifted her glass of wine to take a sip. Unfortunately, the white wine had been sitting by her elbow so long that it had gotten warm. Her face squinched up with disgust and she almost spit the wine back in.

"Too warm?" he asked, laughing at her funny expression as he took a seat across from her.

"Yes. It's disgusting," she replied, chuckling a little herself at how she must have looked.

"I'll get you some more," he said and stood up himself. "No, don't stress," he teased again. "I'll find your kitchen in here somewhere."

She couldn't stop the laughter that escaped her this time because he was teasing her about how small her townhouse was. She didn't care though. It was the perfect size for her. The monthly payments allowed her to put more away towards investments than she spent each month so that was an extra bonus.

He came back with not one glass filled with chilled white wine, but two. And the dratted man sat right back down across from her. "So now you can explain to me why you left work so early when you've never left work early before." His eyes narrowed suddenly as if something occurred to him. "In fact, when was the last time you took a vacation?" he asked gently.

She smiled and shook her head. "That's not fair since you rarely take vacation either. You can't condemn me when you're doing the same violation."

"Touché!" he came right back at her. "So start explaining."

He leaned back in the comfortable chair and watched her. She didn't answer his question, but they did have a lively debate about another issue, one he couldn't even remember and which segued from one topic to another. He didn't care either. He simply enjoyed being here with her.

They used to talk like this, he remembered. Until that bastard had come to pick her up for a date. He'd been so furious after seeing her with another man, he'd gone straight to the gym that night and knocked out one of his sparring partners. He hadn't been allowed back into the gym for a week after that incident.

Now she was here, the afternoon sun fading into darkness and he watched the light play off of her beautiful features. He liked her like this, relaxed, in her own domain and feeling more confident. He'd had a hard time lately. His mind vacillated between memories of her being hit by the brute and then the way she'd looked as she'd climaxed in his arms. He hadn't been sleeping well either because every time he fell asleep, he'd feel her again, only to wake up and find that she wasn't there.

It had been tough when he'd only fantasized about her being in his bed. Now that he had the reality as a memory, it was ten times worse. He wanted her back, in his bed and in his arms. And he wanted to figure out how to keep this camaraderie going. He wasn't sure if he could have both, but he was determined to figure out how. Their kiss this afternoon proved that she wasn't as immune to him as she was trying to pretend.

Xander couldn't believe how comfortable her backyard was with the small lights intertwined into the tree branches that came on automatically as they talked about everything and anything. He loved watching the animation on her beautiful features and thought he could spend the rest of his life just sitting here in her backyard watching her and listening to her talk about all of her hopes and dreams, arguing with him about politics, or just telling him he needed to get a grip on whatever he was arguing about with her.

He liked that about her. People didn't normally argue with him. His clients came to him furious with their spouse and told him to make the marriage that they'd worked so hard for just disappear. He told them what to do, how to protect themselves from their spouse's lawyer and they did it. They followed his instructions to the letter, never even questioning his expertise.

Autumn would argue with him about the sky being blue simply because that was who she was. And it turned him on like nothing else could. As the night slowly descended and the twinkle lights showed off her laughing, brown eyes, he had to shift in his seat to adjust his hardening body as he watched her.

Why had she run away the last time they'd been together? What had he done wrong? His other lovers over the years had told him that he was a good lover, and he knew with absolute certainty that she had enjoyed their night together. But ever since that morning, she'd pulled back, put space between them. It was as if she were now embarrassed that she'd given in to the temptation. Which really rankled since he hadn't regretted a single moment. Except, perhaps, that it hadn't lasted longer. Fifty years longer, he thought with irritation.

She shook her head about some political viewpoint he'd just discussed and told him point blank that he was wrong. He laughed, but didn't contradict her claim, enjoying the confidence that was such a part of who she was. She hadn't spoken to him like this in…years! Ever since she'd been the receptionist, not knowing what she wanted to do with her life. She'd been so fresh and eager back then. Well, she still was, he thought as she laughed at his comment about the latest politics. But there was something different about her now. A hardness about her eyes and her mouth that had evolved over the years. And every once in a while, he saw something in her eyes, a hurt that made his stomach clench. When he saw that look, no matter what angry words she was spewing in his direction, all he wanted to do was pull her into his arms and make her tell him who or what had hurt her. He wanted to protect her, to make her life happy and erase all the anger and frustration, except when it was directed towards him!

He picked up the bottle of wine, intending to fill up her glass again. He'd only had half a glass, enjoying her laughter too much to muddy his focus by drinking wine. But when he realized that it was empty, he knew that it was time to leave.

Hell, he didn't want to leave. He wanted to lift her into his arms and make love to her right here on the soft grass of her back yard. And then he wanted to carry her into her house and make love to her on every horizontal surface he could find.

"I'd better head home," he said instead of pulling her out of her chair so she would land on his lap. When she looked down at her hands instead of at him, begging him with those warm, chocolate eyes, he got the message. "Get out of here," he read in her body language.

Damn! After that kiss in the conference room, he'd thought that perhaps she might be as interested in exploring this chemistry he knew they were both experiencing. For so long, he'd wanted her. Initially, she'd been too young. Fresh out of college, wonder in her eyes and excitement at all the world had to offer her. He'd stayed away. But she wasn't fresh out of college any longer. And the way she'd looked at him earlier today after their kiss, not to mention the way she'd responded to his touch… No, he chided himself. She hadn't been herself that day. He'd taken advantage of her after the fight. He knew perfectly well how the adrenaline rushed through one's system after a fight and he'd kissed her right after that. She'd been reacting to the fight, not to him.

But this afternoon…there hadn't been any fight. There hadn't been any adrenaline. Well, until he'd walked away from her. He'd wanted to fight someone, to punch them so hard he could actually do damage when he'd had to walk away from that conference room.

With a sigh and a groan of determination, he rose from the chair. "I'll leave you alone now. But thanks for the wine," he said. "And I enjoyed talking with you. It was just like old times."

He got out of there as quickly as he could, almost running from the house now. Because if he didn't get out now, he wasn't sure he'd have the strength to do it later. Not when she was looking so sweet and sexy sitting there in the big chair, her legs curled underneath her with those cute pink socks. She always looked so sophisticated at work with those killer heels and her skirts so tight that they left nothing to the imagination where her legs or bottom were concerned.

Actually, correct that! Her butt was even better when it was uncovered, he remembered. He hurried faster, almost diving into his car before he changed his mind. He could easily convince himself to turn around and drag her into his arms. He could get her wanting him again. He was sure of it, but would that be fair? She didn't want him normally, so pushing his attentions on her was inconsiderate.

His tires almost squealed as he pulled out of her parking lot and drove home. His hands gripped the steering wheel, white knuckling it all the way home until he reached his apartment complex. When he finally reached his own place, he went straight to his great room and… stopped in his tracks.

"What the hell are all of you guys doing here?" he demanded as he realized all three of his brothers were sitting in his apartment. And they were drinking his best scotch!

"We're celebrating!" Ash called out, standing up and handing him a glass.

Xander didn't hesitate. He took the glass and downed the amber liquid, then held it out for his brother to fill it up again. "Why was my place the designated celebration zone?" he asked, downing the next glass as well.

"Because it was closest," Ryker responded as if that were the most obvious answer, lifting his glass up for Ash to fill it as well.

Xander sat down in one of the deep chairs, his brothers draped over his sofa or the other chair. "And?" he prompted, needing more of an explanation. Although, it wasn't like his brothers to need much of an explanation to celebrate anything. There had been occasions when they'd all congregated simply to celebrate Tuesday or whatever day of the week it happened to be.

All four of his brothers looked like he felt and they were all slamming down the scotch at an alarming rate. No one explained why they were celebrating, but they joked and teased each other just like brothers were prone to do. It felt good, drinking like this after being in Autumn's company. He needed the release, the ability to just kick back. It was either get drunk with his brothers or head right back to Autumn's townhouse, picking her up into his arms and making love to her against the wall. He didn't think she would be very receptive to that option so he kicked his feet up onto his coffee table, forcing himself to stay put.

He laughed as the four of them got drunk, ribbing each other for the way they lived their lives or the lack of a lady love in their lives. When that subject came up, Xander was silent, staring at the liquid in his drink while he thought about the most frustrating woman on the planet. He had women throwing themselves at him at social events, showing up at the office constantly. Rarely could a business meeting be conducted at a restaurant now because women would stop by his table, dropping barely veiled hints that he should ask them out, or not even bothering to wait, but offering themselves up for one party or charity event or another. It was irritating, especially since Autumn was the only woman he wanted on his arm.

"Well, it isn't like the resident monk would know anything about that," Axel was saying.

Xander had no idea what they were talking about, but he looked up and all three of his brothers were looking directly at him. "What?" he asked.

The three of them rolled their eyes. All of them knew about his infatuation with their office manager although none would come out and say it for fear of Xander's anger at the sensitive subject. But they also knew that Xander had rejected women's advances ever since Autumn had walked into their office and started working for The Thorpe Group.

"When was the last time you got laid?" Ash asked.

He wasn't about to tell any of his brothers about his afternoon and evening with Autumn that had surpassed all of his fantasies. They might be close personally and definitely professionally, but his relationship with Autumn was private. "You're a crude ass, did you know that?" he said. Turning to Ryker, he brought up another subject, not bothering to wait for an answer from Ash, nor did he expect one.

"Hey, whatever happened with that altercation in the deli where Autumn was hurt?" Ryker asked. "I got the police report, but I think the police were still waiting for you and Autumn to go down and make a statement."

Xander had completely forgotten to take Autumn down to the station. "Did that jerk get released?" Xander asked furiously, sitting up straighter in his chair. "If he so much as comes near her..." he left the sentence hanging since all three of his brothers were quick to reassure him that the culprit that had started the fight had been sentenced to community service and anger management classes as well as two years' probation.

In Xander's mind, he didn't think that was strong enough of a punishment, but he couldn't really go to the judge and demand something worse. The jails and prisons were packed already with criminals; they wouldn't pay much attention to a guy who took a swing at a woman.

Maybe Xander could. He mentally made a note to have their lead investigator, Mark, look into the guy's background. Anyone who was willing to pick a fight in a public place in the middle of the afternoon had to have some skeletons in the closet. Perhaps it was time to become the fellow's worst nightmare. In Xander's experience, someone like that had a lot more issues that had been swept under the rug. It was time to bring them out, make the man accountable, he thought with relish.

"Any idea why Autumn didn't fight the new accounting software decision today?" Axel asked, shooting for what he thought might be a less explosive subject.

Ryker looked over at Xander who was staring down at his glass. Xander had no idea that his brothers were waiting for a response. He was too caught up in his plans to make the brutish man's life a living hell. So when he lifted his glass to drain the remaining scotch, he realized that all three of his brothers were staring at him oddly.

"What?" he asked, standing up and pouring himself another glass of scotch. He needed something to dull the memory of Autumn, both last Monday as well as this afternoon when she'd looked so soft and warm sitting in her tiny but cozy backyard.

Ash chuckled at his brother's irritated expression. "We were talking about the staff meeting earlier today," he said. "Obviously you're as much aware of our current conversation as she was this morning."

Since the four of them had killed the first bottle, Xander was grabbing another from the sideboard where he kept the liquor. But at the first mention of the staff meeting, he dropped the bottle of scotch. The very meeting after which he'd kissed Autumn for the first time since he'd made love to her.

He looked up at the others warily, trying to hide his reaction. "What about it?"

Ash, Axel and Ryker all looked at each other curiously, then back at Xander who was wiping up a puddle of thirty year old scotch before he got another bottle out from his stash. "What's going on?" Axel asked, voicing what was on everyone's mind.

"Nothing," he snapped back and slapped the next bottle of scotch down in the middle of the coffee table so no one had to exert any effort to get up to pour their next round. Himself included. "Why do you ask?" Had he revealed something? He didn't want to do anything to make Autumn feel uncomfortable. Their afternoon and evening together was their private secret. If anyone knew, she'd feel awful. She'd never said it in so many words, but he knew her well enough that it would be an issue in her mind.

Ryker raised an eyebrow. "You didn't think it was strange that the accounting software was approved?"

Xander shrugged and took another sip, not looking any of his brothers in the eye.

Ash tilted his head as he said, "The less expensive software? The one she didn't want us to get?"

Xander's hand froze in mid-air with that news. Had that really happened during the meeting? Damn! He'd really been out of it. He'd been watching Autumn during the meeting, noticing that she was unusually silent. Obviously, he hadn't been very attentive to the meeting agenda. "I think she had something else on her mind. We'll have to run it by her again next week."

Ash laughed and shook his head. "I can't imagine what she was thinking about," and looked over at his brother, trying to prompt him into a reaction. But after so many years of taking sides, Xander was silent. Another indication that something important was going on.

Ash glanced at his brothers, concern written on all of their faces as they surveyed Xander's silence.

Xander knew exactly where this was going. "Not going to talk about it. I have no idea what's on her mind," he said honestly. She might be thinking that their liaison together had been fantastic and she didn't want to ruin it by a second go, or she might have thought he was a complete ass. He had no clue. "So don't give me that look."

"Did you fight with her this week?"

Xander laughed. "Actually, this is the first week we haven't fought about anything." Which, in itself, was odd.

"Do you think she was more badly hurt in that fight than she's letting on?" Ash asked, concern obvious in his eyes.

Xander thought about that, remembering the way she'd moved while in his arms on Monday after the altercation. Yes, she'd been bruised. No, she wasn't more wounded than they all thought. He ruthlessly suppressed his body's reaction to those images and quickly shook his head. "She's not physically hurt. As for mentally?" He shrugged, honestly not sure what her mental state was at this moment. He couldn't even guess which, was part of the problem.

They moved away from personal issues after that. Apparently, all of the brothers were wary of discussing what was going on in their lives and they fell into their old habit of teasing each other over the cases they were handling.

By the time midnight rolled around, all of them were too drunk to head home so each of them found their respective bedrooms while Xander fell into his own bed. But even all the scotch he'd imbibed during the evening hadn't dulled his need for the one woman who constantly drove him crazy. Who had driven him insane with need for years.

Something was going to have to give, he thought. He wasn't sure how much longer he could be a gentleman about the woman. Perhaps he would start his own firm somewhere. Far away from Chicago so he wouldn't be tempted by her sexy figure in those killer heels every day of his life.

Hell, maybe he should just let her move her office to another floor! She'd tried to do that several times in the past but he'd simply vetoed her arrangement, configuring the office assignments so she was still on his floor. He smiled as he stared up at the ceiling of his darkened bedroom, thinking of the time when he'd arranged it so that her office was right next to his. He chuckled in the darkness. She'd only let that set up last for a few months before she finally created a reason to move her office back down the hallway from him.

Across the city, Autumn was laying in her own bed in the exact same position. She'd finished crying about the way Xander had almost run out of her townhouse earlier tonight. The final insult had been when his tires had squealed on his way out of her driveway.

The man had been desperate to get away from her! How pathetic was she that he needed to speed away like that?

She wiped her cheek angrily, irritated that she was still crying. No more, she told herself firmly. She was finished trying to figure this out. She had to figure out how to get Xander out of her heart. They'd had one fabulous, incredible and amazing night together. Even his kiss this afternoon had made her toes curl with desire. But enough was enough. She wanted kids and a husband while Xander had a daily, front row seat watching people tear each other apart.

At this point in his life, he probably didn't believe in marriage. And she didn't blame him. He'd seen the worst and had avoided the state for so long despite numerous women trying to get him to the altar. She had no chance to succeed where so many others had tried and failed.

Xander was probably right to avoid both commitment and matrimony.

That didn't help her heartache a whole lot though.

Sniffing into the darkness, she knew what she had to do. But even the thought of leaving The Thorpe Group made her whole body ache with sadness. She'd worked so hard to get things to their current state of efficiency. She didn't know if she had the energy to start over somewhere else.

But what was the alternative? She couldn't stay so that only left the option of leaving. It was better to just get out of the situation rather than die a slow death by watching him every day.

CHAPTER 6

Thursday night, Xander was working late in his office. He was tired, irritated by a lack of progress on certain cases, his brothers were looking at him strangely and he hadn't seen Autumn all day today. He realized at this moment how much just the sight of her helped him get through the day. When she passed by his office or he saw her in the kitchen or a conference room, it made him feel good. He might not be able to hold her in his arms, but her smile warmed his heart.

Xander tossed the paper to the side of his desk, rubbing his forehead wearily. He was irritated with a client he'd met with earlier in the day who was demanding everything from her husband. The husband had supported his client for the past twenty years, giving her just about anything she wanted. The woman had a huge house on Lake Shore Drive, spent her days shopping and eating in the best restaurants with her friends, throwing elaborate parties, not many of which were for her husband's business connections. Hell, she walked around with a five thousand dollar purse on her wrist and two thousand dollar shoes.

Her husband had cheated, which Xander didn't condone, but now the woman wanted everything in the settlement. But it wasn't in Xander's nature to be unfair. In this case, he suspected that the woman was either having an affair, or didn't even care that her husband had cheated on her. In his opinion, she was only using this as an excuse to divorce him and take him for everything.

He was leaning back in his chair, trying to figure out how to convince his client to leave her husband with at least one set of clothes and a few bucks in his bank account when he heard a noise. It was late enough that the office should be cleared out. There were always the superstar lawyers that were trying to impress by staying later than the boss, but this was going too far, he thought. Everyone needed balance in their lives and staying in the office working until ten o'clock at night was ridiculous.

Getting up, he followed the sounds, finally locating the late nighter in the copy room. And in this particular case, he didn't mind the person working late. Not one little bit.

Leaning against the metal door frame of the copy room, he watched with fascination as Autumn walked barefoot from the copier to the work counter, collating charts and graphs. He had no idea what case she was working on or what system she was going to try and convince the four of them to buy into next. All he cared about was watching her, fascinated by her cute toes that curled up against her calf as she tried to relax the muscles in her legs.

She was shorter than he'd thought. It shouldn't have been such a surprise, since she always wore three inch heels to give everyone a false sense of her actual height. But without heels, he suspected she wouldn't even come up to his shoulder.

She was singing something to herself and it occurred to him that he didn't even know what kind of music she preferred. It sounded a bit like a country song he'd heard recently, but he wouldn't bet on it. Autumn might know how to run an office like a well-oiled machine, but she couldn't carry a tune to save her soul.

"What are you doing here so late at night?" he asked and enjoyed her startled expression. He wished he was closer to her so he could have grabbed her to steady her. He'd use just about any excuse to touch her. Hell, he'd use almost any excuse just to see her. The woman had been avoiding him lately.

"What?" Autumn asked, her eyes searching frantically for someone else to magically appear behind him. Please don't let them be alone, she thought to herself.

He stepped into the room, watching her back up slightly as he approached. "I asked what you were doing here," he repeated. He glanced down at the graphs and smiled. "Are those the results from the survey?" he asked. She'd done an employee survey that he'd initially thought was ridiculous but as soon as she'd explained her reasoning, he'd agreed that it was an important project. That hadn't stopped him from arguing with her. He'd done so only so he could walk into her office and start the confrontation over again after the meetings.

Autumn squared her shoulders and tried to hide the results from Xander. "Yes, as a matter of fact, it is the results. I know you are opposed to silly things like employee morale and trying to ensure that good employees stay with the firm, but I know there are many things we can do to improve the way we do things here, to help people want to stay besides simply giving them more money."

Xander chuckled, loving the way she defended her ideas so passionately. "I agree with you," he said and moved even closer.

Autumn held her breath, leaning back against the work table and barely able to grasp the meaning of his words. "You do?" she asked, feeling like the air had been knocked out of her lungs.

"I do. And I'm very grateful to you for bringing the idea to us, as well as ensuring that the project was put out to all the employees in such a professional and thoughtful manner."

Autumn blinked, completely confused now. "I thought you didn't believe in wasting time and resources on employee morale surveys," she said softly.

"That was then," he lied. "This is now." And he moved closer. He watched her carefully, waiting for some sort of sign. He'd seen it that day in the conference room and he'd acted on it. He hadn't gotten any signals from her that afternoon in her backyard, but maybe he hadn't been paying attention well enough.

He was paying attention now!

When her mouth softened, he moved closer. When he saw her eyes drop to his mouth, he shifted so that his arms were braced behind her on the wall. He wasn't touching her in any way, but when her head tilted back, he couldn't resist leaning his head down and touching those soft, full lips. And when he felt her sweet breath on his mouth, he couldn't stop himself from deepening the kiss.

Autumn couldn't believe how badly she wanted Xander to kiss her. No matter how many times she told herself to avoid this man, when he came close to her, she couldn't banish this need. Damn him! Why wasn't he kissing her? What did a woman have to do to get him to kiss her?

Unable to stop the reckless need down deep inside of her, she lifted her hands, her palms flattening against his chest then sliding upwards. That seemed to be the only signal he needed because his arms wrapped around her, almost crushing her as he lifted her against his body.

"Damn you feel good," he said through gritted teeth as he lifted her up and slid her back onto the table behind her. "And you look adorable without your shoes on," he told her, his hands sliding down her hips, then back up and underneath her tight skirt, bringing the material higher.

"Xander, we can't..." she started to say, but then his hand touched the bare skin at the top of her thigh high stocking and she gasped, unable to speak. Her mouth dropped open, her eyes closed and her head rolled backwards while her hands balanced her weight behind her so she could lift her leg up higher, giving him better access.

"Tell me you want me," he commanded her, his fingers fluttering along her skin, his eyes fascinated by the expression of bliss on her face and his body was already hard and ready to plunge into her heat. He'd wanted her so badly ever since that one night. He'd pushed it out of his mind, thinking it had been a fluke. But then the kiss in the conference room...ah, he'd never forget her response.

Now she wasn't going to get out of it. He wouldn't allow her to deny what they felt for each other. Just the look on her face told him what he wanted to know, but he wanted her to tell him in words. He wanted to hear her say it.

"What do you want?" he coaxed, his fingers discovering the edge of her lace underwear. "Tell me," he commanded.

His other hand slowly worked the buttons on her silk blouse, leisurely revealing the nude colored lace holding her perfect breasts in place. Just for him, he thought. The peaks were already hard, already calling to him. He bent over her and kissed her neck, nibbling on her collar bone while his fingers down lower teased her hips and her breasts.

Autumn thought she might just go up in flames. With his lips and hands teasing her, she was so primed to climax she just…. "To the right," she whimpered.

His dratted hand moved to the left and she bit her lip as her hips shifted that way as well. Arching her back so that his fingers would claim more of her breast, she shook her head as the feelings drove her almost insane with need. "Please Xander!" she inhaled, her hips lifting, needing his fingers just slightly over to the right.

"Tell me you want me," he commanded again, nibbling on her earlobe.

"We can't," she sighed and shook her head back and forth.

"We can and we are. As soon as you say the words," he whispered in her ear.

In frustration, she grabbed his wrist, intending to move his hand where she so desperately needed it but he chuckled and pulled his hand away. Since he was much stronger than she was, there was nothing she could do. "I want you!" she gasped out, needing him so badly. "I need you inside me right now!" she finally said, her eyes open with anger, or passion, shining through her irises.

Xander swallowed hard, his body throbbing with need now. She was right where he wanted her and she'd actually said the words. And those words freed him, gave him all the permission he needed.

"Take off your underwear," he told her almost harshly. When she didn't move fast enough, he ripped them off for her. He opened several buttons on his shirt then took her hands and splayed her fingers over his chest. "Touch me," he told her while he grabbed something out of his back pocket and quickly adjusted his clothing.

With rough hands, he pushed her skirt up around her hips and her silk blouse down off of her shoulders. When that wasn't enough, he almost ripped her bra down so her breasts were freed to his hungry eyes. He bent her back over his arm, holding her in place so his mouth could devour her breasts. He wasn't gentle, his mouth covering her nipple and sucking hard, causing her to scream out and her hips to shift, needing his fingers back where they had been. Xander didn't disappoint. With one hand holding her in place for his mouth, his other hand moved lower, his fingers sliding into that heat that had been tempting him for the past several minutes.

"You're so wet for me," he growled. His fingers came out of her and he heard her whimper once again but her hips weren't still. They were seeking, her whole body arched in preparation for his invasion.

"Open your eyes, Autumn," he told her. When she wasn't fast enough, he yelled at her again. "Now!"

When she followed his command, he held her eyes while he pushed into her. Gently at first, but as she wiggled against him, adjusting her body to absorb his whole length, when he was fully embedded inside of her, he held her eyes while he pushed into her. He wasn't gentle now. He needed her too painfully and the way she was pressing against him was driving him more crazy.

He put her hands on his shoulders then dropped his hands down to her hips, holding her in place while he pounded himself into her, shifting to give her as much pleasure as possible and watching her eyes the whole time, just to make sure he wasn't hurting her.

"Now, Autumn," he coaxed, pressing himself tighter and he held on to that last, tiny thread of control so that she could experience every pulsating second of pleasure possible. He loved the way her body throbbed around her as her orgasm swamped over her, her eyes closed and her body arched, her legs gripping him hard and she cried out with her ecstasy. When he couldn't hold back any longer, his own climax washed over him and he thought he'd rather die than ever leave this moment with Autumn wrapped around him more tightly than he'd ever thought possible.

She had no concept of time or how long they'd been here. She felt like she was floating on a cloud of happiness. Autumn sighed cheerfully, her fingers drifting down over Xander's muscular shoulder to his chest...then lower. She laughed when he growled and grabbed her hand.

"You want another round?" he asked and bit her neck.

Autumn couldn't help the giggle that escaped her and she tried to move away, but since they were still intimately connected and he was much, much stronger than she was, he held her in place.

But then reality started to come back and her mind began to question why something was hard against her back. Looking around, she gasped as she noticed the copier and all the equipment around her.

"Oh no!" she groaned and started pushing against his broad, muscular shoulders, trying not to let her fingertips touch him. If that happened, she wasn't sure she would have the ability to resist the temptation to touch him further.

"What's wrong?" he asked, moving away slightly and helping her sit up.

"We had sex in the copy room!" she whispered frantically, trying to push her skirt down and button her blouse at the same time. She had absolutely no idea where her underwear was! How embarrassing.

Dressing would have been difficult to begin with but her bra was all out of place as well and that added a third layer of complexity.

Xander looked down at her as she tried to dress, adjusting his own clothing while he chuckled at her frantic movements. "Why are you whispering?" he teased, taking over the task of fixing her bra. But she only smacked his hands away when he started taking it off of her more than he was trying to put it back on.

"I'm whispering because I don't want anyone to hear us if they are still in the office! Do you know how horrible it would be if we were caught having sex in the copy room?" she hissed.

Xander's eyes widened with understanding at her reasoning. "Honey, if anyone were still here, they would have heard you a few minutes ago. You definitely weren't quiet then."

She blushed at the memory and glanced at him, surprised that he was already hard and ready for another go. "Please don't tell me that turns you on," she sighed as she finally got her clothes back in order. Or somewhat in order.

He laughed as he slid his tie off of his neck. She'd tossed it behind his shoulder during their lovemaking but he didn't think he needed it any longer. "Are you kidding me?" he asked, astonished that she would even question how turned on he was. It was pretty evident. "Nearly everything about you turns me on."

She was about to start picking up her reports, but her body froze with those words. "Everything?" she asked softly, staring up at him. Was he lying to her? Was this just another one of his lines that he told all the women? Xander was one of those charming men who knew all the right things to say to make a woman feel special and feminine. Had he learned that particular line worked exceptionally well? Because it was definitely making her body warm up, even if it was just a line.

Xander smiled softly and took her hands in his. She only resisted for a moment before she stood up and let him pull her into his arms. "I'll admit this resistance to seeing me, avoiding me in the hallways isn't very exciting. But when I do see you, and get a glimpse of your long, sexy legs in your ultra-sophisticated skirts and those heels – yes, that turns me on." He bent and nuzzled her neck and smiled to himself when her arms reached up to lay gently on his shoulders. "And when I think about what you wear underneath those silk shirts and stiff suits, I sometimes have to go back to my office and hide out until I can get my body back under control." He let his hands slide up her waist, cupping her perfect breasts in his hands, even enjoying the silk of her blouse when he knew that the silk of her skin was even softer.

"We can't do this," she sighed, leaning her head back and pressing her body against his, loving the differences in the way they were made.

"Yes we can," he countered and bit her earlobe.

She shivered, but still managed to shake her head. "No. It would be embarrassing."

He wasn't sure why it would be embarrassing, but he didn't want her to feel uncomfortable. "We're not going to ignore this anymore Autumn," he warned as he moved his hands down to her bottom, pressing her hips more closely to his own. "And I want to know why you walked away from me last week."

She took a deep, shuddering breath, trying to focus. "I need space if we're going to talk about this," she finally said, unable to think when he was holding her so tightly.

He grinned as he leaned down at nibbled on her lower lip. "Then maybe I won't stop touching you," he replied and kissed her, teasing her until she kissed him back. When he lifted his head, she was clinging to him, exactly how he liked her to be.

She laughed nervously, terrified of how easily he could make her want him. "I refuse to be the latest office bet," she said firmly as she pulled out of his arms.

He shifted so he could see her more clearly. "What are you talking about?" he asked, his hands still moving along her body.

Autumn sighed with irritation which was just a mask for how badly she wanted to slide right back into his arms. "Don't you ever go into the kitchen to get a cup of coffee?"

"Sure. What does that have to do with anything?"

She rolled her eyes. "The paper on the fridge?" she prompted then waited a moment for him to get it. But his eyes were still blank. "It's the office betting pool for your current lady love," she finished.

His hands stilled. "What do you mean?"

She pulled out of his arms and moved to the opposite side of the copy room. "The entire office bets on how long your current lover will last. When a new woman shows up, a new pool starts. Hence the new dates, the initials by each of those dates…." She prompted, hoping he would get the picture.

He thought about those for a moment, then shook his head. "You're kidding, right?"

She shook her head, trying to hide the pain she felt every time a new paper went up onto that fridge. "Not at all. When the dates are all filled up, the paper is taken down and someone is assigned control of the money. It's currently five dollars a date," she explained.

Xander threw back his head and laughed, completely amused by the idea of his entire staff betting on how long a woman would stay in his life. Especially since there hadn't really been any woman in his life for so long.

Autumn took that time to gather up her materials, irritated and indignant that he would be amused by someone betting on his personal life. Not a good idea when he was asking to make her the next woman in his personal life. That was SO not going to happen.

Xander knew that his laughter was creating more problems, but he couldn't stop. It was so hilarious that his staff was betting, winning and losing money, on something that wasn't actually happening! Almost from the moment Autumn came to work from The Thorpe Group, the women in his life had been temporary only because he wouldn't, couldn't, give them what they wanted, a real relationship. The ladies became frustrated with how little he would communicate with them, how he barely even kissed them goodnight. Some of them even asked if he was gay because he was so disinterested when they tried to tempt him.

He'd tried often enough, desperate to get Autumn out of his mind. But none of them could compare to her innocent beauty or the energy and passion she put into everything she did. He loved watching her work, getting involved in whatever might not be working perfectly and making it better. She was like the efficiency energy bunny. He'd been entranced from the moment she'd walked in and sat her adorable butt down in the receptionist chair and he'd become more enraptured by her ever since.

But he could see how she might not want to become the latest office gossip. And he would probably need to ease her into the relationship he wanted from her. And then another thought occurred to him. "Are you seeing someone now?" he demanded, furious at the very idea of another man touching her.

She quickly shook her head, which relaxed his muscles again. "Good." He moved closer to her. "So if you don't want the rest of the staff to know that we're seeing each other," and he put a hand over her mouth when she immediately opened hers to argue with him, "And we will be seeing each other," he told her firmly. She stiffened for a moment and he watched her eyes. There was resistance for a long moment, then it seemed like she was accepting his statement so he released her mouth. "How about if we keep the office gossips from knowing about our relationship?" That would give her an easy out if she discovered that she didn't really like him as a man. Okay, so she liked him as a man if her reaction a few minutes ago was any indication, but she might not like him as a person and keeping it quiet would help her if she wanted out. But it would at least give him some time to be with her, to hold her in his arms and enjoy her company. He'd have to figure out how to not pressure her though. That didn't mean he wouldn't do everything in his power to convince her.

"What do you propose?" she asked, thinking she was a fool to even consider a relationship, secret or otherwise, with Xander Thorpe. He was a ladies man, through and through. He was jaded about relationships. He rarely spent any time with a woman before moving on to the next one that caught his eye because, in his mind, relationships didn't last. But maybe she could just take what he gave and tuck those memories into her mind for the future.

He grinned at her response. "We won't let anyone in the office know that we're together. We'll meet at your place or mine and get to know each other."

She wasn't sure she liked the idea. Well, she definitely loved the idea of being with Xander even if it was only temporarily. But the secret thing might be difficult to maintain. "And in public? Or at the office?"

"We can be cordial to each other, right?" he teased.

She bit her lower lip, trying to decide how big of a fool she was going to be when she agreed. Everything in her told her to reject the offer. It was insanity and she couldn't believe it when she said, "Okay."

She was rewarded by his grin which sent shivers throughout her whole body, filling her with decadent anticipation.

"So it's already Thursday," he said, moving closer one more time. "Are you going to come home with me tonight?"

She tried to take a deep breath, but his hands moved to cup her breasts again and it turned into more of a gasp. "It's late," she finally got out although it was hard.

"And?" he asked as if that weren't a good enough excuse.

Autumn knew what he wanted to hear, but she couldn't be that brazen. She wanted to tell him to take her home to his house or hers and start all over on what they'd just done, but this time in private. And slower. More thoroughly.

But she wasn't that confident around him.

He realized where her mind was going and finished his thought for her. "And you should come home with me so we can finish what we started again."

She shook her head and pushed against his shoulders. "If I go home with you, we won't get any sleep." Her nudge wasn't very convincing since she didn't want to sleep alone tonight. Good grief, she didn't even want to sleep!

He laughed, his hands moving higher on her waist. "I don't see a downside to that."

She thought frantically, trying to figure out what was good and bad about the whole situation. She knew this wasn't going to work, but her body wanted him so badly. "You have Ms. Goswin coming in at eight o'clock tomorrow morning."

He groaned at the reminder and his hands stilled although she felt his fingers clench on her hips. "That woman!" he snapped.

Autumn couldn't help but laugh. She'd never seen him express any kind of irritation with any of his clients. They all seemed to love him and he loved them. Some of them were repeat clients, which was truly crazy, but others considered Xander a personal friend after their divorce was finalized. Autumn didn't want to know which of those offers he accepted.

"I thought you and Ms. Goswin were friends."

He quickly shook his head. "Can't stand her," he explained. "She's not a very nice person," he said in a low, irritated voice.

This was a new side to the man and she had to admit that she was amazed.

He looked around, still wanting to figure out how to get her back to his place and into his bed. "How about if I help you clean all this up and then I can take you home?"

She automatically bent to pick up the reports that had fallen to the floor during their bout of passion, trying to hide her blush at the mess that was all over the floor now. "I have my car here," she said as she grabbed all of the papers on her side of the copy room work table while he pulled together the ones on his side.

"It's late and you shouldn't be driving home at this time of the night alone."

She laughed and shook her head. "That's a crazy excuse and you know it."

He laughed as well and they both stood up with all of the gathered papers. "Yes, but it will get me closer to your bed, which is where I want to be."

"It will also leave my car here."

"I don't mind driving you into the office tomorrow morning."

"But everyone will see my car here. And some might see us driving in together. My name would be at the top of the kitchen pool paper by nine o'clock tomorrow morning."

He sighed, realizing what she was saying. "Okay, good point. So follow me home. That way, you'll still have your own car."

Again, she shook her head. "I'm going home alone tonight, Xander." She was proud of herself for being so firm about this.

"Then leave work early tomorrow and come with me. I'll show you my lake house and we can spend the whole weekend together."

Her eyes widened. "You have a lake house?" she asked, interested despite herself.

He shrugged slightly. "Only my brothers know about it," he said. "It isn't big, but it suits my needs."

She smiled, intrigued by yet another side of him. "And what needs are those?" she asked, more than a little curious.

"Privacy."

Her eyes widened. "I thought you were more of an extrovert."

"Normally, I like being around people, but every once in a while, I need the silence of nature." He looked at her cautiously. "I'm not kidding. It's pretty small and rustic."

She loved the idea but didn't want to appear too enthusiastic for fear of putting him off. She had to play it cool, she thought. "What time would you like to leave?" she asked.

He grinned right back at her. "Can you get out of here after lunch? It takes about two hours to reach the house so that will give us plenty of time to get out of here and head to the lake so it won't feel like the weekend is already gone."

She nodded her head, smiling shyly now that she knew his secret. "So that's where you go when you leave here early on Fridays," she said with a grin. "I can be ready tomorrow. And yes, I can get everything cleared off of my desk by lunch time."

"Great," he said. "I'll walk you to your car," he told her as he took her hand and led her back to her office where they both dumped all of the reports.

She grabbed her purse and her coat, leaving the rest of her work on her desk. There was no way she'd get anything else done tonight. She needed a shower and a bed. Preferably his, but she had to be firm about this and sleep in her own bed tonight. Tomorrow, there would be plenty of time to be in his arms.

CHAPTER 7

Autumn nervously packed her bag, not exactly sure what to include but she stuffed a couple pairs of jeans in, a bathing suit, some shorts and a sweater along with both long sleeve and short sleeve shirts. She included makeup, but only because she knew she wouldn't be ready to face Xander without any makeup yet. She might need, oh…maybe ten years, before she would have the courage to face the man with a fresh face. He was too suave and sophisticated and she couldn't imagine sitting across the table from him without looking her best.

She threw her bag into her trunk, then bit her lip as her mind worked through the details. She couldn't leave her car at the office because then everyone would know that she'd left with someone else. But she didn't want to waste time coming all the way back to her place. She lived about thirty minutes away, in the opposite direction from his place. Maybe he wouldn't mind if she left her car in the parking lot of his building, which was only about five minutes from their office.

With that settled in her mind, she dumped her bag in the trunk and slammed it shut.

All morning, she scrambled to get her desk cleared off. Every time she received a new e-mail, she jumped on top of the issue, eager to get it taken care of so no one would be upset by her leaving early. When her phone rang right before lunch, she jumped and glared at it, initially thinking it was another task to get cleared up. But then she saw Xander's extension, she smiled with relief and answered the phone.

"Are you still able to get out of here in say…an hour?" he asked.

"I'll be ready," she replied, feeling silly for the huge grin, grateful he couldn't see her.

"Good. I'll meet you in the lobby."

He was about to hang up when she stopped him. "Wait!"

"What's wrong?"

"Can I drive to your place and park at your apartment instead?"

There was a long pause and then he sighed. "Sure. That will work as well."

Autumn ended the call and turned back to her computer. There were three more messages that had come in just during that short conversation. She quickly opened all three and read through them, then quickly cleared up the issues that needed to be resolved.

Forty-five minutes later, she looked around. Her reports were collated and ready to be distributed, her e-mail was…well, not empty but all the major issues were cleared up, her desk was also clean of any major issues….

Was she really ready to go?

Her stomach flip flopped at the idea of a long weekend with Xander. There wouldn't be anyone around, just the two of them. Was she really going to do this? How stupid was it?

She should cancel, she thought. It was ridiculous to think that she would be any different from all the other women in his life. She would last just as long as they did and then she'd have to watch him with his next woman.

Could she handle that? Did she have the strength to endure him with another woman, knowing how she felt about the man?

Did she have a choice?

Not really.

Before she could come up with a reason not to, she grabbed her purse and headed out of her office.

"I'm leaving early today," she said to Mary, not seeing the surprise in her assistant's eyes as she swung her purse over her shoulder and headed out for the weekend. She was so embarrassed and nervous about what she was doing, afraid her guilt would be written all over her face, that she couldn't look anyone in the eye.

She told the receptionist that she was leaving as well and to talk to Mary if there were any problems, since the receptionist also worked for her as well. When Xander walked out just as she was reaching for the door handle, she cringed when he told the receptionist that he too was leaving early for the weekend.

They stood awkwardly in the hallway waiting for the elevator to arrive, not saying a word to each other. When the doors opened, Autumn stepped in and moved to the opposite side of the cab while Xander politely stepped back from the front to allow another woman to be in front of him.

Once outside the building, she walked to her car, got in and drove away without once looking in his direction. She noticed him pull out of the parking garage right behind her but she didn't even hesitate, too afraid someone from the office might be walking to lunch at one of the many restaurants along this street during their own lunch hour.

She pulled into the entrance of his building and, somehow, the gate for his building's parking garage quickly opened. She supposed he had some sort of electronic opener on his car but she was too nervous about what they were about to do to wonder about it too thoroughly.

She heard her phone ring and answered it from her steering wheel.

"Park in number three," Xander told her. She did so and he moved into space number one.

She was just gathering her purse when her car door opened up and Xander's strong, powerful hands were reaching in, lifting her up and into his arms. "That was ridiculous," he said a moment before he covered her mouth in a kiss that had her knees shaking so badly she couldn't even stand any longer.

When he lifted his head, their breathing was rough and rapid and she didn't want him to move away. In fact, if they weren't in a parking garage, she might be begging him to keep on going. She'd had trouble sleeping last night after his teasing touches and now that desire was right back, just as intense. Possibly more so because she knew what was going to happen.

"Get in my car," he ordered her with a heated look that told her he was just as on fire for her.

"Shouldn't I change clothes?" she asked, smiling. Or at least trying to smile. She wasn't sure she actually made it.

"If you even start to change clothes, I'll have them all off of you and we'll never get to my lake house. And I really want you where no one will be able to find either of us until Sunday night."

She could agree with that. So she pushed away from her car, her legs still pretty shaky, and slipped into his luxurious, black Jaguar sedan. The sleek lines of the exterior were mirrored on the inside and she loved the way the seat hugged her body, keeping her in place.

A moment later, Xander was right next to her and he was pulling out of the space.

"My clothes!" she gasped, forgetting that she needed her bag from her trunk.

"No need," he teased. But then relented when he saw her worried expression. "I got them out already. Your bag is in my trunk so there's no slowing down." He actually stopped at that point and looked at her in the dim light of the parking garage. "Are you sure about this, Autumn?" he asked gently, his hand touching her cheek, smoothing down to her jawline. "I don't want to pressure you into anything you don't want to do."

She almost laughed at that but he was being too sincere. "I guarantee that there isn't anywhere I'd rather be right now," she assured him.

Those beautiful, indigo blue eyes smiled right back at her and he drove quickly out of the garage. In only moments, they were speeding down the highway out of the city. They talked about everything and anything that occurred to them and Autumn couldn't believe how nice it was to have that camaraderie back that they'd had when she'd first started working at The Thorpe Group as a receptionist. He could make her laugh about the silliest things and yet, they argued about everything as well. The arguments this time were good natured, not nearly as heated as they had been before that afternoon in his penthouse. And she discovered things about him that she never would have believed.

The biggest surprise of all was two hours later when they pulled into a wooded, gravel driveway. This lake house wasn't anything like what she was expecting. While his penthouse in the city was gorgeous with all the latest gadgets and designer decorated, his lake house was the complete opposite. The house wasn't enormous and elegant. It was a small cabin, just like he'd told her. And it really was just a cabin. There were rough logs and stones and the edifice stood almost right on the water. The lake wasn't very deep right here, but it expanded out and looked cool and amazing farther to the right. There were pine trees behind the house and a perfect porch with two deep chairs that looked out onto the lake.

She didn't realize it, but Xander was standing behind her while she took it all in. When she just stood there, looking and not saying a word, he couldn't take the suspense any longer. "What do you think?" he asked.

Autumn didn't even turn her head. "It's perfect," she whispered, not wanting to raise her voice for fear that it might break the solemnness of the atmosphere. "How did you get such a perfect spot?" she asked.

He moved closer to her, wrapping his arms around her waist. "I bought up several lots up and down the lake from this point."

She rolled her eyes, shaking her head at how wealthy he was. "Only you," she laughed.

He squeezed her slightly then kissed her neck before releasing her. "Come see the inside."

She followed behind him, feeling warm and protected with his large hand holding hers. It felt like their first, real date, but that didn't make any sense after they'd known each other for so many years. Well, and the fact that they'd made love…um…had sex…so many times.

He led her down a dirt pathway towards the small cabin. There was a double door and a large window looking out onto the lake, but inside, there was only a rustic kitchen powered by solar panels on the roof. Nothing was turned on so Xander had to power up the fridge and small stove so it would at least be ready to use. There was a sitting area filled with deep, rough wood chairs surrounding the large, stone fireplace but not much else other than fishing and snow equipment against the wall. Other than that, there was only one bedroom with more rough wood as the bed and piles of blankets as well as one dresser and a closet in the corner.

"There's only one bedroom," she said as she backed up.

Xander looked down at her, his eyes confused. "Isn't that the whole point?" he asked, matching her step for step.

"Where am I going to sleep?" she asked.

Xander froze, his eyes trying to figure out if he'd completely misunderstood what was going to happen this weekend. Then he saw the teasing glint in her eyes and he growled. "You're not!" he told her in a deep, husky voice, ignoring her squeal as he bent low and tossed her over his shoulder.

Autumn was laughing so hard she could barely breathe but then she found herself on her back, staring up at the man and all her laughter died out while that delirious lust surfaced once more. The time for talking was gone. There was no teasing, no laughing. The only sound either of them made was gasping pleasure as clothes were pulled off and scattered, skin revealed and his hard body finding her softer one.

CHAPTER 8

The weekend was filled with laughter and exploration. Xander showed her all of his favorite places on the lake including a water fall, a secluded field that was filled with sunshine and hiking along the trails and into the forests. Since the water was still warm from the summer heat, he convinced her get into the water with him, but she refused to do it without her bathing suit. By the time they were back up on the front porch of his cabin, she was naked and desperate for him to take her, unconcerned about anyone seeing them because he'd gotten her to the point where she didn't care any longer.

When they weren't exploring the trails and lake, they were exploring each other. She'd never even known that men like Xander existed. He loved cooking and they competed with each other to make better pancakes, each making their own batch then sharing with each other. For dinner, he grilled the chicken and she made a potato casserole and salad. He opened a bottle of wine and they sat in front of the fire, eating, talking and sharing until she couldn't take his distance any longer and she crawled up onto his lap and made love to him the way she'd been thinking of doing ever since she'd seen the fireplace.

They talked and laughed, cooked and made love while intermittently exploring the outside world as well. By Sunday night, she didn't want to be without him, feeling addicted to his large body being so close to hers.

When they were back in the city late Sunday night, he tried to convince her to come up to his place and spend the night with him, but she remained firm in her desire to go home. She didn't have clothes to wear to work the following day and she didn't want to be late, which she would be if she spent the night in his arms and had to rush home the next morning to change.

"I'll make sure you're on time," he coaxed, nibbling on her ear until she was shivering again.

"You'll just keep me awake all night again and I'll be a walking zombie tomorrow, and I'll definitely be late because you might wake me up, but..." she didn't finish her sentence, blushing at the way he'd woken her up the previous two mornings.

He laughed and slipped his fingers underneath her flannel shirt. "You know I'm very good at waking you up," he told her, his sexy voice close to her ear.

"You're incorrigible," she said and sighed as she forced herself to slip out of his arms. She drove home that night but she tossed and turned, not able to fall asleep without Xander's arms around her and his body warming her own.

The following morning, she was late for work because she'd forgotten to put her alarm on and slept through when she would normally have gotten up.

She finally sat down at her desk only fifteen minutes late. When her phone rang at her elbow, she almost didn't answer it, knowing that it would be Xander. In the end, she was too desperate to hear his voice so she lifted the receiver, smiling when she heard his gloating voice.

"I told you to spend the night with me," he said softly and with that deep, sexy voice that she was becoming addicted to so quickly.

"How did you know I got into work late?" she asked, glancing to the open door of her office to make sure no one was coming in or might hear her.

"Are you kidding me?" he laughed. "I've been watching to see those long, sexy legs for the past few hours. I got in about six o'clock this morning."

"You did not!" she laughed, not believing him for a moment.

"It's true. I finally gave up on sleeping because you weren't there with me. By five this morning, I gave up and just came into the office."

She bit her lip since she'd had the same problem. "I..." she sighed, wishing she could be as open with him.

"I know, love. You had trouble sleeping too. But I'll fix that tonight," he said. "Have a good day today." And with that, he hung up, leaving Autumn shivering and smiling like an idiot.

Thankfully, the day flew by and Autumn was frantically trying to clear up the last few issues so she could head home. She wanted to get dinner started so she could surprise him tonight. She stopped and looked around, frozen with the realization that she was just assuming he would be coming to her house tonight.

Her cell phone buzzed and she glanced down, reading the text message. "Leave now!" was all it said.

She laughed out loud as she read it, but she also shut down her computer and grabbed her purse. She was just about to leave her office when she got a mischievous idea in her head. Instead of heading towards the lobby which would take her to the bank of elevators, she turned instead and headed towards the stairs. Xander would probably be heading towards the elevators now as well. He was probably anticipating catching her on the ride down to the parking garage.

She smiled as she waved goodnight to Mary and then disappeared into the stairwell. She slipped off her heels and sped down the stairs, hurrying as fast as her feet could take her. She knew she wasn't going to beat the elevator, but she wanted to beat Xander if at all possible. She had a plan in her mind. She wasn't sure she was brave enough to follow through though.

She was out of breath when she reached the bottom and sprinted to her car. Pulling out of the parking spot, she thought she saw Xander in a group of other people exiting the elevator, but she wasn't positive. She drove through traffic which, thankfully, was lighter at this hour. When she arrived home, she rushed up the stairs, pulled her hair up on top of her head and jumped into the shower. After taking a quick shower, she stood in front of her dresser with her underwear drawer open, now indecisive. If she were calculating things correctly, she didn't have much time left so she grabbed a black, lace bra and matching underwear, pulling them on quickly. She applied a bit more makeup, a pair of black heels (the pair that he'd bought her earlier that week), and stood in front of her mirror, surveying her appearance.

She was pacing back and forth in her room, her hands twisting together nervously. When the doorbell rang, she froze in place, staring at herself in the mirror one more time. Her heart was beating so hard, she could almost feel it in her pulse. But no matter how hard she tried, she simply couldn't answer the door in her black, lace underwear and heels.

When the doorbell rang a second time, she grabbed her robe and pulled it on, tying it tightly at the waist. "You couldn't have gotten a sexy, satin robe!" she admonished herself as she went down the wooden stairs to answer the door. "No, you have to get the frilly, flannel robe that makes you look like a creepy old maid with a hundred cats!"

She opened the door to find Xander on her doorstep. He looked angry and confused, and even surprised to see her.

"Are you okay?" he asked, still standing outside. His hands were on his hips and his broad shoulders looked tense.

Autumn's hands moved to cover herself. She might be wearing a robe, but she knew what she'd intended to be wearing and she suddenly felt vulnerable. He looked like he was now regretting his suggestion that they have an affair. Where was the voracious lover of the weekend? Had he had enough of her? Already? That was so unfair. Other women at least got several weeks with him. But he looked like he was trying to tell her he wanted out after only one weekend.

"I'm fine," she said, her hand gripping the belt of her robe. "Did you want to come in?"

He hesitated for a long moment before he said, "Do you want me to come in?"

Autumn thought she might just burst into tears. In fact, she felt the traitorous tears start to form in her eyes and she blinked rapidly to try and stop them.

Xander saw the look and the wetness in her eyes and he felt horrible. "Autumn," he groaned as he stepped inside her townhouse, his hands coming up to pull her against his chest. "I'm sorry, honey. I don't want to pressure you into something you don't want."

"What?" she gasped, pulling back so she could look up at him. "Something I don't want?" she repeated. "You looked like you were changing your mind."

He looked down at her, his hand moving from her back to cup her face, his thumb rubbing gently against her chin. "I didn't see you leave. I thought maybe you'd stayed at the office to try and avoid me. Then, when you opened the door, you looked irritated, almost angry to see me."

Autumn breathed in a shaky breath, letting her forehead fall onto his broad chest and almost laughed.

Xander didn't understand what was going through her head, but he was tired of trying to guess. "Autumn, if you don't want this, if you aren't feeling anything for me anymore, just say the word and I'll back off."

She laughed softly, but it came out sounding more like a hiccup because she was fighting both the release of her despair and the overwhelming joy that he still wanted her. "I still want you," she said against his shirt. She pulled back but still couldn't look up at him. "Very much so in fact," she whispered.

"Why did you look so sad when you opened the door then?"

One side of her mouth pulled away in an odd sort of grimace. "Because I was mad at myself."

He shook his head, still not understanding. "What's the issue?"

She sighed and stepped back, pulling at the tie to her robe. She couldn't look at Xander, fearful of the amusement she would see in his eyes. "You have women throwing themselves at you all the time. This is a bit harder for me," she finally said. When the tie was open, she held the edges closed with her hands.

"Autumn, I don't think you understand about those other wo…."

He was going to explain about the women in his life, but she slipped the robe off of her shoulders, letting it slither down her body to pool at her feet. Xander was speechless as he took in her slender body with only the black lace covering the important parts.

He didn't say a word. He stared. Hard. Autumn stood there, her nervousness increasing with his silence. Autumn couldn't take it any longer. She had to know what he thought. If he was laughing at her, she'd just shrug off his amusement and pretend to laugh with him.

Slowly, with absolute determination, she lifted her eyes to his.

She didn't see any amusement there. Only heat – and intensity – as he continued to look at her.

He cleared his throat slightly. "You rushed home to change."

"Yes," she whispered.

"You didn't rush back here to avoid me again."

Autumn was so surprised that he would think along those lines that she moved closer to him, relieved when his arms automatically wrapped around her body.

"You're beautiful, Autumn," he groaned a moment before his mouth covered hers in a kiss that demanded complete submission. She was more than willing to give it to him, thrilled that he still wanted her.

When he lifted her into his arms and carried her up the stairs, she wrapped her arms around his neck and laid her head on his strong shoulder, her body throbbing and excited in anticipation of his touch. And she wasn't disappointed. Xander was merciless, kissing every part of her body, teasing her and making her scream out with the need to find fulfillment. When he finally entered her, she sighed with happiness…until he started moving inside of her. Her fingers held on tightly, never wanting this moment to end. When it finally did end, she wasn't sad at all. Just thrilled that he was still here, in her arms. She snuggled close, smiling in the dim light filtering in through the hallway.

"I liked your surprise," he said as he wrapped his arms around her, pulling her back against his chest.

She laughed. "Maybe I'll get confident enough to actually open the door that way in a few years."

He chuckled as well. "I'll look forward to that evolution."

She thought it was sweet that he was even thinking he might still want her in a few years. And it warmed her heart whenever she thought back to the expression in his eyes when she'd dropped the robe. It gave her a bit more confidence sexually to know that he liked her figure that much.

"I'm hungry," she said several minutes later.

He lifted her hair off of her shoulder and nuzzled her neck. "I can oblige."

She laughed and shook her head. "For food," she clarified. She sat up in the bed and looked around, wondering where her robe was.

"It's downstairs on the hallway floor," he told her, reading her mind and then laughing when she bit her lip in consternation. "You're going to have to go down there naked to get it."

She looked at him over her shoulder, eyebrows raised as she accepted his challenge. She slid out of bed and Xander pushed up on his arms to watch, smiling slightly.

She sat on the edge of her bed, debating how she could do this. "It doesn't help if you're staring at me," she admonished him.

"What's the point of walking around your house naked if you don't let me watch?" he asked, pushing a pillow behind his head.

She couldn't figure out how to do it and looked at the floor, wishing she had a throw blanket on her bed she could wrap around herself. And then she smiled triumphantly when she spotted his white shirt on the floor.

"Oh, no you don't," he growled, realizing too late what she had planned. But he was too relaxed and that gave her the head start she needed. She whipped the shirt up off the floor and got her arms into the sleeves before he could stop her. The next thing she knew, she was running down the stair, laughing so hard she almost slipped on her robe when he chased after her, grabbing her by the waist and tossing her over his shoulder. She yelped when he smacked her bottom and trotted right back up the stairs.

"You cheated," he told her and tossed her into the middle of the bed. "For that, you're going to have to pay the price."

"What's the cost?" she gasped through her delighted laughter. But she didn't have long to wait. He kissed her, his body making her crazy.

Several hours later, she laughed as she pushed his hands away. "You can't touch me again until I get some food," she told him firmly. She stood up and grabbed her robe from the floor where she'd dropped it earlier, slipping her hands into the sleeves and tightening the belt around her waist. When she turned around, he was pulling on his jeans, buttoning the fly but he hadn't put on a shirt yet. Even after hours of being in his arms and finding fulfillment over and over again, the man could still stun her with the beauty of his muscular shoulders, chest and stomach. He was cut like a Greek statue and she considered telling him to get right back into bed.

Then her stomach growled and she knew she should focus on getting some food inside of her before anything else. "Right," she said out loud and padded barefoot out of her bedroom.

Xander watched her move, walking behind her so he could enjoy her from the back. "What are you making me for dinner?" he asked as they descended the stairs to the kitchen.

She snorted. "How about a peanut butter and jelly sandwich?" she suggested and opened the fridge.

He was looking in the pantry. "How about pasta?" he suggested and grabbed the jar of sauce and dried pasta. "You get the water boiling, I'll do the rest."

Her eyebrows went up with that. "I'll make the garlic toast," she offered and went into her freezer for the last half of the crusty bread she'd bought a while ago but hadn't used. There was a bit of cheese, fresh garlic and plenty of butter in the freezer which she kept on hand for when the mood struck to bake something yummy and decadent.

"You're on," he told her and reached around her to grab the vegetables that were in her fridge. "Stand back, woman," he said and started opening cabinets in search of the items he would need to make pasta.

For the next hour, they laughed and nibbled on vegetables while they cooked their dinner together. After they'd filled their stomachs with rich, cheese laden pasta, Xander pulled her back into his arms and made love to her once more before they fell asleep in each other's arms.

That started the pattern for the next several days. After work, they would meet at either his place or hers, they would cook, eat and laugh, enjoy each other's company and relax until he took her into his arms and made her so crazy with his touch and his kisses that she was begging him to take her. She had no idea if this kind of passion for another person was normal, but she suspected it wasn't. She'd heard others talk about sex with their spouses in the kitchen and what she was experiencing with Xander didn't have any resemblance to what others discussed. It was like apples and asparagus.

She was walking into the office, feeling happier than she ever had. Until she came face to face with her reality. "He said he had to work last night," a woman draped in a black dress was saying to Diane.

Autumn was about to walk by when something inside her told her to stop and linger for a moment.

"I don't know if he was working late last night, ma'am. But he hasn't come in yet today. Would you like to leave a message?" Diane asked in her kindest voice, which told Autumn that the black clad woman had already been her for a while and was making a stink about something.

"Can I help you?" Autumn asked, stepping forward to help Diane out of the situation.

The woman turned around, swinging her silky black hair in an arc to face the new voice. The woman looked Autumn up and down, dismissing her as unimportant. "I'm looking for Xander Thorpe," the woman explained. "I'm Marcy Duprey."

Autumn waited, expecting the woman to continue. When she finished with just her name, as if that were supposed to mean something, Autumn plastered her 'office manager' smile onto her face. "Do you have an appointment with Mr. Thorpe?" Autumn asked, her stomach starting to twist into knots. She knew exactly where this was going. Had known it would happen but wished it had taken more time.

"I don't need an appointment," the woman stated, preening slightly with a superior expression on her beautiful features. "And I'm just here to hear from him if the rumors are true."

Autumn swallowed, painfully aware that this woman might not be exaggerating. She'd left Xander's house only an hour ago but already she felt cold and rejected. "Mr. Thorpe isn't in the office at the moment. If you'd like to sit down and wait, I can bring you a cup of coffee. Or I can make an appointment for later in the day?" she offered, trying to sound normal and professional, but she suspected she was coming across as brittle and vulnerable, which is how she felt.

The woman waved the option away. "No need. I just need a moment of his time."

"Then you're going to wait?" Autumn asked.

Marcy laughed. "Goodness no. I've been waiting enough for that man. I'm not waiting any more. Besides, if what I read was true, then he has a lot to explain!" She slung her hair over her shoulder and walked out. With one hand on the door, she turned back. "Tell him to call me the moment he gets in," she ordered as if Autumn and Diane were her underlings, here to follow her commands.

Diane blew out her breath and slumped into the back of her chair. "That woman did not look happy."

Autumn knew the feeling. She'd been on top of the world only five minutes ago. The presence of that horrible woman had ruined that wonderful feeling she'd left the house with earlier.

Walking into her office, she had to control the urge to slam the door. She walked carefully and precisely to her desk and dove into the work. She pushed herself harder than ever that day, needing to push the image of that woman out of her mind.

"Did you hear?" Diane stepped into her office, excitement obvious in her eyes.

"Hear what?" Autumn asked, pulling the report off of the printer, her eyes scanning the details to ensure their accuracy.

"Mia Paulson is free! The police were even here to re-arrest her on embezzlement charges but some woman with Ryker recognized the alleged victim."

"You're kidding!" Autumn demanded, standing up and moving out of her office. "Where is she?"

"Down in Ash's office," Diane called back to her.

Autumn didn't wait any longer, running down the stairs to Ash's area. She was so excited for her friend. This was amazing news and it occurred to her that she hadn't even contacted her friend in the past several days. Of all the times when Mia needed a friend, Autumn had been too wrapped up in her own world lately and she was ashamed.

"Where's Mia?" she asked Jean, Ash's administrative assistant.

"She's in Ash's office."

Autumn rushed through the doors, eager to see her friend. It was also a convenient excuse to avoid Xander today, made better by the fact that it was true.

"I just heard the news!" she screamed and grabbed Mia into a huge hug. "I'm so relieved. I told you Ash could get you out of this mess!" she said, rocking back and forth with her arms around Mia's shoulders.

Mia laughed and tried to nod her head, but Autumn's grip was too tight. "You were right. He got everything all cleared up. I can't believe it's actually over!"

Autumn laughed, delighted. "We have to go out and celebrate!" she exclaimed. "Let's go do Durango's!"

"Yes!" Mia agreed, knowing that a margarita was exactly what she needed right now. "I'm totally in!"

They walked out, arm in arm, to the elevators, laughing and giggling as the relief over the past few weeks eked out of Mia's mind.

"Men!" a blond woman grumbled as she pressed the elevator call button over and over.

Mia smiled at the woman with genuine appreciation. "You're the woman who just helped me stay out of jail," Mia said. "Are you okay?"

Cricket Fairchild spun around and noticed the two lovely women behind her. "I'm sorry," she said and took a deep breath while closing her eyes. "Nothing a good martini can't fix," she said, trying to calm down. "Men are just so confusing!" she snapped, the calming breath obviously not working too well.

Mia knew the feeling. "Why don't you come with us? I don't know about the martinis," she cautioned, "but the margaritas at Durango's are perfect for anything that ails you."

"I'm not sure I should be around humanity right now," she came back.

Mia laughed. "That's exactly where I am. I'm Mia Paulson," she said. "And we're heading out to celebrate me not being in jail for the rest of my life."

Cricket smiled back, taking Mia's hand in hers. "That sounds like a perfect start to the weekend. I think I'll join you after all."

As they walked down the street to the bar, Autumn could feel the tension in her shoulders start to dissipate. It wouldn't completely go away, but at least she was out of the office and could avoid Xander for the rest of the day. If he found out she'd left, he would follow her and ask her what was going on. Right now, she couldn't handle a conversation with him. She was too vulnerable and too desperate to ignore the fact that her affair needed to be over with Xander. It had been so amazing, so wonderful and shockingly perfect. But she wasn't the kind of woman who could ignore other women in his life. Nor could she continue to delude herself that she could have an affair with a man who she knew would eventually move on to another woman.

Now that she knew the real man, she also knew that her love for him was stronger than she would like to admit.

She was in love with him. Plain and simple, she loved him with every particle of her being.

Unfortunately, she had to protect her self-esteem and leave before he broke her.

"Wait!" Mia exclaimed and Autumn blinked, about to drown her sorrows in the margarita. Turning around, she watched as Mia walked over to another table and spoke to a woman sitting alone. This was odd, Autumn thought. Mia was talking with one of the newest lawyers on Ash's team.

When the pretty woman came over and sat down with them, Autumn instantly knew that she was going to like this woman. Kiera Ward had a sadness in her eyes that indicated there was much more to her than just a dynamo criminal defense lawyer.

They laughed and drank margaritas, nibbled on the salty chips which just made them drink more. It was a vicious, ingenious cycle, Autumn thought as the conversation swirled around her. This was exactly what she needed. Women who were obviously in the same position she was in. Autumn listened and watched, noticing that Kiera had the same, sad look in her eyes that Autumn did, Mia was furious with Ash, which Autumn suspected was a defense mechanism for the feelings she was fighting and Cricket, the only blond at the table, was furious about something that was happening with Ryker.

The four women here were all victims of the Thorpe brothers' charm. Was there any way to avoid their power? It was shocking that four intelligent, strong women could fall so hard for men who obviously were eager to avoid any kind of commitment.

Xander sat with his brothers at the bar, listening to the four stunningly gorgeous women tear up all of his brothers, himself included. The blond was cute, but really had it in for his oldest brother. Kiera was going on and on about what a ridiculous division Axel headed up and Mia was slamming down the drinks but that was probably okay since she'd just been freed from a murder charge. Embezzlement charges had been pending today, but the whole thing had been dismissed when Cricket, the cute blond, recognized the assumed murder victim. Hard to prosecute a person for murder when the man showed up for meetings designed to commit fraud! What an idiot, Xander thought.

And then his eyes moved over to Autumn. She'd left the office earlier this afternoon. Initially, he'd been worried, but when he'd heard that she'd just gone out to celebrate her best friend's freedom, he took it all in stride. Autumn deserved to get out and have fun. She'd been working extremely hard lately, trying to not let anything slide just in case someone discovered their relationship.

"Should we say something?" Axel asked, leaning back, not looking like he was in the mood to stop any of the conversation. Who would? It was too revealing! These four women were revealing all their deep, dark secrets about the men in their hearts.

"I say we send them another pitcher," Ash said with a chuckle as Mia told the other three women what an obnoxious, untrusting, cynical man he was.

Xander watched Autumn take a long sip of the margarita, his body on fire as he looked at her sexy neck. He loved that neck, he told himself.

"They're going to feel this in the morning," Ryker said with a chuckle.

Ash chuckled as well, pretending to be wounded. "It will be their punishment for all the mean things they're saying about us."

Axel rolled his eyes. "Speak for yourself," he punched his younger brother. "Those ladies might be evil when they're hung-over."

Xander couldn't handle looking at Autumn any longer. He had to have her in his arms. "I think it's time to crash this party. Don't you gentlemen?" he asked and placed his half-finished beer behind him on the bar.

He didn't wait for them to agree, wanting to feel Autumn's softness against him too intensely. "Time to go, love," he said into Autumn's ear.

She turned around, startled to see him so close. "I'm not going anywhere with you," she said and picked up her drink, taking a long swallow.

"Why not?" he asked, pushing her drink away as soon as she put it back down on the table.

"Because Mia, Cricket and Kiera don't go around dating other women all the time. They're nice and fun and we understand each other."

Xander looked at his brothers, all of them trying to figure out how to get the women out of the bar. Ash had the best approach. He simply picked Mia up in his arms and carried her out. He heard her saying something about Ash being an obnoxious brute, but then she put her head on his shoulder and sighed with what sounded like happiness.

He didn't think Autumn would be as amenable to that solution. "How about if we go back to my place and talk about it?"

She snorted and shook her head. "No."

"Why not?" he asked, pulling her chair back and considering the best way to lift her into his arms.

"Don't even think about it," Autumn snapped at him. "Why don't you go find one of those women you've messed around with over the past few months?"

Ryker snorted at that comment. "He wishes!"

Xander glared at his older brother, not wanting his celibacy over the past…who knows how long…to become common knowledge.

Autumn picked up on the statement anyway. "What does he mean by that?" she asked.

"Nothing, love. Let's go."

"No. Because you're going to try and take my clothes off as soon as we get out of here."

He ignored his other brothers' laughter at her comment. "Yes, I am," he confirmed, taking her hands and pulling her up and into his arms. "Any objections?"

She pulled away and slung her purse over her shoulder. "Many."

She walked out of the bar, surprised at how steady on her feet she was after all those drinks. She was proud of herself for how well she'd handled her alcohol. A very responsible adult, she thought with pride.

Xander pulled two chairs out of her way before she crashed into them, then steered her out of the way of one of the tables. She looked pretty cute trying to pretend like she wasn't drunk, he thought. He wasn't going to let her even try to drive home though.

Out on the street, she looked to the right and left, trying to look for a cab so she could get home. She spun around, almost falling onto Xander in the process. "I forgot to pay our bar tab!" she gasped.

"Ryker took care of it," he reassured her, running his hands over her back.

He heard something to his left and almost groaned out loud when he heard Suzy Martin screeching as she looked at him. Suzy was a woman who had tried very hard to entice him into her bed about three months ago. She had long, blond hair, a body that was as thin and flat as a cracker and beautiful eyes.

"I thought you were gay!" she said at the top of her lungs!

Xander's eyes widened and he had to stop himself from laughing out loud. "Um, hello Suzy. How have you been?" he asked, extending his hand awkwardly. He wasn't immune to the hilarity of her comment either.

"Don't you dare ask me how I've been you bastard! You're supposed to be gay!"

He didn't roll his eyes, but it was close. "Why was I supposed to be gay?"

She flung her hands onto her barely-there hips, her cheekbones almost bursting out of her face because of a lack of body fat. "Because you weren't interested! In anyone!" she yelled back at him, obviously furious with him.

He smothered his amusement as the woman he was painfully interested in snuggled against his chest. "I've really got to go," he said, unconcerned with Suzy's opinion of his sexuality.

"What does she mean?" Autumn asked, sighing as she laid her head onto his shoulder. She knew she shouldn't, but he just felt so darn good!

"Don't worry about her," Xander said, leading her back to the parking garage and then gently tucking her into his car.

She was almost instantly asleep and he drove them straight to his place, not even considering heading back to hers. She'd said some strange things and he wanted her here where he could make sure to talk to her in the morning.

CHAPTER 9

Autumn reared up in bed, looking around and then groaned in pain as her head felt like it was going to split apart from the pain shooting across her forehead.

"You're not gay," she whispered.

Xander sat up as well and watched with concern as she worked through the discovery of her hangover. "No. I thought that was pretty clear."

She gripped her head in both hands while still trying to hold the sheet up over her body. "But Suzy said you weren't interested in anyone."

He got up out of bed and went into his bathroom. A moment later, he handed her a glass of water and some aspirin. "I wasn't interested in those women."

She took the aspirin and drank the entire glass of water. "Why weren't you interested in them? And why did she think you were gay?"

She leaned back, unaware that it was onto his chest and not the pillows. All she knew was that she felt wonderfully safe and warm.

"I can't speak for all of the women in Suzy's mind, but as for her, I wouldn't sleep with her. She wasn't happy about that."

Something in the back of her mind niggled at her memory. "What about that horrid woman yesterday?"

He rubbed her shoulders gently, trying to ease the pain of the hangover away but he suspected, from past, personal experience, that only time would ease her pain. "Which horrid woman are we discussing now?"

"The black-haired evil one that came in yesterday morning to speak with you."

His fingers stilled on her shoulders while he went through the people he'd had meetings with yesterday. "Are we discussing Marcy Duprey, by any chance?" he asked.

"I think that was her name." She leaned back, feeling slightly better now that the aspirin was starting to metabolize in her body.

Xander sighed. "Marcy Duprey came in to get her third prenuptial agreement signed. Her husbands have required it in the past."

That was definitely news to her. "Why?"

"Because she's a heartless, merciless woman who goes through husbands like other women go through stockings."

Autumn laughed slightly but then stopped when the pain in her head throbbed. "I think I drank too much last night," she sighed, rubbing her temples gently.

Something else occurred to her and she froze. Pulling away from him, she looked up into his eyes, needing to understand him. "What did your brother say last night?"

Xander rolled his eyes. "Which one? And at what time? They were saying a lot, probably a lot of things you didn't hear."

She shook her head then stopped when it hurt too much. "No, I heard this. It didn't make sense at the time."

Xander stiffened, worried about whatever his brothers might have said that would hurt her feelings. "Which comment, love."

She bit her lip, trying to think through the pain that was still throbbing. "Ryker said 'You wish' after I said something about you dating all those other women."

Xander pulled her back against his chest and resumed his massage. "Ryker doesn't know what he's talking about."

She heard the words, but something about the tone of his voice didn't ring true. "What aren't you telling me, Xander?" she asked, more worried now than she had been last night. "I don't understand you and I'd like to. But I can tell that you're hiding something."

Xander leaned his head back against the headboard slightly. "Are you sure you really want to do this?"

She thought about it for a long moment. "Yes. I think I do. Are you going to tell me something horrible? Like you're a secret serial killer and I'm your next victim? If so, maybe you really should keep that to yourself. If I'm going to die a horrible death, I'd rather not know about it in advance."

Xander was already laughing before she finished her comment. "No, I'm not a serial killer. But then, nor am I a serial dater."

"What's that supposed to mean?"

Xander moved his hands lower, easing the tension along her shoulder blades. "Are you sure you want to discuss this? It's going to change everything and you might not like what you hear."

And instantly, all the tension was right back with her. She pulled away from him and stood up, grabbing his shirt from the chair and buttoning it up before she turned around to face him. "Okay. Tell me. What's going on? What is this big secret?"

Xander leaned back against the headboard again, staring up at the ceiling. "I'm in love with you. My brothers have known about it for years."

She stood there, staring. Not understanding. "But all those women…"

"They were just a smoke screen."

She felt a small little flutter in her stomach. "So when that woman on the street said you were gay, it was because….?" She wasn't sure how to say it.

He ran a hand through his hair in frustration. "Suzy doesn't count."

That was a startling comment. "Why doesn't she count?"

"Because she's too thin. I wasn't even remotely attracted to her."

"And Jessica?"

Xander shrugged again. "Too aggressive."

"Marcy?"

He grinned. "Too mercenary."

She couldn't help but chuckle at that one. "And all the other women?"

His eyes turned wary and he hesitated. But when he saw the vulnerability in her eyes, he sighed and told her the truth. "They weren't you."

She gasped and tried to take another breath, but his words made her heart ache. In a good way this time. "How do I know?" she whispered.

He shook his head. "I can't prove anything to you. My brothers know I haven't slept with anyone for years. Suzy knows which is why she and all of her friends think I'm gay. I wouldn't sleep with any of them, no matter how much they tried to tempt me."

"You weren't tempted?"

"Not even in the slightest."

"But they're all beautiful," she stated as if he were crazy.

"They weren't you, Autumn."

She paced back and forth at the bottom of his bed, ignoring the pain in her head. "This doesn't make any sense. You're a very sexual man."

"I am with you. With other women, they leave me cold."

"We fight all the time!" she said, throwing her hands up in the air with exasperation.

"I like fighting with you," he grinned. "I like fighting and talking and laughing and cooking but most of all, I like making love to you. I love hearing your moans when I do something that you like."

She blushed and looked at her hands. "I moan all the time."

He laughed, nodding his head. "I know that. I like it."

She sat down at the end of the bed, her mind quickly moving through everything he'd told her this morning. "Why?" she asked, trying very hard to understand and believe what he was saying, but it was too hard. Because if he changed his mind, it would break her heart.

"Xander, are you trying to tell me that you haven't had sex with anyone since you met me?"

He shook his head. "No. I can't claim that. I've been with other women in that time. You were too young initially. And then you started dating that ass, Tim or Tom or something like that."

"Tim," she confirmed. "He was a nice guy."

"He was an ass. He had a wimpy handshake and he was afraid of spiders."

She laughed, remembering her telling her co-workers about how he'd jumped up on the kitchen chair when a spider had appeared in his kitchen one night. She'd had to kill it for him and left almost immediately afterwards. "You heard that conversation?" she asked.

"Yes. And went out and killed five spiders that day, just to prove my worth to you."

She laughed hard, even able to picture him going into the woods to find spiders. "You never told me about your killing spree."

He crossed his arms over his bare chest, denying her the view she liked so much.

She bit her lip, trying to figure out if she believed him or not. "So why haven't you said anything in all these years?"

"Because you didn't seem interested in me."

"We used to be friends."

"I want more than a friendship."

And here it was, she thought. This was the brass ring. Dare she ask the question? "What do you want?"

"You," he said without hesitation. "I want you in my home. In my bed. I want you to marry me and make me the happiest man in the world. I want to fight with you and make love to you ten times a day."

Her eyes widened. "Ten times?" she asked, shuddering.

"I have a lot of years to make up for," he explained. He waited tensely for her to respond to the other things he'd said but when she just sat there staring at her hands, he couldn't wait any longer. "Is there any way you might learn to love me?"

She laughed and hiccupped at the same time. "Xander, I've been in love with you ever since you bought me those leather, cashmere gloves after I lost mine."

His face was blank as he said, "Someone dropped them in the parking lot that day."

She crawled up the bed, knowing he was looking down the neckline of the shirt, staring at her breasts. "You bought them at the store around the corner an hour before you gave them to me. The salesclerk had the receipt delivered over to you since you forgot to pick it up before you left."

He grimaced, but since she'd reached him by this point, he helped her by lifting her up and arranging her so she was straddling him, exactly how he wanted her. "So I lied about that. What about the rest of what I told you?" he asked, his hands resting on her thighs.

She tilted her head to the side, considering all that he'd said. "I believe you." She grinned. "Or more specifically, I believe Ryker and Suzy."

Xander froze for a moment, then with a growl, he tossed her onto her back, tickling her in all the places he'd discovered she was ticklish. He didn't let up until she was begging him to stop, laughing so hard she could barely get the words out.

"I love you," he told her tenderly, kissing her smiling lips and looking down at her with all the love in his eyes.

Her fingers reached up to touch his hair and his face. "I love you too. I'm sorry it's taken us so long to realize it," she whispered.

He grinned lasciviously. "That's okay. I'll just have to make up for all the years you were too stubborn to realize what was going on," he said. And he started doing just that.

CHAPTER 10

"Is this your way of ensuring that I don't look at another woman?" Xander asked, leaning against the doorway to their bedroom.

Autumn swung around, her shocked eyes taking in his buff body in the tailored tuxedo. "Goodness," she breathed softly, unable to stop gawking. "Don't do that."

One eyebrow went up in inquiry. "Don't do what?"

"Wear that tuxedo. It's not legal."

He chuckled and walked into the bedroom where she was finishing up. "What's illegal is you, in this dress. I don't think I like seeing you in this dress."

She laughed and smacked his hands away but he ignored her efforts, just like she knew he would. She had just pulled on the blue, satin bridesmaid's dress for Mia's wedding. It was beautiful and sexy and she loved Xander's reaction so she didn't fight his hands too diligently. As if she would ever object to having his hands touch her in any way. "We're going to be late if you don't stop," she said as he bent lower and nibbled along her neck.

"I think I need some handcuffs," he said.

She laughed softly, but the idea had merit. "Who would be wearing the cuffs?"

"You, of course."

Shaking her head, she stepped out of his arms and slipped her shoes on, feeling better now that she didn't feel so short. In her heels, the top of her head at least reached his chin. "There's no 'of course' about it," she argued. "I don't think I should have to wear handcuffs after last night."

He grabbed her wrists and held her in place, just like he'd done the previous evening. "Ah, but you didn't learn your lesson well enough."

"I didn't know there was a lesson to learn."

"There's always something to learn," he came back, lifting her hand so that he could look at the diamond ring sitting there. His finger rubbed over the diamond and he smiled. "We're still not going to announce our engagement today?"

"Absolutely not. This is Mia's day."

He rolled his eyes. "And you think Mia didn't plan all of this?" he asked, indicating the satin blue dress she was wearing which was low cut and sexy as hell. "She's up to something and you know it."

Autumn laughed, agreeing with him. But since she and Xander were already a couple, neither of them minded that Mia was doing a little matchmaking. "So when are we going to announce our wedding?"

Xander shrugged. "Why announce it at all? Why don't we just fly out to Vegas and get married tomorrow?"

She thought about that for a moment, then nodded her head. "Okay."

He pulled her into his arms. "Would you really want to do that? What about a big wedding? Don't you want all of your friends there with you?"

She smiled slightly. "Well, Mia will be on her honeymoon, I can't invite Kiera and Cricket because they're sick of weddings after this one. And I don't want to wait another year or two for them to recover. So why don't we just have a small party when we get back?"

He thought about that for a moment, then shook his head. "No. I want my brothers there with me when I get married. And I want you to have your friends there. I know you've known Mia, Cricket and Kiera for only a few weeks, but the three of you seem like sisters already. They should be there, ready or not."

"We just finished helping Mia. I really don't want to go through all of this again."

He looked at her carefully. "Are you sure? You don't want the white dress and the flowers and all that stuff?"

She grinned. "I can still wear the white dress in Las Vegas. I don't need the flowers or the big reception. I just need you," she said and stretched up to kiss him.

Xander pulled her closer, deepening the kiss even while his mind was working out a plan. He wanted Autumn to have everything, so everything she will get.

MIA AND ASH'S WEDDING

"Do I look okay?" Mia asked nervously, smoothing down the yards of tulle that made up the skirt of her dress. "I probably shouldn't have…"

"You should have," Autumn soothed, pressing a gentle hand to Mia's shoulders while their eyes connected in the mirror. "You look stunning and Ash is going to be so happy when he sees you that he'll be speechless."

Kiera snorted and shook her head. "Ash is never speechless," she came right back, standing behind Mia as well. The sexy blue satin dress was still a shock whenever she looked in the mirror, but at least Axel knew what to expect. She'd dressed at Axel's house and had almost become undressed as soon as she'd walked out of the closet. He'd liked the dress very much.

Autumn and Cricket both laughed at Kiera's comment but Mia was too nervous to see the humor. "He spent too much money doing all of this," she said out loud.

Cricket moved to stand in front of her friend, a stern look on her face. "Mia, you've got to listen carefully. All combined, those Thorpe brothers have more money than a small country so I don't want to hear another word about how much all of this is costing. Ash wouldn't have spent so much trying to hurry this wedding along if he didn't want you to be his wife very much. So here's what's going to happen," Cricket explained with absolute determination. "You're going to go out there and see your man. You're going to forget all about the expense of this entire affair and you're going to have the best day of your entire life. All of your neighbors are out there, your friends, coworkers and a man who loves you so much that he's chomping at the bit to get you next to him. This is your day. Today you are the fairy princess and you're going to have the time of your life. Anything less and I will sneak into your house and do something really crazy and you won't even know I was there until you realize something strange is happening. Do we understand each other?"

Mia's eyes were wide throughout the whole speech until the end. When Cricket came up with that ambiguous threat, all three women laughed outright.

"No you're not. You made a promise to Ryker that you wouldn't ever sneak into anyone else's house."

"Well, except for the businesses and houses that she's paid to sneak into," Kiera teased.

"Yes, except for those," Cricket smiled right back. "I really do have the best job in the entire world." Cricket was hired by Hamilton Securities to join an elite team of ex-military and intelligence personnel who traveled all over the world, testing the security of their clients' buildings and computers. And she was loving every moment of her new job.

Autumn shivered. "I would faint at the first sign of danger," she said, shaking her head at Cricket's crazy skills. "But I'm thrilled that you're happy now."

"Let's get this show on the road," Kiera interrupted. "But Autumn and I are with Cricket, my friend," she said to Cricket, giving her a gentle hug. "We'll be watching. Just so you know, we all have a pact to watch you. The first sign of worry and we're filling up your champagne glass. If you don't take our advice and enjoy today, we'll make sure you're too drunk to remember your stress. Got it?"

Mia laughed but nodded her head. "Got it," she told the three of them. They gave her a big, group hug, then leaned back, all of them checking their mascara in the mirror.

"Okay, let's go find my man," Mia said, tugging her strapless wedding gown slightly higher on her body. "By the way," she said to Cricket, "don't think I didn't notice that huge rock on your finger." She turned and fluffed her dress. "I actually noticed one on everyone's finger. So we're going to have a long chat when I get back from wherever Ash is taking me on our honeymoon."

The three other women looked at each other, then down at each person's left hand. Sure enough, there was a gorgeous diamond ring on each woman's finger.

"I guess I didn't need to go so crazy on those bridesmaids dresses after all," she said. Then she pulled her veil over her head, picked up her bouquet, and headed out of the anteroom of the church.

Autumn, Cricket and Kiera all looked at each other with stunned surprise for a long moment. Then burst out laughing. They looked around at each other, grabbed their own bouquet of flowers, and continued their almost hysterical laughter as they made their way out of the room to take their places at the back of the church.

Ryker, Ash, Axel and Xander all looked at each other when they heard the loud laughing as they stood at the front of the church waiting for the ceremony to start. When neither of them could figure out what was so funny on such a momentous day, they shrugged and looked at the minister who had a very disapproving expression on his face.

Ash didn't care what the minister thought, as long as he performed the ceremony that would make Mia his.

The music started and the laughing stopped. Behind him, he felt each of his brothers stiffen as the women in their lives entered the sanctuary but he couldn't think about them at all, too eager to see Mia.

When she finally appeared, he thought he might have died and gone to heaven. She looked so beautiful in the strapless gown that flared out all around her. She looked delicate, sexy and ethereal all at the same time. No woman had ever affected him like this little lady did. And he couldn't wait to make her legally his own.

She moved into place beside him and he moved her veil out of the way, his breath catching in his throat when she smiled up at him. "You're beautiful," he growled.

Ash wasn't sure what happened during the ceremony because his whole mind was focused on the last few words. "I now pronounce you husband and wife," the minister said with a smile that was warm and approving.

Ash turned to Mia, pulling her close and not even waiting for permission before he pulled her into his arms and kissed her thoroughly.

As they walked out of the church, Ash almost laughed at her trembling response. When they were in the waiting limousine, he pulled her onto his lap, his strong hands encircling her waist as he bent his head and kissed her again, just to feel her response which never failed to drive him crazy with lust for her. When he raised his head and looked down at her, he almost chuckled at the dazed expression on her lovely face. "You're mine now," he said.

Mia grinned and wrapped her arms around his neck more securely. "And you're mine," she whispered back.

Several hours later, Mia was exhausted. She hadn't left Ash's side all night. They'd danced, laughed with family and friends, ate tons of food and drank several glasses of champagne. But now, all she wanted was to be alone with her man, to have him wrap her in his arms and carry her away to some place private and quiet.

"Ready to go?" Ash asked when he felt her lean more heavily against his side. He'd been waiting for her to get her fill of the party before he took her away, but he was growing impatient to have her alone.

"More than ready," she said, smiling up into his blue eyes that she loved so much.

"Let's get out of here," he growled and pulled her closer. He was practically carrying her out of the reception area, wanting her in the car where he could slip that amazing dress off of her lovely figure and have his wicked way with her. "I want you alone."

"Not so fast," Ryker said, stepping in front of his youngest brother.

Ash halted, but only because it was his brother. Anyone else would be mowed down. When Xander and Axel stepped up, shoulder to shoulder with Ryker, Ash knew that he was going to have to fight his way out of this party. "Guys, you're my brothers and I love all of you, but that doesn't mean I won't take you down if you don't get out of my way pretty quickly."

His brothers just laughed, none of them worried about the threat. "We just wanted to say goodbye." Which was an outright lie. The ladies in their group had seen that the couple was trying to slip away unnoticed and had tasked the brothers to slow down the newly married couple so the rest of the guests could get organized.

"Not funny, guys," Ash growled.

When Xander heard the whistle, he gave the signal that everything was set up now. "We'll let you go now. But we'll see you back here in ten days. Lots of things happening."

Ash didn't care what was going on. All he wanted was to get Mia alone. "Clear the way," he told them firmly.

The brothers just smiled and stepped back, causing Ash to look at the three of them suspiciously. He put an arm around Mia's slender waist protectively, then pulled her along behind him.

As soon as they stepped out of the ballroom, a flurry of rose petals was thrown into the air, descending on the couple with delicate kisses of good luck. Mia glanced up, surprised at the shower of rose petals but enchanted nonetheless. She looked over at the three women dressed in similar blue satin outfits, her eyes clouding from the tears that were forming at the touching gesture.

Ash saw the look and stopped, letting Mia enjoy the flower rainfall, enchanted when several of the rose petals fell into her hair, balancing there precariously before falling to the ground.

"I don't think I've told you I love you," he whispered into her ear.

She grinned up into his eyes. "Every time you look at me," she whispered right back to him.

A moment later, they were driving away, Mia unaware of anything but Ash's arms around her, his lips kissing hers and the gentle sway of the limousine as it carried them towards the airport.

KIERA AND AXEL'S WEDDING

"I can't believe this is happening," she whispered. Her hand fluttered around the jeweled waist of her bodice. "Is this really happening?"

Autumn laughed and hugged her friend. "It's been a long time coming, but yes. You are finally marrying Axel."

"Six years!" she whispered. "Six long, miserable, lonely years." She almost started crying as she thought about how much time she'd missed with Axel. "I could have lost him."

Cricket stepped up and took Kiera's hand. "But you didn't. Which only means that this was meant to happen."

"Even the weather agreed with you!" Autumn said with a huge grin on her face.

Kiera shook her head. "I doubt there's going to be another day like today. I can't believe the sun is shining and it is so warm out in November!"

"Axel wanted you to have this wedding," Mia said, handing Kiera the bouquet of daisies and pink chrysanthemums. "And it is pretty spectacular!"

"It will get cold tonight," Kiera warned.

The three women waved away the warning. "Axel has those heaters stationed all around the dance floor under the pergola. We'll be toasty warm. Don't worry about a thing."

Kiera smoothed her hand down her dress one more time. "I don't think I could worry about anything anyway. I'm too excited."

Mia hugged her friend, feeling very relaxed and smug after returning from her honeymoon just the previous day. "It seems like the entire office building has shown up for your wedding. So go on out there and make us proud, girl!"

Kiera's smile widened even more. "You're right. Let's go do this!"

The enormous oak tree behind Axel's house was filled with pink lights, rows of pink chairs were lined up, filled with friends and co-workers, daisies were everywhere and the four Thorpe brothers were once again lined up, but with Axel at the front of the line this time.

When the bridesmaids stepped around the corner of his house, Axel craned his neck to get his first glimpse of Kiera. He even liked the dresses each of the ladies chose, thinking that they looked very pretty in the various shades of green.

But it was Kiera who caught his eye when she stepped around the corner. He'd pictured her so often in his house as he'd built it, refining it over the years but nothing could have prepared him for the sight of her in the blush pink, strapless wedding dress. She was stunning and the most beautiful woman he'd ever seen in his life.

She didn't wear a veil but stepped down the grassy aisle, walking towards him with tears in her eyes. "Are you okay?" he asked when she stepped closer and he could take her hands.

She gave him a watery smile, squeezing his hands as she said, "I cost us six years because of my stupidity. I'll make it up to you."

He almost laughed, delighted that she was still okay. "I thought you were starting to regret not accepting the job in Paris."

"Never. I only regret that we didn't do this the first time you suggested it."

He bent down and kissed her gently. "We have years ahead of us," he whispered. "Don't regret the past. It only diminishes the beauty of our future."

She thought that was the most profound thing she'd ever heard and moved closer to him, resting her head against his shoulder as she turned to face the minister. And when he finally pronounced them husband and wife, she thought her heart might just burst out of her chest with the love she felt for this man.

"You're wonderful," he said as he lifted her into his arms, swinging her around on the dance floor as the music started to play. For the rest of the night, they danced in each other's arms, barely noticing the rest of the guests. She didn't each much, wanting to be with him instead.

But Axel noticed that she wasn't eating anything and stacked food onto a plate from the buffet table that had been set up near his vegetable garden. "Here. You're going to have to eat something."

"I'm not hungry," she said and started to pull him into her arms for another dance.

He shook his head and pushed the plate towards her. "You're going to eat," he said and fed her some sort of appetizer that looked like shrimp and scallops somehow meshed together. "You're going to need your strength for the night ahead."

Kiera blushed, but she opened her mouth to taste the morsel. She ate several more of the delicious appetizers but by the time she'd had enough, she didn't remember anything she'd eaten.

When the party was winding down, Axel was too impatient to deal with the goodbyes. He remembered Ash's wedding and wasn't going to be hindered by his brothers while he tried to make his escape. So instead of announcing his departure, he simply lifted Kiera up into his arms and swept her out of the party. It took the guests another ten minutes before they realized that the bride and groom had already left but they continued dancing on into the night.

Kiera laughed, delighted at his exit strategy and threw her arms around his neck, more than willing to be kidnapped out of her own party.

CRICKET AND RYKER'S WEDDING

"Where are we going?" Cricket asked, taking Ryker's hand but hesitant. He had one of those expressions on his face that told her he was up to no good.

"Do you trust me?"

She laughed and shook her head. "Not when you're looking like that."

His rumbling laughter made her feel all warm and gushy inside. "Well, you're going to have to."

She closed the door on her tiny house for the last time, looking at him carefully. "Why won't you tell me what's going on?" she demanded, pulling her scarf closer around her as the freezing wind whipped around the corner of her house. It had been three weeks since Kiera's wedding and, as predicted, the weather had turned painfully cold, the usual for Chicago's winters.

He shook his head. "You're going to have to trust me."

She laughed and let him tuck her into his car. "I would, if you would give me more information."

He shrugged. "Let's just say I'm taking things into my own hands," he told her and slammed the door shut on her confused expression.

When he was seated next to her, she glared at him. "What are you doing, Ryker?" she demanded more forcefully.

He didn't answer her and she started to become concerned when he drove to the airport. She almost groaned when she saw O'Hare in the distance. "Another job? But I thought I had a few weeks off after the last project," she said. "I'm going to talk to Mitch. He told me he had nothing on the horizon for the next two weeks. I've been working non-stop trying to get things organized..."

"Relax," Ryker said as he drove through the lanes, pulling up into the private parking area of the airport. "This trip is just for you and me."

She liked the sound of that! "Well, if you insist."

"I insist."

She stepped out, slipping her hands into her gloves and pulling her hat down lower over her head. "This is miserable," she grumbled.

"You've been taking too long to organize our wedding," he told her as he led her out of the parking area and straight onto the tarmac where The Thorpe Group's private jet was standing by.

Cricket sighed and hugged his arm. "I'm sorry. I know it's taking too long. I just…"

He stopped and looked down at her. "You don't want to get married in the winter," he said, his eyes understanding.

She smiled, relieved that he understood. "Not really. I don't like the cold and I was hoping for an outdoor wedding. I loved the way Kiera's wedding felt and wanted the same thing."

He smiled and winked down at her. "Come on," he said and squeezed her fingers. "I have a trip to make. You have some time off so you're coming with me. You'll relax, I'll get my mission accomplished and we'll have some time together."

Cricket didn't hesitate. She followed him up the stairs and was relieved when they were able to sit down in the large, comfortable leather chairs. She picked up a magazine while Ryker conferred with the pilot. Ten minutes later, the jet was taxiing down the runway and Cricket fell asleep with her head snuggled against Ryker's shoulder. She fell asleep listening to the soothing sounds of his deep voice next to her and loved it.

She had no idea what time it was when she felt his strong hand shake her shoulder slightly. "Cricket. It's time," he said.

She sat up slowly, looking around to get her bearings. "Goodness," she gasped, releasing her tight hold on his arm as she woke up and took in her surroundings. "Where are we?" she asked.

"Grand Cayman," he told her with a chuckle at her bewildered expression. "You need to change your clothes."

She looked at him as if he'd lost his mind. "Why? Can't I change at the hotel? Or wherever we're staying?"

He shook his head. "Nope. There won't be time."

That was a strange thing to say. "Okay. But what's going on?"

He took her hands and looked down into her eyes. "We're getting married today, love," he said firmly.

She blinked, still not accepting what he was telling her. "Why would we do that?"

He squeezed her fingers slightly. "Your dress is in the bedroom behind you," he explained. "Your friends are already here and we're getting married."

She almost laughed at his expression. "What's the temperature?" she asked, moving closer to him, snuggling up to his big, broad chest.

"It is a balmy eighty degrees."

Her smile widened at the idea. "Mia, Autumn and Kiera are here already?"

"Yes."

"And your brothers?"

"Yes. They all arrived yesterday."

She laughed, delighted with the idea. "You've been a busy boy, haven't you?"

He shrugged. "You're not angry?"

She leaned in and hugged him. "On the contrary. I'm thrilled! I wish I'd thought of this."

"Your parents are impatient to get the thing done with as well. Your mother was very helpful."

Cricket laughed again. "She's pretty good about planning parties. She loves to do it."

"Well, I basically gave her cart blanche but with several stipulations. It had to be in a warm climate and I wanted it done this weekend."

She grinned, thinking of the conversation between this strong-willed man and her mother who always got her way. "I guess I'd better get changed then."

She spun around on her heel, thrilled with the idea of getting married here on the island. When she stepped into the back room of the private plane, she saw her wedding dress already laid out along with the fabulous shoes she'd found last week. This couldn't have worked out better if she'd done all of this herself. But truth be told, she'd been so exhausted trying to move out of her house, put it on the market and work at her new job. She'd been frustrated that she hadn't made more progress on her wedding plans but knew that she'd been procrastinating because she'd wanted a summer wedding. Now she was going to get one!

When she stepped off of the plane, an official looking gentleman was standing at the bottom of the stairs right next to her father and mother. "Ready to get married?" he father asked, taking her into his arms and hugging her gently.

"Very ready," she whispered excitedly.

Her mother laughed and hugged her as well. "I think you're going to be pleasantly surprised."

"Ryker said you'd organized all of this?" she prompted, trying to find out details.

But her mother knew exactly what Cricket was trying to do and she wasn't going to wheedle any details. "I organized it all, but Ryker gave me very specific details about what he wanted. So don't let him fool you. He is the mastermind of this fabulous gala. We just set the pieces in motion."

And that was the only information she was going to get. They helped her into the waiting limousine and off they went. When she stepped out of the limousine on her father's arm, she gasped in surprise. The sun was setting over the ocean and her friends were all standing in a casual grouping right in front of a filmy canopy that had been constructed next to the ocean. The pathway was littered with red roses and lit by candle filled lanterns. And at the end of the romantic pathway, Ryker stood in a white linen jacket and slacks with a white shirt. His three brothers stood next to him in similar suits. And Mia, Kiera and Autumn were also standing there waiting, in flowered sundresses with their hair pulled up off of their necks and held there with flowers. All of them had been in on the surprise, and Cricket wasn't sure if she was going to burst into tears or laugh with delight. So she did both.

A quartet started to play music off to the side and Cricket's father took one of her hands while her mother took the other. They'd never been a traditional family before and she didn't want them to start now.

When Cricket stepped forward and took Ryker's hand, she couldn't stop the tears from falling. "This is beautiful," she whispered up to his handsome face. "I couldn't have planned anything so lovely myself."

"It's okay?" he asked gently, his strong hand cupping her face while his thumb rubbed the tears from her cheeks.

"It's more than okay. It's wonderful."

They turned at that point, and fifteen minutes later, they were husband and wife. Ryker kissed her so gently, deepening the kiss as the waves crashed against the sand. It wasn't until everyone laughed and Xander pounded Ryker on the shoulder that he finally lifted his head.

"Time to party," Xander said and reached over, grabbing Autumn's hand in his. "This way," he told everyone.

They were led over to a wooden patio that was surrounded by lush, green plants and huge, colorful flowers. There was a tropical buffet set up with music and dancing. Ryker had reserved the entire restaurant just for them and they danced, laughed and ate decadent foods with an elaborate chocolate bar for dessert. The cake was all white with delicate butterflies set on the edge, looking like they were about to flutter away. It was so lovely, Cricket almost didn't want to cut it but everyone encouraged her to go ahead and they feasted on lemon wedding cake.

When he took her hand to lead her out the door, he whispered, "I love you," into her ear.

Cricket smiled up into those amazing blue eyes of his, still surprised by how much she loved this man. "I love you too," she finally said, unable to hide the happiness since it was about to burst out of her at any moment. "You make me happier than I've ever been in my life."

He kissed her gently as he led her down the hallway to the suite he'd reserved for their honeymoon. "Ah, a challenge! I accept," he teased her.

AUTUMN AND XANDER'S WEDDING

Autumn zipped the strapless bodice up her side, then bit her lip in anticipation of sliding her feet into her jeweled shoes. She wasn't sure, but she might actually love her silver shoes more than she loved her lace, tea length wedding gown.

The four of them were standing in the enormous suite Xander had reserved for them, ensuring that the Las Vegas hotel was everything Autumn had dreamed it might be. There was champagne chilling for the four of them along with delicacies to nibble on while they prepared for the final Thorpe wedding.

"Oh my," Cricket whispered when Autumn took her wedding shoes out of the shoe box that had been lovingly protecting them for the past six weeks. "How many times have you tried these on?" she asked with reverence.

Autumn laughed and slid her toe into the slender strap that would hold her toes in place. "Every time Xander isn't at home with me," she said, her eyes closing with delight. She opened them up and snapped the chain around her ankle which would hold the shoe on her foot.

"So not very often," Kiera teased.

Autumn nodded her head. "Not often enough but I'd rather have him home with me than trying on these shoes."

"They're magnificent," Mia sighed. "But I don't know how you wear heels that high all the time."

Autumn laughed, having heard that often. "I love them. They make me feel stronger. And I need that when Xander's around."

Kiera's eyes widened at her friend's statement. "Still? I thought you wore them before because he intimidated you."

She nodded her head as she adjusted the delicate chain on the second foot. "I used to wear them because of him. Goodness, he used to irritate me!" she laughed again. "Now I just wear them because he always makes me feel weak in the knees. These help me stand up to him."

Kiera rolled her eyes. "Like you do that very often."

Autumn grinned. "So he's a pussy cat now."

Cricket adjusted the pin in Autumn's hair slightly then stepped back. "I think it's time you married this pussy cat of yours."

Autumn stood up and surveyed her appearance in the mirror. "I would have to agree with you," she said with excitement shooting through her whole body.

"Are you ready?" Kiera asked.

The four women stood together, all smiling, all beautiful and three of them newly married. "Would you have believed that all of us would be married six months ago?" Autumn asked, truly amazed by the changes in the past few months.

"Never," Mia laughed. "Of course, I didn't think I would have been arrested either."

The four of them laughed because she'd met her husband the morning she'd been arrested for murdering her previous fiancé, who hadn't been murdered at all. He was, in fact, serving time in prison with his current fiancée for fraud and embezzlement.

"This is a truly astonishing moment," Cricket said, taking the hands of Kiera and Autumn. Autumn then grasped Mia's hand and the four of them stood in front of the large mirror, three of them in colorful bridesmaid's dresses and one in white lace wedding finery.

"Let's get this show on the road," Autumn whispered. "Otherwise, I'm likely to break into tears."

"That would be bad."

The four of them were about to move, but Autumn stopped them. "Wait," she called out and all four women stopped and stared. "I just wanted to say thank you to all of you. Mia and I might have known each other for years, but it feels like the four of us have been sisters forever. I couldn't have gotten through those miserable months without the support of you three. And I'm deeply touched that I was able to stand with each of you as you married the men you love. But more, I'm honored that you are here with me today, ready to witness my own wedding to Xander."

Mia, Kiera and Cricket all wiped their tears from their eyes quickly then laughed nervously before they melted into a group hug. "You guys are the best," Kiera said fervently.

"Come on, ladies," a deep voice said from the doorway of their suite. "You're going to be late and you know how irritated Xander gets when someone is late."

Autumn stood up and rolled her eyes. "He can just be irritated," she said to Axel who stood in the doorway trying to usher everyone out to the ceremony. But she also hurried out of the room, not looking back for anything. This was her day. It felt like she'd waited so long for this moment to arrive and everything was so much more wonderful than she could have imagined.

Having gone through formal weddings with Mia and Kiera, then a beach wedding with Cricket, Autumn and Xander had agreed that the only way to get married was to do it in style. So they had flown everyone out to Las Vegas for an extravagant wedding at The Bellagio Hotel.

The wedding coordinator was standing outside their door, eager to escort them to the wedding area. When Autumn stepped into the Terrazza do Songo, she couldn't contain her gasp of surprise. It was like they were standing in the middle of a quaint, Italian village with flowers cascading everywhere. And as they looked out over the edge of the patio, the famous Bellagio fountains were dancing to an old Elvis song. She smiled at all the over-the-top details that Xander had arranged, feeling deeply touched.

The music started, swelling to a fabulous crescendo when Autumn stepped out. She walked down the short aisle, her eyes never leaving the tall, handsome man waiting for her at the end. When she stood beside him, she felt like she was floating on a cloud of happiness. And that was before he looked down at her shoes, then poked his own foot out. When she saw what he was silently pointing to, she burst out laughing.

Xander was wearing blue suede shoes!

"I love you, crazy man!" she whispered and leaned forward to kiss him even before the ceremony started.

"I love you to. And I love your shoes!"

It was nice to be marrying a man who knew how to make a woman feel special, she thought. Then they turned to the officiator, smiling as they listened to the beginning of the ceremony.

EPILOGUE

Five years later, Autumn waddled out of their bedroom and glared at Xander as he lifted their three year old daughter up into his arms. "Xander, what did you give Leandra for breakfast!" she demanded, but already knew the answer.

"What did we have for breakfast?" he asked Leandra who covered her mouth with her chubby hands to stifle her giggle.

"Nothing," she said carefully, then looked up at her father for his approval.

"Well, we had something," he corrected, winking at her.

"Oh!" she said and giggled again. "Milk and an apple, Momma," she recited just as she'd been prompted a moment ago.

"And chocolate cake?" Autumn asked, dumping sunscreen into their bag.

"Hello?" someone called out from the foyer.

Leandra instantly wiggled down from her father's arms, eagerly running to greet her cousin Jeremy who was two months older than she was, but still nice about it, she said every time the subject was brought up.

Mia walked in with Abby in her arms, dodging Leandra and Jeremy as they rushed by.

"Don't go out to the pool until an adult is with you!" she called out with a sigh. "Chocolate cake again for breakfast Xander?"

Xander's eyes widened. "How...?"

Ash walked in a moment later, shaking his head. "I'd never be able to get away with that," he said and bent down to kiss Autumn's cheek. "How are you feeling today? Any better?"

Autumn put one hand to the small of her back while the other covered her eight and a half month pregnant tummy. "I'd be better if my husband would stop feeding our daughter sugar for breakfast."

"She's fine," Xander countered and punched his younger brother on the arm before turning back to argue with his wife. "She needs a bit of chocolate every now and then to counter the tofu sausage you're always giving her. She needs a bit of fat." He patted his stomach where the six pack was even more defined than it had been on their wedding day five years ago.

There was more commotion from the side of the house, announcing the arrival of Ryker and Cricket along with their two year old twins, Kayla and Courtney. They constantly wanted to keep up with Jeremy and Leandra, both of whom encouraged the twins to run right alongside them.

As soon as Leandra ran through the kitchen, Cricket shook her head. "Chocolate cake again?"

Xander stared at his sister-in-law, astonished. "How does everyone know about the chocolate cake?" he asked. Unfortunately, he didn't get an answer since Axel and Kiera showed up with their son, Matthew, who immediately raced through the house in search of Leandra and Jeremy.

"You need to get off your feet," Axel said as he bent down to kiss Autumn's cheek, then stole Abby away from Mia, tickling Abby's tummy until she was laughing hysterically. "Why aren't you in the pool? Kiera loved the pool when she was pregnant with Matthew. Took all the pressure off of her back."

"I'm with you," Autumn said and pushed herself off of the chair. Xander was instantly right beside her, helping her up and holding her hand while they herded all the kids out to the pool area. There was a fence with a locked gate, just to make sure little feet didn't get near the pool without adult supervision and the little arm floaties already attached.

Autumn didn't stop in anyway as she lowered her very pregnant body into the pool, instantly feeling relief from the pressure in her back. Mia, Cricket and Kiera joined her, handing her a glass of icy lemonade as well. Xander plunked a wide-brimmed hat on her head, gave her a kiss, then moved off to supervise the kids in the shallow end.

"Goodness, why do men gravitate towards the grill?" Cricket asked as she watched her husband move off to fire up the grill in the corner of the pool area.

The others just smiled and laughed. Xander and Ash were in the pool, tossing kids around, plunking them on their shoulders and making sure they were all having a good time. Ryker was busy cooking their lunch while Axel gave Abby her bottle in the shade.

"Who would have thought," Kiera said out loud as she looked around at the chaos and happiness.

"Not me," Mia said with a smile.

"I'm glad it all worked out so well," Autumn said, sinking lower into the pool and sipping her lemonade.

"I think 'well' is putting it pretty mildly," Cricket said with a sigh of happiness. Ryker must have heard her because he turned in her direction and winked before re-focusing on the burgers and hot dogs.

"Are those tofu dogs?" Mia whispered.

"Yes," Autumn said, laughing at their secret. "I put them into the beef hot dog package so the guys wouldn't know."

The other women couldn't contain their laughter. Four men and five kids stopped what they were doing to survey the laughing women, grins on all of their faces before they turned back to what they had been doing.

"Yes, life is pretty good, even with tofu," Kiera said happily. And the other three nodded their heads in agreement.

COMMENTS FROM THE AUTHOR

For some fun visuals on the Thorpe Brothers and their ladies, go to:

http://www.pinterest.com/elennoxromances/his-captive-lover-mia-and-ash/
http://www.pinterest.com/elennoxromances/his-unexpected-lover-kiera-and-axel/
http://www.pinterest.com/elennoxromances/his-secretive-lover-coming-dec-2013/
http://www.pinterest.com/elennoxromances/his-challenging-lover/

If you have time, please take a moment to write a review on whichever platform you purchased this book. It not only helps guide others who might purchase this book, but I also love hearing from my readers – the good, the bad and the ugly. Some readers tell me there's too much sex, some tell me I should add more, others criticize my grammar and others tell me they love my books. Everything you write, I use to improve my next story. If you love what I write, let me know because I'll continue writing in the same way. If you think I should improve in some way, please let me know. I have a very tough skin and can take it – although I absolutely LOVE the positive reviews/comments.

If you would like to contact me directly, I can be reached at elizabeth@elizabethlennox.com. I try very hard to answer all e-mails because I love hearing from readers so much! It is a thrill to hear from you. But I apologize in advance if I miss responding to your message. Sometimes, things get lost in the inbox. I'm one of those non-techy people so I don't always see things that others might think are obvious. It isn't a slight – I promise. It is just that my mind is off in romance-world and not in the techy-world (much more fun/interesting/exciting in my romance-world even though my husband bangs his head against the desk sometimes when I don't understand the techy-world).

BOOKS BY ELIZABETH LENNOX

Note that all Free Novellas below are available from
ElizabethLennox.com or from your favorite e-book retailer!

The Texas Tycoon's Temptation

The Royal Cordova Trilogy
Escaping a Royal Wedding
The Man's Outrageous Demands
Mistress to the Prince

The Attracelli Family Series
Never Dare A Tycoon
Falling For The Boss
Risky Negotiations
Proposal To Love
Love's Not Terrifying
Romantic Acquisition

The Billionaire's Terms: Prison Or Passion
The Sheik's Love Child
The Sheik's Unfinished Business
The Greek Tycoon's Lover
The Sheik's Sensuous Trap
The Greek's Baby Bargain
The Italian's Bedroom Deal
The Billionaire's Gamble
The Tycoon's Seduction Plan
The Sheik's Rebellious Mistress
The Sheik's Missing Bride
Blackmailed By The Billionaire
The Billionaire's Runaway Bride
The Billionaire's Elusive Lover
The Intimate, Intricate Rescue

The Sisterhood Trilogy
The Sheik's Virgin Lover
The Billionaire's Impulsive Lover
The Russian's Tender Lover
The Billionaire's Gentle Rescue

The Tycoon's Toddler Surprise
The Tycoon's Tender Triumph

The Sheik's Mysterious Mistress
The Duke's Willful Wife
The Sheik's Secret Twins
The Tycoon's Marriage Exchange
The Russian's Furious Fiancée
The Tycoon's Misunderstood Bride

Love By Accident Series
The Sheik's Pregnant Lover
The Sheik's Furious Bride
The Duke's Runaway Princess

The Russian's Pregnant Mistress

The Lovers Exchange Series
The Earl's Outrageous Lover
The Tycoon's Resistant Lover

The Sheik's Reluctant Lover
The Spanish Tycoon's Temptress

The Berutelli Escape
Resisting The Tycoon's Seduction
The Billionaire's Secretive Enchantress

The Big Apple Brotherhood
The Billionaire's Pregnant Lover
The Sheik's Rediscovered Lover
The Tycoon's Defiant Southern Belle

The Sheik's Dangerous Lover (Free Novella)

The Thorpe Brothers
His Captive Lover
His Unexpected Lover
His Secretive Lover
His Challenging Lover

The Sheik's Defiant Fiancée (Free Novella)
The Prince's Resistant Lover (Free Novella)
The Tycoon's Make-Believe Fiancée (Free Novella)

The Friendship Series
The Billionaire's Masquerade

The Russian's Dangerous Game
The Sheik's Beautiful Intruder

The Love and Danger Series – Romantic Mysteries
Intimate Desires
Intimate Caresses
Intimate Secrets
Intimate Whispers

The Alfieri Saga
The Italian's Passionate Return (Free Novella)
Her Gentle Capture
His Reluctant Lover
Her Unexpected Admirer
Her Tender Tyrant (December, 2014)
His Expectant Lover (January, 2015)

The Sheik's Intimate Proposition (Free Novella)